SWING AWAY

by Sam P. DiStefano

DORRANCE
PUBLISHING CO
EST. 1920
PITTSBURGH, PENNSYLVANIA 15238

Dorrance Publishing Co
585 Alpha Drive
Suite 103
Pittsburgh, PA 15238
Visit our website at *www.dorrancebookstore.com*

ISBN: 978-1-6366-1466-3
eISBN: 978-1-6366-1652-0

SWING AWAY

Sweat started dripping off her fingertips as she rotated the softball in her hand preparing for the next pitch, quickly wiping the slight sweat on her forehead with her forearm as she looked back at the runner with a slight lead off second base. The weather was unseasonably warm for a mid-February day, sun beating down, no clouds, not even a slight breeze filled the air. Returning her focus to the batter at home plate, waiting for the sign from her catcher. Ashley Stamper was her name, seventeen years old, about to turn eighteen this upcoming summer, stood about 5'7" tall, weighed around 120 pounds, a very athletic build accompanied by an extremely pretty face. Most people would tell her that she is too pretty to be a softball player, but she knew otherwise. She was one of the top female pitching prospects in the country, given the nickname FIREBALL for having one of the fastest fastballs on record, plays for the Lady Saints of John Franklin High School, a large public school in her home town. As she shakes off sign after sign from her catcher, she hears the unsettling scowl from her teams coach off in the distance.

"Let's go, Stamper! Let's see that tight little ass strike this bitch out!" said the coach as he takes a sip from his silver flask glistening in the sunlight.

Ashley's teammates shake their heads in disgust at their coach's unprofessional and immature heckle. She sees the sign she wants and gives it the nod. Her catcher prepares for the oncoming pitch, as Ashley stares down the batter like a hunter would stare down a deer through his rifle's scope before he fired. Ashley knew this could be the last batter of this scrimmage game, it was the bottom of the 7th inning, with two outs and the score tied at 1-1, pitching a near perfect game, striking out 11 batters with her only blemish being a home-run she gave up in the 4th inning. Taking a deep breath she winds up for what she hopes is her final pitch as the batter already has two strikes on her. Firing an uncharacteristic change-up, the batter expecting an Ashley Stamper fastball, swings earlier but somehow catches the top of the ball with the bat sending a speeding grounder towards short. The team's shortstop unprepared for the oncoming grounder, misjudges it as it speeds pass her outstretched glove heading into the outfield. Ashley puts both hands on top of her head in disbelief as the ball continues deep into the outfield. Their coach doesn't hold back his anger and frustration with his shortstop as the winning run crosses home plate from second base.

"WAY TO GO, YOU STUPID CYCLOPS! barked their coach, referring to the eyepatch she wears from a recent eye surgery.

The shortstop throws her mitt to the ground in anger as the opposing team celebrates their scrimmage win. Ashley's teammates jog off the field in defeat to congratulate each other on a well-fought, well-played game. Making her way off the field Ashley is intentionally shouldered from behind by a passing teammate.

"Nice pitch there, Stamper, were you trying to lose the game?" she said with an unfriendly tone in her voice.

Ashley looked over at her assailant with daggers in her eyes, not in the mood for criticism especially from a teammate. She knows she pitched a great game, but mistakes are going to happen, that's why this is preseason so everyone can work out all their kinks. If anyone deserved to be criticized it should be their coach, who hasn't done much of that since he has been with the team, mostly just there to babysit teenage girls as he works on his apparent drinking problem, his appearance alone would be subject to skepticism, not in the best shape for someone who is in the athletics field, looking more like an out of work truck driver, many of the girls wonder how he ever got the job in the first place. Joining the rest of the team Ashley stood by listening to more of his verbal degrading of his players.

"What are you stupid bitches celebrating for, you lost!" he yelled in anger.

"It's just a scrimmage," responded their shortstop.

"Coming from the one-eyed cunt that cost us the game," the coach said as he moved close enough to be face to face with the girl.

A tear ran down her one exposed eye as she listened to her coach's comments.

"You think I'm going to go through another season of this with you fuck-ing losers! If it weren't for Stamper and Stadtmiller, you baby ovens wouldn't stand a chance," he yelled.

"YOU'RE AN ASSHOLE!" the shortstop screamed having enough of the coach's unprofessional antics.

Before she could even back away, she felt the back of his hand come across her face knocking her to her knees. Stunned, the team looked on in silence as Ashley quickly ran over to her aid giving the coach an unflattering look. Everyone stood there motionless not knowing what to do, used to being mistreated verbally yet this was on a whole different level and they all knew this shouldn't have to be tolerated.

"You pathetic girls better come ready to play next week," the coach scowled in a deep tone. "Get out of my face." Their coach walked away as if nothing happened, being the heartless mean prick he has always been.

The team stayed to converse amongst themselves knowing they have to go through another season with that asshole. Gathering their things the girl proceeded towards the locker room. Before leaving, off in the distance, Ashley noticed a girl from the opposing team standing their holding up her cell phone, thinking nothing of it she headed to catch up with others. The girls showered and changed in complete silence, normally there was some sort of girl chatter going on, even playing for a jerk like him, but today was different, he crossed the line. The verbal abuse was bad enough, now physical abuse is starting. The girls knew they should say something to someone, but it would be their word against his and they can't confront him about it for fear of retaliation, so they all thought for now the best thing to do is deal with it and keep their mouth shut. Most of the girls have left as Ashley was finishing up, getting dressed she could hear the sound of one of the girls crying. Quickly gathering her things she headed off to investigate.

Walking through the locker room she can hear the sound of the tears getting louder so she knew she must be close. Turning down the furthest aisle of lockers, she sees the shortstop Brie sitting on a bench crying, quietly walking over she sits down beside her.

"You okay?" Ashley asked.

"I can't believe that bastard hit me," Brie responded. "Maybe I should just quit. I don't need this."

"You can't quit. If you quit he wins," remarked Ashley.

"Why do you care? You're his favorite," Brie mentions.

"I'm not his favorite, I don't think anyone is his favorite, he can't care less about any of us," responded Ashley. "We need you on this team."

"With the way I've been playing. Yeah, right, I doubt that," Brie proclaims.

"You're a good ballplayer who made a mistake, it could have happened to any of us and we understand about your eye. We know it can't be easy on you going through all those surgeries," assured Ashley.

Ashley continued to console Brie, even having a little bit of girl talk, at one point Brie actually cracked a small smile and laughed a little. She and the rest of the girls knew that Ashley was the leader of this team, most of them looked up to her whether they wanted to admit it or not. However, some girls on the team like Renee Stadtmiller who plays outfield and is arguably one of the best players on the team, sees Ashley as a threat more than anything else, accusing her of hogging the spotlight.

Ashley and Brie end their conversation with a hug, reassuring her that everything will be okay and that he will get what's coming to him. Brie gets her things together to leave, while walking away she turns to say thanks to Ashley, letting her know she will see her tomorrow in school. Ashley remained sitting on the bench for a moment, closing her eyes while taking a deep breath knowing of the upcoming affair about to take place. Grabbing her backpack she heads towards the coach's office, the walk there even though just a little ways down a hallway, feels like a journey of a thousand miles on her body. Her heart begins racing, her breathing becomes irregular, the silence in the locker room is almost deafening. Approaching his office she sees he is already standing against the doorway with his arms folded. She could smell the stench of alcohol on his breath from where she was standing, just the sight and smell of him was enough to make her puke. Verbally abusive, now physically abusive, dressed like he just rolled out of bed, always smelling of booze, she assumed he wasn't married, not because of his appearance, but there was never a ring on his finger, nothing much more was known about him, not that her or anyone else on the team cared to know. He looked at Ashley with a familiar gaze in his eyes, the way a man would look at a woman he was trying to seduce, complete with a haughty grin.

"You want to pitch first game?" he asked.

"Yes," Ashley answered swallowing uncomfortably.

Coach gestured with his head for her to enter his office, as she enters he looks around to make sure no one notices. Once the coast was clear he entered closing and locking the door behind him along with the blinds to cover the one large window to his office.

Ashley enters her car and begins crying heavily, slamming her hands against the steering wheel in disgust. She never used to cry after her interactions with coach, which isn't to say that she didn't hate every second of it, but this time it was different, just couldn't pin point what it was. Maybe it was because this time he finished inside her mouth, he would usually just ejaculate on the floor forcing her to clean it up, but this time he grabbed the back of her head and came in her mouth causing her to spit it, guessing he got a small thrill out of that. She knew what he was doing was wrong, an adult taking advantage of his position of power to get what he wants, but she would keep telling herself it's just oral sex, no big deal, anything to make sure that she gets to pitch every game. It is so important to her to pitch as much as she can so scouts can see her perform and if it meant performing a disgusting act to make sure that would happen, so be it, she will do whatever she has to help her eventually get out of this town. Beginning to compose herself, she wipes away the tears with her hand, preparing to leave her cell phone began ringing. Reaching in her very small purse to see who was calling, she saw the caller ID read STATE PENITENTIARY, with a disgusted look on her face she tosses her phone onto the passenger seat. Her mind processing a thousand different thoughts she sits back in her sit for a moment when a knock on her driver window startles her. Glancing out the window to see that it is her best friend Holley J, who also happens to be the catcher on the team. Not wanting her to see that she has been crying Ashley quickly wipes away the evidence before lowering her window.

"Hey," said Holley J. "What are you still doing here?"

"Hey, I just had to take care of something," answered Ashley. "What are you still doing here?"

"I forgot my history book for Mrs. Knox's class then I was engaged in some really boring conversations with some freshmen," jokes Holley J.

Ashley and Holley J have been friends since second grade, ever since Ashley spilled glue on Holley J's lap during an art project. They are your typical BBFs, they talk about everything with each other, from boys, to fashion, to

5

music etc. They can sometimes finish each other's sentences and sometimes very weirdly, know each other's thoughts. They don't keep secrets from each other or at least they never used to, the two girls know each other like the back of their hands, so keeping a secret from one another would be a hard task to accomplish, but in the back of Ashley's mind she knows she has been keeping a huge secret from Holley J for the past few years. One that she hopes she never finds out and never has to tell her about. Ashley loves Holley J like a sister and would do anything for her and keeping this secret from her kills her every day, but she knows it's for the best and will keep her out of harm's way. Hiding her emotions from Holley J is also a tough task for Ashley, for she can almost always tell if she is upset, mad or just not herself. It is times like this when Ashley must put in extra effort to hide how she is truly feeling.

"That was some shit today, huh?" Holley J asked.

"Yeah," Ashley answered.

"Do you think Brie will quit?" asked Holley J.

"I talked to her, but I don't know," responded Ashley.

"What are we going to do?" Holley J asked.

"I don't know," replied Ashley. "I really don't know."

"I just don't want to go through another season with his bullshit," Holley J stated. "Well, I got to go. I'll text you later."

Ashley acknowledges her leaving with a small friendly wave. Back to being alone again in her car, she goes to start it to leave when she hears her alert for a text message. Not being in the best of moods to want to talk to anyone, she reaches for her phone off the passenger seat. Wondering who it could be from, she looks to see that is from her boss Razz with a text reading, "I need you tonight?"

Ashley sat there shaking her head in disbelief knowing she is in no mood to work tonight, quickly sending a response, "Do I have a choice?"

As quickly as she sent her response, his follow-up text came back, "No, see you at 8."

Again in disgust she throws her phone back on the passenger seat, starts her car and leaves.

A woman aged about early 40s sits on a couch in her robe, her hair is tied in a ponytail, looks like it hasn't been washed yet today, even with her hair tied you can still notice a bunch of the split ends making an appearance. She reaches for a small glass a Jack Daniels sitting on the coffee table in front of her, the open bottle rests close by, a lit cigarette is held firmly in her other hand. She sits there deep in thought with a frustrated look on her face. Taking a drag from her cigarette, she hears the front being opened, focusing hard on the front entryway, she watches Ashley enter the house.

"So where have you been?" the woman asked being totally ignored. "I asked you a fucking question!"

"I told you I had a game today," responds Ashley.

The woman gets up off the couch in an aggravated manner, holding her drink in one hand and the cigarette in the other, making her way over to Ashley in the doorway. Ashley is all too familiar with what is about to transpire, it is like constant Déjà vu for her. The woman is Ashley's aunt, her Aunt Karen, she has been living with her since she was nine years old. Ashley was living with her grandmother for a while, but she passed away just before her ninth birthday. With a father who tragically died when she was just a baby and a mother who is in prison serving a life sentence for murder, her aunt was her only living relative left, who happens to be her mother's older sister. Life for Ashley has definitely not been easy living with her aunt, in fact she would say it is Hell, from the time she starting living there she has been treated more like a slave rather than a niece. Doing things and chores a paid maid would probably not want to do, watching different men come in and out of her aunt's life was not easy for her to deal with either. One dead beat after another coming over high or drunk, sometimes slapping her aunt around. Ashley never said anything because in a sad way she felt like she deserved it, there have been many times she watched her aunt do cocaine and other drugs right out in the open, not to mention what these men have done to Ashley. She has very vivid memories of numerous times she would be asleep in her bed only to be woken up to the feel of a man's hand slowly caressing her young thighs, working their way up between her legs. She would always act like she was still asleep at the time hoping that it would prompt them to just leave, but that wasn't the case on many occasions, horrifically Ashley had her first unintentional orgasm at just eleven years old. One of her worse memories of those nights happened about six years ago, lying in bed trying to fall asleep, blanked by the darkness in her room, she can hear the sound of arguing coming from downstairs between her Aunt and the man she was seeing at the time. She could never really hear what they were arguing about, their voices sounded muffled due to her bedroom door being shut and them being located down stair. Eventually the yelling would stop encasing the house in a weird type of silence, a silence so quiet that you almost want to hear something, anything to prove that you are not going deaf or crazy. That silence would be broken by the opening creek of Ashley's bedroom door, her bed being adjacent to the doorway saw the slight lighting from the hallway enter causing her to squint and slowly open her eyes . As her eyes adjusted to the unwanted break in the darkness, she sees a person's silhouette standing in the doorway knowing right away that it wasn't her aunt. First her aunt never checked on her and second the silhouette was much too big to be a woman. She would quickly close her eyes again trying to think good thoughts like maybe he was sent up here to check on her. Those thoughts were quickly debunked when she heard the first footstep entering her bedroom. The steps on the hardwood floor seemed to get louder as he drew closer to her bed. She kept her eyes closed tightly hoping to not alert him that she was still awake. The footsteps finally stopped indicating that he must now be standing over her, she can smell the combination of alcohol and smoke coming from his breath. Laying there on her side motionless, breathing normally even though her heart was racing. She began feeling the touch of his fingers raking through her hair as well as a small chill all over her body from the covers being pulled off her. Now she laid there in her nightgown with her legs exposed, his one hand started caressing her thigh as the other worked its way up her nightgown pulling down her underwear. Still remaining motionless she closed her eyes tighter, a lone tear escaped sliding down her face. Briefly everything stopped, now laying there with her underwear halfway down her legs. The sound of a belt being unbuckled and a zipper being unzipped resonated louder in a way that didn't seem normal, those sounds shouldn't be that loud or clear even in the dead silence of a bedroom. She felt the density of the bed change when he sat down beside her on the bed, her mind had a million different thoughts racing through her head of what could possibly be happening. That was interrupted by the penetrating feeling of two wet fingers entering her vagina causing more tears to come flowing out of her closed eyes as she felt the fingers moving around inside her. To make matters worse, the sound of skin rubbing on skin can now be heard. Not familiar with the new sound, Ashley cautiously opened her eyes to see what it was, sighting him sitting there masturbating. Ashley's young mind could not comprehend what was happening, she had never seen a male's genitals up until that point or did she care to. The act for which she was witnessing would permanently be burned into her memories, wanting to stop watching yet she couldn't look away. To see the male penis stiff like a pencil and to watch as he would rub and squeeze on it like a large tube a toothpaste was like nothing she had ever seen before. It all culminated with the exiting of the white fluid that came from the tip, squirting out like water from a water pistol. She couldn't watch anymore quickly closing her eyes again, time seemed to standstill for her at times like these, like it was never going to end, but as quickly as it started it was over. It almost seemed like a really bad nightmare, that she dreamt the whole thing even though she knew she didn't. Once again she would find herself in her dark bedroom alone, her face soaked with tears, being one of the many times in her young life that she cried herself to sleep. She never told anyone what was happening, her aunt would just call her a lair and probably punish her more, telling authority figures likes teachers or the police would just draw unwanted attention to her which she didn't want, not even Holley J knows about this, another secret she keeps from her best friend fearing if she knew it might change their relationship somehow. So for all these years she would just let it happen keeping it to herself, bottling up all her anger and emotions, becoming very good at that. She would make a great poker player, her poker face is unreadable, Holley J is the only person who sometimes can see through the mask she wears, but not always.

Ashley stood there in the doorway listening to her aunt rabble on like she always does, she couldn't tell which odor coming from her aunt was stronger, the smell of smoke or the smell of alcohol. Her aunt telling her what chores she still needed to do despite Ashley trying to explain to her that she had homework and she got called into work, her aunt taking another drag from her cigarette nods her head as she exhales the smoke.

"Then you better get your chores done quick, so you are not late for work. You have bills to pay," commanded her aunt.

Ashley not wanting to get into another argument with her, angrily grabbed her backpack and headed up to her room, slamming the door behind her. She goes sits on the edge of her bed where she becomes lost in her thoughts. Ashley's bedroom was your typical teenage girl's bedroom, just not very big. A single bed, a large vanity that doubled as her dresser against the opposite wall, a desk which sits under the only window in her room, stuffed animals which she likes to collect are scattered about lying on the carpeted floor. Most of them sit on a chest she has at the end of her bed, but she likes to scatter a few around the room wherever she can. Her closet which is a pretty good size considering the size of the room is full to the gills with clothes, shoes and other attire, everything from sneakers to hats that she sometimes like to wear. In another corner she has her painting easel where she does all of her paintings, when other teenage girls blanket their walls in posters of their favorite bands, singers, guys they have crushes on from TV or movies, Ashley's walls are covered in paintings that she did. She is a very talented artist, something her art teachers have been telling her all her life. The paintings on her walls are of all variety, from wilted flowers to the painting of a girls face with tears streaming down her cheeks, she paints based off how she feels, you will see paintings of anger, sadness, confusion, fear and from time to time a couple small paintings of happiness which come from her being able to paint and how she feels when she plays softball. Painting, like softball, is her escape from her life, it is like personal therapy, but without having to tell anyone her secrets, she just puts her thoughts and feelings into her paintings. For those seven innings that she pitches or the few hours she invests in a painting, it's the only time she feels happy and at peace, but she hasn't been able to paint to much in months thanks to her Aunt and her unreasonable demands. For as long as Ashley has lived with her she has never seen any of her paintings, mostly because she never goes in Ashley's room, she thinks it's because her aunt sees her room more like a cell than a bedroom and can give two shits about what she has or does in there, especially since everything in Ashley's room was bought by her own money, if it was up to her aunt she would just have a mattress lying on the floor. Holley J has never even seen her room either, due to her not allowed to have friends over, but Holley J knows about her talent in art, on a couple of occasions Ashley has helped Holley J with a couple art projects seeing they are in the same class, one of a few classes they have together, math and history being the other two. She pretty much has to always fend for herself, while her aunt sits back to reap the rewards of having her own personal servant. Doesn't even matter what day or time of year it is, it's always the same, Ashley's birthday is just another day to her aunt, no gifts, not even a Happy Birthday is thrown Ashley's way. Christmas is no different, her aunt not being the most festive type, a regular modern-day Grinch, won't even allow Ashley to put up a tree, but does expect gifts from Ashley, which she treats more like payments for letting her live there, consisting of a expense bottle of scotch, a few cartons of cigarettes and a gift card to her favorite clothing store to some shopping on Ashley's dime, also having to give the same on her Birthday. A teenage girl might feel slighted on days like that, but Ashley doesn't because she has Holley J to celebrate with, and every year they exchange girts on each other's Birthday and for Christmas, being all she really needs.

Sitting there on her bed wondering how she is going to get her chores done in time before she has to go to work, still also having to make something to eat. Looking over at her alarm clock to see that it is 6 o'clock, she has to be to work at 8 which gives her only two hours. Knowing nothing will get done with her just sitting there even though she is exhausted, that softball game took a lot out of her even for a scrimmage. Sucking it up like she always does, grabbed all her dirty laundry from her hamper placing it in the laundry basket she keeps in her room. Leaving to head towards her aunt's room, the sound of a motorcycle draws closer and closer, meaning only one thing, her aunt's current boyfriend Rick is about to make an appearance. You can add him to the list of guys her aunt has dated that Ashley does not care for, just as stupid and obnoxious as the rest of them, but Ashley is old enough now not to take any shit from them. Entering her aunt's room she can see out the one bedroom window that he has arrived, if it wasn't the noise from the bike that gave him away, the smell from the exhaust certainly would have. Her aunt's room definitely doesn't match her physical appearance, it's all neat and organized, simply because Ashley is the one who cleans it, it being one of her daily chores. Luckily it's a very basic bedroom, just a bed, a fairly large dresser which looks rather expensive, hand-carved stained wood and very heavy, Ashley should know, her and her aunt had to carry it up the stairs when she bought it a few years ago. What's in the dresser Ashley doesn't care to know, probably her drugs and stolen goods that Rick sometimes brings over for her to keep hidden. There are probably clothes in there too since there are 6 drawers to the thing. There is a small nightstand next to her bed occupied by an alarm clock and a cheap-looking small lamp. Ashley is not sure what the alarm clock is for since her aunt works all different times of the day and only part time. An old-looking wooden chair that sits in one corner of the room, which is next to the large closet that is over stuffed with her aunt's clothes, shoes and other miscellaneous items. A few pictures cover her walls but nothing of importance, her aunt definitely wasn't the sentimental type, never keeping pictures of family members or friends around the house, any pictures you see up are of just random things, not even any pictures of Ashley, she does know of one picture though, her aunt keeps it in her wallet, it's a picture of her aunt holding her when she was just a baby, she noticed it one time when she had to grab some money out of her aunt's purse. To this day Ashley doesn't know why she has it or even keeps that picture. The room walls are of a light cream color with a white ceiling, Ashley always said the color of her aunt's room was very depressing, no radio, but a 32" flat-screen TV which is mounted on the wall across from the end of her bed. She grabbed the clothes out of her aunt's hamper which is located by the bedroom door and left the room, walking down the hallway to the stairs she can already hear her aunt and Rick going at it. It's the same shit every time he comes over and she is sick of hearing their stupid arguments about nothing, remembering one time they were arguing about how cold drinking water should be. Heading down the stairs carrying the bushel full of clothes, telling by the ambient sound of their voices that they were in the kitchen, which she knew she had to pass through to get to the basement staircase where the washer and dryer were located. Ashley's plan was to just walk on through ignoring both of them, entering the kitchen walking at a brisk pace, trying not to make eye contact with either of them, she feels a pinch on her ass as she walks by the kitchen table where Rick just so happens to be sitting.

"Hey there, Fireball!" Rick said in his signature gravelly voice.

Ashley quickly slapped his hand away, knowing she doesn't have the strength of a boy her age, but she is old enough and strong enough now to hold her own against anyone who tries to be inappropriate with her and just like always her aunt was facing the other way, at the counter in her bathrobe preparing the lines of cocaine the two of them were about to enjoy. Her aunt didn't even try to look presentable even for her apparent boyfriend, her straggly hair still in a ponytail while wearing her famous old beat up slippers and no makeup. Shaking her head and continuing on through the kitchen she was hoping to make it without her aunt noticing her, not to be, as she heard her aunt's raspy voice pierce her ears like so many times before.

"Start paying attention when you are washing my shit, you fucking shrunk a couple of my shirts," barked her aunt.

Standing there listening to her aunt complain about shit like she always does, her free hand makes a fist so tight it actually started turning white wanting to hit her aunt so bad she could hardly contain herself. Many times she visualized herself throwing her aunt to the floor and punching her in the face until her skull caved in, emptying out years of being taken advantage of with never receiving even a single thank you, but she did what she always does, bottles up her anger and walks away heading down to the basement to finish the laundry.

"Man, that bitch has a nice dumper on her," remarks Rick.

"What'd you say?!" her aunt asked angrily.

"You heard me," said Rick watching her aunt walk over getting in his face.

"Say it again, Rick, say it to my face!" her aunt yelled.

"Oh, what's the matter, jealous of your own niece's ass?" Rick uttered pissing her off enough for her to throw his beer in his face.

Ashley was down in the very musty basement of the house. If there was room else where the washer and dryer wouldn't be down there, but since she is the one that does the laundry her aunt doesn't care that she has to go down in that grimy and smelly basement. Other than the washer and dryer the space was filled with old boxes of stuff covered in so much dust if a slight wind were to present itself all the dust would fill the air enough to impair your visibility. Placing the clothes in the washer in a frustrated manner, she can hear her aunt's and Rick's monotone voices arguing again through the closed basement door. She wanted to just stand there and scream at the top of her lungs, if she was alone in the house she probably would, but right now she needed to focus on getting her chores and homework done before she has to go to work.

Ashley drove into the back parking lot of the club where she works, parking in her usual spot right next to the dumpster. She likes parking there because it's close to the back door and no one else ever parks there. The rest of the parking spaces are full, normally from the other workers, it's fairly large for a back parking lot, can probably hold around twenty cars. Ashley has never seen it close to empty due to the fact that she only works at night. One of the surprising characteristics is that its paved, most back parking areas to buildings usually are dirt and gravel or even grass. It also has a sense of privacy from the two neighboring buildings thanks to the wooden fence and cement wall that divides the property which outlines the area, well lit from two corner light post. Ashley exits her car looking at the time on her cell phone which reads 8:15, one thing she prides herself on is to never be late, but sometimes when you are so overwhelmed you lose track of time, however she knows her boss won't be so understanding. Walking towards the back entrance she sees a lot of familiar cars occupying the parking spaces, except tonight she sees something that seems oddly out of place. A long black limo is parked towards the back of the lot long ways taking up four spaces. From her distance she can't really tell if anyone is in there, the light post is only illuminating a portion of the limo, besides it seems to her that the windows are tinted. It seemed stranger because most people with money or the high society types usually park in the front lot. Thinking nothing of it Ashley heads inside, greeted outside the door by one of the bouncers who is leaned up against the wall smoking. Inside she hurries past a lot of the commotion heading for an empty vanity putting her backpack down quickly starting to get ready hoping nobody notice her come in, until she heard the sound of a familiar voice.

"You're late, Show Horse," said the voice.

Ashley pauses putting her makeup on to view the reflection of her boss standing behind her.

"I know, sorry," Ashley responds, her boss creeps closer behind her placing both of his hands on her shoulders.

"When I say eight o'clock, I mean eight o'clock," said her boss.

"I know, it won't happen again," Ashley replied looking into his eyes through his reflection.

Her boss bends over kissing Ashley on the cheek whispering something in her ear.

"It better not," he whispers in her ear after kissing her on the cheek.

"So am I dancing tonight?" Ashley asks still looking at him through the mirror.

"Later, first I have an important client that is looking for some alone time and he specifically asked for you. He is in the limo that you might have noticed in back. Do whatever he wants. Do you understand? Whatever he wants," he said stroking her hair.

"I will," replied Ashley.

"Good girl," he whispers while placing another kiss on her cheek. "Don't disappoint me."

He leaves Ashley to get ready, sitting there for a moment staring at herself in the mirror oblivious to all the commotion happening behind her. Looking into a mirror she doesn't see a beautiful seventeen-year-old girl, instead she sees an ugly trapped vessel of anger and depression, if it weren't for her art and especially softball, she might have eaten a bullet a long time ago.

Trevor Acher, but everyone calls him Razz, the name of Ashley's employer, the owner and operator of the club she works at called Playmates, a very popular and well-known night/strip club in the city. Thirty-five-years old, standing 6 feet tall, medium build, covered in tattoos, short black hair and goatee, also has a long scar on his left cheek from a knife wound when he was a teenager. A master manipulator and business man known for getting people to do pretty much whatever he wants especially females, evidence in the fact that all the girls who work for him as strippers are also prostitutes on the side. He is able to keep it on the down low by having none of the sex done outside of his club, it's all done in house or on his club's property. The club provides a secret hidden basement filled with up to eight rooms where the girls can do their business unseen and in private. Each room is provided with all the necessities, a queen-size bed with just a fitted sheet and no headboard, a small leather couch, leather was chosen for being easiest to clean, a small cabinet placed near the bed filled with condoms, lube or any other product that might be needed. There are no windows in the room and it is completely soundproof, though each room has a hidden camera that the girls know about so he can keep an eye on his girls to make sure they are doing what they are supposed to, also to make sure the guys don't get physical with his girls, Razz will be the one to do that if need be. For a girl to work for him they must meet some requirements, they can't be over the age of thirty, they have to be very attractive, they can't be in any relationships, he wants no boyfriend drama, they must use the protection provided and be on birth control, if by a some small chance they happen to become pregnant they are forced to get abortions followed by the beating he will graciously distribute, as he says, he is not running a daycare here. They must complete mandatory weigh-ins to make sure they are not gaining any extra weight. He also has to be able to test out the goods, one requirement Ashley was able to bypass seeing that she was just fifteen years old when she started working for Razz. She is the youngest girl he has at just seventeen, all the other girls are in their twenties. Razz considers Ashley his golden goose, his cash cow, the object of every man's fantasies, sex with a teen-age girl, that is why she is his most expensive girl. A session with her can run a man between $500 -$1000 depending on who you are or the mood he happens to be in. Her high price tag usually attracts high-profile business men or political figures who are looking to cheat on their wives or just have a good time. Occasionally an uptight college kid will come in looking to blow some of his tuition money to have the night of his life. She is also one of his more popular dancers, one of a select few he lets dance alone. More money rains for Ashley when she has the spotlight then when two or three other girls occupy the stage, combine that with all the lap dances she provides and he sees nothing but dollar signs. Razz and Ashley's relationship is much different than with his other girls. He treats her like he would treat a Lamborghini, he wants to drive it hard, but take very good care of it. This has caused some jealousy from some of the other girls, especially the ones who find themselves on the wrong end of a backhand on occasion. Razz treats Ashley like he would his own daughter, being very strict and over protective, but hands out discipline when it is re-quired, fortunately he has never had to put his hands on Ashley yet, the same can't be said for the other girls. Razz rules over his girls with an iron fist, it is his way and he makes sure all the girls know that, including Ashley. Unlike her the other girls are nothing more than pets who must obey his ever command which include doing sexual favors for him when he wants no questions asked. Leaving is also not an option, they work for him until they get to old or he lets them go, otherwise they will suffer the consequences, his operation is prac-tically flawless, the girls keep their mouths shut and all his customers won't say nothing because they like his place and the services he provides, not to mention they would be scared to go to the cops for fear Razz would have them killed for ratting him out. The club isn't his only business venture, he's also the city's biggest dealer in cocaine and heroin which is also done right out of the club. That side of his business he keeps separate from the girls, on occasion some of the girls will do a few lines of coke with him when he is in the mood for a personal party, other than that he keeps the dealing portion as its own separate entity, all transactions are done right out of his office which is located in the back of the club accessible through a separate door leading to the back parking lot. Some nights hundreds of thousands of dollars pass through his club without a single patron having any idea what is going on. There have been nights when off-duty cops come in for a few lap dances while a fifty-thousand-dollar deal is going down right under their noses. He is very careful with all the moves he makes, the people he interacts with, he is all about the small details. Of course he has his fair share of goons on his payroll, but he likes to take care of transactions himself to skip through all the red tape. Highly intelligent and feared, he has been doing this long enough to know when something sounds legit or if something feels shady.   Ashley makes her way through the back parking lot towards the parked limo, the cool night breeze sends a chill through her body as she approaches. The all-black vehicle looks like a large shadow against the dim light that illuminates the nearby area, whoever is in this limo definitely doesn't want to be seen, why else would they ask for a session in the parking lot. These type of sessions are not uncommon, but most of the girls prefer that comforts of the rooms as opposed to the cramped confines of a car or truck, Ashley couldn't care either way so as long as she gets it done and the quicker the better. The closer she got to the limo the bigger it looked, this car could easily hold fifteen to twenty people, not much else could be made out about the car other than the hubcaps seemed expensive, there was a slight sparkle to them even in the blackness of the night. She assumed whoever was in there was sitting in the back, feeling a bit uneasy as she walked over to the back door hoping the guard standing outside was keeping an eye on her. A couple times she would look over her shoulder to see if she was being followed to make sure no one was going to jump out at her. Highly unlikely since Razz has cameras viewing the back parking lot, but female instincts make it a natural reaction. There was an unusual silence in the air, hearing only the sound of her heels clacking against the pavement. Now standing in front of the back door, she leaned in against the window to see if she could see anyone inside, but her earlier assumption turned out to be true as the window was tinted. Giving the window a quick couple knocks she waited patiently for a response. The slight sound of movement could suddenly be heard from inside when the power window began descending, Ashley leaned over to see if she could get a visual of who was inside, but there was still nothing but darkness filling her eyes. The black evaporated to the sudden entrance of light in the limo putting Ashley in view of a man most likely in his late fifties, wearing what looked like a custom made gray suit smoking a cigarette sitting by the opposite door, he looks over to see Ashley's long brown hair swaying in the light night breeze.

"I guess you are expecting me?" asked Ashley.

"Door is open," the man replied.

Ashley opens the door entering the limo seating herself next to the older gentleman, the once open window begins closing. The gentleman takes a drag from his cigarette blowing the smoke out the partially opened window besides him. She observes the inside with a sense of awe and a bit of nervousness, the awe came from what she saw available in the limo, a large refrigerated area with glass doors filled with enough liquor and booze to get a wedding party drunk, a nice-size flat-screen TV mounted from the ceiling, ending with the plenty of leather-covered sofa sitting outlining the inside, the nervousness coming from being alone in a confined space with a total stranger. Everything surrounding her screamed wealth, from his tailormade suit to the obtrusive gold ring on one of his fingers, to his green gator-skinned shoes.

"Do you smoke?" asked the man.

"No," she answers shaking her head.

"Does the smoke bother you?" the man asked taking another drag.

"I'm okay," she replied intently looking over the man.

He looked very well groomed, shaven face, slick back black hair with touches of gray evident. Ashley notices the little things about people, like how clean his ears were, a very handsome man for his age she thought. Holding his cigarette, the gentleman performed the same routine on Ashley, looking her up and down, sitting there wearing a black skirt with a red silk blouse, no bra visible and black heels, just the right amount of makeup to accentuate her features, her lip gloss covered lips glistened in the light, small hoop earrings dangled from her ears.

"You're very pretty," says the gentleman.

"Thank you," Ashley answers.

"I've seen you dance before," the gentleman said taking another drag from his cigarette.

"Are you a regular?" asked Ashley.

"You can say that," replies the gentleman.

"So what do you want to do?" she asked.

Ashley was never one to ask questions about a client's personal life or even engage in small talk, she would rather just get it over with and totally forget about them, never even getting their names.

"I'm not going to do anything," answers the gentleman looking into her sparkling green eyes, placing his hand on her knee. The touch of a man always triggers memories from her childhood, in her mind it became familiar, it became normal.

Flicking the finished cigarette out the window he starts unbuckling his pants exposing his erected penis, being no stranger to the situation Ashley knew exactly what he wanted. A small feeling of relief came over her as she would rather perform oral sex rather than actually sex, if it's possible to feel any relief from performing sexual acts on perfect stranger. Slowly lowering herself to her knees on the carpeted limo floor, centering herself between the man's legs she grabs hold of the penis placing it in her mouth. The gentleman sat back in his seat with his eyes closed as the euphoric sensation started traveling through his body, hearing the sound of what resembled a little girl sucking on a lollipop as he feels Ashley's lips and tongue massaging his quivering member, occasionally feeling her hand stroking up and down. A million different thoughts run through Ashley's mind every time she is in the middle of these private deeds, sad thing is she knows what she is doing is wrong, but to her it's her reality. As his pleasure intensifies, he grabs the hair on the back of her head, squeezing it as he starts to let out a few pleasurable moans, his breathing becomes slightly heavier as he closes in on climax. She can feel the pressure of his hand on the back of her head while he pushes her head down to get his penis deep inside her throat. Feeling the grip on her hair become tighter and tighter she knew that was the indications he is about to finish. Pushing hard down on her head the man releases a loud moan as he ejaculates in Ashley's mouth, hearing the gargling sound of her choking as saliva is spitted unintentionally. Relinquishing his grip on her hair she quickly gets off the floor wanting to open the door to spit out all the seaman in her mouth. Feeling disrespected, the man grabs her by the back of her head again, also underneath her chin forcing her to keep her mouth shut.

"You're not going to disrespect me like that. Swallow it!" said the gentleman angrily, feeling Ashley's best attempt to escape his grip. "SWALLOW IT!"

With no fight left in her she had no choice but to swallow causing her to gag and let out a large cough. Witnessing her comply with his demand, he opens the limo door pushing her out onto the pavement.

"Fucking whore," remarks the gentleman, notifying his driver who sat up front the whole time silently to take off.

The limo speeds off leaving Ashley there alone on the ground still coughing trying to spit out any access residue, staying there on her hands and knees feeling like some sort of animal, like a piece of gutter trash, grateful that Holley J can't see her like this. All she knew was she was alone again, a feeling that dominates her life more than she would like. The night air was becoming colder sending a chill through her body as she picked herself up off the ground, feeling goose bumps beginning to appear on her exposed legs and arms. Walking that lonely stroll back inside the club rubbing her arms to try to keep herself warm, all she can think about was she needed a drink to get that bad taste out of her mouth.

Twenty-three left, fifteen right, thirty-four left, the combination to Ashley's locker that she has had since her freshman year, taking her backpack off to empty out what she needs from inside and replacing it with contents from her locker that will be needed for her first class. The inside of her locker is rather bare compared to most of the other students at her school, one shelf inside is home to her books, while the one hook would support her jacket if she happened to be wearing one, this morning was rather warm with the sun freely shining without the worry of clouds blocking its view. She has a variety of stickers covering the inside of her locker door accompanied by a small mirror and one picture of her and Holley J together when they won the best pitcher catcher combo two seasons ago. Checking herself in the mirror her eyes seem a little red from her feeling a little fatigued due to having to work past midnight, requesting many times to Razz to not be called in during school nights only to be shot down every time, it's even more frustrating during softball season when she has to really manage her time the best she can to make sure she gets enough hours of sleep. Ashley dresses very casual for school compared to most of the other girls who are more about dressing in the latest styles or trends, she prefers to avoid all that, wearing jeans, a t-shirt and some converse low top sneakers, one reason is for comfort, but the main reason is she already wears all those Barbie type outfits for work and anything she can do to keep that side of her life separate from her everyday life she is going to do. She doesn't really carry a purse, it's mostly a small handbag equipped with a thin shoulder strap just big enough to hold her wallet, car keys, Chapstick and a hairbrush which she pulls out to perform a few strokes, her hair is always down except when she playing softball where it will be put it in a ponytail, it's her one feature that gets the most compliments from other girls. Many days she is asked what she uses in her hair or what's her secret, Holley J being her biggest fan of her locks, usually giving the same modest answer of, it's naturally like that. Girls who have been lucky enough to touch it would describe her hair as soft as cotton with the smell being even more flattering, different all the time depending on what scented shampoo she decides to use. Watching herself in the mirror she sees the reflection of a familiar face.

"Since when do you care how you look at school?" asked Holley J, opening her locker located right next to Ashley's.

"You're late," Ashley replied finishing up brushing her hair.

"When am I not?" Holley J remarked. "I texted you last night."

"I know, I got called into work and I didn't get out until after midnight," said Ashley.

"That sucks, you must be exhausted," Holley J remarked.

"I'll live," stated Ashley.

Holley J quickly got her things situated so the two of them can walk to first period together, simultaneously closing their locker doors they begin their walk to class. The hallways in John Franklin High School are made up of different colored lockers, Ashley's and Holley J's hallway color is purple which happens to be Ashley's favorite color, the different color scheme for the lockers was devised by the school to make it easier for students to find their locker if they knew what color hallway they were in. The before class commotion of the hallways is right on queue walking toward class, students standing around talking, they witness a few couples making out by the lockers, a male student speeds by them in the opposite direction on a skate board, these walks through the hallways area very humbling time for Ashley, looking at all the different kids that she sees almost every day, thinking how they all have pretty normal lives. They all come to school, hang out with their friends, they leave and do normal teenage behavior, have regular teenage jobs like working in a movie theater or a fast food restaurant, they go home to normal parents who scold and punish them when need be, things she will never get to experience, things most people would take for granted or consider normal. But what is normal, Ashley would always think to herself, to her normal is familiarity, her lifestyle would be frowned upon to most of the population, but to her its normal, she feels a weird unconventional comfort from it because its familiar, even though deep down she knows it isn't normal. The girls would have their regular pre-class conversation on their way to class, which mostly consisted of Holley J doing all the talking, she loved to gossip and loved a good rumor, if anything was going down at school or two students starting dating each other, Holley J would know about it, she is like the school journalist who finds out about everything, that's why a lot of her classmates gave her the nickname Scoop because she knows everything that is going on, even some of the faculty acquire her assistance on certain information. Today was no different, she had a large tidbit of information she couldn't wait to share, especially with Ashley.

"Guess what I just found out," Holley J said.

"What?" asked Ashley.

"Coach got called into Principal Davis' office this morning, I think he is there now," answered Holley J.

"Really? Do you know what for?" Ashley asked stopping dead in her tracks causing Holley J to do the same.

"That I don't know yet. Why, what's wrong?" Holley J replied.

Ashley stood there for a moment in deep in thought, wondering what was going down in the principal's office. What are they saying? Is her relationship with Coach going to be brought up? A nauseous feeling came over her worried everything will be put out in the open or worse, everything could be fabricated to look like she was the one making all the advances for her own personal gains. This was one of those times she hopes Holley J doesn't find out anything more, but she had to know what was going to be said in that office, letting it weigh on her conscience all day would be a form of mental torture she couldn't handle.

"I just remembered I forgot something in my locker. Can I just meet you in class?" Ashley asked.

"Yeah, sure, just hurry or you are going to be late," said Holley J.

"I will," Ashley replied heading back in the direction for which they came.

The principal's office was on the other side of the school, if she walked there she would never make it on time seeing there was only ten minutes till class. More thoughts of what could be going down in that office ran through her head motivating her to move faster until she realized she was in a full out run. The more she thought about it the faster she would go, even at her built-up speed, she can still see some of the faces of the remaining students looking at her wondering why someone would be running through the hallways that fast, but she didn't care, she had to know what was going on and what was being said. She couldn't get there fast enough, it felt like time had slowed down, it seemed like the faster she went the further away she was. Turning the last corner she accidently bumps into one of the janitors, apologizing for the mishap she continued on almost knocking over a wet floor sign that was just recently placed. The principal's office is now in her sights, she can feel the contents in her backpack jostling around inside from the impact of her running. Approaching the office she slows down to a fast walk, baring down on her destination the hallways appear more empty as students are entering their classes. Ashley knows she will never make it to class on time, which should be no big deal considering she is carrying a 98 average in first period math, not one to be late for class, but she knows Holley J will cover for her. From her distance she can see inside the office thanks to the large picture window facing the hallway, occupied by Principal Davis, Coach Mabbet and a man she doesn't recognize. Ashley veers out of view from the picture window hoping she won't be seen, planting herself by the closed office door which happens to be slightly ajar giving her a slight view of inside, also allowing her to hear most of what is being said. From her viewpoint Principal Davis is sitting at his desk, Coach Mabbet is sitting in a chair in front and the other man must be standing off to the side out of view. The sound of the first bell echoes throughout the hallways giving her the sense of privacy as now all the students should be in class. Quickly glancing in both directions to make sure no else is coming she sees the coast is clear allowing her to return to her original viewpoint, concentrating her focus on listening intently.

"So now let's get to the real reason I asked you here," stated Principal Davis as he pulls out his cell phone manipulating the device to play a video he has saved. Running the video he looks at Coach Mabbet with tense eyes, similar to a cop when interrogating a suspect they already know is guilty. "You want to explain this?" demanded Principal Davis showing the video.

"Where did you get that?" Coach Mabbet asked angrily, watching a video of him striking one of his players after their last scrimmage.

"You know what? I don't want to even hear your explanation. You're fired," Principal Davis stated with authority.

Still watching and listening, Ashley's eyes widened hearing her principal drop the bomb on her coach, she couldn't believe it, was this really happening? Coach Mabbet valiantly tried to save himself with no success, feeding Principal Davis everything from being stressed out, to his troubles with women, to admitting that he has a drinking problem which should be something you don't tell your boss when you are trying to save your job, Ashley couldn't help but feel a sense joy watching him dig his own grave. The situation escalate when Coach Mabbet stood from his chair in a fit of rage, yelling that it was bullshit and calling all us players a bunch of losers, not helping his situation, he takes a quick swipe with his hand across a portion of Principal's Davis' desk sending various contents flying across the office. Feeling a bit of uneasiness and threatened, Principal Davis quickly calls for security to escort Coach Mabbet out of the school, becoming Ashley's que to find another hiding spot before security arrived. One of the school's girls restrooms was nearby, conveniently right across the hallway adjacent to Principal Davis' office. Making a dash for the restroom Ashley positioned herself behind the door keeping slight visibility on the office hoping another female student doesn't need to use the facilities. A pair of the school's security guards come running into view entering Principal Davis' office, a few seconds later they come out escorting Coach Mabbet out of the school, surprisingly he was cooperative with the guards not doing anything that would cause a scene, he just walked with his escorts with his tail between his legs. Ashley closed the door blocking her view of the principal's office, standing there alone in the empty restroom, closing her eyes for a moment still can't believing what just happened. A very rare feeling of relief came over her, even flashing a small smile to herself knowing that a huge weight has been lifted off her shoulders. He was finally getting what he deserved, something that was long overdue, something she wishes was done a few years earlier when she was a freshman when his inappropriate behavior began towards her. She always blamed herself for letting it go on for as long as it did, if she just had the courage to say something to somebody this could have been taken care of a lot sooner, even preventing the loads of verbal and most recently the physical abuse he bestowed upon the team, but she had to pitch and pitch as often as she could, that was the only way she could get noticed, the only way she could earn a scholarship to a good college and continue to play the game she loved, also her ticket out of here, so she would do whatever it took, whatever she had to do to make that happen. Coach Mabbet sensed that about her and decided to use that in his perverted favor, it never felt right, she always felt awful and disgusting every time she did it, but she was stuck, she was in too far, felt like a fly caught in a spider web with no way out, if anyone found out about their little arrangement, especially the scouts, she could kiss her dreams of a scholarship goodbye. He did promise to keep things quiet which to his credit he did, but she had to make sure he didn't reveal anything to Principal Davis while he was in his office, not even thinking about what she would have done if he did. She didn't want to think about the ramifications if it all came out, all she knew was her already shitty life would have become even shitty, so when she watched Coach Mabbet being escorted out of school it felt like she just dodged a million bullets. In reality there would have never been any reason for him to mention anything, it probably would have just put him in more hot water so keeping his mouth shut was really his only option. Thinking about it now she was relieved one of her many nightmares is over, yet becoming mad at herself letting him walk right out of the school having taken advantage of her and getting away with it Scott free, couldn't help but stand there with a few tears trickling down her face.

Another female student enters the restroom forcing Ashley to quickly wipe away her face with her hand, she didn't recognize the girl who entered, probably an underclassman, however the girl must know who Ashley is as she politely says hi to her walking by. Trying to compose herself she realized there was nothing she could do now, her sexual offender will be long gone in a matter of minutes leaving her to convince herself at least that her tribulations with him are now over and she will hopefully never see him again, but she knows he deserves much worse than just being forgotten. Principal Davis sat at his desk trying to contemplate what just happened, he couldn't believe that someone at his school, under his authority, could pull something that despicable, questioning if he was losing his touch, always one to run a very tight ship. Richard Davis, late forties, medium height, medium build, still rocked a dark brown flattop crewcut from his days serving in the National Guard, did that for nearly fifteen years until a bad shoulder injury forced him to retire. Always wore jeans and a sports jacket with casual boots. Married for twenty years with two daughters, a junior and a freshman that attend a different high school for fear that he might show favoritism. Been the principal for the last fifteen years at John Franklin High School, winning various awards for keeping the school well maintained and getting the best out of his students academically, but this was the worst incident he has seen in his fifteen years at this school. Didn't even give it a second thought about firing him, that type of behavior will not be tolerated, had a student hit a teacher or any member of the facility they would have been instantly expelled no questions asked never regretting his decisions, he makes a choice and never looks back. It helped that the parents of the girl in the video were willing not to get the police involved as long as he was fired, a headache Principal was very much happy to avoid, the less attention brought to the situation the better, but now he finds himself with a dilemma, where is he going to find a coach for the girls softball team in such short notice, most of the school's athletic department is short staffed as it is. Luckily the girls softball team has always operated with just one coach, no assistant, no equipment manager, the coach has always taken care of those responsibilities. Since the girls season starts soon he finds his back against the wall to find a suitable replacement. His compatriot currently sharing his office with him, standing there with his arms folded, offered up a suggestion.

"You're going to have to talk to each girl on the team individually, find out if there was anything else going on that we don't know about, where we might have to get the police involved," says the man.

"I know, that's what worries me," replied Principal Davis. "But I will start that right away."

Kenneth Rivers, a member of the State Athletic Committee, similar to the state's school's superintendents, but for high school sports, mid-thirties, tall, slender black man, shaved head, no kids, not married, been a member of the committee for the past five years, ever since he left the army due to personal reasons. John Franklin High School just happens to be one of the schools in his jurisdiction, his job is to make sure that each school's athletic department is following standard protocol when dealing with their student athletes, fines to the school or suspensions to a particular athlete are handed out if schools fail to comply. Principal Davis unfortunately knows his school is on the wrong end of a fine, the committee should be lenient seeing how Principal Davis took care of the situation right away.

"That still leaves the other elephant in the room," Principal Davis said.

"A new coach," replies Kenneth.

"Season starts in a little over a week, where am I going to found one in time?" asked Principal Davis.

"I might be able to help you out with that," Kenneth answers. "An old friend of mine is staying around here, I was planning on giving him a visit. You might have heard of him, Jake Wheeler."

"Jake Wheeler, the ex-ballplayer?" Principal Davis asked.

"The same," responded Kenneth. "From what I found out he has been living with his brother. What I know he has been sitting around doing nothing for the past year. You need a coach, he needs a job, seems like the perfect scenario."

"Can I trust him?" asked Principal Davis.

"Not only was he a hell of a ballplayer, but a great teammate and a great motivator. If anyone can teach and get the best out of these girls it would be him," Kenneth assured.

"Okay, what do I got to lose, see if you can get him in here for a quick interview, then we can go from there," requested Principal Davis.

"Will do," said Kenneth. "But right now let's focus on you talking to the girls."

Chicken salad again, that's what Ashley is having for lunch along with her usual apple and carton of milk. Eating healthy as possible has always been a main focus for her, she notices a difference in her performance on the mound when she keeps her body well nourished, along with her workouts to keep in shape, at least three to four times a week if she has the time, lately she would be lucky to get one to two workouts in. Sitting in the same spot she always does, staring out at the abundance of students milling around the cafeteria either getting there food or interacting with other students. The school cafeteria is rather large, drawing a good crowd every lunch period seeing it's the school's only one. The standard picnic table style tables with benches won't be found at John Franklin High School, circular tables with plastic back chairs occupy the eating are, typical buffet style serving line with lunch staff is where the food is distributed. Ashley always thought the menu and food quality was always pretty good for being high school cafeteria food, mainly why she buys her lunch every day, also for the convenience, never really having time to put something together at home. Many large windows outline half of the room giving the students a chance to glance outside to see the sun shining on days like today, some tables can be found outside for students to access if they should choose to, but mostly the smokers inhabit those. Currently sitting alone waiting for her table mates to arrive, who include Holley J who happens to be late, which is unusual seeing she is normally the first one there. Waiting for her company to arrive her cell phone rings, lying on the table next to her lunch tray, glancing over to check the caller ID, it shows it's the State Penitentiary calling again, becoming annoyed she swipes to decline the call. As the commotion in the cafeteria builds, more students are up milling around looking for different tables to visit then there are those sitting and eating, two of her teammates who regularly eat lunch with her, approach the table.

"Sorry we're late," said one of the girls plopping her tray of food down on the table. "We just got done talking with Principal Davis in his office."

"About what?" asked Ashley.

"I'm sure you heard that Coach Mabbet got fired," stated the girl.

"Yeah, I'm aware," Ashley responded.

"Well, he is calling in all the girls on the team one by one to talk about what happened with Brie and to see if there is anything we needed to add," the girl said.

"Did you?" asked Ashley.

"I said probably the same thing that all of us are going to say. He was a verbally abusive asshole and what happened with Brie just confirmed it," answered the girl.

"I'm just happy he is gone," the second girl declared.

"That is why Holley J isn't here yet. She was going in when I left," said the girl. "You are probably going to be last."

"Why would you say that?" asked Ashley.

"'Cause you know, you are the star of the team, our captain, you can…," the girl was saying when she was interrupted by a familiar feminine voice.

"Yes, the star of the team," said a sarcastic Renee making an unwanted appearance at their table.

Renee Stadtmiller, senior, eighteen years old, long blonde hair, blue eyes, athletic build, slightly taller and bigger than Ashley, plays center field for the Lady Saints, her boyfriend is the quarterback of the varsity football team. Renee and Ashley have been teammates since freshman year where there has always been friction between the two of them, mainly caused by Renee's jealousy towards Ashley. If you were to ask her, she is the best player on the team and requires more attention, it also didn't help that Renee's boyfriend at one time had a thing for Ashley who graciously declined his advancements. In the back of her mind he has always wanted Ashley, but is just settling for her, knowing Ashley could probably take her boyfriend away from her at any time just adds more fuel to the fire, even though Ashley repeatedly has told her that she wants nothing to do with him. As a ballplayer Renee is very talented, some could argue that she is definitely the second best player on the team, great hitter and a dynamic glove, but not quite at Ashley's level, though feels like she is playing in the shadow of someone who in her mind is inferior.

"What would we ever do without the great Ashley Stamper," Renee remarked standing by their table eating an apple.

"What do you want?" Ashley asked giving her a fiery star, she has never wanted any beef with Renee, but the girl just knows how to push her buttons.

"Can't I just stop over and say hi to some of my fellow teammates?" Renee replied. "Just wondering which one of you losers ratted out the coach?"

"Nobody said anything. Supposedly a girl from Central made a video of the whole incident with Brie," the girl responded.

"Really," Renee said sarcastically.

"Why does it bother you anyway? He got what he deserved," the girl remarked.

"I always knew I was playing with a bunch of prisses. So he was hard on us, big deal, that's what good coaches do," informed Renee.

"So you condone what he did to Brie?" the girl asked.

"Some bitches got to learn," remarked Renee taking another bite of her apple.

"Why don't you just leave?" Ashley demanded hearing enough.

Ashley can feel the tension building at the table and the one thing she does not enjoy is confrontation, luckily their table is set in the corner of the cafeteria so it wouldn't be front and center if things did start to escalate. The ongoing commotion and sound of a hundred voices seem to mask their heated conversation.

"Now why would I want to leave?" Renee asked sarcastically. "You know it's funny, it seems to me that the only person he was never hard on was you, I wonder why that is. Haven't you girls ever wondered that? I will tell you why, because Ashley here is Miss Perfect, the queen bee, the coach's fucking pet."

The tension in Ashley's face became more visible as Renee spoke, it's like she enjoys seeing how far she can push someone until they push back.

"Why don't you leave her alone, Renee?" demanded the girl.

"Maybe you should just shut the fuck up! You need to hear this," scolded Renee. "You're not the only one trying to get a scholarship, but no one seems to notice me when I have to play in your oversized shadow. I am sick and tired of reading about you in the newspaper, Ashley Stamper arm of the Lady Saints. That's because little miss Ashley here always gets whatever she wants," Renee leans on the table with two fist towards Ashley. "Tell me, Stamper, how many times did you get down on your knees…."

Hearing those words being said by Renee sent a surge of electricity through Ashley's body, her brain was trying to calculate reasons why she would start to say something like that, is it possible she knows, if she did why wait till now to say something, how could she possibly know, Coach and her were always extremely careful or maybe she is just an evil bitch capable of accusing her of doing something so wrong and disgusting to get what she wants. Ashley assumed the latter even though she knows Renee is right, it sickened her even more to think about what she did, but there is nothing she could do about it now, the past is the past. Now it became even more crucial that her secret stay a secret, she didn't want to even think about what would happen if someone like Renee ever found out, but the words have been said and she wasn't going to stand for it, triggering something in her mind causing her to snap, standing up in frustration and anger grabbing her carton of milk throwing it in Renee's face.

"You're a fucking bitch, you know that!" Ashley remarked.

Renee stood there in shock with milk dripping from her face, grabs a napkin off the table to try to clean herself up. The other two girls were wiping up some access milk that splashed their way during the random incident. A nearby cafeteria monitor witnessed the episode, yelling in their direction to find out what was going on. Renee assured the person everything was fine, just a misunderstanding. During the minor spat no one noticed Holley J standing there by the table holding her tray of food wondering why Renee was wiping milk off her face and shirt.

"Okay, what did I miss?" asked Holley J.

"I didn't think you had it in you, Stamper. This isn't over," said Renee intentionally bumping into Holley J as she walked away.

"You know, I miss all this quality teammate time, good talk, Renee," said Holley J as Renee departed. "What the hell was all that about?" Holley J asked taking her normal seat next to Ashley, bummed she missed out on the entertainment.

"It was nothing," Ashley replied.

"It was just Renee being Renee," said one of the girls.

"Enough said," Holley J remarked. "Sorry I'm late, I just got out of my little meeting with Principal Davis. By the way, he said he wants to see you next after lunch."

"So what kind of things has he been asking?" Ashley asked.

"Just things like, what did you think of Coach Mabbet? Have you ever seen him do anything to anyone else like what is on that video?" said Holley J.

"Speaking of that video, we should send that girl from Central a thank-you card and a nice fruit basket."

It seemed like to Ashley the rest of the girls were telling Principal Davis everything that needed to be told allowing her to go in there and back up everything that has already been said, which in part will keep the focus off of her, she just wants to go in there answer his few questions and get out as quickly as possible, doing so will close the door on that particular chapter of her life regardless of it not ending the way she would have liked.

"That just brings us to our other problem," Ashley said. "We don't have a coach now and if we don't have a coach by rule we can't play and that can't happen."

"I'm sure Principal Davis is working on getting someone else," replied Holley J. "I don't want to forfeit the season either."

"Yeah, I hope," said Ashley.

This is unfamiliar territory for Ashley, sitting in the principal's office, never having gotten a good look at his office until now, everything was neat, organized and in its proper place. Very little clutter on his desk, just a computer, telephone and a picture of him, his wife and two daughters, who are very pretty Ashley thought, the same could be said for his wife. A few filing cabinets occupied a fair amount of space along with a long wooden table set under the window that viewed outside, which was home to a rather large fish tank with a couple dozen fish of various sizes swimming around, not something you see every day in a school principal's office, but very welcoming. It's probably there to help students relax when asked to appear before him, something she really doesn't have to worry about, her being an honors student and making it a priority to stay out of trouble. Last thing she needs is for the school to have to call her aunt, she gives two shits about her at home, why would she care about her at school, so she finds it best to avoid any potential high school hijinks that would require a call to a parent or guardian. Ashley has always liked Principal Davis, she finds him to be a good guy and a good principal. They never had a conversation together that lasted longer than thirty seconds, the typical hi or good morning or good game yesterday, but she noticed he always had a smile on his face which was very refreshing to her in her world. The man she saw from her earlier stakeout was also there, standing in the same position bringing her curiosity level even higher to who this man is. Patiently sitting there waiting for someone to break the ice, wondering how long this was going to take, she started to feel very uncomfortable even though she really had nothing to worry about, but this was the principal's office, a place no student wants to be in regardless of the situation, Ashley glanced over at the man who flashed her a gentle smile.

"Thanks for coming in, Ashley," said Principal Davis. "This should be quick. I'm sure you have heard the news about Coach Mabbet. So now I'm just talking to all the girls on the team individually to see if there is anything that you would want to add that we might have missed. By the way, this is Kenneth Rivers, he's a member of the high school athletic committee."

"It's nice to finally meet you, Ashley," said Kenneth reaching out to shake Ashley's hand. "I've seen you play before, you are a really great pitcher. Some college out there will be lucky to get you."

"Thanks," Ashley replies.

"So is there anything that you would like to add or tell us?" asked Principal Davis.

"No, only probably what you already know," Ashley answered.

"You sure? You're the captain of the team, he never did or said anything to you that you didn't like or think was inappropriate?" Principal Davis asked.

Ashley couldn't believe what she was hearing, it was almost like everyone knew, but didn't want to blatantly come out and say it. It was like they wanted her to admit it so it wouldn't seem like they were accusing her of anything. Even though she knows no one could have possibly known, the very mention of his name stirs up memories of all the interactions between him and her she would just like to forget it. In her mind the nightmare is over, but it seems like everyone wants her to keep reliving it making her a little irritated.

"I said NO!" Ashley yelled, catching herself raising her voice, quickly apologizing. "I'm sorry. Can I go now?"

"Yeah, you can go now. Thanks for coming in," Principal Davis responded.

Ashley quickly removed herself from her seat avoiding to make eye contact with either gentleman as she left the office. Kenneth stood there looking a bit confused, sensing there might be more to Ashley's story that she is willing to admit to.

"What do you think? You think she is hiding something?" Kenneth asked.

"Ashley is a good student, if she says there is nothing then I got to believe she means it," Principal Davis answers.

The look and smell of this place never seems to change, one of the many reasons why Ashley hates coming here. She checks in with the guard at the front desk letting him know who she is here to see, stating her name and relationship to the prisoner. Awaiting is the standard procedure of walking through the metal detectors where she never has an issue, mainly because she never brings anything in with her, no purse or cell phone, anything to make the process quicker. The State Penitentiary is not a place she cares to spend much of her time at, with its overabundance of guards standing around in almost every direction you look, not the most pleasant people to be around, especially the female ones. Getting a quick pass over with the wand from a female guard who Ashley can definitely tell is a lesbian, with her short crew cut hair and couple weird neck tattoos. The guard took a liking to her instructing her to remain still so she could perform an unnecessary pat down on her. Ashley knows what she is doing, making it even more obvious when she squeezes Ashley's ass with both hands, staring directly at her face cracking a small grin. Finished, the guard directed Ashley to the waiting area, walking away holding a hard stare at Miss Grabby Hands who delivered a quick wink in her direction. She wanted to run over there and punch her in the face for being totally inappropriate with her, it's bad enough she gets this treatment from guys on a nearly daily basis, now it has to come from females too, but she knew it wouldn't be worth it or smart especially since they are in a prison, deciding to just shake it off and take a seat in the waiting area to patiently wait for her name to be called. Sitting there staring out at all the other people who are waiting impassively, some not so much, a few began to raise their voice in frustration of the long wait. Being there sitting among other family members or friends of other prisoners got her to think about why she is even here, this is where her mother calls home, it's been her home for the last eleven years and quite possibly for the next fifty, all because her mother killed a man in cold blood over money with Ashley witnessing the whole thing, another of many bad memories she wish she could forget. Rarely does she come to visit her mother, in the eleven years she has been here Ashley showed her face a total of maybe ten times, not because she doesn't have time, but because she hates her mother, blaming her for everything that is wrong with her life, she basically left her when she decided to take another person's life for selfish and ridiculous reasons, accompanied by the fact her mother won't tell her anything about her father, something she has been trying to get out of her for years, all she knows it that he died in a freak accident when she was a baby. Ashley doesn't want to come here, her mother doesn't deserve a visit from her, but that doesn't stop her mother from calling all the time when she gets the opportunity. Her mother calls more now knowing Ashley is old enough to drive and would be able to bring herself. Before her grandmother, when she was living with her, would bring her even though her grandmother was not too fond of the idea, when she started living with her aunt the visits stopped even though Ashley knows her mother called on many occasions asking her aunt to bring her to see her. It has been almost a year since Ashley has been here, driven by some sense of obligation to come see her every once in a great while even though her mother doesn't deserve it. Sitting there among a sea of many angry and disappointed faces, she was able to self-reflect, wanting to believe she was better than all the inmates currently filling the cells, wanting to believe she was better than the lower end fabric of society that populated the waiting area, but Ashley felt no better and that feeling scared her. It terrified her that she might be on the path to end up like her mother just on the other side of the spectrum, where her mother was into drugs and hanging with the wrong crowd, Ashley is doing what she is doing and that is typically a road no one wants to see the end of. Being a better person than her mother is a small sample of the driving force that motivates her every day, these visits aren't even between mother and daughter anymore, it's more like her coming to spend time with a total stranger who just so happened to give birth to her. Their relationship is so broken Ashley won't even tell her about the sexual abuse she has endured most of her life and what she is currently doing for work. Been waiting nearly twenty minutes making Ashley grow impatient, having got homework and chores awaiting her when she gets home. Times like these she wishes she had her phone with her to keep herself occupied instead of sitting there trying to avoid eye contact with every random person who happens to be in her field of vision. Ashley does lock eyes with a little girl who happens to be sitting across from her playing with a small doll, probably no more than five years old, very cute with blonde hair and blue eyes, wearing jeans and a t-shirt that read "I heart mommy" on it, she looked like a doll herself. The man she was sitting next to Ashley assumed was her father, wearing a gray jump suit with boots, playing on his phone with his grease covered hands, her guess was he was an auto mechanic or something along those lines. The little girl looked at Ashley smiling giving her a small wave, Ashley recanted with a small wave and smile of her own. Looking at the little girl reminded her a lot of herself at that age while also bringing up the memories of that night. A five-year-old Ashley was playing in the living room on the coffee table with her favorite doll, completely oblivious to the lines of cocaine and pack of cigarettes on the same table, the TV nearby was playing *Dora the Explorer*, her favorite cartoon as a kid. Between her doll and her favorite TV show little Ashley was quite content. Staggering into the living room came her mother, her light brown hair tied back in a ponytail, wearing gray sweat pants with a white tank top, eyes red and bloodshot, body very skinny to the point many people began to think she was anorexic, her skin looking much more aged for someone who was just twenty-two years old. Sitting herself down on the sofa, she grabs a rolled up dollar bill lying conveniently on the coffee table where she precedes to snort a line of cocaine, grabbing a cigarette from the nearby pack immediately after, firing it up she lays back on the sofa blowing smoke into the air, looking over at young Ashley who is smiling playing with her doll. A cell phone begins to ring and vibrate wildly on the coffee table, grabbing it anxiously she flips it open to answer it, right away the conversation starts to get heated, continuously taking nervous drags from her cigarette while simultaneously bouncing her fidgety leg up and down. Standing up she begins pacing back and forth continuing to argue with the voice on the phone. Though Ashley was just five years old she can tell something wasn't right freezing herself in place watching her mother walk back and forth like a caged tiger leaving a trail of smoke in the process. The yelling with profanity being thrown over the phone indicated an escalating situation that started to frighten young Ashley, hugging her doll tight as a way to comfort herself. The verbal jousting finally ended with her mother throwing her phone across the living room, sitting back down on the sofa to do another line of coke, rubbing her hands over her face in frustration, again looking over at a scared young Ashley standing there hugging her doll.

"Are you okay, Mommy?" Ashley asked.

"I'm okay, baby, why don't you go play in your room while I make dinner," requested her mother.

Ashley obeyed running off to her bedroom, now alone Ashley's mother begins crying, pounding her fist on the coffee table in anger. Wiping her tears away with her hand, she promptly gets up walking over to the living room closet pulling out a large black duffel bag placing it on the coffee table, opening it up to get a glance of the many small bags of heroin inside.   It   has been about an hour since young Ashley was asked to go to her room, keeping herself occupied lying on her bed with her art pad and crayons drawing random pictures, her favorite doll still right beside her. The bedroom was very small with just enough room for a small bed and small dresser with a few toys sprinkled around on the floor. Nothing on the walls to be seen other than a few holes about the size of someone's fist in random places, young Ashley would sometimes hang her drawings on the walls until she got tired of looking at them. The small closet had no doors with just a few articles of clothing present that belonged to her mother, a few old beat up boxes took up the majority of the floor space, the only window in the room looked out to the dimly lit parking lot of the apartment complex, no drapes or anything on the window other than a few cob webs. Shag carpeting blanketed the floor with its brown and yellow marble color design, its texture stipulates that the carpet hasn't been changed in years with its spots of stiff shags and multiple stains visible everywhere. The enjoyment of her drawing was interrupted by the sound of an unfamiliar voice coming from the living room, a man's voice along with her mother's, despite having her bedroom door closed the voices could still be made out quite clearly benefits to the very small size of their two-bedroom apartment. Stopping what she was doing young Ashley grabbed her doll to stand by her bedroom door to eavesdrop, hearing their voices getting louder just like earlier when her mother was on the phone. Once again she bear hugged her doll tightly to comfort herself as the conversation beyond her bedroom door became more heated, hearing her mother repeat the phrase "Where's my money?" many times angrily.

"Mommy, are you okay?" yelled young Ashley through her bedroom door growing more nervous and scared, wanted to confirm her mother's safety.

"Yes, baby, Mommy is fine, just stay in your room," her mother replied.

The arguing continued convincing young Ashley that the situation was becoming more serious, hearing the deep tone of the male voice arguing with her mother, male voices are nothing new to her, having heard her fair share at her young age due to her mother having an abundance of male friends who come by the apartment from time to time, many nights she has heard her mother screaming from her bedroom. A glimmer of hope fell upon young Ashley when she heard the man yell, "I'm leaving," too young to understand what the argument was all about, but she knew the meaning of those words bringing the frightening situation to a hopeful conclusion, until she heard a sound very foreign to her young ears, a click. Curious to what it was, it compelled young Ashley to open her bedroom door to investigate, stepping out to stand in the short hallway leading to the living room. Her eyes captured a sight of her mother standing there breathing heavy feeling a bit fatigued from the arguing, overcome with much frustration and anger. Sweat upon her brow trickled down her cheeks as her eyes remain focused in front of her, both arms outstretched pointing a gun at the man standing there holding a black duffel bag with his other hand slightly raised to his side.

"Mommy, what are you doing?" asked young Ashley trying to process what is being played out before her.

"Baby, please, go back to your room. Everything is fine. Everything will be just fine, once I get my FUCKING MONEY!" yells her mother at the man.

She wanted to obey and trust her mother, but something kept her frozen in place unable to move, her eyes never left focus on her mother rendering the man invisible to her line of sight.

"You are not leaving here until I get my money," remarked her mother pointing the gun intently at her target, her hands getting sweaty, glancing over to see young Ashley still standing there hugging her doll. "Ashley, go back in your FUCKING ROOM!"

The man takes a step back still holding the duffel bag with one hand raised infuriating her mother even more, inducing her to out stretch her arms to try to raise the intimidation factor.

"You take one more step with that bag and I SWEAR TO FUCKING GOD!" she yells.

"Or else what, bitch," replied the man.

The next moments seem to happen in slow motion through young Ashley's eyes. A large bang rattled the eardrums to her ears, her eyes widened to the sight of the man's head snapping back due to the bullet entering his forehead, making its escape out the back splattering loads of blood and brain matter on the wall behind him causing his limp lifeless body to fall to the floor. The gun weakly falls from her mother's hands, smoke protruding from the barrel as it descends towards the floor, looking over at young Ashley with a face as pale as a ghost, frozen in place herself to what had just transpired, seeing her daughter still standing there with a couple tears streaming down her face as she tightly closes her eyes. Ashley wipes away the couple tears with her hand from her brief stroll down memory lane, hoping no one in the waiting area notices, it's heartbreaking when those are the types of memories she has of her mother. After about a half-hour wait her name is finally called, this time a male guard is there to escort her to the visiting room asking her a couple basic questions to which she replied no to all of them. Entering the visiting room, which is divided up by a large glass wall with small tables and chairs on each side with tall wooden dividers separating each table, prisoners communicate with their visitors through phone receivers located at each table conveniently hanging on the wooden divider. Every table is occupied except for one which is reserved for Ashley, the guard points to the open table where she promptly seats herself. She sits there staring at the emptiness on the other side of the glass waiting for her mother to make her appearance, finding it hard not to overhear the conversations going on either side of her. The overwhelming color of orange from the prison garb worn by her mother comes into view as she is being escorted by a guard to her seat, speaking something into her ear before backing away. The awkwardness started almost instantly as the two stared at each other through the glass as if each of them were looking at a total stranger. Ashley's mother picked up her phone receiver first waiting for Ashley to do the same, looking at her mother's face on the other side of the glass sends nothing but anger and sadness coursing through Ashley's body. Most people would be happy to see their mother after a long time apart, but the woman seated across from her is not her mother, maybe in a biological sense, but to her, her mother died that night she pulled that trigger. Based on first appearance Ashley notices that her mother looks awful, her long hair full of gray, more than a thirty-four-year old should have, skin looks leathery as if she was aging twice as fast as normal people, a far cry from what she use to look like back in the day, back in high school before she had Ashley. She was a knockout just like her daughter, Ashley has seen pictures of her mother before she was born, can hardly believe that it's the same two people, but bad decisions and drugs will do that to a person bringing her once fruitful life full of potential to a screeching halt. Getting tired of just staring at the woman on the other side of the glass, Ashley finally grabs her phone receiver with a distasteful attitude.

"I'm surprised to see you here," says her mother. "You never answer my calls. It's good to see you."

"Why do you keep calling me? What do you want?" Ashley asked.

"I just want to talk to you, hear your voice," her mother replied. "You never come to see me anymore."

"And that surprises you?" Ashley remarks.

"So how is school going? How's softball?" asked her mother.

"Please spare me the act that you give two shits about me," Ashley answered.

"I'm trying here, Ash, I lost a lot in my life, I don't want to lose my daughter too," her mother said.

"Yeah, right, all you ever cared about were those little white lines," Ashley replied.

"Did I ever say I was mother of the year? They don't put angels in here. I know I fucked up. I wouldn't be here if I didn't, but you're all I have left," her mother voiced.

"Don't make me out to be your scapegoat. You always knew what you were doing and why you were doing it," Ashley stated becoming a bit heated.

"You have no idea what I have been through," proclaimed her mother.

"What you've been through!" remarked Ashley shaking her head in disgust. "Do you know that I still have nightmares about that night?"

"That was never supposed to happen, you were never supposed to see that," her mother insisted.

"So if I didn't that would make it okay? What do you want? You want us to have a relationship? What kind of relationship could we have? What could you teach me? What could I learn from you? How to snort lines of coke and deal drugs," a pissed off Ashley ranted.

Ashley's mother sat there pitching her forehead with her free hand, listening to her daughter's tirade knowing every word of it is true. Ashley is old enough now to know what her mother did when she was younger, she was a drug addict and a small time dealer. What she sold and what she used were very different, her drug of choice was cocaine, yet she has been known to dabble a bit with crystal meth, but she was a dealer in crack and a bit of heroin, drugs that was normally very easy to sell if you know the right people. Most drug addicts will usually indulge in any drug they can get their hands on, but Ashley's mother thought it would be better business if she stayed away from what she was selling for fear she would use up her supply.

"What can I do to make things better between us?" her mother asked.

"Tell me about my father," demanded Ashley.

"You're bringing this up again? I told you before he died before you were born," her mother remarked.

"Can you tell me something about him? Can't you give me his name?" asked Ashley.

"I don't remember his name, alright! I don't even know who he was. It was a one-night stand, I got drunk at a party one night and there you have it. Is that what you wanted to hear? Sorry, but I didn't want you to know all that," explains her mother.

Hearing what her mother revealed struck her hard, she didn't think it was possible to feel any more disappointed with her life or her mother than she did at that moment. Always been told that she had a high school sweetheart and that she was on the pill because she was sexual active, but for some dumb luck she got pregnant anyway and tragedy struck when he was killed. The one thing about her mother she always felt sorry for, thinking how tough that must have been for her, now come to find out she is nothing more than a baby that was created in wedlock, by a couple of people too stupid to use a condom.

"I can't believe you," said Ashley with tears running down her face.

"I never wanted you to know that. I disappointed you enough in your life," her mother responded mirroring the tears dripping on the table below.

One of the guards standing on her mother's side came over to tell her that her time is almost up.

"You're right," stated Ashley. "You are a disappointment. Don't call me anymore."

Ashley angrily slams the phone receiver down back in place quickly leaving the visiting room much to the chagrin of her mother who was yelling for her.

The sunlight pierced through the lone basement window like a laser sent from the heavens hitting directly on a slumbering man's face, feeling the heat gradually increase ever second he leaves his exposed skid in the sunlight's path. Squinting from the uninvited light he slowly opens one eye to check the alarm clock located on the bed side end table. Not allowing his open eye to get fully focused, he can see the red digital numbers glowing close by which read 6 A.M. Thinking it is much too early to awaken and feeling much too lazy to get up to shut the blinds on the lone window, he quickly turns over to the opposite side with nothing more than a sheet covering up to his waist hoping to fall back asleep. The sizzling of bacon along with cracked eggs falling into a neighboring frying pan are the sounds currently filling the upstairs kitchen. A young woman standing over the stove keeping a watchful eye on the cooking bacon as she scrambles up the pan full of eggs, the nearby kitchen table is neatly set with plates, silverware and glasses, home to four chairs lining the circular table. Two of the chairs are occupied by twin eight-year-old girls antagonizing each other patiently waiting for their morning breakfast.

"Girls, go downstairs and wake up your uncle," requested the woman.

Cheering with excitement the twins dart out of their seats, heading down the basement steps located in the kitchen, making their way down the wooden steps stomping their shoe covered feet with each step. Both simultaneously reach the bottom, running over to the bed where their uncle lies sleeping, positioning themselves so they both can lean on the mattress with their arms, looking at his slumbering face. The girls continue to stare at their motionless uncle listening to him breathe in a peaceful manner waiting for some sort of reaction. Knowing he is being watched hearing the footsteps coming down the staircase combined with their uncontrollable giggling, the man opens one eye to see his two nieces staring at him.

"Mom sent us down here to wake you up because breakfast is almost ready," one of the girls said smiling.

"Okay," replied the man sitting up, hair a mess, upper body exposed, rubbing his hands on his face to wake himself up, the girls still standing there next to his bed. "I'm naked."

Erupting in a playful scream the girls run back up to the kitchen leaving the man sitting there in bed smiling, the girls reenter the kitchen parking themselves in their original seats reassuring their mother that the task was complete. Preparing their plates with scrambled eggs, bacon, and a slice of toast, another man enters the kitchen dressed in a nice gray suit with a white shirt and dark blue tie carrying a briefcase. Kissing the woman good morning while she gives the girls their breakfasts, he places his briefcase down on a nearby counter to pour himself a cup of fresh coffee, in sync the girls wish their father good morning, he responds walking over giving them both a kiss on the top of the head.

"Where's Jake?" asked the man.

"I sent the girls down to wake him up," the woman replied.

"He's up, he's just naked," one girl commented.

"So are you going to talk to him?" asked the woman pulling the man aside to have a private conversation away from the girls' earshot.

"Vic, we have been over this," replies the man.

"You don't think this whole situation has gone a little overboard?" she asked. "He was supposed to be here for a couple weeks, it has been close to a year."

"Give the guy a break, he has been through a lot," he responds.

"Well, I'm sorry, but that doesn't hide the fact that all he does all day is just sit around and watch baseball. He needs to stop feeling sorry for himself and start taking some responsibility. I mean for Christ sakes he almost got you and your friends killed in that car accident back in high school."

"That was an accident," he remarks.

"Jeff, you know I like Jake, I do, it's just enough is enough. I'm not saying you have to kick him out today, just nudge him in the right direction," Vicki requests.

"Okay, I will talk to him later, I promise," stated Jeff hearing the seriousness in his wife's voice.

"Thank you," she replies.

Glancing at his shiny gold watch realizing he is going to be late, Jeff kisses Vickie on the cheek, quickly leaving the kitchen telling the girls to have a good day at school as he leaves, the girls yell their goodbye. Staggering up the basement stairs wearing just a plain white t-shirt and plaid pajama bottoms with his hair still a mess is Jake entering the kitchen.

"Morning," says Jake walking over to pour himself a cup of coffee letting out a giant yawn.

"Your plate is on the table, eat it before it gets cold," Vickie remarks.

"Thank you," Jake responds. "Jeff leave already?"

"Yeah, you just missed him," answered Vicki.

Jake brings his coffee over to the table to join the girls just finishing up their breakfast, a bus horn sounds from the front of the house indicating their arrival for the girls, quickly grabbing their backpacks which were hanging on the back of their chairs, saying goodbye to their uncle while kissing their mother as they head out the front door.

"I'm going to help out at the flower shop today, so I will probably just pick up the girls after school," said Vickie. "What are your plans for today?"

"Right now I'm just going to finish these delicious eggs," Jake jokes.

"Great," Vicki replies sarcastically.

Kenneth follows the direction of his GPS inside his all black SUV, instructing him to make a left at the next street. He begins to admire this area of town, an area he hasn't had the pleasure of ever seeing. The streets of this suburban part of town are home to many well to do families and individuals, mainly doctors and lawyers call these structures home, housing tracks that are made up of newer homes, either recently built or only a few years old. Kenneth is taken back by how beautiful all the houses are, how he would have a hard time picking out one of them for himself if he was able to afford any of these residents, he would have to work five jobs to pay the mortgage on one of these beauties. Driving down the street to his apparent destination he makes it to the entered address, 1225 Rosewood Dr., which happens to be located on a cul-de-sac, though there is plenty of space in the driveway he decides to park in the street feeling it is the good mannered thing to do, the two vehicles in the driveway suggested somebody was home. Getting out of his vehicle he envies at the sight of the house as a whole, from the architecture, to the perfectly mowed lawn and landscaping, every bush trimmed and shaped perfectly to not a blade of grass out of place, everything looked pristine. Walking up the stone walkway to the front door, he felt like a stranger in a strange land, never been inside a house like this before, especially the house of a lawyer which is what Jake's brother Jeff does, a civil defense lawyer and a damn good one from what he has been told. Finding himself standing face to face with

43

the front wooden double doors, he rings the doorbell which is rather loud playing a fairly odd tone. Patiently waiting for a response he continues to marvel at his surroundings, on the cement made porch area for which he now stands, he sees a nice sized stained wooden table complete with two matching chairs set off to the side under the large picture window. Hearing the locks being undone Kenneth watches the door open up bringing him face to face with Vickie, only the screen door now is between them.

"Hi, can I help you?" she asked.

"Hi, um, I was told that Jake Wheeler lives here, just wondering if he happens to be home?" Kenneth asked.

"Oh, you're looking for Jake. Are you a cop? What has he done?" she responds in a sarcastic tone.

"No, no, nothing that like. I'm just an old friend of his, I would just like to talk to him if I could," replies Kenneth flashing a large friendly grin.

"Yeah, he is here. Come in, I'll go get him," Vicki said.

"Thank you," he responds. "You have a lovely home, by the way."

"Thanks," replied Vicki.

Kenneth enters the foyer of the house continuing to soak in the visual feast that has come bestowed upon his eyes, from what he can see from where he is standing, the inside looks just as good, if not better than the outside. Just above him hangs a large crystal chandelier that doesn't seem out of place to the house's high ceilings. In either direction leads to a couple of large rooms, one he would guess would be the living room seeing there is a couple couches with a love seat, a large flat-screen TV mounted on a wall that hangs above a large brick fireplace, a high staircase and hallway occupy his frontal view, the inside was just as flawless as the outside, he could probably rub his finger across any surface and not find a single speck of dust, even the hardwood flooring everywhere looked shiny and well maintained with the occasional throw rugs scattered throughout. Someone was coming down the main hallway, the lighting produced shadows that covered the person's face as they approached, but the body shape was definitely that of a male.

"Oh my God, is that Kenny Rivers!?" Jake said excitingly.

"Jake Wheeler, how are you doing, buddy?" replied Kenneth as they both embraced in a hug in the front foyer.

"Jesus, how long has it been? You look good," commented Jake.

"A long time," Kenneth answered. "Thanks, so do you."

"What brings you here?" Jake asked.

"I was wondering if we can talk?" asked Kenneth.

"Uh, yeah, sure, this is kind of unexpected, but let's go sit in the living room," Jake suggested.

The two men seated in the living room, Jake seated on one couch, Kenneth on the other, catching up, reminiscing about old times, mainly revisiting their old high school baseball playing days, sharing some laughs, a couple cups of coffee rested close by on the wooden and glass coffee table centered between the couches.

"Those were the days," said Kenneth.

"Yes, they were," replied Jake. "But something tells me you are not here to just catch up."

"You're right. I heard about your knees and what happened with your career, I just want to start by saying I'm sorry," Kenneth stated.

"Thanks, but I'm hoping to get another shot," remarked Jake.

"That's just it, what if you don't?" asked Ken. "Jake, you're a great ballplayer, there is no doubt about that, but maybe it's time to realize that that window is closing."

"I don't think so, I just have to be patient," Jake remarks.

"Patient, huh, let me ask something, how many teams have contacted you in the past few year?" asked Kenneth watching Jake break eye contact giving him the answer without him saying anything. "That's what I thought. Jake, you can't sit around here every day trying to chase something that can never be caught. You're still a young man who has a lot to offer, which brings me to the real reason why I am here. I have a job opportunity for you."

"A job, what kind of job?" asked Jake.

"It's a coaching position, over at John Franklin High School," Kenneth informs.

"They're looking for a baseball coach?" Jake asked.

"Not quite, it's actually girls softball," Kenneth replies.

"Girls softball, are you kidding me?" remarks Jake standing up from his seat laughing, walking to the back of the couch in disbelief.

"Jake, girls softball is no different than baseball, it's practically the same game. The school had to let their old coach go due to reasons that I'm not allowed to discuss, which puts the school behind the eight ball because their season starts next week," Kenneth mentions watching Jake trying to process all the surprising information, knowing he completely blindsided his old friend he goes to stand beside him. "I know this came out of nowhere, but I think this would be a great opportunity for you, a chance to teach your knowledge and skills to these girls. If it makes you feeling any better, you will have access to one of the best female pitchers in the country."

"I don't know," said Jake. "You know girls are a completely different animal."

"The way I see it, you have two choices, you can continue to hang around here hoping a team needs a thirty-something ballplayer with two bad knees or you can start a new career helping young ballplayers chase their dreams," Kenneth preaches, pulling out his wallet to grab one of his business cards. "Here's my card, it explains what I do now, I'm part of the high school athletic committee, my cell number is on it. School is going to need an answer by Wednesday. I'll let myself out. Thanks for the coffee and it was really good to see you." Kenneth leaves, Jake stands there holding his business card briefly thinking about the offer. Coaching has never crossed his mind, especially girls softball, he always saw there was a fine line between the two, a person can either be a good player or a good coach, very seldom can they be both. There have been many professional athletes that went on to coaching careers after their playing days were over, but the results were varied, Hall of Fame caliber players usually made mediocre coaches while average players mainly went on to be a better coach than player. Jake was afraid he would be the former, was always considered a great player, becoming a coach even if it's to a bunch of teenage girls might damage his already small legacy particularly he were to crash and burn. Kenneth was right, though, nobody's knocking on his door for his once generational talent and he can't keep convincing himself that there will be.

During his private moment of contemplating Vickie appeared, having been standing in the other room eavesdropping, something she would admit she is not proud of, but she couldn't help herself, playing it off walking over to Jake.

"What was that all about?" she asked.

"To be honest, something I never really thought about," replied Jake.

Jake is sitting on his small couch down in his room located in the house's finished basement which containing all the necessities one would need for a nice living area, complete with a bedroom and living room area, a full bathroom with stand-in shower, it's like a small studio apartment down there minus a kitchen, drywall, carpeting and a drop ceiling make up the enclosure. He sits watching old videos from his playing days, a time in his life when things were much simpler for him, he was doing what he loved and to him made him feel invincible. Totally admiring his greatness on the screen, watching the old footage though sometimes leaves him feeling depressed thinking about what could have been. Always knew he was going to be a baseball player, the game came easy to him, sports in general did, was the athlete of the family while his brother Jeff was always the brains. Other sports were fun to him, but it was baseball that he had the most passion for, probably because it was his best sport and he enjoyed it the most. He was literally the best player on ever team he played on from little league on up, great hitter, great fielder, shortstop was his position of choice, but he could pretty much play anywhere and be the starter at the position, many scouts were calling him the Mickey Mantle of his generation. Throughout high school scouts would talk to him after almost every game, had offers from three division one schools which included Florida St., West Virginia and Kentucky, ending up committing to Florida St. It seemed his life was on a path which had no forks in the road, this was his destiny, his calling, but sometimes adolescent mistakes can derail you off your familiar path. One night in high school he, his brother and a couple a friends were out partying on Jeff's college campus, they were all drinking, driving around acting like fools like most teenagers do. Their fun quickly turned into a nightmare when they lost control of the car running another car off the road and then crashing into a tree, no one was hurt other than a few cuts and scrapes, except for Jake who suffered a couple banged up knees. The bruising on his knees would eventually heal which would have not hindered him from playing, but the damage was already done. Once the word got out about the accident Florida St. stripped him of his scholarship due to recklessness, drinking and endangering the lives of others, his whole life seemed to change in an instant, the once single path he was once on now was being covered up leaving him without a direction, but he never gave up, knowing he was too talented not to be playing, eventually trying out for a local farm team once all the legal issues, community service and probation were now behind him, a team which he would easily make. Now on a different path from the one he started on he knew his ultimate goal was still in reach, to play major league baseball, which one day came to fruition when he was called up to play for the Cleveland Indians. Despite the obstacles he made for himself he made his dream a reality, but his conquest would be short lived, just fifty games into his major league career he blew out his left knee, an ACL tear that would lay him up for almost a year. Once given the okay by the doctors to start playing again he was back on the field for the next season. Yet that same dark cloud was hovering over him again making the unimaginable happen, blowing out his other knee running into the catcher scoring the winning run in the second game of a double header. This time it was an ACL, MCL tear and doctors were skeptical this time if he would fully recover putting his baseball career in jeopardy. The nightmare would become his new reality as many setbacks during the recovery process including multiple surgeries kept him away from the game much longer than he thought and wanted. Not wanting to wait around for Jake to make a full recovery, which at that point looked bleak, the Indians released him. The farm team was not interested anymore as they saw him as a liability, even though doctors told him he would never play again, he tried contacting other farm teams in other cities, but the news of his knees spread like wildfire with no one willing to take the risk. Having to come to the realization that his career was over, Jake became depressed and started drinking hoping that it would ease the pain of him becoming another one of those great athletes who career and potential were cut short due to catastrophic injuries. As his depression deepened, his drinking intensified, feeling like he had nothing to offer anymore he took every cent he ever made playing baseball to Vegas for a fun filled weekend bender. Hoping to have no one notice him, he wore a lot of hoodies and baseball caps along with sunglasses. Not being in the right mind set for gambling, mixed with the continuous drinking and the few hookers, his weekend of fun proved to be financially costly losing ever dollar to his name. Unable to buy a plane ticket or even a bus pass, he had no choice but to call his parents for help. His return home was met with mixed emotions as he was greeted to an intervention waiting for him at his parents' house. Knowing his life was starting to spiral out of control this was the next logical step. Resisting at first, he finally surrendered to listen to what the group had to say, a group which included his parents, his brother and Vickie. After a long emotional talking to, they finally convinced him to enter rehab and to start seeing a therapist. Jake did his best to live off the grid during this rough stage of his life, the last thing he wanted was for the public to know what he had become which could damage his small but valued legacy, so he did his best to remain isolated, living off the grid for as long as he can until he could get his head back on straight. Rather than risking him being alone he stayed in the house he grew up in for a while until the annoyance of people around town asking to many questions grew to be too much, leading to Jake's brother offering him to stay with him for a few weeks to figure out what he was going to do next, a perfect place for him to stay on the down low, which he gladly accepted and where he has been ever since. A very difficult time in high school left an emotional scar on Jake. He had a girlfriend that he dated his junior and senior year, the relationship was really good for the most part for a high school couple. As Jake's baseball career was taking off it started to leave a void in his relationship, spending more time practicing and at the batting cages it started to drive a wedge between them. They would constantly fight all the time, even to the point where they separated for a few months. When they finally rekindled she wanted to know where she stood in his life asking very bluntly who was more important, her or baseball. Being a realist Jake answered the question being brutally honest with her, baseball was his future and even though he did love her and enjoyed their time together, he couldn't jeopardize his ultimate goal in life, he said it would be best if they just went their separate ways. Hearing those words being uttered broke her heart in more ways than she could handle, becoming furious in a way that he had never seen in her before, yelling things like, you're making a mistake and you're going to regret this, he definitely didn't want to hurt her, but he knew it was for the best. The timing though couldn't have been worse for her especially with the news she was about to bestow upon him. With tears in her eyes she stood before him and spoke the two words no eighteen year old boy wants to hear, I'm pregnant. A look of disbelief and shock appeared on Jake's face as she broke the news, so many emotions were running through him he thought his brain was going to overheat, this was the worst possible thing that could happen especially now since he just ended things. Still very upset with his decision to call it quits, she just walked away saying, I hope you are happy now, not even giving him a chance to rebuttal or state his case in what they should do. He was left standing there like a lost soul who had no answers and didn't know what he was going to do, for weeks after that day he tried to get a hold of her, leaving messages with her parents to call him back, but no luck. Being apart granted him a lot of time to think, he knew this would put a huge damper on his plans, but he knew he wanted to do the right thing. Whatever it took he would help her support the baby the best he could even when he was away at school. He would get a part-time job somewhere when he wasn't practicing and send her most of the money. A couple months went by and he still couldn't get in contact with her until one day she contacted him, a sense of relief came over him that he could now finally tell her his plan to be there and help her out, but this phone conversation was nothing like he expected. She did most of the talking, saying that her and her family were moving out of town for a while due to her father's work and that he would not have to worry about the baby because she was going to get an abortion, stating that she can't have a baby with someone who doesn't want to be with her. Unable to get two words in, he would continue to listen to her release all this pent up anger she had toward him, ending with her saying goodbye and hanging up the phone never to be seen or heard from again. Jake stood there with the phone receiver next to his ear listening to the dial tone trying to process everything he just heard, so many emotions came over him at one time, part of him felt a sense of joy, he now didn't have to worry about altering his plans, now he can keep his focus on his original goal, while another part of him felt an overwhelming sense of sadness, the once baby he was told about was never going to be born and the girl who was going to be the mother he would never see again, it took a while for him to get over the situation and give himself clarity even though to this day he knows a part of himself died during that phone conversation.

Still watching old videos of his playing days, Jake hears the sound of footsteps coming down the basement stairs, not wanting anyone to see him still living in the past he quickly turns off the TV with his remote, sits back waiting for the mystery person to make their entrance. Jeff came into sight, could have also knew it was him picking up the scent of his cologne, saw his brother sitting on his couch looking like a man deep in thought. Jeff walked over seating himself next to Jake, could tell by looking at his face that he had a lot on his mind. Jeff knows that the only reason he is down here is because he promised Vickie, but it's been a while since the two of them had a real heart to heart talk so this was as good an opportunity as any, though he can sense the conversation will probably veer in another direction to what he initially thought.

"Hey," said Jeff.

"I know why you're down here," replies Jake. "Vickie sent you down here to find out when I am going to leave."

"Jake, you know you can stay here as long as you want," Jeff assured.

"What about Vickie?" asked Jake.

"I can handle her," Jeff remarked, being more concerned about what was on his brother's mind. "You seem like you have something on your mind."

"You remember Kenny Rivers?" asked Jake.

"The skinny black kid that used to playball with you in high school?" Jeff replied.

"Yup, he came by here today," said Jake.

"Vickie mentioned something about someone coming here to see you. What did he want?" Jeff asked.

"Believe it or not, he came here to offer me a job, coaching girls softball," said Jake.

"Really, well, that's great, right? You would make a great coach," Jeff remarked.

"Yeah, but girls softball?" asked Jake.

"Girls softball is no different than baseball, really," proclaimed Jeff.

Jake and his brother had a long conversation, about the job offer, the living situation, to life in general. Even though they were very different people they were pretty close as brothers, growing up they always did things together even when they had their different group of friends. Their parents seem to divide their attention between the two of them, Jake's father gave him more attention because he was the athlete and Jeff's mother gave him more attention because he was the intellectual one, but no matter what they always had each other's back when needed and could always confined in one another, trusting the other to keep a secret if need be. One secret they share is the main reason Jeff would never ask his brother to leave, a secret no one else knows about, not even their parents, he owes Jake everything, feeling like he will spend the rest of his life paying him back, a secret Vickie doesn't even know about, If she did know she would definitely not have a problem with him staying here, but Jake asked Jeff not to tell her fearing that she might look at her husband differently. Their conversation deepened, especially about the job offer, Jeff would never tell his brother what to do, but he knows that this job would be good for him both mentally and spiritually, it would once again give him structure in his life, also in a way keep him close to the game he loves, no matter what happens Jeff wasn't going to leave that basement until he convinced his brother to take that job.

"So what do you think I should do?" Jake asked.

"I think you already know my answer to that," Jeff replied. "You have always done the right thing, I don't see any reason why that should change now. Dinner is in ten minutes."

Jeff gets up to leave to let his brother think, once again Jake found himself alone with his thoughts. His brother was right, he has always done the right thing, one of the many perks of being someone with a conscience. Continuing to sit there just staring at the blank TV screen wondering what kind of coach he could possibly be, especially to girls, boys he obviously can relate to, but girls are a completely different animal, they are moody, emotional creatures that have to be handled in a much more delicate manner, not to mention all the flak you can get yourself into if you happen to say or do the wrong things with them, but deep down he wasn't going to let situational flaws scare him away from a new challenge. He started thinking maybe this is supposed to be his new journey, a way to still be part of the game without having to step foot onto the field, the more he thought about it the more he knew he had to do this, it could give his life meaning and structure once again something that has been missing for very long time. Vickie's voice filtered down into the basement letting him know dinner was ready, pulled Ken's business card out of his pocket staring at it for a moment knowing that once he dialed those numbers there was no turning back. Grabbing his cell phone off his coffee table he starts dialing Kenneth's number, waiting for him to answer a small feeling of accomplishment came over him, finally taking the first step to changing his life. A familiar voice answers with a hello on the other end, where Jake simply responds, "I'll do it."

Ashley is sitting at one of the vanities in the dressing room area of the club doing her hair and makeup. One other girl is back there doing the same sitting close by, neither one of them acknowledges the other, Ashley doesn't have much of a relationship with the other girls, preferring not to communicate with any of them, she rather just do her job and leave having enough of her own bullshit to deal with, choosing to rather not hear about any of the other girls problems that she knows they all have, if they didn't they wouldn't be doing what they are doing. There is one girl though that Ashley has grown kind of friendly with, an older girl probably in her late twenties named Nikki, but she is known at the club as Nikki six. Rumor has it she got that name because she supposedly once gave six dudes a blow job at the same time. Tonight happens to be her night off, but she happens to be the only girl Ashley actually talks to, looking past her questionable behavior at times Ashley knows she has a kind heart and has always been kind of a friend to her since she has been working at the club. Finishing up, Razz approaches her from behind giving her a kiss on the cheek.

"Looking good, Show Horse," remarks Razz caressing both sides of her face with his thumbs. "Got someone who is looking for some alone time with you. He is downstairs in room two. Show him a good time for me," he said holding up a bunch of Ashley's hair under his nose to get a quick smell of her scent before walking away leaving her to finish.

"How often do you suck his dick to get that type of treatment?" remarked the girl seated beside her in a jealous tone.

Ashley is alone in the room with her client, a young college kid, not particularly attractive in her eyes but close to her age, sitting in the chair offered in the room with her sitting on top having intercourse. Shirt still on, pants around his ankles while she is completely naked. She prefers they left on as much clothing as possible to deter her from having to look at out of shape, hairy bodies, occasionally she will get a client with a nice physique to look at but not very often. Squeezing her breasts as she bounces up and down upon him, here and there he would caress her whole body with his hands feeling her soft, unblemished skin, very much into it while she is just doing what she can to just get him to finish seeing that he wasn't very well endowed, there was a lot of room left in the condom and she could hardly feel anything. Removing his hands from her breast he grabs her face to pull her in for a kiss which she promptly voids by pushing him back.

"No kissing," Ashley said.

"Oh, come on, baby, let me taste those hot lips," responded the young man.

"Just finish so I can be done," demanded Ashley.

The young man backed off for a few moments getting back to playing with her breasts until he gathered up enough courage to go in for another attempt at a kiss causing Ashley to push him back again.

"I said no kissing, are you fucking deaf?!" yelled Ashley.

"Hey, I paid good money for you, you should do what I want," the young man remarked.

"You paid to fuck me not kiss me!" Ashley declared.

"Come on, a whore like you should be into anything," he replied.

Ashley sat there on top of him motionless hearing those words penetrate her ears like a knife, the one thing she hated to be called more than anything, would rather be called a slut than a whore. She wanted to slap him across the face as hard as she could, but her instincts told her just to leave.

"You know what, I'm done!" she yells as she removes herself from on top of him, quickly grabbing her clothes so she can leave the room.

"Hey, I'm not done!" the man yelled quickly pulling up his pants.

"Finish yourself, asshole," she shouted slamming the door behind her.

Throwing her clothes back on as she returns back upstairs she is followed by the unhappy and frustrated young man, the loud music from the club drowns out his yells for her to stop. Razz happens to she Ashley coming up from the downstairs, her body language depicting frustration and anger literally stomping her feet with every step she takes, followed by her client who is chasing after her. Razz gestures over one of his bouncers as he heads over to intervene. He locates them in the dressing room area, an area the clients are not supposed to be in, Razz has his bouncer grab the client to find out what is going on.

"Why are you back here?" Razz asked the young man.

"She wouldn't let me finish," the young man stated.

"Is this true?" asked Razz looking over at Ashley who appeared not very happy and only partially dressed.

"He wanted to make out," Ashley replied.

"You're disappointing me, Show Horse," Razz remarked.

"If I'm not going to get the chance to finish I want my money back," the young man argued.

"You ain't getting your fucking money back!" yelled Razz signaling to his guard to remove the young man from the club.

"What about my blue balls?" the young man yelled being escorted out. "GET THE FUCK OUT OF HERE!" Razz yelled.

Ashley watched the bouncer lead the man out of the club leaving her alone with Razz, could tell right away by the look in his eyes that he wasn't happy, a look that has never come across his face before when it came to her. She was in uncharted waters now, not knowing what he was going to do or say, doing what Razz wants is always priority number one, Ashley knew that never having a client complain on her before, but she has her feelings on certain situations. Kissing clients is off the table, performing an act that requires feelings and emotions just wouldn't feel right to her. She wants to have a deep connection with someone that she is kissing, that magical feeling that sends shivers down her spine when their lips first touch, you can't have that with total strangers and she will not fake it just because it is what they want. Luckily most clients aren't interested in kissing, but that still doesn't mean she should have to do it if one comes along looking for a long make-out session, she wants it to be with someone special not some horny college kid with a small penis. Sex is just sex, it can be a very emotionless act, it is much easier when she can just lay there while they pump away until they are finished, it's even better when they are a two pump chump and are done in thirty seconds or a minute. Razz looked at Ashley like a father who just found out that his daughter is pregnant, never thought she of all his girls would disappoint him like that. She was hoping that all she would get is a lecture and be done with it, but she has seen what has happened to some of the other girls when they have not fulfilled their duties.

"Razz, I'm sorry," Ashley said standing there in her underwear and silk blouse, hair a little messy from the man's fingers running through it.

"You think I'm mad because I had to throw him out?" asked Razz. "So what, I still got his money." Razz walks over to where Ashley is standing toe to toe with her, begins caressing both of her arms feeling the tension in her body. "I'm mad because an unhappy client is not a returning client," Razz informed.

"Razz, everything was fine until he wanted to start making out and I will not do that," replied Ashley.

"You are so beautiful, Show Horse, I would hate for anything to happen to this face," said Razz caressing her neck and face, staring deep into her eyes.

For a brief moment it seemed like everything was happening in slow motion when Ashley felt the back of Razz' hand come across her face, completely stunning her causing her to tear up, her head turned to the side from the force, breathing became heavier when he grabbed her by the face with both hands.

"Look at me, you're okay," Razz said. "I didn't want to have to do that."

Wiping away the tears from her face with his thumbs, the fear in her face began to excite him, grabbing her tightly on both arms, pulling her in close putting them nose to nose.

"Remember, I own you, Show Horse, you belong to me. Don't make me do that again," Razz proclaimed kissing her on the forehead before letting her go, leaving the dressing room thereafter.

Ashley is left standing there alone crying in her blouse and underwear feeling the chill from the sometimes drafty dressing room, wondering if her relationship with Razz has just taken a turn for the worse, knowing once that physical abuse boundary is crossed it might start becoming a frequent occurrence. At that moment she never felt more trapped then she did right then, after what she has seen or heard about what has happened to some of the other girls, she had promised herself she would do her best not to put herself in that situation, but sometimes that line between do what I say and don't disappoint me is very thin, it especially is for Razz. Ashley understands that he has a business to run and needs to put out the best product, but that shouldn't mean she should stop doing what she believes in so he can make a few extra bucks, all she knew was she wasn't going to succumb to changing her views on her job nor did she ever want to go through what just happened again putting her at a tug of war with her emotions. Instantly things felt different, she always viewed Razz as like a father figure that she never had, was always there and protected her, but the lifestyle comes with a cost. She has noticed a change in him over the years, at least a change when it comes to her, maybe because she is older and more mature, just couldn't quite put her finger on it, whatever it was Razz seemed like a different person from the one she meet nearly five years ago.

A thirteen-year-old Ashley is sitting alone on a park bench looking out over the large pond that sits right in front of her watching the ducks swim and splash each other, most times when she would visit the park she would bring some bread to feed the ducks, but today she came empty handed. It was a beautiful September Saturday, sun's out, not a cloud in the sky, temperature was the perfect warmth, she enjoyed coming to the park sometimes to get away from her overbearing aunt. It was close enough to the house where she could ride her bike or even walk, today deciding to walk given the perfect weather. Like with her paintings, she felt relaxed sitting by the water listening to the sounds of nature, the smell of the fresh air, watching the way the sun would reflect and sparkle of the calm water, the slight breeze that would tickle the many trees surrounding the area would put her in a state of peace, sometimes she would just close her eyes just to listen to the ambient sounds around her which would put her almost in a state of meditation. At these moments even though there were a good amount of people taking advantage of this late summer day, she felt like the only person on earth, time seemed to slow down when she was there, something she needed having started high school this past week, wondering what softball will be like in the spring, more importantly it was a way to get away from her Aunt, to try and empty her mind from all that has happen to her since she has been living there. Being a public park her feeling of solitude would come to an end when an older gentleman arrived sitting on the bench besides her. Ashley made it a habit to not purposely acknowledge people when she wants to be alone, something that is much harder to do when you are in public, part of her wanted to just get up and leave, but she was feeling so relaxed that her body felt weightless and couldn't move. Her curiosity started to get the best of her, without being obvious she made a quick glance over with her eyes only able to see he was wearing a dark blue suit with some very shiny black shoes, didn't get a look at his face nor did she want to, figuring he was a business man or something to that nature, hoping he would receive a phone call or something to keep from engaging with her.

"Beautiful day, isn't it," said the man.

Ashley wasn't in the mood to talk to anybody, especially a strange man in the park, tried to play it off like she didn't hear him, maybe get the hint and end it there. The man looked over at Ashley looking her up and down, watching her long dark brown hair flow in the breeze, glancing at her white graphic T-shirt, pink shorts exposing her smooth hairless legs, down to her pink and white Nike sneakers.

"What's a pretty girl like you doing here alone?" asked the man.

Almost immediately Ashley knew what was happening, wishing more than anything that she was wrong, but her instincts proved correct when the man placed his hand on her knee.

"Why don't you come with me and I will make you feel good," the man proposed.

All those bottled-up emotions started to surface through her body, her mind was in fragments like shattered glass, she didn't know what to do, part of her wanted to just go with him to get it over with because that is all she knew, another part of her wanted to just scream for help causing a commotion that she didn't want to be a part of. His hand gently squeezed her knee caressing it with his thumb, just as she was about to give in and go with him, another man appeared standing before them in front of the bench, neither one of them could tell what he looked like as the glare from the sun was masking his face.

"I don't think you want to do that," said the other man, "and if you don't get your hands off her and leave in the next ten seconds they are going to have to bury you in that suit."

Not wanting any trouble and extremely intimidated by the unknown stranger, the man removed his hand from Ashley's knee, stood up and quickly left. Ashley was amazed at what just transpired, nobody has ever stood up for her like that before, if this man hadn't come along she would have probably left with him and who knows what would have happened. She felt something she has never felt before in her young life, like she actually mattered, someone was actually willing to keep her out of harm's way, it was a good feeling to her, one she hoped she would feel again. The new stranger sat down besides Ashley, this time she actually felt comfortable, she felt safe.

"Are you okay?" the man asked.

"Yes, thank you," Ashley replied slightly nodding her head.

Now that the man was seated and not blocked by the brightness of the sun, Ashley was able to see what he looked like. He was a young man wearing blue jeans with boots, a camouflaged hoodie, very short hair, looked like he had a buzz cut, a goatee made up his facial hair, the sleeves on his hoodie were pulled back on both arms revealing the tattoos that covered both of his forearms, even at fourteen-years-old she could tell he had a young handsome face, would even say he was cute.

"Nice day to be at the park," remarked the man. "Did you know who that man was?"

"No," answered Ashley.

"Well, I can guarantee that he won't be bothering you anymore," said the man. "What is your name?"

Normally Ashley would never engage in small talk with strangers, especially strange men, but this time seemed different, she didn't know how to describe it, but she felt some kind of connection with this unknown person, in a way he was her hero, protecting her from a man whose intentions clearly signified that he had issues.

"My name is Ashley," she replied.

"Hi, Ashley, I'm Trevor, but everyone calls me Razz. It's nice to meet you," Razz said.

"Nice to meet you too, that's a weird name to be called," implied Ashley.

"Well, it's more like a nickname. Can I ask how old you are?" Razz asked.

"I'm thirteen," Ashley answered.

"So what is a girl your age doing in the park by herself? Do your parents know that you are here?" asked Razz.

"I don't have any parents, I live with my aunt," Ashley informed.

"That's good, do you live close by?" Razz asked.

"Yeah, not too far," she replied.

"Now I don't want this to sound weird or anything, but has anyone ever told you how pretty you are?" remarked Razz.

Throughout her short life Ashley has come to the realization that anytime an older man has complimented her on her looks it has led to something that she would later want to forget, but oddly enough this time it felt different, like he was actually complementing her on her looks without wanting or it leading to something else.

"No, but thank you," she said modestly.

The conversation between the two of them continued with them hitting on topics from music, to sports, to movies, to her school life, bringing up that she was a softball player who was going to try out for the varsity team in the spring as a freshman. Other than Holley J or her friends at school, Ashley never had a conversation with someone where she enjoyed the other person's company and was enjoying what was being talked about, never with an adult and especially never with an adult male who simply just wanted to talk. It was the first time in her life that she was around a grown-up man and didn't feel threatened, it was a breath of fresh air for her, something she thought would never happen. The more they talked, the more he began to earn her trust, his voice was very soothing, kind a voice you would like to hear on the radio. Ashley thought he was funny, a couple times she actually smiled and laughed, there was a playfulness to him she found very hypnotic, she could listen to him talk and be around him the rest of the day and not get bored. Once Razz knew he gained young Ashley's trust he proposed a proposition to her on how a girl like her could make some money explaining to her about the club he owns in the city leaving out the soliciting of sex part. Knowing she was too young to dance or to provide services, it didn't mean she couldn't work around the club in other ways while at the same time being groomed and developed into what he knew she could be. Razz had the uncanny ability to see the vulnerability in people, especially in young girls, when she mentioned she didn't have any real parents he knew he caught a bite, another girl with daddy issues, all he had to do was turn on the charm and display a level of kindness that would allow her to put her guard down and be putty in his hands. He was a fisherman always on the lookout for his next trophy catch, if his club was an aquarium all the girls were his exotic fish, when he saw a young girl like Ashley sitting alone on a park bench his instincts could tell she was a prime candidate, never tried to recruit a girl this young before, but he saw something in Ashley that was undeniably rare, like finding the goose that can lay golden eggs, the fact that he had to save her from some random pervert just made his job a little easier. Ashley was caught off guard when he asked her to come work for him, didn't think she was even old enough to work yet, but he explain how he was a private business owner and he would just pay her under the table, something she wasn't familiar with until he described how it worked, kindly asking what she would be doing. Razz simply stated she would just be cleaning off tables and helping some of the waitresses when need be. To Ashley it sounded simple enough, it seemed like less work than what she puts up with at home and she would be getting paid, extra cash to a teenage girl was like hitting the lottery, except for she lives with a very condescending and manipulative woman who will take advantage of her sudden income. Keeping it a secret from her aunt was an option, but when she notices Ashley being gone for hours at a time her intrusive curiosity will entice her to investigate Ashley's extended periods away from home, with nowhere else to go she would have no choice but to oblige by her wishes. However, there could be a silver lining to this, since her aunt hardly buys her anything other than food, which she must cook for herself and her aunt, and the occasional new outfit which is only done out of paranoia that child protective services will come take her live in servant away if she isn't wearing some sporadic new duds. Now if she has her own cash flow coming in it would make her aunt very happy to know that she wouldn't have to buy her anything anymore, Ashley could just start buying her own new clothes, etc. That reason alone would prevent her aunt from absorbing much of whatever Ashley was being paid. Then came the question of how she would even get to the club, she couldn't drive there and her aunt definitely wouldn't bring her, letting Razz to suggest that he would provide a car service for her that would pick her up at her house then bring her back when she was done. It all seemed too good to be true to her, but at this point she was willing to give it a try, anything that would get her away from her house for a while might be good for her, knowing her aunt wouldn't care as long as she answered her phone when she is trying to get a hold of her, the only reason Ashley even has a cell phone. She happily accepts his offer putting a smile on Razz' face, exchanging cell phone numbers at which point he excused himself letting Ashley know he would be in touch. Observing the man who was like an angel walk off into the distance making the beautiful scenery of the park seem to amplify, put a welcomed smile on her face, undenounced to her that the ultimate predator just caught his prey. Ashley stood there in the dressing room area reminiscing about that charming man she met that day in the park, how maybe she might have been wrong these past few years, though she knows Razz is a hard ass, she would never have believed that he would lay a hand on her. She knew everything would be different now, the sight of his face would instill fear in her hoping she doesn't disappoint him again. It was bad enough that she had to walk around that place with constant knots in her stomach knowing that if she gets recruited to play softball in college she was going to have to quit, something she hasn't discussed with Razz yet, making her even more nervous to bring it up considering what just currently happened. None of that mattered at the moment, she just wanted to get back on his good graces and do whatever she could to keep him happy, immediately getting her chance when Razz returned to the dressing room area looking for her.

"Get yourself ready, I need you to dance tonight," ordered Razz.

"Okay," she answered graciously. "Razz, I just want you to know that I am sorry."

Razz walks over to get face to face with Ashley, stroking her hair with his hand, eventually having his hands end up holding the sides of her face. There was a point when Razz' touch use to comfort her in a way she couldn't explain, now his touch seemed tainted and unfamiliar, it sent a sensation through her body that felt foreign and uncomfortable.

"You know you are still my favorite, Show Horse," Razz assured reaching down with one hand squeezing her ass, whispering something in her ear. "Maybe later you could show me just how sorry you are."

"I'd like that," Ashley whispers back, having Razz gently place a kiss on her lips.

Jake's truck pulls into an open spot in the school parking lot. It's about 8:30 A.M., scheduled to meet with Principal Davis at 9. Sitting in his truck looking out at the school it brings back memories of when he was in high school. He has heard of John Franklin High School, but it's a school in a different district from where he graduated, oddly his old school and this one have never meet in any athletic competition before. From the outside he could tell that the school grounds were well maintained, at least from what he could see, the landscaping looked professionally taken care of, there was no sign of property scars like graffiti or weird drawings on the school displaying someone's displeasure of the establishment, it was also multiple floors compared to the one floor high school that he attended. A CD was playing in the truck of some late 90s, early 2000s rock music, stuff he grew up on and listened to back in school. Listening to music helped him relax, a ritual he would perform before every baseball game he ever played in, would always have his head buried in a pair of headphones sitting by his locker, it was a way for him to clear his mind and focus on the task at hand, hoping it works for him today feeling both nervous and anxious at the same time. It was approaching 9 A.M., Jake turned off his truck, exiting checking his hair in the driver's side mirror, not knowing the proper attire to wear to a coaching interview he just dressed casual, a pair of tan khakis with a black polo shirt and black boots. He had no paperwork or anything to bring which Kenneth informed him would be fine. Making his way up the walkway to the front entrance of the school he could smell the aroma of freshly cut grass igniting memories of walking out onto the diamond just after the grounds crew finished with their maintenance. The combination of his nerves and the warm morning sun beating down on him contributed to the small amount of sweat building up upon his brow, what was actually just about a fifty-yard walk seemed like a mile, he had no idea what to expect walking through those doors, this was all new territory to him. Running his own team, especially a team composed of all girls was a scary task, coming from someone who felt more comfortable playing for a coach that way he could just focus on what he needed to do rather than having to make sure everyone else is doing what they are supposed to, but he knew he needed to give this a try, one of Jake's favorite quotes was "*A journey of a thousand miles begins with a single step.*" This was his.

Sitting in Principal Davis' office patiently waiting for him to finish a sudden phone conversation, Jake quickly takes a glimpse of his surroundings while listening in on the phone call which must be to a member of the front office since it was the topic of a student's attendance records. Principal Davis politely tells the person on the phone he has someone waiting for him and that he would call back later ending the call, Jake could tell by his demeanor on the phone that this Principal Davis runs a pretty tight ship.

"Sorry about that," voiced Principal Davis. "I just want to start by thanking you for coming in on such short notice. We just had a situation that we were just not prepared for."

"It's hard to be prepared for any situation," Jake replied.

"By the way, I know who you are. I just wanted to say I'm sorry about what happened with your baseball career," Principal Davis said.

"Yeah, me too," remarked Jake.

"I'm assuming Kenneth Rivers mostly briefed you in on the matters at hand?" asked Principal Davis.

"He basically just said that you had an opening for a coach for your girls softball team," Jake informed.

Principal Davis filled Jake in on what happened with the old coach giving him all the necessary details, Jake couldn't believe what he was hearing, he could be inheriting a team that has gone through verbal and physical abuse for the past few years, listening to all this started to make him question if it was all even worth it. Sounding like to him these girls need a therapist not a new coach, wondering if he was going to be in over his head here. Principal Davis continued on by telling Jake he would have full control of the team and anything else he may need to just ask for provided that he could guarantee that nothing else like this would happen under his watch. Jake knew promises were worth about as much as the person providing them, coming from someone who has dealt team contracts and the promises they were supposed to provide, he knew nothing like that would happen with him at the lead, but that's what they probably thought about the other coach when they hired him. This whole situation felt like he was about to walk through a mine field and every step could be his last, but he knew he needed a job and if he could turn a damaged team of young girls around it would really be saying something about his leadership and character. Sometimes the toughest decisions you make define you as a person, Jake knows he has made plenty of those with this one being right up there.

"So what do you think?" asked Principal Davis.

Jake sat there continuing to weigh the pros and cons even though he knew he was going to accept the job. He couldn't help but realize that Principal Davis had already put his trust in him, maybe it was the recommendation from Kenneth or maybe it was because he was a famous ex-ballplayer and having someone like him on the school's staff would draw the school more recognition, or it could just be he sees something in Jake letting him knew he was the right man for the job, either way Jake started to feel a little more at ease about the challenge at hand.

"Okay, I'll accept on one condition," remarked Jake.

"What's that?" Principal Davis asked.

"That I get a bonus when these girls win the championship," Jake replied smiling.

"I have no problem with that," Principal Davis remarked with the two of them standing up shaking hands to make it official.

Leading Jake out of his office, Principal Davis wanted to show him where his office would be and show him around the school a bit, mentioning that he was going to set up a meeting in the gym after school with the girls so they could all meet. Jake agreed that would be a good idea seeing he was told the girls season starts in about nine days putting him under the gun for preparation.

Jake finds himself standing inside the school gymnasium near a stack of empty bleachers alongside Principal Davis waiting for the girls to arrive who should be making their appearance any minute. Jake was impressed with the school's gymnasium just on its size alone, it was much bigger than the one his high school supported, the hardwood floor looked almost brand new giving off a shine so clear you could almost see your reflection in it, large stacks of retractable bleachers pretty much outlined the entire gym, along with the six retractable basketball hoops conveniently placed around the gym, all at the moment were in the up position. Many championship banners hung amongst the rafters in many different sports, but none were for girls softball which Jake was planning to change, absence of that banner sparked a level of motivation in him he hasn't felt in a long time, being a part of a few championship teams in his day, he knew what it was like to be a part of something special like that and hopes he could do the same for these girls. Coaching these girls is going to be a tremendous challenge considering everything they have already been through, but the one thing he never backs down from is a challenge. While Jake continued to envy his immediate surroundings, the girls starting filing in, seating themselves on the empty bleachers in front of them. Amongst the line of young females was Ashley who intentionally seated herself in front, her more than any of the girls was greatly interested in seeing firsthand the man who was becoming their new coach. She liked what she saw so far, he was younger and much better looking than Coach Mabbet, not that any of that should matter, just worried he might end up having the same intentions as her former coach and she definitely didn't want history repeating itself. As the girls finished seating themselves Jake and Ashley happened to lock eyes, he flashed her a friendly smile propelling her to quickly break eye contact. Once all the girls were present and situated Principal Davis began the introduction process by introducing Jake to the girls, mentioning he was a former major league baseball player, something Jake forgot to ask Principal Davis if he could keep quiet about. It wasn't the fact he once played professional ball, he was worried about them finding out what happened after, even though that is in the past it is still something that he doesn't like to talk about or is any ones business, wanting to just forget that time of his life and focus on moving forward. Principal Davis continued his boosting of Jake telling the girls of the three state championships in won back in high school while winning MVP all three of those years. Most of the girls were too young to have ever seen him play, but that didn't stop them from being very impressed with his athletic resume. Ashley found it both impressive and odd in that a onetime professional athlete would want to coach a bunch of high school girls when he could have gotten a job coaching with a pro team or even a farm club, it seemed suspicious to her, but was willing to give him the benefit of the doubt. Holley J who sat right besides Ashley seemed overly excited to have a coach of his stature lead the team, even going as far as whispering her approval to Ashley. After Principal Davis finished with his flattering introduction he gave the floor over to Jake to speak, he started by thanking Principal Davis for the opportunity to be there, while elaborating more on what the girls heard so far. Handed a piece of paper that contained the names of the girls, he used it to perform a roll call to start putting faces to names. One by one he would call out a name while the girls responded by raising their hand, when Holley J's name was called she responded with an over exuberance of excitement while raising her hand causing Jake to let out a friendly smile.

"And last but not least, Ashley Stamper," Jake announced.

Ashley hesitated a bit before slightly raising her hand.

"So you are the famous Ashley Stamper, I've heard a lot about you."

"What's that supposed to mean?" Ashley asked, receiving a gentle elbow from Holley J.

"Just that I heard you were a great pitcher," responded Jake..

"You have to excuse my friend here, Coach, she has a tendency to speak out when it's not necessary, kind of like Tourette's," remarked Holley J.

"I see, it's okay," said Jake. "Is there any other questions you girls would like to ask?"

"Why do you want to coach us?" Ashley asked as the gymnasium suddenly went silent, asking the question that almost every girl on the team wanted to asked, but were afraid to.

Every girl wondered why he would want to coach a team with a damaged history with their old coach. Sitting patiently waiting for his answer, the girls knew his response had to be genuine or they will figure he is just another washed up old pro just looking to collect a paycheck.

"I know what you all might be thinking," said Jake, "that I am just here for the money or why would an ex-professional ballplayer want to coach a bunch of high school girls when he could probably get a coaching job coaching Triple A or something. Those are all valid thoughts and my reasoning for being here is honestly kind of personal, but let me tell you something today I was told from one of my coaches from my playing days. You can have all the talent and skills in the world, but if you don't have trust, then you don't have a team."

Many of the girls sat there slightly nodding their heads in recognition of Jake's words of wisdom, something they definitely never heard from their old coach who most of the time was too busy yelling or not paying attention to them. They wanted genuine, that's exactly what they got, his posture as he spoke demanded attentiveness, articulated with his words sold the girls on his legitimacy, however some in attendance still remained skeptical.

"Talk is cheap," Ashley remarked, surprised by how sanguinely the rest of the girls were eating up his empty words after all the bullshit they went through with their old coach. "You want us to trust you, then you are going to have to earn it."

"You're right," Jake responded, officially finding the apparent spokesperson for the team, a label he is very familiar with seeing how he was usually the one on his teams holding that position, "and I plan on it."

To avoid any other awkward interactions Principal Davis thought it would be best to end the gathering right then, first allowing Jake to mention there we be practice every day after school starting on Monday until their first game in a week and a half. The girls were dismissed, grabbing their backpacks or whatever belongings they brought, Principal Davis called Ashley over who was greeted by Renee coming down from the bleachers.

"Nice work, Stamper, trying to scare another one away," Renee remarked as she walked by.

Holley J asked Ashley if she wanted her to wait for her, telling her no and would text her later. As the rest of the girls continued leaving the gym, Ashley walked over to stand by Principal Davis and Jake trying not to make eye contact with either of them, shouldering her backpack waiting for one of them to speak wondering if she was going to get detention for speaking her mind.

"I think you owe Mr. Wheeler here an apology," said Principal Davis. "We were lucky to find someone in such short notice and someone with his expertise, now you are not leaving here until you do."

Principal Davis is a man of his word and would make her stand there for hours until she does, Ashley knew to just get it over with, forcing herself to look him in the face locking eyes.

"I'm sorry," said Ashley trying to get a read on the man she will be spending much time around.

"It's okay," Jake assured placing his hand on Ashley's shoulder.

"Can I go now, please?" she asked, wanting to quickly remove herself from the awkward embarrassment of having to apologize to a complete stranger. Given the okay she turns her back walking away.

"I will see you at practice on Monday," Jake shouted watching Ashley leave.

"I'm sorry about that, she is never usually like that," said Principal Davis.

"It's fine. She actually reminds me of someone I know," Jake replied.

"Who's that?" asked Principal Davis.

"Me," Jake answered.

Ashley is walking through a hallway on her way to exiting the school, this time of day the hallways are very quiet, most of the students and a lot of the teachers have left for the day, the only person you might run into is one of the school's custodians working on their after-school cleanups. She makes a quick stop at her locker when she receives a text from her aunt wondering where she is, reminding her that she has her chores to do including getting her dinner ready. The only time her aunt ever texts Ashley is when she needs something done, the cell phone is more like a leash to her and Ashley is on a very short one. Calling her on the phone is not an option for her aunt, would rather avoid any verbal interactions when she can just send visual instructions through text and be done with it. Ashley and her aunt have never had a normal conversation with each other, not that Ashley hasn't tried seeing how she is the only adult female in her life, sometimes a teenage girl has questions that only an adult female could answer or maybe just in need of some advice on a certain subject wanting a female's perspective, but she never got that, she pretty much has had to deal with and figure things out on her own her whole life, to the point now she doesn't want her aunt's help with anything, especially from someone who refers to her as the help which she has called Ashley many times. She just needs to hold out a little bit longer, in about seven more months she will hopefully be away at college never having to deal with her shit again. Right now she just wants to ignore her texts, but if she does she will just keep texting and texting until she answers back, nothing irritates her more than to hear her text notification go off every ten seconds. Texted her back she will be home soon, finishing up getting what she needed out of her locker when she is startled by a familiar voice from behind.

"What was that all about in the gym just now?" asked Holley J watching Ashley jump as she closes her locker door.

"What are you still doing here, I thought you left?" Ashley replied.

"Just wanted to see what was up with you," remarked Holley J.

"Nothing, I'm fine," Ashley said making sure her lock is secure.

"That didn't sound like nothing," insisted Holley J. "Come on, Ash, talk to me."

Ashley wishes she could tell Holley J what's going on, wishes she could tell her everything, it sickens her that she has to keep secrets from her best friend, her best friend since the third grade. Both being only children they clicked from the very beginning, having each other felt like they each had a sister. They were always there for each other during all those special moments in a young girl's life, the first time they got their periods, their first kiss, to their first boyfriend which was all Holley J, there is no place in Ashley's life right now for adolescent boy drama nor do they appeal to her right now living the life she lives, when she is not at the club she would rather just stay away from boys all together as they are a constant reminder of her loss of innocence. Ashley was there to help Holley J through her first break up which was very emotional for her seeing how she was left for another girl. Remembering the many nights she had to sneak out of the house to go over to Holley J's place, watch her go through a box a tissues from all the crying she would do just so she could be there for her. Holley J would have never gotten through that time without her, she has dated other guys, but nothing to serious, won't allow herself to get too attached fearing she might wind up going on that emotional roller coaster ride again, but if it does she knows Ashley will be there for her. To keep Holley J from wondering why she never dates anybody Ashley simply told her she doesn't have the time or hasn't met anyone that gives her butterflies, relying on old love myths as her defense. They are BFFs for life, something they both want to get tattooed on their wrist with each other's name when they both turn eighteen. There is nothing Ashley doesn't know about Holley J, Holley J tells her everything and Holley J thinks she knows everything about Ashley, which she does in a sense except for all the dark times in Ashley's life and especially what she does for a job. If Holley J ever found out it would devastate her and she can't risk losing the respect of the only person in her life that truly matters to her.

"I know, it's just I have been under a lot of stress lately," said Ashley. "I don't know, I guess I just overreacted."

"Well, try to keep those emotions of yours in check, I got a good feeling about this guy," Holley J replied.

"Yeah, we will see," remarked Ashley.

They both chatted for a few more minutes until Ashley brought up she had to get going because her aunt is getting on her case again. Walking out of the school together shouldering their backpacks, each of them headed for their cars. It's seven o'clock P.M., chores and homework are done, not scheduled or hasn't heard from Razz about working, probably because tomorrow is Friday and she always works the weekends, but this is a very rare night for Ashley where she can just sit in her room painting, listening to music. She has been working on a new painting, one of a unicorn standing on the edge of a mountain looking out over the landscape below, sitting at her easel draped in her painting smock, her favorite playlist playing softly in the background, concentrates as the paint saturates the canvas bringing to life her vision with every stroke of her brush, feeling the cool evening breeze as it passes through her open bedroom window. These are the times Ashley wishes she had more of especially now since her aunt has left to go somewhere, where that is she doesn't care, just wants to savor these rare moments where she actually feels at peace, like being on the pitcher's mound during a game, trying not to think about the fact that her aunt will eventually be back, wants to enjoy the time no matter how long it last. The music from her playlist which is playing off her iPod docking station located on her vanity starts to place her in a relaxed state. Singing the words softly under her breath, moving her paint brush gently across the canvas as if she was painting to the music. Holding her palette in one hand, brush in the other, she begins swaying her body on her stool as if she was slightly dancing to the music. This most recent painting is nearly close to completion and probably her best work yet, a definite piece of art worthy of being placed up on her bedroom walls with her other favorites. Thinking nothing could ruin her mojo or break her focus, she heard the loud, growling sound of a motorcycle exhaust pulling into the house's driveway. Ashley knew who that was, her aunt's dead beat boyfriend Rick, hoping he realizes that she isn't home and just leaves, but when the roar of the motorcycle instantly went silent, she determined he was here to stay. The relaxing aroma of the night air was replaced with the stench of the cycles exhaust fumes. Ashley wasn't sure what his intentions were, but she was just going to ignore him, which became difficult when he started yelling her aunt's name. "KAREN," he yelled, the slow delivery and slur in his words clearly validated that he was drunk, yelling her name a couple more times even louder and more stern causing Ashley to believe that he was not too happy with her aunt which she could give two shits about, but that obnoxious, drunk yelling was disturbing her and probably the neighbors. When he still heard no one answer him back, she could hear the front screen door creek open and the front door being unlatched, he was now in the house still yelling for her aunt still getting no response. Ashley wondered if he was too drunk or stupid to see that her aunt's car wasn't here, leaned over to turn off her music so she could hear what she could of him in the house, her bedroom door was open due to the fact that she was alone in the house, if her aunt was there she would keep it shut. Ashley put her painting on hold for a moment waiting to see what his next move was. He had realized by now drunk or not that she wasn't here, but the next sound to echo through the house was one Ashley didn't want to hear, the sound of his footsteps coming up the wooden staircase leading to her floor, followed by his footsteps getting closer and louder coming down the hallway towards her bedroom where he stops, parking himself in Ashley's doorway.

"Where's your aunt?" Rick asked standing there holding the door frame with both hands as if to keep himself from falling over, his medium-length straggly hair and scruffy beard seemed more messed up than usual even for him.

Ashley could smell the alcohol on his breath even at the distant she was at giving further evidence of his current state.

"I don't know, she is not here, so why don't you just leave," demanded Ashley.

"I'm not leaving until I talk to her. She has been avoiding me lately and I want to know why. Is she out fucking some other dude?" asked Rick dragging his feet a couple steps into Ashley's room waiting for a response.

"I just told you I don't know where she is or when she is going to be back and would you please get out of my room," replied Ashley still holding the palette and paint brush in each hand.

Rick looked at Ashley with an arrogant smirk on his face, the way a man would look at a woman when he had devious intentions, has always found Ashley to be incredibly sexy much to the chagrin of her aunt. He has often fantasized about her whether it would be through masturbation or when having sex with her aunt, he has always wondered what it would be like. Even while wearing her paint covered smock with her hair in a ponytail she still looked like a tasty little morsel to him.

"You know I have always found you to be unbelievably sexy," said Rick slurring his words.

"Jesus Christ, will you please get the fuck out of my room!" Ashley said angrily.

Seeing in his glazed over eyes that he wasn't kidding, his stare was making her very uncomfortable, looking at Ashley as if he was already fucking her at that moment. She could only imagine what was going through his mind, the sick thoughts of what he would do to her sexual, the thought of that was making her nauseous. Rick staggered further into her bedroom, his greasy work boots scratching up the carpet, the chains on his leather biker vest dangling in random spots, the smell of garage grease and body sweat which was made apparent to the arm pit stains on his plain white, dirty t-shirt, trumped the smell of alcohol the further he entered. The closer he got to her the angrier she got, wishing her purse was close by instead of hanging on the coat rack by the bedroom door so she could pull out her pepper spray soaking his face in it. This was getting serious as he just kept coming, forcing Ashley to put her palette of paint and paint brush down so she could get ready to defend herself. Continuing to yell at him to leave, she stood up off her painter's stool in an effort to walk by him to exit her room, when she was in reach Rick grabbed her by the arms throwing her down on her bed, quickly jumping on top of her. Ashley frantically tried to fight off his advances, but his strength was overpowering as his body weight held down her legs while he had her arms pinned at the wrist. She screamed at the top of her lungs hoping maybe a neighbor might hear her cries for help, but no one was listening. Rick proceeded to hold both of her wrists with one hand so he could rip off her smock exposing her underneath tube top to begin groping one of her breast while kissing her neck. Ashley pleading for him to stop, but the more she fought back, the more turned on he got, feeling his erection through his jeans rubbing the inside of her pajama bottoms covered thighs, the roughness of his beard scratching her face as his tongue tickles the inside of one of her ears. Releasing her breast his hand worked its way below pulling down her pajama bottoms, the sight of her pure white panties and silky smooth thighs put his loins on fire, quickly trying to unbuckle his pant. During her constant struggle to free herself from this drunk, perverted animal, triggered many unwanted memories of the helplessness she felt many nights being the victim to assholes like this, now a bit older and more capable of defending herself, she wasn't going to just lay back anymore and let scum like this get away with it without a fight. Scuffling with all her might trying to keep him from forcing her legs open, a well-known loud voice was heard.

"WHAT THE HELL IS GOING ON HERE?!" yelled Ashley's aunt standing in the doorway.

Hearing her voice, Rick immediately jumped off Ashley and her bed, standing there with his jeans unbuckled and his erection visible through his boxer shorts, Ashley still laid on her bed, out of breath, sweat running down her face from the immense exertion of energy she used to try and free herself.

"YOU FUCKING ASSHOLE!" Ashley yelled pulling up her pajama bottoms.

"You have got to be fucking kidding me, Rick!" remarked her aunt watching him get his clothing back on.

"It's not what you think, babe," Rick replied, barely able to keep his balance buckling his pants up.

"Get the fuck out of my house," her aunt demanded.

"Babe, listen to me, she asked for it," rebutted Rick.

Ashley's aunt knew he was drunk, but wasn't going to let that go as an excuse, looking over at Ashley, who she can tell was still shaken up, can tell by the look in her eyes that was a lie, her and Ashley may not get along, but she knows Ashley would never do anything like that, especially when she knows she doesn't even like Rick. She realized that if she didn't show up when she did her niece would have been raped by the man that was supposed to be her boyfriend, for the first time she felt sorry for Ashley and was glad she showed up when she did.

"I SAID GET THE FUCK OUT OF MY HOUSE!" her aunt yelled again.

"Come on, babe, I love you," said Rick reaching to touch her face.

"Don't you fucking touch me," she said slapping his hand away in anger, "now get out before I call the cops."

Deciding to obey to avoid any legal trouble, he staggers out of the room, Ashley's aunt avoids eye contact, the sight of him makes her sick to her stomach, had rage building up inside her she couldn't describe. Hoping he leaves quickly, afraid if she doesn't soon get her emotions under control, she very well might kill him.

"This is all your fault, little girl," Rick said to Ashley leaving her bedroom.

"FUCK YOU!" Ashley replied a bit worked up.

"Don't ever talk to me or come here again," her aunt said with tears streaming down her face.

"Fuck both you bitches!" Rick replied making his way to the staircase.

Ashley and her aunt remained in their current positions listening to the roar of Rick's motorcycle being started up, hearing him leaving the neighborhood as the loud exhaust of his bike slowly begins to disappear in the distance. Now that he is gone, her aunt looked up at Ashley, tears soaking her eyes, just staring at her leaning against the doorway with her arms folded. Ashley stared back, could tell her aunt was very upset, wondering what was going through her mind at that very moment, was she generally concerned for her wellbeing or did she actually blame her for what happened. This is the first time her aunt has probably seen the inside of her bedroom, since Ashley's bedroom is the last room of the hallway she never needed to come down this way seeing that her bedroom was on the other end. Ashley never cared where her aunt goes when she goes out, but tonight for some reason she was curious. Her aunt was all dolled up, standing there in a nice pair of black slacks, pure white blouse, a pair of black heels, hair and makeup was done up nice, never seen her aunt look like that before, she looked good, she looked normal. There were only a hand full of places you would go looking like that, maybe there was another side of her aunt she didn't know about, if they could ever have a real conversation with each other maybe she could find out. The real conflict going on inside Ashley at the moment was whether or not she should thank her aunt for showing up when she did, it was a scary thought to think about what would have happened if she didn't, she would have been raped, Ashley knew that, what fascinated her the most was how a seamlessly perfect night could turn into an absolute shit storm in the matter of seconds. Wanting to thank her, knowing it was the right thing to do, but another part of her thought she didn't deserve it, it was the least she could do with all the bullshit she puts her through. Had Rick been able to go through with his deviant intentions before her aunt returned home, it would have been the case of he said she said and her aunt unquestionably would have favored his side, the basis for leaving her aunt in the dark about every horrible behavior that has been bestowed about her, she would just accuse Ashley of lying or trying to seek attention, the comfort and security of family is undeniably absent in this house. A part of her was waiting for her aunt to say something, but she stood there remaining silent, probably still in shock for what she just saw, the silence became almost deafening as neither of them would say anything, so quiet they could hear a lot of the outside commotion coming in through Ashley's bedroom window. It seemed each of them was waiting for the other to say something, but they never did. The stalemate ended when Karen wiped the tears away from her face with her hand then walked away. Ashley got off her bed to grab a t-shirt out of her dresser, sitting back down on her bed, hands were shaking from the shock of what happened, she was almost raped, the thought of that caused her to break down crying. This was her at home where she is supposed to be technically safe, not caught off guard by some man's perverted and immoral advances, felt violated, reminiscent of all the horrible things that happened to her as a young kid in this very room, the main reason she blankets her walls in her paintings, hoping to fill the room with positive thoughts and energy to try to wash away all the negative essence that stains her surroundings. She often wondered why all these terrible acts happen to her when she has never done anything wrong or done harm to anyone else, living a life she never wanted. At times it wouldn't surprise her if her life was the result of some invisible entity sentenced to make her existence as miserable and difficult as possible, dishing out all the mayhem and deviance the human psyche can take until it's subject falls victim to self-termination. Many people believe everyone has a guardian angel that watches over them, Ashley doesn't believe that for a minute, if that were true she would say that her guardian angel was doing a really shitty job and would rather go about it alone, but no matter what happens to her she always perseveres and continues to move forward, she's a fighter who is always going to go down swinging, yet sometimes it feels like she may be winning a few battles, but definitely not winning the war. Sitting on the edge of her bed fighting back the tears, she reaches for her phone located on her nightstand, still pretty early being only eight thirty and normally she would rather just be alone, but she felt like she could use the company to help clear her mind sending Holley J a text seeing if she was home, hoping she could head over there for a little while to hang out. Waiting for a response Ashley debated if she should tell Holley J what happened seeing how it turned out okay, the worse was avoided, but she didn't know how she would react, Holley J has a tendency to overreact even if Ashley tells her nothing ended up happening, everything was taken care of and that she was over it, Holley J still might ask a million questions she wasn't in the mood to answer. The text message alert on her phone sounded from Holley J reading, "I'm home, come whenever you want."

Ashley was greeted by Holley J at her front door, letting her in, the two headed for Holley J's bedroom where they can be alone. Walking through the house to the staircase that leads upstairs, Ashley sees Holley J's parents sitting in the living room watching TV greeting them with a hello which they blindly reciprocated. Ashley's relationship with Holley J's parents was civil at best, though Holley J would never blatantly say it her parents aren't too fond of Ashley for undisclosed reasons. They have felt that way ever since they met her back when she was a little girl, never paying much attention to her when she would come over to visit with Holley J, if she got a verbal hello that would be the extent of their interactions, never has been invited over for a dinner, a normal ritual between best friend households, not that Ashley was interested in sharing a meal at the same table with people that don't like her, the awkwardness alone would ruin her appetite, when the girls would have a sleep over they would just eat privately in Holley J's room. She believes part of their dislike for her stems from their religious lifestyle, both of them devout Christians who use the Bible as life's handbook, their credence with how a conventional home life should be makes Ashley a sinner in their eyes. Living with her aunt, mother in jail, a father who remains anonymous, these are all sins in the world they have created in their own image, not even considering Ashley is not to blame for any of it, using the excuses an apple doesn't fall far from the tree or her family are all part of the same tangled web of transgressions so why should she be any different. Holley J's parents were two hardworking middle-class people, her mother was a secretary for some construction company, father was a fireman. One of life's morals is to respect your elders, which Ashley agrees with to a certain extent, if only they respect you in return, her aunt doesn't deserve any of her respect, however she shows Holley J's parents respect out of respect to Holley J despite their differences. Being their only child Holley

J has always been spoiled by her parents, but has never acted like a spoiled brat, Holley J has always accepted that sometimes money was tight or there were more important things that were needed, one of the many things Ashley loves about Holley J, she was always satisfied with everything she got, never complaining, compared to some of the rich, spoiled girls she knows at school who complain when they receive a brand-new car for their birthday because they didn't like the color. It has always bothered Holley J about how her parents feel towards Ashley, but she wasn't going to let their cynical thinking keep her from having the friends she wants, she may be spoiled but that hasn't kept them from having friction of their own. Regardless of her parents' beliefs, Holley J is a devoted atheist, has been since freshman year, couldn't swallow any more of her parents preaching and the every week trip to church where it's more of the same just on a larger scale, refusing to become another mindless robot programed to spread their evidence less propaganda whenever they happen to meet an apparent lost soul. Holley J has made it perfectly clear to her parents how she feels about that aspect of her home life, wanting them to let her be a free thinker, letting her make her own decisions on personal views and beliefs that come about in one's life, she may be their offspring, but that shouldn't give them the right to strip her of her individuality. Often Holley J thought all the spoiling throughout the years was their way of trying to buy her devotion to their faith, confronting them many times about it, threatening to never speak to them again if they were more interested in bribery rather than doing something specifically for love of their child, she has been giving their word that wasn't the case. To keep the peace in the house and their interactions like a normal family, the subject is off limits out of respect to all those living under that roof, not to say Holley J's parents haven't breached that agreement from time to time.   The two girls are settled in Holley J's bedroom which is about twice the size of Ashley's. Holley J sitting at her desk which is home to her three monitor desktop computer, Ashley is sitting on the edge of her bed. Holley J's bedroom was very technology friendly with her computers which included a laptop, her iPad and few iPods which were all filled with music, her large Bluetooth Echo conveniently resting next to her very large desk equipped with her personally fitted gaming chair. Holley J was into video games, it was her way of relaxing, having everything from competitive keyboards and mice, to top-of-the-line gaming headphones. Her large desktop rig wasn't only for gaming, she was also a wiz on the computer, some might call her a hacker in training, but she would just say she knows her way around the internet. Ashley had a hidden jealousy of the fact that Holley J with all her elaborate high-tech gear has never had to pay for a cent of it. She is not allowed to get a job, her parents would rather she focus on her schoolwork than to succumb to the daily stresses of the workplace, her allowance alone was more than what a typical teenage would receive. Ashley was just glad to have her company right now, hopefully able to get her mind off of what happened earlier.

"I'm surprised you texted me wanting to come over. Is everything okay?" Holley J asked.

"Fine, just wanted the company," replied Ashley, fighting with herself to keep quiet.

"Well, I'm glad you are here because I found out some interesting things about our new coach," said Holley J, manipulating the keyboard to do her bidding.

"I knew you would," remarked Ashley. "What did you find out? He is like a murderer or something."

"No, nothing like that," answers Holley J bringing up some information on her computer screen. "Look, check this out. It says Jake Wheeler was a pro baseball player whose career was cut short due to two catastrophic knee injuries, but after that there is nothing else on him."

"Okay, so," Ashley replied.

"So, if you usually dig deep enough you can find out what he did after baseball, did he work a regular job, was he arrested a few times, you know anything, but there is nothing here, it is almost like he was living off the grid for a while," informed Holley J.

"All I want to know is, if he is another asshole," remarked Ashley.

"According to this he is a well-respected athlete and was a great ballplayer, nothing that would indicate anything like that," Holley J replied, "except for this one little thing."

"What's that?" asked Ashley.

"He was once arrested in high school for drunk driving. Boys will be boys," Holley J said, turns towards Ashley removing the large clip holding her hair hostage, grabbing the brush she leaves on her desk,. "I still have a good feeling about this guy. I think you should just give him a chance, I mean he is all we got right now."

Holley J has always been full of enough optimism to cover the both of them, willing to give anybody the benefit of the doubt. Ashley trusts Holley J's instincts, but it is much more different for her than for the other girls, now she wants to trust her own and the jury is still out.

"Are you going to be working this weekend?" Holley J asked.

"You know I work every weekend," answered Ashley.

"When was the last time we actually spent a whole day together? Maybe I can finally talk my parents into letting me drive into the city so I can come visit you at work," suggests Holley J.

"No, don't do that!" proclaims Ashley in a defensive tone. "I get really busy and I wouldn't really have time to even say hi or anything,"

Since Holley J's parents won't let her drive into the city it makes it much easier for her to keep her job a secret, but it still kills her every time she has to lie to her, even scared to come clean about their old coach's true perverted nature. Holley J only knows the Ashley she sees almost every day, not realizing there is a whole other side to her hidden within the same beautiful exterior she has known most of her life, a side she is scared for Holley J to meet, equivalent to an evil twin Ashley feels like she is protecting her from.

"But I would love a day soon for us to hang out together."

The two of them are lying on their backs on Holley J's bed just staring at the ceiling, something they used to do all the time when they were kids, just talking and gossiping about anything, it brought back many memories of all the sleep overs they used to have when they would do each other's hair and make-up, make up funny dances to their favorite music and watch scary movies to see who would be the one to cover their eyes first, which was usually Holley J who is not to fond of horror movies. Ashley really appreciates the time she can spend with her, tries to never take it for granted, it really is the only time she feels like a normal teenage girl, being some of the happiest moments in her crazy life. One particular crazy adventure the two of them shared happened a few years ago in their junior high days, it was a night much like this one, Ashley was over hanging out, having just finished eating an over cooked pot roast that Holley J's mother prepared. After returning their dirty dishes to the kitchen, Holley J suggested they sneak out and take their bikes down to an old car impound she found one day while riding her bike. Roughly around eight to ten cars were usually stationed there of all models, but nothing exotic or high end, just your basic SUVs, trucks and economical cars, all there because many people refuse to abide by the existing parking laws. The vehicles were kept enclosed by a simple tall metal fence with barb wiring running along the top, but Holley J knew of a secret way to get inside. Thinking it was crazy, Ashley agreed to take a ride down with her to check it out, not knowing what Holley J's true intentions were when they get there. Arriving at the impound which was located directly next to a canal, the girls parked their bikes near the spot Holley J heard about where there is a break in the fencing structure, the whole bottom part of the fence can be pushed in creating a space big enough for the two of them to crawl through. Inside Holley J switch on a small flashlight she brought with her, there was a full moon that night which helped illuminate much of the area, yet the extra beam of light from her flashlight would come in handy. Pointing the light all around checking out what was being stashed there for that week, surrounded by the silence of the late evening and the small breeze coming off the water of the canal, Holley J shined the light on one specific car that caught her eye, a gold 79' Trans Am, neither one of them would consider themselves a car aficionado at the age of twelve, but the color and body design stood out to her compared to the rest of the inventory. Ashley stayed close to Holley J as they walked on the all dirt surface over to the gold beauty, becoming fascinated when Holley J's flashlight shined brightly on the large decal on the front hood, never having seen anything like that before. Investigating the car further, the all leather interior's color seemed to match the outside, a pair of white fuzzy dice and a few air fresheners hung from the rear view mirror, also determining it was an automatic. Close by observing Holley J admiring the car, Ashley grew more and more confused to why they were there, getting a bit antsy trespassing on private property, standing in the middle of a dimly lit car impound during the later hours of the evening.

"Nice car, isn't it," said Holley J.

"Yeah, it's cool," Ashley replied. "So what are we doing here?"

"You want to drive it?" asked Holley J.

"What?! You're kidding, right?" Ashley remarked, knowing her friend all too well that she wasn't.

Holley J was the intrepid type, has always been since they met, seeing kids their age as being invincible and untouchable, a mindset that drives her to sometimes do elaborate exploits to get that rush of adrenaline, blaming the effects of having overbearing parents as the spark that lights the fuse, her way of escaping the cage they want to keep her in, giving her those few moments of juvenile freedom that most kids need from time to time. Ashley is aware what Holley J wants to do is wrong, yet after thinking about it realizes she needs this too, a way to be free for a short time from the shackles she wears at home.

"How do you suppose we would be able to do that? We don't have the keys."

"I know where to get them," answered Holley J with a small grin on her face.

"Aren't there cameras here? Won't they know we have been here?" Ashley asked.

"I took care of the cameras and the security system," informed Holley J. "Back home I hacked into their server and disabled everything, no one will ever know we were here."

Holley J leads Ashley to the small shack like office located by the actual entrance to the impound, two large sliding gates close off the entryway. The office structure was a bit run down in appearance, some of the siding has broken off in certain spots, the windows that surround the layout look like they haven't been washed in years and the few wooden steps leading to the door to enter were warped and misshaped in areas. Pointing her flashlight through one of the windows, Holley J made sure it was deserted, afraid maybe she might spot an employee asleep inside. Nothing other than an old computer, paperwork scattered everywhere and a rack on the wall holding all the keys to the vehicles were the only things visible. Given the coast was clear, Holley J carefully walked to the top step with Ashley close behind her, grabbing the doorknob giving it a shaking to vouch it was locked.

"Now what?" Ashley asked feeling the night air becoming cooler by the minute. Without a word, Holley J pulled out a couple paperclips from her sweat jacket pocket, giving the flashlight to Ashley for her to hold, she bends the two small pieces of metal into specific shapes. Having Ashley point the light at the doorknob, Holley J inserts the two contorted paperclips into the lock, swiftly and carefully she maneuvers the pieces of metal trying to find the sweet spot. After a few minutes of countless fiddling and repositioning of the metal pieces, a click could be heard releasing the lock, turning the knob, Holley J pushed the door open granting them entry inside. Ashley was amazed at the crafty skills Holley J just displayed picking the lock to the door, not the least bit surprised she was capable of something like that, fitting perfectly well with her personality. Staying outside pointing the flashlight inside, Ashley watched Holley J walk over to the key rack trying to figure out which set of keys would be the ones they need, coming across a set with a keychain that had the same decal on it as the car prompting her to grab those. Turning back, Holley J holds up the set of keys in the light jiggling them in excitement, Ashley smiles seeing their risky goal is becoming within reach. Leaving the office room, the girls head back to the gold Trans Am, standing side by side at the foot of the car staring at it as if they were attempting to tame a wild stead. Wasting no time, Ashley snatches the keys out of Holley J's hands proceeding to the driver's seat, followed by Holley J heading to the passenger's. Sitting inside, the girls idolize how they are seated in a car without an adult present, both feeling more mature mixed in with feelings of excitement and nervousness. Wearing shorts, the girls bear the coolness of the leather against their legs, Ashley grabs hold of the steering wheel seeing if she can reach the pedals from her current position, with the very tip of her foot able to touch the accelerator she adjust the seat forward to a better position. Foot now firmly on the gas pedal she tries different keys until finding the one that fits into the ignition, sliding the correct one in she looks over at Holley J who gives her the nod, turning the key the sound of the engine firing was like music to their young ears, Ashley revved the motor a couple times so they can hear it roar, careful not to do it too much, not wanting the sound alerting any nearby civilians. Finding the pull knob for the lights to brighten their path, Ashley presses on the brake putting the car into gear, Holley J sits back in her seat eagerly awaiting takeoff. Keeping one hand on the wheel as the car idols in place, Ashley reaches her right hand out inviting Holley J's to do the same, interlocking their fingers to hold each other tight, Ashley releases the brake pressing hard on the gas, the car peels out on the all dirt surface racing down the somewhat lengthy aisleway of the rectangular enclosure. The girls let out screams of triumph speeding down towards the other end, it was their Thelma & Louise moment only inversed, instead of them driving off a cliff to their demise, they were letting loose and experiencing the freedoms of life. Coming to the end of aisle way, Ashley eases on the brakes turning the steering wheel to take the corner heading back the other way. Holley J found the button on the console to open the sun roof, looking up at the sky full of stars she stands on her seat exposing part of her torso and head to the outside. Feeling the cool night air against her face Holley J raises her arms in the air as Ashley continues to drive through the impound in an oval pattern, skidding around every turn spraying dirt and debris everywhere, the pressure of the wind from the car's momentum reenacted the sensation of being on a roller coaster. After a few more laps the girls switched positions letting Holley J drive and Ashley standing through the sun roof, Holley J not quite as good a driver as Ashley, having a few close calls when turning the corners, almost crashing into a couple of the other cars. The girls little escapade went on for a little while longer until Holley J pressed on the gas and the car began hesitating, eventually leading to the car going dead, rolling to a stop. Holley J turned the key pumping the gas to try to get it to start again, but it was a no go, finally seeing the issue as the gas gage read empty. The car stopped in the middle of the impound way a ways from where it was originally parked, the girls sat laughing in amusement knowing there is no way now they could get the car back in its spot, coming to the decision to just leave it where it is. Turning off the car's lights, leaving the sunroof open and the keys in the ignition, the girls exit the car to head back to their bikes giving a another quick survey of the area to make sure no one was aware of their presence. Their current lives waited for them when they got back, but they will never forget this night as long as they live, even though what they did was illegal and dangerous, for a brief period of time they felt what life was like with no restrictions, to be masters of their own existence, for those moments they were invincible and more importantly they felt free. Despite the fact there was no evidence that they were the ones who left the impound in its current state, the girls never did anything like that again, they got away with this one, next time they might not be so lucky, playing chicken with the law will in the end catch up with you, it was better for them to quit while they were ahead, but they will always have this night which they shared together and for a little while they experienced being freer than they have ever been.

As the two of them lay on the bed laughing and reminiscing, Ashley couldn't help but wonder what's going to happen after this season, after graduation, there is a ninety-nine-percent chance that they will be going to different schools in the fall, she wants to study art, where Holley J wants to study to be a journalist which is no surprise, it scares her to think that after nearly ten years she might not see her on a regular basis like she does now, the only contact they will have is over their phones or social media. Adjusting to the fact that her best friend, pretty much the only person in her life that truly cares about her is no longer just a short drive away is going to be a lot to handle. Change to their common every day interactions was inevitable, yet for so long it seemed so far away, now in their senior year the reality of life after high school is just over the horizon requiring them to adjust to whatever becomes their new normal, promising each other no matter the distance between them they will always keep in contact and be there for each other. There is another matter at stake which is this season and Ashley doesn't want to go out a loser. Time seems to fly by when the two of them are together, Ashley checks her phone to notice that it is almost eleven-thirty, stunned that her Aunt hasn't tried to contact her, but she knows it's getting late and they have school in the morning. Removing herself from Holley J's bed she gives Holley J a hug thanking her for letting her come over, telling her that she will let herself out and she will see her at school exiting the bedroom.

It's a typical busy Friday night down at the club, about thirteen girls on staff including Ashley who just got done dancing her first set. She always gathers a very large crowd when she performs which means more money, sometimes the stage looks like it's carpeted in dollar bills when she is finished, a sight that always makes Razz truly realize what he has in Ashley. Most sets she is dancing to the song "Cherry Pie" by Warrant which Razz picked for her, not a song she cares for but doesn't have much say in the matter. She loves to dance it's just hard to enjoy it when you are completely naked under a bunch of hot stage lights, wearing black heels, finding clear heels very uncomfortable, the black heels go better with her famous school girl outfit she normally strips too, all while the music is playing at an almost deafening level. Having a collection of intoxicated middle-aged men whistling, yelling obscene cat calls, trying to hide their apparent pocket erections doesn't make the experience that more fulfilling for her either. Her sessions on stage cause sweat to beat up on her especially on her face and forehead thanks to the extremely hot lights flashing from pretty much every direction. The sweat serves its purpose for it allows Ashley's body to glisten under the lights which amplifies her sex appeal even more to the on looking men, her body looks like it was chiseled from stone by a famous sculptor, all her main features are the perfect size coupled with the her skin is completely blemish free with no weird moles or beauty marks to be found. She is the main draw when she is scheduled, along with being the most requested for private lap dances.

Ashley climbs off stage to a thunderous ovation while a few of the bouncers start to gather up all the money freely resting on stage. The club's over enthusiastic DJ named DJ Sizzle asks the crowd to give "Angel" another round of applause, Angel is Ashley's stage name also given to her by Razz. She is met backstage by a fellow girl who hands her a robe to put on, standing there wearing a sexy nurses outfit.

"Wow, they are loving you tonight," says Nikki. "I hope I get that type of reception."

"It's not really hard to get dogs to bark," Ashley remarked.

"By the way, Razz wants to see you in his office ASAP," replied Nikki hearing DJ Sizzle announce her name for her set, "wish me luck."

Ashley watched Nikki disappear into the backstage curtain heading onstage for her set. She hurried to the dressing room to put some clothes on so she is not keeping Razz waiting. A couple of the other girls are back there getting prepared for whatever they were called on to perform, knowing her night is not over yet, Ashley dresses in her usual club attire, at times like these she wishes there was time to take a shower to help wash off a lot of the sweat instead of just wiping it off with a towel, quickly sitting down at her specific vanity to fix up her face and do her hair while wondering what it is Razz wants to see her about, hoping she could get through one night without having to have sex with someone, but that would be wishful thinking seeing that she is Razz' hot commodity at this club. Finishing primping herself she leaves the dressing room to head to visit with Razz, the muffled music and commotion of the club can be heard as she walks the hallway leading to his office, as always an armed security guard stands outside his double doors, a large black man at least two hundred and fifty pounds, standing well over six feet wearing a black t-shirts that simply say "Security," along with their matching black jeans and head sets. Their pistols are holstered and completely visible along with their tasers. Ashley is familiar with the guard since she had to have sex with him one Christmas as a bonus from Razz for their loyal and continuous service, letting them pick any of the girls and of course they chose her. The guard recognized Ashley, announcing her arrival over the headset while opening one of the doors for her, she walks into the office to see Razz sitting at his desk with another man who she didn't recognize sitting in a chair in front of him. Standing in front of the desk waiting for Razz to advise why he summoned her, Ashley actually was becoming nervous, girls usually aren't asked to come to his office unless they are in some sort of trouble, since his office is sound proof he is able to deliver his discipline without any distractions, very seldom does he deliver his authority to girls outside his office, but in some rare cases it has happened which Ashley is familiar with. She has been in this office a few times, but not for disciplinary reasons, once was when she first started working here, Razz performed sort of an interview with her, the other time was the night she had danced on stage for the first time, Razz wanted to give her a private graduation gift of sorts to commemorate her now being official, the gift happened to be the car Ashley currently drives, she had recently just turned sixteen at the time, wanting her to be able to drive herself from then on. The gift is one of the reasons there is a lot of tension between Ashley and most of the other girls even though she never asked for it. Now she wonders what the reason is for this latest invitation, just standing there she felt like a squirrel in a wolves den, the only thing putting her at ease was the presence of the strange man in the chair, this call was probably not for her behavior, would never do anything with someone else present. The man looked around Razz' age, sitting there in his blue jeans, timberland boots and leather jacket, sporting a close to the scalp haircut matching his clean shaven face, noticing a tattoo of a dagger on his neck along with him wearing a bunch of rings on his fingers. Whatever they were talking about must have been important, each having a large black briefcase in close proximity to themselves. Ashley knew right away what was going down and knew what the contents of those briefcases were, which surprised her because Razz never does any of his deals or exchanges in front of any of the girls, it has always been something that he keeps close to the chest. Her curiosity was turning to nervousness with every second that passed waiting for Razz to explain the reason for her being there.

"Show Horse, I want you to meet a business associate of mine," said Razz. "This is Hector."

"Nice to meet you," Hector says with a Mexican accent, looking at Ashley standing there in her black skirt, burgundy silk blouse with black heels.

"You were not lying, my friend, she is gorgeous. Are you sure this is going to be okay?"

"She'll do whatever I tell her. Isn't that right, Show Horse?" asked Razz staring dead into Ashley's eyes.

"Yes," answered Ashley not liking where this is going.

"And I can use your office?" Hector asked.

"Whatever you want," replied Razz.

"May I use your restroom to get ready?" Hector asked, receiving a nod from Razz.

Hector enters Razz' private bathroom located in one corner of his office, the two of them now alone for the moment, Razz leaves his seat to approach Ashley to fill her in on what needs to be done.

"This is an important client of mine," Razz says holding her face in his hands. "He wants you, in this room. Do whatever he wants, you understand me?"

Ashley looks into Razz' eyes nodding her head. "I knew I could count on you, Show Horse," remarked Razz kissing her on the forehead. "I'll leave you two kids alone. Make sure you clean up afterwards."

Razz steps out of his office leaving a very overanxious Ashley standing there wondering what kind of fate awaits her, obviously knowing now this is about sex, but why in Razz' office, what did he need to get ready for in the bathroom, this definitely wasn't about simple intercourse or a quick bloodbath only other logical answer she could come up with is this had to be some kind of fetish fantasy she was about to become part of. The sound of the bathroom door unlocking persuading her to focus her attention in that direction, Hector emerges from the darkness of the bathroom wearing nothing but a pair of boxer shorts and a plain white t-shirt covered in a t-shirt shaped piece of plastic. Ashley could tell he was ready to go from his erection hiding behind his drawers. He made his way over to stand in front of her licking his lips, smelling his cheap cologne filled while he asked her to take her top off. Removing her blouse exposing her breasts, he gladly began squeezing them with both hands, feeling his calluses rubbing against her skin as he continues to fondle her chest area.

"Touch me now," requested Hector.

Ashley reaches into his boxers to begin stroking his penis manually, he closes his eyes letting out small moans with every stroke from her soft hands.

"Your hands are so soft," he says reaching down grabbing Ashley's wrist making her stop. "Now for the fun stuff. Lie on your back on the edge of the pool table."

She walked over to the pool table Razz had in his office, the wood seemed to be hand carved with tassels hanging from the leather pouch pockets, highlighted by the lite blue color of the felt on the playing surface. Ashley laid on her back with her legs hanging off the edge like he requested, not a very comfortable position, the felt against her bare skin is rather itchy, feeling like some kind of female sex robot just complying with every command she was given. Hector walked over slowly pulling off her skirt and panties, soaking in the reveal of such a young vagina, throwing the skirt aside, holding up the panties to his nose taking a nice big sniff as if they were a bouquet of roses, proceeding to spread her legs open mimicking what he just did with her panties to her bare vagina. Ashley laid there completely naked with nothing more than her heels on wondering what this man was planning to do, the anticipation was becoming worse than the acts themselves, wishing he would just put his penis inside her getting it over with, but was starting to get the feeling this man was all about the weird kinky stuff, doing things you would only hear about on the internet, whatever he was planning she wanted him to just do it so she could get it over with. Standing there between her legs caressing both of them, he couldn't believe how soft her skin was, so smooth and firm, could feel his erection getting harder with every slide of his hand on her thighs, Ashley laid there is silence while he continues to massage her legs. Doing this for a couple years now she has taught herself to not feel anything, the touch of strange men sickens her so she developed a way to put her mind somewhere else making her turn into more like a sexual prop rather than a real person, feeling nothing, the quicker she can get the men to ejaculate the better, in this case since there hasn't been any penetration to occur she doesn't know how long this will last.

"Just lie there and relax," he said. "I'm going to make you feel good."

Ashley laid there looking up at the ceiling trying to figure out the inner workings of this man's mind, when her head snapped up letting out a large moan, a moan equivalent to that of a female actress in a porno film. She can feel something penetrating her, with each stroke she lets out another moan each one louder than the next, it was a sound she never heard come out of her mouth before, never feeling this way during intercourse, something was off, whatever was inside her felt too hard and too long to be a penis. She can feel whatever it is going deeper and deeper insider her, her nails began scratching the felt on the pool table, it started to feel uncomfortable, tilting her head to view what was sliding in and out of her, to her disbelief the man was using a pool cue, getting more aroused with every stroke.

"Do you like that? Does it feel good?" he asked.

Ashley was slamming her hands on the pool table with every moan finally asking him to stop. He complied pulling out the cue, leaving her laying there breathing heavy. His string of perverted acts continued by sniffing the tip of the cue as she watched with suspicious eyes, her aching vagina never felt more violated, hoping she didn't start bleeding as he laid the cue back on the table. He requested for them to switch places to the chagrin of Ashley, wondering what kind of sick fantasy this guy is trying to play, lifting her naked body off the pool table as he laid himself in her place on his back.

"I want you to get up here and stand over my chest," requested Hector whose whole body laid perfectly flat in the middle of the pool table.

Ashley's confusion grew even more, to not risk injury she took off her heels figuring it would be more comfortable to stand on the table bare foot, also grabbing her blouse putting it back on. She climbs up on the pool table standing over his chest like he requested.

"Turn around and face the other way," he said. "I want to see that ass."

Ashley obliged turning herself around facing the other way, every second that past the stranger and stranger his request were becoming. He reached up squeezing her ass in excitement with both hands to help get himself worked up, laying one arm to his side, with the other reaching down to pull out his erected penis from his boxers grabbing it with his hand.

"Now I want you to squat down over my chest and shit and piss on it," he requested as he started jerking off.

Ashley couldn't believe what she just heard hoping she misunderstood what he just said, but she didn't, she heard him loud and clear. This was truly a sick and disgusting individual who probably has been waiting a long time to act out this gross and extremely disturbing act and she was the lucky female who gets to make his fantasy a reality, wanting nothing more than to tell this guy he was out of his mind, that she would never do anything that despicable even if she was getting paid for it, but she had no choice, if she didn't go through with it causing him to inform Razz of her failure to comply it risked her having a repeat episode of what happened last time she deliberately told a client no. She felt shackled to the moment with no way out, more than ever she wished it was just plain old intercourse, at least that was natural and would have respect for the guy, but this goes far beyond anything she has been asked to do, it would be like asking someone to kill a baby, you know it's wrong and you just don't do it. Right now the best thing for her to do was get it over with, give him just enough to hopefully satisfy his sick desires. She squatted down over his chest while at the same time watching him stroke his penis harder and faster the closer she got to position. He became more turned on when Ashley's asshole was in perfect view of his two starstruck eyes. Luckily for him she had some urine to spare and some bowels to empty, couldn't believe she was about to do this, starting off with dropping some fresh feces on his plastic-covered chest, just enough to hear him yell in delight. What was exciting him more, having it hit his chest or watching it on its way out. Never one to having a heinous odor to her bowels, but it still wasn't something that would tickle the nostrils, he must be breathing through his nose or the scent just doesn't bother him, maybe it arouses him more. Next it was time for her to empty her bladder which wasn't that much, just enough to wet the anus deposit as well as give the plastic shirt a little soaking. He must have enjoyed the sound of the urine stream hitting the plastic, at that moment he blew a load that almost hit Ashley in the face. Figuring this perverted circus act was over she let herself down off the pool table heading to the bathroom to wipe herself grabbing the rest of her clothes along the way, leaving him lying there with almost every execrable substance covering some portion of his body. Ashley exited the bathroom fully dressed minus her heels carrying a roll of paper towels for him to use to clean himself up and to clean any mess left behind, still in the same position as he was when she left walking up to the table.

"What's this?" he asked.

"To clean yourself up," Ashley replied.

"But we're not done, I want to lick your asshole," he remarked.

"Oh, we're done, you sick fuck!" said Ashley leaving the roll on the table. "Now hurry up and clean up. If Razz comes back and sees what you made me do in his office," she said putting her heels back on, walking over to sit in one of Razz' chairs.

"He already knows," he said sitting up with a wade of paper towels covered in shit, urine and semen. "I told him everything I wanted you to do."

Ashley sat there with her legs crossed and her arms folded shaking her head angry that Razz would let a strange man disrespect her like that. He gathered up his clothes to head to the bathroom to change, wasn't in there but five minutes reappearing wearing the same outfit he originally had on. At Razz' desk he poured himself a small glass of Jack Daniels from a bottle Razz must have left.

"I have to say I'm a bit surprised," he said knocking back his drink. "I thought all you whores were into everything."

Ashley's blood started to boil being called that word again, it kept every fiber of her being to keep herself seated in that chair, a rage was building up inside her, feeling like a volcano just waiting to erupt, was willing to offer him a blow job just so she could bite his dick off.

"Look at the bright side, you can think about me every time you got to use the toilet," he remarked laughing.

It was one thing for him to use her in a grotesque manner like he did, making her feel trashy like some gutter whore from the streets, but to make a disrespecting comment like that was the straw that broke the camel's back. She leaped out of the chair as if her body was on fire, darting towards him like a tiger lunging for its prey, her flailing arms caught him completely off guard as she continually connected her small fist with his chest in an attempt to connect with his face, being blocked with his hands to defend himself. Ashley could feel her adrenaline build up throughout her body, felt like an uncontrollable beast of rage wailing on this man when one of her fist happen to contact his jaw. Having enough of the unexpected onslaught, he quickly throws a back-hand hitting Ashley square on the side of the face, knocking her to the floor. Still feeding off her high dose of adrenaline, she quickly picks herself up like a boxer who's not ready to stay down, primed to return to finish what she started. Before she could get close enough to continue her attack, a pair of hands grabbed her arms from behind pulling her back. Ashley yelling obscenities, struggles to break free from the pair of hands holding her back, but their grip is too strong.

"SHOW HORSE, CALM THE FUCK DOWN!" Razz demanded.

Ashley got herself under control hearing his voice, breathing heavy from her sudden outburst.

"What the fuck is going on here?"

"Yo, man, this bitch is crazy," the man replied trying to compose himself.

"FUCK YOU!" yelled Ashley.

"I got what I wanted, I'm out of here," the man says grabbing his briefcase heading to leave the office through the back door. "Be talking to you soon, Razz, make sure you keep this bitch on a leash."

Ashley retaliated by spitting at Hector as he walked by prompting Razz to forcefully throw her into one of the nearby chairs.

"Show Horse, what the fuck are you doing?" Razz asked sternly standing over her with his hands on his hips.

"Why didn't you tell me what he wanted me to do?" Ashley asked a little choked up, releasing a couple tears down her face.

"What's the difference what he wanted? You do what I tell you," he replied, squatting to be in her face.

"'CAUSE I'M NOT SOME FUCKING ANIMAL!" she yelled, more tears descending down her face. "I never felt so trashy and disgusting in my life."

"I've treated you like a daughter, you know you are my number one. We're the same, Show Horse, only difference is I know who I am and where I belong. Do you know who you are? Do you know where you belong?" Razz remarked grabbing Ashley's face with both hands, wiping away her tears with his thumbs. "You're not here to worry about how you feel, you're here to work and do what I say. You want to be happy, make me happy. You know what I see when I look at you, I see the sexist bitch in the world." Razz begins licking and kissing her neck ending with a small peck on her lips.

"You're lucky I'm not going to lose him as a client," Razz said sticking two of his fingers up Ashley's skirt into her vagina causing an unexpected groan from her. "Remember that the next time you worry about how you feel."

Razz pulls out his fingers standing back up, one of his guards interrupts over his earpiece to let him know he has another visitor, Razz replies to let him in, looking back at Ashley always mesmerized and captivated by her natural beauty, letting her know he has more business to take care of, reminding her of their little conversation. Gesturing that she is free to go for the night, without hesitation she removes herself from the chair quickly making her exit from Razz' office.

It is a Monday morning, Jake was in his new office trying to get situated, mainly trying to adjust to the fact he has an office, a mainstream attribute of the modern workplace which he thought he would avoid through a career in professional athletics. With that door now shut he must now embrace his own mortality joining the ranks of the everyday nine-to-fivers, the punch-in-punch-out career, living the life he worked so hard to circumvent, but not many people get chances to reinvent themselves and this was his opportunity. The office itself was left in a pretty good mess, the old coach really didn't take too much out of it after he was fired, clean up would have to wait for another time though as he had bigger issues at hand, wanting to go through each girl's file to try and learn a little about each of them before their first practice together in afternoon. The filing cabinet was an old steel one with a bunch of rust patches appearing in certain spots, opening the drawers was a chore in itself as they seemed to stick forcing Jake to have to really pull hard on them. Succeeding in opening one of the drawers, he took a hand full of files placing them on his desk already covered in sheets of unrecognizable paper spread all over the top, some even covering up the keyboard to the computer found in the corner of the desk. The last coach was a definite slob who lacked any organizational skills, Jake could see the proof throughout the entire office, paperwork piled up everywhere from on top of the filing cabinet, to the one corner of the desk, to even an area on the floor. There wasn't an outside window, just a large window with a set of blinds on it viewing the hallway leading to the locker rooms. There is also a weird odor that manifest in the office which he needs to take care of, the place needed some work, but right now he had files to look at. Seating himself in the desk chair which looked like the only thing in the office that was still in decent shape, Jake began looking through the files. Concentrating hard reading through the information about each of his new players, he almost didn't hear the knock at his open office door.

"Hi, I don't mean to bother you. I'm Danielle Waters, I teach English here. I just wanted to come by introduce myself and welcome you to the school. I actually teach some of the girls on the team," said Danielle standing in the open doorway.

"Thank you, I'm Jake Wheeler," he replied, getting out of his seat to go shake her hand.

Jake firmly believed you can always tell a lot about a person, male or female, with how good their handshake is, hers was firm yet still lady like with her smooth soft skin, telling him that she is a strong woman, yet feminine who always acts like a lady, also finding her to be very attractive, her short dark hair laying perfectly straight and flat complimenting her big brown eyes, just the right amount of make up to accentuate her facial features including her perfect pearly white teeth, large hoop earrings dangled from her ears, wearing a nice silk burgundy blouse with a plain black skirt, nylon leggings down to her black half boots.

"I heard about what happened with the old coach," she remarked. "I couldn't believe he would do something that terrible."

"Yeah, but I can a sure you now these girls are in good hands," replied Jake smiling.

"Really, okay, I'm going to hold you to that," she said smiling back. "Well, I got to get to class, I'll probably see around. Nice to meet you, Jake."

"Pleasure was all mine," said Jake standing in his doorway watching Danielle walk away, looking at her butt as it disappears around the corner. "I'm starting to like this school," he says to himself.

Jake is standing at home plate of the girl's practice field holding a clipboard, wearing his new Lady Saints polo coaching shirt with matching baseball cap and a whistle around his neck, waiting for the girls to arrive which should be in another half-hour or so. He wanted to come out here earlier to draw up what he had planned for today and to check out the field conditions, which he now is equally impressed within relations to the rest of the school, the grass in the outfield is a healthy green perfectly cut, the dirt in the infield is smooth and leveled, showing they keep up with the regular racking needed. The pitcher's mound from what he can see is in great shape, mounded with nice clean dirt with the rubber in the middle, the dugout areas for the home and visiting teams looked in tip-top shape complete with canopy roof to give the players some extra shade during those sun soaked games. The homerun fence in the outfield houses the large electric scoreboard, beyond the fence you will find a wooded area partially cut down indicating some undetermined expansion will be going on.

The afternoon weather is rather pleasant, warm with a slight breeze, sunny with some cloud cover to provide some areas of shade. Jake notices a girl off in the distance making her way to the field, checking his watch he wasn't expecting the girls for another twenty-five minutes, couldn't quite make out who it was, but whoever it is she is running at a good pace. As the mystery girl drew closer, Jake quickly went over his notes for what was on the agenda for his first practice as coach, made up mostly of a lot of speaking to the girls on how he will be running practices going forward, throwing in some calisthenics at the end to start getting the girls in shape, batting and field work will start in tomorrows practice. The overanxious girl finally arrives to the field surprising Jake when it's revealed to be Ashley, just as surprised to see him out here so early as she makes her way to the dugout area.

"What are you doing out here so early?" Ashley asked.

"I was about to ask you the same thing," answered Jake.

"If you must know, whenever we did have practice which wasn't very often, I always showed up early so I could warm up before the rest of the girls got here or I would just practice by myself. Is that going to be a problem?" asked Ashley tightening up her cleats.

"Not at all, I can respect that," Jake replied.

"Okay, but you never answered my question, why are you here so early? I like to be alone when I do what I do," she informed.

"I guess just like you, I'm trying to loosen up," said Jake.

Jake was impressed with Ashley's ambitious manner, showing up early ready to work, knowing every team needs a player with that type of drive, lots of times it can become contagious rubbing off on the other players. She was even ready to go with her attire, hair in a ponytail sticking out the back of her baseball cap, yellow practice jersey, white knee-high socks along with black and white Nike cleats, topped off with her black colored glove.

"You won't be needing your glove today," said Jake.

"What are you talking about? I always bring my glove," Ashley remarked.

"That's great, but today you won't need it," Jake informed.

"Whatever," said Ashley.

Sensing already Ashley was going to be a handful, but the reason why this teams wins, Jake can tell she is the leader of this team and how this team performs will reflect on her. Getting her on the same page as him will be a task, but believes when that happens it will spill over to the other girls creating a well-oiled machine, assuming the rest of the girls can play at a particular level which he hopes to soon find out.

"If I don't need my glove, what am I doing here? What are we going to do today?" asked Ashley.

"I'd rather wait until the rest of the team is here before I announce what I have planned," responded Jake.

Ashley isn't liking how this coach player relationship is starting out, even though Coach Mabbet was a dick, he pretty much let her do whatever she wanted even though it pretty much cost her herself respect. Maybe this was what real coaching was like, maybe this what this team needs to be successful, still though not liking the fact she was going to be treated like all the rest of the girls on the team. Ashley was never an arrogant or cocky person, but knew she was the best player on this team and the best player should be treated differently or at least have some special perks.

"Can I ask you something?" Ashley asked.

"Yeah, sure, I want you to be able to ask me anything," replied Jake.

"Are you married, have a girlfriend or are you single?" she asked.

"That is kind of a weird question, but I am currently single at the moment," Jake answered.

"Do you like younger girls or do you like them older?" she asked.

"I don't think these are appropriate questions," Jake remarked. "Why don't we keep everything to softball-related questions."

"Sorry, just trying to have a conversation," Ashley remarked, her odd questioning was her way of subliminally trying to excrete any important information that might become valuable, yet her attempt fell short, but she didn't get discouraged knowing there will be other opportunities.

Jake looked at Ashley sitting there in the dugout, watching her blow bubbles with the chewing gum in her mouth, wondering if her reputation proceeds her as a ballplayer, anyone he has talked to or asked about her all seem to give the same response, she is one of the best at what she does and judging from her attitude and her body language, most certainly thinks she is going to live up to the hype.

"How many pitchers do we have on this team besides you?" asked Jake.

"Just one other girl," Ashley replied.

"That's it, just one other girl?" Jake remarked.

"You're only going to need me," Ashley responded. "I've never been pulled from a game and I always start."

"I have no doubt that is true, but we might want to consider having at least one more girl be available to pitch just in case, sometimes strange things happen and it's always good to be prepared," suggested Jake.

"I'm just telling you there are no other girls who can pitch on this team," replied Ashley. "Who do you think would know this team better right now?"

"I don't question you know the team better than me at the moment," Jake remarked, "but I bet I can turn one of our position players into a backup pitcher also."

Ashley sat there with her legs crossed and her arms folded listening to Jake make a pretty bold prediction, blowing another bubble while rolling her eyes at the thought.

As time ticked closer for practice to begin, the rest of the girls started arriving, all wearing their practice attire, also carrying their mitts. All the girls joined Ashley in the dugout with Holley J seating herself right beside her. Jake was impressed right away with all the girls showing up on time, gathering together like a team, seeing nothing but a sea of anxious faces sitting there in anticipation for what their first practice with their new coach would be like. This was going to be a learning process for both Jake and the girls since neither party knew hardly anything about the other. Jake started by thanking the girls for coming, then did a quick roll call to verify that all the girls were present, following that up with what the girls should expect at practices going forward, letting them know that practice will be held every day from four to six till the season starts, then practices will be held on days they don't have a game during the season at the same time with one day during the week set aside for rest. Judging from all the reactions he was getting from the girls, it seemed to be they were all fine with his scheduling. Standing before the girls holding his clipboard, hands crossed in front of him, the whistle around his neck sparkling in the sunlight, Jake went down the line looking at each girl individually, giving his head a little nod with each face that comes into his view. All eyes were on him now as he stood there with an aurora that seem to seduce the young ladies, ready to eat out of his hand with every word. Ashley still not convinced, remained sitting there with her arms crossed, shaking her head, knowing all too well how their old coach went about his manipulation tactics, especially on her, something she definitely doesn't want a sequel to, but she was the pitcher of this team and was going to start every game no matter what. Though she doesn't suspect Jake to be that type of person, she has been through enough in her life to realize she can't really trust anyone anymore forcing her to live her life behind an invisible wall.

"Before we get started I just want to tell you girls one thing, no matter how much talent you think this team has, no matter how hard you think you are working, you will never become a team if you don't give a damn about one another," Jake said pointing at random girls.

Sitting at the other end of the dugout was Renee, leaning forward to get a look at Ashley sitting on the other end hoping to make eye contact with her. Getting the feeling someone is staring at her, Ashley looks in Renee's direction, their eyes locked with Ashley receiving a sinister smirk before Renee disappeared back behind her seated neighbor. Ashley shakes her head in a non-worried manner, hoping to get through this season without any issues with her, but Renee has always been a thorn in her side she could never get rid of. The rest of the girls sat in silence, agreeing with slight nods of their heads. Convinced the girls have an understanding, Jake announces practice will now begin, ordering the girls to start running laps along the outside of the infield and outfield and not to stop till they hear the whistle. Their once intrigued faces turned to faces of disappointment as the girls left the dugout, leaving their mitts behind, to begin what was sure to be a grueling run. Observing the girls exiting the dugout, Jake noticed the girl with the eye patch, calling her over to him.

"Can I help you, Coach?" asked Brie.

"It's Brie, right?" Jake asked.

"Yeah," she answered.

"Just need to ask, how long till the patch comes off?" asked Jake.

"Not for another six months," she replied in a worried tone.

"Are you sure you are okay to play?" he asked.

"Yes, I'll be fine, I don't want to miss my last season because of some stupid eye surgeries," she remarked.

"It's okay, I'm not kicking you off the team," Jake replied noticing that the patch is over her left eye. "I just have one question, which way do you bat and what position do you normally play?"

"Well, I bat right handed and I normally play shortstop," Brie answered.

"Okay, just wanted to know," he said. "You can join the rest of the girls now."

Brie left to join her teammates with a small smile on her face, her fear of being taken off the team was dismissed. Jake wrote a few notes on his clipboard regarding Brie's temporary condition with a possible solution if his intuition about her limitations revels to be true. He believes there is a way around any physical defect with being completely blind being the only exception. Still believes he could still play, but the risks definitely outweigh the rewards. Some of the athletes he has witnessed during his playing years never ceased to amaze him, topping the list was the baseball player who used to pitch with only one hand. Now it is up to him to play the mad scientist to help this girl who so desperately wants to play, to fit in with the rest of the team, basically knowing he has the challenge of putting a circle in a square hole, but he was confident he could find a way to make it work. Jake stands there watching the girls run by, clapping his hands throwing out motivating phrases of encouragement. The sound of heavy breathing mixed with the visual of many of the girls doing more staggering than running puts in perspective the type of physical shape this team is in, sweat running down their faces, some of the girls' shirts are even showing signs of perspiration. The one thing that caught Jake's eye the most was Ashley leading the way the entire time, running out in front at a good distance away from the rest of the girls could definitely see now something special in this girl, her no-quit attitude she is demonstrating, running like if he told her to run till morning, he could come back when the sun came up and she would still be there running. Feeling the heat of the sun intensifying, coupled with the look of exhaustion on most of the girls' faces, Jake decided to blow his whistle ending the intense cardiovascular session. The sound of the whistle was music to the girls' ears as they stopped dead in their tracks to catch their breaths, all but Ashley who continued to keep running, having too much on her mind to stop running, all she could think about was what happened at the club over the weekend, the disgusting act she was forced to do, just thinking about it makes her want to keep running until she passed out from exhaustion. She has always heard about something called a runner's high, if you run long enough your body kind of catches a second wind where you supposedly feel your legs go numb and it feels like your running on air along with all the endorphins released in the brain putting you in a state of ecstasy, a feeling she was hoping would take her mind off the recent past. The rest of the girls walked over to the two large coolers of ice water located at one end of the dugout, quenching their obvious and deserving thirst. Jake congratulated the girls on a good first run, requesting they sit in the shaded dugout for a minute to relax. Ashley made another pass when Jake called her back in, acting like she didn't hear him she continued on her way. He dismissed the rest of the girls reminding them of practice tomorrow, telling them to have a good night. The girls grabbed their mitts heading back to the locker room conversing amongst themselves, a sweated up Holley J walks up to Jake, cup of ice water in her hand, watching Ashley running in the outfield.

"You better get used to this," Holley J remarked sipping from her cup of ice water, "she does this all the time."

"Holley J, right?" asked Jake. "Get used to what?"

"Her going above and beyond," said Holley J. "You want to know how much talent is on this team, it's all running right there out in the outfield. I'll see you tomorrow, Coach."

Holley J walks away leaving Jake to wait for Ashley to make her next pass. Just watching her run, the way she pushes herself, it was like looking in the mirror, he was doing the same thing at her age, the first one to arrive at practice and the last one to leave. He very much wanted to applaud her, but still had to get her to respect the coach player relationship. As she made the last turn towards the infield, he filled a cup with ice water to get her to at least take a drink. Ashley saw Jake standing there with a cup in his hand which she very much wanted, throat was so dry every time she swallowed it felt like sand paper. Finally stopping in front of Jake, sweat dripping down her face which she wiped away with the bottom of her practice jersey, happily accepting the drink which she chugged in a matter of seconds, thirsty enough to drink what was left in the cooler.

"Thanks," said Ashley trying to catch her breath.

"You know you don't have to try to impress me," remarked Jake watching the sweat continuing to bead up on Ashley's face.

"Who said I was trying to?" Ashley responded heading over to the cooler to get a refill of water and to get away from the relentless heat of the sun, parking herself in the dugout where she enjoyed her next cup, still breathing heavy and sweating, trying to relax a minute before calling it quits for the day.

Jake walked over sitting down beside her, a little moisture on his forehead from standing in the sun, laying his clipboard next to him an unexpected breeze passes through the dugout appreciating the cool air.

"How bad do you want to win this season?" Jake asked staring out into the empty softball field.

"What kind of question is that?" replied Ashley looking over at Jake with confusion in her eyes.

"Just like I asked, how bad do you want to win? Because if you want to win as bad as I think you do, you and I have to be on the same page. You know the pitcher is like the quarterback of a ball club, they get all the praise for winning, take all the blame for losing."

"What is your point?" Ashley asked.

"The point is you can't do this all by yourself," answered Jake. "If you want to win this season you are going to need my help. No one player, no matter how talented or skilled they may be, no one player is bigger than the team. If you go in with that mindset you will have already lost before you even step foot on the field. Remember that and I guarantee we will do plenty of winning this season."

Ashley soaked in Jake's words of wisdom thinking about the message, strangely she understood what he meant which kind of scared her. She is talented and the rest of the team knew that, even a player like Renee knew it but would never admit it, but her talent alone cannot carry this team which is something she has been trying to do for the past few years without any positive results. He was right, this team was going to need his help, she was going to need his help, something she never got from her old coach who basically put all the pressure on her, never was even a coach, it was more like he was just playing a part and collected a paycheck, he never brought out the best in her or any other girl on the team. Ashley can already tell Jake was the coach this team needed, what she needed, somebody with experience who has been through the fires and who can put all the pieces in the right place. For the first time in a long time she could feel a level of trust building inside her for Jake, even though he hasn't worked on fundamentals yet with them, can feel in her gut this team as well as herself are going to learn a lot, becoming a team would surprise even themselves. The jury is still out on whether she can trust Jake completely, the only person in her entire life she can trust one hundred percent is Holley J, seeing how every adult in her life has acted one way in the beginning then eventually the mask comes off revealing their true colors. It's hard for Ashley to trust anyone, in her mind everyone has a motive or a hidden agenda, it has gotten so bad for her that trust is one of her biggest fears, not a fear she wants or asked for, having gone through what she has been through in her life it would be perfectly understandable to anyone, there was no way she could escape it, it was basically programmed into her mind. If she one day wants to have a normal life, she must find a way to break through that barrier or else she will never enjoy a healthy relationship with a guy or specific people who may come into her adult life that may become important to her.

"I'll try and remember that," said Ashley leaving her seat to make her way back to the locker room.

"Hey, Stamper," said Jake, causing her to stop in her tracks. "Don't forget your mitt," tossing it over to her. "I'll see you tomorrow," Jake remarks flashing a friendly smile.

Ashley gives Jake a nod before running off to the locker room.

Monday night at the club was displaying early week attendance, not that there wasn't a good crowd, but nothing like it gets on the weekends, Razz usually had about six to eight girls working during the week compared to twelve to fifteen on the weekends. He normally saves Ashley for the weekends when it is the busiest, but occasionally he will call her in if there is a special request for her, tonight is one of those nights when he won't need her, the other girls are handling the workload just fine, most of the other girls don't like to work when Ashley does seeing how she steals most of the attention, Razz knows this which is why he doesn't have Ashley work every night because it bothers the other girls, on the weekends though he will tell them it's tough shit and to deal with it, when the other girls start to generate the type of money Ashley usually brings in then they can open their mouth.

Razz is in his office sitting on his couch, shirt off, cigarette in his mouth, heavy metal music playing in the background, doing some background checks on possible new buyers on his laptop located on the coffee table. He doesn't do business with just anyone, he is too smart for that, he'll perform extensive background checks, family history to see if he can find anything suspicious on a particular individual. As far as the transfer of money goes nothing is done over the computer, it's too easily traced, all the transfer of funds are done in person and in private leaving no trail of breadcrumbs for anyone to follow. Razz doesn't even own a credit card to avoid any paper trails, does all purchases in cash, any big purchases he does out of town where he will be most likely forgotten. Banks are another commodity he uses with great caution, he has a personal checking and savings account, along with an account for his club at a local bank, but he only keeps around a thousand dollars in his checking account and maybe triple that in his savings, ever so often he draw out some money or deposit a couple hundred dollars so it actually looks like to the bank that he uses the accounts, all the rest of his money he keeps in a large hidden walk in safe located somewhere on the premises, which he is the only one who knows its location. With each deal he may be handling hundreds of thousands of dollars, to keep the bank from growing suspicious of frequent large deposits he just stashes the money himself, again leaving no trail of the money ever existing. When it comes to the girls they are all paid in cash leaving no evidence that they actually work for him, if something were to happen to any of the girls he could just play stupid, acting like he didn't know who they were. The men on his payroll are paid the exact same way, which include his bouncers and guards, all his other employees, bartenders, waitresses, cooks and DJs are paid normally for tax purposes. Razz loves to stay as much under the radar as possible when it comes to making his deals or working with his suppliers, everything is done through text messages using a code that was created to hide what is actually being said, if anyone were to read the messages they would think he was buying food and supplies for his club, if an actual phone conversation needed to take place, Razz makes sure the call last no longer than thirty seconds to avoid a possible trace. It's these tactics and techniques that have kept him in business for over a decade now with not a single second look from the public or local law enforcement. Razz is much smarter than he looks always having a plan and always having each detail covered, right down to owning property in Canada as a contingency plan. The club was meant to be just a cover for his involvement in the drug trade, but when he saw how much more money he was generating, it became a major fraction of his financial endeavors, not to mention all the sexual benefits at his deposal. A large drug shipment is coming in soon which is going to score him a massive payday, wanting to make sure every detail is taken care of with his suppliers so everything goes through without a hitch, a shipment this size will have all his buyers chomping at the bit. Constantly checking his watch for one of his girls who is over a half-hour late, the rest of the girls are either dancing on stage or downstairs giving their clients personal attention. Tardiness is one of his biggest pet peeves especially from the girls, to him it is a sign of disrespect and he refuses to be disrespected in his own club. Razz hears a knock at his door inviting in the unseen visitor, watching one of the doors slowly open revealing a young woman dressed in regular street clothes, jeans, T-shirt and sneakers, her long blonde hair slightly covering her face to try to avoid eye contact, had a nervous look on her face which grew with every step she took.

"Get your ass in here and shut that God damn door," Razz said turning off the music, angrily blowing smoke out his nostrils and mouth like an angry dragon.

"Razz, I'm so sorry, I was at the doctors and lost track of time," said the woman in a panic.

"Shut your fucking mouth!" responded Razz getting up from his seat, walking over in front of his desk. "Get over here."

The frightened young woman walks over to Razz, head tilted slightly down still trying to avoid eye contact, feeling her body tense up the closer she got to him, stopping within arm's length, swallowing hard waiting for him to say something. He stares at her standing there, taking a drag from his cigarette, a look of irritation in his eyes, knowing this isn't the first time she has done this.

"Why are you late?" he asked, "and look at me when you fucking talk!"

"Again, I'm sorry," she replies raising her head to look Razz in the eyes, "like I said I had to go to the doctor's 'cause I have something to tell you."

"And what is that?" asked Razz.

"I'm pregnant," she stated with tears dripping from her face aware he wasn't going to be happy.

"You better be fucking joking," he remarked, the tension in his face seem to accentuate his facial scar with more definition.

"It's not from a client," she said with closed eyes, tears still seeping out. "I've been seeing this guy for the past few months...."

"SHUT UP!" Razz yells loudly right in her face, some of her hair fluttered back from the wind created by his voice, her tears increased. Razz stood there staring at her, cigarette dangling from his mouth, wiping away some of her tears with his hand, his gentle touch on her face gave her a surprising feeling of comfort resulting in a small smile, until the blunt force of his fist connecting with her gut sent her dropping to her knees gasping for air. Kneeling on the floor coughing, holding her stomach, feeling like any second she could vomit trying to catch her breath, Razz grabs her hair pulling her head back.

"You stupid bitch!" Razz says pulling harder on her hair in anger. "What did I tell you about getting involved with outside men?"

"I'm sorry, it just happened," she responded with tears dripping into her mouth, still feeling the effects from the blow to the gut.

"I don't want to hear your fucking excuses. Get rid of it or I'll get rid of both of you," he says throwing her head forward releasing her hair.

She remained knelt on the floor trying to gather herself together, beginning to breathe normally with her crying starting to subside, wondering if this physical altercation already damaged the pregnancy which she found out earlier in the day was about nine weeks along.

"You're still working tonight, so get your fucking shit together," demanded Razz, "and get the fuck out of my office," bending over to whisper in her ear, "and the next time I see you you'd better be riding solo," he stated blowing smoke in her direction.

The young woman slowly brought herself to her feet still holding her stomach, gingerly walking her way out of the office.

Razz began pacing in front of his desk, his anger has accumulated all this pent-up energy making him feel like a ticking time bomb, knowing what he has to do to release it, quickly leaving his office making his way to the area of the club where the girls give private lap dances, his walk demonstrates a man with determination and purpose. The loud music of the main area thunders on with one of the girls on stage, the above average crowd in attendance clap and whistle with male excitement as he makes his way down the appropriate hallway, checking every single one of the small rooms until he finds one that is occupied. The search ended when he found one of his girls giving a young college kid a dance, without hesitation Razz grabs the girl by the wrist pulling her out of the room leaving the kid with his visible wet spot, pulling the surprised girl down the hallway who is wearing nothing but a thong and a pair of clear heels, takes a shortcut back to his office to avoid passing through the main area. Reentering his office with his companion, closing the doors behind them, Razz drags the girl to the front of his desk where he bends her over the top, ripping off her thong proceeding to pull his pants down exposing his erect penis. The girl braces herself gripping the front of the desk with her hands realizing what is about to unfold. Razz violently inserts his penis into her vagina from behind bringing her to let out a loud moan, continuing to thrust in and out with anger each matched with moans of pleasure, reaching around her with both arms to start squeezing her breasts, hard enough to warrant a few whimpers of pain from her. Moving one hand up to her lips she starts sucking on his fingers, as the intercourse became its most physical, Razz climaxed inside her groaning the release of his pent-up frustration, removing his hands from her body, standing there damp from sweat, removes himself from inside her grabbing a cigarette from off his desk.

"Get the fuck back to work," Razz barks lighting his cigarette.

The young woman without saying a word grabs her newly ripped thong quickly leaving Razz' office. He remained standing there naked puffing on his newly lit cigarette, eventually pulling his pants up, giving his neck a good cracking to each side. Worrying about getting one of his girls pregnant is not an option for him since he had a vasectomy years ago to prevent him from ever fathering a child, never wanting kids, he knew they would just cramp his lifestyle, along with the fact he never wants to be bonded to any one girl. Feeling a sense of relief from releasing that pent-up energy after a good hate fucking, Razz goes behind his desk opening one of the side drawers grabbing a small black box. Cigarette in his mouth, he brings the box over placing it on his coffee table, seating himself on the couch pulling out his wallet. Opening up the box filled with cocaine, he removes enough to create a couple lines, has gotten good enough to grab a couple pinches with his fingers to acquire the proper amount. Closing the box back up, placing it to the side, he grabs a five-dollar bill out of his wallet along with a couple small razor blades which he uses to even out the two lines. When preparation is completed he rolls up the five-dollar bill, snorting each line, one in per nostril. The numbing sensation of each line traversing his sinus column, he can feel the almost immediate release of endorphins in his brain giving him the much welcomed high, leaning back with his bare torso on the leather couch taking a nice long drag from his cigarette, blowing the smoke upwards towards the ceiling, laying his head back closing his eyes.

Tuesday morning, school started like a typical day for Ashley, at her locker transferring contents from her backpack and vice versa, waiting for Holley J's arrival. She has been thinking about what Jake said to her at practice yesterday, been consuming her mind since, with what little free time she had last night at home to do a little painting, she found herself unable to keep her focus, just staring at a blank canvas for over an hour. Holley J is late as usual, Ashley always said she would be late for her own funeral, not something Holley J does on purpose, she is just not the best at managing her time. Waiting for her every morning is one part of the day Ashley dreads most, being surrounded by the overabundance of adolescent chit-chatter mixed with a sea of raging hormones is not how she wishes to start her day, to help block out the overflowing ocean of before class commotion, she will sometimes put in her earbuds letting her music drown out the sounds of morning high school antics. This was one of those mornings, pulling out her earbuds from her backpack while searching diligently for her hiding iPod. The search is interrupted by a male voice she hasn't heard for quite a while.

"Hey, Ash," the male voice said standing behind her shouldering his own backpack.

Ashley didn't have to turn around to know who it was, recognizing Kevin's voice from the many times he attempted to ask her out. It has been months since she bluntly told him she wasn't interested, making her wonder now what the sudden visit could be about, politely turning to greet her unwelcomed visitor.

"Hey," Ashley said turning her focus back on searching for her missing iPod.

"How have you been?" asked Kevin picking up the scent of Ashley's perfume. "I like that perfume your wearing."

"Great, maybe I will get you a bottle," Ashley replied sarcastically with her back to him.

"I've always liked your wittiness," he remarked.

"You know in the interest of saving time, why don't you just tell me what you want," said Ashley quickly turning to face him once again, trying to figure out what annoys her more, her nearby locker neighbors able to eavesdrop in or the fact that this guy can't take a hint.

"I don't know if you know, but Renee and I are kind of on the outs right now," said Kevin.

"Really, does she know this?" Ashley responded going back to looking for her iPod.

"Things with her and I just haven't been the same, her jealousy lately has been driving me crazy, seems like all we do is fight," states Kevin. "So I was just wondering since it has been a while since I asked, would you like to hang out sometime?"

"I'm going to give you the same answer I gave you six months ago, I'm not interested," Ashley said leaning her back against her locker scrolling through her iPod for something to listen to. These are the moments when Holley J couldn't get there fast enough, hoping this situation doesn't come back full circle like it was the last time with him constantly asking her out, it got so bad last time she almost had to complain to Principal Davis. Nothing turns Ashley off more than guys who are persistent, to her it shows a lack of respect and screams neediness, it's not that she thinks Kevin is a bad guy, she just doesn't feel it with him, there's no spark, when she is around him it feels like what it would if she had a brother. It wasn't just Kevin, she had no interest in dating anyone, she doesn't think it would reasonable to bring someone into her crazy fucked-up life, having to keep a partner happy in a stupid teenage relationship that would probably be over before it starts, she has to figure out how to make herself happy before she could do the same for someone else.

"I don't understand, what is it about me you don't like?" Kevin asked.

"Kevin, will you please read my lips, I don't want to go out with you," Ashley replied with an irritated tone in her voice. "Now will you please just leave me alone, I'm trying to be nice here." As the last words of her request left her lips, she was greeted by the one person she didn't want to see at that moment.

"Well, well, well, why am I not surprised to find you here," remarked Renee looking at Kevin with daggers in her eyes, standing there with her backpack on and hair tied back.

"He was just leaving," Ashley replied.

"Babe, I was just saying hi," said Kevin.

"Really, you weren't over here trying to ask her out?" Renee asked folding her arms, Kevin broke eye contact in an attempt to hide his guilt. "You know what, Stamper, you're pathetic, you just can't stand it that I have something you can't have."

"Oh, please! You do realize he came to my locker, right?" Ashley responded.

"Got something funny to say now, Stamper?" asked Renee getting up in Ashley's personal space, the creases in her forehead advertise her displeasure.

"Get out of my face," Ashley demanded looking Renee dead in her eyes.

"And what if I don't, what are you going to do about it?" said Renee in a threatening manner.

This is not how Ashley wanted to start her day, getting shit from the one person at this school who seems to like to start trouble for no reason, feeling it in her bones that the two of them my come to blows, something she definitely doesn't want to do. It's bad enough there would be an audience of students around cheering them on like a bunch of savages, but worse yet she could get suspended for fighting meaning no softball practice and she would lose eligibility to play in the team's first game, the same fate would come to Renee, but she is host to a personality that really doesn't think that far ahead. Standing there face to face with who Ashley considers to be her arch rival, thinking about all the times Renee has intentionally pushed her buttons, accusing her a things that she never did, smelling her cheap perfume, started to make her blood boil, can feel the inability to think clearly, like an overstressed mind about to snap. Her anger started to get the best of her, could feel it taking over her body bringing her to push Renee back enough to draw attention from the curious on lookers. Stunned by Ashley's surprising action, Renee retaliates by pushing her back, slamming her into her locker. Kevin quickly gets between the two girls in an effort to try to defuse the situation before it escalates or a person of authority takes witness. Arriving just in time to hold back a heated Ashley, Holley J gets in front of her friend trying to calm her down while Kevin tries to do the same with Renee. Though the girls are now separated, it doesn't stop them from throwing words like bitch back and forth to each other, even the word cunt was heard by the many students who happen to see the brief altercation.

"Get your own goddamn boyfriend, bitch!" yelled Renee being pulled down the hallway by Kevin.

"Maybe if you took care of him, he wouldn't be barking up this tree!" Ashley yells back with Holley J still holding her back frantically trying to calm her down.

Renee taken away and out of view, Ashley begins to calm herself down, still not happy with a handful of students who were able to witness the dispute, but felt a state of comfort that Holley J was there now. Though Kevin gets on her nerves, Ashley never knew what he saw in Renee, she is a pretty girl and can be feminine at times, but can tell by looking at her she is a jock, maybe that was the attraction, since he was quarterback of the varsity football team.

"What the hell was all that about?" asked Holley J as she opened up her locker.

"I don't want to talk about it," answered Ashley still a bit steaming with how her morning has started.

"Okay, but this should make for an interesting practice this afternoon," Holley J remarked finishing her morning locker routine.

Three minutes until their first class, the two of them leave their lockers, backpacks aboard, taking their normal route through the hallways. Ashley couldn't help but feel the presence of multiple sets of eyes looking at her as she and Holley J worked their way through the busy hallways. The last thing she wants is to be the topic of between class conversations where her name is dragged through the mud like she is some kind of high school deviant, who knows what might have happened if Holley J hadn't shown up when did. The real challenge will be to try keeping her mind off of what happened, luckily she has no classes with Renee, won't see her at least until practice later, like Holley J said this should be very interesting. The final bell of the school day sounded, students empty out of their respected class rooms like a flood, all eager to get to their lockers to make their escape to freedom for the rest of the day, the only ones that stick around are the ones with extracurricular activities or practice for their certain sport. Ashley looks forward to this time of the day even if it is just practice, it's softball regardless, of course she likes the competition of the games much better, but even during practice she is still out there doing what she loves. Practice doesn't start technically for about an hour which gives her time to run to her locker, grab her gear and make her way to the practice field hopefully before any of the girls get there, hopefully before Jake does also. Ashley let Holley J know she was heading to practice earlier during their last class together, something Holley J is not surprised about, would usually join her, but she has to stay after class for a little bit for some extra credit help. Putting her gear in her backpack, Ashley closes her locker door to start her march to the girls' locker room, this is the time of day when she enjoys walking through the hallways at school, it's peaceful with most of the hallways deserted, some of them are so quiet she can actually hear the echo from her footsteps as she walks. A few students still roam the halls as she continues on, but nobody she has to worry about stopping her for a little chitchat. Arriving at the locker room activating the motion censored lights to illuminate the area, Ashley parked herself in front of the locker she has become accustomed to using, quickly changing into her practice attire, always felt a slight eeriness changing in an empty locker room by herself, it felt like she was in a scene in a bad horror movie with any second the killer would pop out murdering her topless body. Getting changed she caught a glimpse of herself in the large wall mirror hanging at the end of the aisle, she stood there staring, hair tied back, breasts exposed, wearing nothing but a pair of pink knitted underwear, the way the light hit the glass seem to make all her features stand out. Ashley never liked looking at herself, hated what was looking back at her, it wasn't anything physical, almost every girl no matter their age would kill to have a body like hers, perfect-sized breasts, flat toned stomach, nice toned legs and an ass that would make Jennifer Lopez jealous. Playing sports, exercising when she can and eating healthy rewarded her with her physique, but it was what she saw on the inside that always made her turn away, she sees is a damaged, abused, ugly monster not worthy of her body, there were times when she wanted to start cutting herself so the outside could match what she sees on the inside, luckily for her she can't stand the sight of blood and who knows what Razz would do if his prize wasn't in showroom shape, one day she would like to look at herself in the mirror and smile. Finishing getting dressed Ashley couldn't help but think about the friction that might bare its ugly head at practice today when Renee arrives, she wasn't going to let her ruin her last season, all they had to be is teammates, they don't have to be friends, but this is the worse it has gotten between the two of them where it started to get physical. It was normally just a lot a trash talking, but this morning was on a whole another level, one that worried Ashley a little bit. She tried to put it out of her mind for there were other things to worry about like getting through this next practice, putting her feet on the aisle bench to tie her cleats, she grabbed her mitt, quickly leaving the locker room to head for the field.

Ashley arrives at the field not surprisingly being the first one there, even beating Jake this time. The weather again is perfect for practicing, warm with the sun shining, a slight breeze to help cancel out some of the heat. Before getting started she walked over to the pitcher's mound to stand quietly by herself, stood there looking down at home plate, closing her eyes to get a smell of the cut grass and dirt of the infield, feeling the wind pass through her body. This is where she feels the most happy, this is where it feels like home, the only place where she feels like she has control and nothing else matters. Opening her eyes squatting down to pick up a handful of dirt off the mound, she held it under her nose sniffing the small sample, afterwards rubbing her hands with the dirt to feel the texture on her bare skin, standing back up digging her cleats into the dirt as if she was getting ready to throw a pitch. Everything felt right as she stood there surveying the infield, picturing being in the middle of a game being watched by the modest crowds that usually attend the girls' games, visualizing the few scouts that would grace her with their presents in the nearby bleachers. Ashley started having conversations with scouts her sophomore year, they knew how good she was, but they always wanted to see how well the team performed throughout each season, since they haven't had a winning record her whole high school career it has put a blemish on her recruiting even though they know she is by far the best player on the team, they want to make sure she can pitch for a winning team, that is what makes this final season so important, Ashley knows nothing short of making it to sectionals will help her cause, being recruited and earning a scholarship is her ticket out of there, the chance to start a new life she so desperately wants and deserves. With the start of practice inching closer, Ashley decides to start her warmups, doing her variety of different stretches to get good blood flow to her muscles, especially her legs and pitching arm, following that up with a run around the field similar to what she had to do yesterday. One of her best physical attributes is her stamina, pitching a seven-inning game can be tiring at times, but feels if she had to could force herself to pitch double that. Many people always wondered why as a pitcher does she need to run a lot, because she is also one of the best hitters on the team as well, being able to run the bases is another aspect of her game, an aspect she is also very good at having very good speed for her body type. There is no aspect to Ashley's game someone would say is just average, she is just an all-around great player and would be a game changer on any team. Her run was at a good steady pace, not too fast and not too slow, just the right speed where she can feel her heartrate begin to increase, fast enough to get her pores to start leaking. After a few good laps she decides to shut it down to stretch out some more, feeling the muscles in her body warming up, becoming more flexible by the second which is good preventative maintenance for preventing injuries, the one bullet of athletic competition she has been able to dodge her whole career, not to say she hasn't had her share of close calls, coming from someone who always plays at hundred and ten percent, but for the most part she has been lucky, one of the few parts of her life where luck has actually played a factor. It does scare her though when she reads stories of athletes whose careers were cut short do to horrific injuries, case in point her new coach, a once promising baseball star now reduced to coaching high school girls' softball. Ashley used to think she would be next, just be another dark cloud hovering over her crazy life, but it hasn't happened and she learned to just put it out of her mind letting fate take care of the rest.

Finishing her stretching over by the shaded area near the dugout to stay cool, she sees someone off in the distance walking towards the field carrying what looks like a couple buckets full of balls while shouldering a bag full of bats. Knew right away it was Jake, his shiny whistle sparkled in the sunlight, seeing him with his hands full Ashley felt compelled to run over to see if he needed some help.

"Need a hand?" Ashley asked, causing Jake to stop dead in his tracks.

"I thought you might be out here," replied Jake. "Yes, please, can you take a bucket of balls?"

Ashley grabs one of the buckets out Jake's hands, walking beside him as they both head toward the field.

"How long have you been out here?" asked Jake seeing the sweat beading up on her face.

"I don't know, maybe a half-hour, I really don't keep track," Ashley responded carrying the bucket of balls with two hands due to the lack of grip from her sweaty palms.

"I just don't want you to wear yourself out before practice even starts," Jake remarked.

"I'll be fine," Ashley responded as the two of them reached the field.

Jake instructs Ashley to leave her bucket by home plate, doing the same with his while dropping the bag of bats by the fence directly behind them.

"Another beautiful day," Jake said, "so I'm assuming you are all warmed up. Grab your mitt, let's play a little catch until the rest of the girls get here."

Jake grabs a mitt he brought for himself from the bag of bats, grabbing a ball out of one of the buckets. Ashley didn't know what to make of the strange request, has never been asked to play catch with anybody her whole life other than with Holley J which would usually happen right before a game to warm up, but never one on one with someone other than her alone in private, it was something she wished would have happened more throughout her life, the lack of suitable or reliable partners may be the reason she missed out on this common activity. With Jake standing by home plate she ran over to grab her mitt relocating herself near third base, with gloves in hand Jake makes the first throw.

"Are you pretty excited for this season?" asked Jake, hearing the softball land inside Ashley's glove with a loud pop.

"Yeah, why wouldn't I be?" Ashley replies throwing the ball back with some gusto on it, hearing the same loud pop when it enters Jake's mitt.

"Nice throw," said Jake returning the ball back, "you're probably wondering what we are going to do today, huh?"

"Is it something other than running?" Ashley asked throwing the ball back.

"Yeah, something other than running," Jake answers making the catch. "Actually for the rest of the practices this week I'm going to find out what positions everyone should be playing, that includes you."

"Excuse me?" she remarked catching Jake's next throw.

"I've heard you can pitch and I believe it, but now it will be your chance to prove it," replied Jake catching Ashley's next throw which arrived with a little extra heat on it/ "Don't worry, you are still the pitcher for this team," says Jake smiling, "but I want you to also be an example, everyone has to earn their spot. Remember, no one is above the team."

Ashley stood there catching Jake's next throw pondering the issue of setting an example, that everyone has to earn their spot, something she never had to do, she was always the starting pitcher for this team. It actually irritated her to think she had to prove herself, wondering if this was a sneaky motivational tactic to get her to show her true worth knowing she is considered one of the best, either way she wasn't going to take her spot on the team for granted, she would show Jake that everything he has heard about her is true and then some.

"I'm not worried in the least," Ashley said returning the ball back to Jake.

"Good," responded Jake catching her recent throw, quickly looking at his watch noticing it's almost time for the other girls to arrive, informing Ashley to take a break and grab some water.

The rest of the team is now present sitting in the dugout waiting for Jake to finish taking attendance, patiently giving him their full attention. Seated at one end is Renee looking down past the other girls focusing all her attention on Ashley who is oblivious to the evil stare. With all the girls accounted for Jake announces what the plan is for today's practice and for the rest of the week, with the girls in agreeance Jake starts them out with a warmup run around the field, topped off with some team stretching. The girls leave the dugout to begin their run which included Ashley who doesn't mind having to run again, leading the pack of girls as Jake watched from afar, the run seemed much easier this time for Ashley seeing she is already warmed up. After a couple of laps she leads the girls over to a grassy part of the infield to lead them in their stretching. Jake takes notice at how Ashley takes charge of the other girls and how they respond to her, can tell she is a born leader, the other girls follow whatever command she initiates and do it without hesitation, except for one girl he noticed doing the complete opposite of everything she said, making a note of that on his clipboard, singling herself out from the rest of the girls with her actions. After a good ten minutes of stretching, Jake was ready to start practice giving the girls the order to grab their mitts, instructing all the starters on the team to position themselves in their normal spots in the field. The starters placed themselves in their regular defensive positions, Ashley took the mound, Holley J now in full catcher's gear, got behind home plate, Renee was alone in centerfield and Brie was in her shortstop position followed up with the rest of the starters. Having all the girls in their designated spots, Jake standing near Holley J, calls for Brie to come join him at home plate. Brie taken by surprise at the call out, graciously leaves her position at short heading towards home plate, Jake instructs one of the girls observing from the dugout to fill in for Brie at shortstop. Jake tells Brie to grab a bat and place herself in the batter's box. Following orders she grabs a bat from the bag she would normally use, being a little on the petite side, she liked to use a low once aluminum bat, finding it easier for her to swing. A bat now in hand, she goes over to stand in the righthanded batter's box, her along with every other girl on the team is wondering why he chose Brie, one of the smallest girls on the team, to come up to bat first. Jake grabbed a ball from one of the buckets, throwing it out to Ashley, telling her to pitch and not to hold back. Every girl was stunned by his request, they all knew Brie could never hit off Ashley, even more so now that she only has one good eye at the moment.

"Excuse me, Coach," said Holley J standing up taking off her catcher's mask, "do you really think this is a good idea? No offense to Brie, but she could never hit off Ashley."

"I don't take offense and she is absolutely right," Brie responded.

"Then just make contact with the ball," Jake said. "Oh, and Ashley, nothing but fastballs, please."

Holley J put her mask back on squatting down in position shaking her head in disbelief, Brie got in her batter's stance taking a couple of deep breaths, choking up on the bat feeling her hands getting sweaty in anticipation of the first pitch, had a look on her face as if she was staring down the barrel of six rifles from a firing squad. Jake signaled to Ashley to fire away, looking at Holley J flashing the fastball sign. Holley J got ready as Ashley wound up firing the first pitch, the ball flew in so fast that Brie swung after the ball already hit Holley J's mitt.

"Again," Jake said.

Holley J threw the ball back to Ashley, Brie takes another deep breath as sweat starts to drip down her face. Receiving the sign again, Ashley winds up firing another pitch ending in the same result, another late swing. Jake instructs them to do it once again. With the ball returning to Ashley, Brie takes yet another deep breath, her hands so sweaty now she can barely grip the bat, waiting for the next pitch to come in, like déjà vu Ashley fires the next pitch resulting in the same ending causing Brie to swing the bat to the ground in frustration.

"Okay, what are you trying to prove?" Ashley asked. "Are you trying to embarrass her?"

"You can stop, I've seen all I needed to see," Jake replied, walking over to Brie who is obviously extremely frustrated. "Why do you think you were swinging late?" Jake asked. "I think I could tell you why. You couldn't see the ball until the very last second which is too late, that sound about right?"

Brie shamefully looks up at Jake nodding her head.

"And you know why that is, it's because the eye you need to bat right handed is out of order right now."

"So what am I supposed to do?" Brie asked.

"I'll tell you what you are going to have to do, for now you are going to have to learn to bat left handed," answered Jake.

"What? I'm a righty, I can't learn to bat left handed," Brie remarked.

"Did you hear that, everybody? Brie said the word can't," Jake said in a loud voice so all the girls could hear him. "If you use the word can't you have already failed. From this day forward that word should not exist in your vo-cabulary, is that understood?"

Most of the girls answered with a slight nod while others answered with eyes at his attention including Ashley.

"For the rest of practice today and for the rest of the week, you are going to take this bat, go off to the side somewhere practicing swinging left handed. And you will keep doing it until it feels like your arms are about to fall off and if they do, we will just reattach them and you will keep swinging left handed. Do you understand?" asked Jake.

Brie answers with a couple nods. "When were you normally hitting in the batting order?"

"Like sixth or seventh," Brie answered.

"If I remember correctly according to your file it says you also run track, is that true?" Jake asked.

"Yes, sir," replied Brie.

"Well, then that means I am going to give you the chance to try and become our leadoff hitter, as far as playing shortstop that will probably have to change as well. I don't need you to become a great lefthanded hitter, all I need you to do is make contact with ball and get on base. I know how much you want to play and this is going to be a hard task to overcome, but sometimes you have to do what is best for you and the team," said Jake. "Look at it this way, when you bat left handed you are three feet closer to first."

Brie cracked a small smile as Jake smiled back at her. Ashley stood there watching and listening to Jake interact with Brie, observing how a true coach is supposed to interact with his players, he saw a problem and he came up with a solution, maybe not the solution she was hoping for but one nevertheless, one that still gives her a chance to play and help the team. Ashley was im-pressed to the point where she felt bad for snapping at Jake who was just trying to prove a point, sometimes players have to make sacrifices for the benefit of the team, corresponding to his point that no one is bigger than the team. Each of these little moments help to chip away at the invisible trust barrier she has put around Jake. It made her excited to see what else he can do with this team as the season inches closer, for the first time in a long time she can honestly tell herself the team may finally be in good hands.

As practice continued, Jake announced he wanted to evaluate the girls' defensive skills, implying he would hit balls tossed to himself from home plate to each of the girls out in the field and outfield, wanted them to make a play at first base, the outfield just needed to make the catch and throw to the cutoff man. Bringing a bucket of balls with him to home plate, he started out by sending a fast dribbler to third, the ball seems to skip effortlessly across the freshly raked dirt of the infield as it approaches the third baseman. The girl gets under the speeding grounder scooping it up in her glove, bobbling it for a second as she prepares to throw, firing a nice frozen rope to first right on target with the awaiting first baseman's glove who could not make the catch as it was dropped upon entry. Jake commended the girl at third for a nice pick-up and throw, telling the girl at first to shake it off, showing her frustration for not making the catch. Yelling to the girls in the outfield the next one is coming their way, grabs another ball out of the bucket, tossing it up, hitting a rocket deep to the outfield, Ashley and the rest of the girls turned to watch the ball go so deep that it sailed well past the outfield fence clearing it by a good two hundred feet, Holley J had to take her mask off to watch the ball disappear in the sunlight. Forgetting how small girls softball fields are compared to the ball parks he used to play in when he was in the majors, he accidently gave the swing a little too much muscle resulting in the humorous outcome. All the girls on the team began laughing, with the girls in the outfield putting their arms up in confusion as Jake sent them his apologies. Ashley was trying to hold back her laughter, but it was too strong causing her to bust out a large smile while shaking her head. Jake promised the girls this time he wouldn't get overexcited with his swings, tossing another ball he gave a full, but weaker swing sending the ball in a perfect trajectory towards Renee in center field. She got under it waving off the other outfielders indicating she has it, might have lost the ball in the sun light if she wasn't wearing her special pair of game sunglasses, the ball descended directly in her mitt which she quickly threw to the cutoff man. Jake sent commending words out Renee's way as the ball made its way back to Holley J's glove, telling Ashley the next one is coming towards her, advising he wanted her to turn two. Hitting another speeding dribbler in Ashley's direction, she ran up on it grabbing the ball still in motion bare handed, firing a laser to second base which was reciprocated back to first where the first baseman proceeded again to mishandle the throw, looking all distraught after her latest error. Impressed with Ashley's extra effort, he couldn't think of anything to say but to give her an enthusiastic thumbs-up, while quickly making a mental note of the continuous flawed play of the first baseman.

Practice continued on with much of the same, even giving the girls who were observing off to the side a chance to play different positions to get evaluated. Brie was still off to the side struggling with swinging the bat left handed, going as far as swinging herself off balance because of the unnatural motion of a righthanded hitter, having to reprogram her body to do something it was never meant to do, a few times she would sword swing the bat to the ground in frustration, but would gather herself and keep on swinging. Jake knew this was only the first day of actual real practice, but he gathered enough metal notes so far as to what changes need to be made for this team to be successful, going to give all the girls the benefit of the doubt, thinking maybe some were just having a bad day, but by the end of the week he should have all the data he needs to put all the pieces in the right place. The two hours designated for practice came to an end forcing Jake to call it for the day, can see between the heat and the constant chasing down of balls for almost an hour and a half, the girls have had enough for the day. Blowing his whistle to dismiss everyone, they all headed over to the coolers for a cup of ice water, Brie showed the most excitement, for now she is done swinging that bat for the rest of the day. Most of them all crammed trying to get their cups filled, looking like a bunch of moths to a bright light. Jake asked a couple of the girls to grab a bucket of balls and grab the bag of bats and the few batting helmets to carry them back to the equipment room. Ashley taking a sip of her water felt a shoulder to her back side causing her to spill most of her drink.

"Oops," said Renee as she continued walking.

Ashley held back from running after her, made it through practice without an incident, but if this is the type of childish behavior she can expect from Renee this season, it is going to take every ounce of self-control not to eventually retaliate. Like a typical bully, girls like Renee feed off your reaction to their ignorant little passive aggressive acts, Ashley knew the best thing she could do was let little incidents like this just roll off her or punch her dead in the face which is what she really wants to do, but she wants to be the bigger person here, dealing with enough bullshit, now it seems like her unintentional rivalry with Renee is mutating into something more.

Ashley sat in the dugout watching the rest of the girls head for the locker room, stopping one of the girls who was asked to carry one of the buckets of balls, to leave it, she would take care of it, the girl obliged leaving the bucket by Ashley. Jake was commending the girls on a good practice as they left, wishing them a good night and he would see them tomorrow. Holley J now with her gear off, sits beside Ashley, sweating heavily from wearing all that equipment, noticed the bucket of balls resting in front of them, meaning Ashley is going to stay a little longer.

"Pretty good practice today," said Holley J wiping some of the sweat from her face with a small towel she always brings to practice.

"Yeah, I guess," Ashley replied, "pretty cool what he is doing for Brie, though."

"Yeah, I was afraid she wasn't going to be allowed to play," responded Holley J. "I see that you are going to stay after again," pointing to the bucket of balls.

"Just for a little while," said Ashley.

"I would stay with you but I got a ton of homework," Holley J said taking a sip of ice water.

"I know, it's okay," replied Ashley, feeling her cell phone vibrate hidden in one of her pockets. One of Jake's rules is no cell phones at practice, they must be kept in their lockers, a rule she would normally obey, she doesn't like to be distracted either when it comes to softball, but she has to keep it on her at all times because of her aunt and Razz, mostly because of Razz for if he sends a text out to one of his girls and he doesn't get a response within ten minutes he'll send out a couple of his goons to find them, which will be easy for them to do because he placed tracking devices in all his girls cell phones so they can be located if need be.

"Then I will just text you later?" Holley J asked.

"You better," Ashley responded, watching Holley J leave.

Quickly pulling out her phone to find out who was texting her, it was revealed to be her aunt, texting her a grocery list for her to pick up on her way home, a list which included beer when her aunt knows she is too young to buy alcohol. It's just another added chore to an already ridiculously over inflated curriculum, putting her phone back shaking her head in disbelief, there is no reason her aunt can't go shopping, she is probably just sitting around getting high or drinking. Now she has to cut her extra practice session short so she will have time to get to the store, get home, do her other chores and do her homework. A good coach never leaves practice until all his players have left, Jake watches his team scurry their way back towards the locker room to finally get out of the hot sun, for some of them it means a date with a nice cool shower, but he knows to expect one to be left behind. Looking over at the dugout he sees what he expected to see, Ashley sitting taking a breather before she did whatever she was going to do, he had some idea with one bucket of balls still remaining. He walked over hoping to get a peaceful encounter, maybe even help her out.

"Looking to do a little overtime?" Jake asked.

"Yeah, and I hope that's not going to be a problem," she replied standing up grabbing the bucket of balls heading back towards the pitching mound.

"Not a problem for me, just wondering if I could help," suggested Jake. "I'm assuming you want to throw some pitches, I figured I could be your catcher for you."

Ashley stood on the mound somewhat taken by surprise by Jake's offer, a coach of hers has never offered to stay after practice to help her, usually it would be Holley J to make such a gesture, all her old coach wanted was to use her, making sure she gave good head so she could get what she wanted. To see Jake offer up some of his valuable time was evidence to her that maybe he did care about this team succeeding, that he cared about her succeeding, has only been the coach for a short time, but Ashley can already tell there is a night and day difference. Her old coach could care less about helping his players or if the team succeeded, he hardly ever held practices and if he did he just sat around drinking while the girls did whatever, she was the one who would try to get the girls to participate in some sort of organized practice, it was okay for a while until most of the girls just decided to blow off practices completely in kind of a strike against their coach. Now with Jake at the helm, she sees so far the complete opposite, he is very organized, is willing to help players with issues that might be causing difficulties with their abilities to play and it definitely looks like he knows his stuff. Ashley always thought of the player, coach relationship to be strictly just business, but now she may be thinking it can be more than that, maybe over time, after chipping more away from that trust barrier, it could grow into a friendship, even though Jake will only be her coach for one season, it would still be nice for her to have someone other than Holley

J to talk to if need be. Holley J is and will always be her go to voice of reason, it was just at that very moment Ashley felt like she was in a different reality, a place she never thought she would ever see or witness, a place she knew existed but wasn't compatible with her messed-up life, now is experiencing it first hand, it almost feels overwhelming like it doesn't belong in her life. Other than from Holley J, acts of kindness have been completely absent from her life unless they were looking for something in return, most likely sexual favors, but this time seemed different, could genuinely tell Jake actually wanted to help without looking for something in return. Overall Ashley still had to keep her guard up, but the trust barrier was getting weaker and weaker by the day, hopefully eventually it will be broken permanently allowing her to do something she has never been able to do, trust a man.

"You don't have to, I don't want to keep you from anything," said Ashley.

"I want to, it would be my pleasure," Jake responded putting his mitt back on heading over to home plate where he squats down into position. "Okay, let's see what you got."

Having Jake catch for her, Ashley wasn't going to need the bucket of balls anymore, grabbing one ball, placing the bucket off to the side. The weather quickly changed with the sun no longer beating down on them, now hidden behind a bunch of rolling in clouds, making it a comfortable temperature with the whole field now covered in shade. Looking at Jake with his mitt open, ready for the first throw, she prepared herself for the delivery, glove up, ball in hand, ready to fire, releasing the throw which rockets towards Jake's open glove, entering at such a velocity it created the loudest slap against the leather of the mitt, Jake could actually hear the ball cutting through the air as it entered his glove.

"Wow! Nice pitch," Jake remarked, removing the ball from his glove, shaking his hand to relieve the sting, "that stung my hand," he said smiling, returning the ball to Ashley.

"Sorry," she replied, "I forgot you are not wearing a catcher's mitt. You want me to back off a little?"

"No, no, no, don't do that on my account," Jake said, "don't worry, I'll live, just keep throwing what you want. At least now I know why they call you Fireball, I thought I smelled smoke as it was coming towards me."

Ashley flashed a small grin shaking her head, preparing for the next throw. Holding the ball in her hand, she shook her arm to help keep it loose, entering her wind up she let Jake know a different pitch was coming his way, flashing the thumbs-up letting her know he was ready. Launching her next throw, the ball made its way towards Jake with much less velocity, but changed direction midway forcing Jake to make a quick reaction.

"Nice curveball," said Jake throwing the ball back. "Where did you learn how to pitch?"

"My grandmother taught me when I was younger, she used to play in high school too," replied Ashley.

"Sounds like she is a good teacher, is she still around?" Jake asked.

"No, she died about nine years ago," answered Ashley.

"I'm sorry," he said. "It's tough to lose a family member, especially when they are good teachers. So what other pitches do you have in your arsenal?"

"I got a changeup," Ashley said.

"Let's see it," Jake remarked holding his glove wide open.

Ashley complied putting her hand inside her glove, positioning her fingers on the ball to allow her to throw the desired pitch, holding up a second to allow a slight wind to pass through. Once in the clear, the next pitch left her hand hitting Jake's mitt with precise accuracy.

"Nice pitch!" he remarked. "I got to say, I am very impressed. Now I'm really looking forward to seeing you pitch in a real game."

Ashley has gotten compliments throughout her adolescences mainly on her looks, which has grown tiresome and an act that has lost its value since she hears it so much, she can't go anywhere without feeling the eyes of horny males of all ages gawking at her, sometimes mixed in with an obnoxious cat call or whistle. It's bad enough she has to deal with that all the time at work, along with many grabby hands, but complements on her pitching, one of her abilities she values most, not as much as someone with her talent would receive, sure scouts have praised her before in the past, along with hearing it all the time from Holley J, acclaim from her has always meant something, but for some reason when it came to outside opinions, their words seemed flat, like they were saying them because they felt they needed to. Jake's words on the other hand felt real, genuine, she believed he really was impressed, for an ex pro ball-player to give such a high praise really meant something to her.

"I told you I'm the only pitcher you're going to need," said Ashley waiting for the ball to be returned.

"It's definitely starting to look that way," Jake replied throwing the ball back. "So what does a girl like you like to do when she isn't playing softball, you have any other hidden talents?"

Ashley felt herself venturing in uncharted waters when it came to interacting with an adult of the opposite sex, most men or a male of any age for that matter, would engage in small talk with her for one reason only, to try to get in her pants. Something about her highlights a girl who is damaged and broken, who can easily be taken advantage of, Razz did it, her old coach did it, they knew how to say the right things to get her to drop her defenses, warping her mind into believing she was meant to be the person she was becoming, having everything she does or happens to her to be normal. Jake taking an interest in her, asking her about other interests she may have outside of softball was a welcome rarity, nobody has ever asked her about her interests, her likes or dislikes, what does she like to do in her spare time, not her teachers, not any of the scouts, not even any of the few people other than Holley J she calls friends, Ashley's own aunt barely knows anything about her and they live in the same house. It's just nice for someone to want to talk to her on a human level, seeing her as something other than a pretty face.

"I actually like to paint," confessed Ashley, Holley J being the only other one that knew.

"Really? Houses?" Jake replied jokingly, catching Ashley's next pitch smiling.

"Canvas painting," she answered smiling as the ball made its return.

"That's very cool, I'd like to see some of your work sometime," Jake remarked. "Do you take art classes here at school?"

"No, I don't, and I would prefer it if you would not say anything to anybody. It's just something I do for myself," Ashley requested.

"I understand, I won't say a word," Jake responded.

She wholeheartedly believes Jake wouldn't making this a major breakthrough for her, proud of herself for partially opening up her door, letting someone like him in on, something only one other person in her life knows. Their private session of pitch and catch went on for another half-hour, until Ashley saw how late it was getting remembering she still had some grocery shopping to do before she could go home. Giving Jake the signal it was time to call it quits, she grabbed the bucket of balls walking over towards him.

Though the sun was absent for most of the duration, she could still feel her body perspiring, Jake had her drop the bucket near him before letting her go.

"I just want you to know, I don't want you to be afraid to talk to me if you ever need to. I know I'm your coach, but I want you to think of me as a friend too," said Jake, "so if you ever have something on your mind and you need someone to talk to, I'm here, my door is always open."

"Does that go for all the other girls too?" Ashley asked, wondering if this is how he sets his trap.

"Of course, I'm here for all of you," answered Jake.

"That's a nice offer, but I think it would be best if I kept my business to myself," she replied.

"Well, if you ever change your mind, you know where to find me. You can leave the bucket, I'll take care of it. Why don't you get out of here and I will see you tomorrow," Jake said.

Ashley gives Jake a small grin jogging off heading towards the locker room, hearing his voice in the distance.

"Hey, Ashley," Jake shouted looking in the opposite direction, stopping her movement, "sometimes you have to take a leap of faith, the trust part comes later, great job today."   Once again his words hit her in a way she is definitely not use too, his phrases of wisdom seem to grab hold of her like a lasso forcing her to decipher the meaning behind what was said. Ashley started to hate the fact he was making her think more, but in a good way, a way her mind needed to be opened up to, not knowing how to respond, she just continued on back towards the locker room.

Pulling into the driveway Ashley noticed a large black dodge pickup truck parked besides her aunt's car, a truck she didn't recognize. It looked pretty new, like it cost a pretty penny, also seemed recently waxed as the exterior shined even in the dimly lit sky of the late evening, complete with vanity plates that read "HARD ASS." Her initial thought was maybe it belonged to that asshole Rick and for whatever reason her aunt took him back even after he tried to rape her, she wouldn't put it past her aunt to take a guy back like that, but Ashley knew his cheap ass could never afford a truck like this. Not even worrying about it she grabbed the few bags of groceries out of her trunk, carrying them all to the front porch, the motion censored front light comes on as she approaches the door. A couple of moths are fluttering around the now lit-up outdoor lamp, having to set a few of the bags down to open the screen and front door, entering with the screen door closing behind her, setting the bags down for a moment due to her arms cramping up from the weight. An unpleasant sound was coming from upstairs, a sound Ashley really wasn't in the mood to hear, loud moans from her aunt, moans of pleasure verifying her aunt was upstairs having sex with the mystery man of the truck. This isn't the first time she has walked into this situation and it most certainly won't be the last with the way her aunt operates, many times she will be in her room doing homework, listening to her aunt being railed by whoever right down the hall, it doesn't help matters that her aunt is a screamer, sometimes loud enough to wake the neighbors, if it wasn't for the mixture of moans and screams the stench of sex in the air would have been enough to give it away. Hoping their act of sexual relations is coming to an end, Ashley picks up the bags to bring into the kitchen. Walking through the living room the evidence of where their little party began is on full display, empty beer bottles accompanied with smoking paraphilia and an open box of Trojan condoms were left on coffee table, along with pieces of clothing spread about from on the couch to on the floor, the smell of weed still lingered in the air as she enters the kitchen. Throwing the bags up on the table she sees more of the same, empty beer bottles on the counter and a sink full of dirty dishes which she has to do on top of the rest of the mess. Putting the groceries away suddenly the house became silent, until the sound of footsteps can be heard from above, judging from their direction they were both heading downstairs. Trying to ignore the coming of unwanted guests, she continued on with what she was doing. To Ashley's dismay her aunt and the truck guy enter the kitchen, she was wearing a red robe with her hair in a ponytail, he was wearing jeans with an opened button-down white shirt exposing his sweaty, hairy chest, his socks along with the rest of his garb probably lay in the living room. Looking like the typical man her aunt would bring home, full of facial hair, smelling of cheap cologne, Ashley tried her best to act like they weren't even there until truck man wanted introductions.

"So this is your niece?" he asked buttoning up his shirt.

"Ashley, this is James," her aunt answered, lighting up a cigarette leaning up against the counter.

Ashley just kept on putting the groceries away trying to block out their presence.

"Hey! Don't be fucking rude!" her aunt remarked, kicking some of the groceries Ashley had placed on the floor. Her aunt loved to embarrass Ashley whenever she had the chance, it seemed like she got a rush out of it, standing there smoking her cigarette like she was some sort of big shot, she wasn't going to let her aunt get to her trying to finish up putting the goods away.

"Don't mind her, she is just shy," said her aunt, an evil look grows in her eyes.

Relaying to her aunt he needed to go, he walked over to give her a kiss goodbye which turned into a deep thirty-second make-out session, the nauseating sound of their tongues slapping against each other with someone else in the room demonstrated the amount of class they both possessed, he even went as far as spreading open the top of her rope to squeeze her breasts. Ashley could do nothing but look in the opposite direction shaking her head in disgust, wanting to just leave the room, afraid they might start fucking right there on the counter. Luckily that fear vanished when she heard him say goodbye, walking out of the kitchen letting himself out of the house, leaving her and her aunt alone.

Finished putting the groceries away, Ashley tried to leave the kitchen to start on her other chores when her aunt grabbed her arm pulling her back.

"You got a fucking problem?" her aunt asked gripping tighter on Ashley's arm.

Ashley wouldn't look at her or say anything, could feel her aunt's nails start to dig into her arm's bare skin with the smell of smoke and alcohol coming from her breath. Seventeen years old still dealing with the same antics she endured since she was nine from her aunt, one to never usually get physical unless she was really pissed, mental abuse was more her forte, Ashley couldn't count how many times she was called a loser or worthless since she has been living there. Ignoring her and her new man toy must have really gotten under her skin for her to grab Ashley the way she did.

"You better start showing me a little respect around here," barked her aunt, "or you're going to find yourself out on the street like the piece of trash that you are."

All the physical abuse she has endured her whole life doesn't compare to how the mental abuse affects her, the physical will heal over time, but the mental stays with you forever. Between the memories of the physical abuse along with the constant degrading, her mind has become oversaturated with quips and vivid pictures she wishes she could delete. Now she is a piece of trash according to her aunt, words like that hit her harder than any punch ever could, a word she can now add to the list of other hurtful words her aunt likes to throw around at her, words like stupid, ugly and a waste of life were most commonly used. Without letting her aunt notice, a single tear fell from her eye, the last thing she wanted to do was to show weakness in front of her aunt, she would just feed off of it trying to break Ashley down more. Being called a piece of trash may have quickly climbed the ranks of words she hates being called the most, along with being called a whore. She knows she is not a piece of trash, but would admit there are times when she does feel like one, mostly when working for Razz, which is why the word hit with such impact coming from her, saying it as a scare tactic knowing her aunt would never throw her out for the risk of losing her live in slave, but sometimes she wishes she did just so she could be free of all her bullshit, then Ashley would realize the streets would probably be no different than what she deals with here, at least here she has access to food and a warm bed.

"So now you are going to finish your chores, cook me my fucking dinner, then get out of my face for the rest of the night," her aunt demanded letting go of Ashley's arm.

Not happy, Ashley stormed out of the kitchen without saying anything, leaving her aunt standing there blowing smoke from her cigarette.

Now later in the evening, Ashley is in her room having completed her chores which included cleaning up after her aunt and her new dude, she is sitting at her desk trying to finish up her homework, music playing softly in the background. She did her best to avoid her aunt while doing her mandatory labor, which wasn't too hard seeing she just sat on the couch watching TV while smoking and drinking more beer. The only time she really had to come face to face with her was when she got dinner ready, Ashley whipped up a bunch of chicken salad to place in some spinach wraps along with some chopped pineapple on the side, it helped her aunt never really complained about the meals Ashley prepares, for one they were healthy and second she never had to do anything but eat, it has made Ashley a good cook over the years, when she has more time she is capable of putting together a nice meal complete with all the trimmings, but some nights she is just not in the mood to cook, which is tough shit when her aunt is hungry. She is happy now she can isolate herself in her room for the rest of the night, her mental exhaustion is about to catch up with her physical exhaustion thanks to her homework. Might have finished sooner if she can only get past what her aunt said earlier, it has been on her mind making it hard to concentrate, it really hurt her, not as though she had any respect for her aunt, but that verbal whip pretty much cemented she will never ever get it from her. Just thinking about it still makes her a little emotional, sitting there at her desk she looks out her open bedroom window feeling the soft, cool breeze on her face, looking up at the clear night sky full of stars with a full lit up moon visible, wondering why certain people end up with the lives they are currently living, a question she knows she will never get an answer to. Deciding she needs a short break from her homework, wanting to hear the sound of a friendly voice, hoping to bring some positivity to an already negative night, grabs her cell phone off her desk to give Holley J a ring.

"Hey," Ashley says after hearing a greeting on the other end.

"What's going on? Are you home?" voice of Holley J asked.

"Unfortunately yeah," Ashley answered in a bummed tone.

"What's the matter? Your aunt giving you shit again," voice of Holley J remarked.

"When doesn't she give me shit, I fucking hate her," replied Ashley getting up from her desk chair to go sit on her bed.

"You know you are welcome to come hang out here for a little while to get out of there," Holley J offered.

"I know and I would, but I still got homework to finish," Ashley said running her hand through her hair, amazed at how the sound of Holley J's voice could always seem to make her feel better, wanting to tell her what her aunt said, but at that moment it didn't seem to matter anymore. "Promise me something."

"What's that?" asked Holley J.

"That we will always be best friends, no matter what we are doing in our lives, no matter where our lives take us," said Ashley as another tear descended down her face.

"Of course, BFFs for life. Remember, we can get our matching tattoos this summer," Holley J said.

"That's right, I can't wait," Ashley remarked smiling with a few more tears running down her face.

The two of them continued to have a nice long conversation, talking basic girl talk from everything to what outfits certain girls were wearing at school to boys Holley J has had her eyes on. Their verbal exchanges whether it be in person or on the phone always seem to flow like a calm river, they could ramble on for hours and never get bored. It wouldn't bother Ashley one bit if the two of them talked all night, the only thing stopping that from happening was the fact she still had homework to finish. It helped her relax to get her Holley J fix for the night, but she really needed to get her homework done. The two of them said their goodnights knowing they will see each other in the morning at school, Ashley hangs up leaving her bed to return to her desk.

It's about an hour later now, the soft night breeze has become a bit cooler entering her bedroom forcing her to close her window slightly. Sitting there at her desk trying to concentrate on what remains of her schoolwork, she looks over at her painting easel with thoughts of Holley J on her mind, coming up with an idea for a new painting. Deciding to abandon her homework once again, gets up to put on her smock, grabbing one of her few remaining blank canvases placing it on the easel, filling her paint palate with the right mixtures of colors needed, while the vision is still clear in her head. Quickly ties back her hair, grabbing one of her many paint brushes out of her storage jar and lays the first drop of paint on the empty canvas.

Another clear warm morning as Jake parks his truck in the school parking lot, already pretty full since teachers arrive about an hour and a half earlier than he needs to be there, but he always seems to find a decent spot. Exiting his truck he leaves the driver's side window open a crack to keep it from becoming too hot inside, throwing his satchel over his shoulder to begin his journey to his office when he hears the soft voice of someone calling for him.

"Morning, Coach Wheeler," says the mystery voice.

Jake turns to see Danielle the English teacher walking up towards him, stopping to greet her.

"Good morning, and you can just call me Jake," he says with a wide smile.

"Okay, Jake," she replies smiling back.

"Aren't you a little late this morning?" Jake asked as the two of them started walking towards the school entrance.

"Actually no, I just came out to grab some notes I left in my car," she replied showing him the folder she is carrying. "So how is the coaching going so far?"

"Um, so far so good, I mean it's still earlier, but I can't complain," said Jake.

"Well, it must be better than okay, Brie is one of my students and I heard about what you are doing for her to help her get a chance to play," she remarked. "I think that's pretty cool."

"It's nothing. I believe there is a way around everybody's personal obstacles," Jake replied.

"I wish a lot of my students had that mindset," she remarked with a friendly smile.   Reaching the doors to the school, Jake pulled open one to allow Danielle to enter first, the hallways are deserted since all classes are now in session.

"Well, I got to get back to class, but it was nice seeing you again," she said with another smile.

"Yeah, you too, you go have a good day," Jake said smiling back, noticing the slight twinkle when looking in her bright brown eyes.

Jake watched Danielle walk away, standing there trying to convince himself to do something he hasn't done in a long time, his mind was flipping through all the possible outcomes like a rolodex out of control, he just didn't want to make a fool of himself this early in their brief correlation, but when she kept flashing her pearly whites, in his heart she was giving him the green light.

"Hey, Danielle," Jake shouted down the hall to get her attention, feeling his heart start racing and his palms getting sweaty.

Stopping immediately in her tracks, smiling before she even turned around, pretty confident to what she thinks is about to unfold, both standing there staring at each other from a distance, Danielle waiting for Jake to speak. He wanted to be smooth as possible with his delivery, but his nervousness mixed with his anxiousness caused him to blurt out the first thing that came to mind.

"You want to go out sometime?" Jake shouted down the empty hallway, which seemed to echo his invitation, shaking his head feeling like a boy asking a girl out in high school, his current surroundings may have influenced his premature request. Standing there expecting the worst, he heard a friendly giggle along with her feminine voice.

"I'd love to," she shouted back with a big smile, quickly walking back over to Jake taking a pen out of her slacks, grabbing his hand to write her cell number on it.

Jake stood there smiling, getting a smell of her perfume as she rolled up the fingers on his hand.

"I'll see you later," she said walking back in the direction of her class.

Alone in the hallway Jake opens up his hand to see what she wrote, it read "You're too cute," with her number followed by a smiley face.

Careful not to smear the ink, he walked the rest of the way to his office with his hand held wide open.

Ten minutes till the end of history class Ashley sat at her desk giving most of her attention to the outside world, tries to pick her seat closest to the windows in the classroom, the different views in each class help bring inspiration to her paintings. History is one of her least favorite classes, can't care less what happened yesterday let alone five hundred years ago. It's not that the class is boring, her teacher a short middle-aged man who seems to enjoy his job way too much, being very animated with his teaching methods, keeps the class lively and partially entertaining, being the main reason Ashley is able to carry a B average in the class. Keeping most of her attention on the sun drenched outside, a bit fidgety tapping her pen on her desk, body language advertising disinterest sitting with her legs crossed, spent most of the class just daydreaming. The sound of the teacher's voice seemed to fade away the more she focused her attention elsewhere, even the nineteen other students that occupied the class seemed to be nonexistent. Growing anxious for the bell to ring so she could head to lunch to meet Holley J and the other girls, Ashley received a tap on her back from the girl sitting behind her. Turning around to find out what she wanted the girl handed her a folded-up piece of paper, pointing to a boy seated on the other side of the room indicating it was sent from him. She made eye contact with her apparent admirer, who proceeded to flash a small smile accompanied with a short wave, knowing before she unfolded the paper what it contained. This happens way more than she would like, not in this particular way, but just in general, Ashley is probably asked out on average around five to six times a week, with every cheesy method they could think of, from passing notes to her in class, to leaving Post-Its on her locker, some have gone as far as to leave a rose with a note on her desk in class. It's not she wants to say no to all of them, some she might actually be interested in, but knows it just wouldn't be a good idea with her lifestyle, referring to Razz' no boyfriend rule, she couldn't see herself being out with a guy and having that weighing on her conscience, along with all the baggage she brings. Ashley would love to go out on a normal date with a guy, would love to experience her first real kiss and sex with a guy she is actually in love with, but fears all the years of abuse may have shattered her perception of what love really is. It depresses her every day that it feels like her youth was stolen from her, all the bells and whistles that were supposed to come with high school life have become tainted and unrealistic. Has always done her best to turn the guys down gently, letting them know she is not interested or really doesn't have the time.

A few more minutes until the bell rang Ashley turned back around unfolding the paper just handed to her, revealing a note stating how beautiful she looked today followed with asking if she is free this weekend. The guy in question she doesn't know personally, but knows of him, he comes with a reputation of being a player, rumor has it he is trying to sleep with as many girls as he can before he graduates, other girls may be stupid enough to fall for his game, but Ashley certainly isn't, so could reject his offer with a clear moral sense. Funny thing was if he were old enough to come to the club he could pay to sleep with her and she would have no choice, but that is not the case, outside the club she can do what she wants. The bell finally sounded, every student raised up out of their seats it seemed in unison, grabbing their backpacks or whatever quickly trying to exit the room, the teacher yelling a reminder of a reading assignment he assigned earlier in class. Ashley shouldered her backpack, following the crowd out the door expecting to see her admirer waiting for her in the hallway. Between class chaos was under way with students clamoring to get to their lockers, having quick small talk with their friends before they head to their next class, after about two steps from exiting history class, Ashley's admirer was waiting patiently leaned up against the wall with his arms folded wearing his letterman jacket.

"So what do you think? Up to having a good time this weekend?" he asked.

"Sorry, I'm busy this weekend," Ashley replied walking away, quickly followed by the boy getting in her path walking backwards.

"Come on, you don't know what you ae missing," he responded. "Other girls at this school would kill to be in your shoes at this moment."

"Just cut the shit," remarked Ashley coming to a stop. "You don't think I know what your plan is, you're never going to sleep with me, you know why because I am never going out with you. Now get out of my way," she said walking right by him.

"You're nothing but a fucking tease, you know that," the boy replied in disappointment.   Ashley walked away throwing up her middle finger backwards in response to his comment, the disrespect from guys seems to never end, they see her as nothing more than a sex object rather than a real person with real feelings, would think after all this time she would be used to it, in a way she is, but doesn't mean it still doesn't hurt her inside. Looking past moments like that have become routine almost like breathing, steering herself through the commotion of the hallways to get to her locker, needing to stop there before heading to the cafeteria to meet Holley J and the others. The activity between classes never seems to change, students by their lockers taking selfies, some are on their phones texting or posting something to Instagram or Facebook, to the couples putting in a quick make-out session before class, sometimes there will be the occasional fight or light skirmish that draws the attention of everyone around, but those are few and far between, it is like reality is in reruns between classes with no new content coming soon. Doing her best to block out the repetitive actions of modern youth, Ashley looks to a new poster on the wall that catches her eye, turning off course to get a closer look. Upon review she sadly realizes it is advertising senior prom, which is in a few months, another aspect of the normal teenage girl's life that haunts her repeatedly. Ashley and Holley J have always talked about doubling up to go to their senior prom, has been something they have fantasized about since they were kids. She wants nothing more than to get the whole prom experience, from the two of them going shopping for dresses, to all the photos ops, to the limo ride. It's not she couldn't find a date, guys would be lined up for blocks to take her to prom, it would be with some random guy who in all likelihood probably would think he would get laid that night. Ashley wants real memories, not ones of some guy who couldn't keep his hands off her, but knows how much it would mean to Holley J for the two of them to experience that night together, so for that reason would risk spending that night with some horny hound dog to make her best friend happy, a bridge she will cross when she gets there, right now she has to hurry to her locker and quickly head for the cafeteria.

Arriving at the cafeteria to find Holley J and the others already seated at their usual table with their trays of food, Ashley usually the first one there is now the late one. Holley J flagged Ashley down in the confusion of the lunch room pointing at the table letting her know she already got her lunch for her. Relieved, Ashley made a mad dash to the table, thanking Holley J in her head after she saw the size of the line to receive your food. Seated at the table, Ashley sets her backpack on the back of the chair, surveying what is on her tray to eat, it amazes her sometimes how well Holley J knows her, every contents on that tray would have been the same if she had bought it herself, a grilled chicken salad with a packet of low-fat vinaigrette, a bowl of mixed fruit and a carton a milk along with bottle of water. Lunch went on like most days with the girls just eating and talking, messing with their phones occasionally and welcoming certain surprise visitors to their table, Holley J seemed more fidgety than normal, sitting there tearing a napkin into a thousand little pieces with her one leg rapidly bouncing up and down. She had a look on her face like she wanted to tell all of them something, a look that Ashley knows all too well, Holley J had some information to broadcast, but she seemed reluctant to share it, which isn't like her, she always loves to relay juicy news or gossip she has found out, it made Ashley wonder if what she had on her mind was bad.

"You got something to tell?" asked Ashley taking a forkful of her chicken salad.

"What makes you say that?" Holley J asked with a big smile on her face.

"Because you are smiling from ear to ear, along with the fact that you just turned that napkin into confetti," Ashley replied.

"Yeah, you do have the worst poker face," said one of the other girls.

"So what is it?" Ashley asked impatiently.

"Okay, okay, okay, you guys are never going to believe what I found out today, it is amazing!" remarked Holley J who could barely hold her excitement in. "Coach asked out Miss Waters today."

"Really? No way," one of the girls remarked.

"I swear," Holley J responded raising her right hand as if on the witness stand. "I got word of it from a very reliable source. So what do you guys think? Our English teacher might end up dating our coach, isn't this like OMG?!"

Holley J continues to live up to the reputation of being the girl who can get the intel on anything, she can probably find out where Jimmy Hoffa is buried. None of the other girls shared her enthusiasm, you would have thought she was the one that just got asked out by a tall, handsome man, thinking the news was very interesting at best, but nothing that exciting. A lot of schools have couples that teacher together or are each affiliated with the school in some way, Holley J is just a sucker for cheesy love stories, loves seeing two people connect, maybe because she knows the two parties involved, her coach and English teacher, it brought a certain sentimental value to it. Ashley remained emotionless, not really seeing the big deal in the news, two adults meeting and feeling some sort of a spark, it happens every day, it just so happens to be her new coach, only worried about if this turns in to something serious, he doesn't suddenly become pussy whipped forgetting about the team. She is not a student of Miss Waters anymore, having her already for tenth and eleventh grade English, but wouldn't hesitate to say she was one of her favorite teachers. Miss Waters' teaching methods were very laid back, would talk to her students more like a friends rather than someone of authority, yet you would always come out of each of her classes having learned something, helping her to generate the highest passing rate in the school. She made education fun and was always willing to go the extra mile to help any student in need of additional help, Ashley being a recipient of that a few times with English being one of her weaker subjects. She found it sad Miss Waters was the closest thing to a mother figure she had in her life, missing her as a teacher, wishing she had her again for her final year. Not much is known about her personal life other than she is not from around here and she isn't married for the time being, her private life was just that, private, until she had a run in with the school sleuth by the name of Holley J. it also doesn't hurt her being very easy on the eyes, probably the fantasy of all her male students.

"What do you think, Ash?" Holley J asked.

"As long as he doesn't lose focus on us, he can go out with whoever he wants," Ashley answered, "and it's probably something he doesn't want advertised all over school, so I would just keep it amongst us for now."

Holley J and the other girls agreed as lunch was coming close to an end, a lot of the other students were already starting to trickle out of the cafeteria. Ashley and the girls grabbed their backpacks along with their food trays that must be returned before leaving, dropping them off at the designated area. The other two girls took off for class telling Ashley and Holley J they will see them at practice later. As the students finished spilling out into the hallway the lunch monitors were yelling out their usual commands which pretty much get ignored by most of the students. Ashley and Holley J were few of the last to leave, the two of them have Chemistry together next which isn't far from the cafeteria, joining the herd occupying the hallway. Holley J tells Ashley she needs to use the nearby restroom, entering leaving Ashley waiting patiently leaning up against the wall. Interrupted by her cell phone vibrating in her back pocket indicating a text message, pulling it out to see who it is from, a message from Razz, telling her he needs her to work tonight and to be there at nine. Quickly texts back okay, leaning her head back against the wall closing her eyes in disappointment.

Practice started like usual with a few laps around the field, followed by ten minutes of calisthenics and stretching. Weather was more comfortable, temperature was nice and warm with no sun due to the vast amount of cloud cover, but a bit more windy than the past few days. Jake started things off by having the girls pair up to do some throwing and catching drills, there was an even amount of girls so no one should be left out as they all scrambled to get a partner. Ashley paired up with Holley J, while Brie had the unfortunate pleasure of being paired up with Renee. He had the girls line up with their partners standing across from them at least a good thirty feet away, starting them off with just a quick game of catch to loosen up their shoulders, to give the girls some incentive to focus, he announced if anyone happens to drop the ball you and your partner must take another lap around the field, if you drop it again it's two laps and so on. Hearing the moans and groans from most of the girls, the sound of Jake's whistle pierced their ears commencing the start of the drill. Jake paced behind one row of the girls shouting out constructive criticisms wherever it was needed, also instructing the girls to throw a little faster and harder. One set of partners suffered their first drop, Jake blows his whistle sending them off for an unwanted lap around the field. Ashley and Holley J have done this millions of times, there was no worry between them about having to run any laps, you can back them up further and further away from each other and they will promise you the ball will never touch the ground. Continuing his observation of the drill, the two girls returned from their run getting back to joining the others. Jake's main focus was on Brie, to see how accurate her throws were and to see if she was able to catch with no distractions, surprisingly she didn't drop one ball, but her throws aren't really at game speed, something he will continue to monitor. Blowing his whistle letting the girls know this drill is over, he tells them to now each move up about five feet closer and to take their gloves off. All the girls responded by removing their mitts placing them on the ground besides them, all standing there waiting to hear what was next for them to do. Ashley happen to look down the line to catch Renee giving her dirty looks, shaking her head wanting to run over to her to tell her to just get over whatever it is that has her panties in a bunch, instead she ignored her bringing her focus back to Holley J. Jake finally instructed the girls, wanting them to toss the ball underhand catching it barehanded, blowing his whistle to start the drill, the girls began with Jake again focusing mostly on Brie, letting the girls know the penalty for dropping the ball doesn't apply here, but he stills wants them to concentrate on what they are doing. Still pacing behind them, he liked what he was seeing making notes on his clipboard, even Brie was handling the drill pretty well, saw her only dropping a few. The drill went on for about five minutes until they were ordered to stop. Practice continued with Jake introducing more drills that would help sharpen and improve the girls' skills, everything from fielding, to base running, to base stealing, to batting practice. Many of the girls seem to be overwhelmed with the practice curriculum, Jake could tell they were not use to this type of training making him wonder what their practices were like before. The only one it didn't seem to faze was Ashley, able to handle anything Jake threw at her, he can tell she is a true athlete who wants to improve her craft as much as possible, some of the other girls like Holley J and Renee were able to keep up to some extent, but not to Ashley's level. Every moment he spends with these girls he is learning they need this and he wasn't going to back down, the more sweat and tears he can get out of them the better, bringing these girls to their breaking point would only benefit them. Ashley became impressed with the way Jake ran his practices, such a night and day difference from the circus she was used to seeing from her old coach whenever they did have practice, finally someone was in control other than her, where she can focus on being a player along with being the spiritual leader, but much of the time today her mind was on having to work later, working during the week throws a wrench into everything, having to get her chores and homework done faster than normal and who knows how late she will be there tonight taking a large slice out of her sleep time, she tries not to think about it, but it will linger in her thoughts until day's end. Between each drill Jake would let the girls take a few minute break to grab some water, none of the girls ever hesitated to throw down a cup of ice water and catch a quick breather. With about a half an hour left Jake sent Brie off with a bat to continue on practicing swinging left handed, telling her to stay within eyesight of him so he can evaluate her progress. Grabbing a bat she felt most comfortable with, located herself on the grassy area in front of the opposing team's dugout, taking swing after swing until she heard from Jake to stop. The clouds above became thicker and darker with the wind picking up a little more speed indicating a storm might soon be on the horizon, it's nothing they couldn't finish practice through, but it might affect some of the girls' performances. It has been a very productive outing so far, even in the sunless sky the girls were sweating and showing signs of fatigue, he was proud of the effort they all have been showing, deciding to end the day with a little game he used to play at the end of practice in little league. Summoning all the girls to line up in front of the dugout, minus Brie who was still off doing her thing, explaining to them the rules of the hitting game they were about to participate in. Each girl comes up to bat getting one pitch thrown to them by Jake, no matter how the pitch comes in they must swing at it trying to just make contact, if they make contact they then go to the end of the line, if they swing and miss then they are out and must go out in the field to chase balls. They all agreed standing there tired, sweat dripping down most of their faces, the first girl makes her approach to home plate, bat in hand with the rest of the girls cheering her on. Getting in her batting stance as a right hander, gives Jake the nod she is ready. Standing on the pitcher's mound with two buckets of balls by his side, Jake launches his first pitch coming in at a weird angle forcing her to stretch and swing at the same time, but was able to make contact as the ball just flew at the ground one hopping onto the dirt in front of home plate, the other girls clapped giving high fives as she made her way to the back of the line. Continuing on, one by one the girls would come up taking their one swing, some would succeed, others failed, joining Jake in the field to chase down any runaway balls, still cheering on the remaining girls. Holley J was up again already making contact twice, standing in the right hander's batter's box waiting for the next pitch. This one is coming in a little faster at a lower angle subjecting her to make a golf swing which she totally misses, tossing the bat aside she graciously joins the other girls out in the field performing a little dance on the way, Jake smiles telling her great job, finding herself a spot in the field. It has come down to the final two girls and to nobody's surprise it's

Ashley and Renee the two best hitters on the team. Ashley was up next, standing there can feel Renee breathing down her neck knowing she wants to pull something, but can't with the abundance of eyes watching her.

"Good luck, bitch," Renee said as Ashley left to take her next swing.

Completely ignoring Renee's cowardly remark, Ashley got back in the batter's box with determination painted all over her face. Jake tosses her a speedy little outside pitch, imagining the ball as Renee's face, swinging at it as if the bases were loaded, sending the ball rocketing over the outfield fence, getting an ovation from the rest of the girls. Turning to face Renee, she arrogantly flips the bat off to the side, walking over to get back in line staring her down. Ashley was oblivious to Jake's compliment on her hit, keeping focus on Renee with fire in her eyes, wanting to see if her big mouth could top that. Renee grabbed her bat entering the batter's box, a lefty, so she is able to still see Ashley standing off to the side in her peripheral vision, the last thing she wanted was to be upstaged by her. This seemly innocent practice drill has suddenly turned into a fierce competition between the two of them, one she surely doesn't want to lose. Eagerly awaiting Jake's next pitch, Renee tries to keep an eye on him while also repeatedly looking back at Ashley, now standing there with her arms folded, a few of the girls cheer Renee on, can tell Ashley's body language is becoming a distraction. Jake's pitch is on its way, coming in rather fast towards her inside, anxious to duplicate what Ashley did she swung a touch early allowing the ball to pass right by her, the girls cheered as Ashley was declared the winner, Renee not happy with herself slammed the bat to the ground looking over at Ashley who had a smug grin on her face. Jake congratulated the girls on a well-played drill, giving extra props to Ashley for outlasting everyone, calling them in for a few words before letting them go for the day. Brie made her way over as well, arms and shoulders are drained from swinging nonstop for the last half-hour. Jake first let Brie know when she is ready she will be participating in the game the next time he suggests it, acknowledging him with a simple nod. He started by telling the girls how proud he was of all of their efforts today, wanting to see a repeat of that at every practice. With the weather worsening by the minute, raindrops can now be felt dripping on everyone, Jake tells the girls to have a good night and he will see them tomorrow. Everyone hurried to grab their things before the apparent downpour arrives, the girls who were assigned to retrieve the equipment grabbed what was expected of them, hurrying back to the locker room as the raindrops became more frequent with thunder being heard rattling the skies above. Ashley was sitting on the bench by her locker preparing to change, wearing a pair of black panties and a dark blue sports bra, Holley J was seated next to her with her locker across the way, almost fully clothed missing a top to cover her pink bra, a couple other girls occupied lockers in their ales, the rest of the girls were scattered about the locker room. The sound of shower heads being turned on, the constant opening and closing of locker doors with the mixture of girls' voices echoed throughout. Ashley still bothered with the fact she has to work tonight, she really wanted to stay after practice to. work out some more, the evident thunderstorm rolling in might have also contributed to the lack of a longer workout. If it was just a steady rain or a little bit of drizzle she would be out there, getting a little wet wasn't going to stop her, Holley J can see frustration in Ashley's face as she just sits there staring into her open locker.

"You okay?" asked Holley J. "You have been staring at your locker for like the last five minutes."

"I got called into work later," responded Ashley, standing up to grab a pair of jeans out of her locker, "and I don't really feel like going in."

"That sucks, if you don't feel like going in why don't you just call in sick?" Holley suggested reaching for a shirt.

"I wish it were that simple," Ashley replied.

"If my parents let me get a job and I didn't feel like working, you can be sure I would call in sick," said Holley J giving her hair a quick brushing.

"Trust me, I really can't," responded Ashley slipping on a pair of flip flops.

"Your boss must be strict, I don't think you have ever missed a day for as long as you been working there," said Holley J.

Ashley wanted so bad to tell Holley J the truth, it literally eats her up inside, the one person she trusts more than anyone in the world has to be in the dark about this aspect of her life, she just couldn't risk how it could affect their relationship, the one thing in her life she cherishes, the only positive thing she has going outside of softball, could never imagine what her life would be like if Holley J wasn't in it, literally scares her to think about that. Their private conversation becomes interrupted by an uninvited and unfriendly voice coming from the opposite end of their aisle.

"I bet you think that you are a bigger shit now than what you thought you were," said Renee standing there just recently coming out of the shower, hair still wet wearing just a pair of boxers, her impressive abs standing out from the dampness of her body, "just to let you know even a blind squirrel finds a nut once in a while."

"Good, then there is hope for you," remarked Ashley, paying no attention to her presence.

"That's right, Stamper the smart ass," responded Renee. "Are you going to be able to keep that wit when eventually the coach's cock is in your mouth?"

"Jesus, Renee!" Holley J remarked.

"What did you say?" Ashley asked looking over at Renee, anger displayed all over her face.

"I mean Ashley Stamper always gets what she wants, you do the math," said Renee sarcastically, holding her hands up imitating a scale.

Losing control of her own body, Ashley lunged at Renee forcing Holley J to step in her path to hold her back.

"Renee, what is your problem?!" Holley J shouted.

"She's my fucking problem," Renee said pointing at Ashley. "I'm tired of her cocky attitude, let her go, I'm not scared of her."

"Will you just get out of here or I'm going to have to go get Coach," Holley J said still standing in front of Ashley blocking her path.

"Oh, you would do that for your little friend, wouldn't you, that's so sweet," remarked Renee. "Just remember, you can't protect her forever. You better watch your back, bitch," she said walking away.

Once Renee was out of sight Holley J backed off Ashley, still steaming from Renee's choice of words, really getting hard for Ashley to keep herself under control around her especially when she says or does stupid shit like that, but needs to be the bigger person if she wants this season to be a success and knows Renee needs to be a part of it to help make that happen.

"What the hell are we going to do about her? If she wasn't such a good ballplayer we could have her kicked off the team," Holley J said watching Ashley return to her locker.

"Fuck her, I'm not worried about her," remarked Ashley finishing getting dressed.

"I mean, we can't go through a season with this much tension between you two," Holley J said. "Should I go tell Coach?"

"If it were anybody else I'd say yeah, I would love to see that bitch get thrown off the team with her tail between her legs, but you are right, she is a good ballplayer and we are going to need her if we want to have a winning season, she may not admit it but she wants to win just as bad as we do, so I am willing to put up with all her bullshit just so we can accomplish that goal," said Ashley throwing her backpack on.

"But she said some harsh things to you," Holley J said doing the same.

"Who doesn't she say harsh things to?" Ashley pointed out as the two of them leave the locker room together.

The club is busier than normal for being the middle of the week, Razz had to almost double the amount of girls on staff to accommodate the workload. The crowd has been loud and vocal with money raining on stage all night with Ashley still to come on next. The wait staff has also been extra busy, every table or booth has been occupied consistently, Razz had to bring on an extra bartender to help with the massive crowd. He loves when the club gets this chaotic, the main showroom is packed to the gills, girls are busy giving lap dances or private sessions, a full house of activity where he sees nothing but dollar signs, providing great cover for when his buyers arrive, making it easier for him to slip away amongst all the commotion letting his bouncers and security deal with any disturbances. A deal going down within the next hour worth about a quarter million, eagerly awaiting that quick text letting him know his buyer has arrived. In the meantime Razz stands out in the showroom waiting for Ashley to come on stage, never missing a chance to watch her dance just to see the crowd reactions and simply because it turns him on. Ashley is one of a couple girls who dance on stage by themselves, a way to keep all eyes are on her allowing him to watch the money start flowing. There have been nights where it looked like an ATM exploded on stage after Ashley has danced, expecting that type of result tonight. DJ Sizzle gets on the loud speakers to amp up the crowd, getting ready to introduce Ashley. Not an empty seat among the chairs surrounding the stage, clapping mixed with whistles and howling are heard in anticipation for the next dancer to grace their presence. Men are sitting there with drinks and money in hand, DJ Sizzle announces the arrival of the gorgeous and sexy Angel to the stage, starting up a new song for Ashley to dance to, "Seventeen" by Winger, appearing on stage in her signature school girl outfit. The chain of intoxicated males began going crazy while Ashley struts across the stage swinging her hair back and forth, bending over to expose her red thong under her red and black plaid skirt. Kneeling in front of a random guy, she rips open her plain white blouse exposing her breasts, tapping the lucky male on the nose with her finger. Money starts flying everywhere onto the stage, getting up to go over to start working the pole, shirt fully off now swinging around and around in various poses, tossing her hair in different directions. Hopping off, she starts waving her ass in front of various men, pulling off her skirt tossing it to the side. Now on stage with only a thong, black heels and plain white thigh highs, getting on her knees grabbing a bunch of cash off the stage floor rubbing it all over her body, her skin glistening in sweat from the hot stage lights. Bringing herself back to her feet, walking with a swagger towards the back of the stage careful not to slip on an ocean of various bills, her back to most of the crowd, she stands there with her legs shoulder width apart in perfect posture. Looking back sucking on one of her fingers, she rips off her thong, twirling it in the air before tossing it into the madness of the on looking crowd, men push and shove to be the lucky one to catch it. One young man snatched it out of the air throwing both his fist up in the air howling in victory. A huge uproar ensues when she turns around to squat, opening up her legs exposing her smoothly shaved vagina, slowly caressing her torso with both hands. Ready to go into her finale, she stands on her hands opening and closing her legs a few times before cartwheeling back upright just as the song comes to an end. At this point she grabs her skirt and blouse, quickly leaving the stage through the back to a rowdy standing ovation.

"Give it up for the incredibly sexy and sensual, Angel!" yells DJ Sizzle to the still uproarious and vocal crowd.

Razz looks on with an arrogant grin on his face watching his prize possession generate more money in a three-minute dance than most of his other girls accumulate in a whole night, assigning a couple of his bouncers to collect all the cash off the stage. Still no word from his contact, he begins to grow impatient, being made to wait is another sign of disrespect, beginning to wonder if he is being stood up which would anger him far more than the waiting. When Razz expects a big payday to happen, it better happen or he will make sure the appropriate party suffers the consequences. Growing more querulous he heads back to the dressing room to visit Ashley.

"You looked amazing out there as always, Show Horse," Razz said standing in the doorway watching Ashley primp herself, sitting at her usual vanity brushing her hair preparing for her private time with a client.

She spots Razz' reflection in the mirror, his voice and presence startled her at first being the only in the dressing room at the moment.

"Is the client here?" asked Ashley touching up her makeup.

"He is down in room four," Razz replies walking up behind her, staring at the two of them in the mirror, putting both of his hands on top of her shoulders, feeling the tension in her body. "Are you okay, you seem tense?"

"I'm fine," said Ashley in a soft tone, feeling Razz rubbing her shoulders. "I better go, I don't want to keep him waiting."

"That's what I like to hear," he said gently pulling her hair back to begin kissing her neck.

Ashley sat there motionless, closing her eyes, feeling Razz' lips and tongue cover a major portion of her neck.

"You taste so good, Show Horse," Razz spoke is a soft, sensual voice.

Beginning to become very aroused, he reached around to squeeze one of her breasts through her blouse, until interrupted by a voice coming over his earpiece informing him his contact has arrived. The only thing that could tear him away from sexual pleasure was money, backing off Ashley still with the blood flowing in all the right places, wasn't going to distract himself from another huge payday.

"I got to go, I got private business to attend to," said Razz giving her one last kiss on the cheek. "Your client is waiting," he says leaving the dressing room.

Ashley approaches room four wearing her standard attire for sexual encounters with clients, black skirt, either a plain white or burgundy blouse, today she is wearing the white and black heels with her hair down. She never knows who she is going to find behind these doors, though she has done it hundreds of times, it still scares her to have what she calls blind sex, especially with some of shit and bizarre request she has had to deal with recently. Even with all the cameras secretly located in the rooms that only the girls know about in case a client starts to get violent or overstays his welcome, she still feels all alone with a total stranger she knows nothing about. Opening the door to enter the room she finds an extremely tall young black man standing by the bed, he had to be at least six feet ten inches in height, smiling when he saw Ashley set foot in the room. This is all new territory for her, never had sex with a black man, let alone some one that tall and if the stereotypes are true, she is in for an experience. The young man begins undressing, bald with a slender body type, tossing his shirt aside not worrying where it fell. Ashley sat on the bed in front of him looking on, watching him remove his pants and boxers exposing the largest erect penis she has ever laid eyes on, just the sight of it made her exceedingly nervous, not knowing what he wanted from this session.

"Begin with those lips on it, baby," he instructed, standing there naked with his hands on his hips.

Ashley unfortunately anticipated that request, getting down on her knees in front of him, grabbing hold of his penis with both hands, inserting the crown in her mouth. The sheer thickness and length proved to be a mouthful for her, trying to cover as much ground as she could without choking herself. The young man getting into it closed his eyes wetting his lips feeling Ashley's lips and tongue messaging his shaft.

"That's it, baby," he says grabbing the hair on the back of her head, pushing down forcing his penis to dive deeper.

Feeling him pushing down harder and harder, driving his shaft deep enough down her throat to almost touch her tonsils, a large amount of saliva began dripping out the sides of her mouth due to the lack of air being denied through her jaw. It was now so deep she began choking, slapping her hand on his bare stomach indicating he needed to stop. Seeing her struggling, he released his hand from her head allowing her to empty out her mouth, coughing once his penis was free.

"It's a mouthful, baby," he said. "Now get undressed and lay on the bed."

Still recovering from the most uncomfortable blow job she had ever given, she takes off her blouse and skirt, kicking off her heels as she lies flat on her back on the bed, reaching over to the end table drawer to grab a condom, luckily grabbing an extra-large size. Handing it over to him, he tears open the package quickly, placing it over his shaft, only able to cover about half the area. He joins Ashley on the bed, pushing her legs open by the knees viewing her clean shaven snatch.

"This will be the first white girl's cave this snake has ever been in," he said, slowly inserting the tip inside.

Ashley laid there, her breathing sporadic, feeling his penis being driven deeper inside her, it was a feeling unlike any she has ever felt, her face grimacing with each thrust he provides. It was painful, even worse than the pool cue, trying to send it deeper and deeper with every motion. She couldn't help but moan loudly, tightly gripping the sheets on the bed in obvious pain, her knuckles turning white from squeezing so hard. He was getting off on her verbal cries, sweat cascading down his bare chest, grabbing both her legs throwing them over his shoulders, grabbing the front of her thighs as handles increasing his aggressive pumping.

"Please stop, it hurts!" she yelled, unable to take anymore, face still grimacing, showing her teeth.

"Almost there, baby," he responded, watching her jostle on the bed in discomfort.

"PLEASE STOP!" Ashley yelled again as he let out a climaxing moan, gripping tightly on her thighs to absorb the sensation.

"That was sweet, baby girl, I think I may like the white chocolate," he said loosening his grasp on her thighs.

Letting her legs down, he exits from inside her, both breathing heavy, Ashley laid there grateful it was over, her insides feeling all stretched out and still in some pain, looking down to notice the condom was not on his penis, causing her to immediately sit up on the bed.

"Where the fuck is the condom?" she asked nervously. "WHERE THE FUCK IS THE CONDOM!"

The young man stood there providing no answers, showing to not be the least bit concerned, thinking quickly, Ashley knew exactly what might have happened.

"You got to be fucking kidding me!" Ashley said removing her naked body from the bed, quickly grabbing her clothes and shoes, storming out of the room leaving him to fend for himself.

High tailing it down the hall to the restroom located nearby if needed, forcefully pushing open the door hoping no one else is in there. Realizing she is alone, enters one of the stalls, closing and latching the door, seating herself on the latrine, spreading open her legs taking a deep breath. Sticking two of her fingers up into her vagina to try to retrieve the used condom, wincing in discomfort, Ashley digs around feeling for the rubber material with no good results, the squishiness of her insides felt like penetrating a warm apple pie.

"FUCK!!" she yells furiously.

Having to keep trying, she carries on determined to not leave the restroom until she removes the construct from her body. A few more minutes go by when finally she feels what she was looking for, reaching in as deep as she possibly can to be able to pinch the foreign object, slowly pulling it out wincing. Once removed she sees almost half of the condom is full of semen, a few drops of blood on her fingers from accidentally scratching herself on the inside. Angrily tossing the prophylactic in the toilet, she flushes it, running her hand through her hair, grabbing some toilet paper to wipe the small amount of blood off her fingers, starts pounding her fist on the stall wall in anger, before calming down, placing her face in her hands. Not worried about any of the semen having spilled, having been taking birth control for as long as she has been working for Razz as part of his requirements. Even Holley J knows Ashley takes birth control, but thinks she takes it to regulate her periods. Sitting there naked on the toilet frustrated and angry, wanting to scream at the top of her lungs, she never felt more alone than she did at that moment. The stall became a metaphor for her life, always feeling like she was trapped in a small square area with no way out, like the walls were constantly closing in on her. At times like these she began to think maybe her aunt is right, she is trash, maybe the only thing she is good for is being society's cum dumpster, having the male sex use her for whatever sick pleasure they want to explore, having no regards for her feeling as long as they can satisfy themselves. Most of her life has been nothing more than one big ongoing nightmare she can't seem to wake up from, sometimes wishing she could just go to sleep and never wake up leaving her life and the sick world she lives in behind. Alone in the stall surrounded by the quietness of her settings, Ashley started to feel the soreness of her latest sexual encounter, between that and having to invade herself for a miss placed rubber, her privates have taken a beating, often wondering how much more her young body can take. Feeling sorry for herself, alone with her thoughts, she hears the sound of the restroom door unlatching, being thrown open with force slamming against the wall. The mystery visitor frantically busts through the other stall door just in time to let out the uneasy sound of someone vomiting, Ashley sat there listening to the spillage splash inside the toilet, the visitor coughing heavily. She couldn't tell who it was, but knew it had to be one of the girls from the sound of her heels clacking on the cement floor as she ran in.

"Are you okay?" asked Ashley, quickly putting her clothes back on, still hearing oral projectile coming from her neighboring stall.

"Huh, who is that?" a voice said in a groggy tone.

"It's Ashley," she answered now dressed, exiting her stall to check on her apparent sick companion.

Opening the unlocked stall door, she sees a girl on her knees with her face hovering over the toilet bowl.

"Are you alright?"

"Do I look okay?" she replied, emptying another load into the bowl.

Ashley feeling like she should help, grabs a hold of the girl's long black hair holding it back for her to keep it from getting more messed up than it already is. The girl made one last deposit before falling over onto her butt on the cold concrete floor.

"I'm good," she remarks, sitting there pinned between the latrine and the stall wall, hair a mess, eyeliner running down her face, traces of puke and saliva encompassing the rim of her mouth. It wasn't a pretty sight as she got some vomit on the rim of the bowl with a few splashes on the back wall. The girl tries to get to her feet, her heels slipping on the smooth surface of the restroom floor, losing her balance trying to brace herself with her hands against the stall walls, Ashley tries helping, grabbing her waist with her hands.

"I said I'm fine," she snaps at Ashley, now to her feet still looking a bit pale, maybe indicating that her bodily pyrotechnics are not over.

"I'm just trying to help," said Ashley grabbing a couple sheets of toilet paper out of the wall dispenser for her.

Looking at her, Ashley is not familiar with the young woman, probably in her middle to early twenties, pretty face with long black hair, a passable figure, a little big in the hips from what Ashley sees, but otherwise a decent body. She must be a new girl Razz brought on or their schedules just never intersected, in all likelihood not quite the first impression the girl wanted to give. Ashley often wondered what led these other girls to want to do this type of work, looking at this girl under the inkling she must be one of those party girls who just likes sex, a nympho possibly, who figures why not get paid for doing what they enjoy.

"Why would you want to help me?" the girl asked wiping her mouth with the toilet paper, still looking a bit groggy. "Have we ever even spoken to each other before? Don't get me wrong, I know who you are. God, I feel like shit," she says running her fingers through her hair," sad thing is I got a guy waiting for me in room three."

Ashley has never had any kind of a relationship with any of the other girls on Razz' payroll, mostly because many of the other girls are jealous of her for whatever reason, but also was never here to make friends, she rather just keep to herself, which might have come off as a little arrogant to the other girls. Though this lifestyle has become normal to her, she has always still felt like an outsider who for some reason wanted to be accepted by her peers. Ashley couldn't help but feel a little sorry for the girl standing there looking sick as a dog, expected to go perform sexual acts with a total stranger.

"What's your name?" Ashley asked.

"Kendra," the girl answered.

"You are obviously in no condition to do anything," remarked Ashley, having a mental fight with her conscience.

"Well, what do you suggest I do?" Kendra asked. "It's not like I can just leave. If he complains to Razz it's my ass."

"What if I do it for you?" asked Ashley, risking more abuse to her body, but there are moments in everyone's lives when they learn something new about themselves and for Ashley this was one of those moments, learning she was cursed with a big heart. She wouldn't say she is a heartless person, but throughout her troubled life she has only really looked out for one person, herself with the exception of Holley J. who she would die for. When it came to strangers or people she hardly knew, would always turn the other cheek figuring she has her own problems to worry about. Pretty convinced none of the other girls working for Razz would ever do the same for her, Ashley felt compelled to do this even though she would get nothing for it other than a more beat-up vagina.

"What are you talking about?" Kendra asked, hit with a dizzy spell causing her to sway in her stance a bit.

"Look, you can barely even stand up," said Ashley grabbing her waist to keep her from falling over. "Why don't you go lie down in one of the vacant rooms for a while and I will go take care of the guy in room three."

"Why are you doing this?" Kendra asked feeling more faint.

"I don't know," Ashley answered honestly, "but let's get you to a room."

Helping her out of the stall, Ashley throws Kendra's arm over her shoulder to help her walk before she passes out. Exiting the restroom Ashley could feel the weakness building in Kendra's body, her shoes dragging across the floor, feeling like her body was going limp, forcing Ashley to hold up all her body weight. Luckily the closest room to the restroom showed vacant on the door switch, opening the door without even turning on the lights, allowing just the light in the hallway to enter, illuminating enough to bring the bed into view. The two girls enter with Ashley placing Kendra on her back on the bed, taking her shoes off for her dropping them on the floor. Kendra fell asleep almost instantaneously when her head hit the mattress, like a switch went off in her body once it was in a horizontal position. Standing there looking at Kendra sleep, Ashley watched her steady breathing became almost hypnotic, for a strange reason it felt like she was looking into a mirror, her body lying there reminded Ashley of herself, she couldn't quite understand why, maybe it was the shadows generated by the small amount of light coming from the hallway manifesting in the small room giving Kendra a different appearance, whatever it was, in a perplexing way it seemed like she was helping herself. Ashley knew she was doing the right thing, whether this girl deserved her help or not may remain a mystery, chances are with the state Kendra is in she may not even remember any of what transpired, possibly not remembering Ashley at all. Not doing her any good standing there observing her while she slept, Ashley left her to rest, closing the door encasing Kendra in total silent darkness, heading over to deal with whoever was occupying room three.

Closing in on midnight, Ashley was in the dressing room changing, gathering her things to leave for the night, feeling completely exhausted and unbelievably sore, a price to pay for accommodating multiple clients in one night, at least her second voluntary service went much smoother than her first, just a middle-aged man who wanted a quick riding, did whatever she could to get him to finish as quickly as possible. A few other girls were there touching up their makeup or changing clothes, Ashley doing her best to keep to herself hoping to leave without any unnecessary interactions, already doing her good deed for the day. Always leaving in the outfit she showed up in, which today was a pair of jeans, a white tank top and a unzipped hooded pink sweat jacket with a pair of blue low-top Converse sneakers, she grabbed her backpack when one of the bouncers entered the dressing room.

"Ashley, Razz wants to see you asap," he said in a deep baritone voice, standing there with his headset on trying to look as intimidating as possible.

Holding onto her backpack straps, she drops her arms in frustration wondering what Razz could want this late, walking aggressively pass the bouncer like he wasn't even there. Walking into Razz' office, one of the guards closes the door as Ashley entered, Razz sitting at his desk smoking a cigarette with no shirt on exposing all his body tattoos, eyeing her down as she walked towards the desk, blowing a heavy puff of smoke into the air. From the expression on his face she could tell something was up, that he wasn't happy, kept staring at her with hollow eyes, spinning and tapping a pen on his desk, the lines in his forehead screaming agitation. Ashley's nerves went into overdrive trying to figure out what this could be about, did everything she was supposed to and more. The silence in the room was just as unsettling as Razz' body language behind the desk, could feel her heart pounding in her chest, her palms became sweaty waiting for him to address why she is standing in his office.

"Would you say I'm an intelligent guy, Show Horse?" asked Razz in a calm relaxed voice taking a drag from his cigarette, "you know, good at what I do?"

Ashley just stood there a bit confused, not quite understanding the question being asked to her.

"ANSWER THE FUCKING QUESTION!!" Razz yelled.

"Yes, you are smart," answered Ashley, a nervous pitch coming from her voice, her body began to perspire in accordance to panicky feeling from hearing the loud delivery of his request.

"You know the one thing I hate more than anything, is when I lose money," Razz said, "especially when it is because of someone else's stupidity."

"Razz, I really have no idea what you are talking about," replied Ashley, still baffled by what this is all about, feeling a knot beginning to form in her stomach as her nerves intensify with every passing second. She has been walking on eggshells ever since that night Razz first put his hands on her, something she thought he would never do considering how highly he thinks of her, yet apparently no one is above his brand of discipline.

"You're beginning to disappoint me, Show Horse," Razz remarked leaving the chair from his desk, putting out his cigarette in a nearby ashtray, walking around to stand toe to toe with Ashley.

Standing face to face, close enough to smell the smoke on his breath, Ashley could detect her body tensing up the closer he got to her.

"Razz, please tell me what this is about," Ashley said as Razz started adjusting her sweat jacket.

"You're about to find out," he replied. "Bring her in," speaking into his earpiece.

Razz' office door opens behind them with one of bouncers manually bringing in Kendra who he is holding by both arms, half asleep still appearing very weak and pale, barely able to stand on her own.

"Do you know who this is?" Razz asked Ashley, walking over to Kendra's limp body.

"Yeah, we met earlier," she answered.

"Hey, HEY! Wake the fuck up," Razz said, Kendra still kind of out of it, lightly slapping her a couple times on the face, still being held up by the bouncer.

Kendra can barely keep her eyes open, almost uncomprehensive to what is going on and who is around her, whatever is ailing her seemed to have gotten worse.

"Do you know where I found her?" Razz asked Ashley pulling something out of his pocket, holding up the mystery object in front of Ashley's face, turning out to be a switch blade, popping up the sharp, steel cutlass. "Now don't lie to me, Show Horse."

"Sleeping in one of the rooms downstairs," answered Ashley, who could see part of her reflection coming from the shiny steel of the blade, a lump begin to manifest in her throat, never having any type of weapon reside directly in front of her face before.

"Right, and how do you think she got there? Considering the state she is in, she could have never made it there on her own," Razz asked, placing the blade flat against Ashley's face just below her left eye.

Ashley's eyes began to water, fighting hard to hold back the tears to hide how scared she was becoming feeling that cold steel against her skin.

"Razz, please be reasonable, look at her, she can barely stand up. You can see she is very sick, I was just trying to help her," Ashley said hearing Kendra cough beside her.

"That is very noble of you, Show Horse, but then who serviced the client she was supposed to in room three?" asked Razz, who could see the fear in

Ashley's eyes, that dread excites him almost like an emotional drug, the more power and control he has over someone the more it galvanizes him.

"I did, I thought I would do it for her so you wouldn't have an unhappy client for not getting what he paid for. She was in no state to do it," replied Ashley feeling the point of the blade pinch her skin.

"And I'm glad he walked out of here happy and satisfied, but the problem is he paid for her services, not yours," Razz remarked angrily, putting his face closer to hers, grabbing her jaw from underneath her chin, squeezing hard enough for her to react. "Do you understand what I'm saying? He got your services for the price of hers, meaning I lost around a thousand dollars on your little Girl Scout act."

"Razz, I'm sorry, I was just trying to do the right thing," Ashley replied, a couple tears streamed down her face, becoming more and more frightened of what he might be capable of doing to her, can feel his displeasure in his grip, the warm air from his breathing gave the skin on her face a subtle itch.

"You think sorry is going to make up the money I lost?" Razz barked. "What if it starts spreading around town that he got the Lamborghini for the price of a fucking smart car? Then every dude in this city will expect the same price and I will not stand for that."

"Razz, listen, when I got to the room the guy was pretty wasted, I'd be surprised if he even remembered who I was," Ashley remarked, hoping he will realize she was just trying to keep everyone content.

Looking deep into Ashley's watery eyes Razz senses she is telling the truth, releasing his grasp on her jaw, pulling the blade away from her face. A sense of relief came over her as he backed off slightly, her tears subsided figuring the worse was over.

"You better pray that is the case," said Razz pointing his finger at Ashley, still holding the blade, directing his attention back over to Kendra, who is still being held up by the bouncer, seeming a little more alert, recognizing Ashley off to her side and Razz standing in front of her.

"Hey, Razz, what's going on?" asked Kendra in a weak-sounding voice, looking over at Ashley. "Hey, Ash, what are you doing here? Why are we in Razz' office? My head is fucking pounding," she said rubbing her forehead, her hair draped over her face.

"Did you ever take care of the client in room three?" asked Razz.

"Razz, I was on my way, but then I started feeling really sick and light-headed, had to run to the restroom to throw up. That's when Ashley found me, brought me to one of the rooms to lie down. She took care of it for me, I was in no condition to do anything, still not. I'm sick as a dog, I need to go home," Kendra said, "and I don't need your goon to hold me up anymore."

Razz gestures to the bouncer to release her, complies by backing away a few steps, staying close by in case he may be needed. Kendra stood there still looking very limp in posture, like any second she could topple over.

"So you are cool with everything that happened?" Razz asked, inching himself closer to Kendra's personal space.

Ashley could hear the sarcasm in Razz' voice, one thing she has learned over the years is it's a sure sign of aggressive behavior coming from him, prompting her to worry about Kendra, would hate to see any harm be bestowed upon her considering how much she is ailing, but knows when it comes to Razz, your psychical or metal state has no bearing on his form of discipline.

"Yeah, everyone got what they wanted, right?" Kendra asked with a bit of confusion in her words.

Razz took a quick glance over at Ashley, his fascial expression spoke louder than any words could, knowing what was about to happened and there was nothing she could do about it. Wanted to tell Kendra to run, but in her state would have never made it to the office door before they would have caught her. Razz brought his attention back to Kendra, holding up her chin with his finger, her green eyes appeared a bit glazed over staring back, cracking a small grin in return. In a flash Kendra felt the back of Razz' hand come across her face from both sides drawing some blood from her lip on the second pass. Blood from her lip trickled down to her chin, feeling something wet on her face she touched her lower lip with her fingers revealing she was bleeding.

"Razz, what are you doing?" Kendra asked, caught completely off guard by his physical outburst.

"What do you mean what am I doing?" Razz asked grabbing the sides of her head with his hands, shaking her as he speaks. "You cost me money, you stupid bitch!" he says throwing her to the floor, standing over her throwing continuous punches to her face as she tries in her weakened state to block the oncoming onslaught of his fists.

Ashley just stood there wanting to intervene, but if she did his rapid punches might be redirected in her direction, could hear Kendra whimpering, her legs flaring about being completely helpless, the bouncer just standing there looking on in amusement.

"Razz, please stop!" Ashley shouted, who couldn't watch anymore.

He concluded his barrage of punches, looking back at Ashley breathing heavy, sweat sliding down his face. Kendra laid there on her back panting and coughing, most of her face colored in blood, an unusual silence overtook the office. Razz placed the blade back in his jeans pocket never breaking eye contact with Ashley.

"Get this bitch out of here," ordered Razz to the bouncer, referring to Kendra's motionless body laid out on the floor like a murder victim, clothes and hair a mess, blood still painting most of her face.

The bouncer picks her up throwing her over his shoulder, her limp body dangles off his torso, hair falling towards the floor, completely unaware of what is going on or where she will end up. Ashley watches Kendra being carried out of the office, wondering what is going to happen to her, she has never watched someone getting a beating right in front of her before, accompanied by the feeling of helplessness knowing there was nothing she could do. Making it worst was the fact any of the girls are liable to be on the wrong end of his fists, positive a few others have already, but those episodes most likely didn't have an audience. She certainly wouldn't want other people around to witness that type of abuse on her if she was unfortunate enough to become Razz' punching bag, wanting so bad to believe Razz would never do anything like that to her, but as time goes on she can't help but realize the once man who has treated her like a daughter, has finally started to show his true colors, a master manipulator who will say and do anything to get what he wants.

"Can I go home now?" Ashley asked with tears in her eyes, wanting so bad to leave after the night she has had, a night she may not recover from for a few days and has school in less than seven hours.

"Not so fast, Show Horse," Razz remarked walking over to her, can tell from her eyes, it was a lot for her to take in. "I still have to deal with you."

"Razz, you don't have to do that, I made a mistake, okay, I get it," Ashley pleaded as Razz placed both of his hands on her face.

"You know I don't want to hurt this face," Razz said giving her a soft kiss on the lips. "But your mistake cost me, so you must feel the repercussions for your actions. I'm the king here, I don't pay you to think or make decisions, you're paid to do what I say and make me money. Don't ever forget I own you, Show Horse, you're my little girl."

More tears streamed down Ashley's face, speculating on how this horrible night was going to end.

Ashley turned on the light in her bedroom throwing her backpack on her bed, looking over at her alarm clock showing a time a little after one in the morning, the rest of the house was silent, most of it covered in darkness. No sign of her aunt who must have turned in for the night, presumably alone since there was no strange vehicle in the driveway. Closing her bedroom door slowly to prevent any unnecessary clamor, she steadily walks over to stand in front of her large closet mirror, briefly stares at herself. Taking off her sweat jacket, right arm coming out first, followed by her left arm, grimacing with every inch exiting the sleeve until fully exposed, dropping the jacket on the floor, getting a good, sickening look at her left arm entirely covered in bruises. The sight of her arm makes her sick to her stomach, never seeing any part of her body look like that before, making her feel like one of those battered wives she hears about on the news sometimes. The more she stared at it, the more reality started to set in, she was given a bruised arm now, what would be next, her ending up like Kendra. With that thought she looked at herself in the mirror and started to cry, a steady flow of tears cascaded down her face, the heaviest cry she has had in a while, feeling a sense of release, having been holding back most of these tears all night. Poking her left arm with her finger to test how tender the skin was, being tender enough for her to wince in discomfort, part of her wanted to stand there crying until she drowned in her own tears, a maddening feeling of depression came over her, a feeling she has felt many times before, but never this intense. Ashley has always known she probably suffers from depression, yet has never gone to a doctor to get fully diagnosed fearing they would put her on medication, which she wants nothing to do with, afraid scouts and these colleges would not want to take their chances on someone who might be a basket case. Overcome with anger and depression, feeling like her life is spiraling out of control, she leaves her bedroom entering the darkened hallway, quietly making her way towards her aunt's bedroom. Every footstep is shielded by the ticking sound of the hallway clock, her aunt's bedroom door is opened a crack saving Ashley the trouble of having to quietly unlatch it. Slowly pushing the door open, the moonlight outside the bedroom window, along with the scented candle burning on her nightstand generates enough light to provide visual aide. Her aunt lying on her stomach sound asleep facing the opposite direction of the doorway with just a sheet covering her up to the waist, a cool breeze coming from the partially open window flickers the bed sheet slightly as Ashley enters the bedroom. Locating her aunt's dresser which is adjacent to the bedroom door, she slowly opens the top drawer barely making a sound, reaching her hand inside to feel around for what she is looking for. Within a few seconds she made contact with the object she seeks, slowly pulling it out closing the drawer at the same time. Having to put all her aunt's laundry in its proper place, she knows what is kept in her dresser drawers. With no hesitation she leaves her aunt's room, closing the door similar to how she found it, making her way back to her bedroom. Reentering she closes the door behind her, walking over to sit on the side of her bed with the object in hand, tears start flowing again looking down at the object, her aunt's silver .38 special. Flipping out the bullet cylinder to see if it is loaded, she snaps it back into place seeing the cylinder was housing the full six bullets. Her tear ducks continue to empty as she cocks the hammer back, taking a couple deep breaths, raising the gun upside down with both hands, placing the barrel in her mouth. Closing her eyes tightly, placing her finger on the trigger, her hands began sweating, rapid breathing commenced feeling her finger slowly start to squeeze the trigger. The beating of her heart escalates just as the trigger pushes all the way back, the sound of gun powder igniting was the last thing she heard as everything went to black, the bullet exits the back of her head splashing blood and pieces of her brain all over the wall behind her, her limp lifeless body falling back onto her bed.

Ashley quickly sits up on her bed in a panic, breathing heavy and sweating profusely, realizing it was just a bad dream. Stricken with many different emotions, she couldn't remember a dream that felt so real, even supporting a small cramp in the finger that would have pulled the trigger. They say you dream about what's consistently on your mind, she would be lying if she said she never considered it, but that it is now happening in her dreams deeply frightens her, like her subconscious is provoking her to do it, identical to self-aware peer pressure. Struggling to get her thoughts in order, she checks the time on her clock, about a half an hour until her alarm goes off to get up and get ready for school, rubbing her face with her hands, discovering she is still wearing the clothes from last night, including the pink sweat jacket, taking it off feeling a bit overheated, unveiling her bruised covered left arm. The pain and discomfort has faded, still the sight of her recently battered arm sends a feeling of dread coercing through her veins. Until it heals it will constantly be a reminder of last night, something she promptly wants to forget, can even still feel the effects of her escapades from last night, extremely sore in her vaginal area. Everything after she left the club seems to be a bit of a blur, doesn't even remember driving home, all she could piece together is when she arrived home it was straight to her bedroom where she dropped her backpack on the floor immediately collapsing on the bed, falling asleep almost instantly. The bigger dilemma now is how she going to keep her arm hidden until the bruises dissipate, primarily from Holley J who would give Ashley the third degree until she knew what happened and if everything was alright, she could lie about it but there is nothing she would be able to come up with that would warrant her entire arm getting bruised, which leads her to believe if no one can see it then there is no issue. At school would be easy to keep her arm hidden, she will wear long sleeves or just keep her sweat jacket on all day, hopefully not becoming overheated. The real problem will be hiding her arm during practice for the next few days, her only solution is to wear a long sleeve crop top, having one in white that were given to all the girls on the team as part of their uniform. Ashley doesn't like to wear long sleeves when she pitches, it hinders her mobility slightly, doesn't feel loose, feels restricted in some way, like she can't deliver what she is capable of, but for the next few days she has no choice, will just have to make due. No point going back to sleep, Ashley elects to just get ready for school now, amazingly feeling pretty awake for getting less than six hours' sleep. Hopefully being at school and around her friends will help clear her mind from that dream seeming to be burned into her memory, just thinking about it sends unnerving emotions through her body. What happened at the club last night isn't painting a better picture, her mind is becoming overflowing with memories she wishes she could just delete from her existence, afraid she might start to lose her mind with a brain full of negative thoughts and horrific imagery. Practice today couldn't come fast enough, the only time she feels she is living a different life is when she steps onto the mound, her own personal therapy, Ashley truly believes that three-feet-wide pile of dirt with the rubber pitcher's plate is the only thing keeping her alive other than her friendship with Holley J. To help keep her psyche in check, she begins her morning routine, consisting of picking out her clothes, jumping in the shower, doing her hair and makeup and making herself a quick breakfast, also having to prepare something for her aunt to eat, something that can just be heated up when her aunt decides to grace the world with her presence.

Ashley at her locker making her necessary book swaps, waiting for Holley J, dressed very casual in an attempt to conceal her left arm, a pair a jean capris, a white t-shirt with a black Nike logo on it, her pink sweat jacket to match her pink low-top Converse sneakers convening her second favorite color, hair tied back in a ponytail. Like every day there is a sustaining ruckus filling the hallway with students trying to get ready for first period, Ashley looking through her backpack is greeted by Holley J.

"Well, you look cute this morning," said Holley J opening her locker, bobbing her head to the music playing through her earbuds.

"You think so?" Ashley asked eyeing Holley J's shirt, a black ruffled top with different colored flowers making up the pattern. "I like that top, is it new?"

"No, I found it buried in my closet, it's cute, right?" Holley J remarked mouthing the words to the song currently playing. "Did you remember to bring your swimsuit?"

"Swimsuit? For what?" asked a confused Ashley.

"We start swimming in gym today. Didn't you get my text last night reminding you?" Holley J asked zipping up her backpack.

"I thought we weren't starting swimming until next week," Ashley replied backing her head against her locker in disbelief. Thinking she might have dodged all bullets, here comes one directly at her, the worst possible scenario that could have come up, swimming in gym class, now she has to come up with a plan by fifth period to excuse herself from a barrage of questions she is not willing to answer.

Ashley pulls out her phone to check her messages, seeing the one she missed from Holley J, not once checking her phone all night with her mind being on so many other things.

"Sorry, I got so busy with work, I hardly even looked at my phone," Ashley remarked. "Shit! This can't be happening."

"Don't worry about it, I got you covered," said Holley J. "When I didn't hear from you I figured you might forget, so I brought an extra suit. It might be a little big on you but it should get you through class."

"It's not about that, I just can't swim today," Ashley said focusing her attention on the sea of students passing by in both directions.

"Why not? You enjoy swimming," Holley J replied, sensing something might be afoot.

"I just can't, okay!" shouted Ashley looking right at Holley J.

"Okay, who pissed in your Cheerios this morning?" Holley J said, displaying her displeasure for Ashley's rude tone.

"Oh my God, I'm so sorry. I'm just got so much shit going on and my mind is going in hundred different directions lately. I know you are just trying to help," Ashley stated, trying to quickly come up with a valid excuse off the top of her head to skip out of gym class. "I got my period last night."

"Well, why didn't you just say that? I can tell something has been bothering you lately, you seem more tense than usual," Holley J remarked.

"I know and I'm sorry, trust me, it has nothing to do with you," assured Ashley.

"You know what you need, you need a girls' day. Saturday we will go to the mall and shop until we can't carry any more bags. Have lunch, maybe catch a movie," Holley J requested smiling. "What do you think?"

Her best friend always seemed to know the perfect way to slow down the runaway train she would call life, what would she ever do without her, even at her not-so-gracious moments, Holley J is always there to try to cheer her up, to bring sunshine to her dark cloud-filled existence. A day together shopping might be just what Ashley needs, it has been awhile since they were able to enjoy quality time together, just to be able to be a normal teenage girl even if it's only for a few hours could really help take her mind off things.

"I think I could definitely use that," answered Ashley putting up a small smile, "but I have to be home by six, I still have to work."

"Great! Then it is settled," replied an excited Holley J.

Joining the mob of students traveling the hallway, the two of them head for their first class, Ashley attempting to walk as distinguished as possible, every step being a reminder of the night before, hoping she doesn't catch a snag proposing her case to get out of gym class. The end of fourth period bell rang throughout the school, Ashley wasted no time leaving her current class, backpack aboard, weaving her way through the chaos that is between periods to get to gym class as fast as possible. Commonly she would wait up for Holley J, but sent a text earlier letting her know she would meet her there. The soreness between her legs continues to be relevant making her way down the hallway, ignoring any greetings thrown her way as she passes by. Arriving at the school's aquatic area, she is greeted with the dewy thickness in the air mixed with the smell of chlorine, the pool room is always kept very warm, the humidity alone is enough to make you sweat. Seeing her teacher standing at one end of the pool dressed in her usual gym teacher attire, white polo shirt with black and gold parachute pants, her authentic whistle hanging freely around her neck. Ashley walks along the edge of the pool, the area lighting reflecting off the water ripples shimmers along all the walls creating a kaleidoscope type effect.

"Stamper, why aren't you dressed for class?" her teacher asked watching Ashley approach.

"Mrs. Powell, I won't be able to swim today, I got my period this morning," Ashley said, trying to deliver her lie with a convincing face, aware Mrs. Powell is a tough costumer when it comes to missing her class, but also is a very reasonable person as well, not one to make you participate if you are ailing or have some sort of injury, "and it is one of those heavy months too."

"Is that right," remarked Mrs. Powell snapping her gum, looking at Ashley as if trying to catch her in a lie, recognizing her as one of her better students, always coming prepared, willing to partake in class, finding it hard to believe she would be deceitful at this time. "So what do you suggest we do?"

"I will just go to study hall. I can always make up the class next week if you want," suggested Ashley, feeling her heart racing inching closer to being in the clear, the other students in the class began filing into the pool area including Holley J.

Mrs. Powell redirects her attention to the twenty coeds lining up along the back wall waiting for class to start, all conversing and engaging in teenage hijinks, boys flirting with the girls, messing with one of the overweight boys whose stomach slightly hangs over his swim trunks. Holley J wearing her light blue one piece, sees Ashley talking with Mrs. Powell, wondering if everything is okay, not even paying attention to the other students as they goof off acting obnoxious.

"Alright, everyone, just settle down!" yells Mrs. Powell blowing her whistle, sounding twice as loud inside the echo filled pool area. "Okay, you better make up this class next week or I will have to give you a zero for the day," she said to Ashley.

"I will, I promise, thank you," Ashley responds in relief.

Walking back around the outside of the pool having to pass by the rest of the students, the annoying sound of deep male voices cackling and whispering obscene phrases begin to anger her, greeted by Holley J on her way out.

"Everything cool?" asked Holley J.

"Yeah, everything is now," Ashley replied, feeling the presence of someone walking up behind her. "I will see you in lunch."

"Hey, Ashley, you too good to swim with us today," said the male voice behind her. "How 'bout I help you with your jacket?"

The boy grabs Ashley's sweat jacket by the shoulders with both hands, quickly pulling down unmasking a small section of her bare arms. Ashley could feel her heartrate increase as the flesh of her bare skin came into the light, hoping nobody caught a glimpse she aggressively shakes off his advances, swiftly throwing her jacket back over her shoulders before anyone could view her bruised arm.

"Fucking asshole," says Ashley, pushing the boy into the pool, walking away cautiously while Holley J and the other students began laughing.

Jake sat at his desk in his office finishing putting together the plans for today's practice, some soft rock playing at a low volume from a iPod dock he has in one corner of his desk, seemed to always concentrate better with so sort of music playing in the background, helping to create a relaxed ambience to his work area. With the season starting in just a week, every practice until then is going to be critical in getting these girls ready, there is still much a lot of these girls need to learn and trying to cram all that into a couple hours every day after school is no easy feat. He has got some good ballplayers on this team, even has some great players on this team, but sometimes that is not enough, many times during the course of his day he would sit back wondering what the old coach was even doing with these girls, aside from all the negative accusations. Did he even teach them anything, a lot of these girls were playing the wrong positions and the old batting orders he found on file, based on what he has seen, are not even close to being accurate with the different skill sets of these girls, it's no wonder they have had trouble putting together a winning season. Looking at old game stat sheets, if it weren't for Ashley's pitching, they might have lost every game. Writing on his clipboard, a small beam of sunlight highlighting many air particles, directly hits the center of his desk courtesy of the tiny window like piece of glass on the wall off to the side, Jake loves the sun, but sometimes he must cover up that small opening, finding that bright patch of light a little distracting. Finished with this afternoon's agenda, he leans back in his chair taking a sip from a bottle of water located on his desk, staring out that very window looking at sun filled sky, feeling the cool air from the small fan he has running on his desk, reflecting on where he is now at this point in his life. Not at all where he pictured himself being, at this time he thought he would have signed a max deal with a team after winning a couple of MVPs to go along with his two World Series rings, probably married with a couple of kids. Life is funny that way, ever since he knew he was good at baseball, he thought he would be playing until he was either too old or his talent began to diminish, never thought in a million years at the age of twenty-eight he would have to retire and seven years later he would be coaching a girls' high school softball team, but compared to where he was just a few years ago, he considers himself a lucky man who has been given another opportunity to showcase his skills in a different capacity. Sticking his left hand directly into the beam of sunlight, slightly wiggling his fingers smiling watching the light sparkle off his skin, many other men don't get second chances like this, understanding he has to do what he can to make the best of it. Deep in thought, leaned back in his chair with his eyes closed, the music still tickling his eardrums, feeling a calming sense of relaxation over take his body, the sound of knuckles banging on wood wake him from his brief trance. Slightly startled from the abrupt interruption, he opens his eyes to spot Brie standing in his open doorway.

"Hey, Brie, what's going on? What brings you here?" Jake asked sitting himself back up straight, turning off the music, trying to shake off his short moment of meditation.

"Are you busy, Coach? Can I talk to you for a minute?" Brie asked standing there holstering her backpack.

"Absolutely. Come in, have a seat," Jake answered.

Brie entered seating herself in one of the chairs in front of Jake's desk, making a rapid scan of the office noticing how much more organized it looks compared to the clutter and disorder is represented in the past. Her hair showcased a long braid in the back, the one uncovered eye hosted a baby blue that gleamed in the office lighting.

"So what's up, everything okay?" asked Jake, intently giving Brie his full attention, he couldn't help but experience a load of jubilation, Brie became the first player on the team to come see him in his office, displaying a level of trust he hopes to build with all the girls.

"Yeah, I'm fine. I just have been doing some thinking in regards to my place on the team," stated Brie. "I just feel like it would be best if I remove myself from the roster."

"Now why would you want to do that?" asked a stunned Jake.

"I just feel like I'm going to be the weak link of this team," Brie responds. "I mean, I know you are trying to help me with my eye and everything, but I don't want to be the one to mess it up for the other girls. They have a future in this game, I don't."

"When you say other girls, do you mean girls like Ashley?" asked Jake.

"Ashley, Renee, take your pick. They are too good of players to have their last season on the team be ruined by my inability to play at the level they need me too," replied Brie slightly lowering her head exhibiting her disappointment.

"Wow, I would have never pinned you for the quitting type," Jake remarked. "But can I ask you one question? Do you like to play?"

"Of course, I love to play," answered Brie reconnecting eye contact with Jake.

"And you do realize that softball is a team sport, right?" asked Jake watching Brie nod her head in response. "What I mean is team sports are not won or lost by one person, you win as a team, you lose as a team. Sure, great players might be responsible for a lot of the credit, but do you know what all great teams with great players have, they have great role players. Players who love to play, but are not there to be in the spotlight, they are there to help the team achieve what they are capable of and that is what you are, you're a cog just like every other girl on this team that is part of this machine we are putting together. You will never be the reason why this team wins or loses and if I didn't think you had it in you I would have never offered you my help. Now if you still want to quit, I can't stop you, but you never even gave yourself a chance."

"I just don't want to let everyone down," Brie remarked.

"If you quit the only person you will be letting down is yourself," responded Jake, telling by her facial expression his words must be getting through to her. "I'll tell you what, I want you to stick it out and continue to do what I told you. The season starts next week, after the first few games if you still feel the same way then you have my blessing to quit. Does that sound like a deal?"

"Okay," Brie answered, her face supporting a small smile. "Well, I got to get to lunch," she says removing herself from her seat, heading towards the doorway.

"Okay, that's more like it. Enjoy your lunch," said Jake, watching Brie exit his office.

"Hey, Coach," utters Brie, stopping herself in the doorway waiting. "Thanks," she says smiling.

"I'll see you at practice," Jake responded smiling back, watching her disappear into the hallway.

Last period coming to a close, Ashley sits in her final class paying more attention to the clock than to the teacher, overly fidgety, rapidly tapping her pen on her desk, finding it hard to concentrate all day, repeatedly thinking back to last night and what she saw Razz do to Kendra and to her arm, which feels better but still looks pretty bad, hopefully it will be visually better in the next couple days when Holley J and her spend most of the day together. She has been spending most of her time in her classes just contemplating about everything in her life, her Aunt, Razz, Holley J and softball, two she loves more than anything and the other two she is desperate to get away from, the fall couldn't come soon enough to start her new life as a college student, just has to really impress the scouts this season taking the first offered scholarship that is presented to her no matter where it is located, as long as it is far from here.

Looking around the classroom at her classmates, completely blocking out the verbal overload coming from the teacher's lips, she can't help but feel overly jealous. They are all living typical teenage lives, most of them coming from upper class households where their parents probably hand them everything, evident to most of the student body's snotty demeanor, with their biggest worry being getting a zit before the big dance. Ashley always thought it wasn't fair, with all the lives she could have been born into this is what she got, drawing the short straw in the pre-birth pool, often thinking maybe she is being punished for a previous life, one she would gladly trade with, but doesn't believe in all that mumble jumble like the afterlife or reincarnation and definitely isn't a religious person. Nobody in her position could ever accept that there is a God, what did she ever do to him to deserve her unpromising existence, if there was anything she would agree with from religious lore it would be Hell because she lives through it every day. Still focusing on the clock, watching every second tick by, Ashley grabs her backpack from off the back of her chair, packing her things inside to be ready for when the final bell rings. With about an hour until practice begins it gives her plenty of time to get to the locker room, change and head to the field to undergo her regular pre-practice ritual. The teacher announces there is no homework for the night bringing the class into a cheerful cackle, especially Ashley, thrilled to hear the good news. The final bell sounded, yet the last bell of the day sounds like freedom to the students as they grab their backpacks or what have you, spilling out into the hallways in a frenzy. Ashley herself didn't waste any time joining the sea of students, weaving her way through the end of day chaos, making a break for her locker to grab what she needed for practice. Earlier she received a text from Holley J letting her know she wouldn't be able to join her for a pre - practice workout due to having to stay after class to work on a project. This may be the only time Ashley felt relieved Holley J was preoccupied, giving the window to not have to change in front of her before practice. Arriving at her locker, Ashley swiftly makes the needed exchanges, ignoring all the commotion from all the other students emptying the school, slamming her locker door shut, shouldering her backpack, she heads for the girls' locker room.

The girls' locker room appeared to be deserted as Ashley passes through a few aisle ways to get to her locker, saw the janitor as she entered emptying the trash cans, but looked like she was on her way out. Dropping her backpack on the aisleway bench, she starts getting dressed into her practice gear, taking off her sweat jacket, followed by the t-shirt she was wearing, her black Nike sports top is all that is covering her upper body, taking a glimpse at her arm. Not knowing if it was the angle she was looking at it or the lighting in the locker room, but her arm seemed to look worse, like the bruises became darker, standing out more. Her self- evaluation of her arm was interrupted by foot-steps coming from the other end of the aisle, quickly turning back to view the janitor standing there holding a full thrash bag staring at Ashley. A short older Spanish woman who could barely speak English, got a full view of Ashley's battered arm, the look on her face resembled someone passing by a car accident on the highway. The two of them stood there for a moment, eyes locked with neither one of them saying anything, ending with the janitor just walking away slowly returning to her duties. Ashley sat on the bench pondering if she should go talk to the her, asking her not to say anything to anybody, then thought who is going to believe an old Spanish woman if she even did say anything, chances are she doesn't even care about the kids at this school, probably just wants to do her job and collect a paycheck, with that Ashley went back to her initial engagement of getting changed.

Walking out to the field in her full gear, including the crop top she is not enjoying wearing, Ashley notices someone standing by home plate, the afternoon sunlight shields the mystery person from recognition blocked by many sun rings inhabiting her line of vision. Making her way closer, putting on her game sunglasses to clear up her view, her new tinted vision she can now verify it's Jake standing there, clipboard and whistle ready.

"Don't you have anything better to do than to be out here an hour before practice starts?" Ashley asked sneaking up on Jake.

"I would ask you the same thing, but I already know the answer," Jake replied, not surprised to see Ashley well prior to the start of practice. "It's a beautiful day, figured I would come out and get some fresh air."

"You could get fresh air during practice," Ashley remarked dropping her mitt to the ground to begin stretching.

"Not alone," Jake responded smiling. "Sometimes I just like to stand in the sunlight, close my eyes and do some deep thinking. I had a feeling you would show up, so how are you today?"

"I'm what I am," Ashley answered putting in her earbuds to begin her run.

"Mind if I join you on your run?" Jake asked putting his clipboard on the ground and tucking his whistle into his shirt. "I haven't run in a long time, curious to see how my knees react."

"I can't stop you," Ashley replies, "but don't expect me to slow down for you."

"I don't want you to," said Jake doing a few stretches to loosening himself up. "Aren't you going to be hot wearing long sleeves?"

"Just try and keep up," Ashley remarks taking off running.

Caught off guard by her quick absence, Jake hurries to catch up, turning his baseball cap backwards, his black basketball shorts flapping in the breeze, following her path along the outside of the field moving at a comfortable pace. His knees seemed okay at the moment, stiff at first, but appear to loosen up more with ever stride. Wanting to give his knees a real test, he turns on the jets, speeding up to come side by side with Ashley, who looks over to view a smiling Jake. Matching her pace, the two of them run side by side for the next few laps, seemingly in sync with their arm motion and stride. A couple more laps in Jake stopped at home plate feeling his knees beginning to ache, slowing Ashley down seeing him come to a stop, but she was waved on to keep going. Watching Ashley continue on, breathing heavy, sweat dripping down his face, he sits himself down on the infield dirt, legs out straight, leaning back using his arms to hold himself up, allowing the throbbing in his knees to subside. Running in the outfield, Ashley sees Jake laid out in the infield, his body language advertising exhaustion or discomfort, decides to bring her run to an end, feeling the running start to aggravate the soreness in her vaginal area. Jogging over to the water cooler feeling extra sweaty due to the crop top, wanting so badly to take it off, she grabs a couple of cups of ice water, walking over to where Jake has positioned himself to hand him a drink.

"Thank you," Jake said, sitting up to quench his growing thirst. "Join me down here for a second."

Ashley seats herself on the infield dirt next to Jake, sitting Indian style putting her sunglasses on top of her ball cap, face wet with sweat, quickly taking a sip of water.

"What happen, you run out of gas?" Ashley asked sipping her water.

"I wish that's all it was," replied Jake, pulling up his shorts on both legs revealing the two six-inch scars residing on both knees. "I was just curious how long I could go until they both started acting up."

"So that's why you can't play anymore," remarked Ashley.

"Among other things, yeah, that is the reason," said Jake. "You know, every time I look at those scars it reminds me of the life I once had."

"You miss playing, don't you?" Ashley asked.

"Every day, I'm not going to lie, I'd give anything to be playing again, but life dealt me a different hand and I like to think everything happens for a reason," answered Jake.

"Do you think coaching us is part of that reason?" she asked looking at Jake, her face covered in shade from her ball cap.

"Maybe," he responds smiling, receiving a small return grin from Ashley.

"Can I ask you something? What happened after baseball, I mean there was a gap in there between then and you coming to coach us," wondered Ashley.

"Are you asking because you tried to Google search me and it gave you nothing after my pro career?" Jake asked.

"I'm sorry, I really don't mean to pry," Ashley said playing with the dirt in front of her.

"It's okay. What I'm about to tell you though not to many people know about," Jake replied.

"Really, you don't have to tell me if you don't want to," insisted Ashley.

"It's fine, I trust you," remarked Jake.

Ashley sat there, knees bent, arms hugging her legs, listening to Jake tell his story, the drinking, the depression, the gambling, all culminating to where he is now, she had no idea someone like him could go through a dark period like that, pro athletes to her were viewed as invincible, like superheroes, nothing bad could ever happen to them, but the more he spoke, the more she realized almost everyone has personal demons they are battling with in secret, a topic she knows all too well about. Her battle has been lifelong, behind closed doors, where every day seems to delivers a new obstacle for her to clash with. The one thing Ashley always tries to do is not feel sorry for herself, that is not the pathway to a better life, it just leads to a longer sentence in your own personal emotional prison, but couldn't help feeling sorry for Jake with everything he went through, a top tier athlete who seemed to have the world by the balls only for it to be taken away from him thanks to a case of bad luck. Jake even explained what happened with his apparent arrest back in high school, a story that left Ashley virtually speechless, concluding with his moral victory over his demons, relaying that he hasn't had a drink in over five years or gambled, his only downside is he has to take depression medication every day for the rest of his life. Listening to Jake open up to her made Ashley feel more and more comfortable, someone she could relate to in a way, giving her hope there is light at the end of the tunnel, just the journey there won't always easy. Feeling so comfortable, she opened up to him about certain aspects of her life, her strong relationship with Holley J, the situation with her mother and her aunt, not knowing who her father was, even her rocky feud with Renee. Hearing herself spill her guts about portions of her life to someone was a huge breakthrough for her, having never trusted anyone other than Holley J, to garnish this information to, especially a man, Jake may be the first male in her entire life she can actually trust, who would never take advantage of her or ask her to do inappropriate things. Wondered what her high school career would have been like if Jake was the coach of this team all four years, how really close they could have become. Very much wanted to tell him about what her old coach made her do, but held her tongue, not wanting to stir up a team controversy that would put more attention on her she really doesn't want. Sitting there with the sun beating down on their shoulders, an occasional breeze to cool them off, not another soul in sight, at that very moment she felt like her and Jake were the only two people in the world, fitting for one of the few great events in her life, the day see was able to open up to a male figure and feel good about it. Ironically it happened coming off one of the worse nights she has had in a long time, but no matter what she will always remember the day she sat on the infield dirt, with the sun shining, alone with an adult man and feeling safe. The monumental moment even briefly took her mind off the grisly dream from last night, finally having a good memory, the start of many to hopefully begin to drown out the negative ones.

Jake was moved with Ashley willingly discussing some of her life issues, couldn't help but feel bad for her, hearing how her aunt treats her broke his heart, no one should have to go through that, let alone a teenage girl. He wished there was something he could do for her, but didn't think it was his place to get involved. All the day to day stress she must go through at home, at school, he now understands why she puts in the effort she does, the time before and after practice and the time she probably trains on her own, she needs an outlet, somewhere she can pour all her pent up anxiety and that's where softball comes in. Jake was now motivated more than ever to help get this team on the right track and to get Ashley where she wanted to go. Knowing now his coach-player relationship with Ashley was going to be different, stronger than it was before, now can only hope it stays that way. With a little bit of time before practice starts, the two of them stand to their feet, stretching out to relieve their relaxed muscles from being stationary for a bit, Jake suggests Ashley throw some pitches until the rest of the girls arrive to loosen up. Getting no argument from her, she plants herself on the pitcher's mound while Jake places himself behind home plate, engaging in the pitcher, catcher version of catch. Holley J has always been Ashley's catcher, whether it be at practice, in a game or just the two of them practicing on their own, but now having Jake step in for a second time gives her an alternative if she so choses to have one. Seizing the time to resume conversation, in between Jake's many compliments he consistently tosses out Ashley's way on her pitching.

Strangely the crop top doesn't seem to be bothering her today, but still wishes she didn't have to wear it. As the start of practice grows closer, Holley J emerges in the dugout carrying her duffle bag full of her catcher's gear, could hear the slap of Ashley's pitches hitting Jake's mitt halfway to the field. Waving Holley J over to take his place, she grabs her mitt to go replace Jake to do what she has done probably a thousand times before. With no offense to Jake, having Holley J squatted down behind home plate makes Ashley feel complete, the two of them have a chemistry that is unmatched, she would not want anyone else catching for her during a game, they know each other's strengths and weaknesses, even little tells have become like a secret language between the two of them, they have done this so much together they could probably do it with their eyes closed. Girl talk ensues, Jake gives Ashley the thumbs-up in reference to their earlier talk, also praising her pitching, she responds with a nod as he grabs his clipboard off the ground, untucking his whistle preparing for the rest of the girls to arrive.

Practice began like any other, Ashley leads the team in a run, followed by a round of warm up calisthenics, ending with a few minutes of stretching. Jake then taught the girls more fielding and hitting drills until it came time to send Brie off alone again to practice swinging left handed. Under Jake's guidance and teachings, Ashley could see the team gelling better and better together with every practice, becoming more impressed with his uncanny ability to spot every girl's strength and weakness and to use it towards the team's advantage, like she is playing for a completely different team than the one she has played for the last three years, a good sign seeing the season starts in less than a week. Jake blows his whistle ending practice for the day, another successful outing, can see improvement across the board in various areas from a lot of the girls, they are working hard, evident to all the sweat and heavy breathing surrounding him as the girls gather around to take a knee. Ashley positions herself front and center with Holley J by her side eagerly waiting on Jake's post-practice lecture, starts by telling the girls to give themselves a round of applause for a great practice which the girls happily oblige. During Jake's talk Ashley looked back at all the girls, observing the expressions on their faces which were those of purpose, every girl had their eyes locked on Jake soaking up every word. Their demeanors were like soldiers listening to a general before they were sent into battle, he had every girl's full attention, displaying something that was always missing from this team since Ashley has been a part of it, unity, the girls were buying what Jake was selling and it showed with their reactions to Jake's words, even Renee located in the back, showcasing her signature snotty look, was totally focused. Holley J looked up at Jake, still in her catcher's gear, with a huge smile on her face, typical of a girl who is crushing on someone, it's no secret most of the girls on the team find Jake attractive, including Ashley, who isn't afraid to admit to herself when a man is nice looking despite her not so great history with them. Reminding the girls about their first game of the season next week which means they have only three full practices left until then, but he believes this team will be ready.

"I just want you girls to remember one thing before I let you go today, a little quote that my high school coach once told us. It's not how good you want to be, it's how good you are willing to be," Jake stated scanning his eyes to cover all the girls, ending with eye contact with Ashley. "Now everybody, stand up."

All the girls climbed to their feet, their attention never wavering.

"Most teams always do the traditional hands in to show unity, but this team is going to be different," Jake explains. "We are going to show team unity a different way, a special way, our way. Put one fist in the air."

The girls all select a fist, promptly thrusting it upward, still keeping their focus on Jake.

"This is our sign of unity, whether we are all gathered together or separated on the field, when one fist goes up they all go up, understood?" asked Jake, the girls all answer in unison with a loud, clear yes sir. "Keep those fists up, team on three," he requested. "One, two, three."

"TEAM," shouted the girls.

Jake dismissed the team, telling them to all have a great weekend and will see them on Monday. The girls all grab their gear, walking back to the locker room as a group. Ashley and Holley J hung back, deciding to stick around for a little while longer to work on some more pitches, Ashley had a little time before her aunt would start blowing up her phone with unwelcomed texts. Jake was the last to leave, walking away he turned back to see Ashley and Holley J congregated around home plate, the girls took notice of Jake's watchful eyes from a distance. Walking backwards as the girls took notice to him, Jake gingerly throws one fist in the air, getting an immediate response from Ashley and Holley J doing the same.

Ashley sounds her car horn in Holley J's driveway signaling her arrival, another beautiful spring morning, waiting patiently with her driver's side window down to catch some of the daytime breeze, supporting sunglasses to counter the bright early sun. Again wearing her pink sweat jacket, the bruises on her arm are starting to fade, but are still very noticeable. Ashley has been looking forward to this time with Holley J and doesn't want any distractions, keeping her arm covered will not only benefit Holley J, but herself as well, if she doesn't see it she won't dwell on it, out of sight, out of mind. Listening to the sound of her car idling, she sees someone pull back the drapes in the picture window, the glare on the glass from the sunlight made it hard to decipher who was standing there, her only guess was one of the disapproving parents. Holley J excitedly exited the front door saying goodbye to her mother, who must have been the one in the window, boisterously heading for Ashley's passenger door. Entering the vehicle promptly throwing on her shades while the car slowly backs out of the driveway, her passenger window open, the car drives off down the street. The girls drive to their destination, shades on, hair flapping in the wind, Holley J is singing and dancing in her seat to the music coming from the car's CD player, a mixed CD given to Ashley from Holley J of what she would call must have driving tunes. Holley J always plays DJ when the two of them drive together, a title agreed upon by both of the girls since Holley J is known for her great taste in music. Singing the recently playing song word for word, her angelic voice overpowering the roaring clamor of the speeding car cutting through the air, Holley J gestures for Ashley to join in, who motions back waving her hand, mouthing the word no, sticking her tongue out indicating awfulness. Holley J retaliates with a big bright smile, resuming on alone. Ashley has always told her she has an incredible voice and should have joined the glee club or make some demo tapes, but like Ashley with her paintings, Holley J just likes to sing for herself. Just as Holley J's mini concert ends, the girls arrive at their nearby mall.

Walking together through the shopping center, each carrying a small retail bag along with their purses, the girls noticed the mall seeming overly crowded even for a Saturday. The mixture of families, groups of teenagers, many from other schools, couples, variety groups and the collection of mall walkers make up the traditional clientele. The ominous mall soundtrack plays overhead, loud enough to be heard, but at a low enough volume where no one really knows what song is playing, especially on a busy day like today. The two of them come upon a store they both are into, ducking inside to start their conventional browsing process.

"Oh my God, tell me this isn't the cutest freaking shirt you have ever seen," raves Holley J, holding the top against her chest looking in the nearby mirror. "It would probably look better if I was a little more busty, but it is so adorable. What do you think?"

"I don't know, I like the color," Ashley replies skimming through some clothes on a neighboring rack.

"Are you saying you wouldn't wear something like this? I'd wear a shirt like this every day if I had your frame," jokes Holley J, giving the shirt a second look in the mirror.

"If you like it so much, buy it," said Ashley reviewing a pair of black yoga pants.

"Maybe I will," remarked Holley J checking the shirt's price tag, "Whoa! Looks like I'm going to have to put you back before I break it."

"What's the matter?" asked Ashley draping the yoga pants over her arm to be purchased.

"A, this is the matter," Holley J responds showing Ashley the price tag. "That is pretty steep for a shirt and my parents would kill me for spending that kind of money on just a top."

"Do you really like the shirt?" Ashley asked, recalling how Holley J's eyes lit up when she first laid eyes on it. Holley J has the worst poker face, can always read what emotion she is feeling simply by looking at face, making it hard for Holley J to hide her feelings from her.

"Does a bear shit in the woods? Yes, I like the shirt!" answered Holley J hugging the top against her chest.

"Then I'm going to buy it for you," said Ashley grabbing the shirt from her, piling it on top of the yoga pants.

"Wait, what?" said a confused Holley J. "Ash, I can't let you buy this for me, it's too much."

"It's okay, I want to," insisted Ashley.

"Oh my God, you're going to make me cry," Holley J remarked, her eyes beginning to water, hugging Ashley like a little kid. "Thank you, thank you, thank you!"

"Thank you," Ashley responded.

"Lunch is on me," said Holley J releasing her from her grasp. "This is the best friend any girl could ask for right here, this girl right here," she shouted to everyone shopping in the store, pointing to Ashley, who places her hand over her face in embarrassment, shaking her head.

Ashley and Holley J are at the food court preparing to have lunch, the area is becoming overpopulated, empty table and chairs running scarce. Finally locating a place to sit and eat, they park themselves to get some much needed rest from walking the mall for the past few hours, enjoying some overdue nourishment as well. Holley kept her word, buying lunch for both of them, knowing Ashley likes to watch what she eats, diverting her to purchase a couple grilled chicken salads with a pair of bottled waters to wash it down. Their conversation while eating focused mainly on the team, both giving praise to Jake's coaching prowess, filling them both with excitement on the upcoming season. The day together with Holley J was much needed, giving her a chance to be free even just for a few hours knowing work loomed in the distance. Though the food court was oversaturated with mall patrons, Ashley could only hear the sound of Holley J's voice, blocking out the concoction of a hundred strange voices that surrounded them. Discussions together were always so fluid, like a running waterfall, they understood each other and could finish each other's sentences, they could almost tell what the other was thinking, feeling like they could tell each other anything, bringing Ashley back to the heart to heart she recently had with Jake. Listening to Holley J talk, always with a smile on her face, looking deep into her eyes, seeing the most trustworthy person she has ever known, feeling like she had a revelation after her unexpected opening of her life door, being it only a crack, to someone other than Holley J, she determined, amongst the scourge of local society, it might be time to let Holley J in on her most deepest and darkest secrets. Something that has been eating at her since they meet doing that art project together back in third grade. Just the thought of the words coming out of her mouth began to put knots in her stomach, only her time at the club could compare to the overwhelming feeling of nervousness and fear swirling relentlessly through her body, about to cross a bridge she hoped would have burned down before she got there. Sitting there holding a plastic fork inside an empty plate, nervously tapping it against the side, going over in her head all the possible reactions she could expect from Holley J, feeling like a prisoner in her own mind, at odds with her thoughts to the point she was trying to talk herself out of it, but realizes Holley J is going to find out eventually, so would rather have her hear it from her than someone else.

"Holley J, I have something I have to tell you," said Ashley, feeling her heart pounding almost out of her chest. Alone and in private would probably be a more suitable place to air out her dirty laundry, but the sudden surge of courage overtaking her might dissipate soon, wanting to take advantage of the window while it's open. Being in a crowded food court seemed irrelevant, no one can predict when the best time to do anything will come upon them.

"Yeah, what is it?" Holley J asked. "Is it about what happened with Steven last week, because I already know and from what I heard he deserved it."

"No, it's not that," replied Ashley taking a deep breath. "You are probably not going to like what I'm about to tell you."

"Why, what is this about?" asked Holley J, looking at the serious demeanor on Ashley's face, halting the consumption of her lunch. "Okay, Ash, you are starting to scare me."

Ashley about to open her mouth letting out the first words to her confession, gets interrupted by a stranger's voice.

"HOLY SHIT, IT'S YOU!" said the strange voice.

Ashley looked over to view a few guys in their earlier twenties standing next to their table, a glancing Holley J also looked on at their unwelcome visitors with a suspicious stare.

"Excuse me," remarked Ashley, not familiar with any of the young men.

"You're Angel, the stripper down at Playmates," says one of the young men. "This is the girl I was telling you guys about. Yo, I've seen this chick naked, bro, she's a smoke show."

"I think you have me confused with someone else," Ashley repented, afraid if she doesn't get rid of these dudes they are going to blow her cover.

"I don't think so, you have one of the hottest faces I have ever seen," the young man remarked. "With a body to match."

"I'm sorry, it's not me," Ashley scolded getting irritated.

"Guys, she just told you she is not who you think she is, so why don't you just leave her alone. There are plenty of other girls here to bump your boners," snapped Holley J not happy with their persistence.

"There is one way to prove it," offered the young man. "Show me your tits."

The young man and his friends start laughing, slapping hands in a celebratory manner, Ashley jumped out of her seat to confront the annoying trio.

"I told you, you got me confused with someone else and I'm not going to say it again," Ashley said getting in the young man's face.

"Fine," responded the young man arrogantly. "Let's get out of here, guys, but you know I heard for the right price you can fuck this bitch."

Enraged by the young man's disrespectful comment, not even caring she was in the view of a lot of people, Ashley angrily shoved the young man hard enough backing him into a nearby table that was luckily vacant. Many of the surrounding food court visitors brought their attention to the unpleasant scene, an onlooking mall security guard witnessing the confrontation swiftly heads over to intervene.

"What's the problem here?" asked the large black security guard, his muscular arms seemingly popping out of his short-sleeved shirt.

"No problem here," stated the young man composing himself, a look of aggravation displays on his face. "We were just leaving. See you tonight, sweetie."

"Are you girls okay?" asked the security guard, watching to make sure the young men disappear into the crowd.

"Yeah, everything's fine," Ashley replies, sitting back down in her seat.

"You should have thrown those three idiots out of here," suggested Holley J, clearly unhappy with what unfolded.

"They willing left on their own terms, other than that there's nothing I can do, unless they were harassing you and you would like to fill out a report," remarked the security guard.

"That won't be necessary," Ashley replied, clearly still upset about the situation, more so that she drew unwanted attention to herself, the nosey stare of strange eyes looking on getting their free entertainment of public drama.

"Then you girls have a great rest of your day," said the security guard heading back to his post.

"What the hell was that all about?" asked Holley J, seeing Ashley is still bothered by the three young men's immature behavior.

"Like I said, they got me confused with someone else," replied Ashley, disturbed by the fact she once again has to lie to Holley J's face.

"Some guys just won't take no for an answer. Kind of funny, though, they really thought you were a stripper. I mean you are definitely pretty enough, but any girl willing to expose themselves like that, I don't know, I couldn't have any respect for a girl willing to do that, pretty disgusting in my book. Anyway, didn't you say you had to tell me something?" inquired Holley J.

Listening to those honest words coming out of Holley J's mouth, Ashley began to feel sick to her stomach, feeling like at any second she could have a panic attack, a punch to the gut like she never felt before.

"It's not important," Ashley remarked feeling her tear ducts filling up.

"I'll be right back, I got to run to the bathroom," announced Holley J getting up to leave.

Watching her best friend walk away, in her mind symbolizing the outcome of her buried confession, a couple tears streamed down her face in validation to the response she would receive from Holley J if she would have told her secrets. Ashley sat there heartbroken, like she just got a glimpse into the future, wanting to believe Holley J would understand and be by her side no matter what, but it is a chance Ashley can't afford to take. In some sick way today's events were a way of the universe telling her to keep certain details to herself, determined now to never lose her best friend, vowing to herself to take these secrets as far as she can, hopefully to the grave.

Off in the distance Ashley sees Holley J returning from her trip to the bathroom, quickly grabbing a napkin off the table to wipe away her few shed tears, regrouping herself to not let on something is wrong. A day that started out to have so much great potential, quickly turned into a day she was not looking forward too from here on out, amazing how suddenly fortunes can change in the matter of seconds. Holley J makes her return to the table, seating herself, letting out a gratifying sigh.

"I feel so much better after that," said Holley J, peering across the table at Ashley, worried she might not be in good spirits to finish with their day together. "Are you sure you are okay?"

"I'll be fine," Ashley answers, caught in a tornado of emotions.

Finishing up the last few bites of her salad, Holley J glanced up to notice Ashley's sweat jacket has dropped off her left shoulder revealing portions of her bruised arm.

"Jesus!" said a shocked Holley J, reaching over the table to pull down more of Ashley's sweat jacket exposing more bruising. "What the hell happened?"

Quickly pulling up the sweat jacket to cover herself, not making eye contact with Holley J. When it rains, it pours, Ashley couldn't believe how drastic a turn the day has taken, now having to come up with an excuse that would be valid enough to explain the condition of her arm, the last person she wanted to ever see it got a front row view of it.

"It's nothing, I just fell down the stairs at home," Ashley said, hoping Holley J buys her fib. "I didn't tell you because I didn't want you to worry."

"That must have been quite a tumble," Holley J replies suspiciously.

"Got to watch when you are carrying that laundry basket, you know," remarked Ashley, feeling like she is about to be interrogated.

"Did you get hurt anywhere else? Are there bruises elsewhere?" Holley J asked.

"No, just this arm," answered Ashley, mad at herself for not being more careful hiding her arm, having to spin a web of lies now to cover for herself.

An apprehensive Holley J couldn't help but wonder if Ashley was keeping something from her, lately picking up on some weird vibes, it could be nothing, but her instincts are usually pretty honed in, finding it strange Ashley fell down a flight of stairs only injuring one arm, no bruising or injuries anywhere else, something didn't add up, but had no reason to suspect Ashley was lying, they have always been straight forward with each other, only this time she had some uncertainty.

"Will you look straight into my eyes and swear to me that is what happened?" Holley J asked, wanting so bad to believe her.

"I swear that's what happened," Ashley replied, looking directly into Holley J's baby blues, her reflection in Holley J's pupils staring back at her. She just looked into her best friend's eyes and lied directly to her face, it felt like she was being stabbed with a thousand knives in her heart, having to rigorously fight back tears that would have shown her guilt. In her mind Ashley was calling herself a terrible friend, from her point of view their entire friendship could be seen as being based on lies, an inner struggle she deals with every day, hurting Holley J is the last thing she ever wants to do, to her that would be emotional suicide she would never be able to handle. The only thing giving her some sort of emotional comfort is she truly believes keeping that side of her life dormant from Holley J is the right thing to do, at least until the time is right.

"Alright then, well, you need to be more careful, you could have broken your arm. Could you have imagined if that happened, I don't even want to think about it," said Holley finishing up her lunch. "So then you are up for some more shopping?"

"Sure," replies Ashley, trying to portray a believable grin on her face.

Another extremely busy Saturday night at the club, the main show area was completely filled, there wasn't a table or booth available, standing room only, the bouncers outside working the front entrance had a roped off line of people still waiting to get in, even the bar area was overrun with customers, to the point Razz had to schedule three bartenders to handle the load. He brought in double the amount of girls, a couple are on stage dancing, the rest are either giving lap dances or are downstairs for their more private, personal sessions. The clientele tonight appeared to be more rowdy than usual, the bouncers and security guards have been extra busy, already had to toss out a few guys for their drunken disorderly conduct, some were escorted out for being inappropriate with the girls during their lap dances. Keeping a club full of mainly drunk, horny men under control can sometimes be no easy feat, but the security at Razz' club seem to thrive the more out of control it gets, the more regular patrons no matter their intoxicated state, have grown to respect Razz' lackeys cause they don't fuck around, they handle ever situation as quickly and quietly as possible, the last thing Razz needs is his place swarming with on duty cops. With the music blaring, all the waitresses moving rapidly around the club delivering food or taking orders, it's an atmosphere filled with testosterone and libidos working overtime, the overpowering mixed scent of sweat, alcohol and various body sprays and cologne filled the air. This was the kind of night Razz lives for, money rolling in from every direction, with the best part being it's still early.

Sitting in his office on his couch shirtless, smoking a joint, Razz texts details to one of his buyers. Usually on a busy night like this he tries to spend much of his time out on the main floor overseeing all the loud commotion, but has other business to attend to and knows his crew can handle his operation. Was out there a little earlier to see Ashley on stage, never misses when she dances, something about her is just a visual feast for his senses that no other one of his girls can seem to replicate, wants to taste the goods with her very badly, it's just for some odd reason he can't explain, just won't pull the trigger on it. Receiving his latest text confirming his latest deal is a go, Razz tosses his phone on the coffee table, lays back with the joint in his mouth, spreading both of his arms out across the top of the couch with a sinister grin appearing on his face in total delight. Basking in his newest financial conquest, he hears his office doors open with two of his girls entering, one being Ashley, walking over to stand by the coffee table. The girls could smell the marijuana entering the room, watching Razz take another hit. Signaling to the one girl, he unbuttons his jeans as she positions herself on the floor between his legs, pulling out his erect penis where she begins to perform oral sex on him, looking on awkwardly Ashley waits for the reason she was called to his office.

"There is a client waiting for you downstairs, Show Horse, in room four," instructed Razz blowing smoke into the air. "He said for me to tell you, he has a surprise for you."

"What's that supposed to mean?" a confused Ashley asked.

"How the fuck should I know, all that matters is that he paid for you," Razz responded. "He seemed pretty eager for you, though. HEY, EASY WITH THE FUCKING TEETH!" Razz yells to the other girl, slapping her across the head.

Having seen enough of the other girl giving Razz head, a sight that turned her stomach, she turned to leave, wondering who awaits her downstairs. A few steps into her departure she hears Razz' voice call for her.

"Hey, Show Horse," Razz calls out.

Ashley turns to acknowledge him.

"The makeup on your arm is smearing," he states with a smile on his face, hearing his sarcastic laughter as she leaves his office.

Infuriating Ashley listening to Razz take joyous pride in his handy work, because of him she had to arrive at least a half-hour early to have enough time to apply the coverup which is now evident it's not holding up, deciding to stop back in the dressing room for a quick touchup.

Downstairs has been the major hot spot of the night with every room being used at a consistent rate. Most of the girls hate nights like these, being so busy there is hardly any time for the girls to properly maintenance themselves before they have to repeat their services. Room preservation also suffers, not allowing for suitable sanitizing of the already over used mattresses forcing the girls to perform on recent excreted bodily fluids. Proceeding down the hallway towards room four, Ashley can smell the stench of sex filling the brightly lit corridor, a couple girls emerge from their respected rooms totally naked, swiftly heading to the downstairs bathroom. Standing right outside room four, Ashley grabs the doorknob, hesitant to turn it, hating every time she walks up to these doors it's always a mystery of who is on the other side, no matter their age or what they look like, her feelings and values are non-existent when entering these rooms, becoming that living breathing sex doll expected to perform at the drop of a hat, like a soulless android. Being told the client had a surprise for her was weighing heavy on her mind, what could they have meant by that, what could the surprise be, either way she knows in this business whatever it is probably wasn't going to put a smile on her face.

Wanting to get this over with she unlatched the door entering the room, to her utter dismay, triggering a strong case of nausea and disbelief, standing there completely naked supporting an erection, was the young man from the mall. Ashley couldn't believe what she was seeing, hoping real hard she was just hallucinating and there was a different guy actually standing there, but to her disappointment he was real and looking just as smug as he did earlier in the day. Finding herself in a no-win situation, leaving and refusing to engage in what he had paid for her to do would leave her in more definite hot water with Razz, staying to do her job, this guy wins getting the last laugh. The thought of him getting the best of her made her feel completely helpless, feeling like she was caught between a rock and a hard place. The young man arrogantly walked over towards Ashley, his erected penis swinging backward and forth with ever step, that complacent grin flashed over his face.

"Well, well, well, look what we have here. You still going to deny who you are?" the young man asked standing before her, his slim hairy body covered in goosebumps from the slight chill in the room.

"What are you doing here?" asked an angry Ashley, staring at the one person in the world she was in no mood to see.

"Considering my current condition, it's plainly obvious what I'm here for," the young man bolstered, reaching up to stroke Ashley's hair.

"Fuck you, I'm not doing it," Ashley replied, swatting his hand away.

The consequences awaiting her if she refused to do what was expected would probably be harsher than her battered arm, but at that split second she didn't care, would rather take her chances with Razz than to give this guy any formidable amount of pleasure at her expense.

"I don't think so, I paid good money for you," stated the young man. "Now get down on your fucking knees, whore!" he yelled, tightly grabbing the hair on the side of Ashley's head.

That word again, the word she despises the most, being said to her by some arrogant, trust fund having asshole. Ashley's blood began to boil, could feel her adrenaline spiking to the point where she felt strong enough to pick him up over her head and body slam him to the concrete floor below, but felt a more brutal form of retaliation was in order. Giving him the impression she was going along with his request, she slowly descended to her knees keeping her eyes focused strictly on his self-centered grin, his hands still gripping her hair. The cold chill of the bare concrete now pressed against her legs, bringing her within inches of his average-sized hard-on.

"That's it, just like the whore you are," said the young man, slapping her a few times across the face with his erection. "Who's the shit talker now, bitch?"

"Are you ready for it?" asked Ashley in a very sensual voice.

"Goddamn right I'm ready," he responded, gripping tighter on her hair. "I'm going to blow this shit in your face."

Showing a sinister grin of her own, Ashley inserts the young man's penis in her mouth, getting ever so into it, heavily working her tongue to lick the shaft and tip, gaging his level of approval by how much harder he squeezes her hair, his constant low pitch moaning became the green light that she had him right where she wanted him. Ending the perpetual tongue massage, Ashley reinserts the shaft in her mouth to his overwhelming approval, giving it a few quick deep throats, letting out her inner she-devil by exposing her teeth, biting down forcefully, like a vice on his defenseless penis, drawing blood.

"FUCK!!" the young man screams, swiftly pulling his injured organ out of her mouth, her teeth scraping across his flesh on the withdrawal, dropping to the floor in immense pain while holding his penis with both hands, his naked body rolled up in the fetal position wincing in agony.

Ashley wipes away the drops of blood around her mouth with the back of her hand, smearing some of it along her jaw line. Bringing herself to her feet, still all worked up with her breathing becoming erratic, stands over the young man who is still groaning in pain, her hair a mess from his insubordinate and churlish behavior, looking down she doesn't see a defenseless young man, but a hybrid of every male that has ever wronged her. Feeling overpowered with inner rage, as if some unseen force was taking over her body, she let herself succumb to the suppressed anger beginning to overtake her anatomy. Clenching her teeth together, drops of spit sprayed out of her mouth from her heavy breathing, her newly made fists were clasping so tight her hands were white in color, sweat started to trickle down her face and arms as her body became more overheated with her intense physical state. Years of suppressed anger seemed to surface all at once, her conscious mind reached its absolute boiling point. Letting out a scream at the top of her lungs, her mouth open as wide as she could get it, her body so tense veins began to protrude out of her neck, the loud holler lasted what seemed like forever unbeknown to anyone outside the sound proof room. Without warning Ashley kicked the young man in the face with the front of her shoe, the impact broke his nose as blood instantly flew into the air, the next kick rendered him unconscious with more blood arriving on the scene. Her kicks made their way down to his torso area, letting out a yell with every blow. Standing over the young man landing kick after kick, feeling like a different person, a person she one day feared would come out, seeing the faces of every man who has ever molested her, touched her, tried to rape her and fucked her, evening seeing Razz' face, wanting to keep kicking until all those faces disappeared. The young man's body laid limp, totally helpless to the seamlessly endless barrage of kicks, his torso turning bright red in spots from the constant pounding on his flesh, his now flaccid penis still showing traces of blood. Her back to the door, Ashley's vicious beat down came to sudden halt when two security guards aggressively entered the room, one tackling Ashley on to the bed.

Ashley finds herself sitting in the leather chair in Razz' office, a blank expression on her face, eyes appear lifeless staring in an almost psychotic manner. Unaware of what is happening, feels the cool chill of a wet rag against the skin of her jaw line, the damp temperature snaps her out of her hypnotic state. Now fully aware of her surroundings, she slightly cringes in her seat a bit startled, her eyes moving a mile a minute. The cold wet sensation along her jaw is courtesy of Razz wiping away the dry, smeared blood around her mouth, knelt down before her.

"Did you have fun?" asked Razz is a low somewhat angered tone.

Sitting there staring at Razz, Ashley knew this moment was inevitable after what she did to that young man, regardless that he deserved it, he was still a client and all physical altercations are to be dealt by and handled with Razz' security, nothing they saw on camera warranted her behavior.

"He deserved it," Ashley replied in a soft voice, Razz finished cleaning up the blood off of her face.

"You know, you are an exquisite beauty, Show Horse. Even with your hair a little messed and your makeup not at its best, you are still one of the hottest bitches I have ever seen," said Razz fixing some of Ashley's hair. "Hard to believe so much rage and aggression can come from someone so breathtaking. You know you could have killed him."

"Where is he?" Ashley asked, realizing her and Razz are the only ones in his office. The atmosphere felt very strange, almost like she had never been there before, she couldn't explain it, but the look and smell of the room seemed foreign to her despite past visits there before.

"I shot him up with a tranquilizer agent, put him in the alley in the back, called an ambulance telling them we find him there like that. When he comes to he probably won't even remember what happened this entire day," explained Razz. "Do you know the amount of trouble this stunt you pulled could have brought me?" he asked grabbing Ashley's right arm just above the elbow, squeezing almost as hard as he can, matching the tension shown on his face.

Ashley grimaced in pain, feeling his fingernails digging into her skin, only a matter of time before he does some real damage to her throwing arm and she can't have that. Fighting back would only add insult to injury, she had to be smart about this to keep herself out of harm's way. Without even thinking about it she did the last thing she ever wanted to do, leaned in to start kissing him. Caught completely off guard, feeling those young soft lips pressed up against his, Razz released Ashley's arm, picking her up out of the chair, her legs wrapped around his torso with her ass resting atop both of his hands. The make-out session becoming more intense, Razz stumbles backwards into his desk knocking over a couple items, feeling Ashley's tongue in his mouth sent sensations through his body he has never felt before, the soft touch of a teenage girl's lips wrestling with his is nothing more than sexual serenity, for a girl who doesn't like to kiss she is damn good at it. Doing her best job of convincing Razz this is what she wanted even though this whole act is making her sick to her stomach, literally having to fight off throwing up in her mouth from the disgust she feels, can tell through his actions he is definitely enjoying himself, almost choking on his tongue a few times, feeling the constant gripping of her ass the more excited he gets. Heavy breathing mixed with panting starts to escalate, Razz bringing his attention to kissing and licking Ashley's neck, her young soft skin against his lips felt like heaven to the touch, her smell alone was arousing. Throwing her hair to the side to help expose more of her neck, she closes her eyes, not in pleasure, but in revulsion, as Razz' wet, course tongue and lips paints the skin on her neck. Becoming more unbearable ever second longer it went on, she started it, she had to be the one to end it. Putting herself through an uncomfortable, disgusting act was better than any physical abuse she might have received, but promising herself this was never going to happen again, never dreaming her first make out session would ironically be with one of the people she detested most.

"Razz, please, we have to stop," whispered Ashley into Razz' ear.

Hearing Ashley's faint, sensual voice, Razz relinquishes his advances, the two make eye contact looking at each other like hated lovers.

"We can't do this," she said, hoping he agrees, lowering her down allowing her to stand on her own two feet.

"You really think you can get me all worked up like that and just walk out of here?" Razz asked.

"Razz, I just can't do it," she replies, totally worried now this may not end the way she hoped.

"I'm not asking you to fuck me," he responds, unbuttoning his jeans, pulling out his rock hard penis. "You are going to finish what you started. And don't try to negotiate your way out of it and if you even think about pulling that shit you did earlier with me, I'll make sure you never play softball again," threatened Razz, placing both his hand on Ashley's face as she stands there like a statue, feeling paralyzed, tears sipping out of her eyes. "And you don't want that, now do you, Show Horse?" Razz asked, watching the tears stream down her face.

Ashley slowly shakes her head in agreeance, steadily bringing herself to her knees.

Returning home from a very eventful night, another she wishes she could forget, Ashley pulls into her empty driveway, noticing her aunt's car is nowhere to be found, meaning she is probably with her new beau for the night, expecting to find a note left on the coffee table of chores her aunt wants done before she returns home, a ritual she does every time she excuses herself for the night. Ashley exits her car, backpack with her, wearing the outfit she had on at the club, was in no mood to change there, just decided to wear it home, making her ride home a challenge because she hates to drive in heels. Entering the cool night air, she was surprised how awkwardly quiet the neighborhood seemed, parking her car was probably the only thing that broke the silence in several hours. Being a little after two in the morning, the clear night sky was host to a blanket of stars, the moonlight provided some source of illumination, the other being the left on porch light being surrounded by a group of moths. Carefully walking to the front door holding a can of mace she carries in her purse, always wondering if some creep is lurking behind the front yard bushes. Safely making it to the front door, she uses her key to let herself in, greeted to the dominating smell of marijuana. Her aunt's party time must have started here before taking it to a new location. Closing and locking the door behind her, Ashley flips on the living room lamp to bring her aunt's mess into full view. Again empty beer bottles cover the coffee table, joint butts filled the ashtray, there was a couple of Styrofoam containers loaded with chicken wing bones resting on some used sheets of paper towels, even left a couple sprinkles of cocaine with a credit card nearby, the expected note was left in a different spot, taped to the TV screen. Ripping the note off the screen, giving it a quick look over before crumpling it up and throwing it in the trash, deciding to deal with her aunt's bullshit in the morning, she makes her way up the darkened staircase to her room, her mind overloaded with thoughts of today's occurrences, what happened with the dude, with Holley J and her recent affair with Razz. The day became one she would not soon forget for a while, one of many days she will have stashed in her memory banks against her will, but of everything that occurred today, her discussion with Holley J actually bothered her the most, having to lie straight to her face felt like death from a thousand paper cuts, coming within seconds of letting her in on everything. Entering her bedroom flipping on the lights, she tosses her backpack on her chair, walks over to sit on the edge of her bed, kicking off her shoes. Directing herself to the upstairs bathroom where she brushes her teeth to wash away the taste of Razz still invading her mouth, standing over the running water of the sink, watching herself in the mirror, she strokes the toothbrush back and forth, her hair still a little de-poofed and the little bit of make-up she wears is not up to her standards. Swooshing a cup of water in her mouth to spit out the toothpaste, placing her toothbrush back in its holder, she ends with a handful of cold water splashed on her face. Dripping into the sink below, she stares hard at herself not recognizing who is looking back at her, seeing an ugly, angry person full of hate, a stranger, a stranger who she would like to choke the life out of. Returning to her bedroom to change into her sleeping attire, a pair of red plaid pajama bottoms with a white wife beater, she crawls into bed getting her body halfway under the sheets and blanket. Lying on her side facing her bedroom window left slightly open at night, liking the cool night breeze against her face when she sleeps, gazes out at the nighttime sky where the moon happens to be in perfect proximity to her window. Admiring how beautiful the full moon looks all lit up, its light irradiating portions of the darkness in her room, these little moments somehow become her saving grace, as if the mystery of the moon cleanses her soul putting her at peace even if it's just for the night, that in mind Ashley closes her eyes, slowly drifting off to sleep.

Jake couldn't believe how many boxes he had brought with him when he came to live with his brother, a small closet in the back of the basement housed most of them. Looking through a few of the boxes, some of which have accumulated a good amount of dust on top of them, wasn't quite sure what he was looking for, but he would know when he found it. Most of the boxes were filled with nothing more than old clothes or movies and CDs, a lot of which he could probably part ways with. Coming across a few boxes marked "JAKE," he opened one to find a bunch of his old baseball memorabilia, trophies, awards, even one of his uniforms from when he played little league. He held up the old jersey displaying the number nine, which became his number throughout his career, full of grass and dirt stains, a couple tears in various spots, looking at it smiling, being taken back to the innocence of his youth, when baseball was more about fun rather than a job. Returning the jersey back to the box, he opened another finding what he thought he might run into, an old scrap book representing his whole baseball career from the time he was a boy all the way to his time in the majors. Pulling it out of the box, he gave the leather bound cover a quick blow dispersing a minimal amount of dust that rested on top, the rest he wiped off with his hand. Hasn't seen this scrap book in years, was a gift from his father just before he died a few years ago. Starting to feel a little emotional, he exits the closet to sit on an old office chair that was parked near a fake Christmas tree and a couple totes labeled Christmas stuff. There on the chair with the scrapbook resting on his lap, Jake gazed at the cover which read "Jake's Journey" with a picture of him when he played on his first T-ball team. Opening the scrapbook was like taking a stroll down memory lane, seeming to have everything from his baseball life, from pictures, to newspaper articles, to awards he collected over the years, to things like his first batting glove, cracking an occasional smile at his younger self in some of the pictures, flipping through the pages thinking what could have been. Viewing his past in an almost hypnotic state, unaware he was no longer alone.

"Hey," said Jeff, standing close by, witnessing how invested Jake was in his book, "what are you doing?"

"Oh, hey," Jake replied, "just going through some of my things. Came across this old scrap box."

"That the one Dad made for you?" Jeff asked, walking over to stand over his shoulder.

"The same," Jake answered, continuing to flip through the pages. "I never knew he ever did this until just before he died. Looking at everything in here, makes me wonder what it was all for. I mean you work so hard for something only to have it taken away from you. I have always felt bad about what happened, I still blame myself every day," said Jeff.

"Jeff, we have been over this a thousand times, what happened wasn't your fault," Jake remarked. "We were kids, we did stupid things and there was no guarantee that was the cause of it."

"Yeah but, that one stupid thing might have cost you a long, hall of fame career," Jeff remarked.

"I never tried to stop you, it doesn't matter anymore, what's done is done," Jake said, continuing to flip through the pages, coming up on a picture of him, Jeff and his father when Jake was playing in his first major league game. "Wow, I totally forgot about this picture."

"I remember that day, you hit a home run at your first at bat," recalled Jeff. "We were both so proud of you."

"I remember giving Dad that home run ball, him asking why I was giving it to him, saying should keep it," said Jake.

"And you were like, why? I'm going to hit more," Jeff and Jake said in unison, both smiling and laughing at the memory.

"I really miss him," Jake remarks, their father passing a few years ago from a sudden stroke, leaving their mother to reside alone in the house they grew up in.

"Yeah, me too," agrees Jeff.

"You want to hear something weird. Since I have been coaching these girls, it has kind of relit the fire in me. I know I can't physically play anymore, but being sort of around it again just makes this whole process harder sometimes. I miss playing so much," Jake said with a single tear sliding down his cheek.

"Look at it this way, you get to do something much greater now," Jeff replied. "You get to pass all your knowledge on to these girls."

"Yeah, they are good girls," replied Jake.

"I'll let you be alone for a few. Dinner is in ten minutes," Jeff said, patting both his hands on Jake's shoulders before walking away.

Jake returned the scrape book to its box, feeling happy he found it, realizing sometimes the hardest thing to do is let go of the past and make way for an uncertain future. Recovering the box, placing it back on the pile, he exits the small closet closing the door behind him.

Monday's practice, two days before the first game of the season, Ashley early as usual, going through her before practice routine, the days inching closer to the opening day, has her feeling more and more anxious for the day to arrive. Never feeling this way before the start of a season due to the lack of real coaching during years past, now under Jake's coaching and guidance, there has been real team unity bringing excitement to the girls on the team, especially Ashley who has waited her whole high school career to play on a team this well coached and focused. She sees big things happening for this team and for her, expecting this to be her best season yet, which would be saying a lot considering she has been one of the few bright spots on this team over the years when they were in such disarray.

About a half-hour into her pre-practice workout, finishing up her run and exercises, Holley J can be seen in the distance jogging towards the field carrying the bag with her catcher's gear. Perfect timing for Ashley, they could get in a good twenty minutes or so of pitching practice before the rest of the girls arrived. Patiently waiting on the mound rotating a softball in her hand, ready for Holley J to assume her position, thankful the bruises on her arm have just about completely vanished allowing her to wear her regular short-sleeved practice shirt. Holley J drops off her bag in the dugout, removing her catcher's mask and mitt, running over to park behind home plate so the two of them can begin their private workout. Squatting down, lowering her mask, Holley J gives Ashley the thumbs-up she is ready, punching the inside of her glove awaiting the arrival of the first ball. The next twenty minutes or so the two of them pitch and catch while working on signs and pitch placement. Their chemistry Ashley would describe as magical, they are so in tune with one another as teammates they believe one wouldn't be able to work without the other. Every pitch she throws, Ashley looks at her best friend squatted down at home plate, her partner, not just on the softball field, but also in life, she thought she might look at her a little different after what Holley J said at the mall, yet she doesn't, still sees the same girl she has always known and that will never change. The partly cloudy skies has made way to a blanket of blue with the sun in full display, yet it was the perfect temperature, not too hot, not too cold with a small breeze, still warm enough for Ashley and Holley J to work up a nice sweat during their session. Winding up for her next pitch, Ashley could see Jake walking towards the field out of the corner of her eye, indicating practice will be starting soon. Greeting the girls approaching home plate, he is greeted back, deciding to have a little fun with the girls. Jake stand behind Holley J pretending to be an umpire, wanting to call out all of Ashley's pitches, electing to join in, Holley J gives Ashley the sign she agrees to, the ball slams into Holley J's mitt, glancing back awaiting Jake's call, he answers giving an amusing strike signal with over-the-top vocals. The girls share a short chuckle at Jake's expense as Holley J returns the ball back to Ashley. Over the next few pitches Jake responds to each pitch with a more over-the-top performance than the last one, the girls laughing harder at each one, Holley J toppled over from laughing so hard and Ashley stood on the mound holding her gut. She couldn't remember the last time she laughed like this, there have been times her and Holley J have shared a laugh together, but nothing to this extreme, it felt really good and to be doing it at the one place she calls her sanctuary makes all the more special. These are the moments she wants more of in her life, not just on the softball field, but everywhere, these are the moments that give Ashley hope life is still worth living, needing more laughter in a life that is no laughing matter. Watching Jake's antics with her and Holley J, showing he can easily be a fun guy along with being a great coach, makes Ashley appreciate him more, bringing her level of trust with him to even greater heights, something she hopes continues to grow. Fun with the girls extended on the next pitch, pretending to be a batter, standing there holding his imaginary bat, shaking his behind. Trying not to laugh, Ashley throws the next pitch a little inside, brushing Jake back a step, gesturing throwing down his invisible bat, taking off to rush the mound where he playfully tackles Ashley who is laughing hysterically, Holley J decides to join in by scampering to the mound, falling to the ground laughing with her best friend and coach. Finishing their laugh session together the rest of the girls begin to arrive. Ashley finished leading the girls on their run, exercises and warm-ups, Jake asked the girls to gather around him taking a knee, looking over his team hearing the heavy breathing exiting their lungs, sweat dripping down most of their faces, making eye contact with a few girls, one being Ashley who is knelt down in front like normal, the two swopping smiles with each other. Standing there with his hands behind his back, his whistle sparkling in the bright sun, tells the girls today's practice will be a little different, instructing them to get in position in the field, but wanting Brie to stay behind. The girls stand to go grab their mitts, with the regulars getting into their defensive positions without Ashley taking the mound, Holley J puts on her full catcher's gear before returning behind home plate.

"Okay, kid, let's see how much that practice has paid off," Jake says to Brie. "Grab a bat and let me see you bat left handed."

"Yes, sir," Brie replies, going over to grab a bat.

"I didn't want you on the mound for this," Jake explains to Ashley, standing next to him observing the rest of the team. "She won't be facing you during the season, I think it would be best if she faced someone she would have a chance of hitting against."

"I get it," Ashley responds.

"You do? So you are okay with this?" Jake asked.

"I think it's a great idea," answered Ashley, clapping and cheering Brie on as she approaches the batter's box.

The rest of the girls chime in with Ashley, clapping and cheering, showing their support for their teammate, her batting helmet on, Brie gets into her batting stance taking a couple deep breaths.

"HOLLEY J," Jake yells. "Call it."

Giving him the nod, Holley J flashes the replacement pitcher the first sign. Brie anxiously awaits the first pitch taking a couple more deep breaths, sweat trickle down her face, her gloveless hands feeling a bit clammy gripping the bat. Jake and Ashley look on in anticipation, the pitcher winds up, tossing a speedy pitch towards Holley J, Brie's exposed eye focuses solely on the ball, swinging with no contact, hearing the sound of the ball hitting leather.

"Again," Jake instructs. "Brie, you are fishing. You are holding the bat like a fishing pole. Hold it more towards your chest."

"Okay," Brie replies, still hearing the cheers from Ashley and the rest of the girls.

Holley J returns the ball to the pitcher, flashing the next sign, giving her the nod the pitcher winds up for the next pitch. Taking a couple more deep breaths, taking Jake's advice holding the bat closer to her chest, Brie watches the ball come soaring in, swinging again, this time hearing the sound of the softball colliding with an aluminum bat. Ashley and the rest of the girls cheer as the ball sails over the third baseman's head landing in the outfield, Brie throws her arms up in victory, Jake smiles clapping, looking over at Ashley who smiles back. Now that Brie's batting test is over, Jake has one more test for her, telling her to go relieve the girl at first base. Taking off her batting helmet, grabbing her mitt, Brie positions herself at first base. Jake grabs a bat, walking over to home plate asking for the ball. Ball in hand, he announces to the shortstop the ball is coming her way and to make the play at first. Giving him the nod, Jake hits a speedy dribbler in that direction, the girl at short uses flawless technique scooping up the fast rolling ball off the infield dirt, quickly throwing in the direction of first base where Brie awaits with an outstretched mitt. The ball enters Brie's glove with a good smack remaining firmly in her grasp. Receiving a thumbs-up from Jake and verbal confirmation from the rest of the girls, Brie grins from ear to ear throwing the ball with perfect accuracy back to Holley J. Wanting to see more, Jake hits a few more infield balls, telling the girls to make the play at first or to turn two, each time Brie making the catch with no problems. One last test, Jake hits a swift grounder towards first, telling Brie to make the play at third. Standing there with her knees bent and legs apart, she captures the ball off the smooth laying infield dirt, in one continuous fluid motion, throws a frozen rope to the third baseman. Ashley elated with Brie's play, throws one fist in the air, relaying Jake's gesture to show team unity, the rest of the girls follow suit, all except Renee standing in center field with her arms folded. Happy with what he has seen, Jake tells the girls to take a ten-minute break, calling Brie over.

"Well, it looks like you have definitely been practicing," said Jake, commending Brie on her performance.

"Yes, sir, every day like you said. I really want to play," Brie replies, standing before him with a serious look on her sweat-soaked face.

Looking at the determination on Brie's face, it reminds him of him in that position when he was younger, doing whatever it took to impress the coaches. Natural talent will only get you so far, it's the ones willing to put in the work that puts the eyes on them.

"You definitely have the fastest legs on the team and your catching and throwing has improved," Jake remarks. "I got a question, are you here to help the team or help yourself?"

"The team," answers Brie.

"Okay. I'm going to let you start at first base and be our leadoff batter," informs Jake, watching the huge smile appear on Brie's face, jumping up and down with her hands together in excitement, "but, if you start to struggle or have any problems, I'm going to have to make a switch, deal?"

"Yes, sir, deal," she answers, still bubbling with elation. "I will not let you down."

"I'm sure you won't and I'm glad you decided not to quit," Jake said.

"Me too," agrees Brie smiling.

"Now go get some water," orders Jake.

Running over to join the other girls, Brie informs them of her good news, where she is greeted with hugs and high fives, the happiest for her being Ashley, giving her the biggest hug and congratulations, always Brie's biggest supporter and the one that believed in her the most. During their moment of bonding, Renee silently approaches, having been quiet as of late.

"I never thought Coach would do it," Renee remarks, standing beside Ashley and Brie with her hands on her hips. "I guess he's not interested in winning. By the way isn't the expression, keep your eyes on the ball, not your eye."

"Why don't you just shut up and leave her alone," barked Ashley, positioning herself to get in Renee's face.

"Oh, how cute, you are coming in the aid of the handicapped," Renee responded, the rest of the team drawing their attention to the two of them. "This is a fucking joke and you know it."

"You know, Renee, you're a really bitch," Brie shouted standing behind Ashley.

"It's a good thing you got two ears so you can hear when I tell you, I don't care what you think. I didn't sign on to play on a team with a Goddamn charity case. I thought Coach would have enough sense to put her on the bench where she belongs or even the equipment room," snapped Renee.

"I'd take her over you any day," said Ashley, "just do yourself a favor and walk away."

"Is that a treat?" Renee asked. "How come I get the feeling you had something to do with this? I get it, you and Coach still...," she finishes making the blow job gesture.

Not thinking about her actions, Ashley throws Renee to the ground where the two begin rolling around on the infield dirt in an unfriendly scuffle, full of slight hair pulling and light punches. Before Holley J or any of the other girls can step in, Jake hurried over to break the two of them up, having watched the blow up unfold. Pulling Ashley off Renee separating the two, standing between them telling the rest of the girls practice was over for the day except for the two involved in the altercation. Grabbing their things, the girls began leaving, Holley J decided to stick around waiting for Ashley, staying out of sight in the dugout.

"Neither one of you say a word, you know I've noticed there was some tension between you two for a while, hoping it would just blow over, but I guess I was wrong. This is not a good look for the two best players on the team. You two are seniors, is this how you want to spend your last season, at each other's throat, fighting over some stupid, petty, teenage bullshit," Jake states, keeping each girl at arm's length away from him, both covered in dirt, breathing heavy, eyes still locked on each other trying to calm themselves. "This is the last thing we need right now with the season just a couple days away. We can't have this, any riff between players is never good for a team, I know, I've seen it firsthand, next thing you know the tension spills over to the other players, the team becomes divided and that's all she wrote, a team can't win broken up into fractions, it has to be whole, one unit. You two are going to ruin the season before it even starts, you think that is fair to the other girls who have worked hard to get ready. Now I don't know what it is that has driven a wedge between you two, I don't care and it's not my business. What is my business is seeing that this team performs at the level you guys are capable of and we will not be able to do that if you two can't get along. I'm not saying you have to be best friends or even have to like each other, but you are going to have to learn to coexist. Not everyone on a team is going to like each other, that's just how it is, but on the field you are not friends and you are not enemies, you're teammates, teammates with a common goal. This is not up to me to figure out, but don't make me have to give you two an ultimatum."

"Sounds like you just gave us one," Renee remarks wiping some dirt off her face with the back of her hand.

"You know, if you have a problem with how I run this team, you have two options, either you live with it or get out," Jake states. "Now am I going to have any more trouble from you two from here on out?"

The two girls look at each other like a couple of mortal enemies in a stare down shaking their heads no.

"I'm sorry, there are no silent answers allowed on this team," said Jake folding his arms. Ashley responds with a no, followed shortly after with a low tone no from Renee.

"No what?" Jake asked.

"No, sir," Ashley answers.

"No, sir," replies Renee hesitantly.

"Good, Renee, you can go. Ashley, stay, I need to talk to you," Jake orders.

Renee flashes Ashley a smug face leaving, stopping at the dugout area to grab her mitt where Holley J waits patiently for Ashley.

"Hopefully now you will learn to keep your mouth shut," said Holley J as Renee walks by.

"Eat shit," Renee responds leaving the dugout.

Alone with Ashley, Jake pulls a wet nap out of his pocket which he always carries just in case, handing it to her. Ripping it open, she using the dampness to clean some of the dirt off her face, the smell of lemon radiates from the soaked cloth.

"Am I in trouble?" Ashley asks, now wiping her hands with the wet nap.

"You know you can't put your hands on another player," Jake replies, "but if I don't discipline you, it will look like I'm choosing favorites. I'm going to call for another practice tomorrow because this one got cut short. You can come, but you can't participate. Does that sound fair?"

"Yes, sir," answered Ashley. "I promise it won't happen again."

"It better not, then I will have no choice but to suspend you for a game and I know you don't want that," states Jake. "You know since I got you here. Ever since you told me about your mother and how things are with your aunt, I've been a bit concerned, how is everything going at home?"

"The best it can be, I guess," she responds.

"Look, my offer is still on the table, you ever want to talk, don't hesitate to just shoot me a text or call, I'm here to listen."

"I know. Can I go now?" Ashley asked.

"Yeah, get out of here, I will see you tomorrow," replied Jake.

Ashley hustles over to meet up with Holley J so the two of them can head back to the locker room together, always there waiting when she needs a friend, sitting in the dugout with her legs crossed and arms folded like a concerned mother would be for her child.

"Everything okay?" asked Holley J, wondering what their little meeting was all about.

"Yeah, I'm fine. He is going to hold another practice tomorrow, I can come, but I have to sit it out," Ashley answered. "You ready to go?"

Holley J grabs her duffle bag and the two of them begin their slow walk back to the locker room.

"So what now?" Holley J asked.

"About what?" Ashley remarked.

"About Renee?" wondered Holley J.

"I promised myself I wasn't going to let something like that happen, but that girl really knows how to push my buttons," Ashley remarked.

"Well, between you and me, I'm glad you did it. More glad that coach only sentenced you to a missed practice," Holley J states, the two of them walking side by side.

"Yeah, me too," said Ashley.

"I just hope she really does want to win and doesn't do anything to jeopardize our season," said Holley J.

"She may be a bitch and I can't stand her, but I know she wants to win," Ashley remarked, both entering the locker room.

Ashley is in the kitchen hovering over the stove preparing her aunt's dinner for the night, the smell of marinated chicken sizzling in the pan and sautéed vegetables fill the kitchen air, her music playing off her docked iPod to help lighting the mood. Her Aunt sitting at the kitchen table partially buzzed, smoking a cigarette, polishing off another beer, watching Ashley maneuver around the stove, dressed casually, hair tied in a ponytail, the red nail polish on her fingernails are all scraped up and uneven. Exhaling a breath of smoke observing Ashley working diligently, cooking three pans at once making sure each one is at the right temperature, mixing and stirring the vegetables while giving the chicken breasts the appropriate amount of turn overs. She can feel her aunt's eyes on her, watching every move she makes, normally her Aunt is not in the kitchen when she is cooking, usually in the living room watching TV smoking a joint, waiting for her dinner to be served to her, but today for some reason she is front and center, watching over Ashley like a hawk.

"Is that shit almost done, I'm hungry," barked her aunt, blowing more smoke towards the open kitchen window located adjacent to the table.

"It's done when it gets done. Do you want to eat raw food?" Ashley remarks, expertly working a spatula and wooden spoon.

"Oh, you trying to be a smart ass. You better watch your tone, little girl," said her aunt. "It's not like your cooking is that good anyway. And turn off that fucking music, who would listen to that crap, you want me to turn into a fucking low life like you."

Over the years Ashley has trained herself to block out almost everything her aunt says to her, especially anything degrading, but when you hear it over and over again she starts to believe maybe it is true. She does everything for her aunt and gets treated her like some gutter trash from the streets, her own flesh and blood. On the outside Ashley plays it off like it doesn't bother her, but on the inside it tears her apart, every word is like a bullet to the chest, if she was able to cry on the inside she would have drowned years ago. Grabbing a couple plates out of the cupboards, slamming them down on the nearby counter in anger, she keeps her back to her aunt, not wanting to see her self-satisfied face. Ashley's demeanor just went through a total makeover, not even enjoying her favorite music anymore playing in the background, but won't turn it off to spite her aunt. The food can't cook fast enough, having to stand there being a verbal target, it boggles her mind that they are related, even her mother was never like this.

"By the way, James is coming over soon. We will probably end up fucking later, so if you don't want to hear us, I suggest you bury your head in some headphones or something. He's got a dick that would make an elephant scream. You know about dick, don't you?" her aunt asks letting out a complacent laugh.

Ashley retaliates by turning her music up louder preparing the plates of food, one for her aunt and one for herself which she always eats up in her room. Putting the designated portions into each plate, she can hear her aunt trying to talk over the louder music.

"I said turn that shit off!" her aunt shouts, Ashley putting her plate of food in front of her. "I know you can hear me, bitch!"

Her anger growing by the second, Ashley walks back over turning the music up louder to just about maximum volume, the staticky noise protruding from the small iPod dock speakers was irritating to the eardrums, but didn't bother Ashley one bit as she finished preparing her dinner plate. Extremely aggravated, her aunt puts out her cigarette, rapidly getting up from her seat to walk over to where the iPod dock is stationed, grabbing it ripping the cord out of the socket, forcefully throwing it across the kitchen against the wall where parts of it shattered to pieces.

"Now what?" asked her aunt standing within inches of Ashley, staring her down like a boxer before a fight, the stench of alcohol intensifies with every word she speaks.

Without saying a word, Ashley walks over to the location of the destroyed iPod dock to examine the damage. Reviewing the dock it is determined it is no longer salvageable, but the iPod itself seems to be intact. Rescuing her iPod from the wreckage, she grabs her plate of food.

"Enjoy your dinner, I hope you fucking choke on it," Ashley mumbles under her breath, leaving the kitchen with her plate of food to head for her room.

"What was that?" asked her aunt, following her through the living room to the upstairs staircase. "You are going to find your loser ass out on the streets."

Without a break in her stride, Ashley continues on up the stairs towards her room completely ignoring anything her aunt is saying.

"Don't forget you have to come clean up the mess in the kitchen, you dumb bitch!" shouts her aunt.

Her verbal outcry is met with a loud, violent slamming of Ashley's bedroom door, forceful enough to rattle the pictures hanging along the staircase wall.

It's been a couple hours since the unfortunate interaction with her aunt in the kitchen, working now on a new painting, one that symbolizes what it's like to live in this house with a soulless, heartless human being. Isolating herself from the outside world, she is able to concentrate on the project at hand, earbuds in place, listening to some music to drown out the moans and screams of her aunt's apparent session of rough sex from down the hall, keeping her bedroom door shut hoping not see her aunt again for the rest of the night. Spreading her paint across the canvas, becoming lost in her thoughts with every stroke of her brush, thoughts like, graduation is in the near future and she still hasn't heard back from any colleges, finding it strange since Holley J already received her acceptance letter to Florida State months ago. Even more odd is that a few colleges were ready to offer her a full scholarship to play softball, letting her know they would get in touch with her by mail, but haven't seen anything delivered to the house. Ashley understands sometimes things get lost in the mail, but from four different schools, what are the chances of that. The more she thought about it, the more it started to bother her, something is not right, there had to be some explanation, going away to college is her only escape from this hell she currently resides in. Mixing a few more colors of paint for her palette, wondering who she could possibly talk to too maybe get some answers. In times like these Ashley would always call Holley J, but this seems to be a situation that would be better suited for someone who knew about getting scholarship offers. Listening to her favorite SiriusXM station, during one of the music breaks a member of a band is on air to introduce the next song, greeted all the on air listeners with his name, which happened to be Jake. Hearing that name, Ashley saw it as a sign of who she needs to talk to. Thinking she could wait till tomorrow to talk to him, but knew she wouldn't be able to sleep with this hanging over her head.

Deciding to take a short break from her painting, Ashley hung up her palette on its designated spot on her easel, grabbing her cell phone off the nightstand. Sitting on her painting stool staring at her phone, contemplating if this was a good idea, realizing she was about to call a man, something she is very unfamiliar with and in ways scared to do. Going through all the reasons to herself it is okay, for one he is her coach and players call coaches all the time, except for her ex-coach who she avoided like the plague whenever she could, also was given the okay by Jake to call him if she ever wanted to talk about anything and this was something important. Fearing she might sit there trying to talk herself out of it, she just gave in, dialing his number, knowing she could use his help. Hearing the phone ringing on the other side sent her nerves and her stomach into a tailspin, feeling so nervous she began hoping he didn't answer, until she heard a voice on the other end.

"Hello?" asked Jake, who is sitting on his couch watching TV.

"Hey, Coach, it's me, Ashley," she replies in a very nervous sounding tone.

"Hey, Ashley, how are you?" Jake asked.

"I'm okay, I hope this not too late to call," Ashley remarked.

"No, not at all, is everything okay?" he responds, hearing the tense tonality in her voice causing him to sit forward on his couch, taking his attention off the TV.

"Yeah, I'm okay, I just had a question for you," she replied.

"Sure, no problem, shoot," he reinsured her.

"Is it normal to not hear back from colleges you were offered scholarships to at this time of the year?" she asked, hoping he would have an answer for her.

"Well, that depends, when did you send in your letter of commitment?" Jake asked.

"I haven't gotten any letters from any of the schools," answered Ashley.

"When did you get these offers?" asked Jake.

"I got most of them last year," Ashley replied.

"Then you should have received something by now," Jake informs.

"That's what I thought, but I haven't received anything," said Ashley.

"That is very strange," Jake responded. "I'll tell you what, why don't you text me the names of the schools and I will make a few phone calls, see what I can dig up."

"That would be great, thank you," Ashley said, feeling more relieved.

"No problem," Jake replies smiling. "I'll see you tomorrow then, unless there is something else."

"No, that's it, thanks," said Ashley, when her bedroom opens up revealing her aunt standing in the doorway wearing a black Victoria's Secret negligee with her hair all messed up.

"Who the hell you talking to?" asked her aunt.

"None of your business, can you please shut the door," commands Ashley, not realizing she forgot to cover up her phone, allowing Jake to hear the unpleasant banter.

"You know you're a fucking asshole. By the way, you are going to have some sheets to wash tomorrow, they are a little wet," barked her aunt. "Think you can handle that, you stupid bitch?"

"Just shut the Goddamn door!" Ashley yells, her aunt slamming the door shut, loud enough for Jake to hear the bang over the phone.

"I got to go, I'll see you tomorrow," Ashley relays to Jake before hanging up.

"Ashley, wait," Jake shouts, hearing the dead silence of a disconnected call.

Stunned by what he had just heard, sits back on his couch deep in thought, the sounds of the show on the TV make up the ambient noise in the room. Definitely not a psychiatrist or a parent, but he is intelligent enough to know when he sees or hears signs of physical or mental abuse, no way was that acceptable behavior he heard over the phone, no child, no matter what age should be talk to like that. Obvious now Ashley wasn't lying, figuring she was over exaggerating as teenagers tend to do, but clearly it is worse than she had described it. Jake stared ahead only able to feel sorry for her that she has to live in an environment like that, understanding why she works so hard to be great at her craft. Within a few seconds he received a text from Ashley listing the schools he requested.

The new season starts the day after tomorrow, the way practice ended yesterday Jake wanted to hold one more to go over some things with the girls to make sure they are also mentally prepared. Because this wasn't an officially scheduled practice, he had to send out a teamwide text to all his players to inform them of the extra get together. Ashley already knew about the practice, but knows she can't participate as punishment for her actions for the previous day, doesn't mean she can't still show up at her usual early time to go through her workout routine. Making her way to the field carrying her glove with one softball inside, a much cooler day than the recent ones due to the overcast that has been obstructing the sun's presence, even the wind is making its existence known with heavy gust passing through at random times. Placing her glove in the dugout to begin her stretching before her run, she wondered if Jake was able to find anything out, being on her mind all day. Having about thirty minutes before Holley J shows up, she sets out on her run. This run she can tell is going to be more intense having to run against the wind in certain directions, but is nothing that will stop her from finishing. During her runs, besides focusing on her breathing, it gives her ample time to think, which she is doing a lot of throughout this circuit. Thinking when Holley J told her a few months ago to look into why she hasn't heard anything back from those colleges, which she planned on doing, but with everything going on with her in her day to day life, it just kind of slipped her mind. Thinking how her aunt is drinking more, doing more drugs, increasing her already hostel and mean personality, doubling her hatred for her, making life in house just about unlivable. Thoughts of Razz, how he preyed on a vulnerable young girl, manipulating her into thinking he was everything she saw that day when they met in the park, feeding on her weaknesses to turn her into a person she thought she was always meant to be. And thoughts of her mother, the ringleader who was responsible for setting into motion the events leading to where she is today. The more she ran, the more the thoughts raced through her mind like a mental rolodex, just jumping from thought to thought, to the point she lost sight of the environment around her, only seeing what she sees in her mind, but never drifted off course. Getting that second wind she pressing on, feeling her leg muscles contracting with ever stride to the resistance of the wind, sending a cool chill down her spine. With her lungs reaching full capacity, Ashley puts an end to her run, feeling both tired and energetic at the same time. Takes a short breather walking over to the coolers for a quick drink of water before she begins her exercise portion of her workout, includes body squats, lunges, push-ups and various other exercises. Standing just outside the dugout doing her workout on the freshly cut grass, still battling the wind at times, she exerted herself harder than normal, using those earlier thoughts as fuel to push herself to her limit, in her mind feeling her body getting stronger, leaner and more flexible. In the distance she can see Holley J walking towards the field carrying her duffle bag, she too feeling the effects of the wind moving forward. Finishing up the best, most intense workout Ashley has had in a while, stands there with her hands on her hips breathing heavy, sweat dripping down her face, observing Holley J entering the dugout, heading over to greet her friend, also getting another cup of water.

"This wind is brutal today," snaps Holley J, tightening the laces on her cleats.

"Wait till you have to run in it," Ashley remarks sipping her water, her heavy breathing catches Holley J's attention.

"Sounds like you had a good workout just now," Holley J says. "You heard anything from Coach yet about the letters?"

"No, I'm hoping he has something to tell me when he gets here," replied Ashley.

"Well, I'm glad you finally took initiative to find out what is going with that, clock's ticking," Holley J said, geared up and ready to begin their private practice. "Now let's see that fastball of yours cut through this wind."

Holley J leaves the dugout to walk over to home plate, followed by Ashley heading for the mound. Like clockwork the two engage in their customary pitching workout, complete with flashing signs and verbal communication. The mental connection between the two of them is unrivaled, knowing what each is going to do before they do it, staying in sync with each other is what makes them one of the best pairings in the state, contributing to just about almost flawless play. It breaks Ashley's heart this is going to be their last season playing together, once in college she is going to have to adjust to a new catcher as Holley J will be at a different school not even sure if she is going to play now that her sidekick won't be on the mound looking back at her. Holley J would be okay not playing the game anymore for she saw it more as something her and Ashley could do together, but knows Ashley needs to keep playing for as long as she could because she is a once in a generation talent. Whether it's during practice, an actual game or these private workouts with Holley J, these are the times in her life when Ashley actually feels free.

The slap of the softball hitting the inside of Holley J's glove echoes through the air as Jake makes his way to the field, quickly becoming an expected sound for him to hear during his walk to the diamond. Every few moments he hears that crack of leather get louder the closer he gets, even the wind has a hard time drowning out the familiar sound. Déjà vu sets in every time he arrives to the field seeing the same visual as the last time, as if they never left. No one could ever question these two girls' work ethic, especially Ashley's, Jake knows players like these are hard to find on most teams and he is certainly glad he has a couple of them.

Approaching the infield not wanting to mess up the girls' rhythm, he lets them complete a few more pitches before intervening. Seeing Jake standing there, Ashley held up letting Holley J know they are good for now, both girls leave there current position to walk over to Jake. By the look on his face Ashley could tell she was about to get bad news.

"So I was able to contact all four schools," said Jake.

"And," Ashley responded, standing there wiping some sweat off her forehead with the back of her hand.

"They all said they sent out letters to you months ago and they were curious why they haven't heard from you yet either," Jake stated. "I explained you said you never received any letters."

"Well, this doesn't make any sense, is it even possible all of them got lost in the mail?" asked Holley J standing there in her catcher's gear, mask flipped up onto the top of her head.

"Highly unlikely," replied Jake. "So then I asked them to give me the address they have on file, maybe they got the wrong information," Jake pulls out a small piece of paper from his short's pocket handing it to Ashley. "Is that your correct address?"

"Yeah, that's the right address," Ashley remarks looking at the piece of paper. "Now what?"

"Well, that's where I got some good news and bad news, the bad news is that two of the schools are backing out, saying regardless of what happened to the letters they needed an answer ASAP. The good news is the other two schools are still interested, but they are going to send scouts out to watch you play again just to make sure they are still making the right decision," stated Jake.

"Well, of course they are making the right decision, Ashley is one of the best players in the country," responded an angry Holley J.

"I'm not disputing anything, just telling you what they told me. Trust me, I tried to haggle with them to be reasonable, used my name to try to build some rapport, but once these big time division one schools make up their minds it's a winless battle," informed Jake.

"I just want to know what happened to those letters. I mean shit like that just don't disappear," said Ashley, frustrated her hard work could almost be for nothing.

"I know you're mad and you have every right to be, but if you want my advice, I would just concentrate on having the best season of your life and impressing the hell out of those scouts again which I know you will do," Jake replies, seeing the disappointment on Ashley's face.

"I'll make sure she has her best season ever," Holley J states.

"That makes two of us, we've got your back and I'm sure the rest of the team will as well," responded Jake.

"I guess I have no choice," an upset Ashley remarks. "Thanks for the help, I appreciate it."

"You're welcome," said Jake. "Holley J, could you give me a moment with Ashley alone?"

"Sure," she says, heading to the dugout to grab a drink of water.

"Now that I got you alone for a second, how are things at home?" Jake asked.

"What do you mean?" Ashley responds, remembering their phone conversation from last night and the unpleasant bickering he must have heard.

"Just wondering if you are okay," wondered Jake.

"No offense, whatever goes on in my home life is really none of your business, I know what I told you before, but I'm fine, just worry about me on the field," Ashley insists.

"It's just I overheard what your aunt said to you and that's no way for her to be speaking to you...," Jake replied.

"And I can handle it, can we please just drop it?" demanded Ashley.

"Okay," Jake answered, able to see the sadness behind her eyes, an emptiness that radiates from an unhappy person, perceiving everything isn't okay at Ashley's home, but will respect her wishes at least for now. "You know you have to sit this practice out."

"Yeah, I know," Ashley said, seeing the rest of the girls arriving out of the corner of her eye.

Even with the uninvited wind, the finally practice before their season opener was another success. Ashley spent all of practice in the dugout observing, wanting so badly to be out there, but respected Jake's decision. Watched as Holley J lead the team on their run and exercises, saw her backup pitch decently enough to examine the team working as a unit like Jake stated. She was really liking what she saw from the girls, from the drills, to fielding practice, the effort and hustle they were exerting was a sight to behold, this is without a doubt the best the team has ever looked, making the opener in a couple days even more exciting. Surveying Jake coaching from the outside really put things in perspective for her as to how good a coach he really is, almost like he was born to do this, learning just as much sitting in the dugout viewing Jake at work as she would have being out there with the rest of the girls. But sitting there laying witness to the team becoming what she always hoped they become, ruminations of what could have happened to those letters continue to weigh on her mind. Jake ended practice like he always does, calling the girls in to take a knee before him. A lot of them tired and out of breath, hearing all the panting and heavy breathing, giving them a second to catch their breath. Looking over at the dugout seeing Ashley sitting there patiently with her legs crossed, hands resting on her lap, he waves her over to join the team inferring her punishment is over, quickly leaving her seat, jogging over to take a knee at her normal spot right in front of Jake and next to Holley J.

"Okay, now that we are all together, I want you girls to give yourselves a nice round of applause for another exceptional practice," requested Jake, hearing the clapping of almost two dozen hands. "I don't think I have to remind you that our first game is Thursday, right here on this field. Do I think you girls are ready? Absolutely, I am so proud of how hard you all have worked to get ready. Now I can bore you with motivational speeches or tell you you're the greatest girls' softball team to ever step onto a field, but I'm not going to do that. I'm going to let you do that for me, you girls have an opportunity to do something great, this team has more talent than you realize, you all bring something special and unique to the table, you are in possession of the greatest weapon a team could ever have, unity. A team that plays together, succeeds together, you are not a bunch of individuals, you are one, we are one. Play for the name on the front of your jersey, not the name on the back. Some of you after this season will never play this game again, so don't you owe it to yourself to go out and be a part of something special, to go out playing like a champion. Now I can't predict the future, but I can promise you, if you all go out there every game and play your hearts out, play to the ability I know you are capable of, leaving everything on the field, no matter what happens, you will always leave the field a winner," Jake said to the girls, each of their faces stern, keeping eye contact with him the entire time soaking in every word he spoke. "They say you play how you practice, I think you girls are going to be just fine."

Jake smiled ending his post-practice speech, judging by the reactions he was seeing from all the girls, he knew they understood and were ready to go. Even Ashley, with all that's going on with her, could see the unbelievable turnaround of this team, just the aura given off when all the girls are together now is something she never thought was possible with this group. She was ready and knew the team was ready, this year was going to be something historic, something special, she could feel it in her bones. Hearing Jake's speech got her fired up, her adrenaline was going so much, she was ready to play a game right now. These are the points in time Ashley wished happened more often, where nothing else mattered and her world outside the grass and dirt of this field doesn't exist, all she cares about is this team, doing what is necessary to pile up the wins and to impress the hell out of those scouts, convincing them it would be a travesty if they didn't offer her what she knows she has already earned.

Instructing the girls to get to their feet, Jake advised them to be at the field preferably around an hour before game time so they would have ample time to warm up and so he could go over the line up and batting order along with some last minute game preparations. Before he could utter another word Ashley turned to face the girls throwing one fist in the air, followed by every other girl on the team including a hesitate Renee who was the last to join in, veering her eyes in another direction. With all the girls' fists in the air, Ashley leads a chant that sent chills down her spine. This was it, the next time they take this field it will be for real. The chant ended with all the girls getting fired up, standing in place clapping rapidly. Feeling the abundant surge of energy from the girls, Jake chimes in to remind them to get rest and he would see them on Thursday for their season opener, declaring they were free to go. All the girls scattered, most heading to the dugout for a drink of water, others just headed back to the locker room. Ashley and Holley J were planning on sticking around for a little while longer, wanting to work off some of their newfound energy. Jake was a bit wary about the girls' elongated practice, fearing Ashley would wear herself out before game time, but his concern was quickly put to rest when Holley J reassured him Ashley has been doing this since she has known her, never having a problem with fatigue before a game. Trusting the girls' judgment, he left them to do what they had planned, would have stayed to help, however he had a lot of prep work he wanted to get done before their first game. Telling Ashley and Holley J to have a good session and not to stay out too long, he left wishing them a good night. Alone again the girls were ready to pick up where they left off, neither one of them cared, the weather kind of took a turn for the worst as the wind picked up even more with the temperature taking a significant drop indicating a probable storm coming.

Willing to brave the elements, the girls took their spots at their positions, feeling so revved up they feel like they could practice during a hurricane. Getting back into it, Ashley nods the sign from Holley J, her wind up is interrupted by the vibration of her phone hidden in her back pocket stopping her dead mid delivery. Signaling to Holley J she needs to hold up a second, grabs her phone to learn she received a text, she didn't even have to read to know who it was from, the once burst of energy she felt completely dissipated like air being let out of a balloon. Looking at the text it is revealed she was right, it was from Razz letting her know she needs to work tonight. It's a few hours before the club opens, Razz is in his office sitting at his desk smoking a joint, a briefcase full of bags of heroin and a silver Desert Eagle pistol lies before him, heavy metal music plays loudly in the background, waiting for the arrival of a new buyer he recently came in contact with. Normally complacent on taking on new buyers, rather do business with regulars seeing how there is a well-oiled process that goes down with usual clients, everyone knows what to do so all deals go off without a hitch, clean and under the radar. Too many clients draws attention, having just enough to keep his products moving while not looking suspicious. The only reason he took on this new buyer is because one of his regulars vouched for him saying he was legit. Not to impressed with him already, being thirty minutes late, disrespecting Razz before they even have met. Now worried he won't follow his instructions, he gets up from his chair too began pacing back and forth behind his desk, joint dangling from his mouth passing through clouds of smoke. Instructing this dude to send him a quick thumbs-up text when he arrives and to use the parking lot and entrance in the back to avoid onlookers. Growing more and more anxious and frustrated as the seconds tick away, begins to ponder if he made a big mistake agreeing to meet up with this guy. His waiting comes to an abrupt end when his cell phone starts ringing, using a remote to turn down the music, he grabs his phone off the desk to answer it, standing dead still with an agitated look on his face, a voice on the other end confirms his identity as the one Razz has been waiting for, relaying his location as being in the back parking lot standing in front of the sign labeled private. Quickly hanging up, Razz grabs the Desert Eagle off his desk tucking it in the back part off his jeans, covering the rest with his black t-shirt. His guards and bouncers not showing up for a couple hours yet, knows he is on his own with this one, not that he was afraid of anybody, the extra man power just seemed to put is mind at ease knowing there was someone to watch his back, the pistol he has hidden in his back side was his bodyguard for this one. Walking over to the special door in the back of his office that leads to the back parking lot, Razz peers through the peep hole to make sure he is actually out there, visually confirming the man's existence, he unlocks the large deadbolt securing the door, opening the entrance way, slightly blinded by the late afternoon sunlight to unveil his new buyer, a medium height, stocky built man with black slick back hair, wearing jeans, a leather coat and sunglasses, securely holding a large duffel bag with both hands in front of him. The man produced a pouch oozing odor, it was strong, almost pungent, seeming to just hang in the air unrecognizable, Razz couldn't tell if it was from cheap cologne or the man's pheromones working overtime.

"Well, it looks like we finally met," says the man.

"You were supposed to text me, don't ever call me on my phone," Razz explained, unable to see his eyes through the darkness of his sunglasses.

"Let's not get caught up with the details, bro, I have what you want, let's do this," responds the man, judging from his tone is in an obvious hurry.

Wanting to just get this over with, Razz gestures him inside, taking a quick look around outside for any potential onlookers, determining the coast is clear, ducks back inside closing the behind him. His new client stood by his desk with the same demeanor he displayed outside, still leaving his sunglasses on despite now being indoors.

"Let's see the goods," requested the man, standing with perfect posture, like a statue, yet seeming very relaxed.

Razz opened the briefcase on his desk displaying the contents inside. Moving from his stationary position, the man peeks inside grabbing one of the bags of smack to put under his nose to get a good whiff of his potential purchase. Satisfied with the product being legit, the man tosses the bag back in the case.

"We've got a problem, my friend," says the man, returning to his statue like stance.

"There's no problem, that's a hundred percent smack in that case," Razz responded, getting more and more bothered by the fact he couldn't see the man's eyes. You can never trust a pair of eyes you can't see, one of the few things he learned from his father, hidden eyes equals hidden agendas, he had to contain himself from ripping those sun glasses off his face.

"I know it's the real shit," the man replied, "but I have a hundred fifty thousand dollars in this duffel bag, but you aren't showing me a hundred fifty thousand dollars' worth of product."

"I beg to differ, in fact I'm actually cutting you a deal. Normally I would ask for two hundred, but I thought I would be a nice guy, cut you break seeing this is our first transaction and all," Razz said, seeing his reflection in the man's eye wear.

"I would say you got balls asking for two. I'm willing to part with one hundred thousand," the man says, still standing there motionless.

"I don't give a fuck what you want to pay, I set the prices here," Razz remarked with a sarcastic giggle, placing both his hands behind his back, one grabbing the stock of the pistol.

"Well, it seems we have come to a bit of an impasse," says the man.

"Not really," Razz states, pulling the gun out from behind him, holding it with both hands pointing it directly at his guest, the shiny silver of the pistol gleams in the light of his office. None of his other deals have ever come to this, knowing it's not a good look for business, but when things don't go as smoothly as he would like he gets agitated causing him to go to the extreme and pulling a gun on a man he has never met before would qualify as just that. If life taught Razz anything, it's better to be the intimidator then the one being intimidated, something he has grown to be quite good at.

"I'm going to make this very simple for you. You can either leave the bag and take the case and get the fuck out of here or you can leave the bag and the case and I throw your ass out. All I know is I'm getting every fucking dollar that is in that bag, one thing I can't stand is having my fucking time wasted and take off those Goddamn sunglasses."

"I've heard you were a tough cookie, not much for negotiating," the man says, dropping the duffel bag to the floor and removing his sunglasses exposing his dark, beady eyes, "but I always get what's coming to me. I've heard you got a nice place here, hate to see something happen to it."

"You want to bark threats at me, go ahead. If you are expecting me to panic or lose sleep, it's not going to happen. In fact, I'm willing to bet I won't see your ugly face around here again. Now I'm going to give you one more chance, you either take the case or you take a bullet...and you better make your decision quick or I'll make it for you," threatened Razz, holding the pistol calm and steady.

"Well, I guess I really only have one choice," the man remarks, reaching over to close the briefcase, picking it up off the desk. "I still think I'm being cheated."

"And I'm telling you, you are getting what you paid for, you know where the door is," Razz responded, keeping the gun on the man making his way towards the door.

"You are right about one thing," the man says stopped at the doorway, looking back at Razz who is still pointing the gun, "I definitely won't be showing my face around here anymore, but I do know a lot of other faces," he remarks putting his sunglasses back on.

"Get the fuck out of my club," instructed Razz, watching the man disappear into the back parking lot sunlight.

The man now gone, Razz returns the gun to his backside, walking over to the doorway to see if he actually left. Hearing the sound of a car engine combusting, he looks out to the parking lot smelling the fresh exhaust of a recently started motor, watching the car of his unwanted guest drive out of the lot, tires squealing turning onto the side road speeding away. Satisfied he is long gone listening to the engine noise fade away in the distance, Razz closes the door behind him. Thinking about what the man said just before he left, threats come with the lifestyle they are nothing new to him, sometimes he welcomes them, it's a sign of respect, very rarely does anyone ever follow through, but he is always prepared for any type of retaliation. Lighting up a cigarette he took from a pack lying on his desk, Razz picks up the duffel bag off the floor, walking over to place it on his empty coffee table. Sitting down on the couch, opening the bag to view the many wrapped stacks of hundred dollar bills. Flipping through the cash, a sense of relief came over him, the man wasn't lying about the amount the bag contained. Counting the money before every transaction is always a priority, something that has become automatic to Razz, like breathing, would make sure every dollar was accounted for and if it happened to be short, would make sure he would get what's coming to him, but thankfully that has never been a problem for him, his clients are good with paying the prices he sets, charging a little less than street value has made him the go to supplier in the city, still making huge profits on every deal. Business skills have always come natural to Razz, from the time he was a youngster stealing loads of candy from the corner store and selling to all the neighborhood kids. He always knew when and how to steal it so he would never get caught, it became routine, soon he was hitting other stores, stealing other items to build up more supply. At one point he was making more money than a teenager working a part-time job. Always doing it alone, he never needed help and that was the way he liked it, bringing on a partner would mean having to split the profits, why split them when you can have it all. What makes him so successful in his endeavors is his attention to detail, what comes with being a perfectionist, once he finds what works, he never strays away from it, he'll just improve his methods until they are perfected.

Complacent with the money, Razz picks up the bag, putting out his cigarette in the nearby ashtray, surrounded by the silence in the office, takes the bag over to one of the side walls housing a small abstract painting of a woman holding a baby. Standing before the wall, Razz places his hand on a certain area pressing inward triggering a portion of the wall to crack open like a door. Fully opening the secret door, he enters a short hallway consisting of a low drop ceiling, low enough where he could touch it jumping with minimal effort. Motion censored lights illuminate his short walk down the hallway, stopping amidst the large steel vault resting in front of him. From the outside the vault resembles one you might find in a quality bank, the large steel door stands taller than he does, equipped with a thumbprint scanner for entry, Razz was never a fan of combination locks, considering them weak and penetrable, he wanted a way to assure he was the only one that could access the vault and a print scanner was the most reliable feature he could think of. Placing his right thumb on the scanner, he waited patiently for his thumbprint to be read, culminating in the scanner flashing a bright green light under the glass indicating he is granted access. Spinning the large spindle wheel, Razz pulls the heavy vault door open revealing the inside. More motion censored lights irradiate the interior stepping foot inside. Front and center in the middle of the vault, he is surrounded by shelves upon shelves full of stacked bundles of cash, one shelf is home to a large steel box lined in red felt full of loose diamonds and jewelry, another is accommodating his supply of narcotics, ranging anywhere from heroin, to cocaine, to crystal meth, there is even a large stock of marijuana he keeps for personal use. A few automatic weapons along with a couple shotguns hang neatly on wall brackets at the back of the vault. Walking over to one of the shelves full of cash, Razz places the contents of the duffle bag to its new home.

Emptying the bag, he takes a step back to look around at his surroundings admiring what he has built for himself, under the lights of the vault you could see a twinkle in his eye as he pans over all that encompasses him. Nobody else knows about this vault and if they did they would never be able to find it, Razz paid a lot of money to have such an elaborate setup, but knew it was money well spent with all of his valuables safe and secure. Knowing no one will ever have access to the contents of his vault is a huge moral victory, if he were to die tomorrow everything inside would just lay dormant maybe never to be found and even if by chance it were to be discovered, it would take high tech qualified personnel to access what rested behind that large steel door. Done idolizing himself, Razz exits the vault slamming the door shut.

It's the night before the first game of the season, Ashley finished her chores and making dinner for her aunt, wanting some alone time, but wanting to be out of the house for a while she decided to go for a run. Standing on the front porch wearing black spandex shorts with a matching black tube top, Nike running sneakers and her hair in a ponytail, the cool evening air felt refreshing against her exposed skin. Popping in her ears buds she set out down the porch steps to begin her run down the street. The light orange color in the sky specifies there is about an hour of light left making her way down the street.

Neighborhood seems deserted, not another soul or passing car in sight, just the way she likes it, music playing softly in her ears to drown out any outside noise or disturbance that might distract her on her run. Turning down another street she realizes it has been awhile since she has been through this part of the neighborhood, long enough to where all the houses and sights appear new to her, like she just entered a foreign town. Even though the late evening air is brisk, Ashley can still feel the sweat beginning to bead up on her bare skin, her forehead enduring the blunt of the dampness. Further on she ran the more she missed these late evening runs, especially on nights like these, perfect weather and a surrounding quietness making the workout more intimate. Ignoring any of the scenery as it passes by, she is fully aware of the landscape approaching, coming up on the park where she met Razz, a place she hasn't been to since that day. What once was a place where she would go to escape and clear her mind, be alone even when occupied with other pedestrians, now became this dark place even if the sun was shining, tonight though she was in a different state of mind, willing to run through fire if she had too. Without breaking stride she enters the park, running down the path running alongside the water. Still a good half-hour or so of daylight left, the scattered light post throughout the park begin to illuminate. Running along the water fills the air with a soothing aroma, one she wishes she could stay and appreciate more. Only a few other people were spotted in the park as she ran towards the other end. Staying on the current path, out of the corner of her eye, Ashley sees the bench she was sitting at that day coming up on her left. Drawing closer, memories of that day flashed through her mind, like a TV flickering multiple images. Running by she views a girl around the same age she was at the time sitting there alone, looking out at the water, her blonde hair in pigtails, a lonely look on her face, Ashley remembers supporting the same expression right before that strange man sat beside her wanting her to go off with him. Wanted to stop running and watch over the girl to make sure she wasn't lost or a runaway, instead turns herself around to run backwards at a slower pace, keeping an eye on the young girl the further and further away she gets. Ashley's concern was put to rest when she spotted a woman approach the bench seating herself next to the girl, handing her something and getting a hug in return, preferably her mother, breathing a sigh of relief knowing the girl was going to be okay, Ashley turns back around, running out the other end of the park.

Making it to a street home to a variety of stores and restaurants, a street Ashley is very familiar with having been to a few of these establishments many times, mainly the grocery store located a little ways down. Some of the smaller pubs triggered some unpleasant memories of her aunt dragging a very young Ashley to accompany her to the active night life that manifest after dark, remembering many nights watching her aunt getting completely shit faced while strange, obnoxious, desperate men tried to seduce and grope her. Barely ever had to buy a drink, would flirt constantly with these men, many of which became sexual partners, unfortunately for the both of them. Sitting on bar stools is not how a child under ten years of age should be spending some of their nights, her aunt would make her bring a small toy to keep her occupied, but Ashley's young eyes would just sit there observing what all the adults in the room were doing, the loud music playing in the background, the smell of various liquors tickling her young nostrils, the many grown-up conversations going on simultaneously, witnessing couples making out, some of the same sex, each night culminating in her aunt driving the two of them home drunk, sometimes followed by a man she had just met or had been seeing.

Not too busy at the present time for a street populated with small businesses and eateries, normally when people drive down here they have to look hard for a place to park, now there is spots available all over the place, maybe just catching the area at a down time. Deciding to stay running mainly on the sidewalk rather than the road, she proceeds onward down the street, the road lit up from the outside lights coming from the various businesses, a décor of color from the mixture of lights resembles an amusement park lit up at night, the brightness generated is enough to drown out the many street lights inhabiting the area. Slight fatigue begins to set in the further down the road she went, viewing the darkness slowly beginning to blanket the outside world. Determining she has traveled far enough, Ashley comes to a stop taking a break on a nearby bench for a breather. Breathing heavy, sweat dripping from her face, feeling the cool chill from the incoming night air, the touch of a masculine hand is felt on her shoulder. Startled by the uninvited contact, she quickly turns to look back over her shoulder to view the perpetrator, surprised to lay eyes on Jake standing there.

"Hey, thought that was you," said Jake with a smile. "Didn't mean to scare you."

"Coach, sorry, just wasn't expecting…what are you doing here?" asked Ashley, totally relieved the hand didn't belong to some random creep off the street.

"I was going to ask you the same thing, but it's obvious you are out for a run," Jake replied. "May I?" asked Jake, wanting to share the bench.

"Of course," answered Ashley, Jake seated himself beside her.

She couldn't help notice how Jake has always spoken to her, kind and respectful, always a true gentleman, something she is certainly not use to, at first it made her fell a bit uncomfortable, when you a use to being treated a certain way everything else seems strange, but now receiving that respect and chivalry on a more consistent basis, understands this is what she deserves and it's okay for it to feel good.

"I was just running some errands and thought I would stop and get something to eat," Jake said looking over at Ashley. "Hungry?"

The two of them share a table for two by the large window of the bistro they currently reside in, being late evening the restaurant wasn't too busy, being seated right away. This was one of the many restaurants on this street Ashley has never been to, there are a couple diners on this road that serve a great grilled chicken salad that her and Holley J visit occasionally, but this bistro appears to be a little on the high-end side, a place where one might bring a date to. The dim lightning, the candles and empty wine glasses on the table, the soft vocal less music playing throughout made for a new dining experience. Appreciating the artsy and melodic tone of the interior with its very soft mood color scheme to the bizarre artwork hanging on the walls, it had a very mellow and easy going vibe, a place where one could visit alone and feel like they were the only one there. Part of Ashley felt like a misfit compared to the swank upper-class individuals making up the rest of the clientele, even wondering why Jake would have selected a place like this, maybe he has been here before and likes the food, maybe he wanted to take her somewhere nice rather than your typical greasy spoon for burgers and fries, maybe he was just trying to impress her with dinner at a classy place, either way she felt under dressed and out of place. She asked herself what she was doing there, sitting in a fancy restaurant with her softball coach dressed in workout clothes, thought she may be dreaming and at any second she was going to wake up still sitting on the bench by the road, yet everything felt too real to be a dream, but couldn't help admit to herself despite feeling out of place, she was comfortable and felt safe in Jake's presence. Looking over the menu Ashley realized this isn't the place one comes to for a quick meal, everything sounded complicated to make taking a lot of effort, she considered herself a good cook, but the selections on this menu appeared out of her league of cooking expertise, all sounding delicious, different makes of chicken, fish, even beef. Technically she already ate dinner, but her nice long run help build up another appetite, eyeing the chicken French with mushrooms and asparagus.

"You come here a lot?" asked Ashley, continuing to survey the menu.

"I've been here a few times, the food is really good here," Jake answered, taking a sip from his water glass. "You think this place is a little too much?"

"No, it's fine. It's just I've never eaten in a place like this before," she replied.

"See anything on the menu you like?" asked Jake. "Just order what you want."

Their waitress came over to take their orders, Ashley found the female wait staffs outfits to be cute, a black ruffled skirt with black nylons and black loafers, topped off with a black and white, short sleeve latex top, ending with a black and white bow in their hair. Jake gestured for the waitress to take Ashley's order first, already knowing his order, the place makes a mean stuff peppers dish that actually melts in your mouth, becoming his go to meal here. Ashley informs the waitress she is interested in the chicken French with just ice water to drink, getting the nod from Jake on a good choice, relaying he also wants ice water to drink. The waitress grabs the two sided laminated menus from them, leaving to put in their orders.

"So how was your run?" asked Jake.

"It was fine," Ashley responded. "I didn't think I would come out this far."

Ashley was caressing both her arms due to the cool temperature inside the restaurant, the air conditioning must be on full blast, not helping she is sitting directly under a vent. Jake can see she is a little on the cold side, not just from watching her rub her arms, but from the goose bumps visible all over.

"You cold?" Jake asked, seeing her trying to hug herself to stay warm.

"I'm okay," she replied, feeling goose bumps popping up on her legs now.

Without saying another word, Jake unzipped his fleece jacket, getting up to remove it, stepping over to place it upon Ashley's shoulders before returning to his seat. Instantly she felt the warmth of the jacket against her bare skin, mainly coming from the jacket's saturation of Jake's body heat, promptly causing the goose bumps to dissipate.

"Thank you," she said, snugging it tightly atop her shoulders, the scent of Jake's cologne protrudes off the fabric, finding the fragrance appealing.

Another gesture of chivalry Ashley is not accustom to, always thought men and boys like this were extinct at least in her world, a world where they all wanted was one thing. Never has she ever been treated like an actually lady, someone who has actual feelings and not just a piece of meat, it felt new, it felt different, it felt nice. It was clear Jake wasn't like the other men who have passed through her life, really has become a friend, someone she could trust, never thought she would see the day when she would be sitting alone in a nice restaurant with a guy who wasn't trying to get into her pants, not that she ever been on a real date before or that this is a date, but it feels gratifying to experience something simulating a social engagement without the other party wanting something in return.

"Feel better?" Jake asked with a smile on his face.

"Yes, much," she answered. "I guess I'm not really dressed for winter."

"It does get kind of cold in here sometimes," Jake replies with a chuckle. "So what made you decide to go out for a run the night before a game, you nervous about tomorrow?"

"I usually don't get nervous and running helps clear my head, plus I enjoy it," Ashley remarked. "What about you, you nervous about tomorrow?"

"Unlike you, yes, I'm very nervous about tomorrow, not that I don't think you girls are going to do great, it's more about me having to prove sometime to myself," he expressed, "besides, being nervous is good for you, it loosens you up. But seriously I have all the confidence in the world in you and the rest of the team, I guess that makes me partially excited too."

"Okay, maybe I am a little nervous," added Ashley. "I just have so much riding on this season with the scouts and then everything you have done for us, I don't want to disappoint you."

"I think you would be the last person that would disappoint me," Jake noted. "I believe you are the heart and soul of this team and we will go as far as that arm of yours will take us. I have a feeling the words I'm about to utter you probably have never heard before, you're an extremely talented girl and any team, this one or a team at the college level would be lucky to have you."

"You really believe that?" she asked, looking Jake right in the eyes.

"Yeah, probably more than I should," he declared.

Jake watched as Ashley's face lit up like a Christmas tree, seeing a smile come across her face he has never seen before, has always known she was a very pretty girl, but witnessing her reveal her perfect teeth and the way her baby browns seem to sparkle amongst the candlelight, he was looking at what only could be called a living porcelain doll. The hardest working teenager he as ever met, guys on his high school team wouldn't come close to her dedication and fire, having all the attributes and work ethic of someone who knew what they wanted and wasn't afraid to go after it, the true characteristics of a winner. He saw a lot of him in her, feeling like he was having dinner with a female version of himself, but he still had major concerns about certain details in her life. That night she called and he overheard her aunt talk to her the way she did set off extensive red flags, he hasn't been able to get that phone call out of his head, Ashley is a tough girl, but he still worries for her. Remembering his parents fighting a lot, though they kept the harmful words to each other, never directing them to him or his brother, couldn't imagine how he would have felt if one of his parents spoke to him like that, both were always very supportive and encouraging, proud of his accomplishments, would have never thought less of him had he ever come up short of his goals. Jake can read the writing on the walls, Ashley doesn't have support or encouragement coming from home or any other place for that matter, Holley J might be the only one. Reaching your goals is hard enough in and of itself, but to do it completely on your own without the support of friends and family must take an extremely strong willed person. He could tell Ashley was that person, she wasn't going to let anything stand in her way, yet doesn't mean she should have to do it alone. Definitely routing for her and would help her in any way he can, part of him though believes there is more to her than she is letting on. Remembering her opening up a bit that day on the field, yet he suspects there is a lot more to her story, keeping things very close to the chest is something Jake has noticed about Ashley, a very private person, one who likes to keep things to herself, which could be a blessing or a curse. Not one to pry in other people's lives, however he feels a sense of responsibility to her as her coach if he possibly conceives something might be wrong.

"Now that we are kind of alone, I wanted to talk about what's going on with you," Jake remarked.

"What do you mean?" asked Ashley, partially distracted from the glare coming off the window.

"Just in general, how are things?" responded Jake, trying his best to subtly get her to open up without actually being to forward.

"The same," she declared, looking at the expression on Jake's face, portraying a look of someone who wanted to ask something difficult, but was hesitate to inquire. "You look like there is something on your mind."

"Look, Ash, I'm going to be honest with you. I can't get what I heard that night on the phone when you called out of my head. I know it's not my place to pry, trust me I'm not that type of person and it's none of my business, but I feel like in a way it is. I mean I'm your coach, you're technically a student of mine and I'm just looking out for your wellbeing," commented Jake, looking directly at her waiting for a response.

Staring back at Jake, looking at a man who has become the first one in her life she could trust, knowing there is sincerity in his words, confessed to some of what goes on at home to him before, but wasn't even scraping the surface. Peering back at him sitting there waiting for her to say something, the sudden silence between them seemed deafening almost awkward. She won't even tell her best friend everything, why should she tell a guy she has known only a couple weeks.

"All I can tell you is this, if I ever need your help, I'll ask for it, I promise," Ashley voiced.

"I guess that will have to do for now," Jake uttered. "I just want you to know that I'm here if you ever need me."

"I know," she replied, there are times when people say things like that, yet when you need them they are never there. It was different with Jake, he carried himself as someone who is an honest person, trusting he meant what he said and would be there if she needed him,

"Can I ask you something?"

"Sure," Jake answered.

"That day on the field you were telling me a little about a girl you were dating in high school that had a major impact on your life. Can elaborate more on what you meant by that?" Ashley asked, no way a great guy like Jake should be single, rumors surfaced he has been talking to Miss Waters at school, if any of the speculations are true the two of them are doing a great job keeping it on the down low.

"Well, that's kind of a long story," Jake stated.

"Our food isn't here yet," remarked Ashley, stipulating she is interested in hearing the whole story.

Leaning back in his chair taking a quick gaze outside at all the lights from the various other businesses, Jake can see his faint reflection looking back at him through the window, beginning his story as if he was talking to himself through the mirroring he saw through the glass. Ashley could depict the changes in his emotions with every transition of the tone of his voice, listening about the break-up, the pregnancy, the girl moving away and the abortion, could hear in his voice how much that affected him. When speaking of the abortion is what began hitting him the hardest, where she saw this masculine former professional athlete actually shed a few tears, seeming to shine as they ran down his face. The more he spoke about it the more choked up he became, once had a baby he was willing to help take care of, but was taken away from him for selfish reasons. Ashley couldn't detour from her eyes getting misty, tear ducts ready to overflow hearing about these sad events in Jake's life. It was depressing to her for many reasons, particularly since he was willing to be a man even at a young age, stepping up to his responsibilities, but also because some baby who is no longer with us missed out on having someone who would have made a terrific father, ending the sad tale stating he hasn't heard or seen the girl since. Wiping the few tears away with her hand, Ashley realized under all that manly exterior lives a broken man who, despite all he has been through is trying to put back together the shattered pieces to his life, having to over-come a huge loss in his early years, still finding a way and the strength to ac-complish what he set out to do. Hoping she is that strong emotionally and internally to not let anything stand in her way, believing she is and believes Jake would too. Jake apologized for his emotional outburst wiping the tears from his face with his napkin, worrying he ruined their evening, bringing Ash-ley to apologize for bringing up what was a touchy subject and for his loss, suggesting conversation through the rest of dinner would be of the upbeat va-riety, Jake agreed with a small smirk as the aroma of their dinners grew closer in the hands of their waitress. Their meals before them, they enjoyed a pleas-ant, quiet dinner together, discussing matters of softball and random pop cul-ture, even sharing a few laughs along the way. Ashley sedentary, eating a free meal, one she didn't have to cook for herself, having pleasurable chit chat, at that moment felt like the rest of the world didn't exist, the other patrons in the restaurant seemed to go silent as if they were mere vessels just there to take up space, felt like she was in a different reality, a better reality, the only thing on her mind was what she was going to say next to string along their topics of dialogue. She felt like a different person, a better person, one giving her demons the night off in hopes to appreciate the moment and to realize nights like these are possible. Ashley couldn't believe how good her meal was, having never tasted Chicken French this good before, the chicken was so tender she could cut it with a fork, the asparagus were crunchy and seasoned to perfection, part of her wanted to find out the recipe so she could try making it for herself, but knows these eateries are stingy when it comes to giving away their secrets. By far the best meal she has had in a long time and it wasn't just about the food, she had great company, Holley J was the only other person she enjoyed having a private meal with. Everything was perfect, where she didn't want the night to end, wishing she could freeze time and just live in this moment for a while, the only thing that could make things better was if Holley J was there to join them. Eventually having to go home never even crossed her mind, was living in the moment, something she has never done outside of standing on a pitcher's mound. They finished up their meals with great satisfaction, both at a loss for words at the quality of the food, Ashley used some of the bread to sponge up the remaining sauce in her plate. Jake flagged down the waitress for the check, Ashley viewed the time on her phone displaying a little after ten, still early enough for her to get home and do a little painting before turning in. Paying the check by tossing a bunch of cash on the table, Jake commented to the waitress how great the food was.

The two of them exit the bistro, standing outside momentarily being blinded by the bright lights inhabiting the long stretch of road, the chilly night air prompted Jake to let Ashley continue wearing his jacket. The night life appeared to have picked up in the time they were nestled inside, the flow of traffic increased significantly, many people wandering the sidewalks trying to decide which watering hole to enter to drink their sorrows away, many were just standing around smoking. Not wanting Ashley to run home alone at night, Jake insisted on giving her a ride which she gladly accepted. Following him a little ways down the street to where his truck was parked, she observed the growing number of people filling the street, having been a long time since she has been down in this area at this time of night, nothing seemed to have changed, only thing missing was the drunken street fight with the appending arrival of the cops. Arriving at his parked truck, Jake opens the passenger door for Ashley, another chivalrous act new to her, closing it behind her once safely inside, she always pictured Jake to be a truck guy, to her guys that drove trucks showed a sign of masculinity, sports cars or luxury cars were typical with insecure or douche bag men who were usually compensating for something else. Inside of the truck was neat and orderly aside from a few papers and brochures laying atop the dashboard, the smell of pine resonated from the air freshener hanging from the rearview mirror, the truck was definitely an older model, but still in great shape. Jake entered the driver's side as she buckled her seatbelt, this night has turned out to be a night of first for Ashley concluding with her being inside a man's vehicle and not required to perform a sexual act, reminiscent of the countless automobiles that have been the set piece for her services at Razz' club back parking lot. Safely inside, Jake starts the engine, driving off down the road.   Jake's truck pulls up next to the curb in front of Ashley's aunt's house, neighborhood is quiet with a few houses supporting light from their front door fixtures including her residents, the headlights cast enough light to illuminate the front yard putting her aunt's car into view letting Ashley know she is home. A majority of the house is covered in darkness negating Jake from commenting on its appearance, all he could tell was the house didn't look very spacious, barely large enough for two people. As the truck sat there idling, Ashley wanted to tell Jake to just take off and keep driving never looking back because she knew her perfect night was coming to an end.

"Thanks again for dinner," she expressed, taking off Jake's jacket placing it beside him.

"My pleasure," he replied watching her exit the truck. "Get some rest, got a big day tomorrow."

"I will," she said, standing outside the truck with the door open.

"Okay, I will see you tomorrow, goodnight," added Jake.

"Goodnight," Ashley said, slamming the truck door shut.

Jake drove off waving back at her, standing there in the street by the end of her driveway, she watched as Jake's tail lights faded away into the blackness of night.

Feeling a chill from the cool air, began her slow walk up the walkway to the front door, seeing no other strange car parked in the driveway signified her aunt was home alone. Placing her key in the lock, Ashley peered over at the picture window, the drapes were drawn shut and not a hint of light was visible through the glass. Opening the door, stepping into the entryway completely surrounded in blackness, overwhelmed by the silence in the house, only sound that could be heard was the ticking of the small clock hanging in the kitchen. Flipping on the living room lamp, Ashley is startled when the presence of light unveils her aunt sitting leaned back on the couch motionless wearing clothes indicative of someone who was planning on going out, one hand was holding an open bottle of Jack Daniels, probably using that to wash down the four empty beer bottles sitting on the coffee table. Even from where Ashley was standing, could identify how lightly glazed over her aunt's eyes were sitting there staring into nothingness, her limp body looked like someone who was either hypnotized or possessed. From the gathered evidence Ashley assumed her aunt must have had a date and he canceled or this guy broke things off with her, best guess being the latter, however her aunt would use any excuse to drink.

"Where the hell have you been?" Ashley's aunt asked, finally showing some signs of life, turning her head to put Ashley in her sights, the skin on her face looked like it was sagging the way the light was hitting her dermis.

Not interested in having another heated exchange with the lush residing on the couch, Ashley ignored the interaction directing herself to the staircase.

"HEY! I'm talking to you!" her aunt shouted sternly, leaning forward to throw the bottle of Jack Daniels in Ashley's direction, shattering against the closed front door, swiftly removing herself from the couch to quickly stagger her way over to Ashley's position.

Ashley stood there in shock having that solid bottle of glass explode inches away from her, the grasp of her aunt's hand on her upper arm pushing her back against the wall.

"When I ask you a question you better fucking answer me," utters her aunt pointing a finger in Ashley's face.

"What, you going to take it out on me because your man finally realized what a bitch you are," Ashley stated, physically feeling the tension between the two of them in part to the slap she received across her face.

"Don't you ever fucking disrespect me in my own house," barked her aunt, feeling unsympathetic as Ashley holds the stricken side of her face with her hand.

In the tens years Ashley has lived with her aunt verbal abuse was always the culprit, however she is no stranger to physical abuse at her aunt's hands, sober or drunk, many encounters in her earlier years have left her bruised from wooden spoons to dictionaries. As a small child she was good at hiding the marks from everyone around her, as she got older the physical abuse slowly tapered off in favor of the verbal and metal variety, which Ashley finds to be much, much worse. It was taking every molecule in her body to refrain herself from retaliating, holding back years of built-up anger and aggression, yet she felt frozen, unable to move, all she could do is stand there looking at the person who delivered the blow, feeling the struck side of her face tingled in irritation.

"You're the reason my baby sister is rotting in a cell somewhere, if she would have just gotten rid of your stupid ass when she had the chance, I wouldn't be stuck taken care of a pile of white trash like you. You're the biggest mistake this family ever made," her aunt declared, in full view of the impact of her words, watching Ashley's eyes water releasing a stream of tears down her face.

Wanting to stand strong, show her aunt she is unbreakable, but her spoken words caused more damage than any physical trauma could have, each word felt like a thousand more slaps across the face, she couldn't think straight, her mind felt like a Rubik's cube being scrambled vigorously. Without thinking about it, as if something else was in control of her body, Ashley just turned running up the stairs towards her room, slamming the door shut as she entered, seating herself on her bed where she began crying heavily. Tears continuously dripped from her face, her emotions in a whirlwind feeling like she could cry forever. Hearing what her aunt said, the tone in her voice, the expression on her face, the hollowness in her eyes like she didn't have a soul when she spoke, reassured her she meant every word she said, not just tonight, everything she has ever verbal directed regarding her. This is first of Ashley hearing her aunt blaming her for her mother's current predicament, like it had nothing to do with her mother's own actions, like anyone has a choice to not be a fetus growing inside a woman's uterus. After altercations like this with her aunt, Ashley wishes her mother would have aborted her, it would have saved her from this sick game she calls her life, maybe even postponing her birth to a more deserving mother. For her aunt to have an agenda like that against her, to hold a grudge with someone who was never old enough to be held responsible for their own actions, who was dragged through life on a lease held by someone who wasn't in control of their own existence, who made bad decisions after bad decisions, really demonstrated the mentality Ashley has had to deal with over the years. Grabbing her phone wanting to call Holley J, even considered calling Jake, staring at the phone screen seeing her dark reflection looking back at her, eyes a little puffy from all the tears shed, decided she wasn't in the right state of mind right now for human interaction, would be best if she was alone. Hooking her phone to its charger located on her nightstand, Ashley lays down on her side, not even breaking down her bed, still wearing her workout clothes, trying to unravel the mystery that is her being. The residence that should be home feels more like a prison cell where she is doing time for transgressions she didn't commit, feeling lost in her own existence and every directions was the wrong one, afraid the darkness will be too great for the light to overcome. Wishing she could go back to where she was earlier in the evening, where she felt like a young lady and not a piece of trash, where she was respected and not disrespected, where her life felt meaningful and not expendable. It's remarkable how drastic ones place in reality can change so radically from moment to moment, from one of the best nights she has had in a long time, to in a blink of an eye, wanting to lock herself in her room and never come out. Plans to do a little painting have to wait with her not being in the right mind set. Lying there with her back to her open bedroom window, receptive to cool breeze filtering through her room, she closed her soaked eyes until she drifted off to sleep.

Ashley stands upon the mound, game gear on, eyes closed, soaking in the scattered rays of sunshine appearing sporadically through the random breaks in the clouds, as if in a state of meditation, all she can hear is the sound of her own thoughts, her breathing is slow and steady, alone in a place where she knows she belongs. Jake wanted all the girls at the field an hour before game time, which would be a half-hour from now. She was here a half-hour ago doing her workout and warm ups, now standing on the mound rotating a softball she borrowed from the equipment room in her right hand, letting her feel the texture of the leather and stitching against her fingertips. All day in her classes this was all she could think about, at lunch Holley J commented on how determined her demeanor looked. Opening up her eyes to look around the field at the empty bleachers and dugouts soon be occupied by players and spectators, and hopefully a few scouts. Pounding the softball in her mitt to loosen it up, the sound of a distance voice permeates through the air catching Ashley's attention. Looking out beyond the field, sees Holley J approaching carrying her gear filled duffel bag, moving rather swiftly as if in a hurry. Entering the home team dugout, Holley J drops her bag on the ground to sit on the bench to retie the laces on her cleats. Ashley leaves the mound to visit with her in the dugout, hearing her heavy breathing working on her footgear.

"Game hasn't even started yet and I'm already ready for a nap," Holley J mentions jokingly, grabbing her glove out of the duffel bag,

"I ran into Coach in the hall, he said he should be here any minute. I take it you're ready."

"Aren't you?" asked Ashley seated next to Holley J.

"I follow your lead, if you're ready I'm ready," responded Holley J fixing the ponytail in her hair. "I have to tell you, I got a really good feeling about today."

"Just today?" Ashley asked.

"You know, I'm now psychic, just be happy I got this feeling for today," Holley J remarked. "Are you okay? You seemed kind of out of it all day."

"I'm alright, just got a lot of stuff on my mind," Ashley stated.

"So when were you going to tell me about your dinner with Coach last night?" asked Holley J.

"How did you find out about that?" Ashley replied, thinking how she forgot to tell her best friend, the one person she tells almost everything to, about the chance meeting with Jake. She was going to tell her, however the unpleasant run-in with her aunt when returning home must have over shadowed the enjoyable evening she spent with Jake, the bad always seems to outweigh the good when it comes to what comes to her mind first.

"Ash, it's me. A guy in my Psychics class said he saw you there with him last night," Holley J answered. "As far as I know no one else on the team knows, especially Renee, I mean she already accuses you of being a kiss ass."

"Do you think that's what I am?" asked Ashley.

"Of course not," a reassuring Holley J answers. "But I am curious how the two of you ending up having dinner together."

Seated beside her best friend, Ashley explaining how the chance encounter happened, from her going out for a run, to running into Jake who was on his way to get something to eat, asking her for some company. Holley J believes one hundred percent she is telling the truth, specifically because she knows Ashley to go out for runs at night.

"I think it would be best if we kept it between us," suggested Holley J.

"Yes, please, I don't want the team to pull apart over something like this, especially since we are more together than we have ever been," Ashley remarked. "I swear I was going to tell you."

"I know you would have," Holley J responds with a smile. "Ready to warm up?"

The two of them left the dugout heading for their designated spots to get a few minutes of a warm up till Jake and the rest of the team arrive.

About fifteen minutes till game time, parents and friends are filling the bleachers, score keepers and scoreboard operators are getting ready, umpires position themselves, one locating himself behind home plate sweeping off any unwanted dirt. Jake has the girls gathered in their dugout after completing their pregame warm ups, going over starting positions and batting order, ready to give his pregame speech, the opposing team is over in their dugout appearing to be doing the same.

"Okay, this is it. This is the moment all you girls have been preparing for. Every error, every hit, every run scored is going to count from here on out. Some of you may be nervous which is totally fine, in fact I encourage it, nervousness heightens focus and if you are not nervous then I'll be nervous for you because I am anxious myself. There is going to be mistakes made, not just by you girls, but by me as well, there is going to be some highs, there is going to be some lows, but no matter what happens, we are all in this together. Over in the other dugout they are probably being told they are a better team than you, you don't have to be the better team, just be the better team today. You girls are ready and are good enough to play with any team that steps out onto that field with you, now just go out there and prove it," Jake speaks with passion, every girl on the team never pulled their eyes away from Jake as he spoke, particularly Ashley who was enthralled by ever word.

"Now I'm just going to ask you girls for one small favor, just kick their ass."

The faces of the girls all lit up with Jake's friendly request, a clapping brigade ensued amongst the team lead by Ashley getting them fired up, all but Renee who sat at the end of the dugout with her legs crossed and arms folded, popping a large bubble made from the gum she was currently chewing, her eyes hidden behind a dark pair of sunglasses. With the game just minutes away, the girls carry that enthusiasm out of the dugout gathering around each other and Jake, ready to get going. Ashley instructs the girls to put a fist up with Jake joining in, the team obliges with various fists pointing skyward, Renee who strategically put herself at the back of the pack, stood there with her fist barely up in the air looking away from the rest of the girls. A chant started, led by Ashley with all the feminine voices responding in unison, breaking away with the game about to start. As the home team they take the field first, all the fielders head to their designated positions, clapping and encouraging verbal heckling ensue as the girls run out onto the field, Ashley hangs back to receive the game ball from Jake.

"I don't want to put any undue pressure on you, but those scouts are here, I figured you would want to know," said Jake holding the game ball over Ashley's mitt. "This is it, this is your time, don't worry about the crowd, don't even worry about the scouts, just put all your attention to the batter at the plate, just be yourself and the rest will follow," he adds placing the ball in her mitt. "Give 'em hell."

"Yes, sir," responds Ashley, receiving a nod and smile from Jake before he returns to the dugout to monitor the girls play.

Making her way to the mound where Holley J is waiting for her, Ashley's infield teammates utter motivating words as she nears the rubber, cheers from anonymous fans also rain down upon her.

"Okay, let's do this, let's have our winning streak start today," suggest Holley J standing there with her catcher's mask laying atop her head. "We all got your back."

"Yeah," Ashley replies looking out into the outfield seeing Renee standing there flashing her the finger. "Everyone."

"Let's you and I just play catch," Holley J stated. "Make believe the batters are in the way."

"I'm ready," said Ashley, giving her the nod.

Holley J returned to her location behind home plate, giving the umpire the go ahead before pulling her mask back down, squatting herself into position. The umpire yells out the signature "PLAY BALL," initiating the start of the game.

Ashley stands patiently upon the mound rotating the softball in her hand waiting for the first batter to approach home plate. Glancing over at the bleacher area to see if she could spot the scouts, surprised at the amount of people viewing the game, normally the stands are never full, yet today they are jammed pack with people spilling over to sitting on the grass next to the bleachers, some are just standing, mostly faces she does not recognize. The regulars in the stands are parents to some of the girls on the team, something Ashley can't relate to, not one family member has ever seen her throw a pitch in a game, which is to be expected since her mother is in jail, her aunt can't care less and her father is a roulette wheel of options, but she is use to it, making it this far on her own, she plans on finishing it on her own. Bringing her attention back to home plate where the first batter of the game makes her way into the batter's box. These are the moments Ashley lives for, there is no other place in the world she rather be at this particular section in time, this is where she knows she belongs, where she feels the most alive. Just the atmosphere of this athletic competition brings her to a state of euphoria, the feel of her game uniform against her bare skin, the scent of the grass, the continuous chatter of the spectators, the sound of the ball coming off the bat, the whole game experience brings her in contact with a whole new world, one where she never wants to leave. The first opposing batter enters the batter's box, a lefty, Ashley loves pitching against lefthanded batters, being right handed it is more natural when she wants to pitch away from the batter not having to cross her body. The batter stands in digging her cleats into the dirt trying to give herself a good stance knowing Ashley's reputation, making sure her batting gloves are secure she chokes up on the bat ready for the first pitch. Ashley takes a deep breath rotating the softball in her hand waiting for the sign from Holley J. Receiving the sign she expected, gives Holley J the nod, one fastball coming up, typically how Holley J likes to start every game, show the batters early what they are in for. Preparing for her wind-up time seems to stop, all the surrounding outside noise literally goes silent as if she is standing out on that mound all alone, generally nothing enters her mind when she is in this Zen like state, but thoughts of last night's encounter with her aunt seemed to slip through the cracks. Those distressing thoughts reignited her anger, afraid her emotions might throw her off her game, decided to use her anger as fuel, use the ball as a vessel to empty out all the resentment and rage she is housing. Ashley can feel a sudden rush of adrenaline coercing through her body making her feel powerful and invincible, this batter and every other batter that comes up to the plate is in for a rude awakening, she wouldn't want to be the other team right now. Ready to deliver her first pitch, Ashley keeps focus on only Holley J's glove, like she said, they are not even there, let's just play catch, exactly what Ashley intends to do. Winding up her eyes see nothing but her intended target, swinging her arm in her pitching motion, the ball launches out of her hand like a cannon ball leaving a cannon, rocketing through the air on a direct course for Holley J's mitt, in what seemed like less than a second the ball slapped against Holley J's glove with a large thump leaving the batter to swing late and awkwardly causing her to lose her balance.

"Strike one," the umpire announces, her teammates continue with the encouraging chatter while Holley J shakes a stinging gloved hand before returning the ball.

Jake applauds her start voicing for her to keep it up. The ball back in Ashley's possession she stomps her foot into the mound dirt to create better footing for her upcoming pitches. Ready and awaiting the sign from Holley J, again blocking out all the outside noise eyeing her focal point. The sign is flashed with Ashley giving the nod, a change-up is now ordered, strategically placing her fingers in position on the ball to allow for the pitch to be executed, beginning her wind up cues Holley J the pitch is on its way enabling her to slightly shift her position, opening her glove wide to accommodate the destination of the pitch. With a fluid motion the next pitch leaves Ashley's hand heading towards a puzzled batter unsure on how to react, thinking the ball would be coming in rapidly like the pitch before, the batter swings well before the ball reaches her appropriate swing zone permitting the ball to slide right by her safely landing in Holley J's glove.

"STRIKE TWO," the umpire announces.

More motivating chatter and cheering come from Ashley's teammates, Jake stands by the dugout clapping, favorably nodding his head, feeling confident on what's ahead for the rest of the game. The ball is returned, Ashley looking for her first strikeout of the game and season. The batter, who appears discombobulated, digs her cleats back into the dirt, repositioning her hands on the bat in hopes of a different outcome, takes a couple deep breaths before returning to her batter's stance awaiting the next pitch. Receiving the next sign from Holley J, Ashley shakes it off specifying the pitch she wants to throw, like clockwork Holley J knows instantly what means and what is coming. Preparing herself Holley J slightly shifts her body position opening her mitt up wide, sending Ashley the nod letting her know she is ready. Without hesitating Ashley goes into her wind-up letting the next pitch go, leaving her hand at a velocity surpassing her first pitch, in a blink of an eye the ball enters Holley J's mitt with another loud thud leaving the batter standing there dumbfounded not even having a chance to swing.

"STRIKE THREE," announces the umpire while the batter walks back to her dugout all distraught and a tiny bit embarrassed.

Holley J stands up to return the ball back to Ashley giving her vocal recognition, followed by her teammates as well as Jake, looking over at him she is greeted with an approving fist pump. Starting to feel settled in striking out her first victim, her confidence was growing, this is what she was born to do, over the last few minutes her life was perfect, rotating the ball in her hand she awaits the second batter, brimming with self-assurance, ready for a repeat performance with every hitter that dares come to the plate.

Ashley retired the next two batters including another strikeout, a great start for her and the team as they come off the field for their first go around at bat. Entering the dugout the girls removed their gloves in preparation for their turn at swinging the sticks, Jake congratulated them as they entered, primarily Ashley who he overly complimented on her strong showing. The first one up was Brie, placing her helmet on and grabbing the bat she wanted, walked out of the dugout where she was stopped by Jake talking privately in her ear, doing a lot of nodding in concurrence to his insightful words. Leaving Jake's side she heads to home plate to enter the batter's box, clapping mixed with motivating phrases are sent her way courtesy of her teammates with Ashley leading way. A majority of the girls are standing, leaning on the small chain-linked railing residing in front of the dugout to watch Brie at the plate, Ashley and Holley J being two of them. Brie stands in the batter's box left handed, remembering what Jake had told her, getting a good stance and a good grip on the bat holding it close to her chest, letting out a couple deep breaths the opposing pitcher sends her first pitch which comes in low and outside leaving Brie to let it go by for a called ball. More clapping with shouts of "Good eye" come from Jake and the dugout, the snapping sound of bubble gum bubbles popping resonates from a few of the girls. Brie gets set for the next pitch, her good eye rapidly looking around at her environment before putting complete focus on the oncoming ball which happens to be on its way. Liking the current direction of the pitch, Brie swings in a slight upwards motion making flush contact with the ball sending it soaring over a leaping shortstop's reaching glove on its way deep into the outfield where it lands several feet in front of the left fielder. Immediately dropping the bat, she hustles towards first being waved on to go towards second, blowing past the first baseman, she gets on her horse to speedily head for second where the second baseman is waiting for the throw from the outfield. Brie's speed allowed her to slide feet first through the dry dirt causing a small dust cloud into second well before the ball reached the second baseman's mitt. Standing up brushing off the crud from her pants she hears the uproarious clapping and cheering coming from Jake and the dugout as well as the energetic crowd. Ashley stood there against the railing clapping, probably the most proud of Brie, thanks to Jake she found her perfect place on the team, after last season's never-ending barrage of verbal and then physical abuse, even before she had the surgery on her eye, happy to see Brie smiling and having fun playing again.

It is now Ashley's turn at bat after their second batter grounded out, Jake put her batting third right in front of Renee having their two best hitters up towards the top of the lineup. Grabbing a helmet, she heads to select a bat, being very superstitious when it comes to picking the right one, it must be a certain weight and length and it can't have any wording of any kind anywhere on the bat, Ashley had one of her best hitting performances as a freshman using a bat like that, telling herself she would never use a different type of bat ever again, luckily the team has a few sticks that match that description. Finding the one she wants she heads for home plate entering the batter's box, scraping out some of the dirt with her cleat, quickly adjusts her batting glove, only wearing one glove on her non-dominate hand, likes the feel of the rubber gripping against her skin on her dominate hand believing it gives her better grip. Slightly choked up on the bat, arranging her feet to accommodate her preferred stance, where she loves to crowd the plate, awaits the delivery of her first pitch. Ashley approaches batting as if someone was playing chess, while most batters just try and keep their eyes on the ball, she always tries to anticipate the type of pitch and where about it will be heading giving her a jump on her opponent, it's the pitcher in her that commences the mind games, softball may be a team sport, but everyone knows it's always a one-on-one battle between the pitcher and batter, who can get the best of the other. Standing steady and stern with a serious demeanor on her face, moderately swaying the bat back and forth, she watches the pitcher go into her wind-up. Predicting a fastball, possibly low and inside, a standard first pitch to a batter trying to shallow up most of the strike zone, sending a message to the hitter of who owns the inside of the plate. Her eyes watch as the ball comes darting in the exact direction she had foreseen, a little more inside than she thought causing her to jump back a hair letting the ball brush by just missing her stomach area.

"BALL ONE" is signaled by the umpire, her enthusiastic teammates led by Holley J, applaud her great vision, Jake sends words of approval her way.

Not even the least bit intimidated by the pitcher's attempt to back her off the plate, Ashley plants right back in the same spot placing her feet in the exact divots her cleats left in the dirt. Sensing the pitcher knows she means business, Ashley awaits the next pitch, telegraphing it might be some sort of off speed pitch, possibly low and outside, if that is the case she will be ready to take her first swing. Eyeing Brie with a good lead off second, observes the pitcher once again go into her wind-up, Ashley's eyes notice the angle of her throwing shoulder stipulating her assumption might be on point. The ball leaves the pitcher's hand placing a small smirk across Ashley's face, liking what she sees in the ball's speed, trajectory and direction. Very seldom does she see a pitch she likes so earlier in her at bat, leaving her no choice but to take a swing. Holley J watching from the dugout spots Ashley raising her left heel off the ground, her tell she is about to take a swing, something Holley J only knows about. Making contact with the ball flush on the butt of the bat, sending it rocketing high and deep into the outfield where the centerfielder must try to run it down. Running out of real estate, she approaches the outfield fence where she watches the ball clear the structure by a good twenty yards. The dugout erupts with clapping and cheering as Ashley and Brie round the bases to cross home plate, the many spectators, including the scouts, give Ashley a much deserved standing ovation. Running the bases, Ashley underwent a surge of confidence she has never felt before, in part to the greatest start she has ever had to a game in her life, striking out two batters, hit a two run homerun at her first at bat. Rounding third she tries to pin point where this sudden boost is coming from, knowing she's good, but feels like a different person out here, a better version of herself, and to be doing it in the first game of the season in front of the on looking scouts just makes it that much sweeter. Wherever it's coming from she realizes she has to ride this wave for as long as she can, if only the rest of her life could have moments like these, even if they are just sprinkled in from time to time, where she feels high above the world and she can do no wrong. Times like last night with Jake and the times she spends with Holley J are great, it's just those are different types of moments, ones where she feels like she needs the aid of someone else to have an exceptional blip in time rather than doing it on her own, something that is hard to explain. Returning to the dugout, the girls are greeted with high fives and a few hugs, Jake especially gave Ashley the biggest praise making her return. A distraught Renee kept to herself as the team celebrated, being up next she witnessed again Ashley stealing her thunder. Now late into the game, Ashley back on the mound with two innings left to play and her team up 2-0, she has pitched a brilliant game so far having given up only two hits and has already struck out eleven batters. Right now she sees herself in her first jam of the game, a runner on second with two outs and the opposing team's best hitter is coming up to bat once again. Last time she was up Ashley struck her out, but good hitters always learn from their previous at bat. Standing on the mound going through her pre-pitch routine, her next challenger enters the batter's box, a right-handed, big-bodied girl capable of a lot of power. Getting into her batter's stance, she takes a couple quick practice swings, Holley J gestures to Ashley what she wants the next three pitches to consist of, nodding back she digs into the rubber preparing to throw the first pitch, briefly looking back at the runner on second who has a decent lead off the bag. Ashley looks back towards Holley J rocketing a high fastball that cuts through the air with ease in the direction of home plate, caught off guard by the elevation of the pitch, the batter swings late completely missing the ball landing safely in Holley J's mitt with a loud thump. Clapping and cheers once again flood her way while the ball is returned to her, already knowing the next two pitches to throw, wasting no time into getting ready for the next pitch. Swiftly rotating the ball in her hand, adjusting her fingers for the called pitch, she goes into her wind up sending an outside curve ball towards the plate. The batter's eyes widening watching the pitch come her way, registering it's a curveball, the batter vaguely reaches forward while swinging making good contact sending the ball high towards centerfield where a ready Renee awaits. Mistaking the ball's trajectory and angle, Renee runs full speed in the balls direction, reaching up with an out stretched arm, the ball hits the top of mitt before falling unexpectedly to the ground. A disbelieving Ashley throws her arms up in distress, watching the runner from second cross home plate to score, Renee urgently picks up the ball throwing a rope to second base where the batter slides feet first safely. Hands on her hips, Renee stands there looking off in the distance through her dark sun glasses, shaking her head, receiving reassurance from Jake and the other girls.

Acquiring the ball back from the second baseman, Ashley feels the pressure for the first time in the game. The score now 2-1 with the tying run on second, still with two outs. Knows if she can get past this next batter everything will be okay, but she can't fall victim to the pressure, something she has a tendency to do from time to time if she lets her emotions get the best of her. The last play wasn't her fault, repeating it over and over again in her head, observing the next batter making her way to the plate. Holley J sensing the frustration in Ashley, standing on the mound with her hands on her hips, the obvious body language of someone a little annoyed, calls time out to the umpire, heading out to the mound to meet with her.

"You okay?" asked a concerned Holley J.

"That bitch probably dropped the ball on purpose," declared an angry Ashley.

"It doesn't really matter now, the play is over with," Holley J responded. "How about you just relax and let's worry about taking care of this next batter. I know how you get, you're pitching a monster game, don't let someone else's mistake ruin that."

"Okay, so what are we going to do?" Ashley asked, still bothered by that last play.

"Let's go with our bread and butter, fastballs, high and dry," Holley J suggested leaving the mound to head back behind home plate.

Back into position, Holley J pulls her mask back down giving Ashley the nod, the umpire signals to resume play. The girls get into sync with each other giving the green light to proceed, fueled by Renee's mysterious blunder, Ashley is ready to finish the game off the way she started it. Holley J was right, shouldn't let someone else's mistake rattle you, just keep focus on what you are supposed to do. Jake called out to Ashley asking if she was okay, responding she was fine. Wanting to show his support, he raised one fist into the air hoping to start a chain reaction. Almost instantly every girl on the team, from the ones out on the field to the ones in the dugout, followed suit raising one fist into the air, including Holley J doing it from a squatting position, Renee stood in centerfield with her hands on her knees shaking her head. Ashley raised her fist, ball in hand, showing team unity, knowing Jake and the girls have her back. The next batter is ready and waiting in the batter's box, hoping to drive in the tying run. Set to deliver on Holley J's bidding, Ashley winds up to throw some smoke, one, two, three, three pitches, three swings and a miss giving her twelve strikeouts for the game, but more importantly saves the lead for the team heading into the bottom of the inning. Coming in from the field for their next at bats, Ashley walks gingerly, in no rush to get off the field. The girls situated themselves in the dugout, Renee returns back towards the end, throwing her mitt in frustration on the bench before sitting down with her arms folded and her legs crossed. Jake halted Ashley before she could enter the dugout, still detecting vexation on her part.

"What's going on? You alright?" asked Jake, who can clearly see the irritation in her eyes.

"There's no reason Renee couldn't make that catch," Ashley mentioned.

"I'm not arguing that, but everyone makes mistakes, and you backed her up by striking out the next batter, like I said just leave it on the field," Jake noted.

"Yeah, well, she put me in a position that I hate being in," she said. "Every time someone makes a mistake the pressure is on me to bail everyone out."

"The pressure is only there because you put it on yourself, trust me, I know all about that, I used to put so much pressure on myself I thought for sure one day I would turn into a diamond," he replied. "You didn't do anything wrong and putting unnecessary pressure on yourself is going to lead you to making more mistakes. That's what great players and leaders do, they back up their teammates whenever they can no matter what, and you will come to see acts like that can be very contagious. Greatness just doesn't happen, great players make themselves great. You're pitching an incredible game, why don't you just focus on that right now."

Jake has such a way with words you can't help but listen, Ashley heard what he was saying, but she needed to confront Renee to find out if it really was just elapse in judgment. Walking away from Jake, entering the dugout, she works her way past the rest of the girls finding herself standing before a very disinterested Renee.

"What was that out there? You can usually make that catch in your sleep," Ashley stated, standing there with sweat dripping off her face.

"What's it to you?" a smug Renee asked, refusing to make eye contact, keeping her eyes hidden behind her sunglasses, body language continues to be very closed off.

"We could have lost the lead," noted Ashley.

"Then why don't you go back to the locker room and cry about it," Renee uttered, showing no remorse for her unlikely slip-up.

Feeling the tension starting to build being in Renee's presence, Ashley just turned to walk away leaving her to sit by herself to drown in her own personal pool of self-loathing. Some people just don't care about their actions or take responsibility for them, they'd rather just sulk and close themselves off from the world. Returning to the other end of the dugout, she rejoins Holley J and a few of the other girls to cheer on their upcoming batters. Laying her head on her rested arms upon the railing, Ashley all of a sudden seems detached from what's going on around her, really bothered by Renee's complacent attitude. Usually vocal, cheering on her teammates, now finds herself just staring out into space ignoring everything and everyone around her, letting Renee's childish action get the best of her again, there is just something about that girl, her snotty behavior just gets under her skin. Thinking about what Jake said, she is not going to let her wreck the terrific game she is pitching and the only way to do that is to be the bigger person, not let Renee's actions dictate hers. Dominating the game so far, there is no reason to think she can't finish that way. Lost in the vastness of her own thoughts, the emitted sound of more clapping and cheering instantly snaps her out of her self-induced trance, bringing her attention back to the game, viewing one of girls sliding head first into home plate beating out the tag to score them another run. Once again the dugout erupts in joyful jubilation, Jake handing out high fives to the recent base runner returning from her face first dive into the dirt, small clouds of dust emanated from her uniform brushing herself off before entering the dugout where she is greeted with more high fives and hugs, Ashley being the general provider. The team needs Ashley to be focused, giving one hundred percent, every girl on the team knows anything less from her the team will falter and winning will become a struggle, having been the heart and soul of this team since she was a freshman. There are a few good players on this team, but she may have been the only real reason to watch this team back then, probably still is to this day.   Final inning is upon them, the girls return to the field for the last time in the game still holding a 3-1 lead. Ashley returns to the mound with a chance to end the game right here, three up three down, that is the plan her and Holley J discussed trotting back onto the field. Starting the season off with a win would be huge for Ashley and this team, something they have never done before and they are just three outs away from doing just that. Two down due to back to back strike outs from Ashley bringing her total to fourteen for the game, now with a chance to end it right here with the next batter. The opposing team is batting at the bottom of their order normally consisting of their weakest hitters. Ashley remembers the next batter coming to the plate, striking her out earlier in the game, even recalling every pitch she threw at her last at bat. What makes Ashley such a great pitcher is her ability to recollect every batters last at bat, to where she could replay the whole sequence in her head, reminding her of what worked and what didn't. Holley J is the same way too, that's why they are a perfect combo for pitcher and catcher, playing off each other perfectly, out manning the batter 2-1. The batter steps into the batter's box, a right hander, a petit girl who is the opposing team's left fielder. Holley J figures what worked earlier should work again, sending Ashley the sign giving her déjà vu repeating the pattern from the girl's earlier at bat. Five pitches into this at bat, the batter has two strikes and two balls, the last pitch fouled off, Holley J thinks it's time for an off speed pitch flashing the sign for. In agreeance Ashley gives her the nod, winding up to make the throw. Slight fatigue setting into her arm, the pitch comes out of her hand rather late and slightly off target. The batter catches wind of the off speed pitch, swinging when it comes into range, sending a high fly ball deep into centerfield in Renee's direction once again, this time getting a good jump on the ball, able to keep sight of it through the sunlight thanks to the tinted vision of her sunglasses, jogging casually to get underneath it where it falls securely into in mitt ending the game.

An elated Ashley pumps her fist in victory before being swarmed at the mound by Holley J and few other of her teammates. Jake and the girls located in the dugout come onto the field to celebrate the teams win, greeted with a standing ovation from the rambunctious spectators filling the bleachers. Lining up to shake hands with their opponent headed by Ashley, followed closely behind by Holley J, all the girls gave high fives, handshakes or even the occasional hug with Jake filling up the rear. Ashley received many praises from a lot of the girls on the other team regarding her pitching performance, especially from the other team's coach wishing her good luck in the future. After the showing of sportsmanship, all the girls scattered to either meet up with friends or family residing in the crowd or just hung out by the dugout before heading back to the locker room to shower and change. Holley J's parents couldn't make this game because of work, but are usually here when they can be, leaving her to hang out with Ashley amongst all the commotion. Ashley hates watching the end game interactions between everybody, it signifies her better world is coming to an end, having to return to the real world becomes imminent. Still being congratulated by random players and a few spectators that happen to spill out onto the field, she spotted Jake talking to a couple older men, both of which were wearing tan khakis pants with plain red polo shirts, viewing their verbal exchange as friendly and productive, at one point many of the on lookers making up the crowd made their way over to Jake to ask him for an apparent autograph, explaining the overabundance of people attending the game, how often does a former big leaguer coach high school softball. The friendly chatting continued between Jake and the two men, the opposing team gathered their things so they could head for their team bus. Making eye contact with Ashley who was hanging out with Holley J by the dugout, Jake sends her a smile eagerly waving her over to join him and his two visitors. Not wanting to keep them waiting, Ashley hurries over to accept Jake's invitation, an excited Holley J watches from afar knowing already the implications of the small get to together. Jake introduces Ashley to the two men, shaking hands with the gentlemen receiving heavy commendations for her pitching performance, letting her know they have heard of her, admitting to have been following her through her high school career, explaining the original scouts she had spoken to before are no longer affiliated with their school. Graciously accepting their compliments with a smile, some friendly conversation ensued, the highlight being the story of how their school at one time tried to recruit Jake back in high school. The interview portion commenced, listening to their questions, answering them as thorough and well spoken as possible, this isn't her first rodeo with dealing with scouts, knowing there is more to it than just your athletic abilities, they are also interested in your personality and what you plan on studying at the collegiate level. Giving them the same answer she has given other scouts before them, responding with art, wants to study art in some form, giving the two men a brief history of how she likes to paint in her spare time. Jake stood by, watching Ashley handle the two men like a pro, listening to her precise and clear answers to their questions, her great posture along with her charming attitude was the quintessential recipe for winning them over. It was no mystery the two men were very impressed with her, relaying the college softball team could definitely use a pitcher like her, asking her if she would be interested in taking a tour of the campus at some point, something she was never offered before, to see if it is somewhere she thinks she would be happy attending, also throwing in for good measures the school has an excellent art program. Admirably accepting their offer, Ashley received business cards from both men containing their phone numbers in case she ever had any future questions. Letting her know if she has a great season and the team keeps winning, there is no reason for this not to be a done deal. When it came to the subject of the eventual paperwork, Jake chimed in suggesting they send it through email reassuring there would be no mysterious disappearances. A delighted Ashley totally agreed, the men complied with the request, ending the meeting with more handshakes and commenting they'll be in touch. Ashley watched the two men who hold the keys to her getting away from everything is wrong with her life walk away, cementing what she already knew, this is by far the most important season of her life, in more ways than one. Feeling elated and nervous at the same time, not wanting to get too excited, the team they beat today wasn't even one of the better teams on their schedule, with so many games left anything can happen, but she knows this team is different now, they are well coached and better prepared, but if she has to single handedly go out and try to win every game on her own, she is willing to do it. Winning this first game was big regardless who the opponent was, it was surely a confidence booster for the rest of the girls on the team, knowing they can do it and they are better than they always thought. With everything she knows is at stake, Ashley wouldn't want to be doing anything else in the world, this is who she is, who she deserves to be, once she steps off that field she becomes that person she hates the most, the person she waits to kill so she is out of her life forever.

She can see her future in the distance, just needs the courage and guts to get through the fire to get there, a challenge she is willing to accept.

The two men now gone, a curious Holley J comes running up to Ashley and Jake to get the scoop on the private conversation, her energetic and bubbly mannerisms informed the two she was about to hear what she probably already knows. Ashley relaying the news, an overjoyed Holley J embraces her warmly, jumping up and down in excitement. Jake looking on, would have thought Holley J was more excited about the news than Ashley, smiling viewing the two girls having their moment. He coached his first real game to the best possible conclusion, feeling all the emotions and anxiousness he did when he played just from a different perspective. Watching the girls play today reminded him of how much he misses playing, the thrill and intensity of athletic competition he held so dear to his heart, now being consumed through the actions of his players. It's the next best thing, if he can't be out there doing what he loves, then he will live it through the knowledge he pours into these girls, their success is his success, he may have left the game, but the game never left him, like reliving high school all over again during and after the game, only a different gender was on display. Observing the girls' excitement with their victory and the postgame festivities, really took Jake back to a time in his life when things were much simpler, baseball was always easy to him, it just came naturally, the only reason he practiced is because he loved the game so much, all that extra effort and hard work just intensified his talent making him stand out more and more. When Ashley was talking to the scouts, he recalled all his visits and interactions with the college lackeys, there were many, most of the time he didn't need to say a word, they were too busy offering him everything under the sun, some of which were against NCAA rules, yet they wanted him bad enough to risk it. The feeling of being wanted that once surrounded him on a daily basis faded away after his career ended, is now being resurrected working with these girls. That chapter of his life is over and has been trying to accept it, but it's not going to stop him from reminiscing from time to time, especially if he is going to be reminded of it almost every day.

The girls finally part from each other, Holley J suggested the two of them go out and celebrate, proposing dinner at their favorite eatery with her picking up the tab. Ashley who wasn't the least bit surprised at her reaction to the news or the offering of a celebratory meal, the two of them are always ready to acknowledge each other's personal achievements. Holley J was the same way last season when scouts were talking to Ashley, these are big key moments in their lives and they both want to be there to celebrate with each other. Wanting to take her up on her offer, anything would be better than going home, Ashley and her aunt not on good terms even worse than normal, yet feels obligated to do what she is supposed to just to keep her off her back, when she gets this scholarship it will only be a few more months of her bullshit and then hopefully never having to see her again, but she didn't want to disappoint Holley J who by the expression on her face, really wanted to do this. It was still early enough for her to go home, do what she has to do and meet up later, spending time with Holley J repeatedly puts her in a good place, that is if she doesn't get an unwanted text from Razz between now and then. Ashley lets Holley J know she is in for the exclusive commemoration, just has to go home and deal with a few things. A cheerful Holley J speed claps her hands together in eagerness for their night together. Still standing by as the girls plan their evening, a smiling Jake gives the girls one last recognition of a game well played.

"Well, it seems like you girls have your evening planned," said Jake. "Holley J, can I talk to Ashley alone for a minute?"

Holley J complies to giving them their privacy, telling Ashley she will see her in the locker room before leaving the field.

"So much for Renee not having your back, huh," Jake noted jokingly.

"Ha-ha, that was a routine catch, anyone could have made it," responded Ashley with a friendly smirk on her face.

"So how are you feeling?" Jake asked.

"To be perfectly honest with you, I don't know what I'm feeling. I've had scouts talk to me before but this time it seemed different, I can't explain it," proclaims Ashley.

"I understand, I just hope you understand this doesn't mean you have to think you have to be better than you already are. You are going to get better, that's a given, you just have to play your game, be yourself and not worry about what everyone else is doing, eye on the prize. Only one person can screw this up and that's you. They talked to you because they liked what they saw, not because of what they are hoping they are going to see," Jake stated.

The more Ashley listens to Jake speak, the more it has an effect on her, it's a learning experience every time words vacate in mouth, not just a coach, but a true mentor, a real friend, someone her life has needed, someone to help navigate her through the moments in life where she has seemed to have lost her way, she can only hope her coaches at the next level can have as great an impact on her as he does.

"So signing autographs must not be something new to you," remarked Ashley.

"I wouldn't make a big deal out of it, a lot of people love to live in the past," Jake said.

"But you are kind of famous," replied Ashley.

"I was famous, those days are over," Jake informed.

"Still looks like you have a lot of fans, though," said Ashley.

"Let me tell you something about fame, you are only as famous as what you are currently providing to the public," Jake educates. "So that was nice of Holley J to offer to take you out to celebrate," he added.

"Yeah, that's Holley J, that's why she is the best," replied Ashley, feeling bad the plans were made in his presence. "Did you want to come, I mean you are just as much a part of this as she is. I can call Holley J, I'm sure she wouldn't mind."

"No, no, this is something you two should do alone, I have stuff to care of anyway, buts thanks, though," he replies with a warm smile. "I can walk you to the locker room."

Leaving the field, the last of what populated the area for a couple hours, side by side they walk, engaged in friendly conversation, having left the scene of their first victory together.

It's the night before her second outing, Ashley was called into work, the one thing she was hoping wouldn't happen the night before a game. Arriving, the club seemed extra busy, many girls who weren't scheduled were called in to handle the load. The main stage was going nonstop along with extra pole dancing continuously entertaining the roaring suitors from the various mini stages. Waitresses were working in overdrive to try and keep up with the steady demand of mixed drinks that were being ordered and delivered at a consistent pace, their trays full of hardcore beverages, tip glasses overflowing with cash. Every table and booth seemed to be occupied, even the bar area was home to a mass of heavy drinkers, the lap dance rooms went hardly without a break. Razz who routinely stands watching the main floor was nowhere to be found, last seen in the girls' dressing room assigning girls to paid private one on one times, Ashley being one of them. Having already danced earlier, drawing her usual large crowd of horny men, there is unfailingly a man or two willing to pony up the dough to live there wildest fantasy. Making herself up in her customary look when it comes to makeup, outfits are sometimes requested, tonight her client asked for the school girl look, a black and red plaid skirt, a plain white blouse tied in a knot just above her naval, knee high white stockings with black loafers, hair tied into two long braids. The dressing room had girls coming in and out of it all night, Razz stood close by observing all the girls getting ready seeming very agitated, the intensity showing on his face was immensely intimidating to his female employees, causing them to walk on eggshells, worried they may set him off. Rumor was one of the girls never showed up for her shift, prompting Razz to send a couple of his goons to go out looking for her, one of the worst violations to his rules a girl can perpetrate. Every girl there could only imagine the discipline he will rain upon her, specifically Ashley who has seen and been a part of his form of authority, secretly hoping they never find her. Finding it hard to concentrate, her mind elsewhere, full of thoughts about her game the next day, Ashley heads to meet up with her client, walking past Razz who grabs her arm halting her in her tracks.

"You look amazing, Show Horse," Razz softly whispers in her ear, reaching one hand under her skirt to squeeze one of her bare ass cheeks, disclosing she isn't wearing any underwear, giving her a gentle kiss on the lips. "You got me so hard right now. Later," he whispers, softly kissing her on the forehead before letting her go.

Walks away feeling the heat from Razz' eyes staring at her from behind, knowing what he meant when he said later, her night won't be finished after her client, shifting her thoughts to the upcoming unknown with Razz, ever since that night she pleasured him to avoid a physical lashing, his advances have become more and more frequent. Still avoiding intercourse with his prized femme fatale, Razz' claim to sexual ecstasy is a good old-fashioned blow job, which Ashley perceives she will be providing later. The thought of it turns her stomach, having to put her mouth back where probably hundreds of other girls' lips have made their mark, likely explaining the bad taste it leaves in her trap, but knowing Razz it presumably won't end there, with his compulsion for erotica anything is possible. Making her way to the lower level of the club,

Ashley strolls down the hallway to room five where her next mystery client awaits, her bare under carriage feeling the chill of the basement under her skirt, it was requested no underwear stipulating the patron is interested in fornication. Coming up on the room, the hallway was quiet, the sound proofing of the rooms makes walking down the hallway alone sort of a creepy experience, all the other rooms were hosting sexual activity. Opening the door to room five, Ashley enters to find a young man, roughly in his late twenties, sitting up on the bed completely naked with the all-too-familiar self-approving look across his face.

"It's about time you showed up," remarked the young man, looking Ashley up and down getting excited. "You are fucking hot! Bring that sweet ass over here."

Already not too fond of the young man's attitude and tone, she walks over to join him, sitting next to him on the edge of the bed, not the most attractive guy in the world, but not ugly, clean shaven with hardly any hair on his upper body which was a bit on the chunky side.

"What do you want to do?" Ashley asked noticing his penis is still flaccid.

"Oh, I want this school girl on top of me for some extra credit," he replied.

"Your dick is not even hard," she noted, not too impressed with what he's packing either.

"Then do something about it," he remarked placing his hands behind his head in an arrogant, relaxing manner.

Rolling her eyes in annoyance, she leans over to the nightstand next to the bed, opening the drawer to grab a tube of KY Jelly, squeezing a good amount onto her hand before returning it to the drawer. Rubbing the jelly on her hands, she proceeds to stroke his limp penis in an attempt to get it erect, stroking faster and faster, harder and harder with little improvement, her forearms beginning to tire from the rapid arm movement. The young man watches Ashley work his shaft, the friction begins feeling really good, closing his eyes letting out a few low moans. Starting to feel the penis get harder, she starts massaging the head bringing out even louder moans. Now fully erect and hoping he might finish before they even start, she quickly reenters the drawer of the nightstand to grab a condom. Tearing open the package, she places it on his barely five-inch tool, slightly lifting up her skirt to straddle over him planting his erection inside her. Riding the young man who is in a state of euphoria, slides his hands up her silky smooth thighs as she rubs her body against his.

Letting out even louder moans, he works he hands under her skirt to grab her bare ass just as he climaxes, a thunderous roar exits his throat, tilting his pelvis upwards and clutching her buttocks extra tight in reaction to the explosive sensation. Though there physically, her mind remained somewhere else, barley responding to the death grip put on her back side, just happy she lucked out with another minute man. Despite the fact he didn't do anything, a few beads of sweat trickled down his face while he laid there breathing heavy, a pretentious grin appeared on his face as if he was Don Juan. Removing herself from on top of him, without saying another word, grabbed some paper toweling from off the nightstand to clean off her hands and left the room.

Razz had ordered Ashley to come to his office when she was finished with her couple clients, opening his door she is greeted to him shirtless, smoking a cigarette, standing over a girl whose limp body laid on the floor topless, her hair a mess and her face covered in blood. An uneasy feeling came over Ashley, coming to the conclusion this must be the girl who never showed up for her shift. Seeing another girl draped across the floor, beaten unconscious, treated more like an animal rather than a human being, sent shivers down her spine, that could be her one day. One of Razz' guards standing nearby who must have witnessed the unfortunate drubbing, stood like a statue showing very little emotion as if in some sort of trance, his security has always seemed to behave like mindless, unexpressive robots. Razz locking eyes with Ashley, tells his guard to remove the battered girl.

"Just taking care of some business," Razz states, wiping blood off his knuckles with some paper toweling. "I'm glad you showed up, Show Horse, that was good thinking."

The guard picks up the girl off the floor carrying her out of the office, Ashley got a closeup view of her face as the guard pasted by, one of her eyes was swollen shut with blood coming out of her nose and mouth. Razz stuck his hand out inviting Ashley to take it, the smoke from his cigarette cast a small cloud in front of his face. Like an instinctive reflex action, she placed her hand upon his, feeling the course texture of his calluses with her fingertips. Hand in hand, Razz guides Ashley to the couch where they sit side by side very closely, putting out his cigarette placing a hand on her knee, just the touch of him makes her skin crawl, a reaction she never gets from her clients since she doesn't know them personally, it's a totally different uneasy sensation she gets from the touch of total strangers.

"We're going to have company soon, but I wanted you to myself for a few minutes," Razz said starting to kiss her neck. "You taste so good, Show Horse."

Closing her eyes in disgust feeling his wet tongue and lips dampen her skin, continuing the lustful kissing to her naval then her thighs, completing his sensual smooching of all her exposed skin, Razz gently grabs her by the face giving a few soft kisses on the lips.

"I want you to take this beautiful mouth of yours and relieve me of all this tension," he demanded, rubbing her shiny, lip gloss covered lips with his thumb.

He sat back on the couch unbuttoning his jeans, pulling them down just enough to pull out his rock hard erection. This is what Ashley dreaded all night, something she knows is going to become a regular occurrence, he could have this done by any of the girls, but he chose his prize. Looking down at his extra veiny phallus, she slowly leans over grasping the shaft with her hand inserting the tip and then some into her mouth, violently massaging the exterior with her tongue while working in a constant up and down motion, swallowing deep in an effort to get him to finish as quickly as possible. The sounds of pleasure resonated from his intense excitement, giving her audio ques he is getting close, granting her more incentive to work her mouth more intensely over his shaft. With a good grip on the base she can feel the vibrations of the excretion fluid making its way to the top, preparing to pull off, Razz presses down on the back of her head discharging in her throat. It felt like a fire hose went off in her mouth, pulling off, she valiantly tries to hold the pearl jam between her cheeks immediately running for the office bathroom, leaving the door open, hovering over the sink emptying out the waste, spilling out of her mouth like a faucet, drinking a cup of water, swishing it rapidly to try cleaning out any access residue, spitting into the sink when finished. Still had some of the horrid taste of the seaman in her mouth, having to relive a small taste every time she swallowed, frantically releasing more saliva into the sink wishing there was mouthwash available.

"Show Horse," calls Razz.

Ashley looks up into the bathroom mirror seeing the reflection of Razz still sitting on the couch, catching a glimpse of one of the other girls standing there wearing an all-black silk, button-down nighty. Leaves the bathroom not knowing what sick, perverted thoughts Razz had in mind. Walking back over to reunite with Razz and his newest guest, she thought about just running as fast as she humanly can for the door hoping to make her escape, an attempt that would be tremendously high risk, a risk that could conclude with her ending up like the girl from earlier or worse, a thought immediately erased from her mind, mainly because she has a game tomorrow.

"Am I free to go?" Ashley asked, maybe getting lucky and just walks out of there.

"Not quite yet, Show Horse, the party is just beginning," answers Razz lighting up another cigarette. "Have you met Amber before?"

Responds shaking her head no, glancing over at the young lady, her long wavy blonde hair, her small diamond stud housed in her nose lightly sparkling in the light, sporting a small grin on her face.

"That's too bad, because you two are about to become very familiar with one another," Razz responded, cutting up a few lines of cocaine on his coffee table, the small black box full of the white powder rests nearby. "I just hope the show will be as good as the view," he said gesturing to his latest guest.

The young woman walks towards Ashley unbuttoning her nighty uncovering her large, implanted breasts, black satin panties and a large tattoo of a coiled up cobra on the left side of her torso, the same small grin remains on her face. A bewildered Ashley eyes this practically naked woman inching closer to her, fearing already what she knows Razz wants to see. Stopping directly in front of Ashley, the slightly taller young woman leans in to begin kissing her on the lips, gently caressing Ashley's hips with her hands. Struggling to force herself to kiss back, the taste of a female's lips upon hers being very awkward, almost sickening, the kissing became more intense with the young woman's tongue penetrating Ashley's lips. Razz snorts a line of coke observing the two girls go at it, leaning back on the couch exhaling smoke into the air, his bloodshot eyes are glued to the action happening before him. Becoming more aroused, the young woman starts caressing Ashley's body more sensually, grabbing one of her hands, guiding it to the top of her panties, placing it down and inside. Freaked out, Ashley pulls her hand away ending the make-out session.

"Razz, I can't do this, I'm not attracted to girls," Ashley states in a soft nervous tone, looking over at Razz leaned back on the couch, his arms resting upon the top, cigarette dangling from his mouth, a look of sheer disappointment and anger displays on his face. There hasn't been many things in her life she has been certain about, but her non attraction to females is one of them.

Having always known she is attracted to the opposite sex, even after all the sexual and physical abuse she has sustained by their hands, at times she had a suspicion her history with men would alter her sexual orientation in some way, has never even been curious. Girls can be pretty and have good style in her eyes, just not to the point where she gets weak in the knees or gets the goo-goo eyes, girls are just girls to her nothing more, if any girl would have brought it out of her it would have been Holley J, yet she loves her like you would love a best friend. This fascination with males loving to watch two girls sexually pleasure each other has become mainstream, most porn sites feature girl on girl activity which is the ultimate aphrodisiac for most men, Razz is surely no different, but he picked the wrong girl to play out his erotic escapade.

"I don't give a fuck what you are attracted to. I expect you to do what I want," Razz declares sitting forward on the couch. "Don't disappoint me, Show Horse."

"Relax, hun, you may even like it," the young woman added, licking Ashley on the side of the face, taking off her panties seating herself in the chair nearby, spreading her legs wide open unmasking her clean shaven vagina, rubbing high and deep on the inside of her thighs.

Peering at the young woman sitting in the chair spread eagle, her head laid back baring the smooth skin of her neck, playfully squeezing her own breast, the sight of her uncovered pussy deemed menacing, territory for which was to remain unknown to Ashley other than her own. Recognizing what she is being asked to do, the sheer sight of her genitals makes her feel queasy, would rather give head to another client than to put her face between another females legs. Dropping down to her knees getting in position to perform something she thought she would never have to do, Ashley swallowed hard bringing her face closer to the exposed lips, a ripe smell permeates out of the unprotected area which looks beat up and mutilated, evidence this girl has been working for Razz a lot longer than she has. Her eyes tear up swiftly pulling herself back.

"Razz, I'm sorry, I can't do this," Ashley remarked, a stream of tears sliding down her face.

Unhappy and agitated, Razz urgently gets up from the couch hustling over to an upset Ashley. Standing over her he grabs one of her pigtails, yanking on it causing her to wince.

"Now you listen to me, you get this bitch to cum or I'll make you bleed," threatens Razz into her ear, feeling the heat from his cigarette resting centimeters from her face, the smoke irritating her already watery eyes, releasing her hair, throwing her head forward, Razz returns to the couch to snort another line.

"I'm waiting," Razz announces, his soulless eyes leering in Ashley's direction

He isn't kidding around, when he is high he becomes more malicious, just waiting for an excuse to enact physical harm on her. Having no choice but to undertake his demands, despite not having any idea what to do to satisfy a female, this is all unknown territory to her, she doesn't even masturbate, her sexual desires have all been ruined courtesy of her past. It doesn't help she is completely grossed out with what she has been ordered to do, afraid her stomach might not be able to handle it, gags easily to edible food she doesn't like, imagine what the taste of an overused snatch could trigger. All this just enhances what she already knows, Razz stores a cold, black heart in his chest, could have had any other girl perform his erotic exploit, with so many girls on his payroll there was sure to be a few that swing both ways, but it's his infatuation with Ashley and his twisted hunger for watching those do what deems disturbing to them, where he gets his ultimate jollies.

Still reeling from Razz' recent threat, Ashley puts her face closer to the target area, her eyes shedding a few more tears, feeling like she was about to put her face in a bear trap, the genitalia looking more and more intimidating as it creeps up on her. Not totally in the dark with the absence gestures men frequently throw her way, she formed a V with her two fingers placing them on either side of the lips, pressing down while spreading them open, slowly using her tongue in an up and down, swirling motion, holding back a couple gag reflexes. The young woman roughly squeezes her breasts letting out a few sultry moans in accordance with the action down below. Feeling the gyrations in her loins, hearing the passionate groans escape into the air, Ashley sucks on her vagina like a sucker, fighting back more gaging. With the young woman showing a state of sexual pleasure through her bodily movement and verbal cries, it was time to stimulate her from the inside. Wetting two fingers with her mouth, Ashley penetrates the vulva, getting her small fingers as deep inside as she can, the moist, squishy texture of the inner lips dampened the skin of her fingers. Proceeding to slowly motion her fingers in a steady back and forth manner, the young woman gyrates in uncontrollable pleasure, pitching the hard nipples on her breast in unison with her heavy breathing. Tickling the roof of her insides before thrusting her fingers in and out more vigorously, bringing more of a visual response from the young woman who squirms turbulently in the chair, violently embracing her breasts letting out louder moans of pleasure. Razz looks on in delight, his reddened eyes fixated on the action happening before him, smoothly taking occasional drags from his cigarette, blowing the access smoke into the air. Anticipating she has the young woman close to climax, Ashley fights back another gag reflex, tasting the upchuck impulse burning her esophagus, exits her now swampy fingers to tongue the young woman's clitoris. Flicking her tongue aggressively at the bean shaped perineal appendage, the young woman screams as ejaculatory fluid squirts out into Ashley's face causing her to flinch back, tasting some of the released liquid as some entered her open mouth, bringing her cough with a dry-heave. Her convulsing body sprays more fluid like a yard sprinkler, Razz grins watching the young woman leave a small puddle on his hardwood office floor. Ashley backed out of the way of her body pyrotechnics, seating herself on the floor with a few more tears streaming down her face, having just completed one of many uncomfortable and disgusting acts of her life. Razz sits forward on the couch performing a slow, sarcastic clap in appreciation to the girl's performance, with the cigarette still dangling from his mouth, always a fan of girl on girl action especially when he has a front row seat.

"I knew you wouldn't let me down, Show Horse," Razz states, removing himself from the couch to walk over to Ashley, putting a hand out to help her to her feet.

Hesitate at first, wiping away the few tears with her hands before taking on Razz' help. Pulling her up, Razz tugs her close, the smoke from the cigarette initiates burning in her eyes.

"Maybe next time I'll be watching you messing up my floor," remarks Razz, putting his hand under Ashley's skirt, gently rubbing her genitals, slightly squirms in revulsion wanting to pull his hand away, triggering memories of every male paw that made its way down to her forbidden territory seemed to flash before her eyes all at once, suddenly feeling lost in her own body, more tears ran down her face the more he massaged her under carriage. Razz has done things like this before to her, yet she never felt this reaction, the muscles in her upper thighs tensed up to where she thought they were about to burst. Getting his fill, Razz pulls his hand back out, placing it under his nose to get a whiff of her mysterious essence.

"Smells like heaven," Razz says, grabbing her with the same hand under her jaw line pulling her closer, the cigarette now inches from her face. "Until the next time."

Releasing Ashley from his grip, the two stare into each other's eyes for a brief moment trying to read each other's minds, not wavering for a second, she quickly left the office. Hearing his office door slam behind him, Razz walks over to the young woman still draped over the chair, legs open, breasts remained exposed and breathing heavy, waiting for the sensation in her body to dissipate.

"You going to clean this fucking mess up?" Razz asked in a stern, loud voice.

Finding herself home in the upstairs bathroom wearing a pair of white panties and black sports bra, vomiting and coughing, the tiny amount of makeup on her is smeared, her hair drooping over her face into the bowl, not caring if any of it catches some of the puke spilling out of her mouth. The more she thought about what she did tonight, the more sick to her stomach she felt, can still taste the young woman on her tongue, wanting to brush her teeth so bad, but once she entered the bathroom she found herself on the cold tiled floor face first in the toilet unable to hold down the disgust from earlier. Bad enough she has to conduct these various sexual actions on the opposite sex, but to do it to her own made her feel the most dirty and distasteful. Finally finished emptying every last drop stored in her gut, Ashley closed the toilet lid, laying her cheek on the soft, shag carpet like lid cover, bursting into tears. Crying uncontrollably, hoping her aunt doesn't bang on the locked door, even though Ashley made sure she was asleep before locking herself in the bathroom, however when investigating the state of her aunt it was revealed she wasn't alone, her new guy friend was looking awfully cozy snuggled up against her, his arm draped over her, the two of them snoring simultaneously, she didn't even notice the extra vehicle parked in the driveway when she returned home, so focused on just getting herself inside as fast as she can. Collapsed on the small bathroom floor crying, her tears now dampening the lid cover, she never felt more alone in her life, the tiny powder room started to feel like a cell and all the walls were closing in on her. After all she had been through tonight, all she could think about was her game tomorrow afternoon, how at the moment the way she feels, would never be able to pitch a game, could barely bring herself to her feet, completely drained vomiting all the energy out of her body. She has to be hundred percent tomorrow, these games have become the most important moments of her life right now and as dreadful as she feels, must gather what little energy she has left to clean herself up and get her ass to bed to hopefully sleep all of this off. Flushing the toilet before bringing herself to her feet, extremely tired, staggers over to the bathroom sink getting a birds eye view of herself in the mirror, her hands clasping either side of the porcelain sink holding herself up peering at her reflection. The makeup she was wearing is more smudged due to her latest tear fall, her hair is all frazzled, parts of it are sticking up and out, mainly from its time in those tight pigtails, she couldn't remember a time when she saw herself look more defeated, staring at a face she didn't recognize, a face that scared her, wanting to believe that wasn't what she looked like, yet the mirror acted like a screen showing its viewer a glimpse of what the future holds for them, but she was gazing at a version of her in the here and now, the bathroom's bad lighting didn't help matters, the sight of herself was enough to bring her to tears again, looking how she felt, disgusting and nasty, like a cheap floozy that's constantly being used and thrown in the gutter where she belongs. Wanting to stop looking at the monster appearing before her, Ashley turned on the faucet releasing a flow of cold water, filling her hands, splashing it against her face, the chill of the water against her skin sent a quick shock to her system. Opening the medicine cabinet to grab a bottle of ibuprofen, dumping a few pills into her hand to take to combat the slight headache she has been dealing with for most of the night. Grabs the small glass resting in one corner of the sink filling it, tossing the pills into her mouth, sending the water in after to wash them down, turns off the faucet and closes the medicine cabinet, drying her face on the towel hanging on the nearby rack. A shower would be ideal right now, her hair probably smells like puke and smoke and after tonight could definitely use a douche, but is too exhausted, just wanting to go pass out on her bed, deal with everything in the morning, already past one, would like to get at least six hours sleep. Turning off the light in the bathroom, Ashley exits into the dimly lit hallway to drag her dog-tired body to her room, sliding her bare feet along the hardwood flooring of the hallway, her eye lids become heavier looking out into the mostly blackness of the corridor, falling asleep as shuffles along. Hurrying herself onward, afraid she might collapse right there in the hallway, she makes it to her bedroom where she enters the pitch dark area, closing the door behind her proceeding into the darkness, falling over, blacking out onto her bed.

Seven games into the season, Jake and the girls are proudly still undefeated, with every victory seemingly more impressive than the last one, anchored by Ashley's incredible pitching which has become the talk of the high school sports world all over the country, her statistics thus far include three pitched one hitters with two coming back to back, averaging ten strikeouts per game to go along with her section leading six home runs at the plate, the next girl on that list is Renee with five, making regular weekly photo appearances in the sports section of the local paper. These accolades are nothing new to her, but appear to stand out more in part to the team's continuous winning ways, she is on pace to have her best season ever and it couldn't have come at a better time. The past few weeks for Ashley have been a whirl wind, felling like her mind has been going in a thousand different directions at once, has been working more than usual at Razz' meaning many late nights cutting into her much needed sleep, also been affected by the resurgence of her nightmares. Running on pure adrenaline every day, between all the sex, school, her chores at home and softball practices and games, she is afraid her body is being over worked, heading for a physical breakdown, also hasn't had any time to paint, something she has been really missing. It doesn't help her relationship with her aunt is getting worse by the day and her new guy friend has made several passes at her. One such incident involved him walking pass Ashley's open bedroom door naked supporting an erection, throwing her a wink as he proceeded by. Trying not to engage with her aunt whenever possible, just the sight of her nowadays brings her to a level of anger and hatred she can't explain. The workload at Razz' has become ever more rigorous, sometimes servicing as many as five guys in a night, resulting in a recent trip to the gynecologist sparking some controversy when her doctor questioned the state of her vagina, prompting Ashley to give the answer that she masturbates a lot, add in Razz can't seem to keep his skeevy hands off of her lately, looking for head from her whenever he can get it. Quality time with Holley J has suffered, only able to see her at school or softball, barely having enough time to text her out in the real world, let alone see her, of all the bullshit going on lately is what is killing Ashley the most. The time being missed to hang out with her best friend, this is when she could really use Holley J's company the most. Living this double life is starting to become harder and harder on her where she just wants to come clean, yet knows the risk outweighs the reward, an internal struggle she has been dealing with ever since she started working at Razz' club, it kills her every time she looks Holley J in the eyes and has to lie right to her face. Often wonders if Holley J suspects she is hiding something from her, knowing Holley J is the type of person to call people out if she is suspicious of anything, that moment has yet to come, as far as Holley J knows, there are no secrets between them, a situation haunting her every day because she knows the truth. Bothering her that she knows all of Holley J's secrets, the time she made out with a substitute teacher after school sophomore year when they were alone in the classroom supposedly working on extra credit, to the time she explored her sexuality junior year when she slept with a cheerleader she knew from another school, a secret that if her parents found out, she feared they might disown her. Ashley has always questioned her loyalty to Holley J by keeping secrets from her, pondering if she has ever returned the favor of being a good friend.

Jake has remained himself during this time, a teacher as well as a coach, introducing new practice drills and techniques to the girls which test them mentally as well as physically. A lot of what he has inaugurated may seem unorthodox to many people, but like Jake would tell the girls, "*behind every dark cloud there is a blue sky,*" explaining the harder you work, the easier winning becomes. Every practice has become a new adventure for the team, everything he incorporates was shown to him when he was their age just with his special twist on it. The girls' favorite so far was when he borrowed one of the school buses, driving them all to the beach where he had the girls run into the water with their practice uniforms on barefoot, that was waist high to help build strength and speed in their legs from the liquid resistance, also bringing along a bucket of old worn out softballs not worthy of retrieval if they were to get lost, for him to hit from the beach to a group of a few girls standing in the water, chasing them down, trying to catch any balls hit in their vicinity, meanwhile fighting off small crashing waves and the slight chill of the lake water. Every girl at some point got a turn at the exercise, it was a grueling and tiresome experience, yet everyone had fun with it, watching and cheering as girls struggled to pursue the fly balls, some falling into the water, others diving into the air to make the spectacular catch, which many girls did, including Ashley. After Jake emptied the bucket he let the girls enjoy themselves before they left, all running into the water frolicking, splashing each other having a good time. Seeing the smiles and laughter on their faces let Jake know this team would be willing to do anything he told them no matter how intense the practices would get, knowing the results speak for themselves. Standing on the beach barefoot, arms folded, baseball cap on backwards, close enough to feel occasional drops coming off the splashes created by the girls, the soft sand building up between his toes, the sun on the horizon reflecting off the water mixed with a cool lake breeze and the sound of the waves crashing onto the shore line while observing the girls through his dark sunglasses as they played around in the water like a bunch of little kids, a large smile graced Jake's face. He hasn't had a moment like this in a very long time, not since his playing days, everything appeared to be in the right place at the right time, where his recent past felt like nothing more than a distant memory. His moment of personal euphoria was interrupted by the sudden touch of many feminine fingers tugging at him, led by Ashley, who was pulling on his forearms while Holley J and a couple other girls were pushing him from behind attempting to get him to join them in the water. Jake put on a little bit of a struggle feeling those many cool, damp hands on his skin and through his clothing, his feet being dragged through the sand, even if he wasn't willing to oblige, he didn't think he would have a choice, the force the girls were pulling and pushing with would have been too overpowering for him to resist anyway. Feeling the soles of his feet scraping atop the shoreline, Jake looked at a smiling Ashley continuing to pull him towards the water, her hair down and wet, some strains lay harmlessly across her face, encouraging him to join them. His feet finally meet the water, not hiding his open expression with the system shock to the chilly temperature of the lake, Jake playfully picked up Ashley under her legs, jumping out with her into the water, the rest of the girls targeted their splashes in his direction. Ashley and the girls knew they were officially in the water together as a complete team, unbeknownst to everyone, off in the distant, Renee sat wet and alone, hugging her knees by the shore in her shorts and sports bra, peering steadily at everyone through her sunglasses. Continuing to enjoy herself with the team and Jake, horsing around in the waist deep, cool lake water, she started to recollect how much different her life feels since Jake has become her coach, being treated like a normal player, not just some nice piece of ass, for the first time she has been on this team, she doesn't feel threatened to be blackmailed into doing something she never wanted to do just to be able to do what she knew she had to do to get where she wants to go, that feeling of freedom alone may be her greatest victory this season. Also couldn't remember a time she had more fun at a practice, no matter how intense or demanding Jake's practices are, he always has a knack to make them fun at the same time. Splashing around in the water with the warm sun beating down on her shoulders, looking around at the other girls doing the same, watching Holley J take off her practice jersey revealing her white sports bra, holding it up while she twirls it in the air yelling for the rest of the girls to do the same. All the girls living in the moment, Ashley and the others imitated Holley J's act of independence, taking off their jerseys as a sign of team unity, standing in the water wearing nothing other than their sports bras which are damp like a wet t-shirt displaying an outline of what rest beneath, holding their jerseys. Using the moment to again unite the team, Ashley raised one fist in the air, the rest of the girls quickly followed along, Jake looking on pleased with the girls act of unification, yet felt the girls were baring more than he needed to see, blew his whistle ending practicing for the day. Like a herd of obedient cattle, the girls exited the water carrying their soaked jerseys to gather their things to head back to the bus, a still distant Renee removed herself from her inhabited little area, brushing off any sand populating her exposed skin, to join the rest of the team.

Driving the bus back to the school grounds, Jake threw the heat on full blast as everyone sat in their seats soaked and a bit cold, Ashley and Holley J sat together just behind Jake's driver's seat. It was an understandable silent drive back, the girls were exhausted and uncomfortable sitting in wet clothing, yet not one of them complained. The ones with the window seats just gazed at the outside world through the glass, while some of the others sat back in their seats with their eyes closed, a few of the girls conversed quietly amongst themselves. Renee sat alone in the back of the bus with one of her feet pressed up against the back of the seat in front of her, some white earbuds inserted to drown out any unwanted white noise, ignoring the rest happening to populate the bus. Glancing in the rear view mirror to see rows of drained faces, a picture of hard workers, Jake wanted to living up the drive back a bit, turning on what he assumed was the bus's radio, instantly filling the vehicle with outside noise coming from the cheap manufacturer's speakers, the current song playing caught the attention of all the girls, especially Holley J.

"Oh my God, I love this song," announced Holley J standing up in her seat, asking Jake to turn it up, the song petting her eardrums was Seal's *"Kiss from a Rose."* Jake honored her request giving the volume knob a quick turn, Holley J seemingly captivated by the playing music started singing along. Listening to vocal chops of their starting catcher belt out note after note with precise accuracy, the rest of the girls were inspired to join along, all standing or kneeling in their seats, everyone singing in unison with their lead singer Holley J. Renee removed an earbud to investigate what the rest of the girls were doing, not the least bit interested or impressed, rolling her eyes and returning her focus to the scenery flashing by outside her window.

The harmonic vocals of the team singing verse after verse brought a smile to Jake's face making the drive more relaxing, impressed the girls are familiar with a song that was popular when he was a kid, also amazed with the singing abilities coming from his players, sounding like he was transporting a choir disguised as a softball team. Ashley was the only girl still seated, her not being much of a singer, doesn't even like to sing when she is alone, rather one who likes to enjoy music by simply listening, letting the musical notes relax her like a soundwave massage. Having a front row seat to the concert abruptly coming on to the scene, Ashley enjoyed the soft, high pitch voices traveling throughout the bus. Unexpectedly taken by Holley J's public debut, never heard her sing around other people other than her, convinced she never would, maybe it's true what they say, certain music or songs can take over a person's soul leaving them helpless to the rhythms and beats filtering through their minds with the only alternative being to give in and let the music take control. Proud of Holley J for introducing the world to her hidden talent, something Ashley has been pressuring her to do since she discovered her angelic voice, maybe now facing her fear of singing around other people will inspire her to do it more often, Ashley thinks it's a waste to hide your gifts or abilities when they can open so many other doors in your life, if accompanied with the right work ethic and guidance, something she has been trying to persuade herself to do with her paintings. Though there are around twenty female voices circulating in the air,

Ashley finds herself blocking out the rest only concentrating on Holley J's, sitting beside her with a slight grin on her face, glancing up at the rear view mirror making eye contact with Jake's reflection, both greeting each other with a big smile. Only a few minutes from arriving back at school, the bus rides were reminiscent of Ashley's and Holley J's grade school years when they rode the bus together, always sitting with each other, always in the same seat, Ashley wondered if their old school bus still had their marking on it, when they wrote *"Ashley and Holley J best friends forever"* in permanent black marker on their seat.

The ride starts to get a little bumpy due to some of the road construction happening about a mile away from school, forcing the girls to return to their seats, Jake switches off the radio to better focus on the upcoming traffic ahead, sitting in silence anxiously waiting to soon being able to get out of their wet clothes and take a shower. Ashley knew they were close, pulling up to the traffic light to make the left turn down the street where the high school is located. Waiting at the red light, Ashley could hear the clacking of the blinker through the half open window residing next to Holley J, even at a dead stop she can still feel the outside breeze entering the bus, mixed in with the sounds of construction vehicles operating nearby. Almost simultaneously the traffic light turns green and Ashley's phone vibrates in her back pocket.

Another morning for Ashley waiting by her locker for Holley J to make her first appearance, feeling exhausted after another night at the club, these late nights are starting to catch up to her, to where she is making herself a cup of coffee in the morning, drinking it as she drives to school when she doesn't even like coffee, but the caffeine seems to give her system a much needed jolt. With a game this afternoon she is willing to choke down some black sludge as she likes to call it, if it helps make up for any lost sleep. To save time in the morning she just runs a couple strokes with a brush through her hair then puts it in a ponytail, something else she isn't a fan of unless she is on the mound, her hair in a ponytail is such a rare event for school, excepting Holley J to notice it first thing. Rummaging through her locker getting what she needs for her first period class, totally ignoring the rest of the student body continuing their obnoxious morning behavior before the first bell, always smelling the overpowering stench of different body fragrances. Every school day morning is like a mirror image of the day before, aside from that one morning run in with Renee a while back, she can plan on things usually being the same, including Holley J being late. Right on cue, Holley J makes here morning appearance storming up to her locker, backpack dangling from her arm, carrying her to go cup of homemade coffee, French vanilla coffee is her morning beverage of choice, car keys hanging out of her mouth.

"Morning," Holley J mumbles fumbling to get her locker open.

Seeing Holley J's struggling to compose herself, Ashley steps in to open her locker for her, seeing they each know each other's locker combinations.

"Thanks, sometimes I think I should hire an assistant," jokes Holley J, making the necessary locker maneuvers. "What's up with your hair? Since when do you wear a ponytail to school?"

"Another late night at work," responds Ashley leaning back on her locker waiting patiently for Holley J to finish.

"Again? Maybe you should tell your boss to back off on the hours during the season," Holley J suggested, wrestling to retrieve the needed materials for her first class. The difference between Holley J's bedroom and her locker are night and day, her bedroom is always neat and organized, while her locker is in total disarray, it's a wonder how she finds anything in that steel, rectangular black hole.

"Yeah, maybe," responds Ashley in a low saddened tone. "I've been wanting to apologize if it seems like I've been neglecting you lately, it's just I've been really busy with work and stuff…."

"Ash, you don't have to be sorry, everyone gets busy it's not your fault, it's not like we don't see each other just about every day, baring it's at school and softball, but it's still time together. I'll admit it's been awhile since we have done anything that doesn't have the school's name on it, but pretty soon we will have a whole summer to hang out," replies Holley J, "so empty that silly nonsense from your head. And before I forget, I'm going to be sending you an email soon, but you have to promise me you won't opening it until graduation."

"Why do I have to wait until graduation?" Ashley asked looking confused. "Just send it to me after."

"Because I'm asking you to, but mostly because it's kind of a small gift, you'll understand when you see it, just promise me you'll wait," Holley J urges.

"Okay, I promise," remarks Ashley.

"You know I trust you, but I'll know if you peeked. Please look in my pack and tell me that my uniform is in there," Holley J requested.

Quickly unzipping Holley J's backpack to discover her uniform is safely accounted for, giving her the nod. About five minutes until the first bell, Holley J finally gets situated, closing her locker and readjusting her backpack to its proper position, the two of them headed down the busy hallway en route their first class. Sitting in the middle of math class, seated in her preferred spot at the back of the room, Ashley lately has found herself daydreaming more during class, yet is still able to pay attention, a unique skill she has developed over the years. Half the time she doesn't even know or understand the many thoughts that have been invading her mind, usually coming back to thoughts of her aunt and Razz the two biggest thorns in her side, images she can't seem to escape, many times she will see their likenesses on the faces of other people bringing an instant feeling of dread and discomfort through her body. Being one of the few classes she doesn't have with Holley J, she feels alone in this crowded classroom. Classes they have together means they are always seated beside or close by to one another, Holley J's presence helps her to focus more, keeping all the bad thoughts and unwanted visions at bay, Holley J has become her own personal gargoyle perched atop those many churches to keep all the evil spirts away, when they are separated for classes, Ashley repeatedly finds herself where she is right now, trapped in her own head. Listening to the teacher as he scribbles algebraic formulas on the whiteboard with his going dull black marker, she keeps herself busy taking notes, moving her pen across her notepad at a swift pace, trying not to be distracted by the two male students seated directly in front of her goofing off, your typical dumb jocks, she would tell them off, but she already accomplished that feat when they both tried to ask her out earlier in the year and they wouldn't take no for an answer, now they pretty much just ignore each other which is fine by her. Spreading her pen ink across the paper, her mind begins to wander again, bringing up images of the night she was forced to pleasure another female against her will, remembering every intimate detail to her displeasure, mixed in with every other despicable venture that has manifested in her life, one big collage of images and memories she is not wanting to relive again. Her pen makes an erupt stop upon her notepad, gripping it tighter putting more unnecessary pressure on the tip pressing it harder and harder into the paper, tightly closing her eyes hoping to shake away this random wave of imagery her mind decided to bestow upon her. The pen tip snaps from the enormous pressure leaving a small ink puddle on the paper, every visual detail ignites another physical tick, she grins hard showing her teeth, her breathing becomes heavier, feeling like the mind depictions will never end, constantly repeating on an endless loop. A voice can be heard calling her name, clear as if the person was standing next to her, again hearing her name, this time even louder and more clear, precisely as her name is shouted a third time, her eyes open to view the many stares from her classmates listening to the teacher calling her name.

"Ashley, will you come up and solve this equation for us?" the teacher asked standing at the front of the class among the many looking in her direction.

Disoriented, feeling like she just woke up out of a trance, a slight sweat upon her brow, she quickly tries to compose herself. Not wanting to bring more attention her way, Ashley nods getting up from her seat releasing the broken pen from her grasp. Hearing whispers from some of the other students making her way to the front of the class, walking slow between the desks paranoid she might be groped by one of the male students. Greeted by her teacher handing her the whiteboard maker, she walks up to the board, some more whispers and slight laughter can be heard in the background, refusing to look back at the class behind her, Ashley approaches the board immediately beginning to write the answer to the offered equation, with no hesitation she works the marker across the whiteboard filling in the answer with ease, her mind becoming more clear with every drop of ink smeared across the board, when finished she places the maker on the whiteboard ledge and walks back to her seat.

Sitting at a small table for two at a trendy outdoor café, Jake patiently waits for his guest to arrive. The establishment doesn't seem to be too busy for a warm spring evening, the air is still with a slight overcast, the patio's white Christmas like lights outlining the covering canopy shine brightly above being the main source of lighting other than the large candles burning at every table. The only other patron is an older man sitting alone with his cup of coffee reading the newspaper, an activity Jake hasn't seen in a long time, seeing a lot of people get their news from the internet or social media, the elderly must like to stick to what they know rather than burden themselves with ever advancing technology. The old man was close enough for Jake to get a smell of his drink of choice, some kind of dark roast with what smelled like a touch of cinnamon, an unusual combination, but a pleasant smelling one. Years ago Jake would have never found himself in a place like this, always thought of these venues as being kind of tacky, a place for snobby rich people, however since getting out of rehab these spots have become like a safe house for a recovering alcoholic, little chance of falling off the wagon. Waiting patiently he looks out into the busy night life inhabiting the street, a normal crowd for this time of evening, getting a glance of the many different faces, spotting the one standing out like a rose among a field of weeds.

Danielle Waters the English teacher, walking down the sidewalk in her paisley print sundress with her strappy heels, mini hand bag securely across her shoulder, her short dark hair waving slightly in the still air, seeing her walk towards the café brought a smile to Jake's face along with some butterflies, it's been a long time since he has been on an actual date, not that he ever had trouble getting one, his former career and recent life events made it sometimes difficult or awkward at times to meet woman, now that the opportunity has once again presented itself, those old teenage feelings of anxiety have begun to resurrect along with feelings of excitement, haven't feeling this way in a long time, it felt good. Walking with an elegance that could add steam to man's stride, she made her approach towards the café, bringing Jake into her sights. A playful wave and smile is sent in his direction, he reciprocates standing from his seat, greeting her with a friendly hug, pulling her chair out for her to be seated. The waiter comes by to start with their drink order, Jake gestures for Danielle to begin, ordering a strawberry spritz seltzer on the rocks, while Jake follows up with a large spring water with lemon.

"You had no trouble finding the place?" asked Jake.

"Not at all, I've seen it, but believe it or not I've never been here before," Danielle answered. "Since you suggested this place I've been looking forward to it," she adds with a smile.

"You look really nice," Jake noted.

"So do you," she responds.

"I want to apologize for it taking so long for me to ask you to hang out," Jake stated. "Just been busy with the team and everything."

"No need to apologize, I totally understand," replies Danielle. "Speaking of the team, you really got something going with them."

"I guess, I'm just doing the best that I can," Jake remarks.

"I think it's a little more than that, you've built a great thing with these girls, I've seen it, these girls would lay down and die for you, something that team has needed for a long time," Danielle declares. "Trust me, I see it in class, you're all they talk about, especially Ashley."

"Ashley is in your class?" he asked, springing more of his curiosity.

"Not this year, I've had her for two years prior, every now and then she will come by just to talk," she mentions. "She's having a season, a regular on the local sports news."

"Yeah, she's a great pitcher, great ballplayer," Jake remarks. "What else can you tell me about her?"

"Nothing much, she keeps to herself mostly, I mean she has friends, she's was a great student, beautiful girl, really talented," states Danielle. "Incredible artist."

"She's mentioned that she likes to paint, I was always curious to see her work," Jake replied.

"Would you like to see a painting she did for me?" she asked.

"Please," answered Jake, watching Danielle pull out her cell phone from her hand bag, manipulating it to get to her photos.

"She gave me this last Christmas, I mentioned once I have a thing for unicorns," she said, holding out her phone for Jake to view, on screen is a painting of a white unicorn on its hind legs upon a snowy mountain top, a lush rainbow highlights a waterfall backdrop.

"Wow, that's like art gallery good, not something you would think would come from a teenager," Jake replies, stunned by what he just observed.

"I was surprised she gave it to me, it came with a card that said, Merry Christmas, thanks for being a great teacher. Just recently I was able to convince her to major art in college," she adds, putting her phone away.

"What do you know about her home life?" Jake asked curiously, trying to stealthily draw out any information.

"Not much, just that she lives with an aunt. I have a lot of students, it's hard to remember intimate details about each one. You seem concerned about something, what is it?" she asked, staring at the eyes of a man who has an unsettling demeanor to his features.

"You know what, I'm sorry, this wasn't the conversation I wanted to have tonight. Can we start over?" Jake asked, trying to steer the date back on course, rather than trying to play detective, hoping he hasn't derailed completely off the track.

"Sure," Danielle responds with a big smile.

Bringing the conversation to friendly chitchat, Jake and Danielle felt the mood of the evening heading in the right direction, their discussions flowed like a peaceful river, no breaks or any awkward pauses, an example of two people enjoying each other's company. Laughter with the occasional flirting was bounced back and forth between the two, any nervousness either one had at this time completely subsided, enjoying their meals as they talked, hardly ever breaking eye contact with one another. Jake felt like he was living that moment in a dream, as the darkness began to fall around them, the minimal lighting lit up Danielle's face like an angel, her smile shined brighter than the candle burning in the middle of their table, feeling somewhat intimidated by her, a feeling he never experienced with girls, worrying he might not be good enough for her, the emotions of an everyday man beginning to seep out, wondering if this is all part of the transformation process of his new life. He wanted to believe he was the same man he was before his baseball career ended and the downward spiral began, in some ways he was, but in other ways he wasn't, he was a different man, a new man and this pretty young woman was going to be the first adult female to meet him. Their meal continued on being completely oblivious to the increasing company of other customers filling in the other tables, they were sorely focused on each other and the rest of existence didn't matter. Jake was confident the evening was going well, there wasn't a moment he felt like he lost her, sensing she was impressed with the new him. The food was delicious and his personable interactions with the wait staff was sharp and charming as ever. Wanting to continue on the night after dinner, Jake suggested they take a walk, knowing a park nearby. Before he had a chance to fret about her answer, she was already responding she would love to, flashing again that beautiful smile of hers.

Finding themselves walking through the park side by side, the black of night was broken up by the illuminated light posts placed randomly throughout. This night happened to be home to a full moon which could be seen distinctly in the clear night sky, shining brightly from the rays of the now settled sun. They walked a path by the large pond, the moonlight shimmered off the still water helping to light their way, still engaged in deep conversation they barely noticed another soul walking amongst them.

"I have a confession to make," Danielle proclaimed. "My students told me who you are, so of course I had to do a Google search, how come you never mentioned you were once a pro baseball player and a good one from what I saw?"

"That part of my life is over now, I didn't think it was that big a deal," Jake answered, picking up a small rock off the pavement, throwing it into the pond, the park was so silent they could hear the splash of the rock entering the water.

"You seemed like a big deal. I watched a few videos of you on YouTube, you were stated to be the next big thing," she noted. "Then I read about what happened with your knee injuries, I'm so sorry."

"Yeah, me too," Jake replies, throwing another rock into the pond, "but it's okay, just wasn't meant to be, I guess."

"Well, I never thought I would be out with a famous athlete before, you were something special back in the day," Danielle remarked, showing a smile.

"I'm nothing special, believe me," replies Jake, flashing a smile of his own.

"Well, I think you're pretty special," she says, as the two make eye contact sharing much larger smiles.

Exiting a local ice cream parlor, each carrying a small dish of ice cream, he was enjoying a dish of chocolate while she went with mint chocolate chip, taking their desserts to sit down on an outside bench directly in front of the parlor's picture window, seated close enough to where their bodies just about touched.

"How is someone like you not spoken for?" Jake asked, taking big spoonful of his ice cream.

"Well, I thought it would have happened with my last boyfriend, he was everything I wanted except for the being the most important thing," answered Danielle.

"What was that?" Jake asked.

"Single," she replied. "How 'bout you? You know the stereotype when it comes to pro athletes, you haven't fathered a couple kids somewhere?"

"Almost, once," utters Jake in a low tone, going silent, scraping the last bit of ice cream out of his dish.

"Touchy subject," Danielle remarks, realizing she must have struck a nerve.

"I had a girlfriend in high school I dated for a while, when it was closing in on the time to leave school, I thought it would be best if we went our separate ways, I had baseball to focus on, I didn't want the stress of a relationship to worry about. That's when she told me she was pregnant. Anyways to make a long story short, she decided to have an abortion. Now I've always been pro-choice, but you never really know how you feel about something until it happens to you," Jake declares, looking at Danielle with sadness in his eyes.

"I'm so sorry," commented Danielle.

"It's ancient history, although I'd be lying if I said I never thought about it from time to time," he noted, using his spoon to steal some of Danielle's ice cream.

Playfully expressing a stunned look on her face at his desert thievery, Danielle takes a small spoonful from her dish, placing it on Jake's nose, a light-hearted giggle followed. He chuckled wiping the cold substance from his skin with a napkin, looking at the smile on her face which lit up an already bright area under the parlor's marquis, the gentle look of her baby browns staring back at him, Jake could literally feel the rise of positive emotions from her. Gazing into each other's eyes, they both seem to get lost, almost forgetting where they were and what they were doing, sparks would be cascading down to the ground if visual analogies were to manifest in reality. A small gust of wind passed through blowing a couple strains of Danielle's hair to rest in front of one of her eyes, Jake gently reached over to brush the hair aside, softly holding her cheek as he leans in to kiss her on the lips. Closing her eyes feeling his supple lips pressed against hers, she laid her hand upon his clean shaven face. Never more in Jake's life did a kiss feel so right, stirring up feelings of attraction he hasn't felt in a long time, almost forgetting how amazing it felt, could taste the strawberry Chapstick on her pouty lips. Ending the kiss, they once again lock eyes, displaying large smiles to each other. Jake might have found what his life has been missing, he liked Danielle and was very attracted to her, but he must take things slow getting to know each other better, still needing to tell her about what happened after baseball, not seeming like the type of person who would judge him for that, but he just wants to be open and honest about everything with her. Having only been a few seconds, yet he can't stop thinking about the kiss, sensing the feeling was mutual, he leaned in to kiss her again, bringing an excited Danielle to drop her half eaten dish of ice cream on the ground.

Another practice in the books for Jake and the girls, despite the team still being undefeated, he hasn't let up on the intensity of his practices, even though he has been feeling pretty good about himself with the magic that happened last night with Danielle, personal endeavors will not cloud his judgment on how he wants to coach this team, will not let that happen. Has seen it all too often when a team goes on a large winning streak, they grow over confident thinking they should win rather than earning the win, believing you should practice like you're the worst team out there so you play like the best. The girls gathered around on one knee, all of them sweaty with a bunch covered in dirt and fresh grass stains, Jake lectures the girls reminding them of their game tomorrow against another undefeated team they will host on their home field.

"Games like this tomorrow will define you as individuals and as a team. If you go into tomorrow's game thinking they are better than you than you will play like they are. You will approach this game like we have approached every game so far this season, make them feel like they have to earn the right to be on the same field as you, play our game and don't beat ourselves and I believe you will walk off this field the same way you walked on it, undefeated," voiced Jake, looking over all the faces knelt before him, Holley J who always shares the front with Ashley, looks especially giddy, a mysterious grin on her face. Instructing the girls to rise to their feet, Jake lets Ashley lead the team unity chant, directing the girls to raise their fist. Arms reaching towards the sky, all huddled in close, ends practices like they always do, with their team war cry. Jake dismisses the girls, all scattering like puppies being let out of a cage, wanting to be the first back to the locker room for a much needed shower. Ashley and Holley J hang back waiting for the rest of the girls to clear off the field, the two want to verify a nugget of information that has been flying around texts messages all day long at school, initiated by Holley J who broke the juicy story earlier in the morning, Ashley being the first to hear the breaking news. The field gradually empties out leaving the girls and Jake, who is over in the dugout grabbing a cup of water, sipping his drink he notices Ashley and Holley J still standing in the infield as if they were waiting for him.

"Why do I got this feeling I'm about to be interrogated?" Jake asked looking over at the girls smiling, waving them over.

Accepting Jake's invitation the girls scurry over to dugout lead by an enthusiastic Holley J, still supporting a mischievous grin. Stepping out of the dugout to confront his two pantomaths, Jake stands there with his arms folded, looking down eyeing both girls. Holley J clearly being the one who has the questions, standing there with an expression on her face waiting for the okay to talk, Ashley by her side, small smile on her face, basically there for moral support.

"Okay, you two, what is it?" asked Jake, even though he pretty much knew what was about to be asked, it was written all over most of the girls faces during practice, he couldn't expect to spend the night out with a teacher and not have it spread like wildfire throughout the school, especially in a time of cell phones and social media in the capable hands of teenage girls, their ultimate tools when it comes to starting and extending rumors.

"Is it true you went out with Miss Waters last night?" Holley J asked smiling, eyes lit up like a Christmas tree.

"Do I need to answer a question you already know the answer to?" replies Jake.

"So it is true," remarked Holley J, wanting to ask a bunch more questions, yet wants to respect her coach's privacy, main goal was just to find out if her sources were accurate. "This is so great!"

Jake looks over at Ashley shrugging her shoulders declaring her innocence, representing it was all Holley J's journalistic abilities, a regular bloodhound when it comes to finding out the newest and biggest news in school.

"It's not a big deal, we are two adults who shared a nice evening together," Jake proclaimed. "Besides, shouldn't you have your mind on other things, like tomorrow's game?"

"I'm just happy for you two," said Holley J.

"We're not getting married," he remarked.

"Not yet," Holley J responded, hosting a large smile on her face.

Jake shakes his head cracking a smile grin. "Well, I got to get going, I got dinner plans with my parents, Ash, text me later."

Grabbing her duffle bag of gear, throwing it over her shoulder, Holley J headed back to the locker room hearing Jake call for her a few steps into her departure.

"Hey, Holley J, if we could, could we just keep this between us and maybe just this planet?" Jake asks jokingly, viewing Holley J responding with a thumbs-up before heading back on her way.

"She's something else, isn't she? She could probably get a job with the CIA," Jake commented, watching her gradually disappear in the distance.

"To this day I still don't know how she does it," Ashley states.

"So I haven't heard what you think about all this," mentions Jake, curious to hear her opinion.

"I think it's great, Miss Waters is one of the best teachers in school, I'm happy she found a guy like you," expresses Ashley, a small grin appears on her face.

"Look, I just want you to know whatever happens between me and Miss Waters, it's not going to affect my dedication to the team, she knows right now you girls come first," explains Jake.

"I know. So do you like her?" she asked curiously.

"Yeah, she's great," Jake answers. "I just haven't told her everything yet, in time I will. She actually showed me a painting you did for her."

"She showed you that?" Ashley asked, feeling a little embarrassed someone else has seen her work, something she has to get used to if she is going to study art in college. Other than Miss Waters, Holley J is the only other person she has given a painting to. Holley J has a thing for waterfalls, no matter the size or location, she just loves the sound of the water spilling over the crest, descending into the plunge pool, it relaxes her, having been known to play audio of the soothing sound when she has trouble sleeping. For her sixteenth birthday Ashley painted her a large waterfall in a lush forest setting which is hanging in Holley J's bedroom to this day, the painting also includes a symbol Ashley created to show their bond as best friends, a symbol they will get tattooed on their wrist when they get their matching ink.

"Yeah, and I have to say it was incredible, I mean you are really good. When you told me you painted, I have to admit I just figured it was just average stuff, but boy, was I wrong, you really have a serious talent and I'm very impressed," Jake declared.

"Thanks," responds Ashley smiling, completely touched to hear that kind of review of her work.

"I just kind of feel a little left out you know, like when am I going to get my personal painting," suggested Jake facetiously, raising his eyebrows in fun.

"Who says I haven't already started one for you," she replies, telling a little fib that isn't true, however she has been planning on surprising him with one, now more motivated than ever to achieve just that seeing how he feels about her work.

"Well, if that is true, I can't wait to see it," professes Jake with a smile, looking down at Ashley's shade covered face, specifically her eyes, having a mystifying gaze to them as if they were talking to him, disclosing a level of concern. "You seem like you have something else on your mind."

"I don't know, it's about tomorrow," Ashley mentions, the tone in her voice screams edginess.

"What is it?" asked Jake.

"This team, I, have never been in this positions before. We are not accustomed to playing in big games, I mean everything we ever wanted to accomplish as a team is happening so fast, I don't know if we truly are ready for this, if I'm ready for this. I've never been this nervous for a game ever, but right now I'm scared to death. What if the moment is too big for me and I discover something about myself I was never meant to find out, that I'm truly not as good as I thought I was," Ashley conveys, getting a little choked up on her words.

"Ash, easy," Jake remarks, placing a hand on her shoulder to comfort her. "You're ready for this, believe me, you're probably the most ready of anyone on this team. What you are feeling now is totally normal, you know when a team is not used to winning and then they start doing a lot of it, it can be a little scary, like the team is due for a major fall, but I'm here to tell you that is not the case. You and the rest of the girls are where you are because you are all better than you thought you were. You are going to be just fine, I'm willing to bet money on it and this is coming from a recovering gambler. Just treat this one like all the rest and don't get mixed up in all the hype about the match up of unbeatens, go out there and pitch your game and I promise you everything is going to work out for the best, win or lose. I have full confidence in you, I'm not even the slightest bit worried about tomorrow," Jake states, smiling reassuringly, could almost feel the tension in her shoulder through his fingertips. "How do you think the other team is feeling knowing they have to face one of the best pitchers in the country tomorrow, I'm thinking they are way more on edge than you are. These are the type of moments that will define you, just be yourself tomorrow."

"I will, thanks," says Ashley, looking up at Jake's self-assured expression.

Surprisingly the touch of Jake's hand on her shoulder brought about comforting emotions, for the first time a man's touch felt genuine, it felt safe. It really meant a lot to her Jake had that much confidence in her, in the team. Tomorrow will be the biggest game she has ever pitched in, yet thanks to Jake's motivating words feels she will be ready to slay her first dragon.

"Come, I'll walk back with you," Jake offers.

"No, I think I'm going to stay out here for a few more minutes," she mentions, sitting down on the dugout bench.

"Okay, then I will see you tomorrow. Have a good night, Ashley," expresses Jake leaving on his way.

"You too," Ashley replied, watching the best person to come into her life since Holley J walk away, thinking what a shame it is once the season is over she won't have more time with him. Sitting there staring out into the empty field, watching the trees deep in the outfield sway slightly in the wind, her sweaty body producing a modest chill from the current breeze. Overlooking her place of solitude, a place feeling more like a home to her than that miserable structure she shares with her Aunt, a deep sadness comes over her, soon it will be the last time she sets foot onto this field. Wishing she could say all the memories produced on this field were good, no thanks in part to the worst coach she could have possibly have had before Jake came around. Thinking back to what he made her do, how he took advantage of her makes her blood boil, really hated him and is thankful every day that piece of shit is no longer in her life, often rehearsing in her mind what she would say to him if she ever ran into him again. Gratefully this season has become like a new beginning with enough good memories to trump all the bullshit from the past, with plenty of time to add more, including tomorrow. Taking her baseball cap off, letting her hair down, closing her eyes to clear her mind, feeling the cool breeze passing through the dugout, the smell of the grass on the field brings her to a meditated state. Motionless, isolating herself from the rest of the world, hearing nothing but the occasional birds chirping, feeling so relaxed, wishing she could stay in this state of mind forever. Time seemed to stand still, these quiet peaceful moments don't happen too often, being extremely rare occurrences, compelling Ashley to make the most of this solitary time. A sudden vibration breaks her concentration, opening her eyes to grab her cell phone tucked away in her back pocket. Cell phone in hand, it vibrated again stipulating multiple messages. In an instant this tool for social interaction brings her back to reality, without even having to look knows who is responsible for texts, yet after viewing the face of her phone it is revealed the messages are from different parties, her aunt and Razz, reading the texts she throws her phone out onto the field in anger and frustration.

Returning home from practice, Ashley walks in the front door wearing her backpack, carrying a couple plastic bags full of items from the grocery store, greeted by her waiting aunt standing there puffing on her cigarette.

"What the hell took you so long and where are my Goddamn cigarettes?" her aunt said in a loud tone, yanking one of the bags out of Ashley's hand, dumping all the contents on the floor. Locating the carton she wanted, she kicks the other items spreading them across the floor. "Now clean this shit up. I got James and a couple other people coming over in a little while, so when you are done with your chores, you need to put together some snacks for us before you head off to work," she says, looking at Ashley standing there sweaty, a disapproving look on her face, "and you better get that dirty look off your face before I knock it off."

Totally ignoring her aunt's threating words, Ashley goes to gather up the scattered items off the floor. Knowing what it means when her aunt hosts a small together at the house, she can expect a whole lot of drugs and alcohol making their way between these walls, culminating with orgy like sex. Remembering the last time her aunt hosted, her couple people turned out to be more like ten inside this small house. Ashley came home from work to a disaster which she had to clean up. Walking into the house she was greeted with a nauseating odor smelling like the mixture of alcohol, weed and sex, there were empty beer and liquor bottles scattered about, some were even spilled over on the kitchen floor, multiple ashtrays were filled with cigarette and marijuana butts in various spots, blow was being done all over the house, finding white dust on the coffee table, the kitchen countertops and the bathroom along with other drug paraphernalia, mainly syringes which she found on the living room and bathroom floors, also finding used condoms around the house, some even had blood in them. An unfamiliar man and woman were asleep naked awkwardly on the couch, still had a needle sticking out of her arm, her long, dark black stringy hair laid still covering most of her face, some coming close to dangling inside her open mouth, snoring like a barnyard animal. Her anorexic looking companion laid draped over the arm of the couch on his stomach, his bare ass within inches of his sleep mate, those spaghetti arms drooping over the side. Lastly finding her aunt passed out on her back, naked on her bed, seaman glazing her exposed breasts, accompanied by some naked man passed out beside her on his stomach. The sight of everything disgusted her to no end, luckily Ashley keeps her bedroom door locked or she might have found some stripped inbreed junky passed out on her bed excreting some form of bodily fluid all over her bed linen. It took Ashley almost a whole Saturday to clean up that mess, while her aunt just sat on the couch drinking and smoking, barking ridiculous orders, most definitely doesn't want a repeat of that again.

"Also this weekend I need you to clean out my bedroom closet, I can barely close the fucking doors anymore," ordered her aunt, not assumed by Ashley's frivolous behavior, acting like her aunt is not even in the room, finishing picking up the recently purchased groceries. "Are you listening to me?!"

Purposely not paying attention to her aunt, hearing her loud and clear, she takes the refilled bag of groceries in the direction of the kitchen, where she is stopped in her tracks by the hand of her aunt grabbing and yanking on Ashley's arm.

"You know I'm getting real tired of your fucking attitude lately," her aunt speaks softly into Ashley's ear, feeling the warmness of her hot breath on her skin as she spoke. "Look at me when I talk to you!" she demands in a much louder tone.

Completely irate with her aunt's physical advance, Ashley slowly turns her head to come face to face with her aggressor, staring her dead in her bloodshot eyes, seeing nothing but emptiness, a hollow vessel deprived of any sort of heart or soul. This woman has become more physical recently over the years compared to when Ashley was younger, those times her aunt knew she would overpower Ashley, but lately she conducts herself in a more aggressive manner, most likely an arrogant attempt to booster her ego trying to convince herself she can still intimidate, even hold her own against a maturing teenager. Ashley would blame it on her drinking, but her aunt is the same even when she is not intoxicated, the alcohol just seems to intensify her already belligerent personality. In the beginning when Ashley was too young to fend for herself and needed adult supervision, her aunt surprisingly performed her duties as a guardian, however it was tainted by her ungracious attitude, the yelling coupled with her insistence to have Ashley follow her around like a shadow was part of her process to grooming her into what she is today.

Continuing to stare without saying a word, Ashley can tell by the few scrunched age lines in her aunt's forehead she was not amused, influencing her to tighten her grip on Ashley's arm.

"You got something to say?" asked her aunt staring firmly back, her eyes spoke louder than her words. "I didn't think so. Now get out of my face and do what you're supposed to do," she demanded, releasing her grip on Ashley's arm before heading upstairs, closely followed by a trail of smoke from her cigarette.

Now finding herself alone, Ashley took a deep breath to try to calm her hidden, over powering emotions. Standing there holding both bags of groceries looking around at the contents of the small living room, it took every ounce of her will power to keep silent during her aunt's verbal tirade, wanting to retaliate so bad, could feel it in her bones, yet words don't seem to have any effect on the woman, she'll just reciprocate with her usual lexical backlash or deliver a physical solution. The more Ashley looked closely at her living environment, the more it's beginning to look like a prison rather than a place she would call home. Only a few more months until she can walk out that front door, hopefully never having to come back, but it's getting harder and harder to continue to take her bullshit, as time goes on she becomes more and more flabbergasted that they are both from the same bloodline. Not having much time to just stand there feeling like a victim again to her aunt's coldhearted etiquette, Ashley brings the bags into the kitchen to be put away before starting on her chores, hoping to be done and out of there before her aunt's scurvy house guest begin to arrive.

Running very late, Ashley is in the kitchen hurrying to put together a snack platter, grabbing anything she could find, Doritos, some plain potato chips, a half empty jar of Spanish olives, even some saltine crackers to make up the pint sized smorgasbord. Not what you would call a quality snack plate, but that's all Ashley had at her disposal and what could be put together with her afforded time frame. Knowing the type of scourge that will soon be wandering around the house, they will most likely be to drunk or high to even notice or care, it wouldn't surprise her if they tried to eat their own fingers. Placing the completed tray on the kitchen table, she hurries to grab her backpack off the counter to leave, passing through the living room unpronounced to her James had already arrived, seated on the couch engaged in a full blown make out session with her aunt, his hand down the back of her jeans. Walking out the front door Ashley checks the time on her phone, reading seven forty and she has to be to the club by eight with a twenty- to twenty-five minute drive ahead of her barring any traffic. Her nerves begin to escalate entering her car, knowing how Razz feels about tardiness, seeing firsthand what other girls have gotten recently for not being on time. Sending a heads up text was considered, but that would be a waste, Razz doesn't want to hear excuses, if you are told to be there at eight you better be there at eight not a second after. Adding insult to injury, her cell phone starts ringing, grabbing it from her backpack resting on the passenger seat, the caller ID shows a call from the State Penitentiary, not in the mood to listen to her mother's bullshit, letting the call go to voicemail, tossing the phone back on the passenger seat. Starting up the car, Ashley immediately throws it in reverse, slamming on the gas in her flip flops, speedily backing out of the driveway just missing James's truck parked in the street. Throwing it in drive, slamming on the gas again, pressing the pedal down to where it can't go anymore, her tires squealed darting off down the road. Understanding she is going to have to drive faster than usual if she is going to have any chance of making it on time, at the risk of possibly being pulled over by the cops. Never has gotten a traffic ticket, never even been pulled over, always been careful driving especially closer to the city, afraid a cop might recognize her from the club, asking her to do some sexual favor in exchange for not giving her a ticket. This time however she was willing to chance it, a traffic ticket would be much less harsh compared to what could be awaiting her if she is late.

Hurriedly pulling into the club's back parking lot at three minutes pass eight, her car fishtailing through the gate opening, slamming on her brakes skidding into her regular parking spot, tried her best to arrive on time, doing over a hundred on the high way, flying through yellow lights to avoid the red ones, but it turned out to not be enough, she could pretty much expect Razz to be waiting for her in the dressing room. Wasting no more time, she throws the car in park, grabs her backpack, swiftly exits to run towards the back entrance, blowing by the security guard outside enjoying a smoke. Inside she walks down the small hallway leading to the dressing room, hearing voices coming from a few of the girls back there already possibly getting ready. Emerging from the faintly lit back entryway, Ashley totally disregards the other girls heading to an empty vanity. Razz was nowhere to be found, acting as if everything is okay, goes about getting ready, taking a quick second glance around the area to make sure he isn't hiding in the shadows. Thinking the coast might be clear, she grabs her brush out of her backpack, gently stroking it through her hair, watching herself in the vanity mirror having a view of a couple girls whispering to each other while looking in her direction, two girls Ashley has never seen before. Refusing to succumb to childish behavior from a couple of females that don't even know her, just kept on doing what she was doing, keeping the focus on her own reflection. Moving on to putting on her face, grabbing the necessities out of her makeup bag, the flow of girls coming in and out of the dressing room increased causing the area to reek of multiple perfumes and body sprays. Uncapping her eyeliner, her makeup ritual becomes interrupted by a girl who invades Ashley's personal space, leaning on her forearms at the edge of the vanity, her ghetto booty raised high in the air courtesy of her clear stilettos, snapping her mint flavored bubble gum in Ashley's ear. Quickly being reminded why she tries to keep to herself among the herd, being the youngest of all of Razz' harlots it's hard not to stand out. Assuming her visitor has something to say, she makes eye contact with her in the mirror, trying to decide what was worse the constant snapping of her gum or the fragrance it seems she marinades in.

"Razz wants to see you and he doesn't seem too happy," the girl says continuing to snap her gum, her large fake bare breasts resting comfortably on her forearms. "He's in his office."

The girl removes herself from the vicinity leaving Ashley to look good and hard at herself in the mirror, knowing what this is about, somehow he found out or he already knew. Enters Razz' office on edge, hoping he will be reasonable for once knowing she was just a few minutes late. Walking in still wearing her flip flops, Razz stood leaning against the front of his desk wearing a dark blue silk shirt, the top unbuttoned enough to expose his bare chest. Off to the side near the pool table stands a small card table surrounding by four folding chairs which three are occupied by three other girls, all had tears running down their face, leaving one vacant. Standing near the table are two of Razz' goons, one is holding a tray with contents on it too far away for Ashley to see, the other just seemed to be there to lend a hand if needed.

"Welcome, Show Horse, glad you can make it," Razz says meeting Ashley halfway.

"Razz, I'm sorry, I tried to get here as fast as I could, I was just a few minutes late," pleaded Ashley, the tone in her voice displayed her nervousness.

Razz placed a finger over his lips asking for her silence, placing both of his hands softly on her face, giving her a tender kiss on the forehead. Turning to walk away he stops mid stride, holding out his hand wanting Ashley to take it, looking back at her with eyes that spoke a thousand words. Ashley fearful of what is about to happen obeys his request placing her hand inside his, leading her towards the card table, feeling her hand becoming slightly clammy specifying her uneasiness, the closer they got Ashley realized the empty chair was meant for her Seating her at the open chair, standing behind her fondling her freshly brushed hair, Ashley sat there trying to determine what is going on, why is she and these other three girls here sitting there with their heads down, arms to their side, tears still descending down their faces. Ashley only recognized one of the girls, seated right across from her was Kendra, the sick girl she met awhile back in the bathroom, also witnessing her get beat to a pulp at the hands of Razz. All the girls were silent not saying word, their silence seemed premeditated, as if they were afraid to speak. Looking over at the guard holding the tray, she can see what looks like three syringes lying beside one another, yet there is four of them seated at an empty card table bringing her uneasiness to another level.

"Razz, what is going on?" asked Ashley in a soft, confused tone, feeling Razz' hands now resting upon her shoulders.

The other girls lifted their heads hearing Ashley's voice, stunned one of them had the guts to question what was happening.

"You're about to find out," Razz answers whispering into her ear.

Rolling up his sleeves he walks over to the guard holding the tray, feeling extra motivated looking at the residents at his special table, clearly seeing the fear in their eyes. Unquestionably intimidated and scared, Ashley and her table mates watch Razz pick up one of the needles, placing it in the center of the table.

"You know, Show Horse, they say when someone is late they secretly have something to say, is that true? Do you have something to say?" Razz asked slowly circling the table.

"Razz, I'm telling you I'm sorry, whatever you are planning on doing you don't have to do it," implored Ashley.

"Oh, but I do. You are all here for different reasons, yet for the same thing, for FUCKING PISSING ME OFF!" he shouts grabbing the hair of one of the girls yanking her head back. "So now you have to be punished," he states calmly, throwing the girl's head back upright. "In that needle resting before you is an old Japanese chemical they used to use for interrogations. One dose into the bloodstream will cause the victim severe pain throughout their body for up to an hour, you'll feel like razor blades are coercing through your veins, they say the pain at times can be worse than childbirth. As you can see there are four of you and only three needles, which means one of you will leave this table unscathed. So we are going to play a little game, you've heard of spin the bottle, well, welcome to spin the needle."

Razz reaches onto the table grabbing the needle to give it a spin, the girls watch in a panic, the needle twirling swiftly round and round wondering whose fate will come first.

"Razz, please," begs Ashley, tears streaming down her face.

The needle begins losing momentum, in a few seconds a decision will be made, the girls look on yelling for it to not stop pointing at them, Ashley just sat silently. Their cries become louder the more the needle slowed down, a perfect deficiency to human behavior in the time of considerable panic, believing the volume of their voices will somehow interfere with the laws of physics. Razz looked on with the eyes of a man who was eager to put his harsh punishment into motion. These are the moments Razz lived for, the control was the ultimate high for him, the power he was exhibiting makes him feel more alive, his disciplinary tactics have always been severe, but this has to be his most cruel and merciless yet. Barley with enough momentum to make another rotation the needle slowly comes to an evident stop, pointing directly at the girl seated to Ashley's right. Her cries for mercy go unheard as Razz picks the needle up from the table, the guard standing nearby comes over to assist, holding the girl down so Razz can insert the needle into the vein of her forearm. Razz tries to steady the girl's arm, fighting against her squirming in her seat, trying to pull her arm away. Getting frustrated with her non-compliant actions, Razz throws her a backhand across her face, the blow settles her down causing her body to go limp making her arm more accessible. Razz inserts the needle into the girl's arm pumping the fluid into her bloodstream, almost instantaneously the girl feels the effects of the substance entering her body, the pain was beyond excruciating, starting in her arm making its way to other parts of her body the further it travels through the bloodstream. Screaming in agony her body tenses up trying to fight off the affects to no avail, Razz pumps every last drop from the needle before removing it, a trickle of blood marks the insertion point. Ashley and the other girls look on concerned for their fellow tablemate, watching her continue to fidget and twitch in her seat, sweat seemed to start pouring out of every pore in her body. Standing there with the empty syringe in his hand, Razz' facial expression was nothing short of satisfied, the look in his eyes spoke louder than any words, capturing pure joy viewing his target shutter and screaming in pain. Letting out a few more agonizing squeals, she goes into shock passing out right there in the chair, her head flopping over to the side, both arms falling towards the floor, her limp body left in her seat as a visual reminder to the other girls. Second needle is placed in the middle of the table, spun with purpose leaving the other girls more on edge seeing firsthand what possibly awaits them. Starting to feel nauseous, Ashley's heart races feeling like she could have a panic attack peering nervously at the revolving second needle. Waiting for the inevitable, ludicrous thoughts slip into her mind, maybe it will spin forever, maybe this needle is full of a harmless liquid, maybe in the next few seconds Razz will actually grow a heart to show forgiveness to her and the remaining girls. In times of adversity irrational perceptions can cloud one's reality, none of those things will happen, she just has to hopelessly wait for the random outcome. Gradually coming to a stop the needle's point steadily makes a pass by Ashley, closing her watery eyes in overwhelming relief, yet overcome with worry for the other two girls who were surprising silent this go around, their body language articulated all that needed to be said. The needle indirectly stopped angle pointing to the girl on Ashley's left, crying she lets out an obscenity under her breath seeing Razz walk over to her picking up the needle joined by his guard.

"Don't you resist me!" Razz angrily orders grabbing her by the hair, tears causing her mascara to streak down her face.

Without putting up much of a fight she is held back by the guard standing behind her allowing Razz easy access to her arm. Feeling the needle penetrate her skin, she glances over making eye contact with a petrified, tear shedding Ashley mouthing the words *"I'm sorry"* in her direction.

Razz pressed down on the plunger releasing the clear solution into her vulnerable system, feeling the effects almost immediately letting out a loud holler describing her torment. Withdrawing the now empty needle, a drop of blood escapes the entry point, Razz places the used hypodermic back on the tray preparing number three. The newest recipient experiences similar symptoms before her body started convulsing violently in her seat, her eyes rolling into the back of her head accompanied by drool seeping from her mouth, the momentum from the aggressive shaking carried her off of her seat where she fell to the floor. Becoming extremely concerned for her fallen comrade, Ashley wanted to leave her seat to check on her laying on the floor on her side, hair covering most of her face, the shaking had stopped leaving her there motionless. Taking a huge risk, Ashley left her seat to tend to the unconscious girl promptly checking for a pulse on her neck. Establishing she still has a heartbeat, plus the movement of her abdominal area indicating she is still breathing, Ashley felt an immense sense of relief. Though she doesn't have much of a relationship with her coworkers, Ashley feels an unwritten bond with them, a sorority that should look out for one another even if the rest don't feel the same. All working for the same monster, someone who doesn't care anything about them other than the massive coin they continuously produce for him, their wellbeing is of little concern just as long as he can suck as much potential out of all the girls before he has to recycle them. Once you are on his payroll you are his and breaking his rules comes with a cost, believing Razz would have no problem killing one of them if it came down to it knowing they can easily be replaced, having never seen someone take so much gratification in abusing others.

Ashley shook the girl in an attempt to wake her up receiving no response, passed out cold due to the dramatic circumstances her body just endeavored.

"Back to your seat, Show Horse," Razz insisted, testing the third needle with a quick squirt.

"Razz, she might need a doctor," informed Ashley.

"I'll decide what she needs, now get your ass back in that chair," Razz ordered. "Don't make me tell you again."

Keeping eye contact with Razz, Ashley gradually returns to her seat, Kendra looking on in total trepidation with the next round in Razz' sick game about to start. The two girls look across the table at each other knowing one of them will be next with the other remaining unharmed. Wasting no time, Razz places the needle in the center of the table spinning it wildly, putting a little extra muscle into it to raise the tension. Round and round the needle spins hearing the sound of the plastic barrel rubbing against the table's surface with every rotation. Looking over at Kendra whose eyes kept shifting from the center of the table to Ashley, hoping karma didn't intervene with the outcome, last time the two of them were in this office together Ashley watched as Kendra was violently disciplined at the hands of Razz, now the universe may be inclined to settle the score. Neither one of them deserve to be on the wrong end of this needle, yet both are probably secretly wishing for it to point to the other, it's just human nature to want to protect yourself even if you don't want to see it happen to someone else. Somehow Kendra has become like a black cat or a dark cloud to Ashley's world, nothing ever good happens when she is in her vicinity, not blaming her for anything it's just a weird coincidence whenever they are in a room together it's not going to be a happy time, fitting this whole ordeal has come down to the two of them. Ashley wonders if Kendra even remembers that day when they first met in the bathroom, her being very sick and drugged up, going out of her way to try helping her. Not expecting Kendra to volunteer to take the needle, yet in some kind of delusional way of thinking Ashley feels she owes her one, not that she would ever profess that out loud.

With the needle slowing down, the girls look at each other both with tears in their eyes, seconds way from awaiting their fate. Odds are definitely not in either girl's favor this time around with it just being a fifty-fifty chance and the needle just has to point at their half of the table to be selected. The needle now moving at the speed of a second hand on a clock passing by Ashley's half of the table, closing her eyes as tears drip down her face in solace knowing the momentum of the needle won't be strong enough to carry it all the way around towards her side meaning Kendra will be the unlucky recipient. Deep down Ashley wished there was something she could do to prevent Kendra from having to go through this, not wanting to have another front row seat to witnessing her physical assault, yet couldn't help but feel a total sense of relief being the one who will not have to endure the bodily anguish that has been seen from the other girls, feeling like a horrible person taking silent contentment on her victory resulting in someone else having to reap in the agonies of defeat. Coming to a stop the needle points almost directly in front of Kendra, tears start flowing down Ashley's face more heavily, not in happiness, but in sadness for the frightened girl sitting across from her. Kendra sees the position of the needle, lets out a couple tears not saying anything looking across the table at Ashley, not even putting up a struggle or letting out cries for help as Razz sets her arm on the table to proceed with the injection. Never taking her eyes off her, Kendra displays what can only be described as a half grin mouthing the words *"thank you"* once the needle was inserted.

She did remember, hearing her screams of pain as the injected substance starts to run its course. Having to sit and watch Kendra in agony after learning she was hoping the needle pointed towards her to show gratitude regarding Ashley's thoughtful act that night they met, was becoming too much to bear. Kendra vomited on the floor from the pain, wailing louder, grinding her teeth projecting drops of spit with every deep breath she took, her eyes became bloodshot, scraping her long black colored fingernails across the top of the table, raking so hard it left scratch marks even breaking a few of her nails clear off leaving a small trail of blood in their paths, Razz lit up a cigarette looking on in amusement. Letting out more screeches of torment before falling to the floor, Kendra places herself in the fetal position in an effort to try relieving the pain. Immediately Ashley runs over to tend to Kendra, kneeling down beside her placing her hand on her back, rubbing it slowly to try comforting her to the disapproval of Razz.

"Leave her," Razz demanded, watching Ashley remain defiant still attending to Kendra, showing compassion and sympathy for the fallen. Not happy with Ashley's noncompliant attitude, Razz quickly heads over to intervene, showing irritation in his steps. "I said get away from her," said Razz assertively, leaned over getting in Ashley's face.

"I'm just making sure she's okay," Ashley responded, withholding herself from making eye contact, hearing anger in his voice.

"I don't give a fuck if she's okay and you shouldn't either," he replies. "Just another piece of gutter trash who can't obey fucking rules. Now I'm going to say it for the last time, get the fuck away from her."

Ashley could sense being close to Kendra somehow alleviated some of her pain, still partially awake and crying heavily, yet the longer she keeps herself there the madder Razz will get, but something was holding her back, a feeling of morality to care for a person in need, she just couldn't leave her there still awake and in distinct discomfort, the other two girls defensively went unconscious to combat the suffering.

"Okay, sometimes you really disappoint me, Show Horse," proclaimed Razz sucking a drag from his cigarette. "You think what you are doing is helping her, think again," he states taking the cigarette pressing the lit end against Kendra's cheek.

Kendra screams hearing the sizzle of her flesh beginning to cook.

"RAZZ, STOP IT!" yells Ashley looking him square in the face, his eyes reassuring her he wouldn't until she did what he said. "ALRIGHT!" she shouted standing up over Kendra. "Please stop."

Removing the cigarette, Razz comes face to face with a teary eyed Ashley, a small stream of smoke ascends from the freshly burned area of Kendra's cheek. Disposing of the used cigarette, Razz holds Ashley close wiping away her tears with his thumbs, staring at the sadness and fear in her face signifying the whole ordeal was hard on her, yet still furious over her actions.

"I'm glad you're the one who escaped from this game okay, Show Horse, but don't you ever fucking disobey me again!" demanded Razz. "Did you see what you did, because of you I had to fuck up her face, all because you had to play Mother Fucking Theresa. Now every time you see that scar I hope it reminds you it all could have been prevented had you just did what I told you. I hate to see you end up like these three, but if I have to, I'll hurt you bad, now go get to work and don't worry about your little friend, I'll take care of her," Razz stated giving Ashley multiple pecks on the lips.

Free of Razz' grasp, Ashley wasted no time in leaving his office, feeling lousy about herself having to leave Kendra behind, who knows what he is going to do, yet she didn't want to stick around to find out if she couldn't help her. Watching Ashley exit his office, Razz acknowledged his two guards.

"You two clean this shit up and get rid of these three, once they wake up put them to work, I got some business I need to take care of," ordered Razz, the two guards immediately advance ahead with his request.

Ashley reenters the surprisingly empty dressing room sitting down at an empty vanity proceeding to cry excessively, so many emotions gang up on her at one time, how close she came to having to go through what she witnessed with the other girls, to feeling helpless she couldn't do more for Kendra. After all that she is still expected to perform her duties not even being in the right mindset coming off one of the most emotional roller coaster rides ever. Her hatred for Razz was increasing by the minute though her invisible leash was becoming shorter and shorter, the lee way she once thought she had has completely disintegrated, still Razz' number one, but now not above his iron fist anymore, meaning what he said about hurting her and knows it, a far cry from the man she met that day in the park. Letting all that tempestuous waste empty out of her was much needed, not a stranger to a good long cry having had plenty of those in her lifetime, Ashley views them as self-therapy sessions, a procedure to cleanse away all negative energy overpowering her from time to time, lately it's becoming more difficult to free herself from the defeatist attitude that's had a strangle hold on her recently. Usually her self-reflecting periods are done in a more isolated manner, not one to let other people see her cry, however she couldn't hold it in any longer, luckily able to make it to a somewhat private area. Hearing the clacking of high heels coming closer, she quickly wipes her face with her hands trying to remove any evidence of her sulking. A couple of other girls enter completely topless, walking with dissatisfaction in their steps, their skin glistening with sweat and glitter, a couple of older girls both of which Ashley has seen before, one she got into an argument with about six months ago over a parking spot in the back, but have since buried the hatchet, they are by no means friends yet they remain cordial with simple hellos and goodbyes to each other. The two girls congregated on the other side of the room, talking loudly with aggravation in their voices. Not wanting to be so obvious in her eavesdropping, Ashley begins brushing her hair acting like she is unaware of their presences, unsure if they know of Ashley's existence, walking in they didn't even scout the area to determine if they were alone. It was hard to tell if they were arguing with each other or disputing over someone or something, being very animated with their words taking out a lot of their frustrations on nearby clothing and vanity contents, either way they were pretty distraught about something. Soon their voices became muffled and indistinguishable, a defense mechanism the mind uses to filter out any unwanted outside noise which Ashley integrated trying to distract herself from all the loud chatter going endlessly on the other side of the room. Other girls' issues are not her concern, she has her own to worry about, mainly how to get through the rest of this night after such a horrific start, can already tell it's going to be hard to focus with her mind on Kendra's and the other girls' wellbeing. Getting ready more girls entered the dressing room, keeping her center of attention on herself, Ashley wondered how busy of a night was ahead of her, really not in the mood to do anything especially servicing total strangers, doing it on a regular day is bad enough, now she has to do it with her mind clouded, a recipe for an unflattering feeling to feel worse. Nights like these more than ever, would appreciate the premature ejaculators or the two pump chumps making her job quick and easy. Having to go dance first might help a little bit, the bright lights mixed with the loud music hopefully distracts her mind for a short time having to pay attention to her surroundings. Putting the finishing touches on, she is informed through the recent entry of one of the guards, she will be up soon. Ignoring the commotion from the other girls in the room, she stares hard at her reflection in the mirror before leaving her seat to start the second half of an already forgettable night.

Pulling into the driveway close to two in the morning, Ashley anticipated to see a yard littered with cars, yet surprisingly there is none to be found, even James' truck is shockingly absent, all that was there was her aunt's car parked in the same spot as when she left. Leaving her car to enter the house, she was expecting to trip over empty beer cans or bottles that would have decorated the yard a mist a gathering of slobs and uncourteous people, but with some of the yard illuminated by the front porch light that was debunked when the yard appeared empty. Walking up the few steps to the front door the porch was completely vacant, bringing Ashley to one conclusion, most of the damage was done inside. Unlocking and entering the house she overtaken with total silence and darkness, dreading flipping on the living room light to be greeted with a house in total shambles, bracing herself to have a fitting end to her night. A flick of the switch the light overtakes the blackness uncloaking the nearby surroundings revealing the unexpected, the room was just how it was when she left earlier aside from a few empty beer bottles and a full ashtray resting on the coffee table. Curious, Ashley headed for the kitchen wondering if she would find the same, turning on the light it was more of the same, a couple beer bottles on the counter and the snack tray she left on the table looked to be barely touched. Too tired to wonder what went on here tonight or even care, most important was she didn't return to a disaster she would have to clean. Extinguishing the lights in the kitchen and living room, Ashley heads upstairs, her aunt's door must be slightly open hearing her snoring. Quietly latching her bedroom door shut to obstruct the annoying sound, she enters her bedroom tossing her backpack on the chair. Going directly to sleep was not an option, tired yet still wound up she felt like a quick bath, hoping soaking in the warm water would relax her.

Running the bath filling the tub, Ashley de-robes unmasking her naked body, hoping the sound of the falling water resides strictly in her location, its temperature begins steaming up the bathroom mirror. Reaching the desired volume, she shuts off the nozzles bringing the room to a sudden quiet, slowing sliding herself into the freshly poured water. Totally emerged, she lays her head on the edge closing her eyes feeling the liquid warmth against her skin, feeling much needed after an insane night. Soaking her emotions, still couldn't help but think about what had happened to Kendra and others, so caught up in the state of their welfare Ashley was never able to texts Holley J this night, something always making her feel distressed forgetting about her best friend, making herself feel more horrible than when she first entered the water. A single tear streaked down her face in guilt, not just for Holley J, but for Kendra and company, feeling like she didn't do enough. She can't go to bed with all this on her conscience, thoughts racing through her head, a deep sleep would be impossible, deciding to slide her body forward allowing her to submerge her head under the water in an effort to use the warm liquid to relax her mind. Remaining motionless, other than a few air bubbles rising to the surface, the water above becomes perfectly still like a sheet of plate glass, eyes open holding her breath, she motioned the idea of staying plunged until she closed her eyes for good, remembering in less than fifteen hours she would be playing in the biggest game of her life.

Ashley and Holley J walked towards the field not having to be there for about another hour giving them some time to go through their pregame ritual. Their conversation was normal mainly focusing on the game, however Holley J sensed some uneasiness all day from Ashley. First her apologizing for not texting her last night, which wasn't a big deal to her, to her being rather quiet most of the day, at lunch she hardly said two words. Asking her if everything was okay, Ashley simply replied, she must be nervous, having never played in a game before with this much at stake. Holley J could understand being on a team that is not used to winning this much, but she reassured Ashley if anyone should be nervous it should be the rest of the team not the best player probably in the whole country. Holley J feeds off of Ashley's energy, if she is nervous it makes her nervous, but the two of them have always gotten through any challenge that has been put in front of them on the field together regardless of the outcome good or bad. Carrying her duffel bag full of gear, Holley J struggled to keep pace with Ashley who only had her mitt to bring along, she offered to lug the bag for her but was turned down, Holley J considers hauling the bag the only weight training she does. Arriving at the field everything looked pristine, all the grass was freshly cut, the infield dirt evenly raked and smoothed out, the smell of a recently mowed lawn is one of Ashley's favorite aromas, true to many ballplayers. This was also a big deal for the school hosting a game like this, wanting everything to look presentable advertises a lot about what you represent.

Entering the dugout Holley J unloads her bag on the floor, Ashley kneels down to securely tie her cleats, both girls put their earbuds in to enjoy some music from their iPod when they warm up with a run. Signaling to each other they are ready, both head out, staying side by side the two run at an equal pace keeping their speed to a minimum, not too fast to tire out but not to slow to not feel their muscles loosening up. Holley J is not much for working out or much of a runner, but she will do it if accompanied by Ashley, one of many things they enjoy doing together, it helps her be a better catcher something very important to her when it comes to Ashley, wanting to give her best effort so she can to help her be the best pitcher she can be.

During Ashley and Holley J's pitching warm up session Jake approaches the field seeing a familiar sight, appreciating the drive on display, always reminded of himself back at that time. Ashley likes using Jake's arrival as a timer letting her know it's getting close to game time, typically bringing her and Holley J's collaboration to an end, a good time for a break anyway. Meeting up with Jake in the dugout the girls grabbed some much needed water, working up a bit of a sweat in the warm afternoon sun, catching the sporadic cool breeze kept the temperature comfortable, perfect weather for a ball game. Having quenched their thirst with a nice ice cold drink, the girls prepared themselves, Holley J began putting on her catcher's gear, Ashley sat at the end of the bench bouncing her one leg up and down, nervously rotating a softball briskly in her throwing hand, catching the eye of Jake standing nearby.

"You okay?" Jake asked seating himself beside her.

"Yeah, I'm fine," answered Ashley just staring out into the field.

"You sure?" he asked a bit concerned.

"She's been like that all day, Coach," Holley J chimed in, strapping on her chest protector. "She keeps telling me it's nerves and her being nervous is making me nervous."

"Just give me a minute," Ashley requested, the rest of the team begins to pile in.

Moments before game time, Jake has the girls gathered just outside their dugout kneeling on one knee ready to give his patented pre-game pep talk.

"Today's talk is going to be short, I think I said all I needed to say at practice yesterday. Now I'm just going to leave it up to you girls, if you believe you belong at this moment you'll do just fine, don't let what this team has done in the past dictate what happens here today. Strength doesn't come from what you can do, it comes from overcoming the things you once thought you couldn't. This is your chance today to prove that," Jake proclaimed. "You have a chance today to leave this field the only undefeated and number-one team in the section. Just go out there and win it."

Giving Ashley the nod allowing her to lead the girls in their pre-game chant, hearing the passion in their voices sent a chill down his spine, they want this just as much as he wants it for them, their first big test of the season and they are ready as they'll ever be. The team congregation ends with some enthusiastic clapping pumping themselves up before taking the field, Jake asked Ashley to hang back a moment letting the rest of the girls take their positions. The large crowd filling the bleachers show their energetic support cheering on the girls as they jogged onto the field, whistling and an overpowering blow horn are a few of the encouraging sounds emanating from the spectators.

"Okay, it's time, you sure you are alright?" Jake asked concerned, placing the softball in Ashley's mitt.

"I'm fine," she replies, getting the nod from Jake.

Ashley walks towards the pitcher's mound to an uproarious volume of cheering watching their star pitcher take her place. Her stroll to the mound put her in view of the larger than normal crowd, a sight beginning to overwhelm her. Both sets of bleachers were filled to capacity, many onlookers were spilled out onto the grass sitting in personal park chairs, many were standing, even noticing faces she has never seen attend one of the team's games including Principal Davis and Miss Waters among others. Also spotting that league representative who knows Jake very well standing off to the side with a group of about five other men, most likely the other scouts she heard would be in attendance. The atmosphere didn't feel ordinary, it felt strange, it felt foreign, her otherwise familiar sanctuary felt like it was being invaded by some abnormal entity causing her to feel like an outsider in her own home. Reaching the mound, putting her in the center of everyone's attention, Ashley looked down the way at Holley J standing behind the batter's box ready to go, a sweeping sensation passes through her body making her feel very nauseous, her throwing hand became clammy, pressure began to build in her stomach elevating whatever was left over from her lunch rerouting it to her throat forcing her to turn, leaning over to vomit on the dirt encircling the mound. Observing Ashley's episode, Jake immediately runs out to the mound to check on her status, met promptly by a concerned Holley J sprinting from home plate. A sudden hush comes over the various spectators looking on with great worriment, Kenneth and the scouts began chatting privately amongst themselves, not what everyone expected to see to start this contest, all were sitting on pins and needles awaiting news on Ashley's condition.

"Ash, are you okay!?" Jake asked in a slight panic.

"Maybe she's sick," suggested Holley J.

"I don't think she's sick, I think it is nerves," remarked Jake, yelling over to the dugout for one of the girls to bring out a cup of water.

Many of Ashley's teammates gravitated towards the mound checking to see if she was okay. The ensemble grew in size as even girls off the bench made their way to check on the situation, Jake signaled to the home plate umpire to give him a few minutes, instructing his players to return to where they came from including Holley J, appreciating their concern for their fallen teammate, yet there was really nothing they could do.

"Oh my God, I have never felt like this before," Ashley states, the vomiting seems to have come to a stop. "I feel so embarrassed."

"Don't be," Jake says handing her the cup of water. "I know exactly what you are going through."

Alone on the mound together, every pair of eyes in attendance is locked in on the private discussion happening at the center of the diamond.

"Sip some water and I need you to just relax and breathe. There is no shame in being nervous, okay, it happens to everyone and everyone reacts to it differently. I was just like you, I threw up when I got real nervous too, but the real question is, why are you so nervous?" Jake asked.

"I don't know," Ashley replies surveying the area, a hint of sadness in her words   .

"Hey, look at me, don't look at them," ordered Jake, anxiety written all over her face. "It's just me and you right now. Now tell me what's really bothering you."

"What if I'm really not ready for this, these big game moments, what if I'm just a regular game pitcher who is just a fraud, someone who caves when the pressure is on. I really don't think I could handle learning that about myself," she responded.

"You're right, maybe I should just take you out," he suggested, standing firm folding his arms.

"Wait, what? You're kidding, right?" asked Ashley, her anxiety quickly switched to confusion.

"No, you just said you might not be ready for this and I have to do what's best for the team, right?" remarked Jake.

"You can't be serious. Who are you going to put in? Jess? Nothing against her but she has never pitched a full game. You want to win this game you have to leave me in," Ashley demanded.

"I think you just made my point for me," noted Jake smiling. "You are ready for this, more ready than you know, you are probably the most ready person that will step out onto this field today. You want to be out here, you need to be out here, these are the moments players like you are made for. And don't pay attention to the crowd or the scouts watching, ignore all the outside noise this isn't about them, sometimes the biggest obstacle standing in your way is you. All you have to do is be yourself, just be yourself," commented Jake, his words already having a positive effect on Ashley's emotional state, the once fear in her eyes drastically turned to fire.

Leaving the mound, Jake gestured to the umpire they were good to go, the crowd clapped in support relieved Ashley was fine, hearing it from her teammates lead by Holley J standing at home plate raising one fist into the air, instantly followed by the rest of the team besides an unresponsive Renee who stood arrogantly in centerfield, capped off with Ashley doing the same looking over at Jake who reciprocated the action giving her the nod. The day belonged to Ashley and her teammates from beginning to end they were in total control of this matchup. Playing a school that hasn't been on their schedule in nearly a decade known for being one of the top girls softball teams year in and year out, yet on this day than ran into the best pitcher they would face all season.

Ashley could not have been more dominate in her play, allowing only two hits while striking out fourteen batters and hitting two homeruns. The rest of the team rallied around Ashley's performance putting on a good showing of their own, Brie was a perfect four for four at bat, adding two stolen bases, Renee hit her own homerun combined with great defensive plays out in the field including robbing an opposing player of a homerun, up to Holley J catching and calling a flawless game. Overall the entire team played near perfect inspired softball lead by Ashley and Jake's proficient coaching resulting in a seven to nothing win clearly promoting who the best team in the district was. However this moment belonged to Ashley and her masterful pitching, on full display every inning, from her velocity to her command, she was like a skilled surgeon out there unquestionably catching the eyes of the scouts who spend most of the game taking notes and conversing amongst themselves. What they considered her most impressive feat though was overcoming the earlier episode before the start of the game, a true testament of will and the ability to execute under pressure, a characteristic all great athletes possess. Ashley and the team received a standing ovation from the crowd, their excitement was nothing short of authentic, vocal from start to finish, showing they were behind the team no matter what. After the final out which occurred from a strikeout, Holley J flipped off her mask sprinting towards the mound to embrace Ashley, the two best friends shared a moment telling each other how much they loved each other and how proud they were to be a part of this historic win together smiling and shedding a few happy tears. Soon the rest of the team ran up to join them to celebrate the victory sharing hugs and high fives, all except Renee who was absent from the on field jubilation, slowly walking past the commotion to be with herself in the dugout. The happiest person of all might have been Jake who was so proud of how his team played never once showing an ounce of fear or panic a true showcase of a well-coached team, running out to congratulate the girls passing out his share of high fives and congratulatory remarks. Making his way through the on field gathering, found himself face to face with Ashley, a large smile graced his face mimicking the one staring back, propelling him to grab her in the biggest hug picking her up off the ground. At first Jake's act startled her, not used to sharing hugs with people other than Holley J, especially from a man, yet his embrace felt warm, genuine, in a weird way father like allowing her the comfort to hug back putting her close enough to discover how good he smells. Sharing that welcome hold with Jake further emphasized how much of a better player she has become since he has arrived in her life, not knowing what would have happened earlier if he wasn't there to help put her mind at ease, something she really doesn't want to think about. He has helped her uncover things about herself she never knew were there, it saddens her to think how hard it is going to be to leave this team and Jake after this season, he has quickly become one of the greatest people to come into her life in a very long time, a life very much in need of his presence.

During the postgame team handshakes, Ashley watched Miss Waters come over to Jake giving him a big hug and peck on the lips obviously to compliment him on the big win, shortly joined by Kenneth and the scouts, many handshakes were exchanged before they got down to the business in a social interaction. Ashley received many praises and commendations from the opposing coach and a few of the players demonstrating good sportsmanship after a hard defeat, a team they could very well see again later on in the season. Witnessing a lot of the players interact with a majority of the crowd reminds her how alone she usually feels after a game despite being surrounded by many familiar faces including Holley J. Before she knew it she was being summoned over by Jake to be introduced to the scouts, greeted by Miss Waters with a quick hug to plenty of handshaking with the scouts. Ironically it can to be known a couple of these scouts came from the same school that once tried to recruit Jake, in spite of his short pro baseball career, Jake still remains quite popular around town and in the baseball world. The one scout was actually the one that spoke to Jake those many years ago, reminiscing about the conversation they had reminding him how he thought Jake was one of the best prospects he had ever seen, reiterating he saw the same enormous potential in Ashley. Telling a few funny stories, sharing a few laughs the discussion generally stayed professional, all stood around for about twenty minutes prior to ending with more handshakes and one last sales pitch to entice Ashley on the benefits of attending their university, saying their goodbyes the scouts departed leaving a lasting impression. An overly excited Holley J reemerges initiating another hug, so proud of Ashley drawing the recognition of more schools, her joyous attitude sparked a proposal for another girls night out to celebrate. Never one to turn down quality time with Holley J, Ashley gives her approval looking forward to hanging out together giving her at least one night of normalcy. The once loud and boisterous crowd vanished, small amounts of trash hidden under the bleachers marked the only evidence of their existence, leaving a silence that hasn't been about in a couple hours. Opposing team silently made their departure exiting the field to a disappointed bus ride back to their school, most of Ashley and Holley's teammates have already made their way back to the locker room leaving the field more deserted, leaving Jake, Miss Waters and Kenneth behind. Jake gave his final praises to Ashley and Holley J, never overstating how proud he was, mainly speaking in Ashley's direction, telling them to hit the showers to go out and commemorate their big achievement.

"Ash, before you leave, I want you to use this game as a lesson, that no matter what hurdle is put in your path, you have what it takes to overcome it, just like I knew you did," commented Jake. "That goes for you too, Holley J."

"Hey, I'm just delighted to see you and Miss Waters together," Holley J shares with a big smile.

"Get her out of here," Jake responds. "You two go and have some fun."

"You as well," Holley J replied giving Jake a friendly wink.

"Thanks for everything today," Ashley added, saying their goodbyes to Miss Waters and Kenneth, she walks away with Holley J.

"You're welcome," Jake said with a smile.

"I just want you to know you two make a cute couple," Holley J shouted from a distance.

"Goodbye, Holley J," Jake yelled back, shaking his head with a smile.

"I guess our secret's out," Danielle said with small chuckle.

"It was never in," Jake responds jokingly. "I'm sorry about all that."

"It's okay, I think it's cute," a smiling Danielle replied.

"Well, I have to say this day turned out to be a huge success for you," added Kenneth. "Also proving you were definitely the right guy for the job, amazing turn around, already talks of a district and quite possibly state championship."

"Jake, that would be incredible," said Danielle with a huge grin.

"It would be, but right now I want my girls to focus on one thing at a time, which would be next game," Jake stated.

"I agree and I would never question any of your methods, you have done an unbelievable job so far," stated Kenneth. "But I think we should go out and celebrate ourselves, this is just as big a win for you as it is for the girls."

"What did you have in mind?" asked Jake.

"I've heard of this club in the city, you know a real gentlemen's club, always wanted to check it out, what do you say?" Kenneth asked.

"What do you think?" Jake asked looking over at Danielle.

"I think you should do whatever you want to do, go have a good time," she replied giving Jake a kiss on the cheek. Danielle has always considered herself an independent woman who never needed the help of a man in her life, yet when she is attracted to someone she puts one hundred percent effort into it, she really likes Jake and could see something materializing in the future, taking things slow would be the best strategy right now with both being busy with their jobs at the moment, also with her history of being burned in past relationships. Thirty-five and not married is not where she thought she would be at this point in her life, her womanly instincts assure her Jake is legitimate, someone who isn't into playing games, a man who knows what he wants. Showing she may be a tad bit jealous would come off as clingy and a bit needed, not the look she wants to project so earlier on in their courtship, especially with a man she plans on keeping around. Truly enjoyed getting a glimpse of him in action today, would have done it sooner, but being a part of a few after school programs takes up a majority of her time, today she was able to get another teacher to cover for her and she is so glad she did. Observing Jake coaching the girls was nothing short of impressive, in full command of the team, viewing every little detail that transpired out on the field to continuously calculate what his next move would be, a definite leader, a character trait she always found sexy in a man.

"When did you want to do this?" Jake asked.

"I'm free in a couple nights, I'll text you then, where and time," answered Kenneth.

"Then it's a date," agreed Jake

It started out as a normal Saturday, Ashley was doing her usual weekend chores which differed from some of her regular ones being she has more time not having to go to school, her aunt doing what she always does, sitting on the couch in her robe watching TV smoking, an open bottle of beer waiting on the coffee table. Cleaning the oven is one of her weekend duties, spending the last hour almost elbow deep in rubber gloves scrubbing the inside, wearing a paper face mask to keep from inhaling the strong fumes of the oven cleaner, finding it ironic she has to clean an appliance her aunt never uses when she does all the cooking. Having finished most of her other tasks this was the day she was to clean out her aunt's bedroom closet, a job she is not looking forward to, who knows what her aunt has stashed away behind those doors. Closing the oven door, removing her cleaning accessories, Ashley wanted to get started on the closet so she could have some time before having to go to work to finish the painting she has been working on for Jake. Going through the living room Ashley must walk past her aunt, hoping to do so without any purposeful inter- action, getting about three steps in the bitch on the sofa decides to speak.

"Getting started on my closet soon, I want it done today and while you're at it I need my sheets washed, I got James coming over later and clean yourself up, you look like a pathetic housewife," her aunt remarked, referring to Ash- ley's cleaning attire, an outfit consisting of old worn-out jean capris, an old black and red flannel unbuttoned to reveal her plain white t-shirt, sleeves rolled up, hair in a bun, pair of black crocs on her bare feet. Hearing her aunt's words, she refuses to make eye contact advancing through the living room to the stair- case, trying not to say much to her as of recently, rather just do her obligations while avoiding her as much as possible.

"I know you can hear me, bitch! Don't you fucking ignore me!" her aunt yelled, watching Ashley disappear up the stairs.

If her aunt's verbal lashings left marks, Ashley's body would be full of vis- ible scars, would rather have her aunt physically abuse her, at least physical abuse heals over time, metal abuse truly never heals and can stick with you forever. Climbing to the upstairs proved to be harder, having her aunt add to the list of tasks, having to do a special load of laundry to do the bed sheets in- furiated Ashley even more, hates washing her aunt's bed sheets, finds it dis- gusting being the linens are marked with mostly blood and cum stains. Entering her aunt's bedroom, Ashley is greeted with a familiar stench of fish and cheap perfume, a smell that doesn't sit well with her weak stomach. Cov- ering her nose she hurries over to the bedroom window opening it as wide as it can go letting the warm outside air circulate throughout the room hoping the scent of nature can vanquish the overpowering funk. The scenery in the room hasn't changed, an unmade bed littered with dirty clothes besides a nightstand with a large box of condoms and a tube of KY Jelly sitting next to an alarm clock appearing to be ten minutes fast. Breathing in the fresh air pro- vided from outside made the working conditions a little more tolerable, having no curtains on the window kept any breeze from being obstructed from entering, keeping the air flow consistent. Opening one side of the sliding closet door, Ashley came into view of an overstuffed, unorganized mess, everything from an abundance of shoe boxes, some on the floor, others on the upper shelf which might not even contain shoes, to clothes laying on top of boxes or draped over other clothes happening to be on hangers. From what was visible at first glance, a lot of the clothes were old probably ready to be either thrown out or donated. Her aunt was never one to have a sense of fashion nor does she ever expect her to, wearing what is comfortable to her or she thinks will grab a guy's attention. Digging through some of the clothes, she was surprised to find a couple tops she thought was cute, even finding some still having the tags on them. Believe it or not this was the first time since she has lived here she has been in this closet, not that she has ever cared to search it, always assumed it was forbidden territory, now here she is having to organize this cluttered closet of disorganization, this was going to take a lot longer than she thought making her more irritated.

One hour into the reorganizing process there is a bunch of clothes laid out on the bed, most of the boxes that were occupying the floor, many covered in a small layer of dust and cobwebs, were consolidated to decrease the volume. Filled with everything from old papers to greeting cards, some even contained old photo albums. Ashley's curiosity getting the best of her pulled out one of the albums, sitting on the end of the bed to take a glimpse at the saved photos. Flipping through the pages, the pictures were mainly of her aunt and her mother when they were around Ashley's age, showing no emotion when glancing at the pics, one picture caught her eye, though, it was one of her mother holding Ashley just after she was born with her aunt standing beside her, strangely enough they both had smiles on their faces as if they were actually happy with the new life that will connected to them forever. For a brief moment Ashley felt a little emotional, quickly passing reminding herself what they both have become. Placing the album back after reaching the end, discovered a small music box, pulling it out admiring its shiny, silver tint, flipping it open to unveil a tiny plastic ballerina spinning in place to the soft musical notes created by clockwork mechanism hidden inside, the charming little melody put a small, surprising grin on her face, a little stunned her aunt would own an item like this, definitely not a device matching her personality. Closing the top she returned it to the box where she found it, folding the flaps in to keep it closed. Some of the boxes housed old cassette tapes and CDs, all of musical acts Ashley never heard of. The small amount of shoe boxes actually did accommodate pairs of shoes, a few had sneakers, restacking all the boxes on the closet floor more orderly leaving more space to spare. Many shoeboxes populated the top shelf, some were even stacked two or three high making it a bit of a struggle to reach some of the boxes, even on her tip toes her five-foot-six frame had to stretch with all her might to make contact with her fingertips try to slide the boxes over the edge of the shelf. Balancing the first stack, she was able to safely lower them to the floor deciding to check their contents after. Reaching up for the next stack her calves started burning being up on her toes, a feat proving more difficult wearing the crocs. Getting the next stack off the shelf didn't go as smoothly as the first, clearing the shelf the top box wasn't evenly leveled with the others causing the stack to sway slightly ending in the top box falling over spilling on the ground, the small packet of papers settled inside were now scattered around the floor. Ashley got on her knees to retrieve the loose paperwork, disapprovingly shaking her head for making more work for herself. Not interested in what information each sheet offered, she just placed them back in the box, however one leaf residing a glossy insignia in its corner intercepted her attention bringing her to quickly reach for it. Examining the details of the paperwork tears began to build up in Ashley's eyes, now completely distraught she began looking through the others to see if there are any more like it, to her dismay a few others were located baring different emblems. Looking over each sheet the tears commence pouring out of her getting more and more upset and angry. They were the college letters she thought never came, her aunt must have saw them when they came in the mail and hid them from her which all makes sense since her aunt is always there before Ashley to get the mail. Why did she keep them, why not just throw them away? Whatever her motives were, Ashley could bet her intentions involved hurting her in some way, she couldn't believe what she just found, her aunt must have forgotten they were hidden up here, obviously never wanting Ashley to find them.

Devastated at what she discovered, Ashley crumpled the papers in her hand holding them up to her face getting them soaked with her tears, slightly rocking herself back and forth. This was her future her aunt was messing with, there was no limits to the deceit she was willing to go to too fuck with Ashley. This was the straw that broke the camel's back, soon Ashley's sorrow turned into rage throwing the dampened papers to the floor, swiftly getting herself to her feet storming out of the room. Making her way down the hallway to her room, entering to grab her softball bat leaned up against the wall, exiting she hurried down the hallway to the staircase, bat firmly held tight in her right hand. Every step she took bringing her closer to confronting her aunt, the rage inside her intensified, stomping down the stairs with attitude, could feel her adrenaline raising trying to be loud enough to grab her aunt's attention. Reaching the bottom of the staircase there she was just as she left her, cigarette in hand, sitting back on the couch like she was the shit. Just the sight of her enraged Ashley more, like putting gasoline on a fire, without hesitation she grabs the bat with both hands walking up towards the television swinging at the screen with all her might, like trying to hit a homerun during a game, making contact the screen cracked in various directions leaving a large hole in the center as the display went black.

"WHAT THE FUCK!?" her aunt stands up yelling, in total disbelief of the behavior happening before her.

Ashley took a couple more swings at the TV with each swing being more forceful than the last, the pressure from the impact caused the fairly large set to fall off its stand to the floor where it about broke in two. Completely infuriated Ashley turned her wrath onto the rest of the living room, swinging and smashing the lamp right of the end table sending the lampshade and pieces of its base airborne. Riding the wave of her violent emotions, turns her attention to the coffee table, swinging the bat over her head like a lumberjack shattering the glass sending all the fragments and items that were resting atop to the floor below. Her aunt in complete bewilderment watching Ashley savagely destroy her living room, became a bit frightened at her sudden violent outburst, fearing she might be next on the hit list.

"WHAT THE FUCK IS WRONG WITH YOU?!" yelled her aunt, standing inches away from a heavy breathing, bat wielding Ashley.

"SHUT UP, SHUT THE FUCK UP!" Ashley shouted. "Why are you trying to ruin my life?! Why did you hide those college letters from me?"

"Is that what this is about?" her aunt asked with a chuckle. "You want to know why? I'll tell you why, because you don't deserve a good life, you belong in the gutter with all the other whores and you're going to pay for all this shit, YOU HEAR ME?!" her aunt angrily replied.

"I FUCKING HATE YOU!" yelled Ashley, reinitiating her fury swinging the bat at various knickknacks hanging on the walls, leaving large holes in place of the once hanging novelties. "I'M TIRED OF TAKING YOUR FUCK-ING SHIT."

Ashley's relentless path of destruction continued, swinging the bat at any-thing within reach. Every swing was fueled by years of pent up anger, aggres-sion and hatred, a human volcano that just erupted, willing to swing that bat until she couldn't lift her arms anymore, screaming obscenities picturing her aunt's likeness as every target. The living room now in shambles, a scene of maniacal conduct, Ashley's aunt needed to try to put an end to this disastrous rampage. Bravely stepping in front of the bat, grabbing it mid swing, the two of them engage in a power struggle to gain control of the situation. The stand-off pursued, screams of exertion were exhaled by both, each clasping the bat so tight their fingers were turning white. Her aunt exhibited strength neither were aware of, still Ashley was able to out muscle her enough to forcefully press her up against the wall, the impact induced a picture to fall to the floor. Desperately trying to rip the bat from her aunt's grasp, refusing to allow her the position of dominance, pulling her away from the wall slamming her against it a second time her aunt's grip begins to weaken, Ashley tugs fiercely on the aluminum stick releasing it from her grip, sweaty hands combined with aggressive exertion loosens Ashley's hold on the bat sending sailing through the air finally smashing the living room picture window. Grabbing each other the two begin to scuffle knocking over various end table accessories, their mo-mentum carried them into the kitchen colliding with glasses and empty beer bottles staged on the countertops, the sound of repeated glass shattering mixes with their grunts and groans. Their melee shifts them in the direction of the kitchen table, strenuously pushing the chairs and all out of position. Ashley has her aunt bent backwards with the small of her back pressed up against the edge of the table, her one hand pushing up on her aunt's chin. Unnaturally bent over her body provokes a scream of discomfort trying to retaliate, under estimating Ashley's physical strength. Her body pinned upon the table unable to free herself, her aunt raises one of her bare feet pushing into Ashley's gut driving her backwards ramming her into the refrigerator, Ashley's weight drives it out of its spot sending the couple boxes of cereal resting on top to fall and spill on the floor. Unbound and furious, her aunt charges after Ashley deploying a rebel yell, the veins in her neck protrude through her skin, her now unfastened robe uncovering her plaid boxers and bare breast, flutters like a cape. Coming at her like a bull seeing red, Ashley prepares to defend herself from the ungrateful, selfish bitch heading her way. Balling her right hand into a tight fist, waiting for her to reach the right spot, throws a ruthless right hook catching her square on the jaw also making contact with her nose, a punch filled with years of anger and built up hostility, thrown with the intention to equal all the metal and physical anguish Ashley has experienced in her years under her aunt's roof, a battle cry soundtracks the strike. The enormous force generated from Ashley's hundred-and-thirty-pound frame sends her aunt stumbling backwards revisiting the kitchen table breaking her fall. Lying back on the table top dazed, blood leaking from her nose and mouth, feels the tight grip of a pair of hands around her neck.

"I FUCKING HATE YOU!" Ashley utters with tears streaming down her face, squeezing hard on her throat like a pair of vice grips, feeling the esophagus beneath the skin, her tears dripping on her aunt's bare chest.

Standing over the person who is supposed to be her family not her enemy, someone who was to take her in and protect her, provide her with a decent life so she could grow up into a successful young woman was now gasping for air, latching onto Ashley's wrist in an attempt to loosen her grip.

"Why do you hate me some much?" asked Ashley crying profusely. "You let them steal my innocence. I want you to die."

Turning blue in the face from the lack of oxygen, eyes wide open moistened with tears, her aunt vigorously flailing her arms trying to grab at anything, from tugging on Ashley's shirt to reaching for her hair desperately trying to free herself. So much rage and hatred siphoned through Ashley's body consolidating at her fingertips responsible for the sudden increase in her hand strength. Feeling a pair of legs kicking wildly about below, the once erratically swinging arms began to go limp, specifying to Ashley she is now in total control, her aunt currently completely helpless, within seconds of losing consciousness. Wanting so much to put an end to her selfish and abusive ways, wanting to validate to herself what she is doing is completely justified, Ashley's conscience reveals its ugly head bringing her to the realization that continuing down this path will make her no better than she is, despite everything she is the better person and always will be and living with the blood of her aunt on her hands would thoroughly diminish that. A mental switch went off in Ashley's head bringing her to release her aunt's throat leaving imprints from her hands covering most of the skin on her neck. Listening to her coughing and gasping for air, Ashley stood motionless, a blank expression on her face staring deep into her aunt's eyes, hands shaking registering she came within inches of taking her life.

"Get out," her aunt mumbles, struggling to get oxygen to her lungs. "GET THE FUCK OUT!"

Still shaken up, Ashley silently walks out of the kitchen stepping on broken glass, walking through fallen debris passing through the living room, making her way upstairs to her bedroom, the previously loud ruckus has shifted to an awkward silence throughout the house. Entering her room in tears, a wave of unknown emotions comes over her, she is being kicked out of the place she has called home for almost ten years, though it hasn't been the most pleasant and in certain situations down right awful place to stay, it was still the site where she laid her head. She has always wanted to leave, but not like this, not knowing where she is going to go and what she is going to do, it couldn't have come at a worse time especially when she has to work in a few hours. Grabbing a couple large duffel bags out of her closet, Ashley starts filling them with the bare essentials and anything she can fit, mostly clothes, toiletries and most importantly her softball gear. With every article of clothing or item stuffed in the bags, the more the reality sets in, she is possibly about to be homeless, dropping to her knees breaking down momentarily. So many thoughts raced through her mind she could barely think straight, all she knew was her time here was coming to an erupt end, once she walks out the front door it will be for the last time, there was no coming back from the incident that just occurred. Coming off the biggest win in her softball career, to the unnerving exploits that went down at the club, to what transpired today, the more walls Ashley seems to break down in her life there is always a bigger, thicker one there to replace it, fearing eventually she won't have the strength anymore to even put a dent in the next one. Back on her feet to finish packing, face soaked from the shed tears continuously dripping onto her bedroom floor, takes a look around her bedroom at all she has to her name, everything she has purchased with her hard earned money, it's disheartening to her she has to leave most of her belongings behind at least for now, particularly her paintings. Every painting covering her walls represents a different chapter of her time spent in this house, each painted with emotions she felt at the time of conception, every stroke of the brush was her way of talking to the canvas, emptying her feelings through the spreading of the paint. She would love to take all that hard, sentimental filled work with her, yet she is willing to trade in a room full of paintings for her sanity if it meant never having to deal with what most of her art represents again, her love for painting means all can be replaced one day. Packing what she can of her painting supplies she decides to take one painting with her, the one currently stationed on her easel almost finished, the one she was working on for Jake. Zipping up the bags stuffed to gills, both packed so full there isn't a single wrinkle in the bags material, Ashley throws a strap over each shoulder before taking her unfinished work. Stopping at the doorway, she turned to give her bedroom one last look not knowing how she should feel about this sudden departure, this was the site of many horrific happenings in her life, yet it was the only room in the house that felt like home to her. During her last second moment of reminiscing she catches sight of the framed picture of her and Holley J on her nightstand, couldn't believe she almost forgot the one thing in the room that has true sentimental value and couldn't be replaced. Taking the picture, she exits her room closing and locking the door out of habit, lugging her baggage to the staircase, descending towards the front door. At the bottom, Ashley looks over with tears in her eyes to see her aunt back sitting on the couch smoking a cigarette amidst all the devastation around her, robe remains wide open, the blood from her nose and mouth still visible. Making eye contact with Ashley, the two undertake in a tense stare down, each waiting for someone to say something but never did, very rarely are the two in the same room together without the exchanging of words, mostly initiated by her aunt spewing out her daily dose of hurtful, obnoxious commentary, yet this silent interaction speaks louder than any swapping of words could have, punctuated with the symbolizing blowing of cigarette smoke into the air.

Ending the awkward and tense engagement, Ashley walks out slamming the door behind her, putting her bags and canvas in her trunk prior to getting into her driver's seat, taking out her cell phone to call the one person she could.

Just finishing up with dinner, Jake helps Vicki clear off the kitchen table as the twins scurry away to do their own thing. Jeff is away for the weekend on a business trip to prepare for an upcoming trial, has also worked late most of the week prompting Vicki to appreciate Jake being around to help out with the girls. Since Jake started coaching Vicki has been a lot more lenient about him staying at the house, letting him wait until the season is over to look for a place so he can focus on the team, relating being a former high school basketball player herself never letting anything distract her during the season, even their relationship has benefited from the extra time alone together giving them more time to talk, allowing them to be more civil with one another. Vicki doesn't hate Jake, she just doesn't agree with many of the choices he has made throughout his life, giving way to having his brother, her husband to carry most of the burden. There has always been a bit of friction between him and Vicki ever since the day she heard the story of how he drove drunk back in high school with some friends and Jeff in the car inducing her to see him as an irresponsible and careless person, granted things recently between them has gotten better, but the enmity is still there. Filling up the dishwasher with the dirty plates once holding pasta with meat sauce, Vicki wipes down the table surface with a damp, soapy rag, the area where the twins were seated being the most filthy. Lately when they are alone together they would break out into some small talk or polite conversation, yet this proceeding remained silent. Completing redressing the table, Vicki's cell phone located on the kitchen's center island begins to ring, a song by Pink is her ringtone of choice. The caller ID displays "Husband," answering she steps aside to greet Jeff with a welcoming toned hello, launching into their long private discussion. Jake can only hear the muffled sounds of words from where she is standing, but can see the large smile on her face appear ever since she picked up the phone, watching her giggle and relishing in whatever it was they were talking about. They aren't the best of friends as in-laws, yet Jake has always respected Vicki as a wife to his brother, most women would complain or put up a fuss about their husband always working late or having to take business trips, but knows he has a demanding job that could require long hours and frequent times away from home, still she handles it like a trooper disdaining herself from adding any more hassle to probably an already stressful job and he is sure Jeff truly appreciates it. Many women may even stray under these conditions, but if there is one thing Jake candidly knows for sure about Vicki is she is not that type of woman, it's never been about money or social status they just have an unbreakable connection and she wouldn't be stupid enough to risk everything she has for one act of infidelity. He knew Vicki was the one before Jeff did, the way he would never stop talking about her after they first met, to Jake he is witnessing true love right in front of him, secretly jealous of his brother for finding the perfect girl he could the one, someone he is still on the lookout for, maybe it's Danielle, he really likes her and she checks all the boxes of what he is looking for, but only time will tell. Tonight was the night Jake was to accompany Kenneth to that gentlemen's club, just waiting for a text or call to confirm, having already spoken to Danielle early on the phone to make plans to meet up with her tomorrow afternoon. Firing up the dishwasher Jake's phone begins to vibrate wildly on the counter top, the caller ID shines Kenneth's name, quickly drying off his wet hands with a nearby dish towel he answers. Exchanging macho hellos, Kenneth goes about explaining the plan for the night consisting of them meeting at the club with the time of arrival being around nine o'clock. Agreeing with the arrangement, Jake lets him know he will be there anticipating a fun night. Normally he would be worried attending a place like that, filled with mostly testosterone driven men acting a fool looking at well portioned naked female bodies, might be tempted to have a sip of the juice, yet now he finally has his life going in the right direction, the team, meeting Danielle are big contributors to that and falling off the wagon could put him back at square one, something he never wants to go through again, self- retribution completely out weights the urge.

After a few minutes of small talk the two hang up in preparation for their meet-up later. Driving down the lit up city streets following the directions Kenneth provided, Jake realized how long it has been since he has made a visit to this part of town. Was always fascinated with big city life, the grouping of the buildings, the many neon lights that lit up the landscape, all the diverse people wandering the streets, it was a different world, a world he once saw himself being a part of during his playing career, now he just sees it as a catacomb of enticement and seduction, a nice place to drop in on, but that formerly desired life has taken a back seat to a new, better, simpler one. Turning down the street accommodating his destination, traffic increased indicating he must be close. Driving cautiously he can see in the distance the large, vivid, radiant sign making up the marquis, the title Playmates with the outline of a female glowing brightly, changing colors every few minutes to keep it fresh.

Pulling up Jake viewed the long line stretched a little ways down the sidewalk, velvet ropes kept everyone in a single file making it easier for the bouncer working the door to handle the incoming crowd. A fair amount of women made up the awaiting patronage, most are escorted by a male companion possibly boyfriends who were nagged to take them along or it's a couple's unique bonding experience. One of the many drawbacks to the city is the lousy parking situations, it isn't allowed on the street in front of the club or on the other side of the road, a public lot just up the way or the side street on the corner is where most cars are being held. Jake decides to use the large lot paying the five-dollar parking fee, finding a space towards the back up against a tall chain-link fence. Checking his watch exiting his truck reading eight-fifty-five, wondering if Kenneth has arrived yet, starts his walk to the front of the club. A few other cars pulled into the lot as he weaves his way through to the exit noticing some flashy rides amid the collection of vehicles, a few Mercedes, a couple of Jags, Porsches, and Lexuses, even a couple BMW sports cars, speculating the lot must be under heavy surveillance to have expensive cars like that parked out in the open, justifying the reason the lot is so well lit. Walking on the sidewalk leading towards the club, Jake receives a text from Kenneth letting him know he is standing outside the front entrance waiting, informing Jake he isn't standing in the line so he will be easy to spot. Approaching the busy area under the marquis, he locates Kenneth standing off to the side, dressed very causal supporting a dark blue sports jacket. The two embrace in a man hug being the only people not standing in the line to get in to the dismay of the impatient patrons waiting for their time to enter. Kenneth explained he got them a couple of VIP passes granting them insist access to the club including their own private booth, a couple complimentary lap dances, half price on drinks and front row seating around the main stage. Taken back by Kenneth's generosity, Jake thanked him in advance relaying he didn't have to do all that, would have been happy just showing up and enjoying the show. Wasting no more time they head inside, Kenneth telling the bouncer they have a reservation, the large guard checks his iPad to be sure he is on the list, getting the nod the bouncer calls for assistants on his headset, another well-built guard comes out from the front entryway to escort Jake and Kenneth inside. Learning what they are eligible for the guard directs them inside, Jake couldn't help but notice both of the guards were strapped and not in a concealed way, but resting right on their hips in plain sight, having never been to a club where the bouncers or guards carried leading him to come to two conclusions, either this place has a history of trouble or this place has never had a problem because of the visual repercussions that are walking around surveying everything. Jake assumed the latter, no place would attract high society type clientele if it had a reputation of being a haven for disorderly conduct. Inside Jake and Kenneth were in awe of what they were seeing making a quick scan of their surroundings, all the topless girls pole dancing on separate little stages, the overwhelming lighting and music being showcased, to the pure energy being generated from all the vitalized libidos. The place was definitely a man's playground, you couldn't turn your head anywhere and not see a pair of bare breasts or a voluptuous booty, a couple of the girls were dancing fully naked showing off their shaved under carriages. The guard directed Jake and Kenneth to their private booth having to dodge a few waitresses dressed in skimpy outfits, some were wearing just a skirt and a pair of heels. More armed guards stand motionless in various spots around the club, their demeanors was like that of a robot, showing no emotion just positioned there surveying the area. Reaching their roped off private zone, the guard briefs them the main stage show starts in less than thirty minutes and will send a waitress right over. The two of them look over to see a whole row of private booths, all of which were occupied, from where they are sitting they have an almost complete overview of the entire club. Jake has been to his share of strip clubs in his day, back when he was playing remembers during his rookie season sometimes after road games he and a few of his teammates would check out the local night life hitting up the preferred hot spots, the renegade actions of someone young and single, but none of those places were anything close to this, the sheer scale of the place, the diverse clientele, to just the overall look which resembled ahigh end nightclub, many of the clubs he remembers visiting were shitty hole in the walls with patrons to match. Their waitress arrives, a well-proportioned short haired blonde girl wearing a short, black skirt barely covering her buttocks, no top putting them in plain view of her evident fake breasts, a pair of white high-top Converse sneakers were her footwear of choice, standing there half naked in front of two strange men exhibiting a bubbly and friendly attitude, displaying a large smile that never left her face. Kenneth ordered a Jack and Coke executing some playful flirting, Jake went with his go to, ice water with lemon, typing in their orders on her iPad she gave some recommendations for a few of the appetizers on the menu, responding they were good for now she left to obtain their drinks. A few minutes until the main show the DJ makes an announcement the night headliners were coming up, an uproar of cheering manifested amongst the crowd complete with heavy clapping, Jake and Kenneth carry their drinks to their seats around the main stage. The remaining chairs began to fill up, many supporting overanxious adult males, a few women joined the front row, drinks in hand, anticipating the upcoming festivities. The rest of the eager crowd was standing room only gathering up behind the seated spectators. The main stage was dimly lit with black lights giving off an enough glow to see the large mirrors making up most of the background, an apparent black curtain was at the center, a T-shaped architecture housing a pole towards the end of the long runway. Sitting patiently waiting, Jake noticed a nearby hallway constantly being entered and exited, another strapped robot like guard stands watch controlling the flow of traffic, most likely the area of the club where they perform the lap dances, probably offering private chambers for the deed, a distinguished looking man comes over to stand by the guard, arms folded with his attention extensively on the main stage, his body language and demeanor accentuates a domineering personality, one of someone with power or ownership.

"The premier girl here is one called Angel," Kenneth says taking a sip of his drink. "I hear when she is on the bill this is the type of crowd she draws. We are in for a treat tonight, my friend."

"I'll be the judge of that," responds Jake smiling, bringing his attention back to the mysterious hallway watching a man exit nonchalantly zipping up his pants. "What else do you know about this place?"

"Well, there is a rumor you can engage in extracurricular activities with the girls for the right price," explains Kenneth.

"You're kidding?" asked a stunned looking Jake.

"I don't know how true it is," Kenneth answers, "what's the big deal? You never had a massage with a happy ending before?"

"I plead the fifth," Jake replies.

"I wouldn't worry about it, we probably couldn't afford it anyways," added Kenneth. "Let's just enjoy the beauties about to put their bare asses in our faces."

Unannounced the stage lights illuminate, shining brightly giving everybody's eyes sitting around the stage a sudden jolt, crowd erupts in cheers and clapping given the signal the show is about to start. The DJ informs the crowd of the first girl coming to the stage playing her regular jam loudly through the speakers, stage lights continuously change between white, red and blue as the first girl bursts through the center stage curtains wearing a revealing cowgirl outfit complete with cowboy hat and boots. A loud roar encompasses the onlookers mixed with many sounds of whistling and catcalls, many applauds can be heard at various points during her routine. Cash from the stage side patrons began being tossed on the runway, an assortment of bill dimensions were used. Kenneth and Jake contributed what they could, needing to ration out their generosity to support the other girls yet to come on stage. The young woman executed a few physical feats in an attempt to increase her earnings, one involving an older man placing a twenty dollar bill between her butt crack, squeezing her glutes together to hold the bill in place, twerking excessively inches from the gentleman's face keeping the bill firmly in position. Blaring hooting and hollering commences practically drowning out the music, Kenneth and Jake are among the rowdy, whistling inducing crowd enjoying the entertainment thus far. Sending the second girl off stage to tumultuous applauds, a pair of guards come over to clear off all the cash left behind during the performance. The overly energetic DJ's voice returned in preparation for the night's headliner, first making a few announcements in regards to drink specials going on and reminding everyone to tip their waitresses. During the brief intermission, Jake's cell phone vibrated in his back pocket startling him slightly forgetting he even had it with him, usually when coming to places like this he would just leave it in the truck. Checking out the alert it's a text from Danielle, saying hi, hoping he is having a good time, not wanting to be one of those guys who texts back right away, decided he will respond to her in a little while, though touched she was thinking about him. Surprisingly also noticed he had a missed call from Ashley from about a few hours ago, wondering how he could have missed it, becoming a bit concerned pondering why she would call him on a Saturday night. Has an open door policy for all his players, but when it comes to Ashley he holds her to a different standard and worries about her the most, increasing his curiosity to know why she would have called, however convinced himself to the theory, if it was important she would have called back or there would have been multiple missed calls from her, being courteous Jake sends Ashley a quick text apologizing for missing her call and he will contact her tomorrow. With the push of the send button, the DJ gets the crowd hyped for the long awaited headliner.

"Alright, everybody, it's the moment you all have been waiting for, coming to the stage right now is your headliner, the super sexy, superhot and super sultry, Angel," introduces the DJ starting up her music.

A thunderous roar ensues mixed with heavy applauds and ear piercing whistling overpowering the newly started music. Appearing from behind the curtains as her alter ego is Ashley dressed in her famous school girl ensemble down to the ponytail, immediately going into her dance routine. Her athletic build and background allows her to perform moves and feats of flexibility most of the other girls can't achieve, reasons for her being the most popular dancer. Seeing young Ashley execute many of her provocative dance moves, mainly keeping her back to the onlookers to start her routine, sends the crowd into a frenzy, especially the lucky few having a bird's eye view. Kenneth and Jake aren't shy with their yells and boyish catcalls, talking amongst themselves how they are into the school girl outfit. Pulling off the scrunchie to her ponytail, flinging it blindly into the crowd, whipping her hair around, playing with it with her hands, revving up the motors of all the male spectators even more, preparing them for when the wrapping comes off. Her back still to the up-roarious mob of desirous, alcohol induced men, Ashley rips off her red and black plaid skirt uncovering her plumb bare ass, slightly bending down to wave it back and forth seductively. Kenneth and Jake are seated close enough to view the beads of sweat trickling down the unblemished skin of her buttock, the two enjoying the visual treat like a couple of sailors on weekend leave. Been a long time since Jake has been able to get out and be a man doing man things, was always a little hesitate to put himself back out there fearing the pressures of modern society when it comes to male bonding might be too much for him to handle being around all this testosterone, power drinkers and the adult an-tics of the present-day male, yet he feels totally in control and not the least bit tempted, just appreciating a good time with an old friend. Continuing with their private philanthropy, Kenneth and Jake leave their contributions onto the stage, though not as generous as some of the fellas seated around the stage, with fifty and hundred dollar bills appearing everywhere. Jake was grinning from ear to ear thoroughly captivated by the young lady's sexy showing, thirsty for more, yet his night of unbridled fun quickly fizzled away eyeing the young woman pirouetting around ripping open her white polyester blouse exposing her perky, white breasts, getting a view of the girl's face.

"Oh my God!" Jake said shockingly realizing it was Ashley, becoming frozen, his grin morphed into a look of confusion mixed with a look of disbelief, wanting to believe it was just a girl who looked like a spitting image of her, but was sitting to close to not recognize that face. His heart sank into his stomach, feeling sick almost disturbed at what he was seeing, leaning over to a just as mortified Kenneth to verify if he was witnessing the same thing. The two of them just sat there not knowing what to do, wondering if maybe it was just a dream and any second they would wake up and the real girl would be up on stage dancing half naked, but it wasn't a dream and it was really Ashley up there with nothing on other than a thong and some thigh high white stockings. Making it worse the thong came off, being hurled into the crowd, Jake closed his eyes shaking his head not wanting to see anymore, feeling like he is doing something wrong, wanting it to be over knowing on a professional level he is seeing something he shouldn't be seeing, trying to fathom how this girl on stage flaunting herself is the same girl who just the other day pitched her best game of the season. The lights on stage must be bright enough to affect her visibility or she just doesn't pay attention to who is seated around her, Jake thought for sure he would be spotted or even Kenneth, dancing literally right in front of them with her back turned, squatting down to shake her bare ass close enough for them to smell her body spray. Ashley jumps on the pole swinging herself round and round igniting the over excited onlookers even more, Jake who once was part of the zealous crowd feels himself getting worked up wanting the yelling and whistling to stop, the same way a father would want to protect his daughter. Wanting to remain in the shadows, Jake backed his seat away from the stage requesting Kenneth to do the same, assuming Ashley's time is coming to an end. Performing more acrobatics moves in her finale, Ashley leaves the stage through the back curtain to deafening yelling, applauds and ear-piercing whistling, leaving behind a stage littered with an abundance of cash. While the DJ makes a couple more announcements, the same pair of guards swiftly scoop up all the green blanketing most of the stage, the lights around the main platform darken, all the patrons gathered around began to scatter. Led by his clouded instincts, Jake climbed on stage heading for the curtains inferring it would lead him to Ashley's current location, Kenneth followed behind acting as backup if need be. Before he could enter Jake is halted by the same gentleman who he saw overseeing all the recent activity, standing in the entryway blocking his path.

"Can I help you, bro? Are you lost?" asked Razz leaning against the overhang with his elbow, taking a puff from his cigarette, gesturing to one of his guards to assist him.

"I need to go talk to that last girl that was on stage, I know her," Jake replied in a concerned tone.

"Yeah, so do most of the guys in this city," responded Razz arrogantly.

"Do you realize she is underage?" Jake asked a bit worked up.

"Not that it is any of your fucking business, but I don't give a fuck how old she is. She puts asses in the seats and money in my pocket," Razz gloated. "How the fuck you know her anyway?"

"That's none of your business," replied Jake starting to get angry, registering he must be talking to the owner. "You understand you could be in a lot of trouble?"

"Oh, yeah, what are you going to do, call the cops?" asked Razz. "Go ahead, in fact there is a couple of them sitting in a booth right over there. Now I don't know what your deal is, but do you think you're the first guy to say you know who she is or know her on a personal level, I don't care if she is your fucking niece, she works for me and if you want to still see her standing upright, you'll turn around and walk away and forget this whole misunderstanding ever happened and forget what you saw."

"I can't do that," insisted Jake, wanting to grab this guy by the collar, slamming him to the ground.

"Let me make it very simple, I don't care who you are to her, but when she is scheduled to work she better be here and if you decide to try and be a hero and keep her from me, I will find her and then I will find out who you are and I will find you, so be a smart boy and let it go," threatened Razz. "You don't know the world you're in, my friend."

"Jake, let's just go, we'll deal with this later," commented Kenneth tugging on Jake's shoulder from behind.

"Listen to your friend, I'll have one of my guards escort you out, don't let see your face around here again and you can take that to heart because I don't ever forget a face," added Razz. "Get them the fuck out of here."

Honoring Razz' demand, the guard softly pushes Jake to get him to proceed in the direction leading to the front entrance, holding the butt of his pistol from inside its holster as a scare tactic in case they try any funny business. Following behind Kenneth and Jake making their way through the busy confines of the main floor, girls are back to dancing on the smaller stages drawing the attention of most of the crowd, bumping shoulders with the occasional drunk weaving their way to the exit. Guided right out to the front marquis, Kenneth and Jake are left to the freedom of the outside world, their escort informs the outside guard of the situation implementing their actions to keep them from returning. Not wanting to cause a scene, Kenneth and Jake walk away to gather their thoughts soon arriving back at the parking lot, coincidentally the location of Kenneth's car. The lot was now close to capacity, yet completely empty to any other human life, the two men were alone under the lights with only the sounds of periodic traffic driving by. Kenneth stood leaned up against his trunk arms folded, Jake pacing back and forth like a caged tiger directly in front of him, if the two of them could see each other's thoughts they would learn they were identical, what they recently saw wasn't a joke or a dream and they couldn't unsee it, the images were branded into their memories.

"What the hell did we just see?" asked Jake, obviously confused and upset, hard for him to think straight.

"I don't know, but what I do know is this isn't good," Kenneth stated.

"I know," Jake replied, "I just don't believe it."

"You really had no idea about this?" asked Kenneth.

"Of course not, she told me she worked as a waitress," Jake answered. "Everything changes now."

"What do you mean?" asked Kenneth.

"I mean she lied about this, who knows what else she could be lying about," responded Jake.

"There is a bigger picture here," Kenneth noted. "Jake, if any of these schools find out about this they will re-track their scholarship offers and you can forget any other schools lining up to sign a stripper and this puts me in a very awkward position, I'm supposed to report incidents like this, you know she can be banned from playing softball again."

"God, that would kill her," said Jake.

"I know and I don't want to see that happen," remarked Kenneth.

"All I know is I didn't sign up for this, to find out my star player is an exotic dancer," Jake states.

"What are you going to do?" Kenneth asked seeing the uncertainty in Jake's face.

"You have to let me handle this my way and promise me you won't say anything to anybody," insisted Jake.

"Jake, I don't know if I can do that," Kenneth replied.

"Ken, please, she's a good kid and I want to try and help her. You heard that asshole in there, he threatened her," noted Jake.

"What if she has been lying about other things?" Kenneth asked.

"Then I will deal with it," answered Jake.

"You know you are really putting me under the gun here, I could lose my job," Kenneth commented, wanting to help his friend, but this is a circumstance where he would being taking an awful risk, yet he believes in Jake and is willing to stick his neck out for him. "Alright, I won't say anything, but I can't promise you for how long."

"I understand," Jake said, "thanks."

Saying their goodbyes for the night, Kenneth makes his way to the diver side door to leave.

"Jake, I'm sorry all this is happening," said Kenneth, a sympathetic tone in his voice.

"Yeah, me too," Jake replied.

"I'm going to be out of town for a while for work, I'll touch base with you when I get back," informed Kenneth.

Entering his truck, he leaves Jake to stand alone in the combination of unnatural light and the just recent moonlight. Waving to his friend leaving the parking lot, Jake starts his thought heavy stroll to his truck. He couldn't remember a night or time when an occurrence took such a drastic turn, maybe the day his pregnant girlfriend told him she was going to have an abortion was the only other occasion that came to mind. This was something he was really going to have to think about the rest of the weekend, considering postponing his lunch with Danielle tomorrow, worried when he sees Ashley again it's not going to be the same, he's going to see her differently in a way he doesn't want to, yet couldn't help but feel sympathy for her, deep down he wants to help her, knowing she has such a bright future ahead of her and he would hate to see it get derailed by extremely egregious adolescent choices. He has to do whatever it takes to get her to talk even if it takes devilishly excessive measures, thankful he didn't get the opportunity tonight, confronting her with a clouded mind could have only ended in disaster. Adding fuel to the fire was Jake's brief interaction with Ashley's boss, a man who only seems to value what will benefit him and gathering people around him that will help make that happen. Her boss meant everything he said, could see it in his eyes this wasn't a man who fucks around, there is nothing more menacing then one who is sure of themselves. Fearing he might have made the conditions for Ashley a dire one, sparking even more motivation to confront her. Right now he just wanted to go home and sleep on it, hoping a good night's rest will clear his mind allowing him to figure out what he is going to do. Entering his truck he remembers the missed phone call from Ashley furthering his curiosity about the nature of that call, also remembering the text he sent her stating he would get in touch with her tomorrow, something he is not ready to do yet, but must be prepared in the event she tries to contact him again which he is ready to deal with if by chance that happens.

In the driver's seat staring out the windshield at the clear night sky, not a single cloud in sight, just a sky brimming with an overabundance of stars, Jake gazed at nature's living portrait trying to recall the last time he witnessed a night sky like this. Nothing but the recognition of irony surfaces, beholding one of the most beautiful night skies he has seen in a long time on an evening where he observed a very shocking, unpleasant sight. Keys were in the ignition, yet he couldn't start the truck, a sudden overwhelming feeling of emotions came over him resulting in a lone tear sliding down his face, gripping the steering wheel tightly, laying back against the head rest knowing the second he drives out of the parking lot it will become an entirely different ballgame. His once flawless and enjoyable coaching job was just hit with an atomic bomb and he's the soldier trying to survive through the aftermath. Succeeding in his moment of deep thought, Jake perceived what he has to do, starting the truck he leaves the parking lot to make his way home.

Jake just ended a phone call with Danielle postponing their lunch date together, very appreciative of her understanding, promising he will make it up to her. Just not in the mood to face the world and have a good time, his good night's sleep became nonexistent, tossing and turning all night seeing repeated visions of Ashley's naked body up on that stage. All morning he has just kept to himself wanting to stay away from the rest of the world, even skipping breakfast after numerous attempts by Vicki to get him to come upstairs. Being alone, locked in his room felt like the best option to get some serious thinking done, the kind of thinking that could give someone a headache as if their brain was overheating. So unwavering in his efforts, he refused to even get dressed for the day, hair a mess, still pacing in his plain white t-shirt and plaid pajamas bottoms, bed still unmade, most of his other morning regimens like shaving, taking a shower and brushing his teeth have been completely ignored, been pacing so much Jake started getting rug burn on his bare feet, one of his uncontrollable nervous ticks when his anxiety begins to act up, often happening before big games during his playing days, however that was more excitement than nervousness. Keeping himself trapped in his downstairs room for the day sounded like a good plan for the day, other than what he had arranged with Danielle the rest of his day was wide open. Growing a bit fatigued from all the constant short distant walking, Jake sits on his couch to gaze at his blank television screen, not even in the right frame of mind to enjoy a little TV, could likely see himself just zoning out all day viewing the furniture and material things staying alongside him in the basement.

The constant silence Jake has surrounded himself in is sometimes interrupted by heavy footsteps coming from the floor above, though it was the ringing of his cell phone located on the table set across the room breaking his self-induced trance. A bit alarmed from the unexpected ringtone theme, he slowly rises from his stationary position to walk over to the alerting sound pondering who would be calling, not expecting to hear from anyone. Standing close enough to the table to put his phone in eyeshot, Jake sees on the caller ID it's Ashley calling. Seeing her name on screen caused his heart to drop, feeling totally unprepared for any verbal interaction with her. His first instinct was to not answer it, let it go to voicemail, that way if she happens to leave a message he could listen to it at his leisure, yet a little voice in his head was telling him to answer, to face this dilemma head on now rather than later. Listening to his conscience like he has always done in the past, Jake picks up his phone to answers it.

"Hello," greeted Jake in a low unenthusiastic tone.

"Coach, I need to talk to you, it's important, can we meet somewhere?" Ashley asked.

Hearing the sound of her soft, feminine voice broke Jake's heart, it felt like he was talking to a stranger or someone who is owner to a lot of secrets, even through the phone their once rapport felt different.

"Are you okay?" asked Jake.

"Not really, can we please just meet somewhere to talk?" insisted Ashley.

Jake conceived something was wrong from the timbre in her voice, she sounded upset even a little worried. The opportunity has arisen for him to confront her and get the answers to his many questions rather than put it off having to agonize over it until a later time.

"Want to meet at the field in about an hour?" Jake asked, suggesting a place where he knew they would be alone in case things got a little heated, saving themselves from causing a scene in public, furthermore it would only be appropriate to have a conversation like that in private without the fret or distraction of strange ears.

"Yeah, I can do that," replies Ashley. "Thank you, see you in an hour."

Her voice fades away through the cellar air space, Jake hangs up suddenly with a purpose to his day, accompanied with an instant feeling of nervousness, curious what emotions will overcome him when he finally sees her face to face.

Time being short, he quickly prepares to shower and to dress accordingly, hates having to rush to get ready, not one who enjoys going against the clock, probably why he always gravitated towards baseball nothing in the game is timed, the clock was never your enemy. Hustling around, putting his clothes out, all he could think about was what he was going say to Ashley when he finally sees her.

Standing with his arms folded on the pitcher's mound facing the outfield, Jake breathed in some of that fresh early afternoon air, the sun was nowhere to be found behind the thick overcast blanketing most of the area. The weather perfectly mirrored Jake's emotions to the upcoming meeting, deliberately showing up early to gather his thoughts together, a baseball diamond or a replica of it will always be his equivalent to a virtual thinking cap, the look and different scents associated with the area simply puts his mind at ease making it easier for him to think clearly, figuring it will always be that way up until the day he dies. Staring out at the outfield watching a number a birds fly from tree to tree, the crunching sound of footsteps on the infield dirt alerts Jake he is no longer alone. Knowing who it is, taking a deep breath he slowly turns around coming face to face with Ashley, standing there with sadness in her eyes and all over her face, a knot began to form in his stomach, it was her yet she felt like a stranger.

"Hi, thank you for coming," Ashley said, dressed as though she just threw something on, jeans, T-shirt, pink sweat jacket, hair in a ponytail wearing flip flops.

"What's this about?" asked Jake, judging by her body language and facial expression, he assumed it was something important, maybe serious.

"I don't know how to say this, I got kicked out of my house yesterday," she reports, tears started flowing down her face. "My aunt and I got into a huge fight because I found out she was hiding all my college acceptance letters. It got physical and she through me out."

Not what Jake thought he was going to hear, closing his eyes shaking his head slightly in disbelief.

"Where are you staying?" he asked, though he had a good idea.

"I'm at Holley J's right now," she answered. "Holley J knows what happened, but her parents just think I'm there for the weekend. Her parents are like super religious and they don't like me very much, I mean they are civil to me, but if they knew what happened they would never let me stay there. I just don't know what I'm going to do, I can't go back home, I can't go back to that."

Jake felt like all his emotions were being put into a blender, couldn't remember ever feeling sorry and disappointed by someone at the same time, yet through all of it, still wants to help her, but to do that he has to get the truth.

"Ashley, I want to help you, but for me to do that you have to be totally honest with me," Jake stated.

"I am, I told you everything that happened," responded Ashley confused by his statement.

"Honest about everything," he repeated, taking a step forward invading Ashley's personal space.

"I don't know what you are talking about or what's going on, but this is becoming weird, I think I should just go," Ashley replied, turning her back to Jake to start walking away.

"Where are you going, Angel?!" yelled Jake, few strides into her getaway, watching her stop dead in her tracks as if she just hit an invisible barrier.

She stood frozen trying to comprehend if she heard what she thought she heard, pivoting slowly around to face Jake once again, eyes overflowing with tears.

"Where the hell did you hear that name?" asked Ashley in utter bewilderment.

"Why don't you tell me?" Jake asserted.

"How did you find out?" she asked, in shock from what's transpiring.

"I saw you last night," answered Jake, choking a bit on his words. "I was there."

Ashley's complexion went from her normal skin tone to almost a milky white as if she just saw a ghost, covering her mouth with one hand in total embarrassment, turning to start running away only to be stopped in her tracks by Jake's sturdy grip on her arms.

"Get your fucking hands off me!" Ashley yells, trying to wiggle her way loose from Jake's clutches, sobbing excessively.

"I'll let go if you promise not to run away, I want you to stay here and talk to me," requested Jake, her body began to settle, reaching a relaxed state suggesting it was safe to release her.

Free from Jake's grasp, Ashley had a window of escape, but remained stationary, like she couldn't move almost paralyzed, unable to look Jake in the eyes. Been seen naked by hundreds of men, probably thousands, yet she has never felt this humiliated or uncomfortable before.

"I wanted more than anything to believe that wasn't you up there, that it was someone else," noted Jake. "Are you going to tell me what's going on?"

"I can't," she responds shaking her head.

"Then you leave me no choice," commented Jake. "You're off the team."

"WHAT?!" replies Ashley in a fiery tone. "YOU CAN'T FUCKING DO THAT!"

"I can do whatever I want. I don't want to do it, but I swear you will never step foot on this mound again if you don't talk to me. This is your chance to come clean, I want to help you but I can't if you won't let me in," Jake states, "and you have to quit, do you realize if anyone else finds out about this all those scholarship offers will be taken away and they will make sure you never play softball again and there will be nothing I can do about it."

"What do you want to fucking hear? That I'm some sleazy piece of gutter trash that likes to flaunt her shit in front of men because I think it's fun, WELL, SURPRISE, I AM! And it gets even better," noted Ashley.

"I don't understand," remarked Jake.

"Come on, Coach, what would guys like you love to do to a girl like me?" she asked, tears continuing to stream down her face.

"Ashley, please tell me that's not true," a choked up Jake responds.

"That's right, I'm a fucking SLUT! I fuck guys for money, is that what you wanted to know, is that what you wanted to hear," she remarks.

"Why?" Jake asked, eyes getting watery.

"Because I like money," Ashley answers sarcastically. "Maybe I'm just that type of girl."

"I know you are not really like that," replies Jake.

"You don't know anything about me, all you know is from what I've told you. My life has been hell," an upset Ashley exposes.

Breaking down to spill her guts to Jake, describing every graphic detail about all the sexual, physical and mental abuse she has endured over the years, all the way back to when she was a child, even recounting a suppressed memory of the very first time the abuse started, five years old living with her mother well before that infamous night. Her mother had a friend over, she was passed out on the couch while her friend worked his way to Ashley's room where she was sitting on her bed wearing a yellow little girl's nightgown playing with her doll, the uninvited individual walks in to an oblivious young Ashley, her back to the bedroom door. Slowly he approaches her from behind, inching closer his shadow engulfs her obstructing the light generated from the small, rusty old lamp sitting on a foldable dinner tray next to her bed. The sudden enclosed darkness notifies her she isn't alone, turning around to view the creator of the mysterious shadow, young Ashley comes in eyeshot of the man standing by her bed with his pants down, his erect penis within arm's length of her reach. The man's face was masked by shadows keeping his identity hidden, telling her to lick it like a lollipop, that it was okay all little girls do it.

The more Ashley opened up, the more Jake questioned if this was really happening, wanting to believe he was still in the middle of his sleep battle and this was one of the crazy dreams he was experiencing where any second he would wake up in a cold, damp sweat relieved it was only a projection of his subconscious, but it wasn't a dream, it was happening, this was reality at its most hard hitting since his downward spiral after his pro career ended. Jake really couldn't believe what he was hearing, his heart broke with every word she spoke, couldn't imagine going through life on the receiving end of countless heinous and despicable acts, the once anger he was feeling quickly transformed to pity having to hear what this beautiful young girl has had to endure throughout her life. Not in a million years he expected to hear something like this, he knew her home life wasn't the best, familiar with stories of many athletes whose childhoods were full of struggles and hardships, but this was on another level of fucked up. The more Ashley confessed, the harder it became for him to keep listening, so much darkness in a life full of so much potential, an incredible ballplayer and talented artist battling more demons than any one person should have too, speaking from experience having overcome his fair share of demons to get where he is today, but nothing like the ones she has been struggling with.

Thinking the worst had been said, another devastating revelation became relevant when she opened up about her relationship with her last coach, a subject matter that embarrassed her, choking on her words characterizing the specifics of their private sessions together, tasting the salty tears having leaked steadily into her mouth. Hearing the details about the coach he proceeded, Jake could hardly keep his reaction in check, what a piece of shit he thought, taking advantage of a damaged soul for his own personal gratification, wishing he could have five minutes alone with this scum bag. Went on to explain why she never reported him, a clarification he didn't agree with, but understood. Firing him was just a slap on the wrist for what he just heard, sickening him men like that could behave in a malicious manner and get away scot free, probably already on to his next victim.

From the emotion in her voice to the choice of her words, Jake could identify she has always wanted to open up about this rather than keep it suppressed, but was probably held back by the fear of judgment, how the rest of the world would perceive her. A sense of guilt came over him having made her empty all the skeletons in her closet at this time and in this manner, but he would be lying if he said he wasn't happy it happened this way.

"Ashley, I'm so sorry," said Jake overcome with emotion.

"Don't be, I did what I had to do," Ashley responded, "and I'm going to continue to do what I have to do."

"It doesn't have to be like that," Jake remarked. "If you are serious about your future you will let me help you."

"What are you going to do? You think you are just going to come along and be my fucking hero? You have no idea the position that I am in. You just have to accept that this who I am," Ashley insisted.

"Why would you want to keep doing this?" asked Jake.

"Because it's all I know and I'm sorry your perception of me has changed," Ashley said, unable to look Jake in the face, looking over at the empty bleachers.

"I want you to look square into my eyes," ordered Jake, grabbing Ashley tightly by the arms. "Do it."

Refusing, keeping focus on what's in her line of sight.

"DO IT!" Jake yells with purpose, alarming her by the loud angered tone in his voice, she obeys shifting her focus to his concerned gaze. "Now look deep into my eyes and tell me you don't want my help," Jake instructed. Staring extensively, more tears descended down her face, seeing kindness and trust peering back at her.

"Please help me," Ashley whispered breaking down crying, Jake embraces her allowing her to extinguish years of suppressed emotions, talking under her breath squeezing clumps of his shirt. Listening to her break down, emptying out so much negative energy, her body trembling against his physically feeling how frightened and lost this young girl really was, couldn't help but to start tearing up himself, holding her tightly, Jake knew the first thing he had to do. Not wanting her to end up living in hotel rooms or worse on the streets alone, offers her to come stay with him for the time being. Taken back by his generous offer, Ashley having no other better options willingly accepts.

Leaving Holley J's was hard, but Ashley knew it was the right thing to do, would prefer to stay with her best friend, but the elephant in the room constantly looms large. Spending time alone with Holley J is always enjoyable, wishing she could do it more often, but since her parents haven't always been too fond of her, it would make for an awkward living arrangement. Always being that way ever since Holley J introduced Ashley to them, something about her has always rubbed them the wrong way. Thought it might be the reaction to her home life, not having a mother or father around giving off the vibe she is some troubled orphan and would be a bad influence on their daughter, yet they never tried to keep her and Holley J apart. Then there is the religious aspect, two devout Christians following the bible like its life's personal handbook, church every Sunday morning, a ritual they try to drag Holley J along too. Visits to their home many times resulted in distressing ventures to convert her to Christianity, preaching heavily about the need to have Jesus in your life and the many consequences of a life empty of God's love, finding it very awkward and demoralizing, yet politely rejecting their undesired teachings in a way showing respect to their home and beliefs. Most visits the two girls escape to Holley J's room for the duration of Ashley's stay, a safe house from all the Jesus and God malarkey, something Holley J knows unnerves her best friend. This latest dilemma with Ashley and her aunt emanating in her recent stay could only last for the weekend, they would never allow her to stay on a long term basis on the account of her history, if it were up to Holley J, she would be able to stay there as long as she needed, yet was thankful for her opening her doors when she needed it. Though Holley J was stunned when learning where Ashley would be staying, she understood really having no choice due to a lack of options, also promised not to mention it to anybody else, especially the rest of the team, assumptions of favoritism could be the wrench in the cogs that derails their season. A sudden silence surrounded the kitchen table where Jake, Jeff and Vicki sat each with a coffee mug in front of them, wrapping up a lengthy household meeting, a serious discussion on the topic of Jake inviting Ashley to stay with them for a while or at least until he finds a place of his own. Always appreciating his brother and Vicki allowing him to stay with them until he got back on his feet, now asking to bring another person, a stranger to them to live in their house would be a lot to ask anybody, but after presenting the situation and deciphering the facts she would have nowhere else to go other than the streets, Jeff and Vicki felt it was the only humane thing to do regardless of how either of them thought of the circumstances. Jeff was the first to agree to letting her stay, having only been back less than an hour from his latest business trip, his luggage still sitting at the front door entryway, when Vicki after greeting him with the usual kiss and hug, informed him that Jake needed to talk to them about something very important. Jeff unfailingly trusts his brother's judgment and didn't even think twice about lending a hand in helping this girl who happened to be one of his players. Vicki at first was more hesitant, already opening her home to Jake was now being asked to do it a second time to a complete stranger, not wanting to come off as a heartless bitch, she came around giving her blessing on the condition she is Jake's responsibility, doesn't mind serving an extra plate at the dinner table, but everything else he must handle. Accepting the terms, Jake graciously thanked them for their help, notifying them she would be arriving soon. Space was definitely not an issue, the house having two extra guest bedrooms upstairs, neither one of them have been used in quite a while, normally saved for out of town family members or friends needing a place to crash, however it has been some time since they accommodated any special guests. When Jake first moved in he was offered one of the rooms, but Jeff insisted he stay downstairs so he would have more privacy. Lack of usage had Jeff and Vicki considering turning one of them into a storage room, yet since they are mostly out of sight out of mind they are just left alone. Vicki excused herself wanting to go prepare one of the guestrooms making sure it was presentable, giving the bed some clean linens, opening the bedroom window to circulate some fresh air, whether she agrees with the state of affairs or not she never wants anyone to say she wasn't hospitable, with the twins spending the day at her parents she can get the room ready without any interruptions. Giving Jeff a quick kiss before exiting the kitchen, she leaves the two brothers to have some alone time, has been awhile since Jake and his brother had a private conversation together, even being under the same roof few opportunities seem to arises. Looking over at Jake who was fiddling with his empty coffee mug, his eyes peering at the center of the wooden table, the lawyer side of Jeff repeatedly has the ability to read body language, facial expressions and eye movement, he would tell you you can learn almost anything about a person just from reading their eyes, one of the reasons why he was always such a good poker player, viewing his brother he could instantly tell there was something weighing on his mind, something he wants to reciprocate, but doesn't think he should. Their relationship as brothers has always been good, even as kids they have always looked out for each other, never kept secrets, were willing to talk about anything from girls, to the crazy shit they would do with their friends, yet whatever was concerning Jake this time was something different, something beyond asking to provide a bed for someone in need.

"Something on your mind?" Jeff asked, breaking the silence, knowing there was, just wanted to throw out a line to see if he would bite.

Jake knew his brother could see right through him, you would have to be a stone cold statue to hide any information from him, could feel Jeff's eyes looking him over. Now that Vicki has made herself absent, Jake felt more secure in letting Jeff in on what was really going on. Gaining his brother's full attention, Jake relays every detail he could remember on what's going on with Ashley, even her exploits at the club. Nobody Jake trusted more with the information he was bringing forward, having another point of view, along with Jeff's legal advice could come in useful to what was a very dicey situation. Hung up on every word Jake spoke, with a demeanor resembling one normally showing up in the courtroom from listening to many witness testimonies, Jeff thought he had heard everything, but this was something he never expected to hear. The concerned tone in Jake's voice, the readable tension in his face as he spoke, brought general apprehension to Jeff, mainly from hearing about the exchange with the club owner who Jake described as a real hard ass and a first rate asshole. Getting the police involved wasn't an option, most likely they were paid off to keep quiet while at the same time able to enjoy the finer offerings of the facility. Pleased Jake let him in on this unique predicament, Jeff was one hundred percent willing to help out in any way he could, worried his baby brother might be in over his head, it's not every day a simple coaching gig turns into a deliberate rescue mission. There is always strength in numbers and this is one of those times trying to go at it alone might be too much for anybody to handle. Letting Jake know he doesn't have to go through this solo and he has his up most support, Jeff reassures them both they will figure it out together, an alliance which put Jake temporarily at ease. Knows he did the right thing telling his brother, who better to ask for help from than a legal mastermind, trying to put into words how to thank him for being there. Wanting no part of any thanks, there was not enough he could do for Jake to make up for what he did for him that life changing night so many years ago, will always feel indebted to his brother, yet Jake specified once this is over they would be even. Ending their private conversation, Jake made Jeff promise to keep this between them, meaning he couldn't tell Vicki, word of this could change her mind about letting Ashley stay there which could potentially drive a wedge between him and her. Jeff has never lied or kept secrets from his wife, yet certain circumstances trump the sacred vow of honesty amongst spouses keeping her best interest at heart, what she doesn't know won't hurt her. Agreeing to secrecy, Jeff checks his watch realizing its time for him and Vicki to head over to her parents' house for dinner to reunite with the twins. Leaving the kitchen to reconnect with her so they could be off on their way, Jake remained in his current position recollecting the conversation him and his brother had just moments ago, mixed with thoughts of how things are going to be once Ashley's presence is felt, continuously sliding his one index finger over the rim of his coffee mug showcasing some unsettled nerves. With Jeff and Vicki pursuing their plans for the evening there was nothing left for Jake to do other than patiently wait for Ashley's arrival.   Standing over the kitchen sink with the faucet running, soapy dish cloth in hand, Jake cleans the coffee mugs left from earlier, an alerting sound comes from his cell phone lying on the counter space next to the sink. Quickly shutting off the faucet and drying his hands, he checks his incoming text message which is from Ashley stating she is in the driveway. Wasting no time, Jake swiftly heads for the front door to greet her, feeling he nerves begin to flare up again not knowing what to expect from this agreed arrangement. Opening the front double doors there he sees Ashley standing on the anterior patio holding two duffel bags while wearing a backpack, her expression mimics that of what Jake is feeling. Grabbing one of her bags, Jake invites her inside. Showing Ashley the bedroom she will be using during her stay, allowed her to drop her bags off inside. Entering the room, she stops a few steps in to overlook the surroundings, everything looks brand new, the bed appears to be almost twice the size of her regular bed, a mango smell comes from the deodorizer placed on the nightstand, the breeze from the open window helps to circulate the scent. Appreciative for the homey room, she places her bags upon the bed, a small smile could be seen on her face.

"Let me show you the rest of the house," Jake states.

The tour of the house began with the rest of the upstairs including the large attic, making their way downstairs to the main floor where the brunt of the house is located. Being shown room after room, Ashley was in awe of the sheer scale of the home, everything was beautiful and expensive looking, the type of house she imagined some of her clients probably lived in, her comfort factor started to slowly deteriorate feeling out of place, like she didn't belong, a girl like her would be a stain to the elegance of a home of this nature, surely not use to being around a structure screaming of money and full of happiness. Holley J's house was nice, but nothing like this, if she had somewhere else to go she might have reconsidered Jake's offer, already feeling like a burden. The next room which Jake described as a sitting room, a term Ashley never heard before, a room indicative to what its title states housing wicker furniture and coffee table with its main show piece being a black grand piano stationed in one corner of the room, large windows make up one whole wall putting in view the large in ground pool in the back yard. Noticed every room she was greeted with a different pleasing aroma, the type of fragrances one might smell at a high end day spa. They both stood in the center of the room, Jake expressing how this was his favorite room in the house, loving to sit there some nights just staring out into the darkness in total silence. Losing track of Ashley's position, his moment of self-reflecting was interrupted by the melodic sound of a piano being played bringing his attention to the source of the music. Facing the piano, Jake sees Ashley sitting on the bench effortlessly tickling the ivories, playing some familiar pieces mixed in with some original melodies. Feeling drawn to the elegant music, he makes his way over to stand next to the piano to witness her fluid finger work with the keys, her eyes were closed, body slightly swayed as if hypnotized by her own musical tapestry, a modest grin inhabited her face. Being impressed with every note she played, feeling like he was trapped in a musical spider web spun by her melodic tones. Been quite some time since he heard someone play this particular piano like this, it pretty much remains dormant, nobody living in the house even knows how to play, Jake tried to learn as a kid, was told it would help with his hand eye coordination, however he lacked the patience required to learn a difficult instrument like the piano. Jeff and Vicki keep it because it's a sophisticated piece and it really accentuates the room. Continuing to be moved by her flawless playing, Jake stares at her current peaceful existence trying to piece together the puzzle of how someone with so many talents as her was dealt the hand in life she was. Suddenly the music ends leaving the room silence.

"That was incredible," Jake said.

"My grandmother taught me when I was younger," replied Ashley. "It came pretty easy for me, I use to love to play, I found it very relaxing. I haven't had access to one in a while, when I saw this one I couldn't help myself, guess I wanted to know if I could still play."

"I think you got your answer," responded Jake in a low enthusiastic tone.

"I still have to go to work tonight," Ashley mentions, keeping eye contact elsewhere.

Jake's formerly peaceful mood quickly eroded away hearing Ashley remind him of her current profession, sickening him he has to let her go off to continue with what he now knows, putting him on edge for the rest of the night wondering if she is okay.

"I need you to promise me you won't say anything to anybody, especially Holley J," requested Ashley.

"Don't you think you should tell her? Eventually the truth always comes out," Jake remarked.

"I can't," she answered.

"You told me," Jake noted.

"That was different, you didn't give me much of a choice," said Ashley.

"She's your best friend," remained Jake.

"That's right and I want to keep it that way. Just promise me," Ashley insisted looking up at Jake.

"Okay," Jake responds with hesitation.

Thinking ahead to tomorrow when they are back at practice to prepare for a couple games this week, how it is going to be? Can he still coach with this now continuously weighing on his mind? Afraid he will constantly be looking over his shoulders, yet he has no other option, everything will have to run normally until he can come up with a plan.

"We're going to figure this out," Jake declared.

"I hope so," Ashley commented.

Practice went on like usual with the regular sight of sweat soaked practice jerseys and heavy breathing coming from the girls. Jake was his normal self, preaching and educating, being around the team seem to take his mind off what has been occurring lately despite the fact Ashley was always in eyesight. She was her normal self around the team as well, the same leader and motivator he has witnessed all season long, still hard for Jake to believe the on the field Ashley and the off the field one are the same person in spite of both versions having the same personality, it was more of a light and dark side. Even the weirdness of both of them now staying under the same roof was nonexistent, each of them were able to maintain the typical coach, player relationship for the sake of the team, however they both would be lying if they were to say there wasn't some awkwardness there between the two of them, Jake contributes much of it to the events of the last twenty-four hours. A considerable amount of last night, he spent just lying in bed with the inability to fall asleep, on his back looking up at the ceiling wondering and worrying about Ashley, wasn't until well after midnight he heard the footsteps of her climbing the staircase to the upstairs reassuring her safe return, trying not to think about what she was probably doing most of the night as he was now able to slowly fall asleep. The rest of the house had already turned in for the night leaving the introductions for a very tense morning breakfast. Jake made sure to get up a little earlier than normal setting his alarm to go off an hour premature to keep Ashley from walking into a kitchen full of unfamiliar faces. Waking up before the sun, something he hasn't done in a very long time, making a point to get dressed and ready for work before everyone else woke up despite the fact he barely got any sleep. Between his anxiety waiting up for Ashley, to what would be an interesting morning when the rest of the household finally meet her, he felt sluggish and still tired, thankfully a nice cold shower helped him to feel more arouse. Wanting to make Ashley's first morning as comfortable and welcoming as possible he decided to overtake the kitchen to put on a pot of coffee and to begin preparing breakfast for everyone. Soon the kitchen was occupied with the famished appetites of the family, each making their appearance one after another, greeted to the appetizing aroma of sizzling bacon, scrambled eggs and French toast. Vicki who is usually the breakfast chef embraced her rare morning off, for the first time in a long time was able to sit with Jeff and the twins and enjoy a nice breakfast together before they all had to run off to work and school. All that was missing was Ashley who was in the shower Jeff reported, hearing the water going in the spare bathroom on his way down. Though it felt like a typical Monday morning, any minute their mystery guest was about to make her first emergence to Jeff and his family bringing their intrigue level to an all-time high adding a slight discomfort to their morning meal. The wait ended as a very nervous Ashley entered the kitchen to the stares of her curious hosts. Standing with closed off body language, she greeted everyone with a good morning, Jake leaves his cooking duties for a moment to introduce her to everyone, feeling her anxious energy encompassing the kitchen. One by one, Jake identifies everyone, greeting her with handshakes and friendly smiles, the twins who were informed of the upcoming living conditions even complemented Ashley saying how pretty she was. Taking a seat at the table, she remained closed off, still feeling like the center of attention, wanting to crawl out of view to hide, Jake's presence was the only thing keeping her together. Not wanting to be rude, she gave thanks to Jeff and Vicki for allowing her to stay, relaying how beautiful their house was, offering to help with any household chores to show her appreciation. Seeing Ashley for the first time Jeff can see the correlation between her and the industry she currently is employed in, referencing how easy on the eyes she is, though years of abuse is the main culprit for girls her age to fall victim to that lifestyle, ashamed how someone so stunning physically can be so damaged. Vicki instantly felt threatened by Ashley's looks, having her in the same house as her husband all of a sudden felt like a bad idea, not that she didn't trust Jeff, it was Ashley she was more concerned about, hearing all those stories about teenage girls seducing older men for money or their own sexual pleasure, generally those with daddy issues a profile she corresponds with after hearing the story of her parents or lack thereof, for all Vicki knew Ashley could be trying to play Jake as well doing her research to find out he lives with his finically secure brother putting her in the perfect scenario. Being way past changing her mind on agreeing to these conditions, leaving her know choice but to keep a close eye on the young vixen, showing smiles to camouflage her female intuition.

Passing out everyone's food, each plate contained what that particular person was known to enjoy, Jake asked Ashley what she would like, though very hungry, her stomach felt in knots from nerves, simply requesting a glass of orange juice and a small portion of eggs. Awareness to social restlessness in the room as they all sat eating their breakfast made for a quiet meal together, even the twins who are regularly restless and antagonizing each other before their bus comes were well behaved. Jeff decided to be the one to break the ice, asking Ashley questions a typical teenage girl would find comfortable and friendly, mainly questions about school and softball. Learning from experience with many clients, asking the right question or questions that are universally considered good-natured, can help make a person feel more relaxed in any situation, Jeff noticed the change in Ashley's body language the more their exchange continued, sitting more open as she ate the rest of her breakfast. The sudden barrage of questions caught Ashley off guard at first, but started to find it welcoming as if Jeff was truly interested in her. Vicki's attention focused mainly on the twins, yet couldn't help but listen in on the cordial banter between her husband and their new house guest, already sparking flames of jealousy. Mostly sitting in silence, Jake wanted to allow everyone to get comfortable with the extra body at the table, his nerves could probably compete with Ashley's, anticipating it might be a few days until the novelty wears off. Breakfast ended with the sound of a school bus horn loudly blaring from outside, Vicki scrambled to get the girls ready, helping them with their backpacks and handing them their lunches while saying their goodbyes as they raced for the front door. Jeff was next to depart, checking his watch viewing he was running late, throwing on his suit jacket, he gave his customary kiss goodbye to Vicki before grabbing his briefcase off the counter, exiting the kitchen. The abrupt dispersal of everyone gave Ashley a glimpse of real family life, the husband running off to work, the wife leading the kids to the bus for school, all aspects of life that have always been absent from hers, her normal is vastly different than the normal being displayed before her, this is a new reality she stepped into, one where happiness is as standard as the air she breathes rather than some unattainable magic you only hear about in fairytales. At the table wondering if one day she could have all this, a husband, kids, a nice home full of love and warmth, the things every young girl dreams about, yet the path she is on now doesn't lead to what she is looking for, it is leading her to a much darker future one where she fears will possibly end like her mother's. Though it was extremely awkward, she couldn't have gotten through it without Jake by her side, knowing more about her now than even Holley J, never imagined somebody other than her best friend would learn of her darkest secrets. Trusting Jake has been one of the smartest decisions she has made in a very long time, the road to redemption begins with him the unlikeliest of places compared to the coaching she has received in the past. Right now all she can do it take everything day by day and regardless of how uncomfortable things are at the moment to just be grateful she has a place to stay for the time being, what doesn't surprise her is the fact she hasn't been contacted by her aunt since she left the house, more evidence she never cared, for all she knew Ashley could be dead in a ditch somewhere. Coming up on time to have to leave for school, now a few miles further away she will have to leave a bit sooner than normal.

Getting up from her seat, she grabs her backpack resting next to her chair, Jake gets up to began clearing the table, he doesn't have to be to the school for another hour giving him a little extra time. Thanking Jake for breakfast, Ashley hand carries her backpack out of the kitchen on her way to her car, getting wishes of a good day at school from Jake.

Hearing a form of etiquette she never once heard while living with her aunt made it more clear how utterly deprived she has been most of her life.

Most of the girls vacated the field to head for the locker room, Jake, Ashley and Holley J hung back in the dugout. Ashley let it be known to Jake that Holley J knew she was staying with him for now and it will be left between the three of them. This is the time after practice when Ashley and Holley J go off doing their own thing for a while, but today they had to take a raincheck, Holley J had a doctor's appointment with her dermatologist. Packing her gear back in her duffel bag, Holley J suggest the two of them hang out later perhaps grabbing something to eat. Agreeing to the proposal, always in favor of any chance for them to be alone together, advising Holley J to text her when she is done with her appointment. In agreeance, Holley J shoulders her bag bidding her adieu leaving the dugout. Jake and Ashley were left, sitting side by side staring out into the now deserted field both recalling what came to pass the last time they were alone there together. After an intense practice this would be the time a coach and his or her star player would reflect and throw strategic ideas back and forth, yet this wasn't one of those times.

"Have you heard from your aunt?" Jake asked.

"No and I don't expect to," answered Ashley. "And I don't care either, I never want to go back there."

"I get it," Jake said.

"So what now?" asked Ashley, keeping her eyes forward.

"You have to quit there," Jake replied.

"I told you I can't," she remarked.

"Then I need you to give me the name of the owner of the club," requested Jake.

"I don't know if that is such a good idea," Ashley remarked.

"Ash, listen, if you want my help you are going to have to work with me here," informed Jake.

"I don't really remember his name, I think he told me once before, everybody just calls him Razz," states Ashley.

"Think," Jake insisted.

"I think it's Trevor, I don't know his last name," responded Ashley.

"So Trevor," Jake said.

"There's something else, I think he is into some other business on the side," she proclaimed.

"What kind of business? Like drugs, does he sell drugs?" he asked intently.

"I don't know, I know he smokes a lot of weed and I have seen him do cocaine before," she notes.

"Okay, that's a start," he remarked. "Let me ask you something, has he ever done anything to you?"

The question pierced through her like a razor sharp arrow, already given him all the specifics about everything else, there was no reason for Ashley to lie about some of the disciplinary measures she has been a part of or has received. Bowing her head, she confessed all the physical abuse she has sustained at the hand of Razz, mentioning all she has seen happen to other girls as well. Sorry he asked, but Jake knew what he was about to hear wasn't going to be pleasant, only infuriating him more learning this piece of shit puts his hands on Ashley in a violent way, any of the girls for that matter, wanting nothing more than to see this scum bag get what he deserves.

"What are you going to do?" Ashley asked, looking over at Jake, an unsettling look appeared in her eyes.

"Whatever it takes," responded Jake.

Back at the house with some time to kill before having to leave to meet up with Holley J, Ashley is in her temporary room putting her clothes in the empty dresser provided. The first bedroom she has occupied in a while she can safely say isn't the sight of assorted heinous acts done against her, giving the clean, wonderful smelling room an odd rapport, mentally afraid it could never feel like home until she has been violated against her will between these walls. Not the way a personal bedroom should feel, hopefully this can be the first one that feels like home without it being corroded with dark history, a feat well within possibility judging by the congenial atmosphere of the rest of the house. Stepping out into the hallway, Ashley walked up to the stained wood banister overlooking some of the downstairs, a peaceful and quiet stillness surrounded her, still in admiration of the overall elegance being displayed throughout, thinking about what it would have been like to grow up in a house like this. Enjoying the view, she is interrupted by a couple pairs of eight year hands tugging on her shirt, looking down to see the twins urging her to follow them, each grabbing a separate one of Ashley's hands to lead her to their bedroom. Going along with her pint sized kidnappers, Ashley is pulled into the twin's room which was a sight to behold, being three times the size of any bedroom she ever had or saw. Decorated like a girl's room you would see in a high end home and gardening magazine, pink, purple and yellow being the dominating colors. Bunk beds each dressed in unrelated color schemes rested in one corner of the room, the bottom bunk housing two large drawers underneath, with a large embellishing chest placed at the foot of the structure. A large flat-screen TV was mounted on the wall opposite of the bunks, granting the girls optimal viewing experience while lying in bed. Each girl had their own hand carved dresser complete with their name engraved in big bold letters, a child sized wooden table and chair set sat comfortably in the middle of the room, covered mostly in coloring books, crayons and markers, a plethora of stuffed animals, plushes and dolls were located all over, many Disney posters and various pictures filled some of the walls, the soft thick carpeting blanketed the floor. This was the type of bedroom every little girl would dream about having, one of many benefits of getting to grow up in a well off family. Led to the center of the room where the twins politely ask Ashley to have a seat on the floor. Unable to resist their young adorable faces, she plants herself Indian style waiting to see what their young minds have in store. The twins inform Ashley they would like to play beauty salon, doing each other's hair and makeup. With some time to spare, she happily accepts the invitation, instructing one of the twins to sit front and center with her back to Ashley. Beginning to braid the one twin's hair, the other goes to stand behind Ashley, playfully dressing up her long, soft locks with multiple clips and old school barrettes. Spending this time with the twins became more enjoyable than she had anticipated, not having much experience with kids, never having really been around them, yet she felt comfortable. Engaging with the young girls as they made up fun hairstyles and mischievously did each other's makeup, Ashley felt like she entered a time warp and was transported back to a time to encounter the innocence she sadly lost as a child, able to relive these moments of childhood she never got to through these two little girls. Though she was twice their age, she was appreciating their company, making small talk she discovered they were both very smart for being just eight years old, laughing together and just enjoying the moment, Ashley needed this, to see life from a different perspective. Knowing the twins are growing up in a household like this, loved dearly by two wonderful parents, it made Ashley happy to know these girls will most likely never have to go through what she has, still it depressed her that these are the things she missed out on throughout her life.

Walking up the staircase to the upstairs hallway, Jake could hear the giggling and laughing coming from the twin's room. Initially going up to check on Ashley, he felt compelled to investigate the laughter coming from the twins' room, hearing Ashley's voice among the guilty perpetrators. The bedroom door was open wide enough to see all three girls inside having a good time with each other, yet closed enough for Jake to hide himself from being seen. Looking on at Ashley laughing and smiling with his nieces, being the little girl she never got to be, brought an unseen smile to his face.

Ashley and Holley J are seated outside their favorite outdoor café enjoying some fine cuisine and each other's company, the atmosphere was light hearted many of the other outside tables were unused giving them a small sense of privacy, though their table rested directly next to the sidewalk, the flow of traffic from passing bystanders was surprisingly light for this time in the evening. Eating their meals, Ashley spent most of the time answering questions about what it is like staying at Jake's brother house, even though it has been less than a full day since she has been there. Holley J being Holley J wants to know ever specific detail from how it looks to what kind of food they eat. Wondering sometimes if Holley J is some kind of human computer for the fact she loves to store as much information as she can for later reference. Kindly feeding her whatever particulars she deemed appropriate for her mental files, Ashley was careful not to tell her anything that would be classified as nobody's business, even to her best friend. Every fork full Ashley consumed made her realize more how much these hang out times with Holley J mean to her, sometimes catching herself looking across the table at her watching all her hand gestures as she rambles on about the latest gossip, yet not hearing any of the words just seeing someone who has been by her side for so many years, someone who has made seeing tomorrow worth it, at that moment she pledged to herself one day she would do something big for Holley J to say thanks for always being there, any promises Holley J would ask her to keep no matter how big, she would honor them.

Coming to the end of their dinner, the girls drew their attention to the sudden increase of patrons now milling the area, mainly comprised of over caffeinated and liquored up town folks, tables around them once empty were now becoming occupied. The temperature became unexpectedly cooler forcing the girls to throw on their sweat jackets feeling the chill evening air pass through the café patio. Turning into a charming nightfall, all the outside lights from all the stores, bars and eateries illuminated almost in unison, from her seat Ashley can see off in the distance over a close by rooftop the reddish orange tint to the sky mixed with a few clouds as the sun gradually makes its descent for the remainder of the night. Staring at that peaceful night sky, Ashley thought it would make a great painting, soaking in as much of the visual to her memory banks as she can, loving these unanticipated moments of inspiration, a subtle way of bringing meaning to her life. Their waitress stops by the table to drop off their check, swiftly confiscated by Ashley before Holley J had a chance to glance at it, representing dinner was on her. An appreciative Holley J insists on leaving the tip, claiming the next one will be her treat. Digging through her shoulder satchel for her wallet, Ashley is suddenly greeted by a shadow enveloping the opening of the purse in total darkness restricting her vision, looking up to see who or what is causing the unexpected shade, sees a young man, roughly in his mid-twenties, standing on the sidewalk beside their table.

"It's you," said the young man, a bit of excitement in his voice.

"Excuse me," Ashley replied, drawing her attention to the young man.

"You're the girl from Playmates, the stripper Angel," he commented enthusiastically.

"Ash, what is he talking about?" a confused Holley J asked.

"Nothing, he's lying, he has me confused with someone else," Ashley stated in an angry tone.

Eagerly pulling out his cell phone, the young man brings up a picture of Ashley on stage in the buff, the lighting in the shot perfectly captured her face.

"Look, check it out for yourself," says the young man, showing Holley J the photo.

"Oh my God," Holley J utters, snatching the phone from the young man's hands to get a better look. "Ash, is this really you?"

Showing Ashley the photo of her wearing an open white blouse exposing her breasts and her bare shaven under carriage, the tears building up in Holley J's eyes glistened under the patio lighting. Seeing that photo of herself seemingly baring it all sent a wave of unflattering emotions surging through Ashley's body, never before has she seen with her own eyes the visual of what she looks like on stage, it was her meeting her other persona for the first time, like Dr. Jekyll meeting Mr. Hyde, instantly detesting what she saw, looking at an image created by lies and manipulation alongside years of abuse.

"Holley J, listen," Ashley pleaded, building up moisture of her own in her eyes.

"Just tell me the truth!" ordered Holley J, standing there like a deer in the headlights.

"Yes," answered Ashley, looking Holley J square in the eyes, tears sliding down her face.

Grabbing the phone out of Holley J's hands, Ashley violently presses it against the young man's chest pushing him away, yelling at him to leave.

"You're a waitress, huh," remarked an upset Holley J.

Storming off, knocking down her chair, Holley J walks briskly down the sidewalk trying to avoid oncoming patrons heading towards her car. Promptly Ashley chases her down in a frenzy, accidentally bumping into approaching foot traffic, catching up she grabs Holley J by the arm bringing her to a halt.

"Holley J, I can explain," Ashley said with sadness in her voice.

"I just want to know one thing. How long?" asked Holley turning.

Turning to face her best friend in the middle of the crowded sidewalk, more tears streaming down her face.

"Holley J, please," replied Ashley, suppling her own wet works.

"HOW LONG?!" Holley J asked, raising her voice drawing the attention from nearby bystanders.

"About three years," a hesitant Ashley answers, nearly choking on her words responding.

"Oh my God! I don't believe this. You've been lying to me for the past three years? That bruise on your arm that time, it wasn't from falling down the stairs, was it?" asked an angry Holley J.

"Holley J, you have to let me explain," Ashley pleaded.

"Explain what? That my best friend is secretly a whore!" uttered Holley J.

"Please don't say that," Ashley voices, the words hit her like a punch to the gut.

"What hurts me the most is the fact you lied. I can't talk to you right now," declares an upset Holley J, running off disappearing into the darkness of early night.

"HOLLEY J!" yells Ashley, tears profusely streaming down her face, her loud stern holler catches the recognition of many people passing by, undeterred by the countless eyes fixated on her outburst.

After a few minutes of hoping Holley J will reappear out of the blackness of night, Ashley finally realized she was gone and not coming back. Overcome with an abundance of sadness, she backs herself up against the building wall behind her, crying heavily, slowly sliding down to the ground below hugging her legs burying her face between her arms. Ashley has always dreaded what Holley J's reaction would be if she ever found out the truth, reacting the way she always thought she would, but this wasn't how it was supposed to be, would have wanted it to be on her own terms, coming from her mouth not from some strange guy from the streets. Jake was right, the truth always comes out, yet mostly always at the wrong time. This will be by far the toughest test their friendship will ever endure, understanding now she has to come clean about everything and it must come from her not some outside source.

Sitting on the cold concrete wrapped in a blanket of depression, her heart ached thinking about what must be going through Holley J's mind, what it's going to be like when they see each other again, Holley J can't avoid her for too long having another game in a couple days. Keeping her head down refusing to view the immersive nightlife happening around her, hearing the many footsteps and chatter of those passing by, she became lost in her thoughts wondering what is going to happen between them. Holley J doesn't believe in many of her parents' religious beliefs, but she does gravitate to some of their opinions on certain types of people including their judgment of what society calls exotic dancers, that they're the lowest of the low, ones who tease the opposite sex for money, whores who are a penetration away from being prostitutes. Knowing how Holley J feels about girls like her and being friends with one is probably not an option with her which is what scares Ashley the most. Even with all the activity going on around her, she never felt more alone, convinced soon some stranger would ask if she was okay, yet no one ever did, a picture of today's society where they must have seen her as a young kid consumed with teenage drama, if you are not covered in dirt and blood it's not worth anyone's time to get involved. The longer she sat there soaking her shirt in drops of overwhelming sorrow, the greater her panic became Holley J could possibly garner the title former friend and no matter what she had to do whatever it takes to make things right.

Sitting on a black wicker chair of the front patio enjoying some of the fresh night air, a tall glass of iced tea rested on the small wicker table placed adjacent to his position, Jake recently got off a phone conversation with Danielle. With everything that has been going on as of late, the two of them haven't had much time to spend together, making up excuses for the reason he has been so distance lately which she has been accepting, but sooner or later he is going to run out of explanations and he hates to have to keep lying to her. Contemplated on telling her everything despite the fact he promised Ashley he wouldn't brief anyone else in on her confidential lifestyle, a promise already broken by informing Jeff with the details. Breaking a promise if done in hopes of helping the opposing party is completely justified according to Jake, though promises are an agreement built on trust often times there are bigger things at stake than keeping ones word. Been sometime since he has appreciated the solitude of sitting alone in the still and silence of the night with only the glow of the overhead patio light to provide some sort of visibility, Jeff, Vicki and the girls are attending some school function and should be back soon. Lost in the glimmer of the other houses surrounding the cul-de-sac, felt like he has been sitting there for hours yet it has been only around thirty minutes, trying to escape the main basis for why he decided to enjoy his own company, patiently awaiting Ashley's return. She went out with Holley J and work supposedly was not on the agenda, but when she is not scheduled, she is on call which could explain why she isn't back yet, a thought that still brings a sickening knot to his stomach. Since Ashley's interrogation at his hands, he has felt compelled to be more protective of her, an instinct of his character when it comes to his friends and family.

Having another sip of his iced tea, off in the distance a pair of headlights emerge from the darkness making their way steadily towards the cul-de-sac. The closer the beams of light got the more glare they produced making it difficult for Jake to make out the vehicle, watching the lights steer in the direction of the house's driveway, from the sound of the engine, he determined it wasn't Jeff as it slowly pulled up parking behind his truck. The lights vanish and the engine sounds off, Ashley appearing from the driver's seat, slamming the car door with a little extra behind it, walking up the walkway with her arms folded reminiscent to someone trying to close themselves off to the world. Entering the light of the patio, her eyes glistened indicating she had been crying, also evident from the fresh tears wetting her face.

"Are you okay? What happened?" Jake asked, leaving his seat to greet her.

Looking up at Jake with so much sadness in her eyes, Ashley immediately starting to cry again, after consoling her for a brief moment, he guided her over to one of the wicker chairs where she took a seat. Returning to his seat, Jake intently waited to hear what caused her current emotional state, wondering if she is even going to tell him seeming pretty upset at the moment. Too early for her to be home had she been at the club, so he assumed it had to be something with Holley J, thinking maybe they had a fight. Ashley sat there trying to control her emotions, saw Jake was all ears ready to listen, right now he might be the only friend she has left.

"Holley J knows," Ashley said, wiping away some of the tears with her jacket sleeve.

"Everything?" asked Jake.

"No, but enough," she answered still emotional.

"Ash, I'm so sorry," Jake remarked.

Sitting on the dimly lit patio, Ashley explained how everything went down.

Standing by her locker overcome with anxiety, Ashley waited and wondered if Holley J was going to make her regular morning appearance. After her much needed talk with Jake, she spent the rest of the night in her new room trying to text and call Holley J, sending so many texts her thumbs actually got sore, reverting to calling her consistently resulting in the calls going straight to voice mail which she filled up rather quickly. For the last four years they have met every morning at their lockers before first period like clockwork unless one informed the other they weren't going to be there for a specific reason. Today Ashley fears might be the first day Holley J doesn't show up on purpose just to avoid them coming face to face. Watching in the direction of the hallway Holley J would regularly come down, seeing nothing but the usual student commotion and interactions, the faces of normalcy she sees almost every day except for the one that would stand out the most. Checking the time on her phone the first bell will ring in less than three minutes, they would have commonly left for first period two minutes ago bringing to light she will be making the walk alone this morning. A single tear slid down her cheek leaving her locker to head for first period, walking slow and sluggish compared to the rest of the student body's frantic tempo through the hallway. Keeping to herself trying to avoid any interactions with anybody, even completely ignoring many morning greetings thrown her way, at her current pace she was going to be late, something she really didn't care about at the moment, even having thoughts about ditching school entirely not being in the right mind set to concentrate on schoolwork or to listen to other classmates bullshit all day, but she can't, Jake would find out and most schools have a policy, no school, no play and she wasn't going to let that happen. The hallways began to empty out as students entered their appropriate classrooms leaving Ashley practically solo in the hallway, going from complete chaos to almost complete silence in a matter of seconds. Sounding of the first bell projected loudly through the loud speakers, Ashley still had to turn down one more hallway to get to her class, fittingly seeing her teacher standing outside the doorway waiting for any late stragglers to make their arrival, unfortunately for Ashley, she seemed to be the only one, entering the classroom swiftly heading for her desk slighting all the eyes from the other students.

Now fourth period, Ashley is sitting at her desk at the back of the classroom with her anxiety on the rise, this is the second class her and Holley J have together, a no show for first period, got Ashley pondering if Holley J is deliberately missing classes they share together, a ploy that can only go on for so long, eventually she would have to come to class. The rest of the class is still filing in with Holley J nowhere to be found, Ashley knows she is here asking earlier classmates if they saw her. All the desks become occupied except for the one directly besides Ashley which is the one reserved for Holley J, about thirty seconds till the bell and still no sign of her. Just as the bell sounds, Holley J enters the classroom abruptly as if she had been running, instantly heading for her desk restraining herself from making eye contact with Ashley. Planting herself at her desk, Holley J deliberately keeps her eyes forward, the tension between the two of them has reached discomforting levels, both knowing they are in uncharted waters with their friendship, a place neither of them thought they would ever get two, yet Ashley knows this is all her fault, feels like a knife through her heart seeing her best friend seated alongside her completely ignoring her.

"Are you really going to keep ignoring me?" whispered Ashley, peeking over at Holley J who's looking more like a stranger rather than her best friend, like a totally different person, not displaying her ordinary bubbly personality ready to regurgitate the latest gossip or rumors she managed to get the inside scoop on.

Holley J remained eyes forward fighting the urge to respond, physically feeling the uneasiness and sadness being radiated from Ashley's direction, though she may not show it, this is hurting her just as much as it is hurting Ashley. Not wanting to sit through class unnerved, Holley J raises her hand to grab the teacher's attention, asking to come to the front to speak privately. Waving her permission to proceed forward, Holley J makes her way to the head of the class for a quick one on one. Too far away for Ashley to hear what was being said, Holley J doing most of the talking, the teacher just stood there leaned up against his desk with his arms folded. Her name must have come up because the teacher looked in Ashley's direction immediately catching her spying eyes, the short meeting ended with a head nod to Holley J, gesturing to an empty desk at the front of the class left by an absent classmate. Returning to her desk, Holley J grabbed her backpack still avoiding eye contact with Ashley to reseat herself at the vacant desk to put some space between the two of them attempting to make it easier for her to concentrate. Watching Holley J sit at the head of their row putting her out of view, Ashley was stunned by her actions since Holley J hates to sit in the front, even going as far as having small talk with the guy seated next to her. Many of their classmates took notice to the surprising change in the seating arrangements. Several began whispering amongst themselves, others just eyed Ashley knowing those two are generally joined at the hip. Nothing Ashley hates more than to become the subject of gossip or a rumor, yet when day after day you are surrounded by other millennials with ownership to the best in cell phone technology, it's only a matter of time until you become the meme of the day. This will be the first time ever they are in the same class and not sitting together or seated next to each other, perfectly clear now Holley J is serious about needed some time, it's how much time that scares Ashley, feeling an emptiness in her life even though it's only been a couple days, how is this code of silence going to affect their ability to play softball together, they have a game to two days, more importantly how is this going to affect her personally when she is out on the mound looking down at home plate to see her peering back. A quote Ashley once read comes to mind, *"A true friend accepts who you are, but also helps you become who you should be."* That friend has been Holley J throughout the years, just now she is asking to be accepted for who she really is.

The teacher starts class writing on the whiteboard with his back to the class, Holley J slowly looks back to try catching a glimpse of Ashley while at the same time Ashley leans her view to observe Holley J.

A busy early afternoon occupied Jake sitting in his office doing some back paperwork, a small radio on his desk softly plays some classic rock, music has always helped him focus, still getting use to the fact part of his job is behind the desk, a place must athletes in their prime hope to never find themselves, yet it's better than the place he could have been headed too. Doing a little computer work his cell phone begins to ring, laying within reach by his keyboard. The caller ID shows Jeff is calling prompting him to put a hold on what he was doing to give it an answer.

"Hey," said Jake, turning away from the computer to give his brother his full attention.

"Hey, are you busy?" Jeff asked, sitting in his office at the law firm.

"I'm good, what's up?" Jake replied.

"Well, I got some information on that club owner," states Jeff.

"No shit," responds Jake in a somewhat stunned tone.

"His full name is Trevor Archer, originally from Los Angeles, was an only child, father was killed in the military, mother still lives back in LA, a real head case, spent most of his youth in and out of juvie for robbery, grand theft auto, destruction of property and weapon charges, has also done time for multiple assault charges. Since then, however, he's done a pretty good job keeping a low profile, not on social media, if he has a cell phone it's under someone else's name, no tax records, any bills he pays he must pay in cash, no trace anything is done online. Has one checking account, no credit cards, no record of a residence other than his business, has become really good at covering his tracks," mentions Jeff. "Jake, this guy is bad news."

"Jesus," said Jake, shocked learning of this guy's apparent resume. Leave it to his brother to dig up some dirt on somebody, always said if Jeff never became a lawyer he would have made a great detective, similarly good at getting in contact with the right people,

"What about the possession of the cocaine?"

"It would be her word against his, even with probable cause he could just dispose of it, but if he is selling then that's a different story, problem is no obvious evidence. If he is selling, he is doing it to outside parties, at the club would be too risky, like I said before, he probably has a few cops on his payroll to keep the rest of the police from snooping around," Jeff added.

"And the prostituting?" asked Jake.

"Like I said he's great at covering his tracks, if it's all done inside the club and the girls aren't the ones physically taking the money, unless you catch it in the act, he could just have the girls say it's consensual," Jeff mentions.

"So what now?" a concerned Jake asked.

"I don't know, let me keep doing some research and we will figure it out, but in the meantime, Ashley has to keep doing what she is doing, I know you don't want to hear that, trust me I don't want that either, but we can't let on that we may know anything and risk her safety, for now it's the safest play," urges Jeff.

"Why can't we just explain to the police what is going on?" asked a slightly agitated Jake.

"I wish it was that simple, like I said he's probably paying some of the cops off. This could be a very touchy situation if we don't handle this properly," Jeff insists.

"You know best," replies Jake, would never doubt his brother's judgment, more equipped to give the best advice in a circumstance like this, but bothering him having to prolong Ashley's involvement in such a dangerous lifestyle, working for a real son of a bitch. "Thanks for the insight."

"No problem, we'll talk about it more later, see you at home," Jeff said, hanging up on his end.

Hanging up, resting his elbows on the desk, putting one hand over his mouth engaging in deep thought, just a week ago all his focus was on getting the team better heading deeper into the season, now with everything going on with Ashley, Jake is starting to feel overwhelmed wanting to put just as much focus on helping her, finding it hard to discover that middle ground mentally. Add on the unexpected disturbance to Ashley's and Holley J's friendship, two of his best players, escalates the mental stress to unknown levels. Starting to have flashbacks of the conceptual torment he struggled with when his playing career ended which led to the drinking. He would be lying if he said he didn't feel like he could polish off a full bottle of Jack Daniels right at that very moment, alcohol was the only thing that really relaxed him, a liquid solution flushing away all the negative thoughts, yet ruining five years of sobriety would be the biggest mistake of his life right now. Thinking about what he could do to take some of the edge off came a knock on his partially open office door, looking over at the doorway, Jake sees Danielle standing there, the sight of her puts a smile on his face.

"Hey," greeted Jake. "Come in."

"I hope I'm not bothering you. If you are not too busy I just wanted to know if you would want to go grab some lunch?" Danielle asked.

Seeing her standing there felt like he just took a shot of adrenaline, some alone time with her was just what he needed.

"I'd love too," Jake answered. "And I have something I need to tell you."

The rest of Ashley's school day was nothing but her trapped in an invisible suit of anxiety, barely able to concentrate on any schoolwork, spending most of the rest of her classes in a foggy haze thinking about their first run in with each other, how Holley J just ignored her and asked to be seated somewhere else. Lunch was more of the same, Holley J was a no show, first time since they have known each other they didn't spend school lunch together bringing her other table mates to questioned where she was, persuading Ashley to tell them the truth, briefly explaining her and Holley J have hit a bump in the road and needed some time apart. Not worried they would see Holley J and she would tell them the real reason for the sudden scarcity in communication, no matter how upset she may be or if the friendship was truly over, Holley J would never spill on any of Ashley's private life. The third class they shared together was much like the first, only this time Holley J asked to sit somewhere else immediately upon entering the class room, striking up conversations with classmates she would never normally talk to. Taking every fiber in Ashley's body to hold back tears seeing her best friend act like a completely different person, watching her interact with others knowing that was them just a few days ago. At the end of school they would always meet up at their lockers discussing the rest of their day, Holley J also updating Ashley on any new developing high school drama, yet today ended the way it started with Ashley alone at her locker, didn't even bother to wait around this time recollecting the track record of the day so far, knowing it was a done deal Holley J wasn't going to show. Making matters worse, she received a text last period from Razz summoning her into work tonight which didn't surprise her thinking it would be the perfect ending to an already fucked up day.

Slamming her locker shut, Ashley walked out of school, arms folded, refusing to make eye contact with anyone taking her long journey to her car. Despite walking with body language showcasing someone disinterested with the rest of the world, it doesn't stop a couple male classmates from attempting to ask her out, responding by just continuing on her way and not saying anything. Reaching her car most of the student parking lot was empty except for a few cars, one being Holley J's parked across the way. Unlocking her door, Ashley sees Holley J walking towards her car with a male classmate, both smiling and laughing with each other, whatever they were saying echoed through the parking lot yet it was hard to make out what was being said, ending with Holley J giving her companion a hug before entering her vehicle and driving away. To Ashley, it was like watching a different reality, what Holley J's life would be like without her in it, from what she just saw it didn't look too bad and that really scares her. Seating in the driver's seat, placing both hands on the steering wheel lowering her head to have a quick emotional moment, she takes a couple deep breaths before starting the engine and driving away.

Pulling into the house's driveway, Ashley didn't see Jake's truck meaning this will be the first time she will be in the house without Jake present, a situation she is really not comfortable with seeing how she has only known them for less than three days. There was a red SUV parked up towards the garage most likely belonging to Jake's sister-in-law, of all the residents of the house, she's the one who gives off sort of bad vibes whenever Ashley is around, leading her to believe Mrs. Wheeler is no to fond of her staying there. The feeling was mutual if Ashley had somewhere else to go, she would have gone there instead, not the type of person who likes to become an inconvenience, but when you have a lack of options sometimes you have to take what is offered to you, though she does feel safest being around Jake. Entering the front door carrying her backpack, a strange silence is in the house as if no one was home, not even the ruckus noise of the twins eight playing and wreaking havoc could be heard. Seeing the opportunity to just head up to her room to do some homework before she has to leave for work, Ashley climbs up the staircase only to be greeted by Vicki at the top carrying a bushel of laundry, the awkwardness between the two of them was apparent immediately. Vicki looked at Ashley as if she was staring at an old high school rival, the girl everyone would say was better looking, had the better body, the girl with the rep for stealing boyfriends just because she could. Being alone together for the first time, they both felt handcuffed to engage in some sort of chit chat or small talk seeing how they will be under the same roof for a while.

"Hi," Ashley opened with. "How are you?"

"I'm fine, just doing some housework," replied Vicki.

"Are the girls here?" asked Ashley, unable to think of anything else to say.

"They are in their room," Vickie answered. "I have a lot to do and I still have to get dinner ready...."

"I'd be happy to take care of the laundry so you can get dinner started, I really would like to help out whenever I can, it's the least I could do," Ashley mentioned, not really having the time to do it at the moment, but felt it was necessary to help deviate any beef Vicki was having towards her.

"Okay," agreed Vicki. "The laundry room is right off the kitchen, there is a load in the washer right now, then you can put these in."

Placing the full bushel on the floor, Vicki proceeded downstairs leaving Ashley to fend for herself. At first it felt like being back at her aunt's all over again, however that feeling subsided quick cause she is not being forced, there is a difference between being a slave and helping out a generous act whenever you could. If any good came out of her time living with her aunt it's she knows her way around household machines and is very comfortable performing any household chore, dropping off her backpack in her room she returned to grab the bushel to get started. Getting done rather swiftly with the laundry, having finished washing and drying, leaving every article folded on the large wooden table located across from the washer and dryer, Ashley now sits Indian style on her bed doing some homework. Definitely missing the comfort of her old bed, her current one is a little too soft for her taste, a more firmer mattress is more to her liking. Would be extremely selfish of her to start nit picking about certain things, just needs to be grateful she has a place for now to lay her head. Typing away on her laptop, feeling the outside breeze coming from the open bedroom window, causing the laced curtains to flutter in the air, comes a knock on her door, giving permission to the outside resident to enter.

"Hey, can I come in?" Jake asked, noticing Ashley working diligently on her homework.

"Sure," answered Ashley, happy to see Jake is finally home.

"I heard you did some laundry earlier, that was nice of you," commended Jake entering the room, closing the door behind him.

"Well, it's the least I can do," she states.

"How are you doing? How was school?" he asked.

"It sucked today," Ashley answered with some sadness in her voice.

"Holley J still not talking to you?" he asked standing at the end of the bed.

"No," she replied shaking her head.

"Just give her some time, she'll come around," Jake commented.

"And what if she doesn't?" Ashley responds teary eyed. "I decided I'm going to tell her everything, I'm not going to lie or keep things from her anymore."

"How are you planning on doing that?" he asked.

"With this," answered Ashley, pulling out a sealed envelope from her backpack with Holley J's name on it. "I wrote this letter today in study hall explaining everything. I'm going to give it to her tomorrow after the game. It was the hardest thing I ever wrote."

"I know you may not want to hear this, but you are doing the right thing," mentioned Jake.

"Then why do I feel like this could be the end," she responded, tears running fully down her face.

Jake grabs a couple tissues from the box on the nightstand to hand to her. Wanting to say something that would put her mind at ease, but he couldn't come up with anything. Doesn't know Holley J as well as Ashley does, people's beliefs and views are sometimes impenetrable and some are willing to lose everything for what they stand for. Jake wants to believe a friendship and bond like these two girls have could overcome anything, yet secretly to himself hopes everything works out, Ashley is unquestionably a girl who doesn't need any more disappointment in her life.

"I doubt it will be the end," Jake remarked.

"I have to work tonight," Ashley expresses in an unenthusiastic tone.

Jake lets out a disapproving sigh knowing for now there is nothing he can do about it.

"Soon hopefully you'll never have to do that again," Jake asserts, before walking over to open the bedroom door. "Dinner will be ready in five minutes."

This night at the club started on par with the rest of the day for Ashley, when first arriving, the dressing room was over crowded with girls trying to get ready resulting in a lot of pushing and shoving, some escalating to heated arguments. To avoid the mayhem, Ashley did her best to get ready in her car, turning out to be quite the feat. Returning inside most of the area had cleared out leaving just a couple of girls getting ready, one happened to be Kendra who looked like she fully recovered from that night aside from the cigarette sized scar now settling on her cheek. Before Ashley could even go over to see how she was doing, Kendra left to perform her duties acknowledging Ashley by flashing a small grin leaving the dressing room. She couldn't remember when there was that many girls gathered together in one space at one time, all that estrogen in a small area combined with everyone trying to make a good buck is enough to make tempers flare from time to time, especially working for someone like Razz who expects nothing sort of perfection. This is one night she wishes she didn't have to work, her mind is elsewhere and her mood is more unpleasant that normal for being at the club, certainly not in the right mind set to hear the abundance of whistling, hollering and cat calls regularly come her way. A few minutes before she has to go on, standing backstage waiting for the other girl to finish her set, all Ashley could think about was Holley J and what could possibly happen after she gives her the letter tomorrow. Zoned out just staring at the black curtains in front of her, unable to even hear much of what is happening on stage, feeling floaty as if her body was as light as a whisper. Sudden flash of light coming from the opening of the curtains stuns her glossy eyes snapping her out of her self-induced trance, feeling the slight wind created by the girl coming off stage briskly walking past her.

Hearing the DJ making his between set announcements, Ashley feels a pair of hands grabbing her butt from behind, hot breath breathing on her neck. Only one person would creep up behind her and grope her like that, his gravelly voice speaking softly to her.

"I'm looking forward to watching you dance again, Show Horse," Razz murmurs in her ear, swiping her hair aside to start kissing her neck. "There will be a few clients waiting for you after, one in particular, let's just say is a good friend of mine and I'd like to see him taken care of. He also has special perks."

"Razz, I'm not feeling very good tonight, I would like to leave after this, please," requested Ashley, suddenly Razz' hand grabs her below the jaw line squeezing tightly pulling her in close, feeling his humid breath on her face.

"Well, you better figure out a way to feel better, because if you don't do what you are told, I'm going to make you feel much worse," threatens Razz. "I know you won't disappoint me, Show Horse," giving her a gentle kiss on the cheek prior to releasing her from his grasp.

Leaving back stage to go enjoy Ashley's set from his usual vantage point, Razz looks at the crowd around the stage being jam packed, almost claustrophobic, a sight that tickles his money hairs, lighting up a cigarette he stands with his arms folded waiting for the DJ to introduce his golden goose. Back stage Ashley feels a bit tense, can almost still feel Razz' presence near her, like any second he could appear out of the shadows.

All she can think about now was the few men she would have to gratify after with her mind in a state of complete disarray, not even sure she has the will to push through her set, yet while she tries to put herself in some sort of functioning state, she hears her introduction to make her appearance. Ashley doesn't know how she did it, but she made it through her set, ending a short while ago, doesn't even remember any of it, as if her body was on auto-pilot and her mind was going along for the ride. Completely oblivious to all the standard noise pollution she hears when on stage, seemed like she was performing in a vacuum and sound didn't exist, all that was current to her senses were the bright lights of the stage. Leaving without as so much as a bow or wave, she scampered her nude body off stage to relocate back in the dressing room, where surprising she was alone.

Getting herself together for her waiting Johns, she persisted on how much she hated Razz, unable to think of a time when she didn't, but her fear of him out weighted her hatred becoming the driving force for her to obey. Already feeling tired, she could only hope her upcoming sexual escapades have a similar out-of-body experience granting her immunity from the serviced events, not remembering what she did would make the rest of her night a little more bearable. Touching up her makeup at the vanity, comes face to face with the person she never wanted Holley J to know about, stopping what she was doing to stare at herself in the mirror, her eyes looked upon what she saw with resentment, even more than what she has for Razz, the harder she stared the more she could feel her blood boil, clenching her fists so tight they began turning white. Standing up from her seat she leaned in closer to the glass, her breathing became more erratic, closing her eyes she mumbled quietly unidentified words, reopening them letting out an enraged yell at her reflection before punching the glass cracking it severely.

Finishing up with her second client, Ashley walks the hallway to the downstairs bathroom to gargle some mouthwash having just given back to back blow jobs, the taste in her mouth beginning to make her gag. Considers those easy appointments, doing oral means she only has to be with her expected customer for like five to ten minutes, teaching herself techniques to get these men to ejaculate quicker. Entering the bathroom she is greeted by a couple other girls freshening up, one is completely naked leaning over one of the sinks spitting semen into the drain. Leaving one sink free, Ashley opens the cabinet hanging above to grab the bottle of mouthwash stored inside with various other items the girls may need. The other girls leave exchanging derogatory comments about Ashley, going as far as giving her the evil eye as they exit. Spitting out the mouthwash, she checked the state of her left hand, luckily not cutting it up real bad after its run in with the mirror, just a couple small scratches are left with hardly any bleeding. Razz will most likely find out about the mirror, but she will just play dumb and say it was an accident. Washing her hands quickly, she dries them off, leaving to head for her final deed of the night. Entering the room to see a young guy with a slender build sitting up on the bed with a pair of jeans on and no shirt, his upper body completely covered in tattoos with a few on his face, smoking a cigarette. Body art on guys was nothing new to Ashley having seen her share of ink on clients, but found this guy's look rather intimidating, reminding her of Razz in a way, even the way he smokes his cigarette staring at her comes off as menacing.

"So you're the prize senorita that's going to entertain me for a while," the man said in a heavy Mexican accent. "Razz wasn't kidding when he said you were a fine-ass bitch."

Moving towards the bed to get a better look at what she's going to be dealing with, Ashley got a closer look at his body paint made up of satanic and Nazi imagery, highlighted by the large swastika on the left side of his chest, his face ink made an already unattractive face even more so. The man sits up with the cigarette in his mouth reaching out to grab one of Ashley's hands pulling her in closer, where she smells an overpowering amount of cologne. He runs his index finger from the bottom of her neck all the way down through the cleavage in her blouse getting a preview of her soft, smooth skin. Putting the cigarette out, he leans in closer to get a sniff of her feminine aroma, positioning his nose close to her neck, smelling her up and down getting turned on by her luscious scent. Liking what he sees, he grabs Ashley's shirt with both hands ripping it open exposing her breasts, the couple buttons that were holding the blouse closed fly off in various directions. The man quickly grips each breast squeezing vigorously, Ashley stands motionless showing no emotion, looking off staring at anything other than the wretch fondling her chest, can feel his calluses rubbing against her skin. Her bare stomach became his next target for his sexual appetite, releasing her breasts to glide his hands down her sides to her hips grabbing hold tightly, lowering his head to come face to face with her naval, dragging his tongue along her dermis until he reaches just under her breasts planting wet kisses randomly around her torso.

"No kissing," states Ashley in an irritated tone, pushing the man back.

"Says who?" asked the man, angered by Ashley's physical retaliation.

"Says me," Ashley replied. "Now just shove your dick in me so we can get this shit over with."

"Bitch, I don't think you know who you are talking to," he responds, getting in Ashley's face, the nauseating smell of smoke and bad breath permeates around her personal space.

"I don't give a fuck who you are," she states, feeling a swift backhand come across her face, the sudden blow startled her, putting a hand on her face to ease the sting, a trickle of blood seeps out of her lower lip. "YOU MOTHERFUCKER!" she yells ready to react back, but her effort to counterattack was viciously interrupted by gun pointed directly at her face.

"You got something to say now, bitch," he utters, grabbing the hair on the back of her head with his free hand.

"How did you get that in here?" a nervous Ashley asked, frozen in fear staring down the barrel.

"I told you, me and your boss have an understanding," the man answers. "Like him, I always get what I want. Such hostility for an exquisite beauty, whores like you need to be taught some manners. So this is what's going to happen, you're going to fuck me until I'm sick of your face or there is going to be another dead whore in the streets. Do you understand? DO YOU FUCKING UNDERSTAND?!" he yells, pulling on her hair yanking her head, the cold steel of the gun barrel pressed up against one of her cheeks.

Ashley never thought she would ever be looking down the barrel of a gun unless she was pointing it at herself, feeling a sense of panic she never felt before, the last time she was in a room with a gun present she watched her mother kill a man in cold blood. Now finds herself on the wrong end of a heater with no idea what this guy is capable of, yet his appearance and attitude alone would indicate he is probably competent to do anything. Even worse Razz or a couple of his goons are watching this unfold right before their eyes and there hasn't been any attempt to defuse the situation, expecting someone to bust through the door to rescue her from this piece of shit, but it never happened, she was on her own and left to do exactly what he said or this room and this guy's ugly face could be the last thing she ever sees, responding with a slight nod as a couple tears streamed down her face.

Ending the longest session Ashley has ever had with a client, she leaves the room running down the hallway naked carrying her clothes to the bathroom, her chest and stomach coated in spots with semen. Bursting through the bathroom door, a couple girls are occupying the sinks with an unseen girl locked in a stall making her self-known hearing the toilet flush. The girls at the sinks stop what they are doing to look at Ashley's reflection in the mirrors getting a clear view of her non glamorous state, not in the mood or interested in any of their dirty looks or childish remarks, Ashley just walks past them heading down to the far end of the bathroom where the single shower awaits, hardly ever used due to its poor maintenance and half the time it doesn't work, but she is in no condition to travel to the up stair showers. Throwing her clothes on the floor, she steps inside the door and curtainless entryway, the tile based flooring feels a bit gritty under her bare feet trying to turn on the water, looking up at a few cobwebs hanging in the corners filling out the uneasy décor, one had a live spider crawling around in it. Fiddling with the wall nozzles, a gargling sound emits from the plumbing as the water makes its way to slightly rusted shower head. Feeling a couple drops land on her back, the water ultimately escapes gushing out soaking Ashley in the face. Grabbing an old bottle of body wash left sitting on a shelf indented in the shower wall, squirts a handful to quickly relieve herself of the bodily fluid permeating around her stomach and chest. The body wash has a lavender type scent to it, lathering all over, scrubbing with her hands letting the rather lukewarm water spray steadily.

Rinsing off, she presses her hands against the shower walls keeping her head down letting the water rain down upon her, crying quietly to herself, her tears were camouflaged against the water dripping from her body and dangling hair, never in her life has she felt more like a piece of meat than she does right now. This man treated her like a soulless blow-up doll, keeping his gun in hand as he fucked her every way possible resulting in his four orgasms during the three-hour pounding she took making her worried she might be sore tomorrow. The lowest point in her life happened when the man stuck the barrel of the gun in her mouth while he ejaculated on her face making her begin to feel like the word she hates being called the most, a whore. When he was done he just threw his pants and shirt on leaving the room without saying a word, leaving her lying on the bed like some sort of cum sponge, not even a person.

Standing under the soothing temperature of the water helped her to relax a bit, clearing her mind breathing in some of the steam from the occasional hot water that decided to filter out, realizing she hasn't thought about Holley J since she had a gun pointed at her face, becoming more concerned about not pissing this guy off. Switching off the water, Ashley tosses her wet hair back, stepping out of the shower onto the cold concrete to attempt to air dry standing by her pile of clothes, the warmth she felt inside the shower has been replaced with the cool air of the basement walls, not even the bad lighting above the shower generates much heat. Shivering, hugging herself to try to warm up keeping her head down, paying no attention to the other end of the bathroom, Ashley hears the sound of heels clacking on the floor coming closer, suddenly the noise stops replaced by a female voice.

"I thought you might need this," said a girl, standing in the shadows of the small walk way towards the shower.

Looking over to see the girl who was at one of the sinks when Ashley first arrived, handing her a towel. Taking it from her, the girl turns and leaves before Ashley can even thank her. Coming to the end of one of the worse days she can remember, odd she would receive a kind gesture from an unexpected source, it was the first time another girl at the club actually looked out for her, always assumed most of the other girls are not too fond of her, but maybe it's because she never really gave any of them a chance. Regardless of what the other girls' stories are or why they are working there, they all have the same amount of chance to fall victim to Razz' authority, something that should unite all of them, not put them at odds with each other. Alone once again, Ashley quickly dries herself off feeling the dampness and chill evaporate the wetter the towel became, her clothes probably got some dirt and grim on them from sitting on the unswept bathroom floor.

Getting dressed all she could think about was how she was left alone in a room with a strange man being held at gunpoint, so angry she forgot she wouldn't be able to button her blouse closed, having to improvise tying the bottoms together the best she could. Sliding on her heels she hung the wet towel over the showerhead before storming out of the bathroom to go confront Razz.

Walking back upstairs, Ashley knew where Razz would be, this time of night he routinely would be in his office either fucking one of the girls or doing some blow. He doesn't like anyone coming to his office unless he calls for them, right now she doesn't care, equivalent to her walking into the lion's den and asking for trouble, but right now her anger trumps her fear. Arriving at Razz' office seeing the normal guard standing by the doors, watching Ashley approach knowing she wasn't given reason to be in the vicinity, spotting a demeanor and attitude in her strides indicating she meant business. Reaching out to grab her arm to stop her from entering, Ashley forcefully yanks it away bursting through door.

The unexpected interruption catches Razz off guard, sitting on his couch he springs from seat to rapidly investigate the disturbance, surrounded by a couple other men each wearing business suits seated nearby. In a panic, the men quickly close two briefcases resting on the coffee table full of heroin or possibly cocaine, another briefcase full of money was sitting directly in front where Razz was seated which Ashley got a glimpse of before she was grabbed viciously by the arm and pulled aside by an angry Razz, the guard who chased Ashley in was given an ear full before being told to return to his post.

"What the fuck do you think you are doing, Show Horse?" an enraged Razz whispers in her ear. "You know no one is allowed in here without permission. You better have a good reason because I'm about two seconds from making you have a very bad night," he states gripping her arm tighter.

"I had a fucking gun pulled on me tonight!" Ashley declares.

"So," responds Razz. "Don't you think I know that?"

"Then where the fuck were you?" she asked. "I was scared to death."

"I told you he was a friend who has special perks, he likes to use extreme intimidation methods when he is with girls," Razz explains. "He wasn't really going to do anything, don't be a fucking baby. Do you really think I would let him shoot you in my own fucking club? I watched the whole damn thing, I got off watching him fuck you like some sort of animal."

"What the fuck is wrong with you?" Ashley asked completely unsettled from what she just heard.

"Are you questioning me?" Razz asked, slapping her lightly across the face back and forth with one hand. "Huh, are you fucking questioning me? Just do as your told 'cause if anyone is going to shoot you around here it would be me, don't forget that and you better keep that pretty mouth of yours shut about what you have seen here, do you understand?" he asked clenching her arm tighter. "I said do you understand!?"

Ashley answers with a small nod.

"Now get the fuck out of here," he demands, releasing her from his grasp.

Returning to his comrades, Razz lights up a cigarette apologizing for the intrusion, sitting back down giving Ashley the evil eye, waiting for her to exit the office.

Standing there looking back at those soulless eyes realizing she wasn't looking at a man, but the devil or some embodiment of him, the ring leader to the rest of the demons in her life, yet she came into sight of what she always had a hunch about, without another word she leaves slamming the door behind her.

The clock is a few ticks away from striking one o'clock in the morning, everyone in the house was asleep, Jake was sitting by the front picture window drinking a cup of coffee. He couldn't go to sleep until he knew Ashley was back safe, waiting anxiously for a pair of headlights to emerge from the darkness, every couple minutes peeking through the curtains like a concerned parent. Sipping his room temperature Joe, his next glance out the window is rewarded with bright lights heading right for his location, the beams light up a portion of the cul-de-sac as they drew closer. A sense of relief came over Jake observing those headlights pulling into the driveway, still keeping an eye on Ashley exiting her car, though they live in an exponentially crime free neighborhood, you can never be too careful when it comes to teenage girls walking alone in the dark no matter where they are. Seeing her head towards the front door, Jake quickly abandons his post to head for the kitchen with only a few nightlights to brighten the way. Dumping the rest of his coffee in the sink, he hears the front door open, pouring himself a glass of water, the sound of the faucet running echoed through the house intriguing Ashley to investigate who could be up at this hour. Removing her flip flops and dropping her backpack, she walked barefoot to the kitchen to find Jake standing over the sink.

"What are you still doing up?" Ashley asked, trying to keep her voice down.

"I couldn't sleep," answered Jake. "Are you okay?"

"If you are asking about what happened tonight I really don't want to talk about it, in fact I really don't want to ever discuss what goes on at the club, besides you really don't want to know. If I make it back, it was a good night," she replies. "I just want to good to bed, I'm so exhausted."

"Okay, I understand," Jake said.

"Um, one thing, though, Razz does deal, I saw it tonight even though I wasn't supposed too," added Ashley.

"Are you sure?" Jake asked.

"Yeah, I'm sure," she answered. "Well, I'm heading to bed, I'll see you in the morning," walking out she stops for a moment, keeping her back turned. "I know you mean well, but you don't have to wait up for me," she proclaims exiting the kitchen.

It's about a little over an hour before game time, Ashley is out on the field preparing like she normally does, luckily it's a home game so no need for an awkward bus ride to the opposing school. The school day went just like the other day, a mirror image of it like in the movie *Groundhog Day*, Holley J still avoiding her to the point Ashley has given up texting or calling her. Her biggest concern is what's going to happen come game time, she has to communicate with her catcher or could it be possible Holley J will ask to sit out and have her back up play, there has never been another girl playing catcher when she pitches, just the thought of that makes her feel quite uncomfortable, either way this is going to be a huge test to Ashley's mental toughness. Sitting in the dugout tying her cleats, she puts a rubber band on to hold her hair back, the weather at game times calls for overcast relieving her of having to wear sunglasses, but will keep them on top of her cap just in case. Exiting the dugout to begin her run, she sees Holley J off in the distance coming towards the field carrying her standard large duffel bag, at first Ashley thought her eyes were playing tricks on her seeing a sight that has become almost automatic before a game, however her theory of a visual mirage was discredited when Holley J entered the dugout in the flesh. This was messing with her mind, why would Holley J ignore her all day, yet show up like normal when she could arrive a little before game time. Holley J dropped her bag on the dugout floor seated herself on the bench, alone together for the first time since their quarrel began, the two girls stared at each other waiting for one to speak.

"I'm not here to work out with you, you can do that on your own, I'll do my own thing," Holley J said in a serious straightforward tone. "I'm here to warm you up when you are ready. Let's get one thing straight, the only conversations we are having from now until the end of the game will be about only the game. I'm not going to jeopardize your great season or the team's over our recent differences."

"Can I say something?" Ashley asked, happy to just hear Holley J's voice again.

"Unless it's about softball I don't want to hear it," remarked Holley J, seeing the hurt in Ashley's eyes so immense it's like it's on display on a large billboard.

"Then take this," replied Ashley, pulling the letter she wrote out of her uniform's back pocket. "I was going to give it to you after the game, I guess now is as good a time as any."

Hesitantly reaching out to grab the envelope addressed to her, a small instruction is written under Holley J's name, *"Read when you are alone."*

Not saying anything else, Ashley takes off to start her run. Holley J stays seated holding the letter on her lap watching her best friend do what she does best, get prepared to be the best player on the field. The letter has got Holley J curious making her tempted to read it now being technically alone at the moment, however the unknown contents might affect her emotionally and she wouldn't be able to play if she is all emotional, deciding to wait till she gets home to read it, she places it inside her bag. Wants so bad to be out there working out with Ashley like she always does, but keeping secrets from her especially one so disgusting in her eyes is really hard to get past, making her question if Ashley has been lying to her about other things. It's hard being around Ashley right nowhence the ghosting act, needing her space to comprehend it all, missing telling her all the latest gossip and rumors that have surfaced around school, can't even talk to her about the new guy she has been cordial with which deeply upsets her the most, Ashley invariably gives the best advice when it comes to boys, for someone who isn't into the high school dating scene, she seems to read boys like a book preconceived to knowing if their intentions are pure or adulterated. Dwelling on the situation now will only hinder Holley J's ability to perform at her best, wanting to keep her focus on the game for the sake of the team and for Ashley. Throwing in her earbuds, Holley J goes off to do her own warmups. Even with the relative distraction of her and Holley J's recent differences, Ashley is pitching a game worthy of her talents. When game time came the two of them were right back to their old habits on the diamond, Holley J signaling the right pitches with Ashley executing perfectly, en route to another ten plus strikeout performance, however Holley J limited how much they verbally communicated during the game, completely dismissing all mound visits. Jake took notice of Holley J's discrete measures to distance herself from Ashley as much as possible, not even sitting near her in the dugout between innings. Ashley may not show it on the field, but he knows what's going on between the two of them is eating her up inside, proving how mentally tough this girl is when she needs to be. Like it was for him, the diamond was the only place that felt right, a setting free of judgment where they feel like they belong, being among the dirt and grass was their safe house, in between those lines nothing else in the world mattered, they were free.

The game ended on another Ashley strikeout giving her and the team another win via shutout. Though most of the attention is on Ashley and her pitching, the rest of the team contributed as always, Brie's batting average is better now left handed then it ever was right handed with two good eyes, also leading the team in stolen bases. Renee is tied with Ashley for most homeruns on the team and in the district, also her center field defense has been stellar as of late, sacrificing her body on many occasions to insure a tough out, even her attitude has tone down a bit over the last few games making her presence around the other girls more tolerable. Holley J has been masterful catching for the team, along with her improved hitting, is having one of her best seasons. Since Jake took over the team, a few other girls including some underclassmen have been catching the eyes of a few scouts, a testament to their hard work and play, making it more impressive is the fact they are teammates with probably the best player in the country in Ashley. The team still being undefeated has brought a lot of recent publicity to the school and Jake himself, being the former all-star ballplayer who turned the team around, no stranger to attention, he rather have the recognition go to the girls, his days of being in the public eye are in the past and would much rather be a spectator now. Sometimes attention is just unavoidable, it comes with being great as an individual or a team, when you have a team that is number one or close to number one in every major statistical category, it's going to raise a few eyebrows. All the team's recent success also has accumulated to a growth in home game crowd attendance, every game is filling the bleachers with onlookers spilling over to the grass watching from personally brought fold up chairs, many believe Jake being the coach has a lot to do with the spike in the team's popularity, something he thinks is utterly ridiculous, a matter he has addressed the team on before, nobody goes to a game to watch a coach or manager no matter who they are, they are there to see great team work and athletes perform their craft at the highest level. Ashley is thrilled the spotlight is shining on others too rather than just her.

Regular after game festivities developed, Jake talking to a few parents getting what he would call unwarranted congratulations, signing the occasional autograph which he can't believe people still want. All the girls scatter to do their own thing, except for Holley J who quickly entered the dugout to take off her gear and immediately head for the locker room, wasn't kidding when she told Ashley the lines of communication are cut after the game commences, not even willing to stay to celebrate with other teammates. Talking to a couple of parents, Jake witnessed Holley J's early exit in his peripheral vision, ignoring most of the words being said to him, looking over to check on Ashley who was sitting in the dugout with her head down. Most of the girls came over to commend her on a well-pitched game, patting her on the back, throwing a few complements her way. Endearing as it is to be recognized by her teammates, the one opinion she cares most about walked away without even a goodbye, once the game ended her thoughts redirected to Holley J and the letter.

After a very uneventful dinner with her parents, Holley J retired to her room for the night, listening to her mother and father speak about political taboos and what the government needs to do to ensure citizens remain patriotic to flag gets somewhat annoying after like the thousandth time you hear it, filter in how they occasionally use the dinner table as an excuse to preach on religion makes for a sometimes awkward dining experience. Holley J loves her parents and would do anything for them, just wishes they would realize not everyone is going to share in their views and beliefs even when it's their own offspring. Locking herself in her room, finally alone to do what her mind has been on all through dinner, to read the letter Ashley gave her. Picking it up from her nightstand where she left it when she got home, leaning up against a picture of her and Ashley. Sitting Indian style in the middle of her bed, briefly staring at the front side rereading the applied wording, for as long as they have been friends they have never exchanged a letter, especially one instructing to read when you are alone, a far cry from the small notes they would pass each other during classes. According to pop culture, receiving a letter can go one of two ways, its contents are either really good or really bad, there is never no middle ground, wondering what side of the spectrum this letters falls into makes Holley J immensely nervous. Understanding why Ashley went this route with her refusing to talk or answer any of her texts and phone calls, they say written letters are a sign of respect to those who receive them regardless of what is said on the paper, something about hand scribed words makes it much more personal, a level of intimacy an email or text can never achieve. Tearing open the letter, Holley J's anxiety increases, the thickness of the envelope warns her of multiple pages. Evaluating the lighting in her room, there seems to be a significant amount coming from her three brightly lit computer monitors on her desk as well as from the lamp on her nightstand illuminating Ashley's fine penmanship, nothing left to distract her Holley J begins to read.

Susan Lendroth once said,

"To write is human, to receive a letter: Devine!" a quote Holley J remembers hearing from learning about literature in English class, a quote that suddenly popped into her head while reading Ashley's letter, she couldn't be more wrong. Holley J found this to be the hardest and most despicable thing she

has ever read, the details shared made her feel sick to her stomach. Every sentence became more shocking than the last one, holding her hand over her mouth continuing on. The more she read, the harder it was to carry on, a couple times she had to stop to collect herself, learning about Ashley's childhood and the way their ex-coach blackmailed her. This couldn't be true, Holley J thought, how could these things happen to someone so close to her and not know about it. Her emotions felt like they were being twisted into knots, eyes tearing up she didn't know if she was angry or upset. Learning Ashley not only strips, but engages in sexual acts for money became too much for Holley J to bear, feeling like she didn't even know her best friend anymore having this secret life, a life Holley J could never agree with or would want to be a part of. She watched movies and seen the news, girls like that are subject to a multitude of sexually transmitted diseases even if they are careful or even worse end up dead at the hands of some street thug who is just looking for a good time. These and many other thoughts swirled through Holley J's head making her question the friendship she has with Ashley, wondering if it can ever go back to the way it was. The end of the letter clarifies bluntly why Ashley does what she does and why she kept it from her all this time, even apologizing for lying to her, the explanations she provided for were both heartbreaking and heartfelt, closing with Ashley being adamant about her decision to keep all of it from her, not wanting to worry or burden her with her issues, admitted wanting to tell her a few times, but chickened out or felt it wasn't the right time, being sorry she found out the way she did, defending herself by saying it's not the type of life you want to broadcast about to anyone. The last thing written was how much she loved Holley J and no matter what she decides, she was the best friend she ever and will ever have.

Dropping the letter beside her in disbelief, Holley J closed her eyes and began sobbing, overwhelmed with confusion and uncertainty, feeling she needs more time to process all of what she had just learned, would be a lot for anybody to handle, finding out dark secrets about your best friend, remaining in the isolated silence of her room, Holley J dove deep into thought of what she wants to do.

In his office sending a quick text to Jeff relaying Ashley confirms her boss is dealing, an immediate response comes back stating, okay and they will talk later. Picking up his desk phone, Jake calls one of the administrative assistants requesting a student be sent to his office. Granting permission, they informed him they will send for the student right away, hanging up the phone Jake leans back in his chair patiently waiting for his guest to arrive.

The bell sounded, releasing students to the hallway mayhem of between classes, something Jake gets a firsthand view of through his office window, among the frantic commotion he sees Holley J, backpack aboard, walking alone gingerly staring at the floor totally disregarding the other students, stopping at the office door.

"You wanted to see me, Coach?" asked Holley J standing in the doorway.

"Come in, close the door and sit down," Jake ordered.

Closing the door, Holley J sits in one of the empty chairs in front of Jake's desk leaving her backpack on, full of nothing but curiosity to why she was asked to come to his office.

"So how are you doing?" asked Jake.

"Okay, I guess, been better," Holley J replied, total confusion in her voice.

"Look, what I'm about to say and what we talk about does not leave this room, understand?" he asked, resting his forearms on his desk.

"Yeah, sure," she responded, her curiosity turned to slight nervousness.

"You seem upset about something," Jake said, reading the obvious expression on her face, this is not the Holley J he has grown to know, the bubbly, energetic, full of tenacity, say what's on her mind girl seems to have been replaced with an exact replica who is the total opposite or this is a girl who just found out something about her best friend that she is still in shock from.

"I'm okay," she replied shrugging her shoulders.

"Look, I know there is a bit of a misunderstanding going on between you and Ashley, I mean you made that quite obvious to everyone at the game the other day" stated Jake. "I just want you to know that I know everything."

"What do you mean?" a confused Holley J asked.

"Did you read the letter?" he asked back.

"How do you know about the letter?" Holley J responded stunned.

"I didn't read the letter, I just know Ashley gave you one. You have to know everything you now know, I already know," explained Jake.

"How do you know?" asked Holley J, upset someone knew before her.

"She told me," he answered.

A distraught Holley J angrily leaves the chair shaking her head making a break for the door.

"Holley J, sit down, please!" ordered Jake, his deep masculine voice stops her in her tracks.

A bit hesitant Holley J slowly returns to her seat.

"Look, how I know or why I know is irrelevant right now, what's important is that she needs our help. I can't imagine how you are feeling, you have known her much longer than I have, but right now she needs her best friend, not another enemy."

"This isn't easy for me, you know!" a crying Holley J expresses. "It's like I don't even know her anymore."

"Oh, I think you know exactly who she is," declares Jake. "She is still the same person you have known all these years. How she feels about you hasn't changed, she just thought she was doing the right thing by not saying anything. Let me ask you this. Has anything you learned changed how good of a friend she has been to you?"

More tears streamed down Holley J's face, slowly shaking her head no.

"I'm not saying you can't take the time you need to process everything, but at least let her know," suggested Jake, handing her a couple tissues from his desk. "Okay, you can go."

Leaving her seat drying her eyes heading for the door, wasn't the visit Holley J was expecting, however it was comforting for her to know just how much Jake cares for the girls on the team, certainly not used to coach loyalty or the actually coaching he provides, compared to what they got from their old coach and what he did to Ashley, getting away with it seems totally unfair and pisses her off more than she can explain.

"Holley J," Jake calls out, waiting for her to look back,

"Think about what I said."

Giving a couple light nods, Holley J exits the office.

Arriving home the earliest Jake has since he got the job coaching the girls, primarily because there is a break in the schedule, don't have a game until Tuesday giving him and the girls a much needed rest, being Friday gives everyone a four day layoff. On his way home he received a text from Jeff to meet him in his office when he gets back, surprised his brother is already home from work most days he's commonly home later. Asking to meet in his home office specifies they are going to be talking about some serious topics, only has important discussions in the confines of his private four walls.

Parking his truck behind Vicki's SUV leaving room for Ashley for when she has to go to work later, something he hates to admit is still real, Jake entered the house wasting no time heading for Jeff's office. Giving the closed office door a knock, he enters to see Jeff sitting at his desk talking on his cell phone, the conversation must have been significant being totally engaged in what was being said even raising his voice a couple times. Being inside Jeff's home office, Jake realized how foreign the room actually was, probably the only room in the house he hasn't seen regularly, really never having any reason to go in there until now, everything about the room was new to his eyes. Definitely looked like your typical office, hardwood flooring, large wood stained desk, two leather chairs in front of his desk for any invited guests, massive bookshelves located adjacent to Jeff's position filled to capacity, most likely housing law books with a few general reading material sprinkled in there, topped off with the sizeable window located directly behind the desk, no drapes just venetian blinds in the up position at the moment. The walls were decorated with a few pictures, one was from his wedding day hanging beside a recent picture of the twins, the décor catching Jake's eye the most was the large framed action poster of him during his major league days, seemed out of place with the rest of the room, but seeing it on the wall meant a lot to him knowing his brother remembers the man he once was. Jeff's call came to an end, tossing his phone on his desk in frustration. Sitting in one of the empty leather chairs, Jake is taken back by the disappointed look on his brother's face.

"Work never ends," Jeff said leaning back in his chair. "So going by your text earlier she saw a deal going down?"

"That's what she said," replied Jake, sensing doubt in Jeff's voice. "I'm getting the feeling you're not convinced."

"I believe her, it's just was she sure it was drugs being sold?" asked Jeff. "I'm not saying it wasn't, but we have to be certain and even if it was, I'm afraid it's still not enough. Right now it would be her word against his."

"So what do we do?" Jake asked.

"I know a couple guys at the police force, I'll give them a call, see if they know anything about this place, maybe we can find out which cops are on his payroll," responded Jeff. "I know how bad you want this taken care of, but we have to go at this the right way cause this could easily blow up in our face and could potentially make things a lot worse for her and us."

"I know, I just feel helpless like I should be doing more," Jake stated, voicing his resentment for the whole situation.

"Hey, you've done a lot already," assured Jeff. "You got her to open up to you, you've given her a place to stay, I know you're thinking it's my house, but what's mine is yours."

Nobody was a better talker when it comes to getting someone to see the glass as half full then Jeff, always had a way with people, Jake couldn't count how many times when they were kids Jeff talked their way out of definite punishment from their parents, always knowing what to say and how to say it sometimes making their parents feel guilty for even considering disciplinary actions. They were always close since they were kids, pretty much taking care of each other, though they are two different people, Jake being the jock and Jeff being the brain, some may have thought a rivalry would have consumed them, but it never surfaced, instead a brotherly bond formed where each one made sure the other would always succeed in whatever it was they were pursuing in life, there was no one Jake would rather have in his corner at a time like this than his brother.

"I assume Ashley will be working tonight?" Jeff asked.

"Yeah, it's the weekend, these are her three mandatory days," answered Jake.

"You're going to get through this," assured Jeff.

Ashley was sitting on her bed doing some homework, finding it hard to concentrate thinking about Holley J, wondering what her reaction was to the letter, figuring she would have heard something by now, fearful the silence is Holley J's eventual decision, doing all she could do the ball was in her court now. Wanting to jump in her car to drive over to Holley J's to force her to talk to her, but invading her space at the moment could make things worse. Many times she became distracted by redirecting her focus to the unfinished painting she had started for Jake resting against the wall under the bedroom window. Veering over at it more and more brings to life how much she has been itching to paint again, having been awhile since her brush has touched a canvas and right now she could use that personal form of home therapy. All the rest of her supplies are back at her aunt's house, if she hasn't already destroyed or burned everything. Buying all new supplies was an option, but why should perfectly good stock, just rot away in a house where it is under appreciated, it was her stuff and she has every right to reclaim it.

Her mind clearly somewhere else, Ashley lowers her pen and closes her laptop to take a break from her homework. Considering doing something she said she would never do, thinking about when would be the best time to do it. Checking the time, her aunt would still be at work for at least another hour, if she went now she could run in and grab everything while avoiding running into her which she really doesn't want to do. Still having a key to the house, not worried her aunt changed the locks because she was too lazy to do anything like that. The thought of going back there though sends a feeling of uneasiness through her body, yet she was just going to get what was already hers, after she could stop by the grocery store to grab a few things. Making up her mind now was the right time, she left her room. Downstairs she seemed out Vicki, found in the kitchen preparing dinner, politely informing her she was on her way to the store, asking if there was anything she needed. Secretly still not a fan of her young guest, Vicki did need a couple things, seeing this as an opportunity to use her as a delivery service, telling her the items she wanted. Grabbing her purse off the counter, Vicki searched for her wallet, Ashley advises her that wouldn't be necessary, it was on her. A bit suspicious of the gesture, Vicki lets it go, hearing her cell phone begin to ring, picking it up off the counter to answer it, nothing left to say, Ashley leaves the kitchen to be on her way.

Turning down the street where her aunt's house is located, Ashley can feel her anxiety growing, returning to the scene of many crimes would be hard for anybody. Pulling up, she decides to park by the curb preventing the unlikely event of her being blocked in the driveway. The outside of the house looked the same, staring at it through the driver's side window, feeling like it's been years since she has been back, yet it's been only a week. Not wanting to waste time, she exits her car heading up the walkway to the front door, the sights of the yard have remained the same, empty beer bottles left on the porch steps along with a full ashtray, the lawn in need of a good mowing. Standing at the front door seeing more empty beer bottles by the rusted steel chair nobody ever sits in. Putting her key in the lock, it opens like always encouraging her everything should go smoothly. Entering the house, she is reunited with the smell of weed and other odors she could never quite identify. The inside was a mess viewing the living room from the entryway, much of the damage from their fight still was visible and hasn't changed. The smashed in TV still was resting on its stand, cracks and holes in the walls haven't been fixed, the fallen pictures still remained on the floor, the glass from the coffee table has been replaced with a piece of wood that just lays on top, more empty beer bottles and ashtrays occupy the thin piece of lumber with the main eyesore being the large piece of broken glass resting atop the wood covered in left over cocaine, a very redneck, white trash look right down to the cardboard covering up the broken glass of the front window. Most of the furniture has clothing draped over or hanging off it, a sad sight to see even in Ashley's absence her aunt still won't lift a finger to take care of her own home. Though standing in the house again felt disturbing and uneasy, Ashley couldn't help but be curious how the rest of the place looks. Walking through the living room to the kitchen, she would sometimes hear this crunching sound beneath her sneakers, the unvacuumed carpet must be infested with fragments of potato chips evidence by the couple of empty bags just thrown on the floor. Entering the kitchen was more of the same, beer bottles on the counters, the sink over flowing with dirty dishes, the table was back in place, however the couple of broken chairs haven't been removed. Ashley could only imagine what the inside of the refrigerator looked like, but withheld her interest seeing enough of the disorder already. Consumed by old habits, Ashley picks up a crushed beer can off the floor placing it in the overfull trash basket, for a few brief seconds Ashley actually felt sorry for her aunt, how anyone could live in such squalor must really have nothing to live for, making her feel a bit better about herself with how she kept everything in the house in order and looking sharp. Through observing her aunt's living conditions in the wake of her escape, Ashley left the kitchen to go to her old room to get what she came for. The upstairs wasn't much better visually, a few random clothes just dropped in the hallway, some looked like men's clothes explaining the musty smell inhabiting the air. Reaching her old bedroom door she took a deep breath unsure of what to expect when she opens it, part of her believes the room will be trashed and all her painting supplies will be ruined making this trip all for nothing. Slowing opening the door, she is treated to an unanticipated sight, the room is exactly how she left it, not a thing out of place. Walking over, she sits on her bed getting reacquainted with her old mattress, admiring some of her old paintings covering the walls, living in this house was hell, but Ashley missed her room, unfortunately it just happens to be located in the middle of a prison she happen to break free from. Even though she has only been at Jake's for about a week and despite the unwelcome vibe resonating from Mrs. Wheeler, there feels more like home than this house ever did. Checking the time on her phone, she notices she is cutting it kind of close, motivating her to quickly gather what she came for and get out. Folding up her easel, grabbing her paints, brushes and palette, heading to leave the room, becomes interrupted by the sound of a car door being shut. Frantically hurries over to the bedroom window to investigate, to her dismay sees her aunt's car parked in the driveway. Wasting no time, rushes out of the room speedily racing down the hallway and staircase carrying her stuff hoping to exit the house before her aunt enters. Every step, Ashley can feel her anxiety rising inching closer to the front door, leave it to her aunt to arrive home from work early. Reaching the bottom of the staircase, the front opens freezing Ashley in her tracks, preparing herself to come face to face with her old nemesis once again. Her aunt enters immediately greeted by a bothered Ashley standing in her entryway the two lock eyes becoming frozen in each other's gaze. Each of them stared trying to figure out what each one was thinking, Ashley could tell from peering at her slightly bloodshot eyes her aunt was just how she left her, looking rough and tired still smelling like cigarettes and alcohol, amazed she can even hold a job with flaws like that, assuming upon first sight Ashley was there to beg to come crawling back, however her initial instincts were completely dismissed being witness to Ashley carrying a bunch of her stuff to leave with. The awkwardness seemed to intensify the longer they stood there leering at each other, the silence between the two of them spoke louder than any words could. Convincing herself she was desperately waiting for an apology she knew was never going to come, what did Ashley expect from a woman who hasn't even reached out since she left to see if she was okay, they were just two people who had nothing to say to each other and she was fine with that. Breaking eye contact, Ashley steadily walks out the front door, screen door slamming shut behind her, enters her car and drives away.   Walking through the grocery store, Ashley turns down every aisle looking for the last item Mrs. Wheeler requested, normally knowing where everything is located in this store having been there countless times doing shopping for her aunt, but the search for an unfamiliar product can turn your visit into a bit of a scavenger hunt. It would be the last aisle she explored that would have what she was looking for, putting the item in her basket, redirects herself towards the checkout line. Many of the town folks inhabiting the store would recognize her from the local sports page giving her praise and congratulations, appreciating the kind words and support, but would much rather be left alone, feeling undeserving of their gracious comments. It was a busy Friday afternoon, many of the checkout lines had numerous patrons waiting impatiently for their turn, some with carts overflowing with groceries. Getting into what she thought was the shortest line, Ashley held her full basket firmly with both hands hoping the few customers ahead of her would notices she only had a handful of items, letting her go ahead, but it was not to be, even with her given status as a high school sports star she was meant to wait like everyone else. Luckily her patients paid off as the nearby closed express lane opened up with the cashier waving over any potential shoppers meeting the criteria, Ashley being the closest became first in line. Exchanging quick greetings with the cashier, Ashley proceeds to empty her basket onto the belt, items being rung up as she grabs one of the various magazines for sale of the shelf to take a peek at. Flipping through the pages, she hears her name being called from behind.

"Stamper?" the voice asked.

Literally dropping the magazine to the floor hearing the all too familiar voice sending a surge of disbelief and edginess through her body, didn't even have to turn around to know who it was. Coach Mabbet is standing behind her, convinced he would have left town or something after being fired never to be seen by her again, a slap on the wrist compared to what he truly deserved, however life has a funny way of bringing things full circle. Ashley's first instinct was to just ignore him, maybe he would assume he had the wrong person, but something came over her, the universe was giving her the chance to say to him what she always wanted to regardless of the place and time. Slowly turning around coming face to face with one of the most hated people to ever come into her life, just the sight of him makes her feel nauseous sending shivers down her spine.

"I thought that was you," Coach Mabbet said, placing a hand on Ashley's shoulder.

"GET YOUR FUCKING HANDS OFF ME!" yelled Ashley knocking his hand away, drawing the attention of everyone around, the cashier ringing out Ashley's stuff was standing there holding her receipt unsure of what was going on. "I JUST WANT EVERYBODY HERE TO KNOW THAT THIS SON OF A BITCH SEXUALLY ABUSED ME FOR THREE YEARS AND

GOT AWAY WITH IT!" she continued yelling taking her receipt and few bags removing herself from the line.

Every customer stood silently, some had their cell phones out to film the next big viral video, all the cashiers stopped working to hear what Ashley had to say. You could see the mix of embarrassment and fear all throughout Coach Mabbet's face feeling every set of eyes directly on him like a deer caught in the headlights.

"I know what you are all thinking, why didn't I say something or turn him in, it's because this asshole blackmailed me, threatened to take away what I loved most. I always wondered what I would say to you if I ever saw you again!" Ashley stated, standing behind the checkout lanes keeping direct eye contact on Coach Mabbet. "I know now that it really doesn't matter, all I know is that you are a piece of shit and I hate you and I hope you die and I hope, I fucking hope that the next girl you decide to prey on realizes that nothing in this world is worth losing your dignity over. TAKE A GOOD LOOK, EVERYONE, THAT'S WHAT A SEXUAL PREDATOR LOOKS LIKE!" Ashley adds, pointing straight at Coach Mabbet before leaving the store.

Jeff was still in his home office on his cell phone talking with a couple acquaintances at the police department, having left earlier after receiving a phone call from Danielle, Jake wanted to give his brother the privacy to do what he does best. Being busy with his phone calls Jeff lost track of time, the once sunny outside has faded to the black of night prompting Vicki to enter his office unbeknownst to him, deeply engaged in the current conversation. A displeased Vicki stands in front of his desk, arms folded, an annoyed expression on her face, waiting for Jeff to acknowledge her presence. Growing impatient, Vicki loudly clears her throat to grab his attention, a technique that worked seeing Jeff hold up a finger asking for a second. Writing some information down before ending the call, Jeff tosses his phone onto his desk, leaning back in his chair rubbing his eyes prior to bringing his awareness to his visibly unhappy wife.

"What are you doing?" Vicki asked a bit put out.

"What do you mean?" replied a confused Jeff.

"We were supposed to go out together tonight, remember, Jake is watching the girls," said Vicki.

"Oh, shit, that's right," Jeff responded. "I totally forgot, I was doing a favor for Jake and just lost track of time, I'm sorry."

"There you go again, everything is about Jake," she uttered, anger in her voice. "When are you going to stop coddling him, when it comes to your brother you drop everything, I mean for Christ sakes we have a strange girl living in our house because of him, who I don't trust by the way."

"Vick, I told you, I owe Jake more than you know," Jeff said.

"You always keep saying that, what do you owe him for?" an irate Vicki asked.

"I promised him I wouldn't tell anybody," he replied.

"Damn it, Jeff, I'm your wife, if you want me to continue going along with all this bullshit you better tell me what is going on," demanded Vicki.

Rubbing his forehead, feeling backed up against a wall, Jeff felt Vicki was right, she was his wife and deserved to know everything, hoping when he hangs his dirty laundry she will finally understand.

"You better sit down," Jeff suggested.

Vicki complies sitting intently with open ears.

"This isn't easy for me to say, you remember how I told you back in high school Jake drove me and our friends drunk and crashed the car. Well, it wasn't Jake that drove, it was me."

"What?!" a stunned Vicki voiced.

Jeff remembered that night like it was yesterday. It was a late spring night, every star seemed to be out that evening accompanied with a full moon, glowing brightly in the clear sky lighting up many of the normally darkened roadways. A black '91 Dodge Charger being driven by a young Jeff speeds down the road, was the last day of his first year in college, out celebrating with Jake and a couple of their friends. Recently leaving a party held on campus, they were heading to meet some girls down at the beach for a late night swim. All four of them had been drinking, but Jeff insisted he was okay to drive, especially since it was his car. Jeff worked the whole summer before as a mason to buy the vehicle he called his steel beauty. As the speedometer climbed to over a hundred miles per hour, the four passengers head banged to the metal music blasting on the radio. Well after midnight, they hadn't seen another car for a few miles, thinking it would be smooth sailing all the way to their destination. Driving steadily down the two-lane road with nothing but woods flashing by out their glare filled windows, Jeff repeatedly rubbed his eyes hoping to wipe away his blurry vision, a couple times the car drifted over to the shoulder haphazardly putting the passenger side tires in contact with gravel and dirt making it a bit harder to steer. Regaining control placing all four wheels back on the asphalt their back seat riders laughed it off, lighting up a couple joints in the process. Jeff let out a spirited laugh still trying to shake his eyesight clear.

"You sure you are okay?" asked a smiling Jake from the passenger seat.

"I'm okay," Jeff answered. "I'll be better when we are face to nipples with those girls at the beach."

The backseat explodes into uproarious hollering puffing on their roaches, smoke be sucked out the cracked open back windows. Turning the music up louder to get the four of them amped up, just a few minutes away from being naked with the girls in the moonlit water, Jeff was still fighting with the glare and blurry vision causing the car to slowly start to coast over into the other lane. Jake had his head back and eyes closed, the two in the back were completely oblivious to anything that was going on outside the car. The vehicle's speed slowly declined the more it faded over into the opposite lane, Jeff unaware of his position on the road tiredly closed his eyes for a split second only to be alerted by the blaring sound of a car horn. Reopening his eyes, he was greeted by two headlights directly in the center of his windshield. Frantically swerving out of the opposing headlights path waking Jake from his cat nap, Jeff slams on the brakes producing the car to skid uncontrollably until it smashes head first into a tree. Everyone inside was shaken up, once surrounded by the sound of a roaring engine and loud music has been replaced by complete silence as they all try to recompose themselves from their near death experience. Removing his laid head from the steering wheel, Jeff asked everyone if they were okay, remarkably nobody suffered any serious injuries. Jeff had a few bloody cuts on his face and forehead from the impact, the back seat passengers sustained some minor whiplash from the sudden jolt due to the seatbelts, Jake had both of his legs slightly pinned from the knees down against the now caved in dashboard. The windshield shattered in place, one good kick would send glass fragments everywhere, the smashed in front end was bellowed in so much the hood was bent into the shape of an upside down V, smoke escaping from the damaged area. Attempting to open his door, taking a couple hits with his shoulder to jar it loose, Jeff gingerly steps out for a second wiping some of the trickling blood from his forehead with his hand. Standing by the wreckage, he sees the other car a little ways down the road sideways up against a tree, too far away to see how many people were in the vehicle, could only make out the possible model of the car which looked like a BMW. The moonlight shined on the car like a spotlight, its waxed white exterior made it visibly easier to see on the streetlamp less road, Jeff watched the driver's side door open with the driver removing him or herself from the car talking on what must have been a car phone as the party on hand's voice echoed about the silent roadway, most likely calling the cops. Not wanting to be seen Jeff ducks back into his mangled car worried and upset.

"Oh my God! I am so fucked!" Jeff announced.

"Okay, calm down, it was an accident," said Jake freeing his legs.

"If I get a DWI that's it, they will revoke my scholarship and then I can kiss law school goodbye, you know Mom and Dad could never afford the tuition," uttered Jeff.

"That's not going to happen," assured Jake.

"What are talking about? Look at me, I'm drunk as shit," Jeff proclaimed, a glimpse into his rearview mirror highlights the arriving red and blue glow of oncoming police sirens. "Oh, shit!"

"All of you get out of here," ordered Jake, pushing his brother to exit the car so he could slide over into the driver's seat.

"What are you doing?" asked Jeff.

"You weren't driving, I was," stated Jake.

"Jake, no, I can't let you do that," Jeff remarked.

"Get the hell out of here, I'll take care of it. You're going to law school, you're going to become a lawyer. You're on your own getting back, now get out of here before they see you," Jake demanded.

Jeff hurries to the other side of the car to help let out his friends, opening the passenger door to grab a flashlight out of the glove compartment.

"Jake, you sure…," asked Jeff.

"It's okay, get out of here now, GO!" Jake screams.

Jeff and his friends hustle to hide in the darkness of the woods until it was safe. Jeff and company disappear to conceal themselves amongst the trees while the area quickly becomes overrun with the flashing lights of cops, firemen and EMS. Looking on to make sure his brother was nowhere to be seen, Jake patiently waited to be visited by one of the on scene officers, rubbing down his knees he's approached with a bright flashlight to the face, greeting it with squinted eyes.

Listening to the unexpected truth come out, Vicki sat there dumbfounded, the whole time she has known Jeff, was lead to believe it was Jake driving the car that night always giving her the impression he was reckless and careless.

"Jake ended up getting arrested and was sentenced to six months' probation and his license was suspended along with community service," Jeff said. "It was a risk for him too of losing his scholarship, but he knew he could get to the major leagues another way. So my friends and I walked about four miles to a gas station where we called a cab. Jake made me promise that I would never do anything like that again, because of what he did I kept my full ride to school and eventually got one for law school. Everything I am and everything we have today is because of what he did that night. The worse part of it, even though his injuries to his legs in time healed his knees were never the same. I ruined his playing career that night, his career was cut short because of me," added Jeff with tears in his eyes. "That's why I owe him."

With this recent revelation, Vicki became emotional witnessing Jeff break down talking about what his brother did for him, understanding now why Jeff is always there for Jake no matter what the circumstances, selfless acts should never go unpaid especially if they change a life. Knowing her husband he will be indebted to Jake for as long as he lives and she can't blame him. Wishing she could take back all the times she has been hard on Jake knowing what she knows now, yet she now can have a better relationship with him starting at this very moment. Wiping her tears away with her hands, Vicki leaves her seat to go over to console her husband, the two embrace in a loving hug exchanging I love yous.

"There is something I got to do," Vicki whispered to Jeff.

Leaving Jeff's office, she walks through the living room, seeing through the picture window Jake standing outside on the front patio, something he has been doing a lot lately, leaned up against one of the post resembling someone deep in thought. Exiting the house, standing before him with a subtle grin on her face, feeling like she is staring at a completely different person, the old image she once had for him peeled away leaving behind what she now sees.

"Hey," said Jake, conceding Vicki's presence on the patio.

Without saying a word, Vicki hugs Jake giving him a tender kiss on the cheek, holding him tightly, wanting each second of the embrace to reflect how sorry she was for any of the indifferences they may have had in the past. Before

Jake could react to the surprising show of affection, she released him from her clasp, returning into the house.

Turning out to be a very different Friday night for Holley J, generally spending the night isolated in her room playing her computer games, a tradition she started when Ashley began working every weekend. This particular night, she wasn't in the mood for games or fun in general, even turning down a date with her new friend, all she wanted to do was just sit on her bed in her dimly lit room, hugging one of her pillows thinking, which she has been doing for the past few hours. With nothing to distract her, Holley J fell deep into thought becoming lost in her perceptions, Ashley dominating the majority of her thinking. Recalling what Jake said to her earlier, Holley J tried to look past everything she just learned, focusing predominately on everything she already knew about her best friend. Jake was right, reminiscing about all the good times they shared together, all the times Ashley was there along with the many things she did for her since the day they met, carried way more weight and meant so much to Holley J, she could see herself forgetting the other side of Ashley didn't even exist. During her moments of reflecting, Holley J found herself conflicted between the reasons why she was so upset, was it truly because Ashley lied, hiding it from her or was it really because she was scared for her best friend living that type of life. Everyone has skeletons in their closet, how you react to discovering them determines whether or not you should continue on with a certain relationship. Believing Ashley when she said in the letter she always wanted to tell her, but fear of ruining their friendship kept holding her back, just hurt that her best friend wasn't able to talk to her about it, they have always told each other everything. Will never agree with what Ashley is doing, but Holley J understands why she does it, she misses her friend and wants to help her, asking herself the big question, can she see her life without Ashley in it?

Answering the question, Holley J grinned hugging the pillow tighter ready to forgive and forget, grabbing her cell phone off her nightstand to send a text to Ashley saying she wants to talk. After typing a couple letters to her message, she erases all of it, feeling anxious, not wanting to wait until tomorrow, Holley J comes to the conclusion she needs to do this now and in person, deciding she was going to drive up to the club to talk to her face to face. Throwing her pillow aside, hopping off her bed to throw on a pair of sneakers, puts on a light jacket, grabs her phone and car keys, exiting her room. Her parents would never go for her driving into the city, Holley J would have to be very discrete leaving the house, if worse comes to worse she will just tell them she is going to run to the store. Favoring her parents are doing what they normally do at this time of night, fleeing the house shouldn't be a problem. Coming down the staircase, Holley J peeks into the living room to confirm her parents are doing their usual routine, each sitting in their specific recliner, glasses of wine at the ready on a small table located between them watching their Friday night regulars on TV. Slipping by unnoticed, she quietly departs for her car, entering the driver's seat starting the engine hoping her parents will assume it's the neighbors, waiting to turn her headlights on until she is clear out of her driveway, looking free and clear she ignites her lights driving off. Driving downtown is a new experience for Holley J, unfamiliar with all the connecting intersections and multiple one way streets, thankful she has access to GPS on her cell phone which sits securely in her dashboard phone holder. Definitely wouldn't want to be driving around in this area blind, very easy to get lost and judging by some of the inner city dwellers she sees wandering the sidewalks, probably not a good place to ask for directions. Being an avid follower of current events, Holley J knows most violent crimes towards women happen mainly in the city. Not the type of person to drive in areas she is not well acquainted with, especially by herself only having a small can of pepper spray on her keychain for protection, understanding now why her parents didn't approve of her driving downtown, particularly at night. Normally Holley J would take an opportunity like this to get a glimpse of some big city living, but she is not here to sight see, just wants to get to her destination to surprise her best friend. According to the GPS, she should be arriving any minute, being instructed to turn down the next street, she can see off in the distance the bright neon lights of the club's marquis. Coming closer, she saw the long line of people waiting to get in, driving by looking out her driver's side window she caught a glance of the inside when the outside guard opened the door for the next group to enter, the few seconds of visual intel didn't give her much information other than the place had a good crowd present and buried within all the ongoing commotion was her friend. Locating the parking lot just up the street, from her view it looked like she might be out of luck finding a stop, nevertheless she pulled in anyway hoping to get lucky, not wanting to park to far away, already on edge being in the city at night alone. Making her rounds in search of an empty space, she got lucky finding one directly under a lamp post putting her car in full illumination, couldn't decide if that was a good or a bad thing, either way she was happy to find a spot in good proximity to the club.

Immediately leaving her car, Holley J grabs her phone starting her walk towards the front entrance, passing by a couple having sex on the hood of car, other than the man's pants being down to his ankles exposing his bare ass, they were both fully clothed, not a good first impression on her first trip to the city, figuring stuff like this must happen all the time around here. Walking the sidewalk, Holley has her keys in her hand with the pepper spray at the ready, after what she just saw, she wanted to be prepared for anything. The walk gave her time to try to figure out how she was going to go about this, knowing she is too young to enter a place like this, her only option would be to ask the front guard for help. Arriving at the front entrance, Holley J can hear the music coming from inside, the volume increased every time the doors opened to let people in or out. Standing there she can feel some of the eyes from the waiting patrons focused on her, probably wondering what someone her age is doing at a place like this. Wasting no time, Holley J approaches the towering guard handling the line.

"Excuse me, I'm looking for someone who works here," Holley J said.

"You can't go inside, it's twenty-one and older," replied the guard letting more people enter.

"I don't want to go inside, I just need her come out here so we can talk, please, it's an emergency," stated Holley J.

"Who are you looking for?" asked the guard.

"Ashley Stamper," Holley J answered.

Talking into his headset, the guard relays Holley J's request to someone inside waiting for a response back, letting her know it might be a few minutes. The longer she waited, the more uncomfortable she got, the atmosphere of this place wasn't sitting well with her, yet watching the front doors repeatedly open and close giving her a few seconds to view the inside, peeks her curiosity. Looking around to observe her environment as she waits, Holley J catches sight of a man in a leather jacket leaned up against a parked car at the side of the road, a small duffel bag laid beside his feet, smoking a cigarette. His body language, along with the subtle way he puffed on his smoke, made him seem rather sketchy to Holley J, his eyes never left the club entrance. Normally not the type of person to stereotype, but the heart of the city is probably a haven for most shady people, uninterested in sticking around to see the outcome of this stranger's visit, she was hoping the wait wouldn't be much longer.

"Okay, she is not allowed to come out to the front, if you want to talk to her you have to meet her at the back of the building," informed the guard.

"How do I get to the back?" Holley J asked, relived she no longer has to stand in the middle of everyone's line of sight.

"Just go around the corner here, walk a little ways down and you will see a smaller parking lot, there will be two doors, don't go to the red one, she will be coming out of the other one," the guard instructed, pointing out the valid route.

"Okay, thank you," said Holley J, swiftly heading in the required direction.

As Holley J disappears around the corner, the mystery man flicks away his finished cigarette, picking up the duffel bag walking steadily to the front guard.

"I'm here to see Razz," said the man in a stern tone.

"Business or personal?" the guard asked.

"Business," answered the man, showing the guard a peek of the bundled money occupying the duffel bag.

"Razz wasn't expecting anyone tonight," said the guard looking the man up and down.

"He knows my associate, I'm just here to deliver what we owe and then I will be on my way," the man stated.

"Let me let him know you are here," the guard remarked.

Again the guard relays the current information to the inside while still continuing to let groups of bystanders inside. Waiting for confirmation, the guard firmly stands his ground not letting his eyes off the unannounced stranger standing there supporting an odd grin perfectly matching his slicked back hair and chiseled jaw line. All the guards at Razz' club take their job very seriously and would hate to disappoint their boss in anyway, good pay and special perks could make any man trustingly loyal. The awaited verification comes through the guard's headset receiving detailed instructions.

"You have to go around back, there is another parking lot, go through there and look for a red door, Razz will meet you there," instructed the guard. "Put your arms up."

The man complies dropping the duffel bag and raising both arms straight out preparing himself to be frisked, the guard pats the stranger down finding no evidence of a firearm, letting the inside know he is clean, the guard sends the man on his way. Reaching the back parking lot after a nerve wracking walk down a very dimly lit side street, Holley J jumped at every little ambient sound that echoed from the darkness. Entering the lot there had to be at least twelve to fifteen cars parked there, yet noticed Ashley's right away sitting beside a large dumpster. She figured this must be mainly the place where all the girls park, seeing it's the closing to the building and many of the make and models of the vehicles are stereotypical of what female drivers are seen in from small compact cars to the SUVs. The lighting wasn't much better in this area with only one post lamp stationed towards the back and a couple overhead lights illuminating the two back doors, one being bright red, which are spaced about thirty feet apart. Remembering what the guard told her, stay away from the red door, Holley J anxiously walked to the other door to wait. A multitude of moths and some other flying insects fluttered around the bright light of the door frame, some even decided to annoy Holley J, standing patiently waiting for the door to open, causing her to back away a few feet from the light to free herself from the bothersome onslaught. Her nerves overcame her entire body standing there in the chill air of the late night, any second her best friend is about to walk out that door to see her standing there and all Holley J could think about is what Ashley's reaction is going to be. Very uncomfortable being here, Holley J convinced herself she is doing the right thing, couldn't wait, had to make amends as soon as possible or it was going to drive her crazy for the rest of the night. Waiting was coming to an end, hearing the latch on the door coming undone, Holley J stood tall watching the door slowly open allowing Ashley to reveal herself. Completely shocked to find Holley J standing on the other side of the door, the last person she expected to see, yet despite the location of her unanticipated visit, Ashley couldn't help but feel a sense of happiness seeing her best friend standing there.

"Holley J, what are you doing here?" Ashley asked, walking away from the light of the door to join Holley J standing in front of some random car.

Holley J got her first glimpse of Ashley in what she would call her work uniform, seeing her in the black heels and skirt wearing a little bit of makeup made her almost unrecognizable, it was her other personality live in the flesh.

"Ash, please let me talk," insisted Holley J.

"Make it fast, 'cause I have to get back," Ashley replied.

"I just want to say I'm sorry, but you have to understand this isn't easy for me, seeing you like this, the fact that you lied and kept it from me. We're supposed to be best friends, we tell each other everything," Holley J said.

"You're right, but I never wanted you to see me like this. This is who I am, this is what my life turned me into. Do you thing I want to be here? Do you think I want to do this? I have no choice," stated Ashley, eyes becoming watery.

"I know," Holley J responded, "that's why I'm here, I'm behind you no matter what and we are going to figure out a way to get you out of this."

"You mean it?" asked Ashley, tears streaking down her face.

"Of course, you're my sister and I love you," Holley J answered, the girls embrace in a heartfelt hug, tears running down both of their faces.

"I love you too," Ashley whispered holding Holley J tight, ecstatic she got her best friend back, almost feeling like she was someplace else rather than in the back of one of the places she hated most, "why did you come here, you could have waited till tomorrow."

"I couldn't wait, I wanted to see you," replied Holley J, the two releasing each other, "besides, I can't have our star pitcher being more distracted with all this girly dramatic shit."

Ashley lets out a small giggle in reference to Holley J's witty comment indicating her friend is back to her old self.

The man walks down the sidewalk carrying the duffel bag, his dark clothing camouflages him in the darkness resembling a shadowy figure lurking in the night, moving with purpose totally comfortable within his environment reminiscent of someone who is a product of the streets. Turning into the lot, the man walks straight for the lit up red door, learning he is not the only one amongst the empty vehicles catching sight of a young girl standing alone as if waiting for someone. Thinking if he didn't have business to take care of, she was of the age for the opposite sex he would pursue for a good time. His presence went unnoticed, blending in the shadows, the rubber soles of his black boots kept his footsteps quiet walking up to his designated door. A large wooden partition on the right side of the door frame hid him in the bright overhead light as he knocked to declare his arrival. The door slowly swings open bringing the man face to face with another guard, again patted down before being allowed to enter. Walking inside with the duffel bag in hand, the man does a quick survey of his surroundings, three men occupy what he determined was a large office, two of them guards, one standing by a pair of doors on the other side of the room, the other he met upon entry, both strapped. The third man standing nearby smoking a cigarette would likely be the man's person of interest, his associate's description of Razz was spot on.

"Who the fuck are you and why are you here?" asked Razz, inching closer to his mysterious guest.

"A while back you did business with an associate of mine, he said you weren't happy with his payment. I'm just here to give what's coming to you," the man said, his eyes shifting to try keeping taps on the position of the nearest guard.

"And what associate would that be? I deal with a lot of people," Razz said taking a drag from his cigarette, reaching behind him making sure his concealed piece was at the ready.

"Hey, what difference does it make? You going to question the delivery of payment?" asked the man.

"Well, when you put it that way. Come on in have a seat," invited Razz, walking over to his desk to light up another cigarette.

"I'm fine right here," the man replied, trying to keep a close eye on his host and his goons.

"See, the problem is I don't know who the fuck you are or who the fuck you work for. I wasn't expecting anyone tonight, I don't have people show up without an appointment, so it got me to thinking that maybe everything you are telling me is bullshit and you are here for a different reason," Razz stated, "the big question is, what is that reason?"

"I'm just here to drop off," said the man, opening the duffel bag to show Razz the bundles of cash inside. "I was told this is what was owed."

Getting view of the money in the bag, Razz registered maybe this stranger is telling the truth, yet his instincts are steering him to believe the situation doesn't feel right. However when someone walks into his club with a bag full of money, they better be prepared to leave without it, gesturing to the guard nearby to confiscate the bag from his unknown guest.

"My associate also wanted you to have something else," said the man, reaching into his jacket front pocket to pull out a pair of sunglasses. "He said you liked these and he wanted you to have them."

Throwing the sunglasses in Razz' direction, the man quickly stuck his hand inside the duffel bag to pull out a pistol he had buried under the money. Gun in hand, the man fires first at the approaching guard tagging him in the shoulder, blood erupts from the wound knocking him down to the ground. The man's sights turn to Razz, ducked behind his desk to get out of the line of fire, drawing out his piece to retaliate, the sound of bullets puncturing the wood of his desk and pieces of debris from stricken desktop items keeps him hidden in place. The guard at the double doors takes cover firing back, missing his target as the man flees aggressively out the door he entered in with the bag still in his possession.

"MOTHERFUCKER!!!" yells Razz, as he and his unwounded guard chase after him.

Ashley and Holley J stand face to face in the middle of a small darkened parking lot in the back of a strip/night club located deep in the city, a setting the two of them never thought they would ever share together, yet here they are making amends in the most unlikely of places.

"I hate this, but I have to go back," said Ashley, seeing Holley J and the two of them clearing the air felt like a shot of adrenaline to get her through the rest of the night. "I'm so happy you came...."

The girls' interaction was interrupted by what sounded to them like large fireworks going off.

"Did you hear that?" Ashley asked, looking in the direction of the back of the club, the sound was close by seeming to be originating from Razz' personal door.

Just as fast as the girls heard it, the origins of the sound came to fruition observing someone running vigorously from out of the building firing a gun in the direction from which he came. The man's identity was kept hidden in the dullness of the night with the only thing seen clearly was the muzzle flash from his gun after every pull of the trigger. Heading in the girl's vicinity, the man swiftly ducks behind one of the parked cars, followed by more guns shots coming from the opposite direction. Ashley yells to Holley J to get down, both taking cover behind a separate parked vehicle, Ashley sits on the ground with her back to the car door, Holley J on her knees with her hands over her ears in an upright fetal position, letting out screams of panic and worry hearing the bullets shatter numerous car windows, some of which are directly over them showering them is broken glass. A majority of the bullets were being absorbed by the steel frames of the vehicles acting as shields, a few tires were the recipient of some off targets shots. Between the gun fire, Ashley can hear Razz' voice yelling for the perpetrator in a threatening manner, making it very clear he might not make it out of this alive. Becoming more aware of how fortunes can change in the matter of seconds, Ashley kept herself fixed in her current position, just a few minutes ago she and Holley J were sharing a tender moment and in the blink of an eye, the two of them find themselves in the middle of vicious shoot out, both scared out of their minds. Coming to the lot entrance on foot is another of Razz' guards called over for back up, his weapon drawn, keeping his back to the wooden fence in hopes to remain anonymous. The guard peeks around the corner to see if he can get a view of the target, but it is too dark between the spaces of the cars to pin point his exact location. Feeling pinned down, the man quickly reloads his piece, frantically trying to devise his next move to escape, his options limited too where he came in which would put him directly into the line of fire or he could scale the concrete wall find right next to him, the only obvious choice is to get over the wall. From the ground it's far too high to make it over even with a running start, however using the hood of the car just in front of him could be used to springboard himself over. Keeping his head down, the man waits for a break in the bullets whizzing by, standing up to provide himself some cover fire, leaps on the hood of the car firing rapidly to buy time to jump over the wall with his bag in hand disappearing into the darkness. Glancing again around the fence the guard gets a glimpse of some movement in the middle of a pair of cars, swiftly turning out of cover he fires three shots in that direction, ducking back into cover in anticipation of return fire, yet is greeted with the sound of silence. Assuming he hit his target, the guard slowly removes himself out of cover aiming his gun down sight in preparation for a sneak attack.

Walking gingerly into the lot in the path of his bullets, the guard voices over to Razz and the other guard standing outside Razz' door by the partition, that he thinks he got him. Razz angry and worked up, breathing heavy, orders the two guards to make sure before reentering the building slamming the door behind him. Realizing the firing has ceased, Ashley stands up calling for Holley J walking a parking spot over to where she had been hiding, screaming when she sees Holley J on her back clothes soaked in blood.

"OH MY GOD!!" yells Ashley, running over to kneel down beside her, blood seeping out of her mouth. "Holley J, you're okay, you're going to be okay. HELP! SOMEONE HELP!"

Racing over to Ashley's cries for help, the two guards see the realization the bullets struck the wrong person, verifying the intended target got away. The guard who fired the shots shouted furiously in disappointment, recognizing her being the girl earlier from the front entrance, the other got on his phone to call 911.

"I'm right here, help is coming," whispers Ashley crying heavily, putting her hand over the wound to try to stop the bleeding appearing to be in Holley J's abdomen.

Holley J tries to talk, yet instead of words a series of coughs are released. Feeling helpless looking down at her best friend in obvious pain and discomfort, though Ashley wasn't wounded the sheer visual of Holley J on the ground, blood pouring out of her generated an aching in her body she has never felt before. It almost didn't seem real, was like a bad dream she would have as a kid where her friend becomes hurt or in trouble yet would feel paralyzed, shackled by some unseen force not allowing her to intervene, forced to stand by watching them suffer until she would awaken in a cold sweat. But this situation was very real, blood seeping between Ashley's fingers and the tears dripping off her face was evidence of that.

"Don't try to talk," Ashley said, feeling Holley J's blood on her hand continue to pour out of the punctured area. "You're going to be okay," she said laying her forehead upon Holley J's hoping the ambulance arrives soon.

Ashley sits in the emergency room in a daze just staring at whatever happens to be in her line of sight, eyes still glossy from all the crying, still wearing the clothes from the club, her one hand along with much of her outfit soaked in Holley J's blood. Her blood soaked hand worriedly and nervously taps rapidly up and down on the wooden arm rest of her seat, loud enough to draw the attention from the few individuals sitting, waiting patiently nearby. Looking at Ashley with curiosity, wondering how a girl like her dressed in such flattering clothes would be covered in blood. Feeling the gazes coming from the surrounding on lookers, she totally ignores their stares of intrigue, used to having eyes on her for different reasons, any other day or place would tell people to mind their own business. Not even concerned she left the club before getting permission to do so, jumping in her car to follow the ambulance once they picked up Holley J, telling the two guards waiting with her she was leaving, guaranteed they passed the news to Razz. Can only imagine what he will do to her next time she has to work, but right now she doesn't care, willing to take anything Razz can dish out if it means Holley J will be okay, being the only thing on her mind at the moment.

Seeming like Ashley has been sitting in the waiting area for hours, yet it's only been about thirty minutes, growing impatient wanting to know what is going on with Holley J. The last time she was at the hospital was when Holley J broke her leg skiing in eight grade on a trip with her parents, riding her bike nearly twelve miles to visit her, seeing her aunt would never have gone out of her way to bring her. Remembers how in good spirits Holley J was, despite the rest of that school year she spent on crutches leaving her to be Holley J's aid whenever necessary, a job she would do again in a heartbeat. The first to sign her cast drawing their created BFF symbol on it, staying by Holley J's side in the hospital until she was ready to be discharged. Now Ashley finds history repeating itself, this time with a far more serious and dangerous injury, still, like her broken leg, will not leave Holley J's side until she knows she is okay.

A few other random to be patients sporadically came rushing into the emergency room looking for assistance, one middle-aged man came stumbling in wearing a white dress shirt, half of it was covered in blood from an apparent stab wound, keeping constant pressure on the open gash with both of his hands. Minutes later Ashley sees Jake running in through the electric sliding doors, the first person she called to explain what happened even before Holley J's parents who she couldn't get a hold of, leaving a voice mail on their phones. Without exchanging any words, Ashley gets up from her seat crying, greeted by Jake with a strong embrace.

About ninety minutes have passed, still no word on Holley J's condition, the emergency room waiting area is now occupied by all the girls on the team after Jake sent out a massive group text to all his players before he arrived, the fact that they all showed up at this time of night leaving whatever it was they were doing or not doing in support of their fallen teammate meant a lot to Jake and Ashley as well. Renee even showed up being the last one to arrive, passing through the sliding doors dressed in attire indicative of someone who was most likely out on a date with her boyfriend, it's the first time she has shown any compassion or interest in anyone other than herself, going as far as to sit amongst the other girls rather than away on her own. The waiting area was completely silent, everyone just sat there with worried and concerned expressions on their faces, no one wanted to speak, words seemed irrelevant, what could be said that would make the circumstances any easier, many girls sat side by side holding hands, others had their own private rituals to help cope with the situation, not every day a teammate gets accidentally shot. Ashley and Jake sat together, grabbing her hand resting on the arm rest giving it a soft squeeze, vindicating he's going to be by her side. Having Jake there, seeing all her teammates, Ashley felt the unity of her real family, they have been backing her up all season, but now she needs them more than ever and it means the world to her they are here to offer their support, with fatigue setting in from all the waiting, Ashley gently rests her head upon Jake's shoulder. A little more time has passed, a few of the girls have fallen asleep in their seats, Jake now up pacing back and forth drinking a cup of coffee. Coming through the sliding doors is Danielle, who came as soon as she got Jake's message, greeting him with a large tender hug. After what seemed like an eternity, a doctor finally makes an appearance looking for a parent or guardian to speak with, an anxious Ashley alertly jumps from her seat hoping to hear what the doctor has to say. Knowing Holley J's parents haven't arrived yet, Jake felt he was the next suitable alternative, gesturing to Ashley to hold back. Approaching the doctor, he can tell by his body language and the unenthusiastic expression on his face, what he had to say wasn't going to be easy.

"Are you the father?" asked the doctor, pulling Jake off to the side prohibiting anyone else from hearing what he had to say.

Ashley did her best to get within earshot of the conversing men without seeming like she is eavesdropping.

"No, her parents are the way. I'm her softball coach," Jake answered, matching the doctor's low tone. "So how is she?"

"She's bleeding internally, we tried but we couldn't stop the bleeding," the doctor said, "the bullet ruptured her...."

"Wait, what are you saying?" asked Jake.

"There's nothing more we can do for her, I'm sorry," informed the doctor. "She wants to talk with someone named Ashley."

Seeing Jake's reaction to the news the doctor is telling him, putting his head down rubbing his forehead with his hand, never the behavior of someone receiving good news, tears start flowing down Ashley's face, a horrific feeling consumes her body, her gut in knots slowly stepping forward to try hearing what is being said.

"Coach, what is going on?" asked Ashley very emotional. "Is Holley J going to be okay?"

Hearing Ashley's inquiry coming from behind him, not knowing how to tell her, Jake keeps his back to her not acknowledging her cries for answers.

"TELL ME!" Ashley shouted at the top of her lungs, the loud outburst gets the attention of all her teammates and everyone else seated in the waiting area, hearing a deep emotion in her yell, sends a feeling of sadness throughout everyone that heard it.

Excusing himself from the doctor to confront a very emotional Ashley, the short walk Jake took to where she stood felt like a journey of thousand miles, each step the panic and fear on her face became ever more clear.

"Coach, what is happening?" Ashley asked, tears pouring out of her eyes.

Jake stood before her trying to hold back his emotions, reaching down to grab one of Ashley's hands, holding it gently in his, he looked in her soaked filled eyes contemplating how to break the news to someone who's whole life was already a series of horrific events. Trying to read Jake's blank expression, spotting a lonely tear coming out of his left eye slowly cascading down his face, learning in biology, a tear coming from the left eye first represents sorrow.

"The doctor said….," Jake started, not having the heart to tell her, just relayed the doctor's other message, "Holley J wants to see you."

Without hesitation Ashley left to follow the doctor to the room Holley J is being held in. Standing there with his head hung low, hands on his hips being approached by a concerned Danielle, Jake makes eye contact with her, without saying a word he slowly shakes his head to deliver the devastating news. Ashley enters Holley J's room to the sight of her lying on her back at a slight incline, various tubes and wires connected to her along with an IV, a blanket covered her from the waist down, the steady beeping of her EKG the only sound that could be heard. Walking up to her bedside, Ashley got a better visual of Holley J's condition, looking pale and sickly, her breathing was slow and weak sounding, eyes closed trying to sleep. Seeing Holley J in this state was the worse sight Ashley's eyes have ever bare witnessed too, usually a teenage girl seeing her best friend at her worst would consist of a bad hair day, poor clothing choices or a makeup mishap, not the brutal reality of them lying helplessly in a hospital bed.

"Holley J, I'm here," Ashley said softly, grabbing Holley J's closest hand.

Hearing Ashley's voice, Holley J's eyes slowly began to open, sluggishly turning her head to put her in eyesight.

"Hey," said Holley J, her voice frail as if strenuous to talk. "I guess I've looked better, huh."

"Yes, you have," Ashley replied with a small giggle, mixed in with her weeping. "You're going to be okay."

"I want you to lay with me," requested Holley J.

"Okay," said Ashley, kicking off her shoes, lowering the side bar to climb up atop the bed, being sure not to interrupt any of the tubes or wires laying herself on her side facing Holley J, a darker version of the many times they would lie together on Holley J's bed goofing off having quality girl time. "I'm right here."

"Are my parents here?" Holley J asked.

"They are on their way," answered Ashley. "Coach and the rest of the girls are here waiting for you."

"I wish I could see them all one last time," Holley J remarked in a weakening tone. "I just wanted you here so I could say goodbye."

"Don't say that, you're going to be okay," responds Ashley crying heavily.

"You're the best friend I ever had and I love you so much. I want you to go be great, be the person I know you are, you're living a dangerous life and I'm so scared for you," replied Holley J. "I'm so sorry for everything."

"You don't have to be sorry and I love you too, just get better, okay," Ashley remarked, soaking the sheets underneath her with her tears. "Please don't leave me."

"I want you to promise me something," requests Holley, tears slowly seeping from her eyes.

"Anything," Ashley declared.

"Don't be next," said Holley J looking over at a grieving Ashley. "Don't be next," she said taking a couple deep breaths. "I love you, BFFs forever."

Holley J takes one last breath, her eyes slowly shut, the steady beep of her EKG flatlining echoes throughout the room.

"Holley J, HOLLEY J!!!" shouts a heartbroken Ashley, her cries for a response go unanswered, bottom lip quivering watching her best friend's eyes close for the last time.

Putting her arm over Holley J's lifeless body to give her one last hug and tender kiss on her cheek, Ashley holds her tight crying loud and uncontrollably.

Reentering the waiting area, Ashley walks gingerly displaying barely enough energy to keep herself upright, Jake, Danielle and the girls looked on watching Ashley make her return seeing the redness in her eyes and blank expression on her face. There wasn't a dry eye amongst them being passed on the news earlier, Jake rose from his seat to approach Ashley, never seen looking more broken. Standing toe to toe, the two make eye contact spawning Ashley to breakdown crying once again, Jake immediately hugs her holding her close as the tears run down his face.

"NO, NO, NO! Not Holley J," Ashley cried. "I just want Holley J back!"

The rest of the girls leave their seats to join in with Jake embracing Ashley and one another in one giant group hug to mourn together as a team. Ashley's loud cries over shadowed all the silent weeping being administered by all the girls, Danielle grieved silently alone in her seat, allowing the team to share the moment amidst themselves. The other few guests waiting patiently for their friends or family looked on in respect and heavy hearts watching all the girls exhibit an emotional unity for their fallen friend. After a few minutes mourning as a unit, the girls disperse to take the sadness home with them for the rest of the night, all of them giving their condolences to Ashley before they departed, hugging each of them individually. Jake shared a quiet moment with Danielle telling her it's okay to go home and get some sleep, Ashley seated herself in the closest chair still trying to get over the traumatism of the nights events. Staring blank faced at the floor, tears still pouring down her face, she becomes unaware of footsteps approaching from the side, putting into view a pair of well pedicured feet wearing black strapped sandals perfectly contrasting the bright red polish on the toe nails. Ashley looks up to see who the expertly groomed feet belong to, being surprised at the sight of Renee standing there, not use to seeing her all dressed up looking girly.

"Hey, I just wanted to say, I know I've been a bitch for as long as I can remember and I know you and Holley J were tight, for what it's worth I'm sorry," expressed Renee, holding out her hand to call a truce.

Standing up to be eye to eye with Renee, the first time the two of them were this close to each other without verbal bashing or a physical altercation breaking out, the one girl that has been a thorn in her side all throughout high school stands before her trying to prove she has some sort of heart beating in that chest of hers. In no condition to elaborate if Renee's comment were genuine, Ashley ignored her out stuck hand, grabbing her to share a friendly embrace instead, feeling Renee hug her back, the tears start flowing once again.

It was a Saturday morning unlike any she has ever had in her life, Ashley woke up from barely three hours sleep, spending most of the night crying, what she started at the hospital, she finished back in her room, her pillow case soaked with hours of eye leakage. Didn't even bother changing out of her blood stained clothes, just came home and collapsed on her bed, physically and emotionally exhausted, yet she couldn't fall asleep, completely terrified of facing the first day of her life without Holley J, wasn't just her who died last night a part of Ashley died too, in a life where moral decency and love have been extremely scarce, the only person that has ever shown her either is now gone leaving her to face this cruel and unforgiving world on her own. Jake has been great, the first man that has come into her life she can actually trust, after everyone left the hospital, she cried more in his arms listening to him console her with words very heartfelt and meaningful, his strong masculine voice spoke of philosophy on loss and how to cope really helped put Ashley's mind at ease at least until they returned home and she was alone again. Growing up without a mother and a father, it was the first time since her grandmother was alive, she was given some sort of parental advice, wouldn't leave her side until she was ready to say goodbye and leave, but he's not going to be around forever. One of the hardest parts of the night for Ashley was facing Holley J's parents when they finally arrived, explaining what happened, having to tell them they loss their only child. Holley J's mother had to be admitted after passing out hearing the horrifying news, though they never actually said it, Ashley could tell from the expressions on their faces, they blamed her for what happened to Holley J. Most of the night laying there crying in bed, all she could do was think about how different her life is going to be now, how Razz is somewhat responsible for Holley J's death, having all the memories of her and Holley J flood her mind making her grieving even more difficult. The little sleep she did get was interrupted by the morning sunlight hitting her square in the face through her bedroom window, hoping everything that happened last night was just a horrible nightmare, but the blood on her clothes and skin reminded her it wasn't. Had no idea what time it was and she didn't care, just continued to lay there on her side looking out the window watching the curtains flutter from the breeze.

Completely void of energy or any ambition to do anything other than stay in her current position, Ashley reached up to grab the picture she brought back from her aunt's house of her and Holley J from off her nightstand, staring at it releasing more tears, running her fingers down the glass overlapping the image of Holley J as if to touch her one last time. Returning the picture to the nightstand, she cried in the cusp of experiencing the worst pain she has ever endured in her life, wondering if the hurt will ever go away. Being unfamiliar with the grieving process, too young to grasp the concept of death when her grandmother died, Ashley was feeling emotions she has never felt before, kind of scaring her prompting her to believe she might be having a nervous breakdown. Definitely not feeling herself, at times she felt light headed, stomach felt full though she hasn't eaten in hours, wondering if it's normal to miss someone who's been gone less than twelve hours. So much going through her mind all involving Holley J, everything they were looking forward to doing together throughout their lives has quickly become an illusion, evaporated like a puff of smoke. Being together when they graduated high school, visiting each other at their particular college, being each other's maid of honor at their weddings, being the good aunt to each of their future kids, getting the matching tattoos they have always talked about. Life is never fair and it's never been more apparent to Ashley than it does right now, a world will take away a decent, wholesome, incredible person like Holley J, but leave pieces of shit like her aunt and Razz who do nothing but make everyone else's lives miserable, what would a cruel world be without monsters and Ashley knew two of the worst. Jake told her to live her life as if she were honoring Holley J, one of many words of wisdom he passed on at the hospital, also replaying the promise Holley J asked her to keep just before she passed, telling Ashley not to be next referring to her dangerous lifestyle, a promise igniting her motivation more than ever to leave that part of her life behind her, but it's not going to be easy, Razz most likely has it in for her, but there is nothing he could do to make her feel more pain than she is feeling right now. If there has been any time she deserves a night off it would be tonight, yet Razz' heartless, money and power hungry mentality won't feel the slightest sympathetic her best friend was shot on his club grounds in a shootout he was involved in. Nothing angered her more than the thought of having to work a minute longer under Razz' regime, has to try whatever it takes to free herself from his clutches or it will be a stain on Holley J's memory. Many of her isolated moments of silence became interrupted by the constant buzzing of her phone going off, not really ready or in the mood to interact with the outside world, Ashley just let the messages pile up, most likely they are messages from her teammates checking to see how she is doing. Besides her phone is Holley J's, which she confiscated from her just before she entered the ambulance, holding it until she was able to use it again, now that Holley J is gone she wants to keep it as a memento.

Growing tired of lying down and having cried what seemed like every last tear she could muster, Ashley sits up to a slight feeling of dizziness brought on by her equilibrium being off from her hours of immobilization in the same position, rubbing her eyes to help regain her clarity, decides to check the messages on her phone. Twenty-five text messages were received with most of them coming from, like she suspected, the girls on the team, however a few were from Razz noting clearly his unhappiness and anger with her, mentioning she better not think of not showing up tonight for her sake.

Wanting so bad to tell him to fuck off, yet to keep the peace for the time being she simply responded she'll be there. Sitting on the edge of the bed, looking over at her recently reclaimed painting supplies, the easel supporting the unfinished painting for Jake, remembering when he once told her, a busy mind is a clear mind. Tossing her phone onto the bed, Ashley stands up to go gather all her needed toiletries and clean clothes to lay out on the bed from the supplied dresser, exiting the room to enter the upstairs bathroom, its door wide open suggesting it is not in use. Snatching a towel out of the linen closet, Ashley enters the bathroom closing and locking the door behind her, wasting no time turning on the water in the shower, getting undressed waiting for it to warm up, sticking her hand in to test the temperature of the water, she enters the shower letting the door close itself shut. Pressing her hands against the marble interior of the standalone shower, lets the warm water wet her hair as it cascades down her body seeing the red coloring from the blood on her hand and legs find its way down the drain. Tilting her head back letting the water rain on her face, feeling the warmth against her skin, felt a sudden calming sensation, the urge to start crying again evaporated allowing her to lather up her body, smelling the fragrance from the body wash helped her to feel more relaxed giving her a few minutes of much needed jubilation.

Returning to her room robed in nothing but a towel, hair completely dry and brushed, Ashley always blow dries her hair after any shower regardless if she is going anywhere or not, can't stand her hair being wet. Inside her room Ashley catches a slight chill from the light breeze coming from her open window, also noticing the bed tray left on her bed. The tray contained a plate with an egg white omelet the way she likes it, full of onions, broccoli, mushrooms and a little cheddar cheese, a few strips of turkey bacon and a small bowl of mixed fruit along with a tall glass of orange juice to wash it all down, a Post-It note was also attached. Seating herself next to her surprise breakfast, Ashley peels off the note which read, *"I know you are going to need some time alone, but I'm here if you need to talk, enjoy your breakfast, Jake."*

The gesture brought a lone tear to her eye, certainly not used to these small acts of kindness coming from within a place she currently resides, this sort of goodwill would have never happened at her aunt's house. With the shower helping to relax her, a bit of her missing appetite made a return, even feeling her stomach growling while she was cleaning up. So hungry, Ashley decided to eat before she got dressed, sitting there wrapped in the towel, grabbed the fork off the supplied napkin and enjoyed her favorite breakfast. The food was delicious and much needed feeling the nutrition give Ashley a sudden boost of energy.

Setting the tray aside, gets off the bed to get dressed, going extra casual for her outfit, not even putting on a bra or any socks since she doesn't plan on leaving the house until she has to go to work later. Now dressed, she grabs her smock hanging on the back of her easel, puts in her earbuds to listen to her usual pop and soft rock music, begins mixing her paint, palette in hand, brush at the ready, places the first stroke of paint on the canvas.

Another swing and crack of the bat sends the machine pitched fastball soaring back at the safety netting hung high behind the pitching machines.

Jake stood in his signature batter's stance awaiting the machine to send the next pitch his way, these old batting cages were where he would come back in the day to think, it's been years since he set foot inside any batting cage, let alone the one he spent most of his youth in. Coming to the cages not only gave him great practice, but it also helped him think clearly, everyone has their little activity or secret place that helps them focus better. The place hasn't changed a bit since he last was here, everything is still old and worn in, still used old-fashioned pitching machines which was part of its charm and what Jake liked about it, the machines were known to breakdown a lot, but when they were up and running they were the most accurate and well-paced pitching machines you could use, also in the perfect location for being outdoors to where the sun was never directly in your eyes. Cage number seven was his go to cage, Jake felt cage seven's machine threw slightly faster pitches than the rest having tried them all. Every time he would swing his personally brought bat, many memories of all the times he spent here as a kid and younger adult would come flooding back. Mainly memories of his father standing outside the cage critiquing his stance and form on his swing, he was the one who got Jake started coming here, would bring him anytime he had some free time and would stay until Jake could make contact with all sixteen balls from a single token. Later when Jake was able to bring himself, he started to come alone to practice and would still stay until he made contact with all sixteen balls. A couple of the other cages were occupied with young teenagers, one actually recognized Jake, asking for his autograph. Working on his third token worth of balls, hitting every pitch coming his way is now routine, the only time he would miss one is if he let it go by purposely because he didn't like the ball's trajectory. Unsure how long he plans on staying, might go through fifty tokens with everything he has on his mind, spending much of the night trying to get his feelings in check, still figuring out how to react to all that's happened. A player on his team was killed, every time he thinks about it, he swings the bat with enough force, if the safety netting wasn't there the ball might end up on the moon. Holley J was a good girl who had a bright future ahead of her, now just like that she is gone, in some ways he feels like he let her down, a coach is supposed to protect his players and he wasn't able to do that.

Ashley is in shambles over the loss of her best friend, now fearing she could be next, what started out as a coaching job has turned into so much more.

Waiting for a pitch, Jake senses the presence of someone walking towards his cage, assuming it might be another fan looking for an autograph.

"You still got that smooth swing," said Jeff, leaning against the fence part of the cage. "I thought I might find you here. You okay?"

"I didn't sign up for this, Jeff, this was just supposed to be a simple coaching gig," Jake said, still keeping his focus on the incoming pitches.

"I know," remarked Jeff, "and what I have to tell you is not going to make anything easier. There is nothing they can do about the shooting, it's going down as self-defense, the stand your ground doctrine. They'll just say she was at the wrong place at the wrong time."

"You're kidding me?!" Jake replied, removing himself from his stance to face his brother, a baseball flies by striking the fence where Jeff stands. "GOD DAMNIT!" he shouted, swinging his bat in a sword like motion, connecting with the concrete ground snapping the bat in two.

Tossing the broken bat piece aside, Jake leaned his back against the fence divider sliding himself to a seated position on the ground, the last few pitches whiz by with not so much as a flinch, beads of sweat trickle down his face.

"Jake, I know what you must be going through, but if you don't want anything to happened to Ashley, we have to take care of this now," suggested Jeff, squatting down to talk to Jake through the fence, "that idea you had might just work."

"I thought you said it could put her in more danger," Jake replied.

"It could, but what choice do we have," said Jeff, "as long as she is willing to go along with it we have to try. I know you don't want nothing to happen to her, I don't want her to end up like her friend either, but think about all the other young woman we could be helping by nailing this asshole. I know you didn't ask for this, all you were trying to do was get your life back together and then all this happened, but it did happen and now you are a part of it."

"You know my sponsor once told me, *If you want to see the rainbow, you gotta put up with the rain,* for the longest time I never knew what that meant, but with everything that has happened, I'm beginning to understand it now," Jake remarked. "I'm scared, Jeff, not just for Ashley, but of what I might become after this."

"You're going to be fine, you're the strongest person I know," reassured Jeff, "right now there is a girl back at the house who is in morning and needs our help. Let's give it to her."

A couple hours have passed, Ashley still working diligently to finish the painting for Jake, hasn't left the room since she has started, doing her best to keep her mind on the task at hand. The bubble she has created for herself in her room, wanting to stay away from human contact for a while seemed to be helping a bit, however sometimes a song would come on her playlist Holley J was a fan of, blanketing her again in sadness causing her eyes to tear up. Despite some emotional hiccups, her focus has remained steady, being a little while since she has picked up a brush. Segregating herself to this creative state is what Ashley needs right now, it has always been an escape for her, an alternative for when she can't be on the mound. She couldn't count how many times these type of sessions have gotten her through many bad days living with her aunt, the blank canvas gave her the opportunity to create pieces of a better world than the one she unfortunately exist in. Putting some of the finishing touches on her recent project, comes a knock at her bedroom door, the low playing music filtering through Ashley's ears drowned out the secondary noise, leaving her to not see the door opening and Vicki making a stealthy entrance. Wasn't until Vicki's shadow immersed itself over Ashley and her easel that she was aware someone else was in the room with her. A bit startled, Ashley turned to see Vicki standing close by, quickly tapping one of her earbuds to pause her music.

"I'm sorry, I didn't mean to scare you," said Vicki, "I knocked, I just don't think you heard me."

"It's okay," Ashley replied in a very soft tone.

"I heard about what happened last night and I just wanted to tell you how sorry I am," stated Vicki, seeing the pain in Ashley's face and eyes.

"Thanks," Ashley responded.

"Look, I know I haven't come off as the most welcoming person in the world, it's just this whole arrangement is kind of odd for me, but I do know how you are feeling and what you are going through," Vicki mentioned. "I lost a close friend of mine back in college."

"What happened?" asked Ashley, hearing true sincerity in Vicki's voice for the first time since she has been here.

"Accidental drug overdose, she used to take pills for migraine headaches and one night she took way more than she should have, died that night in her sleep," informed Vicki, seating herself on the edge of the bed, "the pain and hurt you are feeling right now, I know it doesn't seem like it, but it will go away. Now you just have to learn to live with her vicariously through your memories, as long as you have those she will never go away, I think about my friend every day."

Seeing the tears forming in Ashley's eyes, made Vicki mad at herself for ever secretly accusing her of being something she is not. Remembering a time when she would have been jealous of a girl like Ashley, her beauty was stereotypical of girls who never had any problems and always got what they wanted, but now she sees a beautiful girl who is lost and now recently alone. The old Vicki wouldn't have cared, now it breaks her heart to see anyone like this.

"This may sound a little strange, but sometimes after a tragic loss the world has a way of sending you someone that will change your life. What I mean is, two months after my friend's death I met Jeff," Vicki said, standing back up bringing herself closer to Ashley, "and if I had to go through that again just to meet him, I would."

Hearing Vicki share her story, the tenderness in her voice made Ashley reconsider her thoughts and feelings about her. She was a good woman, asked to invite a total stranger in her house, Ashley could see herself acting the same way if the roles were reversed, doing what all women looking out for their family would have done.

"I'm here if you ever want another female to talk to," said Vicki, watching a couple tears stream down Ashley's face.

Being in the moment, the two of them embrace, Ashley let the tears flow feeling the warmth in Vicki's arms. This hug generated a different sensation compared to other hugs Ashley has experienced, knowing what it was like to be hugged by Holley J, but this hug was filled with more emotion, something you might feel from a mother hugging her daughter. Never having that adult female to have real talks with, that mother figure which has been obsolete her entire life, Holley J was always her shoulder to cry on or have deep conversations with. Her tears of sadness became mixed in with tears of acceptance, for a brief moment the compassion a person would feel from a mother's love was being felt by Ashley for the first time, part of her didn't want to let go, it felt good, it felt needed.

"Is that a painting of Jake?" asked Vicki getting a glimpse of Ashley's work.

"Yeah," Ashley answered.

"It's beautiful," Vicki commented, positioning herself in front of it to get a better view. "You are really talented, I love the action shot you created. You giving this to him?"

Nodding slightly in response watching Vicki marvel over her work, not many people have seen what Ashley can do with some oil based paint and an empty canvas, if she keeps getting feedback like this that might have to change. Again feeling that motherly presence in the room, compared to when her Aunt would come into her old bedroom, filling it with hate and anger completely siphoning out all the creative juices, hovering over like a dark cloud.

"He's gonna love it," reassured Vicki. "I'll let you get back to finishing. I was going to make myself a grilled chicken salad for lunch, would you like one?"

"That would be great, thank you," Ashley replied.

Flashing Ashley a friendly grin, Vicki leaves the room closing the door behind her. Back in front of her painting, Ashley grabs her palette and brush and continues on.

Later now in the evening, Ashley is getting ready for work, having spent all day in her room other than when she had to use the bathroom, packing up her backpack with the essentials and extra clothing to get ready for a typical Saturday night at the club. Having no idea what to expect from Razz when she arrives, already prepared for him to be furious, capable of anything which is the scary part. Wishing she could take the night off, her mind and emotions are so tangled, performing tonight will take extra effort she really doesn't want to give, all she wants to do is just curl up in bed to continue grieving. Getting out of the house for a little while would be fine if it was to do anything else, more than ever she wants out and to never do it again. Going away to college was supposed to be her out, but since the school she is interested in is only a few hours away, Razz will make her drive back every weekend to continue on with her duties or he will send a search party of a few of his goons to find her. He better just be prepared for an emotionless robot to show up tonight, a mindset of someone who doesn't care about anything at the moment. Standing over the dresser taking her daily dose of birth control, she hears a knock at her door. Having already received a visit from Vicki earlier, she had a good idea who was behind the door, being in the same house your bound to run into the other residents a few times in a day, today she hasn't seen or heard from Jake yet other than through his note this morning.

Giving her permission for the knocker to enter, the door opens revealing what she already knew. Jake walks in to find Ashley sitting on the edge of her bed, her head down being still as a statue, letting the minutes and seconds pass before she has to leave for work.

"Hey, how are you doing? You okay?" asked Jake, seating himself on the bed beside her."

"I'm how I am," Ashley answered in a depressed sounding voice.

"Have you heard anything about the funeral arrangements?" Jake asked.

"No, nothing yet," replied Ashley.

"I was going to call the league on Monday to see if we could postpone are game on Tuesday…," noted Jake.

"No, we are playing, it's what Holley J would have wanted," said Ashley.

"Are you sure you're going to be up for that?" Jake asked.

"I'm going to have to be," Ashley proclaimed.

"When do you have to leave for work?" asked Jake, a bit of disgust in his tone.

"Soon," she answered. "I know what you are going to say."

"What if I was going to say I might have an idea to free you from all this," he declared.

The mentioning of a possible out sparked interest from Ashley, making eye contact with Jake in response, conveying he has her full attention. Gazing back at her, Jake could see the heavy sadness in her eyes, a girl emotionally and mentally drained, completely deprived of any motivation looked like a different person, this whole incident with Holley J has totally taken the life out of her, now is expected to go do what she does at that club. At times like this Jake knew it was in her best interest to be entirely honest with her, even if it meant a possible loss of trust between them. Informing her he had something to tell her first, confessing to her Jeff knows everything and wants to help, explaining he only told him because he needed his advice, if he didn't think Jeff could help he would have kept his promise and not said anything, proclaiming he only did it because he wants to help her.

Ashley sat there unexpressive, struggling to comprehend what was just admitted to her, knowing what she knows about Jake, he wouldn't maliciously just tell anyone after he promised he wouldn't, his actions very much imply he wants to help communicating to her, his breaking of his promise was with good intentions, responding with a couple slight nods indicating she is alright with his decision. Getting Ashley's blessing for his breach of her trust felt like a weight was lifted off his shoulders, figuring she knew his heart was in the right place. Now with all that out in the open, Jake elucidated what his proposal was, describing what would need to be done. Listening intently to Jake, piecing together what was being explained, mentally doing calculations of a success rate to the plan at hand, nothing at this point would mean more to Ashley than to see Razz finally go down, but what is being asked of her to do seems simple enough, yet would put her in a very dangerous position. This was real movie type scheming, she can do many things, but being a pawn in some elaborate course of action may be a little bit out of her comfort zone, however this may be her only chance and she made a promise to Holley J, her hatred for Razz burns hot enough to fuel her motivation to go through with this. She is scared and angry, a combination that may help level the playing field when dealing with someone who is totally unpredictable. Only thing worrying her is can she put herself in the right mind set to pull this off, her emotions have clouded her ability to think clearly at times, hoping the haze clears up when the target is before her.

Agreeing with the plan, Ashley returns to her original posture, eyes looking down towards her feet. Recognizing a sense of worry, mixed in with her heartache, Jake puts his arm around her shoulder pulling her in close allowing her to rest her head on his shoulder as they wait together silently for her time to leave. Having some drinks out on the backyard deck, Jeff and Vicki oversee the wet twins playing on their wooden playset in their bathing suits, just coming out of the water after a quick evening dip, once the sun starts to go down the girls know access to the pool is down for the day, the activated self-propelled vacuum starts its daily traversing of the pool as the automated lights illuminate a bulk of the backyard.

Jeff and Vicki's drink of choice is some sweet and dry red wine only consumed when they can enjoy a glass together, the wine holds sentimental value for it was a drink they shared on their wedding night. Time spent in their backyard is like being at their own personal mini resort, a large in ground pool, massive wooden deck home to many pieces of wicker furniture complete with a giant sized umbrella, a five burner chrome gas grill, used every weekend during the summertime, topped off with a eight foot wooden fence enclosing their yard. This evening though the mood was somber, both displaying expressions as if they just got done watching a sad movie, very little communication between the two of them, the conversation there was focused on Jake and Ashley.

Vicki sat sipping her wine keeping her attention on the twins, Jeff was deep in thought swirling his wine in the glass staring out at the reddish orange altocumulus cloud formation in the sky. Enjoying their time on their swings, the twins giggle and laugh sparking a reaction from Vicki who smiles and claps cheering them on. Watching the normal interaction between his wife and his daughters inspires Jeff to do some investigating, leaving his seat he tells Vicki he needs to make a phone call, kissing the top of the head before reentering the house. Inside he grabs his cell phone out of his shorts pocket dialing his work secretary hoping she is available.

"Hey, Jeff, what's going on?" asked the female voice on the line.

"Hey, Becky, sorry to bother you, but I was wondering if you could do me a favor?" Jeff asked standing in the middle of his living room. "Are you home? Are you near your computer?"

"Yes and yes," voice of Becky answered. "What do you need?"

"I need your hacking skills," informed Jeff. "Can you tap into the State Penitentiary data base and look up a female prisoner, last name Stamper?"

"Sure, I think I could do that, just give me a minute," she requested, getting through about five minutes later. "Okay, there is nobody by that name currently be held there."

"You're sure?" Jeff asked, a look of confusion lines his face.

"Positive, I'm looking at the list of all the women names that are incarcerated right now," she replied. "Who is this woman you are looking for?"

"Just someone for a case," implied Jeff. "Do me a favor and email me that list of all the female inmates to my home email address."

"Okay, I'll see what I can do. Just give me like a half-hour," she said.

"Thanks, Becky, I'll see you Monday," Jeff said hanging up his phone.

At his home office desk awaiting Becky's email, Jeff is being very fidgety, bouncing his right leg rapidly up and down keeping in sync with the fingers of his right hand tapping away on his desk. Befuddled learning Ashley's mother wasn't on the list of female inmates, knowing she has been there to visit her according to Jake. A major red flag in Jeff's eyes, who has become curious about Ashley's birth mother, a gut feeling came over him while sitting out on the deck with Vicki, this woman might have some answers to some of his questions, maybe in some way can help. His wait ended when a new email popped up in his in box with the subject titled *"This is what you asked for."*

Clicking it open, Jeff is greeted to a list occupied by at least two hundred names in alphabetical order. Quickly scanning the S's to double check, finding Becky was right, no one by the name Stamper was on the list. His only other option was to scour through every name on the list to see if any catches his eye. Slowly scrolling down the list, getting about halfway through when one name stands out, seeing this woman's name spikes Jeff's adrenaline, raising his heart rate in disbelief. Clicking on her name to open her file, which included a mug shot of the woman, his pupils dilated as if just seen a ghost, reading through her list of charges, he knows he's got the right woman.

"Oh my God," Jeff said to himself under his breath.

Driving to the club was filled with the most anxiety Ashley has ever had, many times she found herself hastily pressing on the accelerator more than she wanted to, bringing the car's speed up close to ninety miles an hour. Her hands became clammy gripping the steering wheel, often tailgating unexpected drivers causing her to have to brake frequently making her the recipient of a few honked horns due to her unintentional reckless driving. Thinking about what Razz had planned for her and what affairs she was going to put into motion after tonight, knowing once it's done there is no going back. Driving in silence as she repeatedly does when driving to the club, finding music distracting when on her way to hated destination. The drive gave her some time to think about how to approach the objective, deciding to maneuver based on Razz' actions, dealing with someone who seems to always be in irritable mood, if he's ever been in a good mood, Ashley certainly has never seen it. Coming up on the club, she tries to gather the strength needed for the night's events, still being emotionally broken hoping her thoughts of Holley J will give her the stability she is going to need. Pulling into the back parking lot stirred up many emotions, the sight of where the scene of the crime happened the last time Ashley was in this area. Eyeing the very spot where Holley J was slowly dying in her arms brought on some more tears, still able to hear the gun fire as if it was happening in that moment. The lot has become tainted, definitely looking and feeling different to her eyes now, has become Ashley's ground zero, wondering how she would feel being back where it all went down, even considered parking in the lot down the street just so she wouldn't be reminded of the worst night of her life. For tonight she parked in her usual spot right by the building, probably the reason why her car wasn't damaged during the shootout.

Taking a deep breath wiping away the few tears with her hand, she exited her car with her backpack. Walking inside to the dressing room, Ashley was greeted with a few smirks and whispers from some of the other girls that were getting ready, news of what happened probably spread through the club like wildfire, Razz has probably been doing whatever it takes to keep the press and news away. Unwanted attention is the last thing Razz looks for, most likely already dealt with the police, the reason why the place is up and running like nothing ever happened. Another form of evidence Razz has the ability to manipulate the system, a girl gets shot on his property and he can pull the right strings to have it just swept under the rug. Unjustifiable for someone like him to get away with most of the things he does, that's why nobody would ever cross him, he is too well prepared, no doubt he has eyes all over the city.

Trying not to be bothered by all the underserved scrutiny, Ashley heads for an open vanity, when out of the corner of her eye spots Razz walking into the dressing room heading directly towards her, demeanor nothing short of aggressive. Without saying a word, he steps up backing handing her across the face dropping her to the ground. The other girls stop what they are doing to look on, all supporting a similar expression of worry on their faces, Ashley stayed on the ground holding her hand on the impacted side of her face.

"What the fuck you think you were doing, Show Horse? You never leave until I give you permission to leave," Razz scorns, belligerently picking Ashley up off the ground.

"Razz, I texted why I had to," remarked Ashley, totally embarrassed this is being seen by everyone in the dressing room.

"I DON"T GIVE A FUCK WHAT THE EXCUSE WAS!" screamed Razz. "Somebody comes to my club tries to take a shot at me and then you leave because your little friend takes a bullet that I had nothing to do with."

"Razz, she died," said Ashley letting the tears flows.

"Do I look like I fucking care," Razz said, not even bothered by the sorrow being unveiled on Ashley's face.

Hearing those insensitive words coming from the mouth of the most heartless person she knows, lights a fuse inside Ashley she has never felt before, anger grew inside her that made her body tingle as if some foreign liquid other than blood was flowing through her veins. There was no question now she was staring into the eyes of a soulless monster, a person who doesn't give a fuck about any other life other than his own even if those other lives are beneficial to him. This was the green light Ashley needed to know how to go about the night's objective, going to do whatever it takes to bring this motherfucker down. The first step was for her to camouflage her rage by continuing to play the damsel in distress, play off the fear she has for Razz.

"I'm sorry," Ashley said. "I promise, it won't happen again."

"You better not for your sake," threatened Razz, whispering in Ashley's ear. "WHAT ARE YOU BITCHES LOOKING AT? GET TO FUCKING WORK!" yelling to all the girls before leaving the dressing room.

Standing there watching Razz walk away, the fury inside Ashley still blazing, coloring her face a reddish hue, almost hot enough to turn her tears to steam. Looking around the dressing room at the other girls, a few staring back, keeping Ashley the unwanted center of attention, not wanting to cause another scene, just sat at an empty vanity going about her business as normal.

"You want Razz to forgive you, just fuck him, that's what I do," suggested the girl sitting next to her.

Peering over at her not saying anything, getting counsel from someone wearing a bad applicate of cover-up to hide an apparent black eye, dismissing the guidance from her battered neighbor, Ashley returns the focus to herself, face to face with her reflection once again, staring at the person she hopes to kill off starting tonight.

The night hasn't been easy, not that any of them ever are, though this night Ashley was fighting with her emotions over Holley J. At times she felt numb, ready to give in to her emotions. During her dancing, she almost broke down right there on stage, wondering if any of the crowd noticed the build-up of tears in her eyes. Her performance wasn't one of her best, but she got through it, doubting a bunch of drunk, horny men could care less what a naked girl is doing on stage just that she is naked. It was a very handsy crowd on top of that, feeling more than her share of hands on her ass tonight resulting in a few guards having to intervene. The rough time continued with her one on one clients, hoping it would be just a quick few blow jobs, instead she had to perform intercourse every time, one session resulted in the condom breaking forcing her to use some private time in the bathroom trying to clean herself out. Her breasts are sore from being repeatedly squeezed throughout the night, one nipple is especially tender to the touch from one client sucking on it like a baby looking for milk. Random sex with strange men is horrible already, but when you are mentally in another place, Ashley felt in an odd way even more violated, physically being treated like a cum dumpster while the clients use her body for their sexual appetites as she just laid there, at times she would be so far gone within her mind she hardly felt any of the penetration, almost like a victim of Necrophilia except she is still alive. Ashley's last client wanted to fuck her doggy style, her feet on the floor, rest of her draped over the bed, being behind her he didn't see the tears streaming down her face.

Between the sound of their bodies slapping together and his obnoxious moaning, all Ashley could think about is for every second more she lets this happen to herself, she is letting Holley J down. Immediately following her last client, she left one of the downstairs rooms to return to the dressing room to prepare to meet with Razz. The dressing room still occupied with a few girls each keeping to themselves, the mixture of different perfumes and body sprays throughout the night can always be smelled when entering. Giving her hair a quick brushing, taking off her heels to put on her flip flops, Ashley leaves bringing her cell phone.

Approaching Razz' office doors, Ashley could feel a sense of uneasiness come over her, more than normal with what she is going to try to execute. Tonight she chose to wear her plaid skirt which offers a single pocket on the side which is barely noticeable, having her cell phone hidden inside set to voice recorder. She reaches the doors telling the guard she needs to speak with Razz, prompting the guard to communicate to him inside the office he has a visitor requesting entry.

Given the nod to enter, Ashley takes a deep breathe knowing the sight of him will most likely reignite her fury. Grabbing and twisting the doorknob, she realizes she is not entering Razz' office anymore, but a metaphorical room of incrimination, the location for the beginning of a possible ultimate set up. Coming through the door Ashley's eyes spot Razz sitting on his couch with a cigarette in his mouth, counting a considerable amount of loose cash spread out atop his coffee table. Stealthily checking her cell phone to make sure it's working properly, Razz has strict rules about cell phones with the girls, they are not allowed anywhere in the club other than the dressing room. Slowly advancing closer to Razz, wanting to get the cell phone into a good range, coming up to the coffee table, he identifies her out of the corner of his eye.

"What are you doing here, Show Horse?" Razz asked continuing on with his counting.

"I was just wondering if I could talk to you for a minute," answered Ashley, standing directly behind the coffee table feeling her palms beginning to sweat, staring across the way at him arrogantly counting his money not even acknowledging her presence. She felt like there was two separate identities hidden inside her, one was full of absolute anger and the other was drenched in fear, the one caped in anger was fighting to overtake the side covered in fear, knowing she had to disguise the more dominate emotion to not let on to her true nature.

"About what?" Razz asked, still keeping his focus on what he's doing.

"First I just want to say I'm sorry about last night," replied Ashley, fighting back her tears thinking about Holley J, "also I have a business offer for you."

Razz comes to a dead stop in the middle of counting his handful of cash, bringing his eyes up to redirect his attention to Ashley.

"What kind of business offer?" he asked, looking at her with a suspicious demeanor, putting the uncounted money back on the coffee table, taking a drag from his cigarette never taking his eyes off her.

"A biker friend of my aunt, who recently moved here from out of town wanted to know where he could score a good hook up," Ashley stated. "I told him I know somebody but I didn't give him your name."

"So where is he from?" asked Razz sitting back on the couch blowing a puff of smoke into the air.

"What do you mean?" Ashley replied.

"You said he is from out of town, just curious from where," remarked Razz.

"I don't know, it's my aunt's friend, all I know he has a lot of money and he likes to party," Ashley proclaimed.

"I see," said Razz, "does this friend have a name?"

"He doesn't want to give out his name unless you agree to meet with him," mentioned Ashley, getting the uneasy sense that Razz is on to her.

Standing there trying to keep herself calm, feeling beads of sweat wanting to escape the pores of her face being an obvious tell of her dishonesty. Feeling the heat from her recording cell phone on her thigh through the fabric of her skirt, causing some sweat to build up trickling down her leg.

"I can tell you he is willing to pay upwards of a hundred thousand dollars for whatever."

Letting out an obnoxious giggle leaning forward to put out his cigarette, Razz leaves the couch to walk over to stand before Ashley, toe to toe he gently grabs her by the face with both hands.

"Do you really think I'm fucking stupid?" Razz asked in a stern tone, violently ripping open Ashley's blouse exposing her bare chest debunking his suspicion she might be wearing a wire.

Startled, Ashley feels her heart racing due to Razz' unexpected surge, her one hand hovering over the skirt's pocket for extra concealment begins trembling nervously. Razz softly runs his fingers over Ashley's chest, keeping eye contact trying to get a read on her. Doing her best to keep her composure, skin crawling from Razz' touch, she stood strong making sure to not break eye contact. Convinced she is telling the truth, he closes her blouse enough to cover her breasts. Still a bit skeptical, Razz wonders if she has always known about his other business venture, why all of a sudden does she bring a potential buyer to light and why now. Willing to see where this goes, Razz plays along, not one to turn down a possible large deal.

"You tell me right now, Show Horse, you fucking with me?"

"No, never," Ashley responded, keeping her voice tone as firm and leveled as possible, any change in pitch or speaking to fast could reveal unwanted motivations especially to someone like Razz. "I just thought you would be interested and don't worry about him saying anything to anyone else, he's the type that doesn't want to risk losing access to a good dealer if everything goes to your satisfaction."

"You better not be, 'cause I'll do horrible things to you and this beautiful face of yours will going missing," said Razz caressing one side of her face with his hand. "What is your friend looking for?"

"He wanted to know what you got," Ashley answered.

"I got whatever he needs," proclaimed Razz.

"Okay, I'll let him know and I'll text you the details once I let him know you are interested," said Ashley.

"I just have one request," Razz declared. "I want you here with him when he comes to make the deal, is that going to be a problem?"

"I don't think so, no," Ashley replied.

"Alright then, make this happen and don't keep me waiting," ordered Razz.

Giving Razz a slight nod in concurrence to his request, Ashley departs from his office feeling his eyes watching her as she exits through the doors. Clear of the view of Razz and the guard, she stops the voice recorder, successfully getting him to agree to make a deal on tape while coping with the many sensations of almost getting caught. The only blemish being, having to be there with whoever is assigned to make the deal, a demand that Ashley fears suggest Razz might be on to her. Heading back to the dressing room grabbing her backpack to leave, high on adrenaline mixed with her hyper nerves, gets in her car putting the key in the ignition before breaking down crying, clutching the steering wheel with both hands laying her head against the horn releasing all the bottled up emotions she has held in all night.

A very emotional drive home for Ashley crying most of the way, her teary eyes fused with oncoming headlights caused a glare in her vision having to constantly wipe her eyes. Thinking about the risk she just took, combined with her overwhelming heartache for Holley J made for one of the toughest nights she had to endure possibly ever, but her hatred for Razz and her desire to leave that life in the past gives her the incentive and fiery drive to push forward. Anything worth doing is always going to be hard, if this escape from the clutches of a mad tyrant was going to be easy she might have thought about doing it long ago, but double crossing someone like Razz would put her well-being in jeopardy, maybe even her life. Yet Ashley would rather die trying than to stay and continue to slowly terminate what self-respect and dignity she has left, until one day she simply becomes an empty vessel of shattered dreams and a loss of humanity with no reason to remain amongst the living, a future she is scared to face every day.

Pulling into the driveway, Ashley catches sight of the front porch lights shining brightly, spotlighting the silhouette of a large adult male sitting in one of the chairs. Exiting her car, she knew it was Jake again waiting up to make sure she got back safe, despite the fact she told him he didn't have to do that, she couldn't help but feel touched he was willing to compromise some of his sleep to make sure she was okay. Walking up to the porch carrying her backpack another tiny light source was present, a lit scented candle burned on the small table, had the aroma of a bed of roses after a light rain, the kind a scent that could put you in a state of euphoria. Ashley sat in the vacant chair dropping her backpack to the floor, after a night like she had she would generally just head for bed being physically and emotionally exhausted, but this night the combination of her nerves, fear, adrenaline and hatred have her feeling wide awake adding to her briefcase of insomnia. Looking over at Ashley with concern, her slouched posture and defeated manner told Jake everything about her night's experiences, watching her stare blankly at the ground beneath her. Before either of them spoke a word, Ashley pulled out her cell phone from her skirt's hidden pocket, tamely placing it on the table between them, her movement was steady and deliberate as if revealing classified secrets.

"It's done," said Ashley, still looking away from Jake's direction.

"Are you okay?" Jake asked, noticing Ashley won't make eye contact.

"I hate him so much," she answered breaking down crying, "he didn't even care about what happened to Holley J."

Letting more of her suppressed emotions pour out, Jake grabs her hand resting atop her cell phone to try to comfort her, could feel the negative energy permeating from the contact, her hand slightly trembling in his grip.

"For the longest time I used to believe that everything that ever happened to me was my fault, that I deserved it. Everything I was doing was just normal behavior, but normal should feel right and it's never felt right," Ashley ranted sobbing, "because of that I've always hated men, him the most, but then I met you."

Shedding more tears of sorrow and anguish, seeing her pain manifest right before his eyes revealing to Jake just how much more damaged and broken she really is, his eyes teared up squeezing her hand tighter in an effort to remind her she is not alone. In a strange way he saw a lot of himself in her, though their circumstances were different they both shared similar attributes to a pair of lives requiring the means to face their demons whether they were self-inflicted or the result of an outside origin.

"It was never your fault and you should be ashamed that you think that," Jake said, "you never did anything wrong."

"Then why did all this happen to me?" asked Ashley.

"I wish I could give you an answer to that, no one deserves to go through what you have," Jake answered, "but right now you should just focus on making the days ahead better ones."

"So what do we do now?" Ashley asked.

"I want my brother to be there when we listen to what you got, if that is okay with you?" Jake asked.

"Okay," Ashley answered nodding her head.

"For now why don't we try to get some sleep," imposed Jake.

Making eye contact with Jake for the first time since she sat down, Ashley's tear filled eyes glistened in the porch lighting, her glance favored agreement to Jake. Gently wiping away her tears with his thumb, the two stood up, Jake blows out the candle before entering the house together.

Late morning, Jeff, Jake and Ashley are in Jeff's home office preparing to listen to what Ashley got recorded. To ensure their private gathering goes without interruption, Jeff for the first since living in the house locked the door to his office, something he hates having to do with Vicki and the twins in the house, but she is still unaware of what Ashley does for work and would rather tell her when the time is right. Seated at his desk, Jeff looks across his work surface at Jake and Ashley seated in the chairs behind his desk, Ashley coming off another night where her sleep was limited, doing her best to remain wide eyed, fighting off the feeling of surviving fatigue. Her lack of energy showed in her appearance, wearing nothing but a pair of plaid pajama bottoms, a black and yellow t-shirt with the school logo on the front and her hair tied in a ponytail, it was the first time she could remember when she was alone in a room with two men and wasn't looking her best, subconsciously breaking one of Razz' carnal rules, part of his years of manipulative programming. Jake anxiously sat in his chair leaned over resting his forearms on his legs waiting to hear the recording, something that was on his mind most of the night, he to a victim of frequent episodes of tossing and turning in his sleep.

Seeing everyone is ready, Jeff got up from his seat to join Jake and Ashley in front where he leaned up against his desk, a couple times he glanced over at Jake unnoticed with distress in his stare, part of an impulsive reflex due to Jeff's latest possible findings on his computer. Getting the nod to proceed, Ashley pulls out her cell phone from her pajama bottoms pocket, turning the volume up all the way, playing what was recorded from her interaction with Razz, holding the phone up in front of her. Listening to the recording became difficult for Jake and Jeff, getting to hear an inside glimpse of what it's like for Ashley to be around this scumbag, the tone in his voice when he speaks, his choice of words all the way to the verbal threats he throws Ashley's way, they could feel her fear protruding out through the recording. Both brothers took notice of the tension in Ashley's face as the recording played on, sitting as still as a statue having to relive the audio of the intense interaction. Listening intently with the ears of a lawyer, Jeff analyzed every word, every phrase, even using his skills as a voice analyst to decipher Razz' hidden intentions, a skill Vicki knows all too well about unable to keep her true emotions hidden from him at times. Jake on the other hand doesn't need to be a lawyer or a voice analyst expect to know from the contents of the recording, this Razz means business. As the last set of words are spoken through the audio, Ashley silences her phone waiting to hear the guys reactions and thoughts, looking over at Jake, could see the concealed anger in his face ready to go and dish out his own form of justice, Jeff remained leaned up against his desk with a hand over his mouth in obvious thinking mode.

"So what do you think?" Jake asked looking up at his brother.

"I don't know, it's tough to say, this guy is very hard to read, he is very methodical in what he says and how he says it, but he did agree to do the deal," answered Jeff.

"What about him wanting her there when the deal goes down?" asked Jake.

"I can understand that, most dealers when they are given insight to a possible new client from an uncredited source will want both parties there to vouch for one another," Jeff replied.

"I don't know why, but I get the feeling Razz maybe on to this," mentioned Ashley.

"That may be possible, but we are going to have to see this through if we are going to nail this guy, that is if you are still up for doing this?" asked Jeff.

"I am," Ashley answered.

"He threatened her," remarked Jake.

"I know," Jeff responded, "but we are in the deep water now."

"I was told you know a cop that is willing to be the friend I told Razz about?" asked Ashley.

"That's correct, his name is Ray Turner, a great guy and lives to bust people like this," said Jeff.

"So what's the plan from here?" Ashley asked.

"I'll get in contact with Ray, see how he wants to go about this and set this whole thing up," Jeff replied, "as soon as we are ready we will proceed."

"I have to work tonight, what should I do if he asks?" questioned Ashley.

"Tell him the truth, you have been in contact and as soon as he is ready to make the deal you will be bringing a guest," remarked Jeff.

"Just keep in mind Razz is very particular and goes over every detail, he knows how to watch his own back and he always has a plan," proclaimed Ashley, "he is always ready for anything."

"I understand and will keep that in mind," Jeff assured, "we both are impressed with the poise you kept during that whole situation, we both know it could've been easy, you did good."

Ashley couldn't help but sit there feeling suddenly anxious and extremely scared at the same time, this is really going to happen, her escape could be just around the corner, a new life could be waiting her, but it's going to feel like traveling through a mine field to get there, with everything that has been going and with an important softball game coming up in a few days, her anxiety is at an all-time high. Still battling her emotions over Holley J, she asked to excuse herself wanting to be alone for a while, leaving her seat walking out of the office without saying another word.

"Are we sure about this?" asked Jake.

"Jake, you know I'm going to set this up with her safety and best interest at heart," Jeff remarked.

"I know, but what if something goes wrong, you heard him on that recording," Jake stated, standing up from his seat to walk over to the windows looking out at the sun filled sky, "he could kill her."

"No plan ever goes through without a few hiccups, but it's the best plan we've got," remarked Jeff, walking over to be closer to his brother. "Jake, she is a strong girl who has been through a lot worse than this, you want to keep helping her, just keep being there for her."

"When do you think this will all happen?" Jake asked, slightly peering back at Jeff.

"It will probably be a few days," answered Jeff, "there is something else."

"What's that?" asked Jake looking back out into the yard.

"I may have stumbled upon some information you may want to know about, that you are going to want to know about," Jeff replied.

"What kind of information?" Jake asked, turning his focus back to Jeff, look of confusion on his face.

"Let's just say if what I found out turns out to be true, it will change your life forever," declared Jeff.

The early afternoon sun shines bright, only a few clouds scattered throughout the sky, the perfect weather for Ashley to go for a much needed run. After having a self-prepared lunch, Ashley wanted to spend some of her alone time catching up on her running having been awhile since her last run. Coming out of the front door wearing her typical running attire, performing a few stretches to warm up before placing her earbuds in taking off down the street. Run started off with new scenery, running through the new neighborhood passing by the other large houses making up the dead end street. Exiting the housing track, she directed her run on to the shoulder of the main road running against the oncoming traffic, something she feels safer doing. Making her way briskly down the road feeling her heartrate rising, sweat beading up on her forehead and face as well as all the exposed skin in direct contact with the sunlight. Unlike her other runs in the past, this one had no fixed destination, like Forrest Gump, she just wanted to run not worrying where it takes her. Wanting to run until she could clear her mind of all that was going on, while helping to keep her recent emotions in check, focusing on her strides and her breathing keeps her distracted from her overactive mind. Feeling the sun continually beating down on her shoulders, sweat dripping off her skin onto the pavement below, the occasional breeze side swiping her, running without direction letting her emotions guide her. The music from her earbuds plays softly continuing on, completely oblivious to the surrounding landscape having no idea how far she has gone, even the sounds coming from the passing vehicles, including a few horns from some obnoxious men driven cars didn't seem to divert her focus. Her thighs began to burn trucking on, though she felt a bit tired, she didn't want to stop, was thirsty yet wanted no water, she just wanted to keep going running on pure adrenaline. Time seemed to stand still, yet she was running through reality at normal speed, before she knew it, was running through town on a very familiar street. Bringing her running to the sidewalk refusing to reduce her speed, many pedestrians heard her heavy breathing as Ashley passed by. Making her way through town, certain sights she couldn't avoid triggered memories of Holley J, some tears began flowing down her face only to be camouflaged by the sweat dripping off of her. Picking up her speed, Ashley exited town continuing on running blindly. Unsure where she is headed, ran on getting her second wind, as fate would have it the next road she turned down led her right to the school bringing her run onto the grass, leading her to the softball field, specifically the pitcher's mound.

Stopping on the metaphorical place she calls home, puts her hands on her knees breathing heavy trying to catch her breath. The premises seemed deserted as it should be on a Sunday afternoon, even the patrolling campus security was nowhere to be seen. Calculating the distance from Jake's brother's house to the school had to be at least eight to nine miles, a distance she has never ran at one time in her life. Exhausted, legs feeling numb, Ashley decides to lay down on the mound, knees bent, turning off her music just staring up at the sky watching the few patches of clouds pass over, not the least concerned with the dirt sticking to her sweaty skin or clothes or how she is getting back to the house. The sky looked the bluest it has in some time, so clear she could spot any object happening to enter her line of sight including a flock of birds and an airplane so far up it looked like a hyphen moving across the airspace. Though the appearance of the field looked normal, it already started to feel different to Ashley knowing Holley J won't be taking the field anymore with her, wondering how it will affect her when she takes the field in a couple days, looking down at home plate to see another girl in that catcher's uniform. This could be the biggest game of the season yet, the second to last game, if they win they are assured the number one seed in the playoffs, knowing Holley J won't be there to share in the biggest moment in the team's history breaks Ashley's heart even more. Trying to keep her thoughts positive, wanting to have at least five minutes of not feeling emotional, assuming she had shed ever last tear in her body, remembers the last time she had a smile on her face. Coming with the last hug her and Holley J shared together, thinking about that moment, Ashley re-experienced the release of oxytocin through her body, for the first time in a while felt relaxed, so relaxed her body felt weightless like she was floating in the air, before she knew it, was in such a state of ease her eyes slowly closed, laying there still as a board blocking out any ambient sounds only feeling the wind passing through her, fingertips gently raking through the dirt beneath her keeping her in contact with the earth, falling into a meditated state a very small grin appears on her face.

The time has come to get back on the field, retaining her normal routine before a game, Ashley arrived in the dugout about an hour early to go through her usual warm up regimen. It has been a tough couple days back at school, memories of Holley J are triggered constantly throughout the day starting with Ashley's morning stop at her locker where she always waited for a generally late Holley J. Standing there looking at her old locker knowing it will never be opened by her again, Ashley wanted to start a small memorial. The first day back she brought one long-stemmed orchid, Holley J's favorite flower, taping it to the locker door along with a small card which read, "*I miss you and I love you, BFFs forever,*" and a picture of the two of them from last season. By the end of the day Holley J's locker was hoarded with candles, cards, and various flowers, the girls on the team left a softball signed by everyone including Jake, to go with the assorted offerings they all left. The memorial got to be so large, spilling out across a couple lockers and a bit into the hallway. Moved when she saw what she started expand throughout the day, Ashley couldn't think of anyone who could have deserved it more. Brought tears to her eyes seeing the love being shown from Holley J's friends and teammates, something she had to battle with all day.

The morning announcements started with Principal Davis reporting the devastating news to the whole school, asking everyone to bow their heads in a moment of silence. Not seeing her between classes or in the classes they had together, missing her at lunch time with their other table mates who all sat pretty much in silence not knowing what to say. All the teachers she and Holley J shared offered their condolences to Ashley, one even gave a heartfelt speech before class praising Holley J as a student and a person. A few times during the day, Ashley has to excuse herself from class to go sit in a stall in the girls' bathroom so she could cry privately, being totally affected by all the talk of her best friend. Staying focused during her classes was a chore in itself, majority of the time she was daydreaming, thinking about Holley J and the upcoming sting she will be a part of at the club. Though it was only the first couple days back to school since Holley J's death, Ashley could already feel how different the last couple months of the school year are going to be, the look and atmosphere were the same, but the vibes felt during class and while walking the halls seemed so unfamiliar, like she was in an alternate universe, one that didn't contain Holley J which was becoming her new reality. Handling the grieving process is one of the hardest things Ashley has to endure, it is a process everyone will experience one day in their life, you just hope it's not when you are seventeen.

Another tough moment came when Ashley was granted permission by Principal Davis to clean out Holley J's locker, something she did at the end of school yesterday since Jake cancelled practice giving the team an extra day to mourn. A task that proved difficult, knowing the lock combination getting in was easy, it was the items inside bringing out Ashley's emotions, mainly from all the pictures of the two of them hanging on the inside of the locker door from different stages of their friendship, one picture was of the two of them from when they met back in third grade, all of which she would keep for herself. Emptying out all of the other stuff, like her school books and notebooks, some other little nick knacks that were freely thrown inside, coming across a silver bracelet she had seen once before just lying on the ground, examining it further Ashley discovered the engraving on the inside of the bracelet which read, *"To our dearest daughter, we love because he loved us first, John 4:19."* Ashley remembered it was a first day of high school gift to Holley J from her parents which she disapproved of because of its Bible reference, wearing it the morning of their first day complaining about the nerve of her parents, on how they just can't give her something without having some biblical mumble jumble on it. Upset with their insensitive attempt of proselytism, she took it off throwing it in the locker where it remained ever since, another example of Holley J's parents trying to push their religious beliefs on her. Recalls Holley J that day plotting to tell her parents she lost it during gym class, never to be spoken of again. Holding it in her hands, Ashley was torn about what to do with it, keeping it would not honor Holley J's wishes of wanting nothing to do with it, however it was still in good shape to just throw it away, her best option was to hold on to it, later pawning it off. Eventually getting Holley J's locker all cleared out, despite having to maneuver through all the gifts left for her memorial which Principal Davis said can remain for the rest of the week.

Sitting in the dugout tying her cleats getting ready for her warn up run, Ashley could already feel her emotions creeping up again preparing to play her first game without Holley J. Having worked a bit with the two girls that were deemed Holley J's backup during practices at least gave her some comfort knowing they weren't coming in completely blind, they were both decent, however neither one is as good as Holley J was. Whoever Jake decides to put in as catcher, she will trust his judgment, has been right all season long, no reason to believe he will make the wrong decision on this. It's about the time Holley J would show up to warm up with Ashley, later getting into their pitching warm ups, now is left to do it all on her own, going to have to throw balls at an empty home plate, definitely not the same, but at least it will get her arm loosened up. Knowing ahead of time she would be alone, brought it upon herself to bring a bucket of balls with her which are waiting on the mound. Expecting a large crowd of spectators for this game, most likely including more scouts even though she knows the school she wants to commit to, with everything that has been going lately, hasn't had the time to take the campus tour they have offered. Jake assured her she can take a tour any time before the school year is up as long as the college believes she is highly interested. Taking a deep breath looking out at the vacant field, Ashley gets prepared to pitch the most difficult game of her life, both mentally and emotionally, feeling a breeze pass through the dugout courtesy of the partly cloudy skies, emerges onto the field to being her run. Getting closer to game time, many of the girls are making their way towards the field, Jake included, who Ashley hasn't seen all day, normally running into him in the halls at least once during the day, he did send her a text earlier to see how she was doing. In the dugout catching her breath from her warm ups, sipping on a cup of ice water, Ashley watches a few of the girls file in to get ready, Jake follows them in and sits beside her. Seeing the sweat streaming down her face, knowing she was out here doing her thing like always, worried she might have over exerted herself due to her recent emotional state.

"How are you doing?" Jake asked.

"I'm okay, I guess," answered Ashley, still trying to catch her breath.

"You sure you want to pitch today? I got Melanie warming up if you want to sit this one out," Jake said.

"There is no way I'm sitting out. I should be alright," said Ashley, "I got to face this eventually."

"Okay, I'm leaving it up to you, if at any time you think you can't continue you let me know," advised Jake, "I've decided to have Kaitlyn catch today, I feel she is the more ready one."

"Okay," Ashley replied, thinking to herself she would have made the same decision.

"What's on your mind?" Jake asked, reading the face of someone deep in thought, Ashley has a gaze of a person looking out beyond the field as if trying to look into the future.

"I have a lot on my mind, but right now I'm just trying to focus on this game," remarked Ashley.

"If you can learn from the worst times of your life, you'll be ready to go into the best times of your life," Jake said. "It's times like these that will show someone's true character, bringing out an inner strength they didn't know they had. Your life isn't defined by the obstacles you face, it's how you handle those obstacles that defines you. If anybody can do it it's you, 'cause I've seen you do it, I believe in you, but if you don't believe in yourself it's really not going to matter. I've never met a girl as strong as you, you impress me all the time. Now I know you have certain things on your mind and I'd be lying to you if I said I wasn't thinking about that too, but right it's time for Ashley the athlete, the star pitcher to make her appearance."

Jake's motivational words touched Ashley in a way she couldn't explain, only one other person truly believed in her the way he did and she is gone now.

"No matter what happens during this game, don't take me out," requested Ashley, looking over at Jake with a watery eyes.

Agreeing with a slight nod, Jake calls all the girls together.

Minutes away from the start of one of the biggest games in this team's history, Jake gives an emotional pre-game speech in honor of their fallen teammate, many of the girls shaded a tear or two hearing Jake's words, Ashley being one of them, at the end she wanted to say a few heartfelt words having the team's full attention, doing her best to contain her emotions.

"Let's win this one for Holley J," Ashley said sticking her hand out.

Individually each girl stuck her hand in to join Ashley's, including Jake, reciting, "For Holley J."

Being the home team they were taking the field first, the starters trotted out onto the field to a thunderous applauds from the large crowd. Placing the ball in Ashley's mitt, Jake looked directly at her giving her the nod, not wanting to say anything seeing the hurt in her eyes, walking away hoping she will be alright. Ball in hand, Ashley makes her way to the mound hearing the cheers from the onlookers, this trip to the rubber already feeling different, each step she can feel her emotions beginning to take over. Standing at the center of attention, her breathing becomes increased looking down at home plate where Holley J is supposed to be, her heartrate rises, her throwing hand begins to gyrate, feeling like she may be having a panic attack. Looking at the girl in the catcher's gear standing over home plate wearing a different jersey number and carrying a larger body type than she is used to seeing finally hit her causing her to breakdown right there on the mound.

Turning away sobbing, her tears dripping on the dirt below, feeling like she is losing control of her emotions, Jake begins to head out to the mound concerned she might not be ready yet, stopped in his tracks by Ashley yelling at him to stay back. Everyone around looks on with worry in their eyes watching her unravel right there on the field, a voice coming from the outfield grabs her attention.

"HEY, STAMPER!" yelled Renee from center field.

Tears streaming down her face, Ashley looks out in Renee's direction observing her putting one fist into the air, before she knew it every girl on the team had a fist in the air, including the girls in the dugout. Panning around to witness the display of unity surrounding her, Ashley looks over at Jake, their eyes meeting in a gaze speaking louder words, throwing his fist into the air giving her another nod, bringing herself back to position on the mound, feeling the energy and support from her teammates, she stands tall throwing her fist into the air letting the last few tears trickle away. Standing there hearing the cheers from the crowd, mixed in with the inspiring chatter from her teammates, she takes a couple deep breaths trying to regain her composure, digging deep within herself to bring out the person that needs to be on that mound. Letting out screams of aggression to empty out her emotions, she faces home plate signaling she is ready. Rapidly rotating the softball in her hand to feel the leather against her finger tips, Ashley watches the first batter walk to the plate. The girl stands in the batter's box as a righty, waiting for the first pitch, choked up on the bat, her cleats dug deep within the dirt, the girl knows who she is up against, most batter's in the district, even the state would consider it an accomplishment to get a hit off of Ashley. The catcher having watched Ashley's pitching style throughout the season had a good idea of what type of game she should call, flashing the sign for a fastball, Ashley agrees and without hesitation winds up and fires a rocket blowing by the batter so fast, she didn't have time to react. Next two pitches were more of the same, though even faster with the third one getting a swing attempt that was way too late. Hearing the clapping and cheers as the opposing batter walked back to her team defeated, Ashley's emotions were building up again, yet now was going to use them as fuel, feeling something pitching that first at bat, something indescribable.

Suddenly everything around her went silent, like she was standing in a vacuum, everyone was in motion, yet no sound was coming out, like fate was telling her this is about her and she wouldn't need much help. This game became a stunning exhibition of raw talent and empowering determination, every inning Ashley pitched was a showcase to her ever growing pitching skills. Batter after batter, strikeout after strikeout, it was quickly becoming something very special to behold or be a part of. Top of the seventh and final inning, Ashley has struck out sixteen batters and nobody has gotten on base, just three outs away from pitching a perfect game. The crowd and Ashley's teammates were on pins and needles as she approached an historic milestone. She has pitched no-hitters before, but never a perfect game which are more rare than a hole in one in golf.

Jake's squad was up seven to nothing courtesy of a couple multi run homeruns by Ashley and a three run homerun by Renee, who spent most of the game sitting Indian style in center field watching Ashley dominate on the mound, the two hitters that were lucky enough to make contact both grounded out. Jake barely had to say anything all game so far, not even talking to Ashley between innings not wanting to risk breaking her concentration or whatever it was that was driving her. Walking out for her final appearance at the mound, she was greeted to cheers and encouraging chants, an energy was surrounding the field that could be felt by all who was around, just about everyone in the bleachers and the late comers who were designated to personal chairs on the lawn had their phones up to possibly record history in the making. One of the anxious spectators looking on in anticipation was Danielle, watching the game standing behind the home plate fence, clapping nervously. Ashley stood on the mound waiting for the next batter, her body language and demeanor hasn't changed, if she was nervous she wasn't showing it, perhaps so overcome with emotion she doesn't have the reserved energy to feel nervous, so wrapped up in her feelings she seems unaware of what she could feasibly accomplish. The first batter was a victim to another strikeout, being her second one of the game, the girls in the field cheered along with the very enthusiastic crowd. The second batter got a piece of one of Ashley's change ups sending the ball straight up high above home plate, the catcher pushes her mask off waving everybody away, steadying herself under the descending pop up, ball landing securely in her glove initiating more cheers. Throwing out a fist pump, Jake elated Ashley is one out away from perfection, unlike her, his mind hasn't been side tracked all game due to the unbelievable performance she has put on. The third and possibly final batter walks up to the plate, one of the hitters who grounded out earlier, happening to be the best hitter on the team. Wasn't a person seated in the crowd, all were up still with their cell phones at the ready, standing silently to limit any distractions when Ashley is pitching. Jake stood bent over with his hands on his knees trying to hold in his excitement, at times like these he would normally be pacing, however he is one to know spotting movement out of your peripheral vision can interrupt one's focus. Feeling more nervous than Ashley probably does, never having been a part of anything like this before, not in little league, high school or the majors, being part of someone on the cusp of a perfect game. You could cut the tension building with a knife, all the girls in the field stood at the ready with an intensity primed to help Ashley, this wasn't about winning or losing anymore, this was about preserving this monumental occasion they will all be a part of. The batter, a lefty, got in her stance waiting for the first pitch. Rotating the ball swiftly in her hand, feeling some grit from the dirt on her fingers, sweat dripping off her face as the sun made an appearance halfway through the game, shining brightly to Ashley's back. Agreeing with the first sign the catcher flashed her of a fastball, Ashley wound up firing another heater, flying by the batter who swung and missed, quick cheering ensued. Danielle still standing behind the fence near Jake's girl's dugout, hands over her mouth in anticipation to celebrate the prodigious achievement for both Ashley and Jake for leading the team to the playoffs for the first time. Receiving the ball back Ashley heard the hush come over the crowd once more, again rotating the ball in her hand, finally dawning on her she is one strike away from pitching the best game of her life. Closing her eyes for a moment picturing Holley J behind the plate getting ready to catch this historic pitch, a single tear left her eye, Ashley reopened them not even waiting for a sign, winding up firing a rising fastball that within a second was in her catcher's glove after a swing and a miss by the batter. A thunderous standing ovation, complete with whistles and congratulatory chants erupted from the crowd as Ashley, breaking down in tears, was rushed at the mound by her teammates bombarding her with hugs.

Clapping with his eyes watery, Jake sees Ashley getting surrounded by the team, even girls from the opposing team in a show of good sportsmanship headed to the mound to congratulate her. Danielle came around giving Jake a huge hug, being very animated with her praise for Ashley and the team. Was the greatest performance Jake has ever seen on the diamond at any level, a perfect game, eighteen out of a possible twenty-one strikeouts while hitting two homeruns and it wasn't even about the stats, this was the greatest performance for other reasons. Jake could only imagine the emotions Ashley felt stepping out onto that mound, it's tough enough dealing with the competition of the game in and of itself, but then you throw in battling your emotions along with having a heavy heart, the mental anguish she must have felt out there had to be incredible, yet found a way to persevere and have the game of her life. Never has Jake been envious of another athlete before, however that all changed today, having to have lived the life she has and yet demonstrate the strength to accomplish the things she has accomplished without a doubt makes Ashley the strongest person he has ever met.

The congregating at the mound begins to break up, Jake calls all the girls over for his routine post-game talk. First congratulating a still emotional Ashley with a huge embrace surrounded by the sound of clapping by the rest of the team, holding her tight he could feel her body trembling, the game obviously took a lot out of her.

"I knew you could do it," Jake whispers in her ear. "You see, you impress me all the time."

Though the two of them were surrounded by teammates, this moment belonged to Jake and Ashley, with everything that is going on, both wished they could just stand there holding each other until the their worlds changed for the better. Proud of what she just achieved, a showing that will be very hard to ever top, Ashley was grateful to share the moment with Jake, without his guidance and motivational words, might not have be able to accomplish what she did today, bringing out the best in her proving she was even better than she ever thought she was. The glory of the moment should feel more special, but there is a dark stain that will forever be linked to this particular day, the fact Holley J isn't here to share in the acclamation. In a way Ashley feels a little guilty a day like this happened without her best friend present, yet she knows Holley J wouldn't want her to ruin an achievement like this with her sulking over her absence, would want Ashley to celebrate and embrace the moment which she will remember for the rest of her life. Letting Ashley go, Jake watched her get a quick hug from Danielle congratulating her on her amazing performance. The rest of the girls took a knee waiting for Jake to address the team, holding back for Ashley as Captain to take her position in front, Jake engaged in a little small talk with the girls, being humorous and playful, getting some giggles and laughs out of them. Rejoining the team, Ashley took a knee in her designated spot allowing Jake to begin his postgame address. Starting off with the most evident topic, wanting one last big round of applauds for Ashley pitching a perfect game, the girls complied with a thunderous ovation, mixing in some hooting and hollering, Danielle who was standing off to the side, honored Ashley with some more clapping and whistling of her own. Hearing the sound of appreciation and acceptance coming from all those around her, Ashley felt the need to stand and address the team herself.

"I just want to say something to you guys really quick," Ashley said very emotional. "This milestone is just as much yours as it is mine, I could have never done it without you guys, I just want to thank you for having my back and I am so proud to call you guys my teammates and I know Holley J would feel the same way. But the most important thing is, we're in the fucking playoffs."

The girls explode into cheers and applause, Jake listened as they celebrated the hard work they all have put in this season, no matter what happens the rest of the way the season was a success, they were always winners they just needed someone like him to point them in the right direction. Being around the girls this season made Jake realize how much he still missed being on the field and being part of a team, the camaraderie of being with your teammates for a long season of ups and downs, sharing in the thrill of victory and the agony of defeat, but as the season went on that emptiness he was feeling slowly dissipated, he was part of a team just from a different point of view, never would he have thought a group of high school girls would help him in filling that void. Ashley for the first time in a while had a bit of a smile on her face celebrating with her teammates, this is exactly what she needed to get her mind off everything else even if it's only for a short time. The girls were all so hyped up they probably could have played a double header, still having energy to spare, Jake had to calm them all down so he could speak. Now having their full attention, he looked out at their mostly sweaty faces just wanting to say how proud he was of all of them, that he knew they had it in them all the time and it was an honor to be their coach, letting them know they helped him just as much as he helped them. A heartfelt moment between a coach and his players, the sight of the girls' many different expressions of contentment and jubilation was Jake's biggest triumph, giving them the confidence to believe with hard work and persistence anything is possible will serve them well after this season and well after their softball careers. In closing, Jake reminded them the season isn't over, even though one goal has been reached, there still more to thrive for and they will do it together as a unit, leading them off with his fist in the air, all of them mirroring his actions.

Announcing they will have a day off before having practice again, Jake dismisses the girls telling them to have a good rest of the day, offering one last verbal congratulations, before they all scattered going their separate ways. Ashley stayed close to Jake and Danielle as the reality of the situation begins to develop, now that everyone has left to mingle with their friends or parents before heading back to the locker room. Scouts are going to want to speak with Ashley who really isn't in the mood or right state of mind for an interview. It was too late, a pair was already walking in her direction, recognizing those snug smiles and arrogant walks anywhere. Danielle decided to leave letting Jake handle his business, giving him a quick peck on the lips prior to one last hug with Ashley before being on her way.

Reading Ashley's body language as the two men approach, Jake knows she just wants to go back to the locker room, not the time she wants to be overwhelmed with questions from total strangers. The two men offer their greetings with handshakes, coming right out with how impressive a showing that was by Ashley, stating it was one of the best performances they had ever seen from a possible recruit. Not wanting to be rude she extended her thanks, but informed them she has already committed to another school, however gave them good insight on another great player on the team. As luck would have it, Ashley looked over to spot Renee sitting in the dugout with her arms folded looking a bit disappointed, understanding now why she always felt slighted, she was playing in Ashley's shadow, scouts were always interested in her they never even stopped to consider evaluating Renee who would make a great addition to any team. Shouting out her name, Ashley calls Renee over, confused with the request, makes her way to find what all this is about.

"I want you to meet Renee Stadtmiller," Ashley said, introducing her to the scouts. "Probably the best hitter and fielder on the team, she is the one you need to be talking to, if you have any doubts about that just watch any of our game tapes."

"Yes, Renee, I have heard of you," remarked one of the scouts.

A thrilled Renee couldn't hold back her excitement, beginning to ramble on aimlessly before stopping herself, not wanting to ruin her first impression. Jake grinned ear to ear witnessing Ashley's selfless act, even backing her up on her claims, inserting Renee was also the person who has grown most as a teammate. Hearing the praises coming from her teammate and coach, the scouts shifted their attention and questioning to Renee letting Ashley and Jake slip away. Being showered with a prolific amount of congratulations and tribute from the remaining spectators, Ashley headed back to the locker room with Jake by her side hoping to evade anymore interactions, all she wanted to do was get out of her sweaty uniform and take a shower. Looking back at Renee with the scouts, whose interaction seems to be getting quite serious, noticing a lot of smiles and heavy interconnection between the three of them, Ashley catches her glancing over to make quick eye contact. Flashing a smile of appreciation, Renee conveys her gratitude by putting one fist in the air with a nod, receiving the same from Ashley in return.

"You continue to impress me," said Jake as they headed for the locker room.

The past couple days have been a circus for Ashley, the perfect game is bringing her more attention than she would like, local news showing up at school during the team's practice wanting to do an interview with her, which she declined for a couple reasons. Not being a big fan of the media, notorious for trying to dig up dirt on their unsuspected interviewees, bringing out the skeletons in their closet is considered good journalism. She has been on the news before for her play, but in name only, there may have been a few highlights sprinkled in here and there, but nothing where you could see her clearly. Having her face recognized on TV would bring nothing but more problems her way, especially from Razz, who luckily doesn't watch much television, but many of his goons probably do and would notify Razz in a heartbeat. At one point Jake had to step in as the news crew became pushy really wanting to do the interview, letting them know this isn't the best time right now, opting to keep her privacy. It was also headline news during the morning announcements, proclaimed as the greatest sports feat in the school's history, adding to a resume saving her a spot in the school's sports hall of fame, clearly never one of Ashley's goals, but an honor nonetheless which she would accept with grace and pride. Do to the declaration of the past couple days, she has been saturated with more congratulations and praises from her teachers and students she doesn't even know on a personal level, some were even under classmen who view her as a high school sports star. One day after school she was driving back to the house just happening to have the radio on and a local DJ on one of the stations was talking about the perfect game, giving her a shout out and commending her on the amazing feat before throwing in a chauvinistic comment about how hot he heard she was.

Back at the house, Ashley remained in her room still wanting her alone time when she could get it, working on the finishing touches of the painting for Jake. Inspirations for her next couple paintings have recently surfaced, wanting to do one for Jeff and Vicki as a show of appreciation for their hospitality. An idea for a painting that symbolized their marriage and love for one another was what she would try to capture, they even offered to take her out to dinner one night as a way to say congrats to her recent softball milestone which she graciously declined not wanting them to make a fuss. Being around Jeff and Vicki lately gave Ashley the chance to witness what a healthy marriage or just even a healthy relationship is like, could see the amount of love they have for one another as clear as the paint on her canvass, some couples you can tell are going to be together forever just in the ways they look at each other, how they interact, Jeff and Vicki are one of those couples, they are good people who deserve the happiness they have built together. Deep down Ashley questions her own mortality when it comes to intimate relationships, whether or not she could mentally handle the responsibilities and pressures of a one on one courtship, not having the best history of being the recipient of much chivalry or respect. Repeatedly having to remind herself, it's a bridge she will worry about crossing when she gets there, boys and relationships are the last thing on her mind.

Another painting she wants to do is one as tribute to Holley J, but isn't emotionally ready for a project like that yet, her death is still fresh in her mind, needing to deal with the pain of her being gone first before she can honor her the right way. To say this has been a whirlwind week for Ashley would be an understatement, having things happen faster than she can react, an emotional roller coaster with the brakes out and no end in sight. Another unexpected aspect of this week she finds bizarre is it's closing in on the weekend and Razz hasn't asked her to work, most weeks it's almost certain she will be called in for one or two random nights before her weekend shift, yet this week she hasn't heard from him. Not complaining, just funny the things a person gets used to whether it's something they like or not, always having to be ready for a text calling her in became part of her daily routine which made making plans to do anything else rather difficult having no choice but to show up. Thinking in a make-believe type of mind set, was hoping she was living in a different reality, one where Razz didn't exist offering the syllogism for his sudden hiatus. Knowing that not to be true, Ashley wondered if it had anything to do with the upcoming deal he will be making with her so called "Friend," a deal looking like is going too happened on her Friday night shift. Just another ball of anxiety manifesting within her, contributing to her wild ride of emotions, something that needs to be done, however it's still scaring her to death. Right now Ashley doesn't want to think about anything other than how her brush touches the canvas.

Later into the evening, Jake found himself doing what he has been doing lately, sitting out on the front patio with a tall glass of iced tea. Usually sitting out there waiting for Ashley to come back safely from work, yet on this night she is secure inside. Finding himself doing a lot of reflecting and thinking, mixed in with his worrying for Ashley, the big sting going down soon the culprit for most of his feelings of uneasiness. Also curious where Jeff is, normally home by this time even on his late nights, sipping his iced tea the front door opens, walking out with a glass of wine in her hand was Vicki.

"Mind if I join you?" Vicki asked.

"Not at all," answered Jake, gesturing for her to have a seat.

"Where is Jeff tonight?" Jake asked.

"He called me earlier telling me he was going to be late because he had to go to the State Penitentiary to talk to a client, which I find weird," remarked Vicki.

"What's weird about that?" asked Jake.

"He's never had to do anything like that before," stated Vicki.

Sitting on their king sized bed in her pink plaid pajamas reading a book, a scented candle burning on the nightstand beside her with the fragrance of the ocean. Being an avid reader of romance novels, Vicki finds it easy most sessions to dive right into her fictional worlds, able to block out everything around her as she concentrates on the print on the pages. This night, however, she is finding it hard to centralize on her brief exit from the real world, catching herself a few times rereading the same paragraph over and over, still not understanding what she just read, mostly wondering what is taking Jeff so long. Looking over at the alarm clock on the nightstand on Jeff's side of the bed, reading a couple minutes till midnight, beginning to worry, tosses the book aside grabbing her charging phone off her nightstand quickly trying to give Jeff a call, just as she was about to hit dial, she heard footsteps coming from the hallway getting louder the closer they got to their bedroom, the door about fully open, a shadow appears entering the room first.

"Jeff?" Vicki calls out.

"Yeah, honey, it's me," replied Jeff out of sight, seconds before entering, being quiet as possible to not wake the twins or Ashley just down the hall.

"Where the hell have you been? I was getting worried, I was just about to try calling you," explained Vicki, taking notice of Jeff's appearance as he sets foot in the bedroom.

Carrying his brown suit jacket, his vanilla colored dress shirt untucked with his brown loosened tie hanging low, looking like someone who would have spent the night in their car, the exhaustion on his face stood out more than his messy outfit.

"I'm sorry," Jeff said, walking over to give Vicki a quick kiss before seating himself on the large bench stationed at the foot of the bed. "I was going to call again, I just got distracted, it's been one hell of a night," he continues on, taking off his shoes, ripping the tie off of his neck.

"Is everything okay?" asked Vicki, leaving the bed to go sit beside him.

"I found out something tonight and I don't even know how to react to it," Jeff replied, displaying a blank look on his face staring straight ahead. "For the past couple hours I was just driving around trying to process everything. This is huge, Vick, I'm still feeling sick to my stomach, I just can't believe what I found out."

"Jeff, you're scaring me, what did you find out?" asked Vicki.

"Something that changes everything," Jeff answered, reaching to grab hold of Vicki's hand, looking his wife dead in the eyes.

Could tell from years of them being together when something bothers Jeff psychologically, rarely does anything ever surprise him being in the profession he has chosen, curve balls from cases he is involved in happen on a daily basis, yet the shallow look in his eyes forecast a mind in complete stupefaction or complete disbelief. Feeling some of that tensity in his grip, Vicki stare backs with nothing but compassion in her face, an open ended invitation for Jeff to air out his findings, their mastery as a couple of subtle non-verbal communication hit its peck on this night. Turning his body towards Vicki, now holding both of her hands, Jeff explained the dark discovery of his recent investigating. Tears slowly descended down Vicki's face with every word uttered from Jeff's mouth, hearing the shift in his voice's tone indicated the effectiveness of what he found out has on him. Nothing could have ever prepared her for what she is being told, the last thing in a million years she would have expected to hear, tears of mixed emotions suddenly turned into tears of joy, overburdened with jumbled feelings of dejection. Embracing an emotional Jeff, the two sat holding each other, clenching tight enough to feel each other's heart beating, understanding how much this information will affect everyone, both agreeing to reveal the details when the time was right.

Late Friday afternoon, Ashley was in the upstairs bathroom getting ready for another night at the club, also the night the deal she set up was going down. Finished brushing her hair, she stared at herself in the mirror, not even at the club yet, could already feel her heart pounding in her chest, overcome with a heavy dose of anxiety. Already knowing this night will be unlike any other night at Razz', her emotions felt like they were in a blender, a mixture of all a person could feel with fear being the main element, but was ready to take the first step towards her freedom, primed to stand tall against her antagonist in an effort to rid her life of him once and for all. All the times looking at her reflection, never liking what she saw, yet for the first time, she saw someone different, someone who is willing to take a stand, someone who has the backing of good people behind her, someone she actually has some respect for. The monster she always seen was slowly vanishing away, being replaced by the beauty everyone else saw, soon hoping to be able to meet the real her for the first time. Leaving the bathroom, Ashley heads to her bedroom to grab her backpack, having to meet Jake and Jeff in Jeff's office in a few minutes to go over the plan for how this deal scenario is going to go down, slipping on her flip flops, throwing on her pink sweat jacket, heads to meet with the guys.

Standing by Jeff's desk waiting for him to finish up a phone call, Ashley being extra fidgety consumed with curiosity wanting to hear the plan. Jake standing next to a seated Jeff, eccentric himself to hear what the plan of action was for the evening, probably more nervous than Ashley was, wishing it could be him to go about this with her, even though she will be by the side of a trained cop, would still feel more at ease if he was there with her. Ending his phone call, Jeff got right to business explaining to Ashley how all this was going to happen.

"Okay, that was Officer Turner on the phone," said Jeff. "He is ready to go when you give him the signal."

"He won't have a gun or any other cops around, right?" Ashley asked.

"Correct, all he'll have on him is the duffel bag full of money which will be marked bills," replied Jeff. "All he has to do is give him the bag, get the product and leave. Once they have that evidence they can plan a raid when he least expects it."

"How do I send him the signal?" Ashley asked. "What does he look like?"

"You are going to send him a text at this number," answered Jeff, handing Ashley a Post-It with a cell number on it. "Just remember it's very important that you act normal, there is going to be no other eyes or ears in there beside you two. As far as what he looks like, come take a look," Jeff said, bringing up his profile on his computer.

"Okay," replied Ashley, glancing over at Jake, feeling more and more edgy as the seconds tick away.

"It's okay to be nervous," Jeff remarked, seeing the skittishness in her posture. "But you are going to have a really good cop in there with you who does this sort of thing all the time. Right now I need you to send a text to your boss letting him know he will have a visitor later."

Pulling out her phone, Ashley sends Razz a text telling him her friend will be coming by later on tonight to make the deal, the three of them anxiously wait for a response initiating the night's event. Like clockwork when it comes to receiving a text from one of his girls or one about a business endeavor, Razz responds right away.

"He said I'm ready," relayed Ashley.

"Okay then, it starts," Jeff responded.

Coming upon that time, she declares she has to go, shouldering her backpack, walks towards the door being followed by a tense Jake, the two share a moment before she leaves.

"I have to be honest, I wish it was you going in there with me," Ashley said gripping her shoulder straps tightly.

"Yeah, me too," said Jake, putting a hand on her shoulder in an attempt to ease her worry. "Just promise me you'll be careful." The look of concern was all over Jake's face, without him saying it, knew how much he cared about her, filling her with a warm feeling encasing her like a blanket.

Giving a couple nods, Ashley walks away leaving Jake standing there feeling helpless that he couldn't do anything more. Watching the interaction between Jake and Ashley from afar made holding on to his secret even more difficult, eating Jeff up inside he couldn't share the news yet, wanting to wait until this order of action was completed. Wanted to wish Ashley good luck, but as a lawyer knows there are certain phrases you shouldn't say to certain individuals in certain circumstances, saying good luck could infer danger is right around the corner and he didn't want to make Ashley any more jumpy or nervous than she already was, yet in his mind has repeated it over and over since she entered his office.

Night at the club started like any other, Ashley performed as the headliner and serviced a couple clients, for once she kept her mind on what she was doing trying not to think about the matter soon to come, making her hate what she does even more. Sitting in the dressing room, she decides it's now or never, pulling out her phone to texts the cop, instructing him to go to the back of the building, hitting send a lump formed in her throat, looking around at the other girls in the room who are totally unaware of what is about to go down, this would be as much about them as it is about her. Many of the girls Ashley doesn't know on a personal level, but there are familiar faces who all share that same look in their eyes, the silent cry for help. Assuming once this deal is done she will be allowed to leave, Ashley takes off her heals to put her flip flops back on wanting to make herself as comfortable as possible. Expecting her comrade to arrive soon, she leaves the dressing room to head for Razz' office.

The guard standing by Razz' office sees Ashley coming, always a different face standing outside his doors, constantly rotating his guards in an effort to keep many of the club's regulars from remembering identities. This particular guard is new to her, a large black man with a goatee standing tall by the entrance, aware of her appending arrival instructing her to enter. Inside Razz is seated at his couch with an open laptop resting on his coffee table adjacent to an open briefcase full of packets of a white powder, an unopen bottle of whiskey and three small glasses await patiently on one end of the table. A lit cigarette as usual hangs between his lips working in private on his computer, some hard core metal music playing at a reasonable volume in the background.

"So, Show Horse, now that you are here I assume your friend is close?" asked Razz, exhaling a puff of smoke into the air.

"He's on his way," Ashley replied, walking over to the coffee table.

Being in Razz' office is always stressful, yet this time it seems to be amplified, the sooner this guy gets here the quicker they can get this over with. Having only seen one picture of this dude, a headshot while wearing a police cap, the only feature that stood out to her was his stunning green eyes which seemed to leap right off the photograph, could never forget a pair of eyes like that.

"Good," responds Razz. "Why don't you have a seat and relax?"

"Okay," Ashley said, seating herself in one of the leather chairs.

To hide her nervousness, she sat with her legs crossed, body language most common with someone who is placid in nature. Selling her charade even more, she started playing with her flip flop, bouncing it up and down on her foot in a very sensual matter catching Razz' attention. Intently staring at Ashley's smooth and toned looking legs, watching her bobbing the flip flop between her toes, turning Razz on having a major foot fetish. Recognizing the look Razz is staring at her with, the sexual gaze will eventually turn into him wanting some release and her to be the one to satisfy that release. Not wanting to risk having to do something she doesn't want to do, uncrosses her legs to sit with both her feet on the floor putting her hands on her knees, deliberately making the move while not looking in Razz' direction in hopes of it looking spontaneous, wanting to relieve the sexual tension she can feel is building up.

"Come sit next to me," Razz requested.

"I'm okay right here," replied Ashley, still trying her best to look relaxed.

"I wasn't fucking asking," Razz remarked.

Having no choice but to get up and go sit next to him, those couple steps to get to the couch, she can feel her heart pounding sitting down beside him.

Slightly closing his laptop to keep the information on the screen hidden, Razz puts out his cigarette, lying against the back off the couch placing his extended arms across the top.

"Join me back here, Show Horse," Razz said.

Not liking where this is going, fearful her attempt to defuse the sexual tension has failed, seeing herself in the worst position possible. Having to obey, slowly leans against the back of the couch next to him, his one hand begins playing with her hair staring at her face from the side.

"Can I ask you something?" Razz asked, caressing her neck with his fingertips.

"Sure," Ashley answered staring out ahead of her, Razz' touch tenses her up inside, making her feel more uncomfortable than she appears.

"Look at me when I talk to you," demanded Razz, awaiting her to turn and face him, always mesmerized looking at her beautiful face. "Would you do anything for me?"

"Of course," Ashley proclaimed in a soft toned voice, giving the only answers she could, especially now hoping to avoid saying or doing anything that could jeopardize what is at stake. This could be the last time she ever sees Razz and this place again, motivation enough to say what he wants to hear, but anything physical she wants to circumvent at all cost.

"Good girl," remarked Razz, placing his hand on the side of her face to pull her in closer for a kiss.

Wants to resist his advances, but there is nothing Ashley can do, she is trapped, evading his intentions would totally contradict what she just agreed too. In all the acts of sexual desire, kissing someone you don't like or don't have affection for is an appalling feeling, for her it's downright nauseating having already been through it with him before, yet if that's all Razz is seeking to subdue his arousal, she is willing to fall on her sword.

Just before their lips met, Ashley was saved by an incoming call on Razz' earpiece, forcing him to pull back to attend to the message, an instant sigh of relief came over her.

"Looks like your friend is here," informed Razz. "Why don't you go let him in?"

Leaving the couch heading for the office back door, she is pleased to be away from Razz' personal space, her anxiety growing with every step about to put the whole objective into action. Passing by Razz' desk, her uneasiness grew even more noticing the shiny silver pistol lying right out in the open, the sight of his gun reminds her just how prepared he is and how he is ready for anything momentarily filling her with a sense of self-doubt, questioning now if this whole thing is really a good idea. Reopening his laptop while coordinating with his guard over the earpiece, Razz waits to hear if his unknown visitor is clean. Getting the feedback his guest is good, he gives the signal to Ashley keeping a majority of his focus on the computer screen.

Opening the door, Ashley is instantly greeted by those familiar green eyes, seeming to sparkle in the outdoor light, definitely the guy from the picture, though she thought he would be taller, standing there in his jeans, pair of black boots and leather jacket holding a large duffel bag. Making eye contact with her, gives a quick friendly wink cementing their contemporary collaboration, her sudden self-doubt quickly became replaced with a feeling a solace knowing the undercover cop is here finally by her side. Entering, he sees Razz sitting on the couch, doing his best to survey his surroundings without looking obvious, Ashley stood by his side to enforce the allegations they were acquaintances. Escorting her visitor over to Razz being sure to stay close by, this cops track record for situations like this has been highly documented having caught or gotten the evidence for many drug traffickers. Being in his vicinity may be the safest place in the whole club, even without having a weapon on him, he is a man that knows the game and must know what to do in these circumstances.

"Well, if it isn't Show Horse's little friend," said Razz, closing the laptop, turning off the music with a small remote hiding amongst all the other items occupying the coffee table. Inspecting the gentleman standing before him up and down, everything about him seemed legit except for the gold band he is wearing on his left hand. "I mean you are her aunt's friend, correct?"

"You can say that," replied the cop.

"Well, you either are or you aren't," Razz remarked.

"If you must know we are more than friends," said the cop. "Now can we just get down to business?"

"Whatever you say," said Razz. "Have a seat."

The man seats himself in one of the leather chairs on the opposite side of the coffee table, Ashley going back to her original seat.

"Let's see what you got for me," insisted the cop.

Razz turns the open briefcase with the bags of white powder around to face the man. Silently looking on, trying to get a read on the situation, not one to call herself an expert on illegal business transactions, but from Ashley's perspective it seems everything is going smoothly, yet her gut registers something might be off.

Grabbing a bag out of the briefcase, the cop pinches it open to dip his pinky finger inside to taste the goods, dapping a bit on his tongue, assured the product is genuine he returns the bag. Giving Razz the nod, the cop throws his duffel bag off to the side landing near Razz' feet, already unzipped displaying the bundles of cash inside.

"I think it's time we celebrate," requested Razz, cracking open the bottle of whiskey, pouring three separate drinks, handing one to the cop and one to Ashley.

Takes the drink knowing she has never had a drop of alcohol in her life, yet refusing it wasn't an option, being so close to this being over, Ashley would just have to suck it up and drink it down, being more unbothered by the fact Razz is partaking in more illegal actions in front of an undercover cop by serving alcohol to a minor.

"Let's drink to hopefully doing more business in the future," toasted Razz.

The three of them slam back their drinks, Ashley a virgin to the taste of alcohol, begins coughing with her eyes watering due to the intense tang of the whiskey. Finding amusement in her display of discomfort, Razz lets out a mocking laugh pouring himself another glass, pounding that one back just as quickly as the first. Through with her coughing fit, her throat felt like it was on fire, wishing she has a small glass of water to help relieve the sensation.

"You know we are doing business here and we haven't even been properly introduced," remarked Razz. "So what is your name, friend?"

"Why do you need to know my name?" the cop asked.

"It's just common courtesy, we are doing business and if we are to do business again in the future I would like to know who the fuck I'm dealing with," Razz said with a sarcastic laugh.

"Fine, my name is…," the cop started saying before being cut off by Razz.

"Wait! I want her to tell me your name," requested Razz, pointing in Ashley's direction. "So what is it, Show Horse?"

"It's Jimmy," answered Ashley without the slightest hesitation, couldn't use his real name so she blurted out the first male name that came to her, betting on his intellect to know play along.

"That's right, it's Jimmy," reassured the cop.

"Jimmy. Okay then, Jimmy, I guess this is the start of a business relationship," Razz declared.

"You bet," the cop replied, closing the briefcase to prepare to leave.

Watching the undercover cop getting close to being gone with the evidence in hand, once out that door it will only be a matter of days before they come raid the club and Razz will finally be out of her life, just the thought of that could make Ashley instantly cry tears of joy. However they are not out of the woods yet, he still has to physically leave, the tension she was feeling until that actually happened was overpowering as if watching a suspenseful movie she was starring in. Time couldn't move fast enough, seeming like now everything was going in slow motion, all he has to do is grab the briefcase and walk out the door making this whole operation a success.

Observing his most recent financial conquest gather himself in preparation to leave, Razz removes himself from the couch.

"Before you leave I have a special offer I would like to present you as a gesture of us becoming business colleagues," informed Razz, walking over to his desk to grab the pistol, hiding it behind his back making his return to stand behind Ashley still seated in the chair.

"I'm good," the cop replied.

"You haven't heard the offer yet," mentioned Razz, placing his free hand on Ashley's shoulder.

"Look, I got what I wanted, I'm ready to go," said the cop standing from his seat.

"Sit down," Razz demanded revealing the gun, pointing it at his new guest.

Seeing the light shimmer off the shiny steel of Razz' piece, Ashley felt her heart drop from her chest, that gut feeling she had was manifesting right before her eyes, her body instantly went numb with trepidation not knowing what Razz was up to. It wouldn't surprise her if this was just one of his intimidation tactics to demonstrate who really is in control.   "What the fuck is this?" the cop asked, stunned at the current turn of events, slowly sitting back down in his seat partially putting his hands up.

"Razz, what are you doing?" a freaked out Ashley asked.

"Don't worry, Show Horse, this will all be over soon," Razz stated. "Now are you ready to listen to my offer, Jimmy?"

"Sure, whatever," answered the cop.

"What if I told you that I was willing to give you some private time with this fine piece of ass right here, on the house," Razz said kissing Ashley gently on her cheek.

"Now why would I want to do that?" the cop asked. "I'm seeing her aunt."

"I won't say anything if you won't. Are you really going to tell me that you are going to turn down this fine young American pussy, come on, this every adult man's dream right here, the purest of the pure. Guys like you jerk off to girls like this every day, but I'm giving you the chance to have her for real," Razz replied.

"Look, man, all I came for is the drugs. Now you got your money, how about you just let me get out of here," the cop remarked.

"Starting to sound like a little faggot there, Jimmy," Razz said. "It's obvious a man like you isn't opposed to straying a little."

"What is that supposed to mean?" asked the cop confused.

"Are you and her aunt serious?" Razz replied.

"Not that it's any of your fucking business, but yeah, we're pretty serious, why?" the cop insisted.

"How do you think your wife would feel if she knew you had a side piece?" asked Razz. "That's a nice wedding band you got there, by the way."

"So I'm not the greatest husband in the world, sue me," declared the cop, thinking back to all the other undercover assignments he has done, none of which ever got to the point where he felt like he wasn't in control. Many times he went in without his weapon, never at any point would he have ever needed to use it, but right now he wishes he was strapped, the first time during any of his missions he found himself staring down the barrel of a gun. His wit and his ability to smooth talk usually were the only artillery he needed, right now hopes that trend continues.

"I don't care what you do, Jimmy, you can do whatever the fuck you want," said Razz walking back over to the couch to take his original seat, keeping the gun pointing at his promiscuous guest. "I'll tell you what, you want to walk out of here, you just have to do one thing for me."

"What's that?" the cop asked in closer proximity to the wrong end of the pistol.

"Tell me her name," instructed Razz, waving the gun over in Ashley's direction.

See the tension in the man's face increase, sitting there pondering how to respond, he was told Ashley's name once when he was coordinating everything with Jeff, but it must have slipped his mind not thinking is was really important, receiving a picture of her figuring that's all he would need. Every second trying to remember is a second closer to revealing his guilt of having to plead ignorance.

"Come on, Jimmy! If you are messing with this girl's aunt then you got to know her fucking name," Razz insisted. "You don't know her name, do you? You know, Jimmy, the one thing I can't stand is a liar and I won't do business with one and you just lied to me, hell, you have been lying to me ever since you came through my fucking door."

"What the fuck you talking about?" the cop asked timidly.

"Well, actually, you're Turner, right? Officer Ray Turner," Razz stated, opening his laptop to face the screen at the undercover cop, displaying his picture and badge number from Razz' database. Using his facial recognition software when he got a glimpse of him from his hidden camera, strategically placed by his outgoing office door to flag any cops he doesn't have on his payroll.

A deathly panic came over Ashley sitting there stone faced, breaking out in a nervous sweat watching everything begin to unravel right before her eyes. Feeling immobilized in an invisible cage of fear, her only support to getting out of this unscathed was just outed putting both of them in danger, quickly going from certain victory to absolute uncertainty.

"Razz, you don't want to do this," pleaded Ashley, fearing not only for herself, but for the officer who found himself in a demoralizing position.

"YOU SHUT YOUR FUCKING MOUTH! I'll deal with you in a minute," yelled Razz, pointing the gun at her.

Getting off the couch, Razz grabs the cop aggressively by his jacket forcing him to stand up, keeping the gun pointed close to his face. Shoving the cop back a ways, he goes to pick up the bag of money still keeping the gun on his target.

"What is this shit we have in here, huh? Fake money, marked bills?" rants Razz, throwing bundles of the cash at the cop, hitting him in the chest and a couple times in the face. "You just made your last fucking mistake walking in here," he said, firing three shots into the man's chest knocking him to the ground where he laid motionless.

Freaked out and frightened, Ashley watched the cop who was supposed to be her security blanket fall limply to the floor. Tears streaming down her face, quickly runs over to check on the officer's vitals, blood pouring out of each of his wounds checking his neck for a pulse, discovering he was dead. The worst case scenario was playing out, one they didn't have a plan for, finding herself alone trapped in a room with a very pissed off maniac.

Knelt down over the now bloody corpse, Ashley was reminded of the night Holley J was shot, all those scared and helpless feelings she had for her best friend were now being redirected to herself. Staring at the officer's lifeless body, hoping his last thoughts before the bullets penetrated his flesh were of his wife, a last split second moment of happiness, flashing images of her face one last time before everything faded to black. An enraged Razz received calls over his earpiece in reference to the gun shots, ferociously yelling in response for everyone to stay back.

"AND YOU!" Razz shouted viciously, grabbing Ashley off the floor, pulling her up firmly pressing the barrel of the pistol against her forehead, "YOU FUCKING SNEAKY LITTLE BITCH, I KNEW YOU WERE UP TO SOMETHING! YOU THINK YOU CAN BEAT ME? HUH, DO YOU? I should put a fucking bullet in your head."

"Then do it," responded Ashley, feeling the cold steel of the gun on her skin, suddenly not afraid anymore, a rush of adrenaline filled her with the tenacity to want to fight back. If this was going to be her last night alive, she was going to go down fighting, there was no time to be scared anymore, going to let Razz know how she really feels about him, if she was going to die she was going to die with dignity. "I fucking hate you! I'd rather die than have to look at your FUCKING FACE AGAIN! NOW DO IT! DO IT!"

Hearing Ashley's piercing screams towards self-vindication provoked Razz, leading him to pistol whip her across the face, knocking her to the floor on her back. The blow left her dazed, leaving a cut on the side of her face exposing a trickle of blood, a furious Razz stood over her defenseless body breathing heavily.

"I don't think so, Show Horse, you're not getting off that easy," Razz said unbuckling his pants. "I'm going to do something I've wanted to do for a long time."

Getting on his knees he tears open Ashley's blouse unveiling her breast, working his way down to rip off her skirt baring her bottom half completely naked, aggressively spreading her legs open. Fondling frantically to release his erect penis still holding the gun, Razz positioned himself to initiate forced penetration. Still a little groggy from the impact, Ashley regains much of her clarity back feeling the violent insertion into her vagina. The rough and dry probing into her body produces shriek of discomfort, instinctively failing her arms at Razz' head and face attempting to free herself from his nonconsensual advances. Having the flurry of blows rain down upon him Razz is compelled to stop his vigorous thrusting, becoming annoyed and seething with Ashley's form of defense. Able to fight off an opening to the assault, Razz throws another backhand holding the gun, blooding her nose, the impact dropped her arms to the floor allowing Razz to hold them down by her wrists. With her pinned. he reengages in the fierce penetration making sure each ram is harder than the last.

"You make me kill a fucking cop, I'm going to make you feel my hatred," said Razz, hearing Ashley's cries of pain and discomfort, feeling her lower body squirming trying to make his actions as difficult as possible.

Frantically struggling to free herself from Razz' grip, his intense anger giving him a boost in strength, feeling the extreme pressure on her wrist, trying with all her might to break free. The penetration was becoming more and more painful, feeling like a rolled up piece of sandpaper was constantly going in and out of her. The more Razz saw Ashley scuffle, the more aroused he become, wasn't only the force sex, but the power of control he was exhibiting, putting his libido on fire enticing him to make it even more brutal and merciless, can feel the relentless fight in her through the immense insistence to free herself, leaning in so she can feel his hot breath on her partially bloody face.

"Why don't you just lay back and enjoy it like the whore you are," remarked Razz, letting out loud grunts.

Razz in close and within striking distance, Ashley takes advantage, head butting him square in the nose with as much force as she could muster, blooding his nose causing him to release her wrists. Flapping and waving her arms wildly making contact with random areas of Razz' body, she was able to push him over and off her, hysterically getting to her feet. Pissed off and bloody, Razz hurried to his feet wrestling to quickly pull up his pants enough to stand, reaching out to grab for her, clutches her open blouse pulling on it to try to stop her momentum, tearing it off in the process leaving her thoroughly naked. Distracted by the loss of her shirt, Ashley trips over the dead officer slamming her body to the floor, speedily getting upright is stopped in her tracks from behind being pulled back by her hair, Razz clenches a handful tugging hard causing Ashley to let out a scream of torment. Back in Razz' grasp, she suffers a couple more punches to the face while he is holding the gun, her left eye split open immediately beginning to swell slightly obstructing her vision. Blood drips from her nose, mouth and eye onto her breasts, being pressed up against the front of Razz' desk. Delivering one more backhand to her face, Razz flips her around, putting him in view with her back side, Ashley slightly dazed, swipes her arms recklessly across the top of the desk trying to grab something as a weapon, knocking items off in the process.

"You know I've always been an ass man," Razz utters, blood dripping from his nose, directly into Ashley's ear pulling again on her hair.

Dropping his pants again, takes his erection forcefully into Ashley's anus, the immense pressure lets loose a squeal of massive discomfort, Razz grunts mockingly with every slap of their bodies. Overcome with fury, he smashes her face onto the desk a few times to remind Ashley of his dominance and her overall betrayal, shouting derogatory remarks. Battered and in severe pain, the sensation of her anus being ripped open, her face covered in blood dripping on the desk below, all she could think about was wishing Jake was here. In her weakened and woozy state, gathers whatever amount of strength she can produce, swinging her elbow back catching Razz in the side of the head, knocking him back removing him from inside her. Hopping on top the desk to climb over to the other side, she slips on the polished wood falling off the other side landing on her left wrist, breaking it hearing a loud snap. Screaming from the injury, she laid there on the floor on her back, wrist limp and totally useless, attempting to get to her feet was stalled by a crazy eyed Razz kneeling over top of her pointing the gun at her forehead. Looking at Razz with her one good eye, not wanting his face to be the last one she sees, she pictured in her mind the two people she cared about most, Holley J and Jake, awaiting for everything to go dark. Not hesitating pulling the trigger, he hears a click, frustrated he pulls it again to hear another clink. Tossing the gun aside, puts his hands around Ashley's throat squeezing as tight as he can, his eyes wide open displaying a frenzied look.

Trying to pull his hands away, but was too weak, her legs kicking about slowly feeling herself slipping out of consciousness, not the way she wants to go out, being raped and left for dead by the man she hates the most. Able to slightly lift her head fighting to free herself, she was able to see Razz' switchblade out of the corner of her, lying nearby on the floor. Reaching out, Ashley touched it with her fingertips, stretching as far as she humanly can trying to rake it towards her, Razz' grip was getting tighter unable to inhale any air, her vison becoming cloudy full of black spots, only a matter of seconds before she blacks out. Reaching with all her might, almost dislocating her shoulder in the undertaking, the switchblade became fully in her grasp. Wasting no time, Ashley protrudes the blade out, stabbing Razz in the side, pushing the blade in as deep as she can. A wounded Razz falls over to the floor freeing Ashley from his grasp, coughing to suck in needed air, slowly gets to her feet holding her broken wrist. Sore and physically drained, she staggered her way out of the club through the back office door. Her vision restricted to her one good eye, the other now completely swollen shut, enervated and barely able to stand, drags her bare feet along the loose pebbles and grit of the back parking lot slowly tearing up the bottom of her feet. Surprised to see no one standing guard anymore, Ashley hurries her bloody, naked body as far away down the street as she can get, afraid any moment Razz will come stumbling out the door to chase after her. Not knowing where she is headed, teeters out into the road feeling a chill from the late night air across her body, her broken wrist went numb hanging limp in her hold. The silence of the night made Ashley feel even more alone, pushing onward with blood trickling down her legs, overcome with sudden paranoia, crazily looking in all directions for some anonymous night crawler to come out of the darkness to finish her off, comes face to face with a pair of headlights screeching to a halt.

Blinded by the light and the sound of the idling engine, she stands there in an incapacitated state just staring ahead into the unexpected brilliance before dropping to the asphalt below. Passed out in the middle of the road, Ashley is unaware of the older couple emerging from the car to lend her help. Taken back by the disturbing sight of a bloody, beaten and naked young girl lying in the street, the couple acted quickly getting an intimate view of some of the ugliness of the city night life. The gentleman grabbed a blanket from the trunk to cover Ashley's bare body, while the woman dialed 911.

Jake sat alone on the front patio with his standard tall glass of iced tea, a lit small scented candle burned on the end table, eagerly anticipating Ashley's safe return, finding himself checking the time way more than a normal person should. Last checked it was closing in on one-thirty in the morning, a bit later than when she typically comes home. Growing tired, could easily find himself falling asleep right there in the patio chair, yet his constant worrying keeps him awake, has to know Ashley is back safe for him to get a good night's sleep. As the minutes pass by descending them deeper into the night waiting to see that pair of headlights belonging to her car come closing in, Jake couldn't help but feel in his gut something was wrong. Hoping to just be overreacting, knowing there are probably many reasons why she is late, but this night the situation was much different than all the others, most teenage girls aren't out on stings to bring down an obvious drug dealer. Taking a sip of his drink, keeping his eyes fixated out on the horizon wanting to see the flash of lights appearing out of nowhere to put an end to his pessimistic state, Jake turned his attention to the sound of the front door opening. A concerned Jeff steps over the threshold to check on his brother, taking a seat in the vacant chair.

"Heard anything?" asked Jake.

"Nothing yet," Jeff answered, curious himself why he hasn't heard anything yet from Officer Turner, knowing it shouldn't have taken this long.

The sudden silence between them was broken by the ringing of Jake's phone, eagerly picking it up off the center table to check the caller ID. Viewing the number, Jake instantly determines it's one he is not familiar with, however there must be a reason an unknown number is calling him this late at night. Quickly answering the call, listens to the mysterious voice on the other end speaking in a stern and serious tone. Hearing what he is being told, Jake leaps from his seat in total shock, Jeff stands realizing something must be wrong watching Jake hold his lowered head. Thanking the voice on the other end for calling, he hangs up looking back out at the horizon knowing there won't be any emerging headlights anytime soon.

"Who was that?" asked Jeff.

"That was the hospital, Ashley is there, she has been beaten and raped," Jake answered, almost choking on his words, felt close to vomiting right there on the patio.

"Oh my God," replied Jeff, instantly feeling guilty for Ashley's current predicament. "What the hell happened?"

"I gotta go see her," Jake stated at a loss for words, his emotions feeling scrambled.

"Then I will meet you there," informed Jeff.

Running into the emergency room heading straight for the receptionist's desk, Jake is greeted by an overweight middle-aged woman sitting at the desk, showing behavior of someone who is not having a good night, sparking a bit of an attitude asking Jake the reason for his visit. In no mood to call out her terrible customer service skills, informed the receptionist he is there to see a recently brought in patient giving her Ashley's name. Typing on her computer keyboard with a disinterested expression on her face, the woman advises it will be a few minutes, she is being seen by the doctor. Nothing more he can do now but wait, Jake takes a seat in the surprisingly empty waiting area, getting the uneasy feeling of déjà vu from the last visit for Holley J. Looking out the waiting room windows seeing his reflection blending in with the late night glare, the out of focus visual resembles his feelings of helplessness and uncertainty, transporting him back to his darkest days after his career ended. Not a spiritual man, he couldn't help but close his eyes and bow his head to silently ask the universe itself why Ashley? Why does so much innocence deserve the wrath of the unjust? It's the same questions he would ask about himself during his recovery, coming to the realization if the world was fair it would be a better place than the one they are living in today. The sound of the automatic doors sliding open awoke Jake from his meditated state, glancing over he saw Danielle entering, immediately followed by Jeff and Vicki. Having called Danielle on his ride over to let her know what had happened, insisting she didn't have to come up if she didn't want to, yet he couldn't be more happier to see her walking through those doors, was like a small beam of light in the darkest of nights. Receiving sympathetic hugs from both women, Jake introduces Danielle to Jeff and Vicki with the two ladies engaging in a friendly embrace, relaying everything he knows up to this point, just waiting to hear from the doctor. Everyone takes a seat hoping to hear something soon, Danielle next to Jake holding his hand, resting her head on his shoulder, Jeff and Vicki sat across from them, lucky her parents were willing to take the twins for the rest of the night, feeling bad they had to wake them from a sound sleep in order for both of them to be here. Holding Jeff close rubbing his arm, quickly looking at each other, both having decided on the drive over to tell Jake the news

Jeff has found out. It probably isn't the best time or place, but under the circumstances it would have to be now, their only worry is they don't know how he is going to react.

Getting his brother's attention, Jeff implied he has something to tell him, Jake sat in heed, curious to what it could be that it had to be told in an emergency room waiting area rather than back at home, yet judging from Jeff's demeanor and manner it must be something important. Letting out a deep breath, Jeff looked directly at his brother figuring out the best way to say what he has to say. Jake couldn't believe the difficulty Jeff was having in divulging his information, coming from someone who is never at a loss for words, who makes a living telling burdensome details and facts to his clients all the time. Seeing him struggle in getting the words out, Vicki grabs Jeff's hand for support, always being the person to relieve him of any stress just by her touch, squeezing tightly specifying everything will be okay.

Just before Jeff spoke up, a doctor comes out into the waiting area looking for the parent or guardian for Ashley. Promptly leaping from his seat to greet the doctor, followed closely by the others, Jake introduced himself as Ashley's current caretaker. The doctor was an older man projecting years of experience, a pleasant personality yet stern and straight to the point.

"How is she? Is she going to be okay?" asked an anxious Jake.

"She is going to be fine, but this was pretty bad," the doctor informed. "She was beaten up really good, raped violently front and back, had to give her ten stiches in her anus, has a broken left wrist, luckily it was a clean break, so it should heal nicely. We want to keep her here a few days for observation, if you want to see her she is just down the hall third room on the right. Tomorrow we will be moving her to an actually room. I'm just going to warn you it's not a pretty sight."

"Thank you, Doctor," Jake replied as the doctor went on his way.

Wasting no time, Jake and the others walked the hallway towards the room where Ashley is being kept for the time being, hearing the groans and cries from the other patients with the stench of sickness and bad hygiene filling the air. A few nurses wandering the hall crossed their path approaching Ashley's room, one kindly asked who they were looking for, pointing them in the right direction. Stepping into the room, Jake's nerves were running rampant, trying to prepare himself for what he might see.

Spotting her laying in the bed on a slight incline, her left arm in a cast almost up to her elbow, head turned facing away from the entryway. Walking up to the side of the bed, Jake whispers to Ashley he is there, petting the top of her head in a soothing manner. Feeling the gentle contact and familiar voice, she slowly turns her head to face her visitors putting her badly beaten face in full view. The state of Ashley's face left everyone disturbed and bothered, her left eye was swollen shut with the rest of the area covered in small cuts and black and blue marks. Danielle covered her mouth, tears dripping from her eyes, Vicki had to turn away to be consoled by Jeff, closing his eyes shaking his head in disbelief. Jake couldn't hold back his emotions letting the tears run down his face, her once beautiful face was almost unrecognizable. Pulling up one of the empty visitor chairs to sit beside the bed, tenderly placed one of his hands on Ashley's cheek in hopes to put her mind at ease, being careful not to irritate her swollen eye.

Seeing Jake and feeling the nurturing being expressed through his touch, she began crying out of her good eye.

"I'm so sorry," Jake whispered to Ashley, wishing he could have been there to protect her. Looking upon her made him feel so helpless, as if he was in the middle of an unwinnable battle, like punching your reflection in the water, no matter how much you disrupt the stillness, once the water settles your reflection will still be there. Seeing the sadness and regret in Jake's eyes, probably blaming himself for what happened to her, wanting to reassure him she would have never thought that for a second. Getting a glimpse of the others in the room, there to make sure she was okay, expecting to see Jeff and Vicki, it was Miss Waters who was an unexpected surprise, whether she was there more for Jake or her, still meant something for her to be there. Everyone trying to get over the initial trauma of witnessing Ashley's current physical condition, seeing her lying there in the hospital bed, beaten and battered, emotionally drained, there wasn't a dry eye in the room, all wishing they could do something to help take away some of her pain. Her wounds will heal, but the damage has already been done, Ashley looking at everyone by her bedside wished Razz would have killed her when he had the chance, rather than have everyone see her in her most vulnerable state, feeling embarrassed and slightly awkward, but if that would have happened, Razz would have won and she would have died for nothing, more importantly she would have broken her lifelong promise to her best friend.

Weak and exhausted, barely able to keep her eyes open, Ashley felt it was necessary to explain to Jeff and Jake what happened. Going into explicit detail of the traumatic episode she recently lived through, the tears started once again, becoming tired of being a constant emotional wreck, afraid she could possibly dehydrate herself from all the persistent crying, bringing up the factors of witnessing Officer Turner being shot and killed right in front of her. Another innocent cop dying in the line of duty, most likely going unnoticed for his acts of bravery and dedication to protecting his community, another life taken away in her presence. As if the mood in the room couldn't get any more depressing and full of dread, hearing what took place during the attempted bust was more than Ashley's visitors could take, the only high point being her professing the violent attack she distributed to Razz allowing her to escape. Immediately Jeff got on his phone to call his contacts on the police force demanding them to go over to the club, communicating the information he just learned of an officer down and a possible wounded suspect. Enraged, Jake wanted to leave to go to the club himself to possibly finish off what Ashley started, feeling like he has failed in protecting her, something he would never be able to live with had she ended up suffering a worse fate, but an act of vigilante justice wasn't going to erase what was already done, would have had to catch him in the act. Having Jake bedside and everyone else in the room with her, was the safest Ashley has felt all night, yet knows this may not still be over.

"If Razz is still alive he's going to come after me," Ashley said in a weak tone.

"I'm not going to let that happen," assured Jake, softly caressing her hair.

A nurse enters the room to check on Ashley, eluding to everyone she will soon be moved to a new room ending their visit for the night. Sad and scared to see everyone having to go, Ashley pleaded with the nurse to allow them to stay longer, only to have her request denied due to hospital rules, being reassured they all could come back tomorrow. No choice but to honor the hospital rules, everyone said their goodbyes, promising to be back, Jake gave Ashley a soft kiss on her forehead telling her to get some rest and he will see her soon. Watching Jake and the others leave her room, a sudden feeling of panic came over her not knowing how safe she was truly going to be.

On their way out, Jake and Jeff had a conversation with whoever was the person in charge, demanding that no one other than the four names he is given, are allowed to visit the patient named Ashley Stamper. Jeff plays the lawyer card, inferring he could bring a lawsuit upon this place if their demands aren't met, trying to scare them into complying. Willing to implement their plea after hearing the situation at hand, the hospital administrator gave Jake and Jeff his word no other person will be allowed in her room other than them, also promising to pass the information onto all the shift administrators. Confident the hospital will keep to their word, they all left, yet Ashley never left their minds. Back at the house, now almost four in the morning, Jake, Jeff and Vicki are in the living room still reeling over what happened to Ashley, the uneasiness they all felt at the hospital traveled back with them like some airborne entity. All of them tired, yet none of them could possibly go to sleep right now, their minds over saturated with thoughts of the teenage girl lying lonely and scared in the hospital. Jeff pacing by the living room window, had to wait until he heard confirmation on what they find at the club before he could even consider laying down to rest, wants verification on Officer Turner's body, wants to know the status of this Razz character. If Ashley's testimony is true about Officer Turner, this will affect Jeff personally having known the veteran cop for many years, would consider him a friend and would be crushed to know he died the way he did. On the couch sitting with is hand over his mouth, staring out almost in a daze, Jake felt powerless as if his world was under someone else's control, worse than it felt during his darkest days. Every second now he is away from Ashley, the more his anger and anxiety rises, not knowing how she feels at this moment being alone in the hospital, not knowing if she really is going to be safe there, still believing he let her down not having enough water when the fire was burning the hottest. Vicki stood by her husband, expressing to him this is the time to let Jake in on his findings now that they are all alone. Agreeing, since he doesn't know how much longer it is going to be until he hears anything about what went down earlier, Jeff goes to sit across from his brother in the love seat, followed closely by Vicki.

"Jake, I know what you must be going through," said Jeff, "and I don't want to make anything worse for you or Ashley, but I still have to tell you something very important."

"What is it?" Jake asked, hearing the unfamiliar nervous tone in his brother's voice. "Is this what you were going to tell me at the hospital?"

"Yes," answered Jeff. "It's about Ashley."

"Jesus, I don't think I could take any more surprises for one night," remarked Jake, stroking his hand through his hair.

"Trust me, you're going to want to hear this," assured Jeff.

"What is it then?" Jake asked, becoming more and more unsure of the news his brother is trying to tell him.

"Jake…," Jeff said grabbing one of Vicki's hands for support. "Wow, I don't know how to say this."

"Just say it," demanded Jake, still surprised his brother is having a hard time communicating anything.

"Jake, Ashley is your daughter," proclaimed Jeff.

"What are you talking about?" Jake asked, executing a stunned giggle, eyes beginning to water.

"That time I went to the State Penitentiary, I went to see Ashley's mother, hoping to get some insight are things. Her mother is Julie, even recognized me, she never had the abortion. To make sure Ashley really was yours, I conned her into telling me the truth, telling her I might be able to pull some strings to get her a reduced sentence. She admitted to hiding her from you as payback for you breaking up with her. She used her mother's maiden name Stamper to keep who she was hidden, a sneaky ploy in her sick game," Jeff replied. "We will do a DNA test to be sure, but I can tell you by listening to her, I'm convinced she is telling the truth."

"You're not kidding with me now, are you?" Jake asked choking hard on his words.

"Jake, no," answered Jeff.

Hearing the confidence in his brother's voice, Jake instantly broke down crying, sobbing like he has never before in his life. Vicki quickly went over to sit down beside him, rubbing his back in an effort to comfort him. Her eyes teared up hearing Jake cry tears of dismay, not every day you learn you have a child out in the world, especially one he was convinced was exposed of years ago. This was the biggest gut punch he has ever taken in his life, doesn't even know how to react other than initially breaking out into tears. Overwhelmed with emotions, Jake's body felt like a car red lining, his hands began to shake uncontrollably, barely able to see straight, nauseous to where he thought he might throw up. With nothing much more he could do or say, Jeff let his brother vacate all of his vehemences, heartbroken to see Jake suffering through this, couldn't imagine what he must be feeling, to suddenly have your life drastically change in the blink of an eye. The situation wasn't easy for Jeff either, discovering he has a niece that he never knew about, in a way his and Vicki's life was about to change as well, welcoming a new addition to the family.

Mumbling to himself under his breath, Jake uttered many derogatory remarks at the expense of his long time ago ex-girlfriend, furious she lied to him all these years when she knew he was willing to be there for her and the baby. Wondering what kind of twisted person would blatantly remove a parent from a kid's life as part of their revenge for an unpretentious high school relationship, knowing both were on different paths, would have never worked out. The girl lying alone and frightened in that hospital bed, now wasn't just the star pitcher on his girls softball team, it was his daughter, immensely intensifying the hurt his was already feeling, realizing Ashley's unthinkable life could have been avoided if it weren't for someone's selfish nature. Brought meaning to why their relationship grew so close over the course of the season, always feeling a kinship and connection with Ashley, explaining why she is such a terrific ballplayer, that's his blood and his talent flowing through her body, an extension of him past on to his offspring. Knowing the truth justifies those strong feelings he has always had for her, would never admit this to anyone, but she was his favorite player, though he cares very much for all the girls on the team. It would be hard on anyone to suddenly have their life dynamics change in an instant, just a few minutes ago he was under the impression he was a childless bachelor, now learning he's a father.

Getting to the end of his hysterical outburst, Jake takes a couple deep breathes to calm himself, being part of the most emotional and life changing night of his life. For all the anger and hurt he was feeling, there was a sense of happiness starting to creep in between the cracks, has a beautiful and talented daughter who will never be alone again. Letting Jeff and Vicki know he is okay, Jake gets off the couch to walk over to the living room window, looking out at the beginning of dawn slowly surfacing in the distance, the reddish orange of the horizon signifying the start of a new day, for Jake and Ashley possibly the start of a new life.

"Jake, you have to tell her," remarked Jeff.

"I know," Jake replied, continuing to stare of the window. "How could she do this?"

"Julie isn't the issue right now," said Jeff. "You have to keep your focus on Ashley. Once I get the feedback I'm waiting for, we can go from there."

"He's still out there," Jake inferred.

"We don't know that yet for sure," said Jeff.

"What do we do in the meantime?" Jake asked.

"We wait," answered Jeff.

The most exhausting and emotional night turned into a hard morning, nobody in the house got no more than three hours sleep, if they even fell asleep at all. Jake tried to get some shut eye, hoping to give himself a break from reality for a couple hours, but managed only to laid there in bed, staring at the ceiling wondering how Ashley was doing. His eyelids felt so heavy, yet he couldn't close them, so worked up no matter how hard he tried to relax, his body and mind just didn't want to turn off for a little while, prisoner of his own thoughts cycling through his head, even having a private teared filled episode. Jeff and Vicki were able to crash for a couple hours, only to be woken by Jeff's cell phone ringing, bringing the news he has been waiting for. As the mid-morning sun shined brightly through the kitchen window, Jake, Jeff and Vicki sat at the kitchen table, each with a cup of coffee, expecting the caffeine to replace the hours of sleep they all missed, everyone still was wearing the same clothes they had on from last night. The mood in the house hasn't changed much, thinking it would slowly squander away during their brief early morning intermission, only to find it was just waiting for them when they got up. Sipping on their coffees assured the last twenty four hours wasn't a dream, Jeff shared the recent information brought to his attention.

"I got a call this morning from one of my contacts on the police force. It was confirmed, Ray Turner was killed," Jeff said with a heavy heart. "As far as this Razz, he was gone. They found the blood on the floor from where Ashley attacked him, but he was nowhere to be found. They talked to a few of his goons and a couple of the other girls, but nobody seems to know where he is or went. The good news is the place is being shut down and is under investigation, Ashley never has to go back there."

"But he's still out there," Jake remarked, feeling all the uneasiness and anxiety come flooding back.

"Unfortunately, yes," replied Jeff, "and with him having no current residence on record other than the club, he could be anywhere."

"Jesus Christ," Jake uttered. "Ashley is not going to be safe at the hospital."

"If you want to go up there and sit with her for as long as you can, I don't blame you, in fact when Vick and I get the time, we are going to visit her too, we can each take a shift staying with her until she is released or visiting hours are over," suggested Jeff.

"Okay, I'm going to take a quick shower and head down there now," Jake said.

"Alright," replied Jeff, "another thing, they found Ashley's backpack with her phone and stuff. One of the officers agreed to drop everything off here later, along with her car. Jake, he killed a cop, they're going to find this guy."

"I hope so," remarked Jake, leaving his seat to exit the kitchen.

Standing at the receptionist's desk, Jake asked one on the on duty front desk attendants which room Ashley Stamper was in. Felt a bit of security when he was asked what his name was, deducing the hospital staff is holding to their word about who they are allowed to let in. Matching Jake's name with one of the four they have on their list, he is given Ashley's room number and floor, thanking the young lady, heads for the elevator to reach the third floor, room 506.

The elevator doors close leaving Jake to be the sole rider to the third floor, never being a fan of this form of transportation, always made him feel slightly claustrophobic, especially when he has to share the small enclosed space. Watching the digital floor counter slowly tick towards his desired level, Jake couldn't help but realize when he sees Ashley again their relationship is going to change forever, this is no longer a coach visiting an injured player, this is a father going to visit his daughter. That revelation hasn't fully sunk in yet, still having a hard time adjusting to his new reality. The elevator doors open to a sea of anxiously waiting pedestrians, Jake exits having to weave through the over baring crowd, supporting a mixture of visitors and hospital staff, unusual even for a Saturday. These latest frequent trips to the hospital are becoming regular occurrences, hasn't been here this much since the multiple surgeries he had on his knees, now Jake sees himself in the reverse role, the concerned visitor rather than the admitted patient. Whatever his role is, he has never been a big fan of health centers, bringing him nothing but disappointment and heartache throughout the years, considers it the place where dreams come to die.

Walking the hallway leading to Ashley's room, Jake sees the all too familiar expressions on the faces of the staff making their way from room to room to care for the sick and injured, the look of doubt and dismay they try to camouflage with their smiles and perky attitudes. Coming up on Room 506, the change in the dynamic between him and Ashley can already be felt on his end, seeing her for the first time as his daughter will bring a whole new narrative to the situation, she may be the same person physically, but a brand-new aura will manifest when they are together, there will now be an unbreakable bond between them, one Jake hopes will begin when he reveals the truth to her. Standing just outside Ashley's room, Jake can see her lying peacefully in her bed looking away from the doorway, though not in her best physical appearance, couldn't help but get a little emotional, cracking a small smile visually seeing her for the first time as his offspring, gently knocking on the open door to alert her of his presence. Turning her head to investigate the knock at her door, Ashley's one good eye gleams at the sight of Jake standing there, a small smile appears on her face. Entering he observed it's a double room, yet isn't sharing it with anyone at the moment, the other half remained silent and in the dark, already feeling the different energy surrounding them, the closer he gets to her, the more his emotions intensify. Pulling a chair up next to her bed, Jake still finds it hard to look at her in her current state, it was tough when it was just her as his pitcher, but now it's his child lying there making her current condition ever more impactful.

"Hey, how are you?" Jake asked.

"Tired," answered Ashley in a low soft tone. "I didn't get much sleep."

"Neither did I," Jake replied.

"When you see the team, I don't want any of them to come up here. I don't want them to see me like this," requested Ashley. "I feel bad enough that I'm letting them down, I can't pitch the rest of the way."

"I wouldn't worry about that," Jake remarked. "You need to just focus on getting healed up and you didn't let anybody down. If anything, I let you down. I should have done a better job of protecting you and I'm sorry."

"This isn't your fault," Ashley said, her one eye beginning to tear up. "You have helped me more than you will ever realize."

Tenderly caressing her face with his hand, Jake was moved by her words of recognition, despite wishing he could have done more. He was also in the company of the most selfless person he had ever met, more worried about disappointing her teammates, rather than concentrating on herself, the defining characteristic of a true leader, no matter the adversity, she will always put others before her, truly a special person and one Jake will proudly call his daughter.

"There is something I have to tell you," mentioned Jake, finding it hard to get the words out. "When your mother told you about your father, she was lying."

"What? What do you mean?" asked Ashley.

"Remember when I told you about the girl I dated in high school and what happened with her? I never told you her name, her name was Julie," Jake said. "Isn't your mother's name Julie?"

"What are you saying?" Ashley asked, tears streaming down her face.

"Ash, I'm your father," stated Jake, getting choked letting the tears flow.

Hearing Jake recite those words she thought she would never hear in her lifetime, Ashley's first reaction was, she was dreaming and any second she was going to wake up still being alone in her hospital room, a hallucinogenic side effect to hear pain medication. But it wasn't a dream, Jake was right there in front of her, feeling his masculine hand against her face. Her mind was racing trying to evaluate the situation, wondering if this was really happening, just moments ago she was a motherless and fatherless teenage girl laying badly wounded in a hospital bed, now she is being told that the man who has been her coach for the past few months, first man she has ever trusted, the man who in many ways has changed her life, is really her biological father. This declaration would be an emotional bombshell to anyone, but to Ashley it felt like the universe was playing a cruel joke on her, life changing moments of this magnitude don't happened to a person like her, convinced the world has always been against her, already taking away her best friend and the person she loved most in her life. Yet seeing her reflection in Jake's teared filled eyes and hearing the emotional tone in his voice, Ashley knew he was telling the truth.

"What? Are you being serious?" asked Ashley, continuing to let the tears flow.

"I am," Jake answered grabbing her unicasted hand, squeezing it softly, letting his touch reiterate his response. "Your mother lied to you, she lied to me, but now we found each other."

Unable to control her emotions through the realization that this miraculous moment is actually happening, Ashley breaks down crying tears of happiness, so overjoyed the pain from her injuries seemed to subside, leaving her to feel like she is laying on a cloud rather than a hospital bed. The ironies of life sometimes work in funny ways, coming off the worse week she has ever experienced, leading her to the greatest day in her life. The father her mother refused to tell her about, the one she said she had no idea who he was, was now directly in front of her, making her for that brief moment the happiest person in the world, encountering an emotional high not even her current medications could achieve. Ashley always felt a connection with Jake, yet she couldn't explain why, thinking maybe it was because they both had love for the game, but now understands the reasons for those instincts culminating in the results she never thought were possible.

Jake leaned in to embrace Ashley sharing their first hug as father and daughter, crying in each other's arms, a void in their lives suddenly seemed filled.

Holding her tightly, Jake can feel Ashley's body trembling, latching on to him as if never wanting to let go, repairing the desecration on her heart from Holley J's death. Hearing her shed tears of happiness upon his shoulder, Jake was revealed his revelation for the next act in his life, being a father to this special and mistreated young girl, instantaneously feeling that unconditional love a parent feels for their child. Coaching quickly became his new love in the game and he doesn't see himself stopping any time soon, but his true calling was wrapped snugged in his goosebump filled arms.

"So what now?" Ashley asked, returned to her original position in the bed.

"We will have to do a DNA test to confirm," replied Jake. "But we're already a hundred percent certain. Your mother confessed everything."

"I hate her so much," confessed Ashley.

"Yeah, the feeling at this point is mutual," Jake remarked.

"When did you get into contact with her?" asked Ashley.

"I didn't, your Uncle Jeff paid her a visit wanting to get some answers," Jake said.

"My Uncle Jeff," remarked Ashley, flashing a big smile, "this is going to take some time to get used to."

"For me too," Jake confessed, "but now you have a real family, who is always going to treat you the way you deserve to be treated."

Those words sent a warmth through Ashley's body she couldn't describe, smiling, letting out more tears of exultation, she was living her fairy tale ending, only thing that could make it better was if Holley J was there to be a part of it. However the villain of her story was still out there, putting a hindrance on her moments of jubilation.

"What happened with Razz?" Ashley asked, even with Jake by her bedside, a touch of fear in her voice could be heard saying his name.

"They can't find him and nobody seems to know where he is," informed Jake, wanting to be honest with her.

"You know he's going to come after me," Ashley insisted in a worried tone.

"I'm not going to let that happen," declared Jake, gently stroking her hair. "You never have to go back there or see him again. An officer is dropping your car and backpack off from the club to the house later."

"My phone was is in the backpack," Ashley mentioned.

"You want your phone?" asked Jake.

"No, you have to get rid of it," Ashley ordered. "I think he tracks all the girls through their phones, probably why he hasn't found me here yet."

"Okay," replied Jake, igniting various thoughts and proposals to start cycling through his mind. "I'll make sure that is taken care of."

Back home, letting Jeff and Vicki visit with Ashley for a while, Jake was looking after the twins until he was able to return to the hospital later, deciding to leave in hopes of repossessing Ashley's phone. Seeing her car parked back in the driveway upon his arrival, indicated her backpack must have been returned as well. With the weather outside becoming gray and gloomy, expecting a thunderstorm soon, the twins remained in their room to play. Jake sat at the kitchen table sending out a team wide text informing the girls of what happened to Ashley, being as vague as possible, advising them she had an accident leaving her with a broken wrist and a few bumps and bruises, reiterating she was going to be fine, but will be lost for the remainder of the season.

Honoring Ashley's request he mentioned how she doesn't want a fuse, just wants to be alone for a few days, but will be at the next game to root the girls on. In an overreacting type of way, Jake started to wonder if his team was cursed, first what happened to Holley J and now with Ashley, rationalizing with himself that these were just horrible coincidences and the well-being of the rest of his players are no way in jeopardy. Making a quick call to Danielle giving her an update on Ashley's condition, informing her he has some big news to tell, but is going to need to sort some stuff out first and will call her when it is done. Being the down to earth, reasonable, understanding woman that she is, Danielle simply respected Jake's need for some time, declaring she will be here when he is ready. Done contacting all those obligated, Jake leaves the kitchen to head up to Ashley's room. First peeking in on the twins making sure they didn't kill each other, finding them both asleep on the floor for a little afternoon nap, not wanting to disturb them, he closes their bedroom door partially, knowing the girls are safe and sound, Jake redirects to Ashley's room. Inside he finds out he was right, seeing her backpack resting on her bed. Opening the bag, he finds some clothes and a small makeup purse, looking through one of the outer pouches is where he finds her phone along with her keys. Tossing the backpack aside, Jake attempts to open her phone only to discover she has it locked with a finger pattern. Tries various patterns, yet repeatedly is unsuccessful, determined to draw every pattern possible until the phone unlocks. After what seemed like over hundreds of attempts, his fingerprints smeared all over the glass screen, Jake finally draws the correct pattern unlocking the phone. A sense of relief comes over him, worried it would turn out to be a hopeless endeavor, he makes a mental note of right pattern while checking her missed calls and texts messages. No missed calls were shown, however she had a couple of text messages from Razz, neither was long in length, yet both were very threatening. Viewing the time the texts were sent, Jake observed they were sent late last night, confirming that he is still out there. Reading those alarming words directed at Ashley infuriated Jake, realizing this guy wasn't going to stop until she breathed her last breath.

Leaving her room pocketing the phone, Jake swiftly headed to his room, making a quick stop to check on the twins who are still enjoying a peaceful nap. Down in his room, he heads straight for his dresser, opening the top drawer pulling out a pistol, a black .45 caliber ACP which he bought during his playing career. Never a fan of guns, but a professional athlete living alone at the time, needed something to protect himself from the countless unstable fan base that saturates society. The piece had only been fired a handful of times, strictly at firing ranges where he learned how to shoot. Giving the gun a glance over reveals it's still loaded, Jake stands there with his eyes closed taking a couple deep breathes visualizing what needs to be done.

Sometimes there comes a point in a man's life where he must go against everything he stands for becoming, for a temporary moment, a mere shadow of his former self regardless of the outcome. Driven by hatred and the desire to protect what is his, all that matters now is Ashley's safety.

Jeff and Vicki returned home after a few hours in order to let Jake return to the hospital, they would have stayed a little longer, but Vicki had plans to take the twins to the mall to do a little shopping and Jeff had some business to take care of, most of it revolving around Ashley, keeping in constant contact with the police hoping to learn any new news. Reentering the house they find Jake in the kitchen making the girls some lunch, serving them their favorite sandwiches of bacon, lettuce and tomatoes, discovering it to be hard to act normal around the twins when he has so much aggression building up and endless thoughts circulating through his mind. Vicki relieves Jake of his post, taking over so she can get the girls ready when they finish eating, implying she will handle the slight mess, allowing him to go spend more time with his daughter. Giving Vicki an appreciative hug, he leaves the kitchen, being pulled aside by Jeff for a private conversation.

"I see you told her," Jeff said, "she seems still in shock over it."

"Yeah," replied Jake, "I think we all are."

"She is still scared about what this Razz character will do," Jeff said.

"I know and I am too," replied Jake.

"What's on your mind?" Jeff asked, reading Jake's expression and uncontrollable mannerisms like a book, rapid eye movement with rare unfamiliar facial tics, perfect visual evidence of someone with a lot on their mind. He knows damn well his brother is up to something, afraid he is becoming a prisoner of the moment which may lead him to do something he may regret, yet no one, brother or otherwise, should stop a man from being a father, willing to risk more in his short stint as a parent then most other guys would in a lifetime.

"Nothing," answered Jake, totally aware his brother will see right through him, learning many years ago you can't keep the truth hidden from him for very long.

"It's not nothing," Jeff remarked. "Jake, they'll find him."

"This time I don't think so," stated Jake. "I'm going back up there to be with her. I just wanted to say thank you for all your help, I couldn't have done all this without you, but I just have to know that you have my back no matter what."

"What are you going to do?" Jeff asked, looking at his brother who gives him no answer. "Of course, I always got your back," he said as the two of them embrace in a brotherly hug.

Walking away from his brother in a posture and body language emblematic of someone with purpose, displaying a non-pessimistic attitude, Jake heard Jeff call for him.

"Jake," he called out waiting for a response.

Stopping his hasty exit, Jake turned back to look his brother in the face once again, greeted by Jeff sending a couple light nods.

Pulling into the hospital's visitors parking lot, Jake exits his truck carrying a couple of white paper bags, deciding to bring some dinner for him and Ashley, bringing her favorite, grilled chicken salad with a side of fruit. Nobody is ever a big fan of hospital food, thought it would be nice to bring her something she might enjoy. Standing out his truck, bags in hand, he pulls out Ashley's phone he had in his back pocket. Gaining access, Jake does some quick scrolling and key manipulation before slamming the phone to the ground, continually stomping on it with the heel of his boot until it was in a thousand pieces. Taking a deep breath to consume some of the fresh, stormbound evening air, Jake heads for the entrance hearing the gray cloud covered sky starting to talk producing a couple cracks of thunder.

Jake walks up to the receptionists desk in a deliberate and careful stride trying not to draw attention to himself, wearing a burgundy fleece jacket which hangs slightly below his waist, acting as normal and carefree as he can. Checking in, letting the woman peek into the bags to examine their contents, he went on his way to the elevators to head for Ashley's room. Walking away, Jake had a paranoid feeling he was being watched, looking back to find out would only add to his possible onlookers suspicions, favoring to just keep moving hoping he is just overreacting. Standing in front a pair of elevator doors waiting for them to open, Jake spots out of the corner of his eye, a security guard walking the hallway in his direction, bringing him to tense up, tightening his grip on the two bags anxious for the elevator to arrive, keeping his sights forward refusing to make subtle eye contact. As the guard inches closer, the elevator finally opens to the relief of Jake, entering he watches with concerned eyes the guard continue on his way past his location. Taking his private ride to the third floor, more feelings of paranoia surrounded him, thought he was being watched through the elevator camera, rejecting to look at it directly. It felt like the longest elevator ride he has ever been on, even though he was alone, it felt like he was the unintentional center of attention for reasons he may or may not be aware of, afraid when the doors open there will be a group of security guards waiting to apprehend him. But that never happened, arriving at the third floor the doors opened to a number of anticipating passengers, none of which were security or hospital staff members, assuming his over-suspicions are all in his head, Jake departed the elevator to head for Ashley's room.

Dinner was delicious, Ashley thanked Jake for bringing it, wasn't sure how much more she could take of eating the hospital's bland and unappetizing food, luckily only having to stomach it for one more day before being released. Happy to be spending more time with Jake again, though she did enjoy Jeff and Vicki's visit, now knowing the truth, there is something more magical about having her biological father present, there is no way they could ever make up the time they missed together, all they can do is just start fresh to build a strong enough relationship filled with much love and respect to make the eighteen years they were apart an afterthought. Sitting up in her bed, observing Jake cleaning up the minimal mess made by their take-out dinners, Ashley sensed some personal inner conflict in him, saying very little while they ate, seemed nervous, like something is weighing heavily on his mind.

"Are you okay?" asked Ashley.

"Yeah, I'm fine," Jake answered with a slight smile. "I should be asking you that question."

"Jeff seems to think they will find Razz. What do you think? Do you believe him?" asked Ashley with worry in her eyes.

"To be honest, I don't know," Jake replied, grabbing her hand. "What I do know is he will never hurt you again, that is a promise."

"I'm just glad you're here," Ashley remarked, having for the first a true protector and guardian by her side, a couple of many gallant attributes of a true father, this being all new to her, conflicted on what to even call him now, not yet comfortable calling him Dad, "'cause I'm still scared."

"I know you are," said Jake, "but soon it will be over."

Optimism was refreshing to hear, but nobody knows Razz like Ashley does and if you become a target of his that usually translates into your days being numbered, always prepared and always gets what he wants. Letting out a large yawn, becoming sleepy from her earlier medication, she lays back down to prepare to fall asleep, Jake's cue that's it's time to leave, visiting hours were ending soon anyway. Kissing her softly on the forehead, he whispers something in her ear as her eyes slowly close. Seeing the darkness behind her shut eyes, Ashley hears the sound of her room door latching, leaving her alone once again.

Ashley's peaceful sleep became interrupted by the calling of nature, her full bladder needed to be emptied if she was ever going to revisit her slumbering state. Carefully getting out of bed, her bare feet land on the cold tiled floor sending a slight chill through her body, the back of her hospital gown was coming undone exposing much of her backside. Barely awake, she walks to the room's restroom in the mild darkness, only light source coming from the machines near her bed and the light from the hallway piercing through the small window on the room door. Ashley noticed the shower curtain like divider that separates the room was full extended, figuring maybe one of the nurses did it and she didn't remember. There was a strong silence in the room, yet she could hear some of the outside noise beyond her room walls. Entering the restroom leaving the door open a crack, she flips on the light, squinting heavily from the extreme brightness, attentively seating herself on the toilet, still very uncomfortable to be in the seated position. A sense of physical relief came letting the urine flow out of her, cringing a little as her private area is still a bit tender. As the last few drops hit the water below, Ashley grabs a few pieces of the sand paper like toilet tissue hanging on the roll beside her, gently wiping the necessary spots. Getting up, she goes to stand over the sink looking at her messed up face in the mirror, it's the first time seeing it since it happened refusing to look at it before, staring at the person she knew would eventually show up, seeing her face like that hit her harder than any of Razz' punches. No seventeen-year-old girl should ever have their face look like what she is looking at outside of a bad car accident, wanting to cry but couldn't, hard to feel sorry for herself when she knew the possible outcome of the life she was manipulated into living. What she really wanted was a shower, needing to feel the warm water coating her skin, splashing on her face, has felt exceedingly dirty since she has arrived to the hospital, the first thing she will treat herself too when returning back to the house.

Craving the sensation of the liquid warmth against her face, Ashley turned on the faucet getting the water to her desired temperature, using her good hand to splash a couple handfuls at her face, being careful not to irritate her wounds. The warmth of the water on her face felt so good, a common ritual she would perform when she had trouble sleeping, instantly relaxing her. Letting the excess water drip back into the sink, she turned off the faucet looking back into the mirror only to be greeted by the horrific sight of Razz' hooded reflection standing behind her. Before Ashley could even let out a scream, he had her back side pressed up against the sink with a hand forcefully covering her mouth.

"You really thought you could get away from me, Show Horse," Razz whispers. "I'm not going to let some teenage, fucking whore get the best of me. Besides, we've have got some unfinished business," he whispers, putting his free hand under her gown to rub her genitals.

Feeling Razz' fingers start to insert into her vagina, Ashley screams as loud as she could only to have her cries for help muffled by the immense pressure of his hand casing her mouth. Tears escaping from her good eye, she frantically tries to knock away his hand from in between her legs to no avail, rediscovering how strong Razz really is. Struggling to free herself, feeling the cold porcelain of the sink pressing uncomfortably up against the small of her back, Ashley instinctively knees Razz in the groin allowing her to break free for a brief moment, previous to him grabbing her by the hair impeding her escape. Pulling her back, Razz grabs her, angrily throwing her out of the restroom where she slides across the floor on her backside, hearing the squeaking of her exposed skid rubbing against the tile. Racing over to kneel himself over Ashley's body, Razz covers her mouth with his hand once again, pulling out a large switchblade from his backside.

"We could have been great together, Show Horse," Razz said, unveiling the shiny, sizable blade. "Too bad it has to end this way."

Cocking his arm back in a stabbing motion, the sound of close by gun fire was heard, Razz feeling the burning sensation of a bullet penetrating the flesh of his shoulder knocking him off Ashley, who quickly scurries across the floor to sit against the wall next to her bed. Dropping the knife to the ground, Razz slowly turns his injured body over to see where the shot came from, when he greeted to another barrel flash, this time the bullet entering his chest area rendering him motionless. A stunned, crying Ashley looked over to see Jake standing there pointing the gun with an outstretched arm, smoke still protruding out of the muzzle. Immediately going over to tend to her, the two of them embrace as she cries heavily.

"It's over," Jake whispers in her ear, feeling her body shaking, hugging him tightly.

Jake never left, hiding behind the room divider the entire time. It was his plan from the very beginning, ever since he learned Razz was still out there. Hoping to use his one flawed character trait against him, guys like Razz are obsessed with getting what they want and will stop at nothing until they get it. He wasn't going to stop until he got hold of Ashley again, but he wasn't going to do it in a place where they would be alone, fearing it would be a set-up and he would be ambushed. Razz was too smart for that, would rather wait to she was somewhere that had a lot of people, yet can get her alone, what better place than a hospital where he could disguise himself as a visitor and dispose of her silently. If he was tracking her on the phone, then he knew the phone was left at the club for a while, yet she wouldn't be there. Once Razz saw the phone was in a different location, Jake hoped he assumed the phone was back in Ashley's possession. Banking on Razz constantly monitoring the phone's whereabouts, when he saw the phone ended up at the hospital, he would conclude she was there, especially after what he did to her. Using his instincts, Jake would bet with his life Razz would show up there, even giving him an unneeded push through a well strategic text before destroying the phone. Everything after that was just dumb luck, fate was definitely on his side this night. All that mattered in the end is he got the son of bitch and Ashley would be safe, got the rat to come to the cheese.

The past couple of months have been a major life changing experience for Ashley and Jake and the rest of the household. Before being discharged from the hospital, she and Jake had a DNA test done confirming 99.99% that he was her father. Thanks to Jeff's mastery of knowing the law, Jake was only given six months community service for his, what was being called a heroic act and was still able to keep his job as coach of the Lady Saints. Discouragingly Razz wasn't killed that night in the hospital, the first bullet shattered his shoulder, while the second just missed his heart, had to have surgery before he was arrested and convicted on multiple charges, including first degree murder of a police officer. The club has been closed and taken over by the city, all the girls on Razz' payroll spilled their grievances to the cops, finding their liberation finally being free from his dictatorship type regime. News traveled to their ears it was Ashley who sacrificed herself to put an end to his criminal and abusive ways, almost getting killed in the process, all of them wishing they could thank her personally, feeling regretful they never gave her a chance. More of the same came from his guards, most of them sang like canaries in exchange for reduced or no jail time, a few of them got away and are on the run, but it's only a matter of time before they are found and apprehended. One guard even gave up Razz' secret vault, having once seen him enter a particular part of the wall in his office. Bringing in the best tech people, they were able to bypass Razz' high end security system to enter and find a mother lode of more evidence. Some of his security that had been with him the longest showed their loyalty by keeping their mouth shut, but in the end it really didn't matter, Razz was looking at life in prison and the ironic shame a man of his intellect will have to live with for the rest of his life. Through all his perfectly planned criminal exploits, running his business with total command over everyone, to him paying off much of the police, it was a seventeen-year-old girl, his golden goose, that became his undoing.

Attending Holley J's funeral was extremely emotional for Ashley, the alter at the church was beautifully decorated with many bouquets of her favorite flowers nestled on each side of a large portrait of Holley J with the elegant urn housing her ashes stationed front and center. Holley J's parents decided to have her cremated so they could have her remains be close to them, believing having her ashes in the house will bring her spirit home. They could never argue what Ashley meant to their daughter, despite their differences, in an act of goodwill, Holley J's parents gave Ashley a small gift before the ceremony, a small tube about the size of a paperclip, full of some of Holley J's ashes so part of her could be with her at all times. Touched and moved by the gesture, Ashley embraced Holley J's parents thanking them as both parties shared a few tears. So focused on remembering their daughter, Holley J's parents never even question why Ashley had her wrist in a cast and a few cuts and bruises on her face, luckily the swelling of her eye was completely healed. Wishing her good luck on all her future endeavors and their house will always be open for a visit. Giving a touching eulogy that didn't leave a dry eye to anyone in attendance which included Jake and all the girls from the team. Shedding her far share of tears talking about her best friend, Ashley wished so badly Holley J was there to see all that has happened, always be a part of her heart that will be forever broken.

Though Ashley was there to cheer on her teammates for the final game of the season and their first ever playoff game, wearing the small tube of Holley J's ashes as a neckless, the team just wasn't the same without her on the mound, losing both games. Watching the team play and Jake's expert coaching, she knew the team was always going to be in good hands and just fine. Their season may have ended in disappointment, but in Ashley's and the team's eyes it was a huge success, they won in the most important aspect, self-respect, they were shown they were never losers, but winners without the right guidance, Jake was always the missing piece of the puzzle, not just for the team, but for Ashley too, it would be a season they will never forget. Deep down inside she will always feel bad for letting the team down, possibly costing them to miss out on a State Championship, but as Jake would say, her life will always be more important than any game or any great season. The night after the playoff loss, Ashley gave Jake the painting she did of him, bringing elated tears to his eyes, rendering him speechless, totally amazed at the attention to detail presented, one of the most thoughtful gifts he had ever received, knowing the time and effort she had to put in to immortalize him on canvas, promising it will be on full display when he finds his own place for the two of them.

Since the realization of who they truly are to each other, Ashley and Jake have spent as much time as possible together and they couldn't be happier about it, from having private practice sessions at local parks, to just taking a trip to mall or going to see a movie together, Jake even took her to take the campus tour of the college she will be attending in the fall, becoming more and more excited to have this opportunity she worked so hard for. Some of their outings together welcomed a just as happy Danielle, who Jake reconnected with after he was in the clear, explaining everything to her, not leaving out a single detail. Blown away and especially shocked at the acknowledgement Ashley is Jake's daughter, once the initial surprise wore off, she was deeply happy for both of them having found each other after all this time, looking forward to her becoming as much a part of her life as Jake.

Always optimistic and understanding, Danielle stood by everything Jake did, knowing it couldn't have been easy for him, just relieved it was all over so they could be together again.

The last few weeks of school were hard for Ashley at times, certain events came about that she was planning on doing with Holley J, like prom, though she was asked by at least two dozen guys, cast and all, she politely turned them all down having really no interest in going, not just because of Holley J, but because it's a superficial, over exaggerated high school ritual promoted to be every girls dream night, when in reality it's responsible for more loses of a girl's innocence and pregnancies than long lasting memories. Never one to dress like a princess, wearing some over expense garment she would never wear again, if Holley J were there, she would have went because it would have meant so much to her, but since she is gone, Ashley had no reason to go, wasn't going to go with some random guy she has no interest in just for the sake of going, having more meaningful memories to start making, prom night she hung out with Jake and Danielle, going out for a nice dinner, followed by a fun trip to the arcade and miniature golf. Many girls from the team, including Renee, desperately tried to convince her to go, thought it would be a good way to get her mind off things, but totally understood why she preferred not to. Jake and Ashley had been discussing for a while a matter that they needed to face head on if there was ever going to be closure for a particular chapter in their lives.

The security guard scanned the door leading to the visitors' area allowing Ashley's mother to enter and take her seat on the prisoners' side of the glass, coming face to face with Ashley who had a not so pleasant look on her face, peering at her mother with a heated stare that could have burned a hole through the glass between them, each picking up the phone receiver on their side.

"It's good to see you," said Ashley's mother, her aged appearance hasn't changed since the last time the two of them were in this room together.

"I'm not the one that has come to see you," Ashley replied.

"What do you mean?" Ashley's mother asked, watching Ashley get up from her seat leaving her to view an empty chair, quickly becoming occupied by an angry and upset Jake,

"Oh my God, Jake!"

"Why the hell didn't you tell me?" Jake asked with the same heated stare.

Ashley's mother sat there like a deer in the headlights, looking at a face she hasn't seen in nearly two decades.

"TELL ME!" he yells, slamming his free hand against the glass startling her.

Never one to beat around the bush, he could have sat there pointing out all her faults, all the horrible decisions she made, degrade her on what a terrible mother she was, but there would be nothing to gain from exposing the obvious, wanted just to say what he had bottled up inside once he learned the truth.

"You should have never broken up with me!" Ashley's mother said loudly.

Jake shaking his head in disbelief that a person can be so selfish and devious, finding it hard to believe this was the same person he once had strong feelings for.

"You were going to make it big and I was supposed to be there with you!"

"Is that what this was all about, money?" asked Jake. "It wasn't really me you wanted to be with, it was the person I was capable of being, wasn't it? And I was too stupid to figure that out. It sickens me that I ever had feelings for you, true feelings, but you're nothing more than a gold digging bitch and you ruined the life of MY DAUGHTER!!! You had no right to do what you did, I should have been there, I wanted to be there, what happened between us should have never been taken out on her. I just came here to tell you that you are never going to see MY DAUGHTER again, I hope you burn in hell, enjoy your time."

Throwing the phone receiver against the glass, Jake gets up to walk away, hearing Ashley's mother yelling angrily, standing up pounding her fist on the glass. During her mother's tirade, Ashley walks up to slowly and gently place the receiver back where it belongs, displaying a caddie grin on her face while keeping focused on her mother, a metaphorical act of shutting her out for good. Still shouting for the attention of her two visitors, Ashley's mother watches as Jake and her daughter walk out completely ignoring her childish behavior.

A milestone in Ashley's life was recently celebrated, her eighteenth birthday, which became the most special birthday of her life so far, not because she was turning eighteen, but for the first time she was able to celebrate with an actual family, her family. Jake and everybody making a fuss would have been an understatement, treating her like royalty on her special day. Doing everything from leaving happy birthday balloons all around the house and tied to her car, bringing her to the mall for an extravagant shopping spree, where she increased her dwindling wardrobe mainly with athletic gear and few pieces of girlish articles that happen to catch her eye, also adding a few more pairs of sneakers. Vicki and Danielle treated her to her first massage and facial, having a girls-only session, ending the day with dinner at one of the city's finest restaurants, some swanky five star establishment which happens to be world renowned for its seafood, a place that lived up to the hype as Ashley had one of the best lobster bisque and shrimp scampi her taste buds ever had the pleasure of experiencing. One of her many gifts was a new phone courtesy of Jake, being responsible for the destruction of her old one, giving her the newest iPhone on the market, a new phone to a teenage girl gets the same reception and gratitude as if you were to hand her keys to a brand-new car. Overall it wasn't just the best birthday Ashley ever had, but one of the best days in general, the only thing putting a slight damper on it was the fact Holley J wasn't there, it was the first birthday in ten years without her, but she had Holley J's ashes around her neck helping her to feel like she was.

Ashley's life has drastically changed some much since that night in the hospital at times it felt almost overwhelming, but in a good way, everything she ever wanted and everything she always thought she deserved was around her now. Living so long the type of life she had become her normal, readjusting to a life without all the abuse and derogatory and belittling remarks will take time, still having some of her demons to contend with, all cultivating into the hopes of a new normal. The fairytale ending she thought would be impossible for someone like her was happening, her old life was gone, being pushed further and further back with each passing day, taking with it her other identity that died the moment Jake's bullets entered Razz' body. For the first in her life, Ashley can look at herself in the mirror and smile at what she sees, the monster that would once stare back at her was now gone, replaced with the beauty that was never visible, finally being able to view what it was Holley J, Jake and others saw. The world works in mysterious ways, who could have ever thought the man who changed and saved her life would turn out to be her father, someone she believed was going to be absent from her life forever. Happiness was an emotion rarely felt by Ashley when she wasn't on the mound or standing in front of a blank canvas, those brief fixations only occurred when she was around Holley J, eliminating the three people from her existence that made her life a living hell, contributed to the rare emotion happening more frequently, it is the happiest she has ever been and can only see it improving from here on out.

The next stage in Ashley's life will probably be the most difficult yet, full of new roads and challenges, but this time will have the loving support of an actual parent and family. No one can predict the future, but you can guide it in the direction you want it to go, given a new lease on life and nothing now to distract her, Ashley plans on working harder than she ever has before, putting all her focus and energy into being the best possible version of herself, wanting to honor a promise she made to Holley J. During this epilogue portion of her life, Ashley remembered a quote she once heard,

"Hiding your hurt only intensifies it. Problems grow in the dark and become bigger and bigger, but when exposed to the light of truth, they shrink. You are only as sick as your secrets. So take off your mask, stop pretending you're perfect and walk into freedom."

Another tough day on the calendar was upon Ashley, Holley J's birthday, she would have turned eighteen today. Days like these don't make Ashley's pain feeling any better, had a special day planned for her BFF, was going to surprise her with a day trip to a local spa and wellness center, something Holley J always wanted to try, then surprise her with a pair of ear rings she been eyeing for a long time. There are still many moments when Ashley can't believe she is gone and this being Holley J's special day, wanted to honor her memory giving her gift that would last forever.

Parking her car in town, Ashley enters what is said to be the best tattoo parlor in the city, every artist working there is highly regarded and have nothing but positive reviews according to their website. Having made an appointment, she is brought in back by the girl working up front, an obvious regular to the needle as both her arms are completely covered in very colorful tattoos, standing out even more contrasting against her long jet black hair. Definitely not a look Ashley is looking to achieve, always has seen tattoos as kind of tacky, especially when they are overdone, but a small one here or there that has significant meaning behind it can be very special. Greeted by a overweight, biker looking dude with a tattooed bald head and long braided beard, also covered in ink where his skin is exposed, Ashley has a seat in the parlor chair. Explaining what she wants done, pulls out a piece of paper from her satchel, with a symbol she created drawn on it, pointing to the underside of her left wrist as the location.

"Do you want it to say anything?" asked the tattoo artist.

"'Holley J, BFFs forever,'" Ashley said.

Graduation day has come for the seniors of John Franklin High, it's been customary for the school to hold the ceremony on the football field, allowing for use of the stands so family members and friends had access to plenty of seating. Having the ceremony outside is always a gamble, relying on unpredictable weather conditions, but the school always has a contingency plan for such dilemmas. Today, however, the weather couldn't be better, sun shining bright, limited clouds in the sky, warm but not too hot with the occasional light breeze, perfect temperature for outdoor activities. The school's graduation committee did a fantastic job decorating the field and the stage that has to be rebuilt every year for the students to walk across to receive their diplomas, school colors represented everywhere from the balloons, to the streamers and banners, to all the paper décor strategically placed. Ashley and her classmates, dressed in their caps and gowns were waiting anxiously behind the field stands to make their entrance, viewing all who came to watch hurry to get to their seats. Starting off the ceremony, Principal Davis stood behind the podium on the stage to address the crowd, explaining what to expect during the festivities, delivering the clichéd speech of how he never had a group of seniors quite like this and they're the best graduating class he has ever had.

Finishing his opening statements full of bad jokes and purposely placed puns, Principal Davis introduced the graduating class to a thunderous applause. The students walked out single file heading for their designated seats, boys wore black while the girls were in gold, hearing the graduation theme music playing through the outdoor audio system. Ashley coming out towards the end of the line with the S's, looked up into the over packed stands knowing exactly where to look to find Jake and the others, waving up to be captured on video on all their phones, consistent with the mass sea of other phones being held high to snare the memorable moment. Filing into her row to get to her seat, Ashley recollected how often she thought she would never be alive to see this day, yet here she is, sitting amongst her peers waiting for her name to be called to collect the document that will be the start of her new life. More happy she was able to enjoy this day with her face fully healed and cast free. The class valedictorian came up to the podium to give his speech to the crowd and graduating class, saying something that caught Ashley's attention: *"Allow yourself to grow and change, your future self is waiting."* Those words almost seemed meant for her, having a lot of healing to do, yet looking forward to seeing the outcome. Part of his address even paid tribute to their lost classmate, a gesture bringing a smile to Ashley's face hearing Holley J's name mentioned. Looking back at the crowd in the direction of Jake, smiling again, seeing him, Jeff, Vicki, Danielle and even the twins were there to show their support. Vicki was right, though she misses Holley J terribly, wishing she was here and would never trade her life for anything, gained a family in return.   It was time for the handing out of the diplomas. Students were lined up by the small staircase leading onto the stage waiting to hear their name be called so they can have their individual moment of walking alone across the stage, shaking hands with Principal Davis and one of the school's superintendents. Every student heard their portion of visitors in the crowd cheer and yell out chants, some took the opportunity to ham it up, engaging in some sort of goofy dance drawing laughter from the other students and much of the onlookers. Ashley was next in line having gotten to the S's, standing halfway up the staircase in white heels, waiting to hear her name.

"Ashley Stamper," announces Principal Davis.

The sound of her name coming through the speakers resonated as a proclamation of her own personal victory. Walking across the stage, feeling the warm sun against her face, her gown and hair slightly flapping in the breeze, Ashley can hear Jake and the others cheering and whistling loudly as if they were trying to outdo everyone else, while taking videos of her big moment. Receiving her diploma, it's customary to have your picture taken with Principal Davis from the photographers standing in front of the stage, shaking his hand waiting for the okay to exit the stage. Ashley walks off carrying her Leather grain custom diploma cover a high school graduate, an accomplishment meaning more to her than it probably would anybody else considering what she had to go through to get to this point. Heading back to her seat, she holds the diploma high in the air, flashing it to Jake and the others in self-celebration, through all the wins she stacked up on the mound, this was by far her greatest victory.

After another dinner to celebrate her graduation, this time going to a more laid back establishment upon Ashley's request, finding the more upscale dining experiences to be nice and charming, but intimidating at the same time, tonight she felt like going to a regular roadhouse type place for a good steak, finds herself back at the house in her room sitting on her bed doing some web searching on her laptop. Checking her emails, she came across the one sent to her by Holley J a while back, the one she promised she wouldn't read it until after graduation, feeling bad and guilty she almost forgot about it. Dragging the cursor over to open it, Ashley began feeling a bit emotional wondering if she is going to be able to handle what is on the other side of the double tap, coming from Holley J she can expect it to be just about anything. Opening up the email displays a video message, instantly bringing Ashley to tears seeing Holley J again alive and her usual bubbly self, hearing her voice alone gave Ashley goosebumps.

"*Hey Ash, oh my God can you believe we just graduated, also hoping when you play this message we are State champs. It's been a crazy four years to say the least, but we made a lot of great memories together. I'm so glad me and you didn't drift apart once high school started like most friends tend to do. I'm so excited to have us start our new lives after high school, I know we will be going to different schools, but I know that won't stop us from doing our thing. Hoping you will find some nice college boy to finally bring you out of your shell, you are way to pretty to be single all the time. Don't worry, I will keep you up to date on all the juicy details and rumors coming from my campus, you know that part of me isn't going away. I just wanted to thank you for always being there for me, I don't think I could have gotten through high school without you. You've been my best friend ever since I glued my hand to your butt in third grade, I couldn't ask for a better friend or person in my life, you're my hero, my inspiration, I just wanted you to know that. I know you are going to be great playing college ball, I will be following your career there, hopefully I get a chance to make it to a game. Go and be the person I know you are and can be, remember I will always be there for you no matter what, I love you, BFFs forever,*" video ended with Holley J blowing a kiss towards the screen.

Tears streaming down Ashley's face through the whole video, painful to watch, breaking her heart every second it played, yet couldn't help but feel grateful, smiling a few times through her sadness, having documented footage of Holley J being herself, to see her face and hear her voice, something she can keep forever. Wasn't a bit surprised Holley J did something like this, always saying she was born to be in front of a camera, a great talker too, could always make Ashley cry if she wanted to, would have been an awesome journalist.

Wanting to archive this special video, saving it to her hard drive under the caption "Never Delete."

The day has come, it's Friday and college classes start on Monday, time for Ashley to head to campus to get situated. Got her car all packed with everything she wanted to bring, mostly just clothes, a brand-new laptop she bought over the summer and few miscellaneous items that remind her of home in case she starts to get homesick, full tank of gas, plenty to make the short two hour drive. Being a high profile recruit of the school, there is supposed to be an upperclassman to meet with her when she arrives to show her around, scheduled for about three hours from now. Waited all summer for this moment, yet her building excitement is rapidly turning to nervousness, fully coming to the realization that this is really happening, once she gets into her car to start driving, a completely new world awaits her, one she must face alone, even with Jake and everyone just a couple hours away, she will be a stranger in a strange land beginning the building blocks to the better life she has been given the opportunity to obtain.

Wanting to be there when Ashley takes her first steps towards her future greatness, Jake was granted permission to follow her down, being told there was no way she was going to start her first day without him by her side. Everyone decided to tag along to witness the occasion, allowing Jake to ride with Ashley while Jeff, Vicki, and Danielle would follow close behind, it was heartfelt gestures like that Ashley was still getting use too, reminders of what it is like to have a real family be there to support her.

Driving through town on their way to the campus, Ashley needed to make a quick stop at the grocery store to pick up some extra toiletries. Parking fairly close to the entrance, she runs in leaving Jake in the car estimating being only a few minutes. The store not too busy, made it easier for her to grab what she needed and head for the checkout. Carrying just around six items, Ashley was able to use the express lane, dropping what she had on the belt, moving forward preparing to pay.

"Ashley!" said the cashier.

"Oh my God! Kendra, how are you?" Ashley asked, at first not recognizing her, her once dark hair is now a dirty blonde, but knew it was her from the cigarette sized scar on her cheek.

"I'm good, just making an honest living now," answered Kendra.

"I'm glad to hear that," Ashley replied. "I see you dyed your hair, I like it, it looks good."

"Thank you," said Kendra. "I thought it was about time for a change. So what's going on with you?"

"I'm on my way to school, classes start on Monday," informed Ashley.

"That's awesome, I'm happy for you. Look, I was hoping I would get the chance to say thank you for everything and for what you did. I don't think I would be here if it weren't for you," Kendra said, eyes watering flashing a smile.

"You don't have to thank me, I'm just glad you're okay and doing good," said Ashley, giving Kendra a quick hug.

"Hey, text me when you're back in town, we'll do lunch," suggested Kendra.

"I'd like that," Ashley replied, "you take care of yourself."

"You too," said Kendra.

Grabbing her bag, Ashley waves goodbye exiting the store.

Pulling into the campus parking lot she was assigned to, Ashley parked her car in a spot by a curb where she is supposed to meet her guide. Checking the time, sees she is a few minutes early, deciding to sit in the car for a moment to prepare herself for the unknown adventure ahead.

"You okay?" asked Jake.

"Yeah, I think so," Ashley answered. "I'm excited, but scared and nervous at the same time."

"That's perfectly normal," Jake replied. "Take a couple deep breaths, you're going to be just fine."

Ashley and Jake exit her car getting a nice view of the surrounding campus, seeming even more beautiful than when they were there for her tour a few months back. Students were walking about with their backpacks, some were wearing headphones, nobody seemed too much in a hurry as classes didn't start for a couple days. Grabbing her backpack out of her trunk, Ashley goes to stand by Jake, will grab her other stuff later once she knows where her dorm is. Jeff, Vicki, and Danielle, parked a couple spots down, come over to see Ashley off.

"You go be good now and have fun and we are going to see you at Thanksgiving, right?" asked Jeff.

"That's a promise, Uncle Jeff," Ashley replied.

"I want to hear all about it and I'm here if you want to talk," said Vicki.

"I know," replied Ashley, giving Vicki a quick hug.

"Good luck," said Vicki.

"You're going to take care of him while I'm gone, right?' Ashley asked standing before Danielle.

"You know I will," replied Danielle, giving Ashley a hug. "Good luck, honey, see you soon."

Back standing in front of the man who made all of this possible, still amazed when they met in the gym that day he would turn out to be what her life was always missing.

"Well, this is it," said Jake, swiping some of the hair out of her face.

"Yeah, this is it," Ashley replied.

"Remember, you are going to be speaking with the school therapist twice a week," Jake informed.

"I know, I will, I promise," said Ashley, "you coming to my games?"

"I will be getting season tickets," Jake remarked, their moment was interrupted by the sound of a female voice calling Ashley's name.

"Ashley Stamper?" called the voice.

The two of them stared intently into each other's eyes not knowing how to say goodbye.

"Go," said Jake. "It's okay, I know, I will always be here."

Nodding her head with watery eyes in agreeance, Ashley walks away heading for her caller, getting not even ten steps away, turns around running full speed into Jake's arms, engaging in a strong emotional embrace.

"Thank you," whispers Ashley, tears running down her face.

"This is your time now. You go and be great," Jake whispers back, kissing her on top of the head, shedding a few tears himself .

The tender moment being shared by the world's newest father and daughter team brought out the emotions of all that were around them, witnessing an unbreakable bond being established between them, an unconditional love growing every second. They may have only known each other a few months, but already neither one can picture their lives without the other.

Experiencing his first major tribulation as a parent, having to let go, time for her to be the person Jake knows she could be. Releasing their hold on each other, Jake swipes away her tears with his thumb as she smiles, kissing her on the forehead before sending her off to confront her new life. Ashley heads back in her original direction, being greeted by her assigned guide.

"Ashley Stamper, I presume," said an average height, athletic built, dirty blonde haired girl.

"Yes, that's me," Ashley answered.

"Hi, I'm Becca, I've been assigned to show you around and get you situated," said Becca as the two of them shake hands. "It's so great to meet you, I've heard a lot about you. I'm on the softball team too."

"Really, what position?" asked Ashley.

"I'm the catcher," said Becca, sharing a cheerful smile.

"It's great to meet you," Ashley replied smiling, rubbing her fingers on her neckless housing Holley J's ashes.

Briefly looking back in Jake's direction, Ashley smiles giving him a wave. Reciprocating her actions, Jake flashes a large smile of his own, sending her off with their signal of unity, putting one of his fists in the air, observing her doing the same.

"She's going to be fine," said Jeff, placing a hand on his brother's shoulder in comfort.

"I know she will," Jake replied, watching her walk off into the distance.